D0394232

THE MUSE

ALSO BY JESSIE BURTON

The Miniaturist

The MUSE

JESSIE BURTON

ecco

An Imprint of HarperCollins*Publishers*

THE MUSE. Copyright © 2016 by Peebo & Pilgrim Limited. All rights reserved. Printed in the United States of America. No part of this book may be used or reproduced in any manner whatsoever without written permission except in the case of brief quotations embodied in critical articles and reviews. For information address HarperCollins Publishers, 195 Broadway, New York, NY 10007.

HarperCollins books may be purchased for educational, business, or sales promotional use. For information please e-mail the Special Markets department at SPsales@harpercollins.com.

FIRST EDITION

Designed by Shannon Nicole Plunkett
Background art by GreenArt Photography/Shutterstock, Inc.

Library of Congress Cataloging-in-Publication Data has been applied for.

ISBN 978-0-06-240992-8

16 17 18 19 20   OV/RRD   10 9 8 7 6 5 4 3 2 1

For
Alice, Teasel
& Pip

Never again will a single story be told as
though it were the only one.

—JOHN BERGER

CONTENTS

PART III – THE LION GIRLS

PART IV – THE SWALLOWED CENTURY

PART V – RUFINA AND THE LION

PART VI – THE STICKING PLACE

AFTERWORD

THE MUSE

PART I

Cabbages and Kings

JUNE 1967

1

*N*ot all of us receive the ends that we deserve. Many moments that change a life's course – a conversation with a stranger on a ship, for example – are pure luck. And yet no one writes you a letter, or chooses you as their confessor, without good reason. This is what she taught me: you have to be ready in order to be lucky. You have to put your pieces into play.

When my day came, it was so hot that my armpits had made moons on the blouse the shoe shop supplied to every employee. 'It don't matter what size,' the woman said, dabbing herself with a handkerchief. My shoulders were aching, my fingertips chafing. I stared; sweat had turned the pale hair at her brow the colour of a wet mouse. London heat; it never has anywhere to go. I didn't know it, but this woman was the last customer I would ever have to serve.

'I'm sorry?'

'Just *said*,' the woman sighed. 'Any size'll do.'

It was nearing closing time, which meant all the crumbs of dry skin – toe jam, as we called it – would have to be hoovered out of the carpet. Cynth always said we could have moulded a whole foot out of those scrapings, a monster to dance a jig of its own. She liked her job at Dolcis Shoes, and she'd got me mine – but within an hour of our shift, I craved the cool of my room, my cheap notebooks, my pencil waiting by the narrow bed. 'Girl, you got to pick your face *up*,' Cynth would whisper. 'Or you working in the funeral parlour next door?'

I backed away to the stock cupboard, a place where I would often escape, immune as I was by now to its noxious smell of rubbered soles. I thought I might go in and scream silently at the wall of boxes.

'Wait! Oi, wait,' the woman called after me. When she was sure she had my attention, she bent low and slipped off her scuffed pump, revealing a foot that had no toes. Not one. A smooth stump, a block of flesh resting innocently on the faded carpet.

'See,' she said, her voice defeated as she kicked off the second shoe to reveal an identical state of affairs. 'I just . . . stuff the ends with paper, so it don't matter what size you bring.'

It was a sight, and I have not forgotten it; the Englishwoman who showed me her toeless feet. At the time, perhaps I was repulsed. We always say the young have little truck with ugliness, have not learned to mask shock. I wasn't that young, really; twenty-six. I don't know what I did in the moment, but I do recall telling Cynth, on the way home to the flat we shared off Clapham Common, and her whooping with delighted horror at the thought of those toeless feet. 'Stumpy McGee!' she shouted. 'She comin' to get yuh, Delly!' And then, with an optimistic pragmatism; 'At least she wear any shoe she want.'

Perhaps that woman was a witch coming to herald the change in my path. I don't believe so; a different woman did that. But her presence does seem a macabre end to that chapter of my life. Did she see in me a kindred vulnerability? Did she and I occupy a space where our only option was to fill the gap with paper? I don't know. There does remain the very slim possibility that all she wanted was a new pair of shoes. And yet I always think of her as something from a fairy tale, because that was the day that everything changed.

OVER THE LAST FIVE YEARS since sailing to England from Port of Spain, I'd applied for many other jobs, and heard nothing. As the train from Southampton chugged into Waterloo, Cynth had mistaken house chimneys for factories, the promise of plenty of work.

It was a promise that turned out to be harder to fulfil. I often fantasized about leaving Dolcis, once applying to a national newspaper to work as a tea-girl. Back home, with my degree and self-regard, I would never have dreamed of serving any soul tea, but Cynth had said, 'A one-eye stone-deaf limping frog could do that job, and they still won't it give to you, Odelle.'

Cynth, with whom I had gone to school, and with whom I had travelled to England, had become besotted with two things: shoes, and her fiancé, Samuel, whom she had met at our local church off Clapham High Street. (Sam turned out to be a great bonus, given the place was normally full of old tanties telling us about the good old days.) Because of finding him, Cynth did not strain at the bit as I did, and it could be a source of tension between us. I would often declare that I couldn't take it any more, that I wasn't like her, and Cynth would say, 'Oh, because I some sheep and you so *clever*?'

I had telephoned so many advertisements which stated experience was not essential, and people sounded so nice – and then I'd turn up and miracle, miracle! every single job had been taken. And yet, call it folly, call it my pursuit of a just inheritance, but I kept on applying. The latest – and the best I'd ever seen – was a typist post at the Skelton Institute of Art, a place of pillars and porticoes. I'd even visited it once, on my monthly Saturday off. I'd spent the day wandering the rooms, moving from Gainsborough to Chagall, via aquatints by William Blake. On the train home to Clapham, a little girl gazed at me as if I was a painting. Her small fingers reached out and rubbed my earlobe, and she asked her mother, 'Does it come off?' Her mother didn't chide: she looked like she damn well wanted the earlobe to give its answer.

I hadn't scrapped with the boys to gain a first-class English Literature degree from the University of the West Indies for nothing. I hadn't endured a child's pinch in a train carriage, for nothing. Back home, the British Consulate itself had awarded me the Commonwealth Students' first prize for my poem, 'Caribbean Spider-Lily'. I'm sorry, Cynth, but I was not going to put shoes on sweaty Cinderellas for the rest of my life. There were tears, of course,

mainly sobbed into my sagging pillow. The pressure of desire curdled inside me. I was ashamed of it, and yet it defined me. I had
bigger things I wanted to do, and I'd done five years of waiting. In
the meantime, I wrote revenge poems about the English weather,
and lied to my mother that London was heaven.

THE LETTER WAS ON THE mat when Cynth and I got home. I kicked
off my shoes and stood stock-still in the hallway. The postmark
was London W.1, the centre of the world. The Victorian tiles under
my bare feet were cold; my toes flexed upon the brown and blue. I
slid one finger under the flap of the envelope, lifting it like a broken
leaf. It was the Skelton Institute letterhead.

'Well?' Cynth said.

I didn't reply, one fingernail pressed into the floral Braille of
our landlord's Anaglypta wallpaper, as I read to the end in shock.

> The Skelton Institute
> Skelton Square
> London, W.1
>
> 16th June, 1967
> Dear Miss Bastien,
> Thank you for sending your application letter and
> curriculum vitae.
> To thrive, under whatever circumstances life presents
> us, is all anyone can hope for. You are clearly a young
> woman of great ability, amply armoured. To that
> degree, I am delighted to invite you to a week's trial role
> in the typist position.
> There is much to learn, and most of it must be learned
> alone. If this arrangement suits you, please advise me by
> return of post whether the offer is to be accepted, and we
> will proceed from there. The starting salary is £10 p/w.
> With warm wishes,
> Marjorie Quick

£10 a *week*. At Dolcis, I only got six. Four pounds would make the difference of a world, but it wasn't even the money. It was that I was a step closer to what I'd been taught were Important Things – culture, history, art. The signature was in thick black ink, the 'M' and 'Q' extravagant, almost Italianate in grandeur. The letter smelled faintly of a peculiar perfume. It was a bit dog-eared, as if this Marjorie Quick had left it in her handbag for some days before finally deciding to take it to the post.

Goodbye shoe shop, goodbye drudgery. 'I got it,' I whispered to my friend. 'They want me. I blimmin' got it.'

Cynth screamed and took me in her arms. 'Yes!'

I let out a sob. 'You did it. You *did* it,' she went on, and I breathed her neck, like air after thunder in Port of Spain. She took the letter and said, 'What kind of a name is Marjorie Quick?'

I was too happy to answer. Dig your nail in that wall, Odelle Bastien; break apart that paper flower. But I wonder, given what happened, the trouble it led you to, would you do it again? Would you turn up at eight twenty-five on the morning of Monday 3 July 1967, adjusting that new hat of yours, feet wiggling in your Dolcis shoes, to work in the Skelton for £10 a week and a woman called Marjorie Quick?

Yes, I would. Because I was Odelle and Quick was Quick. And to think you have a second path is to be a fool.

2

I envisaged I would be working in a whole atrium of clattering typists, but I was alone. Many of the staff were away, I supposed, taking annual holidays in exotic places like France. Every day, I would walk up the stone steps towards the Skelton's large doors, upon whose panes was blazoned in gold lettering ARS VINCIT OMNIA. Hands on the *vincit* and the *omnia*, I pushed inside to a place that smelled of old leather and polished wood, where to my immediate right was a long reception desk and a wall of pigeonholes looming behind it, already filled with the morning's post.

The view in the room I'd been assigned was terrible – a brick wall smeared black with soot, and a long drop when you looked down. I could see an alleyway, where porters and secretaries from the neighbouring building would line up and smoke. I could never hear their conversations, only watch their body language, the ritual of a patted pocket, heads together like a kiss as the cigarette was flourished and the lighter caught, a leg bent coquettishly backwards against a wall. It was such a hidden place.

Skelton Square was tucked behind Piccadilly, on the river side. Standing there since George III was king, it had been lucky in the Blitz. Beyond the rooftops the sounds of the Circus could be heard; bus engines and honking motor cars, the keening calls of milk boys. There was a false sense of security in a place like this, in the heart of London's West End.

FOR NEARLY THE WHOLE OF the first week the only person I spoke to was a girl called Pamela Rudge. Pamela was the receptionist, and she would always be there, reading the *Express* at her counter, elbows on the wood, gum popping in her mouth before the big fellers showed and she threw it in the bin. With a hint of suffering, as if she'd been interrupted in a difficult activity, she would fold the newspaper like a piece of delicate lace and look up at me. 'Good *morning*, *A*dele,' she'd say. Twenty-one years old, Pam Rudge was the latest in a long line of East-Enders, an immobile beehive lacquered to her head and enough black eyeliner to feed five pharaohs.

Rudge was fashionable, overtly sexual. I wanted her mint-green minidress, her pussy-bow blouses in shades of burnt orange, but I didn't have the confidence to show my body like that. All my flair was locked inside my head. I wanted her lipstick shades, her blusher, but English powders transported me into strange, grey zones where I looked like a ghost. In the make-up department in Arding & Hobbs at the Junction, I'd only find things called 'Buttermilk Nude', 'Blonde Corn', 'Apricot Bloom', 'Willow Lily' and other such bad face poetry.

I decided that Pamela was the kind of person whose idea of a good night out was to gorge her face on a saveloy in Leicester Square. She probably spent her salary on hair spray and bad novels, but was too stupid to even read them. Perhaps I communicated some of these thoughts – because Pamela, in turn, would either maintain wide-eyed surprise at seeing me every day, as if astonished by my audacity to keep coming back, or express comatose boredom at the appearance of my face. Sometimes she would not even look up as I lifted the flap of the reception desk and let it drop with the lightest bang just at the level of her right ear.

Cynth once told me that I looked better in profile, and I said that made me sound like I was a coin. But now it makes me wonder about my two sides, the arch impression I probably gave Pamela, the spare change of myself that no one yet had pocketed. The truth was, I felt so prim before a girl like Rudge.

She knew no other *blacks*, she told me on the Thursday of that first week. When I replied that I hadn't known any either by that name till I came here, she looked completely blank.

BUT DESPITE THE CLUNKY DANCE with Pamela, I was ecstatic to be there. The Skelton was Eden, it was Mecca and Pemberley; the best of my dreams come to life. A room, a desk, a typewriter, Pall Mall in the morning as I walked from Charing Cross, a boulevard of golden light.

One of my jobs was to transcribe research notes for academic men I never saw, except for their nearly indecipherable handwriting, scribbling about bronze sculptures or sets of linocuts. I enjoyed this, but my principal duty revolved around a tray on my desk that would be filled with letters I was to type up and leave with Pamela downstairs. Most of the time they were fairly mundane, but every now and then I'd pick up a gem, a begging letter to some old millionaire or decrepit Lady Whatnot on their last legs. '*My dear Sir Peter, it was such a pleasure to identify the Rembrandt you had in your attic back in '57. Would you consider using the Skelton to help catalogue the rest of your wonderful collection?*' and so on. Letters to financiers and film moguls, informing them that a Matisse was floating around, or would they fancy a new room of the Skelton being named after them, as long as we could fill it with their artworks?

They were mainly written by the director of the Skelton, a man called Edmund Reede. Pamela told me Reede was in his sixties and had a short fuse. In the war, he had something to do with recovering art confiscated by the Nazis, but she didn't know any more. The name 'Edmund Reede' for me conjured up a quintessential, intimidating Englishness, Savile Rowers in Whitehall clubs; eat the steak, hunt the fox. Three-piece suit, pomaded hair, great-uncle Henry's golden watch. I would see him round the corridors, and he would look surprised every time. It was as if I had walked in naked off the street. We studied men like him at school – protected gentlemen, rich gentlemen, white gentlemen, who picked up pens and wrote the world for the rest of us to read.

The Skelton was a bit like that world, the world I'd been taught that I wanted to be in – and just by typing the letters, I felt closer to it all, as if my help in the matter was invaluable, as if I'd been picked for a reason. And the best thing was; I was fast. So once I had finished their letters, I used a spare hour here or there to type my own work – starting over and over again, scrunching up pieces of paper and making sure to put them in my handbag rather than leaving them like evidence in the waste-paper bin. Sometimes, I'd go home with my handbag brimming with balls of paper.

I told Cynth how I'd forgotten the smell of the Dolcis stock cupboard. 'It's as if one week can kill five years,' I said, determined and rhapsodic about my transformation. I told her about Pamela, and joked about the rigidity of her beehive. Cynth paused, frowning, for she was frying me an egg in our tiny flat, and the hob was unreliable. 'I pleased for yuh, Delly,' she said. 'I pleased it going so well.'

ON THE FRIDAY OF THE first week, Reede's letters completed, I was struggling with a poem in a quiet half-hour. Cynth had told me that the only thing she wanted as a wedding gift was 'something written – seeing as you're the only one who ever could.' Touched but agonized, I stared at the Skelton's typewriter, thinking how happy Sam and Cynth clearly made each other. It made me think about my own lack; the foot, but no glass slipper. It also made me realize how I had been struggling with my writing for months. I hated every word that came from me, couldn't let any of it breathe.

A woman walked in just as I lit upon a possible phrase. 'Hallo, Miss Bastien,' she said, and the idea melted away. 'Getting on? Allow me to introduce myself. I'm Marjorie Quick.'

I stood, knocking the typewriter in my haste, and she laughed. 'This isn't the army, you know. Take a seat.' My eye darted to the poem on the reel, and I felt sick to my stomach that she might walk round and see it.

Marjorie Quick came towards me, hand outstretched, her gaze flicking to the typewriter. I took her hand, willing her to stay on the other side of the desk. She did, and I noticed the cigarette scent that clung to her, mingled with a musky, masculine perfume that I recognized from the letter she'd posted, and I would later learn was called Eau Sauvage.

Marjorie Quick was petite, upright, dressed in a way that eclipsed Pamela's efforts. Wide black slacks that billowed like a sailor's as she walked. A pale-pink silk blouse with a grey satin necktie loosely slung inside it. She looked like something out of Hollywood, with her short, silvering curls, her cheeks seeming carved from a fine honeyed wood. She could have been in her early fifties, I supposed, but looked unlike any fifty-year-old I'd ever met. Her jawline was sharp and her glamour hovered.

'Hello,' I said. I couldn't stop staring at her.

'Any bother?' Quick seemed to feel the same, fixing her dark liquid irises on me, waiting for my answer. I noticed she looked rather flushed, a bead of perspiration on her forehead.

'Bother?' I repeated.

'Good. What time is it?' The clock was behind her, but she didn't turn.

'Nearly twelve-thirty.'

'So let us lunch.'

3

She had her name engraved on a brass plate upon her door. I wondered how many women in London, in this year of our Lord 1967, had their own office. Working-class women had menial jobs, or nursed in the NHS, or were factory or shop girls or typists like me, and it had been like that for decades. But there was a world of difference, an almost unnavigable journey, between that and having your name engraved on the door. Perhaps Marjorie Quick was a scion of the Skelton family, here in some honorary position.

She opened the door, the nameplate glinting in the rays of sun through the window beyond, and ushered me inside. Her room was white and airy, with huge windows looking onto the square. The walls were bare of paintings, which I thought odd, being where we were. Three were covered in bookshelves and I spied mainly nineteenth- and early-twentieth century novels, the surprise combination of Hopkins perching next to Pound, and a smattering of Roman history. They were all hardbacks, so I couldn't see if the spines were bent.

From her large desk, Quick grabbed a packet of cigarettes. I watched as she extracted one, hesitated, and then placed it delicately on her lips. I would become accustomed to her habit of speeding up her actions, only to slow them again, as if checking

herself. Her name lived up to her, but whether it was her languor-
ous or hasty side that was more natural was always hard to tell.

'Would you like one?' she asked.

'No, thank you.'

'Then I'll go on alone.'

Her lighter was one of those heavy, refillable silver varieties, to
be left on a table rather than slipped in a pocket. It was the kind
of thing you might see in a country house, a cross between a hand
grenade and something up for auction at Christie's. The Skelton
had a lot of money, I reckoned, and Quick reflected it. Unspoken,
but present, it was in the cut of her pink silk blouse, her brave
trousers, her smoking paraphernalia. In her. I wondered again
what exactly her role here was.

'Gin?' she said.

I hesitated. I never drank much, and I certainly did not like the
taste of spirits. The smell reminded me too much of the men in the
Port of Spain clubhouses – the bubble of rum through the blood,
working to a roar of squalid pain or euphoria heard upon the dust
roads into town. But Quick unscrewed the cap of the gin from a
table in the corner and poured some into two tumblers. She delved
in an icebox with a pair of tongs and dropped two cubes in my
glass, splashed it with tonic to the top, added a slice of lemon, and
handed it to me.

Sinking down into her chair as if she'd been standing for twenty
days, Quick slugged back her own gin, picked up the telephone
receiver and dialled a number. She sparked the lighter and a fat
orange flame appeared. The end of her cigarette sizzled, tobacco
leaf crisping into tendrils of blue smoke.

'Hello, Harris? Yes, whatever it is today. But twice over. And
a bottle of the Sancerre. Two glasses. How long? Fine.' I listened
to the cadences of her voice; clipped and husky, it didn't sound
entirely English, even though it had hints enough inside it of a
draughty boarding school.

She placed the receiver back down, and flicked her cigarette

into a giant marble ashtray. 'The restaurant next door,' she said. 'I
find it impossible to sit inside it.'

I sat down opposite her, cradling my glass, thinking of the sandwich Cynth had made for me, its edges curling in the heat of my
desk drawer.

'So,' she said. 'A new job.'

'Yes, madam.'

Quick placed her glass on the desk. 'First things, Miss Bastien.
Never call me "madam". Nor am I "miss". I like to be known as
Quick.' She smiled, looking rueful. 'Your name is French?'

'Yes, I believe so.'

'You speak French?'

'No.'

'To have and to be confuse me greatly. I thought people spoke
French in Trinidad?'

I hesitated. 'Only a few of our forebears were indoors, speaking
with the French,' I said.

Her eyes widened – with amusement, offence? It was impossible
to tell. I dreaded that my history lesson was too much, too arch,
and I was going to fail my trial period. 'Of course,' she said. 'How
interesting.' She took another slug of gin. 'There's not much to do
here at the moment,' she went on, 'but I expect Mr Reede is keeping you busy with his endless flow of correspondence. I'm worried
you'll be bored.'

'Oh, I'm sure I won't be.' I thought of Dolcis, of how they over-
worked Cynth and me; the way the husbands watched our buttocks whilst their wives slipped on their heels. 'I'm just so pleased
to be here.'

'There's probably more life to be seen in one day at Dolcis Shoes
than a week at the Skelton. Did you enjoy it?' she asked. 'Touching
all those women's feet?'

The question was vaguely shocking, rimed with a sexual sharp-
ness that stung me, virginal as I was. But I would not be cowed.
'In all honesty,' I replied, 'with thirty pairs a day, it was appalling.'

She threw back her head and laughed. 'All the cheeses of France!'

Her laughter was infectious and I giggled too. It was a ludicrous thing to say, but it melted the tension inside me. 'Some people don't mind it,' I said, thinking of Cynth, how I was abasing her for this exchange, this strange game whose rules I didn't know. 'It takes a skill.'

'I dare say. But so many anonymous toes.' She shuddered. 'We have all these beautiful portraits at the Skelton, but we're really just gangling arms, gurgling intestines. The heat inside the liver.' She looked at me hard, and took another drag. 'I've had a lot longer than you to come to that conclusion, Miss Bastien. Toes, the crooks of elbows. Enjoy dignity in them while you can.'

'I'll try,' I said, unsettled once again. There was a restlessness to her; it felt as if she was putting on a performance for me, and I didn't know why.

There was a knock on the door. Quick told them to enter and our lunch arrived on a trolley, pushed by a very small, elderly porter who only had one arm. A basket of rolls, two flat fishes, a buoyant-looking salad, a bottle of wine in a cooler, and something else hidden under a steel dome. The porter glanced at me, startled like a rabbit. His rheumy eyes slid back to Quick.

'That'll be all, Harris. Thank you,' Quick said.

'We haven't seen you all week, miss,' he replied.

'Ah – annual leave.'

'Somewhere nice?'

'No.' Quick looked momentarily disconcerted. 'Just a home stay.'

The porter changed his attention to me. 'Bit different to the last one,' he said, cocking his head. 'Does Mr Reede know you've got a wog in?'

'That will be everything, Harris,' said Quick, in a tight voice. He cast her a disgruntled look and left the trolley, staring at me as he backed out of the door.

'Harris,' Quick said when he'd gone, as if to say his name was explanation enough. 'The arm got lost in Passchendaele. He refuses to retire and no one has the heart to do it.' The porter's word clung to the air. Quick stood up and handed me a plate off the trolley.

'Just use the desk to rest it, if you don't mind.' She carried her own plate round to her side of the desk. She had a slim little back, her shoulder blades slightly poking through the blouse like a pair of fins. The wine had been uncorked and she poured us both a glass.

'It's very good. Not like the stuff we use for the public.' The glug of it was loud and lush and transgressive, like she was pouring me elixir in full daylight. 'Cheers,' Quick said briskly, raising her glass. 'I hope you like lemon sole.'

'Yes,' I replied. I'd never eaten it before.

'So. What did your parents say when you told them you were working here?'

'My parents?'

'Were they proud?'

I wiggled my toes in the confines of their shoes. 'My father's dead.'

'Oh.'

'My mother is still in Port of Spain. I'm an only child. She might not even have got my letter yet.'

'Ah. That must be hard for you both.'

I thought of my mother – her belief in England, a place she would never see; and I thought of my father, recruited into the RAF, gone down over Germany in a ball of flame. When I was fifteen, the Prime Minister of Tobago had declared that the future of the islands' children lay in their schoolbags. My mother, desperate for me not to live a life like hers and Dad's, pushed me to better myself – but for what, when all the land post-independence was being sold to foreign companies who invested the profits back into their own countries? What were we youngsters supposed to do, when we reached the bottom of those schoolbags and found nothing there – just a seam, split from the weight of our books? We had to leave.

'Are you all right, Miss Bastien?' said Quick.

'I came here with my friend, Cynth,' I said, not wishing to dwell on Port of Spain, the death board with Dad's name on it, his empty plot in Lapeyrouse Cemetery that Mama still kept vacant, the Catholic nuns who'd taught me as I grew up in my grief. 'Cynthia's engaged,' I said. 'She's getting married.'

'Ah.' Quick picked up her knife and began to lift a small segment of the sole, and I had the strange feeling of saying too much without having said anything at all. 'When?'

'In two weeks. I'm maid of honour.'

'And then what?'

'Then what?'

'Well, you'll be alone, won't you? She'll be living with her husband.'

Quick always insisted on skirting her own truths whilst getting to the core of yours. She told me nothing about the Skelton, focusing only on finding out about me, and had soon skewered my darkest fear. The fact was, Cynth's imminent departure from our little flat had hung between me and my oldest friend like a silent question, heavy with foreboding. We both knew she would leave to live with Samuel, but I couldn't imagine rooming with anybody else, so I didn't talk about it, and neither did she. I boasted about my new job and she fretted over wedding invitations and made me sandwiches I overlooked. The salary from the Skelton would cover the second room she was going to vacate, and this was my only comfort.

'I enjoy my own company,' I said, swallowing hard. 'It'll be nice to have some space.'

Quick reached for another cigarette, but then seemed to change her mind. *If you were alone*, I thought, *you'd have already smoked three more.* Her eyes rested briefly on my face as she lifted the steel dome to reveal a lemon meringue. 'Do eat something, Miss Bastien,' she said. 'All this food.'

Whilst I ate my slice of meringue, Quick didn't touch a crumb. She seemed born to all this, to the smoking and the telephone orders, the tangential observations. I imagined her in her twenties, raffing round London with a glamorous set, a cat amongst the Blitz. I was piecing her together from Mitford and Waugh, dousing her with a coat of my newly discovered Muriel Spark. It was perhaps a vanity, instilled in me from the education I'd received, which was little different from the model used in English public schools, with its Latin and Greek and boys playing cricket – but I had yearned for eccentric, confident people to enhance my life; I thought I deserved them, the sort of people you found only in novels. Quick hardly had to do anything, I was so sprung for it, so willing. Starved of my past life, I began to concoct a present fantasy.

'Your application interested me greatly,' she said. 'You write very well. *Very* well. At your university, you seem to have been one of the brightest students. I take it you think you're too good to be a secretary.'

Fear ran through me. Did this mean she was letting me go, that I hadn't passed the trial? 'I'm very grateful to be here,' I said. 'It's a wonderful place to work.'

She made a face at these blandishments and I wondered what it was she wanted. I reached for a bread roll and rested it in my palm. It was the weight and size of a small marsupial and I had an instinct to stroke it. Feeling her eyes upon me, I plunged my thumb into the crust instead.

'And what sort of things do you like to write?'

I thought of the piece of paper on the typewriter in the other room. 'Poems, mainly. I'd like to write a novel one day. I'm still waiting for a good story.'

She smiled. 'Don't wait too long.' I was quite relieved she gave me this instruction, because usually whenever I told people I wanted to write, they would tell me how their own lives would make the perfect subject. 'I mean it,' said Quick. 'You mustn't hang around. You never know what's going to pounce on you.'

'I won't,' I said, gratified by her insistence.

She sat back in her chair. 'You do remind me of someone I used to know.'

'I do?' I found this immensely flattering and waited for Quick to go on, but her face clouded, and she broke the spine of the cigarette she'd left on the side of the ashtray.

'What do you make of London?' she asked. 'You came in '62. Do you like living here?'

I felt paralysed. She leaned forward. 'Miss Bastien. This isn't a test. I'm genuinely interested. Whatever you say, I won't tell a soul. Cross my heart, I promise.'

I'd never told anybody this out loud. It may have been the gin, it may have been her open face, and the fact she didn't laugh at my dream of writing. It may have been the confidence of youth, or that porter Harris, but it all came tumbling out. 'I've never seen so much soot,' I said.

She laughed. 'The place is filthy.'

'In Trinidad, we were brought up being told that London was a magic land.'

'So was I.'

'You're not from here?'

She shrugged. 'I've been here so long I can hardly remember anything else.'

'They make you think London is full of order, and plenty, and honesty and green fields. The distance shrinks.'

'What distance do you mean, Miss Bastien?'

'Well, the Queen rules London and she rules your island, so London is part of you.'

'I see.'

I didn't think Quick did see, really, so I carried on. 'You think they'll know you here, because they also read Dickens and Brontë and Shakespeare. But I haven't met anyone who can name three of his plays. At school, they showed us films of English life – bowler hats and buses flickering on the whitewash – while outside all we could hear were tree frogs. Why did anyone show us such things?' My voice was rising. 'I thought everyone was an Honourable—' I stopped, fearing I'd said too much.

'Go on,' she said.

'I thought London would mean prosperity and welcome. A Renaissance place. Glory and success. I thought leaving for England was the same as stepping out of my house and onto the street, just a slightly colder street where a *beti* with a brain could live next door to Elizabeth the Queen.'

Quick smiled. 'You've been thinking about this.'

'Sometimes you can't think about anything else. There's the cold, the wet, the rent, the lack. But – I do try to live.'

I felt I shouldn't say any more; I couldn't believe I'd said so much. The bread roll was in shreds upon my lap. Quick, in contrast, appeared totally relaxed. She sat back in her chair, her eyes alight. 'Odelle,' she said. 'Don't panic. It's likely you'll be fine.'

4

Cynthia married Samuel at Wandsworth Register Office, in a small room that smelled of bureaucracy and cheap perfume, with dark-green walls and steel chairs. Shirley and Helen, two girls from the shoe shop, came along in their finery. Sam's friend from the buses, Patrick Minamore, was best man, and he brought with him his girlfriend Barbara, a fledgling actress and a talkative presence.

The registrar eyed us. The men were in suits, Patrick's tie particularly loud – and everyone looked smart compared to the drab surround. Cynth was beautiful – I mean, she was beautiful anyway, even without love beaming through every inch of her, but in her white minidress, a simple white pill-box hat, and a pair of white shoes, given her by the manager, Connie, as a wedding present, she was radiant. She had a necklace of blue flowers made from ceramic, and two small pearls in her ears, so perfect and round, as if the oysters had made them especially for her.

Patrick, an aspiring photographer, was in charge of capturing us all. I still have some of those snaps. A fountain of rice caught mid-air, white rain upon Sam and Cynth's laughing faces as they stand on the registry steps, their two hands lifted together as the grains cascade.

In marriage, at least, Cynth had triumphed. It was never going to be simple for us to find our way, and Cynth should have had a shoe empire by then, she was that good. It was not easy to sell shoes in Clapham High Street in 1967 as a Trinidadian girl. It was probably easier to write a poem about Trinidad's flowers, send it to the British Consul and be rewarded with a prize. But at least she had Sam, and they had rubbed off well on each other – he serious and shy, she resourceful and determined – how her presence illuminated him as he signed his name in the register!

We went back to Sam and Patrick's flat in black cabs, and told the taxi men that our friends had just got married. The drivers rolled down their windows and played the blues on the same radio station in concert, so loud we were terrified we'd get arrested for breaking the peace. Back in the flat, we lifted tea towels euphorically from sandwiches, found bottle openers, corkscrews, put a record on, and watched as they cut the white domed cake that Cynth had laced with rum.

After a couple of hours, other people turned up – friends of friends. Barbara had summoned up a gaggle of hip-looking folk, girls with long hair and short dresses, fellers in open-necked shirts, who looked like they needed a shave. I only glanced at them; I had long told myself those people were not for me and neither me for them. My back was damp with sweat and the ceiling seemed lower than it had been an hour ago. A couple of Barbara's gang fell into a table, and a little red lamp with tassels tumbled to the floor. Though I'd never smoked it myself, I could smell the marijuana.

When the room was full, the mood was high and Cynth had drunk three Dubonnets and lemonade too many, she lifted the needle off the record player and announced, 'My friend Delly is a poet and she wrote a poem about love.' There was a cheer. 'And she goin' to read it now.'

'Cynthia Morley, *no*,' I hissed. 'Just 'cos you now a married woman, you can't boss me around.'

'Wha' happen now, Delly?' called Sam. 'Why yuh keeping yuh-self so secret?'

'Come on, Delly. For me,' said Cynth, to my horror drawing out the poem from her handbag as another, yet more unstable cheer rippled around the fuggy room. When I had finally showed it to her a week ago, like a schoolgirl walking the long route to the teacher's desk, she had read it in silence and then put her arms around me tight, whispering, *Good Lord, Delly, you truly blessed.*

'Is a very good poem, Delly,' she said now, as she thrust it in my hands. 'Come on, show these people what you have.'

So I did it. A little wobbly from my own Dubonnet, I glanced up only once at all the faces, small moons stopped for nothing else but me. I read my poem about love from the paper, although I knew it off by heart. My words made the room fall silent. And when I finished, there was more silence, and I waited for Cynth, but even she didn't seem able to speak.

I DID NOT SEE HIS face in the crowd when I read that poem. I did not feel his eyes on me, although he told me later he couldn't drag them off mine. I felt nothing change in the room, except the shock of my voice alone and the peculiar euphoria one feels in the wake of applause, feeling at once cheapened and triumphant.

He came up to me about half an hour later, where I was in the minuscule and cluttered kitchen, stacking the empty foil plates in neat towers, trying to make some order out of Sam and Patrick's bachelor chaos. 'Hello,' he said. 'So you're the poet. I'm Lawrie Scott.'

My first thought was to check whether there were bits of egg sandwich on my fingers. 'I'm not a poet, I just write poems,' I said, looking at my hands.

'There's a difference?'

'I think there is.'

He leant against the counter, his long legs straight, crossing his arms like a detective. 'Is your real name Delly then?' he said.

'It's Odelle.' I was grateful for the bottle of Fairy Liquid and the scrubbing pad I began to put to good use.

'Odelle.' He stared back through the doorless arch to where the party had turned without a rudder, sinking into a sea of cigarette butts and shrieks, ring-pulls, discarded hair accessories, and someone's suit jacket crumpled on the floor. Sam and Cynth would be leaving soon – for nowhere but our flat, which I'd promised to vacate for the evening. Tonight, I was to be staying in this pit. This Lawrie seemed lost in thought, perhaps a little stoned, and I noticed small purple smudges of tiredness under his eyes.

'How do you know the happy couple?' I asked.

'I don't. I'm friends with Barbara and she said there was a party. I didn't know it was a wedding. I feel rather rude, but you know how it goes.' I didn't, so I said nothing. 'You?' he persisted.

'I went to school with Cynthia. She is – was – my flatmate.'

'Long time, then?'

'Long time.'

'Your poem was really good,' he said.

'Thank you.'

'I can't imagine what it'd be like to be married.'

'I don't suppose it's much different,' I replied, putting on a pair of yellow rubber gloves.

He turned to me. 'Do you really think that? Is that why the poem was about love, not marriage?'

The mound of bubbles was rising in the sink because I hadn't turned off the tap. He seemed genuinely interested, and this pleased me. 'Yes,' I said. 'But don't tell Cynth.'

He laughed, and I liked the sound. 'My mother used to say that marriage got better with practice,' he said. 'But she was already on her second try.'

'Goodness me,' I said, laughing. I probably sounded so disapproving. Divorce, in those days, still contained the suggestion of debauch.

'She died two weeks ago,' he said.

I paused, scrubbing pad hovering over the sink, and looked at him to check I'd heard him right. 'My stepfather told me I should come out,' Lawrie went on, staring at the floor. 'That I was getting under his feet. And of all places I end up at a wedding.'

He laughed again, but then was quiet, hugging himself in his fashionable leather jacket. I had not had such a personal conversation with a stranger before in England. I could not counsel him, and he did not seem to wish for it. He didn't look like he was going to cry. I thought he might be hot in that coat, but he didn't seem disposed to take it off. Perhaps he wasn't planning to hang around. I registered my regret that this might be the case.

'I haven't seen my mother for five years,' I said, plunging a tray sticky with cake smears into the hot water.

'But she's not dead, though.'

'No. No, she's not dead.'

'I keep thinking I'm going to see her again. That she'll be there when I go home. But the only person there is bloody Gerry.'

'Gerry being your stepfather?'

His face darkened. 'Yes, sorry. And my mother left everything to him.'

I tried to gauge Lawrie's age. He could be thirty, I supposed, but the rapidity with which he was spilling himself open suggested someone younger. 'That's hard,' I said. 'Why would she do that?'

'Long story. She did leave me one thing, actually. Gerry always hated it, which goes to show what a moron he is.'

'That's good you got something. What is it?'

Lawrie sighed again and uncrossed his arms, letting them hang by his side. 'A painting. All it does is remind me of her.' He gave me a rueful smile, his mouth crooked up one cheek. 'Love is blind, love's a bind. I could be a poet too.' He cocked his head at the refrigerator. 'Any milk?'

'There should be. You know, I think it's best you remember your mother rather than try and forget. My father died. And I don't have anything of his at all. Just my name.'

Lawrie stopped, his hand on the refrigerator door. 'Whoa. I'm sorry. Here am I, going on—'

'It's all right. No, really.' I felt self-conscious now, and wished he'd just get the milk out and busy himself. I never usually talked about my parents, and yet I felt compelled to carry on. 'He died in the war. He got shot down.'

Lawrie looked agog. 'Mine died in the war too. But not in a plane.' He paused and I got the sense he was going to say something, then thought better of it. 'I never knew him,' he added.

I felt awkward with this synchronicity of our circumstance, as if I'd deliberately sought it out. 'I was two,' I hurried on. 'I don't really remember him. He was called Odell, but without the "e". When he died, my mother changed my name.'

'She *what*? What were you known as before that?'

'I don't even know.'

This fact about myself sounded absurd and funny – at least, in that moment it did – maybe it was the clouds of pot billowing around – and we both started laughing. In fact, we laughed straight for about a minute, that pain in your stomach when you laugh and laugh – how one mother can rename you, how mad it is another's suddenly dead, and you in a kitchen round the corner from the British Museum wearing yellow rubber gloves.

Lawrie turned fully towards me, the milk bottle lolling in his hand. Sobering up, I eyed it, worried that the liquid would start dripping through the lid at such a terrible angle.

'Listen,' he said, 'Delly.'

'Odelle.'

'Do you want to get out?'

'From where?'

'From *here*, you crazy girl.'

'Who's crazy?'

'We could go to Soho. I've got a friend who can get us in to the Flamingo. But you'll have to take off those rubber gloves. It's not *that* sort of club.'

I didn't know what to make of Lawrie at this point. I could describe him as grief-stricken, but arguably the grief hadn't truly set in. Perhaps he was in shock – it had only been a fortnight. That he was angry with someone, and a bit lost, both certain of himself and yet avoiding himself – these things could be said about Lawrie. He spoke well, and he talked of Gerry and the house and his divorced, dead mother with a practised world-weariness that I wasn't sure he was trying to escape or keep alive.

'I – I'm tired,' I said. 'I can't leave the party.' I pulled the plug from the sink. As the water drained noisily, I wondered how his mother had died.

'The *Flamingo*, Odelle.'

I'd never heard of it, but I wasn't going to tell him that. 'I can't leave Cynth.'

He raised an eyebrow. 'I don't think she needs you tonight.' I blushed, looking into the disappearing bubbles. 'Look,' he said, 'my car's outside. How about we drop the painting off at my friend's flat and then let's go dancing. It doesn't have to be the Flamingo. Do you like to dance?'

'You have the painting with you?' I said.

'I see.' He ran a hand through his hair. 'More of an art girl than a nightclub girl?'

'I don't think I'm either of those girls. But I do work at an art gallery,' I added. I wanted him to be impressed, to show him I wasn't just some innocent prig who chose to wash up crockery rather than fall around on the carpet.

A light came into Lawrie's eyes. 'Do you want to see it?' he said. 'It's in the boot of my car.'

Lawrie didn't try and touch me in that kitchen. He didn't let his hand drift anywhere near. The relief that he didn't, and the desire that he might – I think they are the reasons I agreed to see his painting. I followed him, leaving the dishes stranded in the sink.

I think he wanted me to be impressed by the fact he was driving an MG, but that meant nothing to me, once I'd laid eyes on the painting in the boot. It was not large, and it had no frame. As an image, it was simple and at the same time not easily decipherable – a girl, holding another girl's severed head in her hands on one side of the painting, and on the other, a lion, sitting on his haunches, not yet springing for the kill. It had the air of a fable.

Despite the slight distortion from the orange street lamp above us, the colours of the lower background reminded me of a Renaissance court portrait – that piled-up patchwork of fields all kinds of yellow and green, and what looked like a small white castle. The sky above was darker and less decorous; there was something nightmarish about its bruised indigoes. The painting gave me an immediate feeling of opposites – the girls against the lion, together in the face of its adversity. But there was a rewarding delicacy beyond its beautiful palette of colours – an elusive element that made it so alluring.

'What do you think?' asked Lawrie. His face seemed softer out of the glare of the kitchen light.

'Me? I'm just the typist,' I said.

'Oh, come on. I heard that poem. Make a poem of this.'

'It doesn't work like that—' I began, before I realized he was teasing me. I felt embarrassed, so I turned back to the painting. 'It's very unusual, I suppose. The colours, the subject matter. I wonder when it was painted? Could be last week, or last century.'

'Or even earlier,' he said eagerly.

I looked again at the old-fashioned fields in the background and then at the figures. 'I don't think so. The girl's dress and cardigan – it's more recent.'

'Do you think that's gold leaf?' Lawrie bent down and pointed to the lion's mane, the flowing strands which seemed to glint. His head was very close to mine and I could smell his skin, a trace of aftershave that gave me goosebumps.

'Odelle?' he said.

'It's not your usual painting,' I replied hastily, as if I knew what a usual painting was. I straightened up. 'Mr Scott, what are you going to do with it?'

He turned to me and smiled. The orange light caught the planes of his face and covered him in ghoulish shadow. 'I like it when you call me Mr Scott.'

'In that case, I'm going to call you Lawrie.'

He laughed, and my jaw tingled, threatening a smile. 'I don't think this was done by an amateur,' I said. 'What did your mother know about it?'

'No idea. And all *I* know is, she took it with her wherever she went. At home, it was always in her bedroom. She didn't like it in the public rooms.'

I pointed to the initials on the bottom right of the painting. 'Who's I.R.?'

Lawrie shrugged. 'Not my forte.'

I wondered what Lawrie's forte was, and whether I would ever find out, and why did I want to – and was that the reason I was feeling so odd?

In case he could read my thoughts, I bent my head down again towards the girl in the painting. She was wearing a light blue dress with a dark woollen cardigan – you could even see the cable knit. The head she was carrying had a long dark plait, which snaked unsettlingly out of her cradled arms, towards the red earth floor. The strange thing was, even though she had no body, the floating girl didn't seem dead at all. She was inviting me in, but there was a note of caution in her eyes. Neither figure was exactly beaming in welcome. They both seemed oblivious to the lion, which may or may not have been waiting for the kill.

'I have to go,' I said, pushing the painting away into his surprised hands. Lawrie, the party, the poem, the Dubonnet, Cynth's marriage, the painting; suddenly I wanted to be alone.

Lawrie took the painting from me and closed the boot. He looked down at me, his head cocked to one side again. 'Are you all right? Do you want me to walk you back in?'

'Yes,' I said. 'I mean, no. I'm fine. Thank you. Sorry. It was a pleasure to meet you. Good luck.' I turned away and made it to the entrance of the block of flats, before he called out to me.

'Hey, Odelle.' I looked back to see him jam his hands into the pockets of his leather jacket, hunching his shoulders again. 'I – you know – that really was a good poem.'

'It always takes longer than you think, Mr Scott,' I said. He laughed, and I smiled properly then, nevertheless relieved to be out of the street lamp's glow.

5

When I was growing up, my mother and I would always eat lunch with Cynth's family on Sundays. Four in the afternoon, a big pot on the hob, everyone coming in and out and dipping for themselves – and once the meal was done, we'd draw our chairs up to the radio at seven thirty and listen to the BBC's *Caribbean Voices*, the only broadcast that mattered if you dreamed of being a writer.

Here's the mad thing: poets from Barbados, Trini, Jamaica, Grenada, Antigua – any part of the British Caribbean – would send their stories all the way to Bush House on London's Aldwych, in order to hear them read back again in their homes, thousands of miles across the Atlantic Ocean. There seemed no local facility to enable these stories to be processed, a fact which impressed upon me at a very young age that in order to be a writer, I would require the motherland's seal of approval, the imperial sanction that my words were broadcastable.

The majority of the work was by men, but I would listen enraptured by the words and voices of Una Marson, Gladys Lindo, Constance Hollar – and Cynth would pipe up, 'One day *you* be read out, Delly' – and her little shining face, her bunches, she always made me feel like it was true. Seven years old, and she was the only one who ever told me to keep going. By 1960 that programme had stopped, and I came to England two years later with no idea what to do with my stories. Life at the shoe shop took over, so I only wrote in private, and Cynth, who must have seen the piles of notebooks which never left my bedroom, simply stopped her pestering.

She and Sam had found a flat to rent in Queen's Park, and she'd transferred to a north London branch of Dolcis. Up to that point, I'd never really known loneliness. I'd always had my books, and Cynth had always been there. Suddenly, my thoughts were enormous in that tiny flat, because there was nobody to hear them and make them manageable, nobody cajoling or supporting me, or holding out their arms for a hug. Cynth's absence became physical to me. Do you have a body if no one is there to touch it? I suppose you do, but sometimes it felt like I didn't. I was just a mind, floating around the rooms. How badly prepared I'd been for the echo and clunk of my key in the lock, the lack of her sizzling frying pan, my solitary toothbrush, the silence where once she hummed her favourite songs.

When you saw a person every day – a person you liked, a person who lifted you up – you thought you were your best self, without trying very hard. Now, I saw myself as barely interesting, not so clever. No one wanted to hear my poems except Cynth, no one cared or understood where I was from like she did. I didn't know how to be Odelle without Cynth to make me so. Cynth had done so much for me, but because she was gone, I still managed to resent her.

Her work commitments and mine meant we were only meeting once a fortnight, in the Lyon's on Craven Street round the corner from the Skelton. I barely credited Cynth for the fact it was she who always arranged it.

AT THE COUNTER, THE WAITRESS had slopped our cups so the liquid had spilled onto the saucer, and the bun I'd asked for was the most squashed. When I asked for a replacement saucer, the waitress ignored me, and when I paid for it, she wouldn't put the change in my hand. She placed the money on the counter and pushed it over, not looking at my face. I turned to Cynth, and saw a familiar expression. We walked to find a spare table, as far away from the counter as we could.

'How is it at the work?' she asked. 'You still trailin' after that Marjorie Quick?'

'She meh boss, Cynthia.'

'So you say.'

I hadn't realized how obvious it was, the impression that Quick had made on me over the recent weeks. I had tried to find out more about Quick from Pamela, who could only tell me that Quick had once mentioned the county of Kent as her childhood home. What she did between being a girl and a woman in her fifties was a grey sketch. Perhaps she had been destined for a genteel, Kentish life, a magistrate's wife or some such, but she chose instead to find a different kind of fortune in the rubble of post-war London. Her name was not in *Debrett's*: she was not a Skelton descendant, one of my initial lines of thought. Her impeccable sartorial choices exuded power, a care of herself that was for nobody's benefit but her own. Each perfect blouse, each pristine pair of trousers, was a pre-emptive self-narration. Quick's clothes were an armour made of silk.

I knew she was unmarried and lived in Wimbledon, just off the common. She smoked constantly, and appeared close to Reede in the sort of way that water is close to a stone that it has worn down over decades. Pamela said that Quick had been here as long as Reede had, when he'd taken the directorship of the Skelton, twenty years ago. How she had come to meet Reede, or why she decided to take employment, remained a mystery. I wondered what sort of battle it had been to get to where she was now, and whether she'd read those Roman histories to give her some lessons in war.

'She not like anyone I ever meet,' I said to Cynth. 'Friendly one minute, a sunlight beam. Then she like a hog-brush woman – she bristle so, it pain yuh to be near.'

Cynth sighed. 'We bought G Plan for the flat.'

'G-what?'

'Oh, Delly. Sam work hard hard, so Ah say, leh we buy we a nice G Plan sofa so he can put up he foot at the end of the day.'

'Hmm. And how your feet doin'?'

She sighed, stirring her lukewarm tea with a spoon. 'Oh, let me tell you a thing. So our new postman get the letters mix up, and our neighbour knock with them.' Cynth cleared her throat and put on a posh English voice. ' *"Oh, hell-air. Yes, this must be yours. We saw it had a black stamp."* Is a letter from *Lagos*, Delly. Meh name not on it, and eh know nobody from Nigeria. "Black stamp", I ask yuh.'

Her laugh died. Normally we would have discussed something like this in order to remove its barb, but after the waitress neither of us had the energy.

'Tell me about the feller you was talking to at the wedding,' she said, looking sly.

'What feller?'

She rolled her eyes. 'Lawrie Scott. The white one; handsome, skinny. He friend to Patrick's Barbara. Ah didn't drink *that* many Dubonnets – I saw you in the kitchen.'

'Oh him. He real dotish.'

'*Hmm*,' she said, her eyes taking on a secret glow, and I knew I'd given myself away. 'That strange.'

'Why?'

'Patrick told Sam he been asking about you.' I shut my mouth tighter than a clam and Cynth grinned. 'You writin'?' she asked.

'You only start asking me that, now you leave.'

'I not gone. I on the other end of the Tube map, that is all.'

'Like you worried I got nothing to do these days. Don't worry, I writin',' I said, but this was a lie. I had stopped entirely at this point, believing that the idea of myself as a good writer was laughable.

'Good. I glad you writin',' said Cynth firmly. 'You know, there a poetry night going at the ICA,' she went on. 'Sam's friend is readin', and he's a *real* dotish boy compared to you. His poem does send me to sleep—'

'Ah not readin' at some meet-up, Cynthia,' I said, wrinkling my nose. 'Make no mistake.'

She sighed. 'I not. Is just that you better, Odelle. You better and you know it, and you doing *nothin'*.'

'Eh *heh*,' I said. 'I busy. I work. You go with your G Plan and stop all this foolishness. What, because I got no husban' foot to worry me, I better go speakin' my *poetry* an' ting?'

Cynthia looked distraught. 'Delly! Why you so vex? I only trying to help.'

'Ah not vex.' I drained my cup of tea. 'Is all right for *you*,' I said. 'Don't tell me how to live.'

Cynth was quiet after that. I should have said sorry then and there, but I didn't. She left soon after, pinch-faced with tears, and I felt like a monster come out of the sea to grab her legs.

We didn't meet up the next week, or the one after that, and she didn't ring. Neither did I, and I felt so embarrassed, such a fool – *a real dotish gyal*, as Cynth no doubt described me that night to Sam. The longer she was silent, the more impossible it seemed to pick up the telephone.

All I really wanted to say was that I missed us living together. And I was someone who was supposed to be good with words.

6

*L*awrie found me on the fifteenth of August. It was seven o'clock in the morning, and I was doing the early reception shift. Shops were still shut, the buses that moved along Charing Cross Road less frequent. I walked on to the Mall, and the long thoroughfare, usually busy, was an empty road of greenish light. It had been raining for a week, and the paving stones were wet from a dawn downpour, trees springing in the breeze like fronds beneath the sea.

I'd seen much worse rain than this, so I wasn't too bothered, tucking the copy of the *Express* I'd bought for Pamela into my handbag to protect it from spatters, crossing up Carlton Gardens and over the circular centre of Skelton Square. I passed the plinth of the long-dead statesman adorning the middle point, a blank-eyed fellow whose frock coat was messed by pigeons. In the past, I would have found out who he was – but five years in London had purged my interest in old Victorian men. The statue's infinite gaze made me feel even more exhausted.

I glanced up towards the Skelton. A young man was standing by the doors, tall and slim, wearing a slightly battered leather jacket. He had a narrow face and very dark brown hair. As I approached, I knew that it was him. I could feel my throat tighten, a little hop in the gut, a thudding swipe to the breast. I approached the steps, fetching the Skelton door key out of my handbag. Lawrie was wearing glasses this time, and their lenses glinted in the subterranean light. He was carrying a parcel under his arm, wrapped in that brown paper butchers used to wrap their slabs of meat.

He grinned at me. 'Hello,' he said.

What was it like to see Lawrie smile? I can try: it was as if a healer had placed their hands upon my chest. My kneecaps porridge, jaw tingling, no hope to swallow. I wanted to throw my arms around him and say, 'It's you, you came.'

'Hello,' I said instead. 'Can I help?'

His smile faltered. 'You don't remember? We met, at the wedding. I came along with Barbara's gang. You read a poem, and you wouldn't go dancing with me.'

I frowned. 'Oh, yes. How do you do?'

'How do I *do*? Aren't you going to ask me why I'm here?'

'It's seven o'clock in the morning, Mr . . . . ?'

'Scott,' he said, the joy draining from his face. 'Lawrie Scott.'

I walked past him and put the key in the lock, fumbling as I did so. What was wrong with me? Despite all my fantasies about how this was going to play out, faced with the reality, I was being just as obstructive as I had been before. I pushed inside and he followed me. 'Are you here to see somebody?' I said.

He gave me a hard look. 'Odelle. I have visited every art gallery, every museum in this bloody city, trying to find you.'

'To *find* me?'

'Yes.'

'You couldn't find me in five weeks? You could have just asked Patrick Minamore.'

He laughed. 'So you were counting.' I blushed and looked away, busying myself with the post. He held up the brown-paper package, and said, 'I've brought the lion girls.'

I couldn't conceal the suspicion in my voice. 'Who are they?'

He grinned. 'My Mother's painting. I've taken your advice. Do you think someone will have a look at them for me?'

'I'm sure they will.'

'I looked up those initials you pointed out, I.R. Didn't find a single name. So it's probably not worth anything,'

'Are you planning on selling it?' I asked, head still fizzing, heart thumping uncomfortably as I moved around the other side of the wooden counter. I'd never been so direct with a boy before in my life.

'Maybe. See what happens.'

'But I thought it was your mother's favourite?'

'*I* was my mother's favourite,' he said, laying the parcel on the counter with a grim smile. 'Only joking. I don't *want* to sell it, but if it's worth something, it will get me started, you see. Any minute, Gerry the Bastard – excuse my French – could kick me out.'

'Don't you work?'

'*Work*?'

'Don't you have a job?'

'I've had jobs in the past.'

'The dim and distant?'

He pulled a face. 'You don't approve.'

The truth was, I *didn't* approve of people who did no work. Everyone I knew since coming to London – Cynth, the girls in the shoe shop, Sam, Patrick, Pamela – we all had jobs. The point of *being* here was to have a job. Where I was from, doing your own work was the only wake-up from the long sleep which followed the generations in the fields. It was your way out. It's hard to change the messages that circulate all your life, especially when they've been there since before your life was started.

Lawrie stared into the brown wrapping paper. 'It's a long story,' he said, sensing my disapproval. 'I dropped out of university. That was a few years ago. My mother wasn't – oh, never mind. But I'd like to start something new.'

'I see.'

He looked embarrassed, jamming his hands into his jacket pockets. 'Look, Odelle. I'm not . . . a layabout. I do want to *do* things. I want you to know that. I—'

'Would you like a cup of tea?' I asked.

He stopped, mid-breath. 'Tea. Yes. God, it's early, isn't it,' he laughed.

'Were you going to just stand out there until I turned up?'

'Yes,' he said.

'You're a mad boy.'

'Who's mad?' he said, and we grinned at each other. I looked at his pale face. 'Even without a job, my mother would still think you're perfect.'

'Why would she think that?' he asked.

I sighed. It was too early in the morning to explain.

WE HAD AN HOUR TOGETHER, sitting in the reception hall, the front door locked as I sorted the post and brewed the tea and coffee that Pamela and I had to keep renewing throughout the day. Lawrie seemed genuinely delighted by his cup of tea. It was as if he had never seen a hot beverage before.

He told me about his mother's funeral. 'It was awful. Gerry read a poem about a dying rose.' I put my hand over my mouth to hide my smile. 'No, you should laugh,' he said. 'My mother would have laughed. She would have hated it. She didn't even like roses. And Gerry has a terrible poetry voice. The worst voice I've ever heard. Like he's got a plunger up his bum. And the priest was senile. And there were no more than five of us there. It was bloody awful and I hated that she had to go through it.'

'I'm sorry,' I said.

He sighed, stretching his legs out. 'Not your fault, Odelle. Anyway. It's done. RIP, all that.' He rubbed his face as if erasing a memory. 'And you? How's life without your flatmate?'

I was touched he remembered. 'All right,' I said. 'Bit quiet.'

'I thought you liked quiet.'

'How would you know?'

'You didn't want to go to the Flamingo.'

'Different sort of quiet,' I said.

We were quiet ourselves then, me sitting behind the counter, and him on the other side, the brown-paper package between us, waiting on the wood. It was a nice silence, warm and full, and I liked him sitting there unobtrusive – yet, to my eyes, fizzing with the light I had sensed when we first met.

He was beautiful to me, and as I laid out the *Express* for Pamela, and did a spurious sorting of the desk, I hoped that she would be delayed somehow. Back home, I'd had one or two of what my mother would have called 'dalliances'; holding hands in the dark at the Roxy, hot-dogs after lectures, awkward kisses at a Princes Building concert, a late-night picnic on the Pitch Walk, watching the bluish light of the candle-flies. But I'd never done . . . the whole thing.

I generally avoided male attention, finding the courting business excruciating. 'Free love' had passed us schoolgirls by in Port of Spain. Our Catholic education was a Victorian relic, redolent with overtones of fallen women, irretrievable girls mired in pools of their own foolishness. We had been instructed that we were too *superior* for that exchange of flesh.

My attitude to sex was one of haughty fear, confused by the fact that there *were* girls who did it, girls like Lystra Wilson or Dominique Mendes, with boyfriends older than themselves and secrets in their eyes, who seemed to be having a very good time indeed. How they procured these boyfriends was always a mystery to me – but it no doubt involved disobedience, climbing out of bedroom windows and into the nightclubs off Frederick Street and Marine Square. In my memory, Lystra and Dominique, those daring ones, seemed like women from the moment they were born, mermaids come ashore to live among us, feminine and powerful. No wonder we scaredy-cats retreated into books. Sex was beneath us, because it was beyond us.

The Skelton front door was still locked. I didn't want it to end – the kettle whistling for more tea in the back room, him stretching and folding his legs, asking me what films I'd seen and how could I have not seen that and did I like blues or was I into folk and how many months had I worked here, and did I like being in Clapham. Lawrie was always very good at making you feel like you were important.

'Would you like to go to the cinema?' he said. 'We could see *You Only Live Twice*, or *The Jokers*.'

'*The Jokers*? Sounds about right for you.'

'Oliver Reed's in it – he's excellent,' said Lawrie, 'but isn't a crime caper too flip for you?'

'*Flip*? Why?'

'Because you're clever. You'd take it as an insult if I took you to watch stupid blokes scampering around for the Crown Jewels.'

I laughed, happy to discover that Lawrie also had a strain of nervousness about all this, and touched that he wasn't afraid to tell me about it. 'Or do you want to see one of those French films,' he said, 'where people just walk in and out of rooms, looking at each other?'

'Let's go and see the Bond.'

'All right. Excellent. Excellent! I loved *Goldfinger* – that bowler hat!' I laughed again and he came up to the counter, leaning over to take my hand. I froze, looking at it. 'Odelle,' he said. 'I think – I mean, you are—'

'What?'

'You're just . . .' He was still holding on to my hand. For the first time in my life, I didn't want a man to let go.

Outside, it began to rain. I turned my head, distracted by the rush of water beyond the door, cascading down onto the grey pavement. Lawrie leaned over and kissed me on the cheek. I turned back and he kissed me again, and it felt good, so we stood for some minutes, kissing in the reception of the Skelton.

I broke away. 'You'll get me sacked.'

'All right. Can't have that.'

He moved back to his chair, grinning like an idiot. The rain was thrumming heavily now, but this was English rain, not Trini rain. Back home, aerial waterfalls fell from the breaking sky, week on week of tropical downpour, forests doused so green they were almost black, the neon signs out, escarpments churned to mud, torch ginger flowers so red, like a man's blood had coloured the petals – and all of us, standing under awnings or hiding in houses till it was safe once more to walk the shining asphalt road. We used to say 'it rainin' ' as an excuse for being late, and everyone would always understand.

'What?' Lawrie said. 'Why are you smiling?'

'Nothing,' I said. 'Nothing.'

There was a rapping on the door. Quick was peering through the glass, under the brim of a wide black umbrella. 'Oh!' I cried. 'She early.'

I ran to the door and unlocked it, thanking God she hadn't seen us kissing. Quick stepped inside, and I thought her face looked thinner. She removed her coat and brushed off her umbrella. 'August,' she muttered.

She looked up and saw Lawrie. 'Who are you?' she said, wary as a cat.

'This is – Mr Scott,' I said, surprised at her bluntness. 'He'd like to speak to someone about his painting. Mr Scott, this is Miss Quick.'

'Mr Scott?' she repeated. She couldn't take her eyes off him.

'Hullo,' Lawrie said, jumping to his feet. 'Wondered if I've got an heirloom or a piece of junk.' He put out his hand and Quick, as if resisting a great magnet, lifted her own to meet it. I saw her flinch, though Lawrie noticed nothing.

She smiled faintly. 'I hope, for your sake, Mr Scott, it's the former.'

'Me too.'

'May I see it?'

Lawrie went to the counter and began unwrapping the paper. Quick stayed where she was by the door, fingers gripping the top of her umbrella. She kept staring at him. Rain had soaked her coat but she didn't take it off. Lawrie swung the painting up, holding it against his body for me and Quick to see. 'Here it is,' he said.

Quick stood for four or five seconds, eyes transfixed on the golden lion, the girls, the landscape spiralling out behind them. The umbrella slid out of her grasp and bumped to the floor. 'Quick?' I said. 'Are you all right?'

She looked at me, abruptly turned on her heel and walked out of the front door. 'It's not *that* bad,' said Lawrie, peering over the top of the painting.

Quick was hurrying away along the square, her head bowed, oblivious to the rain soaking her. As I reached for my own coat, Edmund Reede appeared and removed his dripping trilby.

He looked down at me. 'Miss – Baston, is it?'

'Bastien.'

'Where are you running off to?'

'To see Miss Quick. She's – forgotten her umbrella.'

'We were supposed to be having a meeting.' He turned to where Lawrie was now sitting again, the painting on his knees, hastily covered in the brown paper. 'And who's this?'

'Mr Scott has a painting,' I said.

'I can see that. Isn't this all rather a flurry for eight fifteen in the morning? Where's Miss Rudge?'

'I'm on the early shift, Mr Reede. Mr Scott came today because he was hoping someone would take a look at his painting. It was his mother's – her favourite . . .' I trailed off, desperate to follow Quick and see if she was all right.

Reede removed his wet overcoat with slow deliberation, as if I had placed the burden of the world on his shoulders. He was a tall, broad man and he filled the space with his fine tailoring and thatch of white hair, his woody aftershave. 'Have you made an appointment?' he asked Lawrie, his small blue eyes glinting with impatience.

'No, sir.'

'We're not a *drop-in* centre, you know. This isn't really how it's done.'

Lawrie stiffened, the brown paper rustling over his painting. 'I know that.'

'Well, perhaps you don't. Have Miss Bastien make an appointment for you some time next week. I have no time today.' He turned to look back through the door where Quick had fled. 'Why the hell did Marjorie just run off like that?' he said. I'd never seen Reede look worried before. As he turned back, Lawrie stood up, half the brown paper falling to the floor. Reede stopped in his tracks, his gaze on the revealed half of the painting, the golden lion.

'Is that yours?' he asked Lawrie.

Lawrie lowered his eyes and gathered up the paper. 'Yes,' he said defensively. 'Well – my mother's. Now it's mine.' Reede stepped towards it, but Lawrie moved away, putting his hand out. 'Hold on. You said you didn't have time. You said next week. Although by then,' he added, 'I may have taken it elsewhere.'

'Ah,' said Reede. He put his hands up. 'I just want to take a closer look. Please,' he added, which seemed to cost him a great effort.

'Why? A minute ago you couldn't give a damn.'

Reede laughed; a twitchy joviality. 'Look, old chap, I'm sorry if I was blunt. We get a damned lot of people coming in here with Auntie Edna's heirlooms or something they bought for three bob off a bloke in Brick Lane, and you get a bit sick of it. But what you've got there looks interesting. If you let me take a look, I might be able to tell you why.'

Lawrie hesitated, before placing the painting back on the counter. He unwrapped the rest of the paper. Reede stepped towards it, drinking in the image, his fingers hovering over the paint, the second girl's floating head, her snaking plait, the lion's passive stare. 'My goodness,' he breathed. 'Where did your mother get this?'

'I don't know.'

'Can you ask her?'

Lawrie glanced at me. 'She's dead.'

'Ah.' Reede hesitated. 'So – have you any idea where she might have got it from?'

'She bought most of her things from junk shops or flea markets, sometimes at auctions, but this one has been around since I was a little boy. It was always hanging on her wall, whatever house we moved to.'

'Where was it hanging last?'

'Her house in Surrey.'

'Did she ever talk about it to you?'

'Why would she do that?'

Reede gently picked up the painting and looked on the back. 'No frame, just a hook,' he murmured. 'Well,' he said, addressing Lawrie. 'If she always had it hanging up, it might have had particular meaning to her.'

'I think she just thought it was pretty,' Lawrie said.

'Pretty is not the word I would use.'

'What word *would* you use, sir?'

Reede blinked away Lawrie's tone. 'On first impressions, "brave". And provenance matters, Mr Scott, if you choose to exhibit things, or put things on the market. I assume that's why you brought it to us.'

'So it's worth something?'

There was a pause. Reede breathed deeply, his eyes pinned to the picture. 'Mr Scott, may I take you to my office so I can have a closer look at this?'

'All right.'

'Miss Bastien, bring coffee.'

Reede picked up the painting and gestured for Lawrie to follow him. I watched them walk up the spiral staircase, Lawrie looking back over his shoulder, his eyes wide with excitement, giving me a thumbs up.

OUTSIDE, THE RAIN WAS BECOMING a torrent. I scoured the square for Quick, but of course, by now, she had gone. With her rolled-up umbrella in my hand like a lance, I ran along the left side of the square and turned up towards Piccadilly, blindly hoping I would see her. I took another right, unconsciously heading towards the Tube station, and then I saw her, a block ahead. The traffic honked and screeched, and the statue of Eros loomed.

'Quick!' I yelled. 'Your umbrella!' Heads turned to look, but I didn't care. Quick hurried on, so I ran faster, reaching out to touch her arm. With lightning speed she pulled away from me and whirled round. Her expression was fixed on some distant point well beyond the bustling road, the tall and soot-encrusted buildings, the colourful billboards, the pedestrians hopping desperately around the puddles. Then she focused on me, almost with relief. She was drenched, and though her face was sopping wet, I couldn't tell if it was rain or tears.

'I forgot something,' she said. 'At home – I've forgotten – I need to go back and get it.'

'Here,' I said, 'your umbrella. Let me call you a cab.'

She looked down at her umbrella, then up at me. 'You're *soaking*, Odelle. Why on earth did you run out?'

'Because – well, because *you* did. And look at you.' I put my hand on her wet sleeve and she stared at it momentarily. I was surprised by how thin her arm felt to touch.

'Here.' She pulled the umbrella out of my hands and opened it above our heads. We stared at each other under the black canopy, the roar of rain bashing down upon its flimsy structure, people brushing us as they ran to and fro for cover. Her curls were matted to her head; her powder had washed off her face, I could see the true flesh of her skin – and strangely, without the make-up, it looked more like a mask. She went as if to say something, but seemed to stop herself. 'Jesus Christ,' she murmured, briefly closing her eyes. 'It's a bloody monsoon.'

'Shall I call you a cab?'

'I'll get the Tube. You don't have a cigarette, do you?'

'No,' I said, disconcerted, for surely she knew by now I didn't smoke.

'That man – how did he come to the Skelton?' she asked. 'Do you know him? You seemed to know him.'

I looked down. Huge puddles were forming around our shoes. I thought of the coffee I was supposed to be making, how long I could be out here before I lost my job. 'I only met him once before – at Cynth's wedding. He found me again today.'

'*Found* you? That's fairly persistent behaviour. He's not – bothering you, is he?'

'Not at all. He's fine,' I said, a touch defensive. Why was Quick talking about Lawrie, when she was the one acting strange?

'All right.' She seemed to calm a bit. 'Look, Odelle – I have to go. Tell him not to bother you with that painting.'

'Mr Reede has already seen it.'

'What?'

'He came in shortly after you. Said that you and he had an early meeting. He had one look at it and took it to his office.'

She looked over my shoulder, in the direction of the Skelton. 'What did Mr Reede say, when he saw it?'

'He seemed . . . excited.'

Quick lowered her eyes, her expression closed. In that moment, she looked very old. She gripped my hand and squeezed it. 'Thank you, Odelle – for my umbrella. You're a tribune, you really are. But take it, I'm going underground. Go back to the office.'

'Quick, wait—'

She thrust the umbrella into my hand, and turned down the steps of the station. Before I could even call again to her, Quick had disappeared.

JANUARY 1936

I

*S*arah was unconscious, her face turned sideways, her artificial curls crushed on the pillow, the cuts on her bare legs
covered in calamine smears. A soured scent of the night's
last glass rose from her mouth. On the bedside table was an over-
filled ashtray, a pile of detective novels, and her *Vogue* magazines,
their corners curled. Her clothes were everywhere on the dusty
floorboards, here, stockings like sloughed snakes, there, a blouse,
flattened in the effort of escape. Her rouge had melted in its pot. In
the corner of the room, a lizard flicked across the tiles like a mote
upon the eye.

Olive stood at the door, the letter from the Slade School of Fine
Art gripped in her hand. The letter was only two weeks old, but it
had a handkerchief's flutter, the creases almost oiled from so much
refolding. She walked over to her mother's bed and perched on the
end to read it again, although she knew it off by heart. *It is our pleasure to invite you to undertake the Fine Art degree course . . . The
tutors were highly impressed . . . rich imagination and novelty . . .
continuing the rigorous yet progressive tradition of the school . . . we
look forward to hearing from you within the next fortnight. Should
your circumstances change, please inform us.*

If she read it aloud, maybe Sarah would hear her through the
fug, and that would be that; Olive would have to stick to her word,

and go. Maybe a shock like this was best administered under the residual effects of a sleeping pill? When Olive had received the letter, back in London, she wanted to shout from the skyline what she'd gone and done. Her parents had had no idea – they didn't even know their daughter still painted, let alone that she'd applied to art school. But part of Olive's problem was that she had always been used to secrecy; it was where she was comfortable, the point from which she began to create. It was a pattern she was superstitious to break, and so here she was, in this village in the south of Spain.

As she gazed at her mother's sleeping form, she remembered showing her father a portrait she'd made of Sarah from art class at school. 'Oh, Liv,' he'd said as her heart hammered, the expectation inching up her spine. 'Give it as a present for your mother.'

That was all he'd said on the matter. *A present for your mother.*

Her father always said that of course women could pick up a paintbrush and paint, but the fact was, they didn't make good *artists*. Olive had never quite worked out what the difference was. Since she was a little girl, playing in the corners of his gallery, she would overhear Harold discussing the issue with his clients, both men and women – and often the women would agree with him, preferring to put their money behind young men rather than anyone of their own sex. The artist as naturally male was such a widely held presupposition that Olive had come at times to believe in it herself. As a nineteen-year-old girl, she was on the underside; the dogged, plucky mascot of amateurship. But right now in Paris, Amrita Sher-Gil, Méret Oppenheim and Gabriele Münter were all working – Olive had even seen their pieces with her own eyes. Were *they* not artists? Was the difference between being a workaday painter and being an artist simply other people believing in you, or spending twice as much money on your work?

She found it impossible to express to her parents why she'd applied, the portfolio she'd collated, the essay she'd written on background figures in Bellini. Despite all she'd absorbed about women's shortcomings in art, she'd gone and done it anyway. This was what she couldn't understand; where the urge had come from. And yet, even though an independent life was just within her reach, still she was sitting at the foot of her mother's bed.

Turning again to Sarah, she considered fetching her pastels. Once upon a time, her mother would let Olive parade in her furs, or her strings of pearls, or take her for eclairs at the Connaught, or to hear this violinist or that clever poet perform his work at the Musikverein – always friends of Sarah, and always, Olive had gradually realized as she grew up, in love with her. These days, no one knew what Sarah Schloss might say, or do. She resisted the doctors, and often the pills seemed pointless. Olive felt like she was nothing but a dreg, jetsam in her mother's wake. So she drew her, in secret, in ways that Sarah would probably never forgive.

THE LONG WINDOWS WERE AJAR, and a breeze made the curtains dance. The dawn wind had lifted an impressive cloudscape from the mountains beyond Arazuelo, a duck-egg sky striated gold and pink. The letter still in her hand, Olive tiptoed towards the balcony and saw blank fields spanning towards rugged foothills in the distance, patched with scrub and wild daisies, where kites circled and grasshoppers sawed in the empty melon fields, oxen dragging ploughs across the earth in preparation for later seeding.

Oblivious rabbits hopped across the orchard and far off in the hills goats were being herded, the bells on their necks clanking atonally and out of rhythm, a calming sound because it lacked any conscious performance. A hunter's gun rang out, and birds rose in chaos against the baroque Andalusian morning. Sarah did not stir, but the rabbits scattered, expert hiders, deserting the surface of the waiting earth. Olive closed the windows and the curtains dropped. Her mother probably hoped her long-sought tranquillity was to be found here – but there was a wildness under the tolling convent bell, the chance of wolves in the mountains. The futile yaps of a dog in a barn would puncture every silence. And yet, since their arrival, Olive personally found the landscape and the house itself energizing, in a way that was unfamiliar and wholly unexpected. She had taken an old wood panel that she'd found in the outhouse at the end of the orchard, carrying it up to the attic as if it was contraband. She had treated it in readiness for paint; but it remained blank.

Her father strode into the room, his large foot skidding a *Vogue* under the bed. Olive jammed the letter in her pyjama pocket and spun round to face him. 'How many?' he asked, pointing at the sleeping figure of his wife.

'Don't know,' said Olive. 'But more than normal, I think.'

'*Sheiße.*' Harold only swore in German in moments of great stress or great freedom. He loomed over Sarah and lifted a stray strand of hair delicately off her face. It was a gesture from another time, and it made Olive squeamish.

'Did you get your cigarettes?' she asked him.

'Eh?'

'Your *cigarettes*.' Last night, he'd mentioned needing to get cigarettes from Malaga and visiting an artist's studio – hoping to sniff out another Picasso, he'd said, laughing, as if lightning really did strike in the same place twice. Her father always seemed to slip out of the days like this – bored quickly, yet demanding an audience whenever he turned up again. They'd barely been here two days, and already he was off.

'Oh,' he said. 'Yes. They're in the car.'

Before he left his wife's room, Harold poured his beloved a glass of water and left it by her bedside, just beyond the orbit of her reach.

Downstairs, the shutters were still half-closed and the minimal furniture was in shadow. The air had a tinge of camphor laced with old cigar smoke. The finca could not have been lived in for several years, Olive supposed. A large catacomb above the ground, each of its rooms reticent at her presence, long corridors furnished in colonial habits, dark hardwood cabinets empty of homely objects. It felt like everything was as it had been in the 1890s, and they were characters out of time, surrounded by the discarded props of a drawing-room play.

The vague moisture in the air was already evaporating. Olive threw open the shutters and sunlight bleached the room, a day of exposure but no warmth. The view was an uncultivated slope, which led down to the high wrought-iron fence and onwards, to the beginnings of the village road. She looked out; scraggy bushes and empty flower borders, three fruitless orange trees. Her father had said these mansions were always built outside the villages, near to well-irrigated and lush earth, where in summer, he declared, they would enjoy olive groves and cherry blossom, flower gardens of *dama-de-noche* and jacaranda, fountains and leisure and happiness, happiness.

Olive still had on her winter pyjamas and stockings, and an Aran jumper. The flagstones were so cool, it felt as if rain had just fallen on their large smooth squares. *Just do it*, she thought. *Tell him you've got a place, and go.* If only it was easy to act on thoughts. If only it was easier to know what was the best thing to do.

In the pantry, she discovered a tin of coffee beans and an old but functioning grinder. It was all there was for breakfast, and she and her father decided to drink it on the veranda at the back of the house. Harold went to the room where the telephone was. He had chosen this finca as it was the only one hooked up to a generator, but it was a surprise they had a telephone, and Harold was very pleased.

He was murmuring in German, probably to one of his friends in Vienna. He sounded insistent, but he was too quiet for her to make out the words. When they'd been in London, and he'd had news of what was happening in his home city – the street fights, the hijacked prayer meetings – he would plunge into dark silences. As she ground the beans, Olive thought of her childhood Vienna, the old and the new, the Jewish and the Christian, the educated and the curious, the psyche and the heart. When Harold said it was not safe for them to return, Olive could not quite take this in. In the circles they moved, the violence seemed so distant.

He'd finished his conversation and was sat on the veranda waiting for her, on a tatty green sofa someone had left out in the open air. Over his coat, he was wearing a long spindly scarf that Sarah had knitted, and he was frowning over his correspondence. He always had a knack of making sure that his post would be waiting for him, wherever they landed.

Olive lowered herself into a discarded rocking chair, hesitating for fear damp had weakened the glue, woodworm seeing to the joints. Her father lit a cigarette and placed his silver box on the flaking veranda floor. He sucked on the tobacco leaf, and Olive heard the satisfying crackle as his breath intensified the heat.

'How long do you think we'll be here?' she asked, trying to sound casual.

He looked up from his letters. A thin line of smoke rose straight from the cigarette tip, no breeze up here to shift its journey. The column of ash accumulated, curving downwards and scattering onto the peeling boards. 'Don't tell me you already want to leave.' He raised his dark brows. 'Are you –' here, he sought the particularly English word – '*pining*? Is there someone we left behind in London?'

Olive stared listlessly at the January-thin orchard, briefly wishing that there *was* some chinless Geoffrey, with a white stucco house in South Kensington and a job at the Foreign Office as an under-secretary. But there was no one, and there never had been. She closed her eyes and could almost see the dull metal wink of imaginary cufflinks. 'No. It's just – we're in the middle of nowhere.'

He laid the letter down and regarded her. 'Livvi, what was I supposed to do? I couldn't leave you on your own. Your mother—'

'I could have been left on my own. Or with a friend.'

'You always tell me you don't have any friends.'

'There's – things I want to do.'

'Like what?'

She touched her pyjama pocket. 'Nothing. Nothing important.'

'You never made much of London anyway.'

OLIVE DID NOT REPLY, FOR her eye had been caught by two people standing in the orchard, waiting at the fountain that lay beyond the immediate ribbon of grass that surrounded the house. It was a man and a woman, and they made no effort to hide themselves. The woman was wearing a satchel against her body, and she seemed at one in this garden, the canes in the parched earth the only remnant of the tomatoes, aubergines and lettuces that must have thrived here once, when someone cared.

The man had both his hands stuffed in his pockets, his shoulders hunched, chin down, but the woman stared up at the muscular satyr in the fountain, poised with his empty canton. She closed her eyes, breathing in the air. Olive breathed too, the faint wafts of charcoal fire and fields of sage, the emptiness of this place, its sense of desolation. She wondered if there was a means to get that water flowing.

The couple began to approach the house, both of them with a pace as sure as the mountain goats, avoiding rabbit holes and minor rocks in their seemingly inexorable desire to approach. It jolted Olive, this confidence. She and her father watched them come near, their progress punctuated by the light snap of bracken beneath their feet.

The woman was younger than Olive had thought. Her eyes were dark, her satchel bulky and intriguing. She had a small nose and a little mouth and her skin was burnished like a nut. Her dress was plain black, with long sleeves that buttoned at the wrist. Her hair was also dark, thick and braided into a long plait, but as she turned to look at Harold, strands within it glinted redly in the morning sun.

The man had almost black hair, and was older, probably in his mid-twenties. Olive wondered if they were married. She couldn't take her eyes off him. His face was that of a Tuscan noble, his body a sinewy featherweight boxer's. He was dressed in pressed blue trousers, and an open-necked shirt like those Olive had seen on the men in the fields, although his was pristine and theirs were threadbare. His face was fine-boned, his mouth had an agile facility. His eyes were dark brown, and they grazed Olive's body like a small electrical current. Were these two together? Olive was probably gawping, but she could not look away.

'We bring bread,' the man said in accented English, as his companion fumbled in her satchel and raised a loaf aloft.

Harold clapped his hands with delight. 'Thank God!' he said. 'I'm starving. Hand it over here.'

THE PAIR MOVED TOWARDS THE veranda. Although she was about the same height as the girl, Olive felt much bigger than both of them, and uneasy for it – her arms too long and her head too large, her limbs out of control, giving her away. Why the hell was she still in her pyjamas like a schoolkid?

The girl placed a hand on her own chest. '*Me llamo Teresa Robles*,' she said, pronouncing it in the Spanish way.

'*Me llamo Isaac Robles,*' the man said.

'*Me llamo Olive Schloss.*'

She must be his wife, Olive thought, for why else would he be with her at this time of the morning? The couple laughed, and she felt a flare of rage. Being called 'Olive' in Spain might be funny, but it was hardly the same as being called 'Anchovy', or 'Apricot'. Olive had always been teased for her name: first, as Popeye's woman; then as an adolescent, a cocktail nibble. Now, on the cusp of freedom, she was being laughed at for being the fruit upon the Spanish tree.

'Harold Schloss.' Her father shook hands with both of them, and Teresa handed him the bread. He beamed at it, as if it was a bar of gold and Teresa one of the Magi. 'I'm her father,' he added, which Olive felt unnecessary. Teresa knelt down, and with the careless precision of a magician, she produced from her satchel a strong-smelling hard sheep's cheese laced with sprigs of rosemary, a cured sausage, three small quinces and several enormous lemons. She placed each fruit with a flourish on the scarred wood, where they glowed like planets, a solar system in which she momentarily became the sun.

'Having a picnic without me?'

Sarah had appeared at the kitchen door, shivering in her silk pyjamas, wearing one of Harold's flying jackets and a pair of his thickest hunting socks. Even haggard from a bad night's sleep and the champagne they'd picked up in Paris, she looked like an off-duty movie star.

Olive saw the familiar reaction; Teresa blinked, dazzled by the bright blonde hair, the air of glamour that clung to Sarah wherever she went. Isaac knelt and plunged his fingers into the satchel. Something living appeared to be at the bottom, and it stirred, and the satchel began to move of its own accord.

'Jesus!' Olive cried.

'Don't be a coward,' said Sarah.

Teresa caught Olive's eye, and smiled, and Olive felt furious to be so publicly humiliated. Isaac pulled out a live chicken, its loose feathers floating to the floor, scaly feet dangling comically in his grip. The bird's reptilian eye swivelled; fear twitched in its toes, tensing into claws. With his left hand, Isaac kept it still on the floorboards. It was making a muffled cluck, straining for the cool of its mistress's bag. Slowly, Isaac placed his right hand on the back of the bird's head, and cooing quietly, he tightened his grip. With a determined twist, he broke the chicken's neck.

The bird slumped onto Isaac's palm like a stuffed sock, and as he took his hand away and rested the creature on the veranda, Olive made sure he saw her look down at the drying bead of its eye.

'You will eat today,' Teresa said, directly to Olive. Olive couldn't tell if this was an offering or an order.

'I've never seen anything like it so up *close*,' said Sarah. She gave the newcomers a radiant smile. 'I'm Sarah Schloss. So who are you two, then?'

'It's just a bloody chicken,' Olive snapped, her heart contracting as Isaac Robles laughed again.

II

$\mathcal{T}$eresa watched the group move indoors as she collected her offerings from the veranda. She hadn't wanted to come; it looked so obvious to her, so needy. *There's another rich* guiri *turned up with his wife and daughter*, Isaac had said. *You should see the car, the travelling trunks. There's a gramophone roped to the roof.* 'Who is he?' she'd asked her brother, but neither he nor anyone in the village knew. All that was clear was that a week ago, the duchess's old finca had finally got some new inhabitants.

It was not that unusual for wealthy foreigners to come to this corner of southern Spain, bringing their industrial inheritances and discontentments with city life. Indeed, Teresa had worked for two sets of them before. They came down via Paris or Toulouse, Madrid or Barcelona, laden with boxes of paints and novels – and typewriters to write their own novels – and initialled trunks, which sometimes fell onto the road because of their clumsiness with the local mules. They were bohemian millionaires, or, more commonly, the bohemian children of millionaires, from Texas, Berlin, or London, wanting to dip their brush and dissolve in the sierra like one of their barely used watercolour squares. They arrived, they lived for a bit, and most of them departed.

Teresa could see out of the corner of her eye that Olive had not gone inside. The toes of her woollen socks had been inexpertly darned, which Teresa thought was a shame. People like this should dress better. Olive came towards her and knelt down. 'I'll help you,' she said – in halting Spanish, which was surprising. Under the girl's fingernails were crescent moons of vivid green paint. Her bob haircut needed a trim – untamed, it coped her head like the cap of a wide mushroom. When Olive smiled, Teresa was struck by how Sarah's features had been repeated in her daughter's face, but it was as if they had missed a beat and become a jarring echo.

'I'm still in my pyjamas,' Olive said, and Teresa did not know how to reply. That much was obvious, wasn't it? She picked up the floppy chicken and shunted it into the satchel.

'It's beautiful here,' Olive went on, weighing one of the lemons in her palm. 'My Baedeker says North Africa isn't far. *"The Catholic kings wrenched this land from the Moorish Caliphates. Crucifying heat in the summer, and skin-peeling cold in the winter, enormous night-time skies all year round"*. I memorized it.'

She seemed jumpy. Teresa had watched the girl when Sarah had called her a coward; she'd looked as if she had the words to fight back, but was keeping every single one locked inside her skull. There was an urgency in Olive's body, in the movements of her hands. She reminded Teresa of a trapped animal, restless because someone had approached the bars of her cage.

'So,' Olive said, in Spanish again. 'How long have you been married?'

Teresa stared at her. 'Married?'

Olive frowned. *'Casados* – that's right, isn't it?'

Teresa laughed. 'Isaac is my brother,' she said, now in English. She saw the blush spread over Olive's face as she pulled a loose thread of wool from her jumper.

'Oh,' said Olive. 'I thought—'

'No. We have – we had – different mothers.'

'Ah.' Olive seemed to gather herself. 'Your English is very good.'

Teresa removed the lemon gently from Olive's grip, and Olive gazed in surprise at the fruit, as if she had no recollection of taking it up.

'There was an American lady in Esquinas. I worked for her,' Teresa said. She decided not to mention the German family she had also worked for, who, before returning to Berlin merely months before, had given her a rudimentary facility in German. Life had taught her that it was wiser not to play all your cards at once. 'Her name was Miss Banetti. She did not speak my language.'

Olive seemed to awaken. 'Is that why you're here today – you want to work for us? What does your brother do?'

Teresa crossed the veranda and stared out at the skeleton trees in the orchard. 'Our father is Don Alfonso. He works for the woman who owns the land and this house.'

'Is it really owned by a duchess?'

'Yes. Her family is very old.'

'She can't have been in this finca for a long time. The dust! Oh – but I'm not saying it's your fault—'

'*La duquesa* is never here,' said Teresa. 'She lives in Barcelona and Paris and New York. There is nothing for her to do here.'

'I'm sure *that's* not true,' Olive replied.

'You are English or American?'

'Half English. My father's from Vienna. He married my mother, who's English, but thinks she was born on Sunset Boulevard. We've lived in London for the last few years.'

'Sunset Boulevard?'

'Never mind . . . so – you're from Arazuelo?'

'Will you stay long?' Teresa asked.

'That's up to my father.'

'How old are you?'

'Nineteen,' Olive replied, and when she caught Teresa's frown she went on, 'I know. It's a long story. But my mother's not well.'

'She looks well.'

'It's deceptive.'

Teresa's skin prickled at the hard edge that had crept into Olive's tone. She wondered what was wrong with the beautiful, brittle woman in the oversized jacket. 'You will need someone here, señorita,' she said. 'This is not London. You cook?'

'No.'

'Clean?'

'No.'

'You ride a horse?'

'No!'

'I will help.'

'Well, how old are *you*?'

'Eighteen,' Teresa lied, for in truth, she was sixteen years old. She had learned that foreigners often had a romantic, infantilizing attitude to age, keeping their children as children much longer. This girl was clearly a case in point. Teresa herself had never had such a luxury; sometimes she felt as old as stone. 'My brother—' she began, but stopped. She didn't feel like talking about Isaac any more than was necessary. From her pocket, she brought out three envelopes. '*Tomate, perejíl, cebolla*,' she said in Spanish.

'Tomato, parsley, onion?' Olive said.

Teresa nodded. She had not intended these seeds as a gift. She had in fact brought them to the finca in the hope that she could quietly sow them in the duchess's more fertile soil, and ultimately harvest them for herself. 'They are for you,' she said to the other girl. Teresa had never, in sixteen years, given anyone a present.

Olive looked over her shoulder into the dark of the house. From deep within could be heard Sarah's laughter, and the lower bass of the men. 'Let's plant them,' she said.

'Now?'

'Now.'

From the outhouse at the end of the orchard, Olive found two rusting garden forks and handed one to Teresa. Teresa was struck by the other girl's readiness to be here with her, turning over hard earth, weeding as she went. She didn't want to be so happy about it, but she couldn't help herself. Surely it was rare that a girl like Olive might choose to be here, rather than with those inside? When she protested that Olive should put on some boots over those socks, Olive looked down at her feet in surprise. 'Oh, I don't mind,' she said, wiggling her darned toes. 'I like the feeling of the ground.'

Teresa thought that only a rich *guiri*, with more pairs of socks than sense, would ever say such a thing. Miss Banetti, who'd also come for the rustic life, might have said it and appeared an imbecile. But there was something different about Olive, her thoughtless determination, her acceptance that was so whole-hearted, that Teresa not only forgave the girl her whim, but was delighted that she had no care for shoes.

Olive rolled up her sleeves and lugged two huge watering cans of spring water from the well at the end of the garden, and Teresa admired the sinews in her forearms, their pale endurance, the fact that nothing was lost along the way. Up and down the newly furrowed earth they walked with the cans, and as the water fell, Teresa spied a rainbow arching in the drops. If Olive felt the hard soil poking into her soles, she said nothing.

III

Harold invited Teresa to start by cleaning the ground-floor rooms, sweeping away the cobwebs that draped from corner to corner. Using rags ripped from a man's shirt, dipping them in a bowl of vinegar and some of her lemon juice, she scrubbed the windows where dirt had layered round the frames. From the garden, she burned rosemary and sage on the flagstones. In a cupboard in the pantry Isaac found two electric heaters and set them up in the front east room, warming up the bare chalk walls as the sunlight moved over them. He promised them firewood.

Teresa made the Schlosses lunch from the chicken, refusing to eat it with them, although Isaac accepted the offer. By the time the chicken was out of the stove, it was clear to Olive that they had a new servant. But what of Isaac – under what pretence could they keep him near?

The clock in the hall dragged its pendulum four times. 'God!' Sarah said, as they sat at the dining-room table. Her mood was excitable, a great improvement on the day before, but not without its dangers. 'Where's the day gone? It's so cold – I thought the south of Spain was supposed to be hot?' She'd changed into a long-sleeved cream house jacket covering new red woollen trousers, and a blouse in matching scarlet polka dots. At some point she'd painted her toenails, and Olive saw ten small squares of vermilion on the terracotta floor.

'It will get hotter,' Harold said.

From the kitchen, Teresa clanged the tin plates on the draining board, a noise like an armoury.

'Oh well then, I shall fetch my bathing suit,' said Sarah. 'Have you ever been to London, Mr Robles?' she asked, turning to where he sat on her left, pouring coffee into his small white cup. 'Do you smoke? Would you like an almond?'

'Yes, I do. And no – thank you.'

'Please, have one of mine. Harold snaffled some in Malaga. He'll only smoke German ones, so that's all we've got.' Sarah fiddled with the box on the table and pulled out a cigarette; her wrists were burdened with bangles, and they clinked together. Isaac removed the cigarette from her proffered fingers and lit it himself.

'I have not been to London,' he said, weighing the city's name with something like awe. London in calligraphic letters, Henry VIII, the Tower, Middle Temple. Olive's London was not like that – it was a lonely walk through St James's and along the Mall to the National Portrait Gallery to see her favourite Holbein; a penny bun at Lyon's on Craven Street after, or a stroll through Embankment Gardens. That was what she missed – certainly not the other London, the stifling cocktail chit-chat, women's over-rosied flesh, the lemon tang of Trumper's wet shaves fresh on older men; red acne rashes of boys down from Oxford, with nothing much to say.

'London's all right, I suppose,' Olive said, intending to sound jokily arch. 'The people can be ghastly.' Her mother flashed her a look.

'I have been to Barcelona many times,' Isaac said. 'And Madrid.'

Olive thought of their travelling trunks upstairs, the wooden brackets shiny from handling by so many porters, labels from Paris and Buenos Aires, Marseilles, New York; peeling like old skins the Schlosses had shed. She could barely remember any of it now, and nineteen felt like ninety.

'But you have you always lived in Arazuelo?' Harold asked him.

'Yes. I am a teacher in Malaga.'

'What do you teach?' Sarah asked.

'Lithography,' he said. 'At the San Telmo School of Art.' Olive stared hard at her plate.

'Harold's an art dealer,' Sarah went on. 'Kokoschka, Kirchner, Klimt, Klee – all his. I swear he only sells artists whose surnames start with a K.'

'I admire Kokoschka,' Isaac said, and Olive sensed her father become alert.

'Herr Kokoschka painted blue fir trees in Olive's nursery in Vienna,' Sarah said. 'Mr Robles, your English is excellent.'

'Thank you, señora. I taught myself,' he said. 'I have English acquaintances in Malaga, and I practise with Teresa.'

'Do you paint, or only print?' asked Harold.

Robles hesitated. 'I paint a little, señor.'

'You should bring me some of your work.'

Generally, Harold was allergic to people who said they painted. Whenever a hopeful artist got wind that Harold was a dealer, they always misjudged it. Sometimes, they displayed aggression, as if Harold was withholding something to which they were specifically entitled – or they offered a simpering humility that fooled no one. But here was Herr Schloss, asking this young man for his work. Olive was used to how it was when Harold's attention was caught – how he would dog, cajole, flatter, act the father, act the pal – whatever it took, hoping he would be the one to uncover next year's genius. It always hurt.

'What I paint would not interest you, señor,' said Isaac, smiling.

Harold tipped up the pitcher and poured himself a glass of water. 'Let me be the judge of that.'

Isaac looked serious. 'If I have the time, I will show you.'

'The time?' said Harold. Olive's skin tingled.

'When I am not at San Telmo, I am occupied with the workers' union in Malaga. I teach them how to read and write.'

There was a pause. 'Does your father know you're a red?' Sarah asked.

Isaac smiled again. 'I am twenty-six, señora. I do as I must. I supported the workers' strikes. I travelled to Asturias to help the miners. But I am not a red.'

'Shame. That would have been exciting.'

Olive sat on her hands, staring at her mother. Sarah's entire life was predicated on the docility of the workers who propped up her family's famous condiment business. She saw herself as a free spirit, but it was the work of her great-grandfather – starting with his barrel of oranges in Covent Garden and ending up an industrialist with a seat in the Lords – that paid for their travel, the flat in Curzon Street, the cottage in Sussex, the house off the Ringstrasse, the Schiaparelli dresses. Harold's business was certainly successful, but Sarah's inheritance underwrote the lot.

'You are who you are because of the very people you would never deign to consort with,' Harold had once shouted at Sarah, after an evening when she hadn't come home and he'd had to call the police. Sarah, who had in fact passed out on her host's chaise longue and couldn't be roused till the morning, had shouted back that he didn't have a leg to stand on, because he too benefited directly from the family's Finest Cut Marmalade, so he could shut his mouth, unless he fancied finding himself a proper job and a flat in Camden.

'My father and I do not often agree,' Isaac was saying. 'He works for the duchess. All this land is hers. She is eighty-five years old and she won't die.'

'I'm going to be like that,' said Sarah, and they all laughed.

'The people who work her land – how do you say in English? – *tienen un gran hambre—*'

'They're starving,' said Olive.

Isaac looked at her in surprise, and again Olive felt the current that ran through her, the thrill of his attention. 'Yes,' he said. 'Thousands. Across the region.'

'How terrible,' said Sarah.

Olive willed Isaac to look at her again, but he leaned forward and spoke to her mother. '*La duquesa*'s men will give you a job, if you promise to vote for her family and keep her powerful. The poor beg to work her land, for almost nothing, because that is all the work. But she does not remember them if their wife dies, or if their mother is sick. If *they* are sick. She only shows her face during the time of election.'

Teresa appeared at the door of the dining room, and stood with her arms crossed. Her hair had frizzed from the kitchen's steam, her apron covered in bloodied smears. Isaac looked up, seeming to hesitate. Olive noticed Teresa almost imperceptibly shake her head, as Isaac blinked away her warning and barrelled on.

'My father finds her men to work her land,' he said, 'but he only picks the young men, the strong men, not the older ones with families. So more people are starving. And there is no rule on the price for your work here, so *la duquesa* pays you nearly nothing. We tried to change that in the last election, but it has been changed again. And if you complain about how little you get of the harvest – or how bad condition is your house – *la duquesa* and her people will hear. You will not work.'

'But the church must help them,' said Harold.

'Shall I tell you a secret? They say that our Padre Lorenzo has a lover in the village of Esquinas.'

Sarah laughed. 'It's always the priest what done it.'

Isaac shrugged. 'They say Padre Lorenzo wants to make private the fields between the church and the house of his lover, so no one can see him when he makes the journey.'

'Is that a joke?' asked Sarah.

'Who knows, señora? Padre Lorenzo is the cousin of the duchess. He has more interest in territory maps than prayer books.' He sighed, tapping the ash of his cigarette into the ashtray. 'We had a vision. Land, church, army, education, labour – all to change. But we are – how do you say it? *Cogidos?*'

'Caught,' said Olive, and Isaac looked at her again. She blushed. 'You're caught.' She turned away, unable any longer to meet his eye.

'Mr Robles isn't *caught*,' Sarah said. 'He speaks English. He's been to Madrid.'

Isaac inhaled sharply on his cigarette. 'Action may be the only answer, señora. We need the tyranny gone.'

'Tyranny?' said Sarah. 'What tyranny?'

'Most people here are just trying to plant their cabbages and eat them in peace,' said Isaac. 'But many of the children in Arazuelo do not even go to school because they are working in the fields. They need to know who's pulling the sheep over their eyes.'

'Wool,' said Harold. He'd barely spoken, and they all looked at him as he reached into his pocket for his lighter and dipped his head to ignite his cigarette. 'The word you mean is *wool*.' Being Viennese, he pronounced it *voohl*.

'Are you planning a revolution, Mr Robles?' asked Sarah. 'Perhaps we should call you Lenin.'

He held up his hands in surrender, laughing as he glanced at Olive once again. She could barely cope; he was looking at her this time because he wanted to, and she felt as if her head might be on fire. He was the most beautiful man she had ever seen. 'You will see, señores,' Isaac said. 'You are new here, but you will see.'

'*Are* you a communist?' Harold asked.

'No. I am a member of the Republican Union party. And the poverty in our region is visible, it is not in my imagination. Mud huts, ten or eleven children inside them, men asleep on the fields.'

'Isaac—' said Teresa, but he interrupted her.

'It is not just the poor – small farmers, they live on the land, they improve it for the owners – and then they are charged a high rent because they have made the land so productive, that they can no longer afford it. Their labour counts for nothing—'

'You should be careful when you talk about "tyranny", Mr Robles,' Harold said. 'If you insist on being a revolutionary, you will make the people with means to support you fly to the arms of a fascist.'

Isaac lowered his eyes. 'But the people with the means to support us will never support us. I believe there is a way to universal happiness.'

'The coercive redistribution of wealth,' said Harold, looking grim.

'Yes, that will do it. The people—'

'Nothing destroys a country's sense of balance more than the word *coercive*, Mr Robles. But look,' he beamed, 'we are destroying your sister's lunch.'

Teresa stared at her brother. Olive thought of the thin wraiths they'd seen in the fields on their way here, stopping their work to stare at the car like it was a vehicle from a land of fantasy. 'Mr Robles is right,' she said. 'I saw it.'

'Oh, not you too, Liv,' said Harold. 'Not after all those bloody school fees.'

Olive looked to Isaac, and he smiled.

Late that night, after Isaac and Teresa had left, with promises to return in a couple of days with firewood, Olive went up to her bedroom in the attic and locked the door. *Union, onion*; this brother and sister had come with their words and their seeds and Olive had never seen their like. Had she and her parents let them in, or had they simply entered, sensing a weakness in the fortifications? No one was like this in Mayfair, or Vienna; you left calling cards, not chicken carcasses. You spoke of the poor with pity, not anger. You did not plough your own land.

Blood alive, head singing from the way Isaac had looked at her, Olive grasped her easel, pulling open its three legs and fastening them tight. She found the wooden panel she had taken from the outhouse, and placed it on the easel. She opened her window to let in the moon, lit the oil lanterns and switched on the electric light beside her bed. She knelt before her travelling trunk like a pilgrim at an altar, and ran her fingers over the paint tubes hidden under the cottons. As she pulled them out, Olive felt a familiar connection, as if her heart was slotting into place, a moment to breathe. Not one of her colours had burst in transit, all her powders intact, the sticks of pastels not cracked in half. They had always been loyal to her, when everything else was falling out of place.

Moths hurled themselves at the bulbs as she worked, but she paid no mind. For the first time in a long time, all else was eclipsed by a purer sense of purpose and the image that was emerging on the old wooden board. It was a view from the bottom of the orchard, in exaggerated colours, the finca behind it, its peeled red paintwork on every window. It had its feet in the earth, but the sky above was enormous and swirling, with a hint of angelic, silver-grey. The scale of the house made it look smaller in the painting, the trees in the foreground laden with such fruit that in reality was not there.

You could just about call it figurative, but it was not realistic. It had a new form of surreality Olive had never executed before. For all its grounded colours on the fields – ochres and grasshopper-greens, the folkloric tenderness of russet furrows and mustard browns – there was something other-worldly about the scene. The sky was a boon of promise. The fields were a cornucopia of cereal crops and apples, olives and oranges. The orchard was so lush you might call it a jungle, and the empty fountain had turned into a living spring, the satyr's canton now gushing full of water. The finca rose up like a welcoming palace, her father's house with many mansions, its windows huge and open to her gaze. The brush strokes were loose, and colour dominated technical accuracy.

Olive fell asleep beside it at four in the morning. The next day, she stood before the painting as the sun cracked low along the sky beyond her window. She never knew she was capable of such work. She had made, for the first time, a picture of such movement and excess and fecundity that she felt almost shocked. It was a stubborn ideal; a paradise on earth, and the irony was it had only come from this place, this lonely part of Spain to which her parents had dragged her.

Stiffly, Olive moved to the trunk where the letter from the art school was hidden. She pulled it out, read it, smoothed it, folded it neatly, and kissed it, placing it back at the bottom of the trunk, buried deep and out of sight.

IV

*L*ast year,' Isaac said, in English, 'I meet a man waiting for my train at Barcelona station. A journalist. We talk. He tells me, "It is coming. It has happened before and it is going to happen again."'

'What's happened before?' Olive asked. She was standing with Isaac in the orchard, helping gather the chopped wood as he sliced it in half with his axe. She turned briefly towards the house, and saw a shadow move behind the lace curtains of her mother's room. To hell with her; this was Olive's time with him. Sarah always wanted to be the centre of attention, and was very good at it, but Olive loved these stolen moments in Isaac's company.

Out of the corner of her eye she watched his shirt lift, and saw the flash of dark brown flesh, a trail of hair leading away. She felt such pleasure when he handed her the split pieces of wood, as if he were offering her a bouquet. From a decade of devouring novels, Olive knew that charming men were deadly. Their story had been played down the centuries, unharmed through the pages, whilst girls were blamed and girls were lost, or girls were garlanded, mute as statues. Be Vigilant and Prize Your Virginity was a subtitle many of these stories could have taken, most of them written by men. Olive knew all this and she didn't care. She didn't give a damn.

He had been coming to the house with less regularity than Teresa, partly because of his job in Malaga, and partly because he did not have as much of an excuse. It pleased Olive so much to see that their piles of firewood were probably the highest for several miles. If he wanted to tell her about the state of his country, she was more than happy to listen.

He had not noticed her new hairstyle, the gobs of her mother's pomade she had applied, to try and make it smooth and slick. These were not the sort of things a serious-minded man might notice, of course, Olive supposed. Not when his country was in a state of unrest. Not when he was thinking of the people. She decided that to make the most of her time with him, it would pay to be more politically aware.

'What happened before? Chapel tombs smashed open, the corpses of nuns on the ground,' said Isaac. 'Houses like this one, robbed.' They both turned back to look at the finca, and the figure at the curtains dipped rapidly away. 'They say a priest was taken from his sacristy and left hanging on a tree, found next morning with his balls in his mouth.'

'Isaac!' Olive cringed. The word *balls* made her nervous, and she felt childish.

'The newspapers make it seem worse than it is – but they never ask the question as to why the looting happens in the first place. So, this journalist.'

'Yes?'

'He starts talking to me about a polar bear.'

'A *polar bear*?'

'Yes. He tells me he interviewed a duke in his house,' Isaac said, laying the wood blocks on her open hands. Olive saw how the tips of her fingers were stained red. She hadn't stopped painting since meeting him. She was working on smaller canvases, filling notebooks with sketches; it was as if she had plugged herself in – to what, exactly, she wasn't entirely sure – and although she was terrified that this long seam of inspiration was going to end, she felt that as long as Isaac was close, and that she was ready for it, for him, her output might continue.

She knew that by staying down here, she had avoided a confrontation about her true self – no art-school confession with her father was required. And yet, she was happier than she'd been in a long time.

'He told me the duke had a polar bear in his drawing room,' Isaac went on. '*Lo había cazado?*'

'He'd hunted it down.'

'Yes. With a gun.'

Olive curled her fingers up, hoping he might comment on their dyed appearance, so she could say, *Oh, I paint a bit too. Would you like to see?* He would come and see the painting and reply, *This is extraordinary, you are extraordinary. How did I not see?* And then they would kiss, him taking her face in his hands, bending down to brush his lips on hers, full of astonishment at how good she was. She so desperately wanted him to see how good she was.

But Isaac did not notice her fingers, and so Olive turned instead to the anomalous polar bear in her mind's eye, a piece of the Arctic, a grotesquery in the Spanish heat, the barbarity and expense of it, the chill in the heart of the home. 'Why did you tell me about that priest?' she asked, trying to assert herself. 'Were you trying to frighten me?'

'No. I want you to see what's happening here. So when you go home, you will tell other people.'

'I'm not going home, Isaac.'

She waited for him to express his pleasure, but he did not. 'Isaac, you do know I'm not like my parents, don't you?' she said.

'What do you mean?'

'They're frightened of things. I'm not.'

She only wanted to communicate that whatever he thought *they* were, she was the opposite. She didn't see things in black and white, like they did. She was nothing like them at all. It felt very important that he should know this.

'There's a gypsy camp, out in the hills,' he said, as if he hadn't heard her. 'They lost one of their boys. Not *lost*,' he corrected himself. 'They didn't lose him. He was beaten by a gang of men. He was twelve. He died.'

'How awful.'

Isaac put down the axe and walked towards a slope at the end of the orchard. '*Ven aquí*,' he said. *Come here*. Together, they surveyed the land before them. A couple of far-off buzzards wheeled in the sky in search of prey along the ground. The skies were so large, the mountains beyond so solid; it seemed the only violence possible here was the violence of the natural world.

'It'll be all right,' Olive whispered. She imagined slipping her hand into his, the two of them, standing here for ever.

His face was hard. 'The people hold this soil in their blood. That is why the landlords fear them.' He paused. 'I worry for my sister.'

Olive was surprised by this. 'Teresa? She'll be fine.'

At the beginning, Teresa had come every other day to clean and cook. Now she was coming daily. The house still had its dark corners, and its sense of absent occupancy, but it had benefited from her quiet and watchful presence. She never said much, just going about her business through the rooms, taking the weekly envelope of pesetas from Harold with a nod.

'Teresa is not married,' said Isaac. 'She is not rich. She is nothing that fits.'

'What do you mean?'

'She's the daughter of a gypsy—'

'A *gypsy*? How romantic.'

He raised his eyebrow. 'And the sister of a socialist. I do not know which is worse for her.'

'Why?'

'The police, the mayor, the *caciques*. My own father. They do not like me. I've been in fights. And she is too close—'

'Isaac, don't worry,' Olive said, attempting a tone of mature assurance. 'We'll look after her.'

Isaac laughed. 'Until you leave.'

'I *told* you. I'm never going to leave.'

'What do you want from this life, señorita?'

'I – I don't know exactly. I know I'd like to stay here.'

Isaac looked as if he was going to say something, and her whole body willed him to say how glad he was to hear this – but he was interrupted by the sound of crunching leaves. Teresa appeared at the bottom of the slope, her satchel strapped across her body, a flat expression in her eyes. *'La señora te necesita,'* she said to Isaac.

'Why?' said Olive. 'Why does my mother want him?'

Teresa and her brother stared at each other, until eventually Isaac capitulated, sighing as he moved back down the slope, not saying another word.

AS ISAAC MOVED THROUGH THE trees, Teresa imagined for a moment that she and Olive were hunters together, watching their prey before deciding to let it go, preferring instead to stand side by side in the cold air. It was not the thrill of the kill they wanted, but simply the companionship that came from sharing a mutual target.

Isaac was fond of saying that Teresa was the kind of girl who'd sell her grandmother if she had to, not that she'd ever had a grandmother to sell. The worst thing was, Teresa sometimes *did* feel a sort of icy indifference to those around her, who'd never helped her, making it clear that she wasn't worth the bother. She looked over at the furrows she and Olive had made with the gardening forks. The seeds were still deep in the soil, and would not show green shoots for months. Teresa was relieved that she had wanted to hand Olive those seeds. Olive somehow reminded her that she was still capable of feeling something akin to happiness.

'Let's go and smoke on the veranda,' said Olive. 'I stole three of my father's cigarettes.'

ONLY OLIVE SMOKED. FROM ABOVE them inside the house, came the sound of a slamming door. 'Do sit,' she said to Teresa, but only after Harold's motor car had revved down to the rusting gates at the bottom of the slope did Teresa obey. 'That's Daddy out again,' Olive said.

'Will your mother see us? I must work.'

'You don't have to work every minute of the day, Tere. They won't get rid of you for sitting down for five minutes. And besides.' Olive lit the cigarette and took an inexpert drag. 'She's talking to your brother.'

Teresa had seen the empty pill bottles in Sarah's room, the indecipherable stretch of words around the small brown vials. She'd heard Sarah sobbing once, trying to bury the sound in her pillow, and had seen a flash of silvery white scars running down in crisscross lines at the top of her legs. Surmising from the stolen cigarettes that Olive was in a more reckless mood than the last time she'd brought this up, Teresa asked, 'Is your mother very sick?'

'She's a depressive.' Olive sat back in the rocking chair, blowing out a funnel of blue smoke.

'A *depressive*?'

'Smiles in ballrooms, weeps in bedrooms. Ill, in her head.' Olive tapped her temple. 'And here.' She touched her heart. 'She gets worse, gets better. Gets worse again.'

'That is hard,' Teresa said, surprised by the other girl's frankness.

Olive turned to look at her. 'Do you mean that, or are you just saying it?'

'No, señorita. I mean it.' And Teresa did mean it; but really her wish was for Olive to confide in her about everything, and she would say what she had to, in order to make it so. Olive looked out at the orchard. To Teresa, she seemed more at ease in her skin. Her clothes, unusual and boyish, suited her; even her untameable crown of hair seemed intrinsically to fit. Being here in Arazuelo seemed to have brought her out of herself.

'It is hard,' said Olive. 'Daddy calls them her "storm clouds", but that's just a nice way of saying that she drags us around. The doctor says her mind's like honeycomb, chamber upon chamber, broken, rebuilt again. She sees her pain in colours, you know. Steel Blue, Yellowed Bruise, German Measles Red.' Olive gave a grim laugh, and

Teresa tried to process the language. 'It's an illness we've always had in her side of the family. I've got a great-grandmother buried in an unconsecrated grave, an aunt – whom no one speaks of – locked in an asylum. Then there's a cousin, Johnny; he hated boarding school, and tried to drown himself in the Ouse. It's wretched really, and I'm so selfish, I just worry I'm next.'

Teresa could hear the snag of Olive's breath in her throat, before she inhaled deeply again on her father's cigarette. 'I can feel it sometimes, in my bones – just how easy it might be to catch it off her.' Olive turned to her. 'Do you think you can catch it, Tere?'

Worry flickered over Olive's face, the spray of freckles over her nose, her dark brown eyes, her mouth ajar. 'I do not think you will be mad,' she said, and Olive laughed and nudged her, and the touch of her shoulder on Teresa was shocking.

'Well, that's that, then. If you don't think I'll be mad, I won't be. Just my mother.' Olive paused. 'Do you think she's beautiful?'

'Yes.'

'Of course. I think she's a sex maniac.' Olive laughed, but the sound died quickly, because the description had the vague air of medical viability and seemed less funny than she might have wanted. The girls sat in silence for a while, watching the kites circle in the distance. Teresa wanted only that time might cease, that this view, and this strange, confiding peace, be all that existed. To have a friend like this would be to own the world.

'I should be engaged to be married by now,' Olive said.

'There is a man?'

'Oh, no. No. It's just – most of the girls I know in London – I wouldn't call them *friends* – are "taken" now. I'm not. But whenever I see their engagement rings, I feel sad. They're so eager to run away, change their names. It's all so *uniform*. Maybe they all like being the same as each other.'

Olive seemed to be talking to herself now, and Teresa was failing to manage the unstoppered bottle that was Olive's English, pouring out words and words that seemed to have been waiting inside a long time.

'And the fiancés!' Olive said. She hooted ferociously. 'They're so peripheral. Do you know what "peripheral" means?'

'No.'

'On the outside. Not important. They've got interchangeable names, like Philip and Ernest and David. Just one floating face, of a man with no discernible chin. When I said I wouldn't get married, one of these girls said to me, "You wouldn't *understand*, Olive. You've been to Paris – I haven't made it past Portsmouth." Imagine being so idiotic! Imagine thinking being a married woman is the same as travel!'

'Perhaps it is?'

Olive glanced at her. 'Well, there are plenty of miserable wives in Paris. Some of them are my parents' friends. One of them's my own mother.'

'Yes?'

'Marriage is a game of survival,' Olive said, and it sounded as if she had heard this somewhere else, before repeating it herself.

'How did your parents meet?'

'A party. Paris. Mother was seventeen. "An English nettle" – her words. Daddy was twenty-two. It was a bit shocking, her becoming engaged to a Viennese Jew. Her family took a while to accept it, but then they loved him.'

Teresa nodded, thinking this a simplification. Harold was not easily loveable, she thought. He reminded her of a beetle, deep within the wood and plaster of the finca's walls. He needed his hard wings to be kept shiny, his antlers polished with a soft cloth, his body buffed and fed so he didn't bite.

'He was interned during the war,' Olive said. 'They let him out and he worked for the British government. He never talks about that. He represented everything Mummy's life didn't, I suppose. She gets bored so easily, and likes to cause a stir. Condiment Heiress, Cocaine Flapper, Rebel with Hun Groom. It's all so garish,' she added, and although Teresa did not understand the adjective, she could taste its jealousy.

'It's astonishing,' Olive continued, 'how easily she can hoodwink other people that she's whole, when inside she's spiralling, as broken as a shattered pot. I sometimes wonder whether we could have had a stable life – Daddy, walking daily to the Foreign Office – bowler hat, club on St James's, mother at home doing embroidery. I doubt it. Don't you doubt it?'

Teresa didn't know what to say to this fizzing girl, with her plaintive, open face. The Schlosses were so short-handed with each other, that it usually neutralized any depth of reference to their past lives. They were actors in costume, in the moment, performing through the house as if it were a theatre stage and Teresa their sole audience. She desperately wanted to see what happened when they took off their robes and walked into the wings, the darker corners where memories shifted. Olive had now lifted the curtain a little, and shown her the shapes and patterns beyond. Teresa worried that to say something wrong would make that curtain drop again, and break the spell of their solicitude.

'Do you think you'll marry?' Olive said, in the face of the other girl's silence.

'No,' Teresa said, and she felt that this was true.

'If I do, it will be for love, and not just to annoy my parents, like my mother did. Do you think Isaac will marry?'

'I do not know.'

Olive grinned. 'If he does, you'll be alone in your cottage. You'll have to come and live with me and my husband. I wouldn't want you to be lonely.'

'Your husband?'

'Let's call him . . . Boris. Boris Mon-Amour.' Olive laughed and kicked her heels. 'Oh, Boris,' she shouted, opening her arms to the sky. 'Come to me, take me!' Breathless, she turned to Teresa and beamed. 'I haven't felt like this in ages.'

'What do you feel?' said Teresa.

'Happy.'

Teresa drank in the image of this girl, in her Aran jumper and old brown shoes, who didn't want her to be lonely, who had a foolish imaginary lover called Boris, and who had come to the ends of

Spain to discover she was happy. And then she noticed the dried blood, crusted under Olive's fingernails, and she remembered the axe, and Olive out here with her brother, and panic rose. She grabbed Olive's hand.

'What is it?' Olive looked shocked by the contact, and stopped her rocking.

'Your fingers.'

Olive stared down at her rust-coloured nails trapped in Teresa's little paw. 'I'm fine.'

'It's blood. Did he—'

'Did he what? It's not blood, Teresa.' Olive hesitated. 'It's paint.'

'You are in pain?'

'Not pain, *paint*. I didn't clean up properly.'

'I do not understand.'

Olive considered. 'Teresa, if I told you something, would you promise to keep it to yourself?'

It was a risky question, riddled with unknowns, but the alternative was being shut away from Olive, and that was something Teresa could not countenance. 'Of course,' she said.

Olive held up her little finger. 'Put your finger round mine. Do you swear?'

Teresa linked her own with Olive's, feeling the intensity of Olive's gaze. '*Lo juro*,' she whispered. 'I swear.'

Olive reached out and crossed her fingers over Teresa's heart, and Teresa, as if under a spell, lifted her hand and marked Olive with the same gesture, the heat of the other girl's skin coming through her woollen jumper.

'Good,' Olive said, standing up and pulling Teresa to her feet. From inside the house, they heard Sarah's laughter. 'Come on, follow me.'

V

*A*s he sat with Sarah in the front east room, Isaac's gaze flicked up to the ceiling. The room above their heads was the place, eleven years ago, where he'd lost his virginity. His father had just taken the job of estate manager for the duchess, and the finca had been unoccupied. Isaac had stolen the keys from his father's office and crept in with a couple of his schoolfriends. More young people from the surrounding villages turned up around midnight, and he'd got drunk properly for the first time in his life, two bottles of his father's Tempranillo to himself.

In the morning, he'd woken sprawled on one of the covered beds with a woman – Laetitia was her name – fast asleep beside him. When she woke, they started kissing, and in the drugged, dry-headed haze of his first hangover, Laetitia and he had sex. Laetitia, Isaac recalled now, had been twenty-seven years old. He had been fifteen. A vase had been smashed downstairs, and when his father appeared at their bedside with the pieces in his hands, he chased Laetitia out of the room and came back to beat his son. Not for the sex – just the vase. *I thought you were a poof*, his father had said. *Thank God.*

Isaac wondered where Laetitia was now. She'd be thirty-eight, about the age of Sarah, who was pouring out their glasses of lemonade. He looked out of the window, down the slope towards the

village path. He had never been able to hold Arazuelo in propor-
tion. It never stayed the same, and yet it always seemed the same.
It was a self-reflecting place, insular and welcoming by turns. He
was continually trying to leave it, although he could never exactly
say why. Arazuelo was part of his body. Madrid was the moon, Bil-
bao was outer space, Paris a place of biblical fantasy – but Arazuelo could overtake a man like no place else.

'Mr Robles?' Sarah Schloss was talking to him, and he smiled.
He could hear his sister and Olive making their way up the creaking
stairs to the first floor, and then up again to the attic. If Sarah heard
them too, she made no comment. She was smoking again, always
smoking, and her legs were tucked up underneath her as she sat on
the green sofa. 'So, do you think it's a good idea?' she said.

Well, did he? He knew there was something wrong about it, that
he should say no. But he couldn't put his finger on it. 'You must be
terribly busy,' she went on, in the face of his silence. 'But I haven't
had one for years, and it will be such a surprise for my husband.'

'Does he like surprises, señora?'

'Well,' she said. 'He's always surprising me.'

Isaac thought about her offer. That he was a good painter, he
knew. He might even be a great painter one day. As he and Tere
had grown up in the shadows, as Alfonso's illegitimate children,
his father had often bunged them money, on the understanding
that Isaac would grow up and leave all this left-wing, artist stuff
behind. Alfonso, on hearing that his son was now 'consorting' with
union leaders, Anarchists and divorced women, had confronted
him. Isaac had no intention of leaving his work at the San Telmo
school, so Alfonso had stopped his cash flow. He hadn't told Teresa.

He had very little income from the school, as cuts to government initiatives had affected its ability to run classes and pay the
staff. In a few months, Isaac knew he was going to be very poor.
But he could never ally with his father, whom he considered the
biggest hypocrite this side of Seville.

'I pay very well,' Sarah said. 'Whatever you need.'

Although he bristled at the ease with which she thought she

could buy him, he considered what a pleasure it would be to paint a face like Sarah Schloss's. 'Thank you, señora. I accept. But allow me to make this a gift.'

Her eyes closed in a brief pause of pleasure, as if she had always known he would assent. As much as Isaac disliked witnessing this, he admired her self-belief. He felt that he did not want to give her any assurance about her beauty. She clearly knew she had it in abundance.

Sarah smiled. 'Oh, that won't do. This has to be a transaction. How many sittings will you need me for?'

'I think six to eight, señora.'

'And should we do it here, or at your house?'

'Whatever is easiest for you.'

Sarah leaned over the tray as she lifted a glass of lemonade and handed it to him. 'This is your sister's recipe,' she said. 'It's better than any I've had elsewhere. What do you think her secret is?'

'I leave my sister's secrets to her, señora.'

Sarah smiled. 'Sensible. I think it should always be like that – everyone's happier that way. I'll come to you. Harold is in and out all the time, and I don't want him getting suspicious.'

'When is his birthday, señora?'

'His birthday?'

'This is not a present for his birthday?'

'Oh, no,' she said. 'It's just a surprise.' She lifted her glass. 'Cheers. Here's to my painting.'

OUTSIDE HER BEDROOM, OLIVE STOPPED her hand on the old wrought-iron handle and faced Teresa. 'Remember,' she said. 'Keep this to yourself.'

Teresa nodded. She could hear her brother and Sarah talking below. Olive pushed down the handle and let her in.

They were in an unexpected atrium of thick gold light, a huge space that ran along at least half the span of the house, with exposed beams, splintered with age and cracking plaster. Teresa blinked, adjusting her sight, the dust in the shafts of honeyed daylight swirling in Olive's wake. Isaac had been in this house before, running round it like a mad boy, but Teresa had been too young, and so she hadn't known such a room existed.

She stood rigid at the door, looking furtively around for whatever it was that Olive had been hiding up here. She could not smell an animal, nor hear any muffled cries; she could see only travelling trunks, a messy bed, clothes on a chair, books piled up in towers. It was the type of room she dreamed of for herself.

'Shut the door, nincompoop,' Olive said.

'*Nincompoop?*'

Olive laughed. 'I didn't mean it. I just – I don't want them to hear us.'

Teresa was uneasy. Olive was supposed to be the fish out of water, walking round in her socks. But now, standing by the window on the other side of the room, she looked so different. She had walked into the sunlight straight-backed, certain of herself, her arm resting gracefully on the sill, lost in thoughts that Teresa didn't have the ability to reach.

'Teresa,' Olive said. 'Close the door. Come over here. I want to show you something.'

Teresa obeyed, as Olive knelt down under the bed and pulled out a very large, flat piece of wood. When she lifted it up and turned it round, Teresa's breath caught in her throat. '*Madre mía,*' she said, and laughed.

'Why are you laughing?'

'You did this?'

Olive hesitated. 'I did. It's called *The Orchard*. What – do you think?'

It was one of the most extraordinary things Teresa had ever seen. Some of Isaac's paintings were pretty decent, but this one, *this* one, stood before her like a . . . person. It was not a case of thinking, it was a matter of feeling. The painting in its power overwhelmed her.

Her eyes darted all over it. She felt saturated. Who painted like this, a nineteen-year-old in her school pyjamas? Who knew such colours, who could take the land she had only just arrived in, and turn it into something better, and higher, brighter than the sun that flooded the room? For surely, this was the finca and its orchard, reimagined in a riot of colour and dancing shapes, identifiable to Teresa but so essentially changed.

Isaac had talked on occasion about art, about famous painters and what made someone stand out from the rest. *Novelty*, he always said, *makes the difference.* It was the fact that they were unlike the rest. *You can be a brilliant draughtsman*, he said, *but that means nothing if you're not seeing the world differently.* Teresa felt almost a wave of pain run through her. This wasn't just a case of novelty. This was something else, beyond words, an elusive power that was too much for her to comprehend. She didn't know if she believed in God, but she knew this girl was blessed.

'You don't like it,' said Olive, her mouth thinning to a line. 'I knew I should have worked more on those fruit trees. And perhaps there should be figures in it—'

'I like it,' said Teresa. They stood in silence before it. 'Is – this what you do, señorita?'

Olive considered the question, laying the painting on the bed as delicately as one might a lover. 'I got into art school,' she said. 'I sent my pictures and I got a place.'

Teresa's eyes widened. 'But you are here?'

'Yes. I'm here.'

'But you have *un gran talento.*'

'I don't know about that.'

'If I had the money I would buy your painting.'

'Would you?'

'I would be proud to have your painting on my wall. Why are you not at the school?'

Olive looked away. 'I don't know. But it's funny. Just before we left for Spain, I purchased this green, a vivid grasshopper green – and a shade of scarlet, an oil called Night Indigo, a plum and a silvery grey – all colours I'd never used before. I just picked them up and put them on the counter. And it was as if I'd *known* that only here would those paints come into their own, and help me. That they would flesh out my fears and dreams.'

Teresa could not hide her confusion. 'Look, Teresa, it's not easy to explain. My parents, the girls in London . . . Something's clicked down here. It was as if this painting had been stalking my mind and now it's in the light. I've never felt so connected to the *doing* of the thing.'

'I see.'

'But now that it's done and . . . and out of me, I can't help wondering that the paints didn't do it on their own. As if my involvement was nothing at all.'

'No, no. You have done it. If *I* touch the paints, nothing good will happen. But with you, it is different.'

Olive smiled. 'Thank you for being so nice about it.'

'Do you have more paintings?'

'Not here, but I do have these.' Olive went over to one of her trunks and pulled out a large sketchbook, handing it to Teresa.

Teresa opened the pages and saw inside small sketches of hands and feet, eyes and bottles, cats, trees, flowers – completely unlike the painting in their realist, engraved style. Over the next page, she saw a portrait of Sarah, called *Mother, London*, and one of Sarah and Harold together, a still-life sketch in pastel of the lemons Teresa had brought that first day.

She pointed at the lemons. 'I asked you where they went. You said you didn't know.'

Olive blushed. 'Sorry.'

'You stole them?'

'If you want to put it like that.'

'Why is this a secret?'

'It's not a *secret*. I just – don't tell anyone. Except you.'

Teresa glowed, hiding her pleasure in the pages of the sketchbook. The images were extraordinary, as if they might leap off the page. She kept turning, and was arrested by a double page of her brother; *Isaac Chopping Wood, Isaac with Coffee Cup.*

Teresa felt a surge of pain and Olive yanked the book from her grip. 'Just sketches,' she said. Downstairs, Sarah's laugh rang out, a little bell.

'What will you do with this painting?' Teresa asked.

'So practical,' said Olive. 'Not everything has to have a purpose, you know, an end point.'

Teresa flushed, because this was exactly how she thought; pragmatically, like a jackal hunting for a rib. Still, she had detected a defensiveness in Olive's responses which mystified her. If she had half of Olive's skill, she'd be in Barcelona by now, far from Arazuelo. 'You are going to hide it under your bed for ever, where no one will see it?' she said.

'Of course I'm not.'

'So why do you not show it now? You could put it on the wall.'

Olive went rigid, sitting down on the bed next to *The Orchard*. The old mattress gave way beneath her, and Teresa thought suddenly how squalid the bed looked, and how stupid Olive was to put up with such a state of being when she could clearly afford something better. They could even go into Calle Larios in Malaga to buy a new one – she could offer to take Olive, letting her try mattress after mattress until they found the perfect one. But Teresa kept silent, the deft pencil edges of her brother's face reworking themselves in her mind's eye.

'I don't want it on my wall,' said Olive.

Teresa frowned. It seemed a flat protest. She came up to the edge of the bed, her hands on her hips. 'You could sell this in Malaga, señorita,' she said. 'You could make money.'

Olive flicked her eyes up. 'Money? We've got money coming out of our ears.'

Teresa flushed. 'You could go away.'

'But I like it here.'

'Paris. London. New York—'

'Tere. I don't *want* people to know. Do you understand?'

'If that was mine, I would show the world.'

Olive looked over at the painting. 'Say you do show the world. But the world might not like it. Think of that. All those hours, all those days and months – years, even—'

'But *I* would like it, so it would not be important.'

'So why bother trying to please the world in the first place? And, I can assure you, you will never truly like it, if you do it yourself.'

'Then why are you doing it?'

Olive got up, lit a cigarette and stared out of the window. 'I don't *know*. I've never known. I just do it.' She looked over at Teresa. 'All right, I know that's vague. It's just – it feels as if there's a place, a shining citadel of perfection I have in my mind. And with each canvas and sketchbook, I'm inching closer and closer to it, to the place where my paintings will be a better reflection of the person I am, a *different* reflection. And I will fly.'

She rubbed her forehead and came back to lie on the bed. 'Why are we so trapped by the hours, the minutes of every day? Why can't we live the life that's always out of reach?'

Her voice broke, and Teresa reached out a hand to Olive's arm. 'I'm sorry, Tere,' Olive said. 'I'm probably mad. But it's how it's always been. I just wanted to show someone. I'm glad you liked it.'

'I love it. *Me ha encantado.*'

'Here.' Olive was brisk again, leaping off the mattress with her cigarette still in her hand. 'Take these. You might like to look at them.' She reached down for a book on Renaissance painters, and an old *Vogue*, and handed them over. 'The magazine is my mother's, but she won't mind.'

Teresa flicked through the Renaissance book, colour plates of men and women in their finery, their skin taut as boiled eggs, bulging eyes, delicate ringed fingers and swathes of damask on their shoulders. Strangely elongated Virgin Marys, darted with a yellow beam of the Annunciation; nightmarish scenes of mythical beasts; men with five legs; women turning into pomegranates. She read the names silently: *Bellini, Bosch, Cranach.* It was another language to learn and assimilate, to wield like a weapon.

The *Vogue* was well out of date, but Teresa didn't care. It was hers. She was glad it was already a year old. Sarah barely glanced at her magazines before dumping them on the floor of her bedroom, their colours and allure a siren that Teresa was astonished her mistress couldn't hear. But she didn't want Olive getting into trouble.

'Are you certain your mother will not mind?' she said.

'She won't even notice. Isaac is still here I think,' Olive said, putting away the sketchbooks and *The Orchard* under the bed. 'We should go and see what my mother wants with him.'

Teresa pushed down the cloud that rose in her chest at the mention of Isaac, closed the Renaissance book and followed Olive out.

Isaac picked up the second glass of lemonade and clinked it against Sarah's. He was used to women being like this around him; feline, flirtatious, sometimes giddy. He never encouraged, but this only seemed to make their behaviour more pronounced. It was almost clownish – and yet he had learned not to assume immediately what women wanted from him. It might look like one thing, but it was quite often another.

He thought of how essentially different Olive was from her mother, so innocent, reaching out to him like a drowning girl, more obviously than she probably imagined. And yet she intrigued him in a way that Señora Schloss did not. Sarah dazzled immediately, but there was something supple and interesting about Olive, beneath her awkwardness. She was a survivor of her parents' marriage. He wondered whether if Olive stayed with them indefinitely it might work out badly for her.

He heard footsteps, and Olive appeared at the door, switching her attention between him and her mother, as if she was trying to work out a difficult sum. Teresa was peering from behind Olive, with a strange look of triumph on her face that made Isaac wary.

'Liv,' said Sarah. 'Guess what?'

'Do I have to?'

'Mr Robles is going to paint my picture.'

'What?'

'As a surprise for Daddy,' Sarah went on. 'I've given Mr Robles a commission.'

'But he hates surprises.'

'Well, so do I, Olive. But Daddy is getting this painting, whether he likes it or not.'

Olive came forward, seating herself on the moth-eaten arm-chair, left at a careless angle to the sofa. 'Have you got time to paint this, Mr Robles?' she asked. 'With all the work you have?'

'It will be an honour,' he said. Olive looked towards the unlit fireplace, filled with logs that Isaac had piled up for their convenience. Teresa remained in the doorway. She was sneering slightly at him, and he felt irritated with her. She lived in a bubble, she had no idea how many times over the years he'd protected her.

'I should be in the painting,' Olive announced.

'Livvi,' said her mother after a pause, realigning the crease of her trouser leg. 'It's my surprise.'

'I think Daddy would like us both to be in the painting. We sat for one years ago. We should do it again.'

'We did?'

'You've forgotten. Yes, we did. Mr Robles, don't you think that would be a good idea?'

Isaac felt the pressure of the women's attention like a physical weight. 'You must decide,' he said. 'He is your father, your husband.'

Sarah picked at a bobble. 'Mr Robles, if I agreed to sit with my daughter, would you need to paint us together?'

'Not always, señora.'

'Well then,' she sighed. 'We shall work it out between us, won't we, Olive?'

Olive tipped her chin in Sarah's direction. 'Yes, Mother,' she said. 'We will.'

VI

*O*live and Sarah were to have three initial joint sessions, arranged when Isaac was not teaching in Malaga. Teresa was to guard the secret. 'Tell Harold that we're at the market in Esquinas,' Sarah had instructed her. 'Or seeing the local doctor. You can think of something, Teresa. You're so clever.'

By the second session, as Isaac painted Olive and her mother in the dimming light of his cottage kitchen, Olive knew something was wrong. Sarah, in a semi-sheer lavender blouse and a brown silk skirt, kept her spine continuously at a slight arch, one arm draped behind Isaac's kitchen chair. She was concentrating on being her best self for the artist, but Olive could see how bleak and drawn Isaac looked.

She thought he should be happy; his party had just won the national election. It had been on the wireless, on the front pages of the newspapers her father brought back from Malaga. A left-wing coalition was in power, something that surely must make him feel triumphant.

'What's wrong?' she asked, when Sarah excused herself for a moment.

He looked up from where he was painting, with a surprised expression. 'Another boy was killed,' he said. 'I knew him a little.'

'Killed?'

'Last night. A local boy called Adrián, a member of the Anarchist party. He worked in a factory in Malaga. Started by tying red ribbons on donkeys and bicycles, and ended up burning his boss's property records. He had a loud mouth, but he was only a kid. Some bastards shot him and tied him to the back of a truck.'

'Oh, Isaac. That's awful.'

'They are calling it a crime of passion, which is a joke. He didn't have time for love.'

'Have they arrested anyone?'

Isaac's expression darkened. 'No witnesses. He tied himself to the truck, of course. He didn't have any feet left by the time they'd finished.'

'Good God. Who would do such a thing?'

'Everyone, no one. The Civil Guard are saying it was a Communist gang, mistaking him for some rich kid. Others are blaming it on the gypsies. Anarchist, Communist, Falangist or Socialist, *oligarco*, *gitano* or what? Maybe his father did it?' Isaac spat.

Olive wanted to comfort him, but she knew her mother would be back any moment. She tried to be steady. This was a one-off, she told herself, a hideous thing, but still unique. The boy was a symbol of nothing, just an unlucky human put out too soon. But she remembered what Isaac had told her – the polar bear, the priest swinging from a tree, the soil of the land coursing through the people's veins. She thought of *The Orchard*, waiting in her attic, her perfect, multi-coloured paradise, and felt ashamed of her ignorance, her foreign and insistent make-belief.

The next evening, Teresa sat at the kitchen table in the cottage, whilst Isaac skinned rabbits he'd shot for a stew. She had before her the *Vogue* which Olive had given her, and she handled it as delicately as if it was a first edition of a precious book. The woman on the cover stared delicately back. She was blonde, wearing a long cream cape, one black-and-white-striped beach shoe peeping out. She was leaning on the side of an open-top car, shading her eyes against the sun but looking upwards nevertheless, at some invisible point. The sky behind her was deep blue. HOLIDAY – TRAVEL – RESORT FASHIONS ran along the bottom of the picture in a clean, attractive font.

'You've been quiet,' Isaac said. 'Are you worried about what I'll do?' When she remained silent he said, 'Jesus, Teresa. You should be worried *for* me.'

'Just be calm about all this, Isaac. Nothing you do will bring back that boy Adrián. Stealing honey from the duchess's beehives is one thing, but putting yourself in danger is another—'

'I could say the same to you.' He pointed at the magazine with his knife. 'You should behave, too.'

'But I'm not in danger.'

'Are you sure? Remember last time, Tere. I won't bail you out twice.'

'I haven't taken a thing. Olive gave me this.'

Teresa remembered how it had been with Miss Banetti. The loneliness, the drudgery. The woman had had so many belongings that she didn't even notice when they began to disappear. It had been so tempting, so easy. Small things first, a ring, a silver matchbox. Then on to empty scent bottles, and finally a necklace of emeralds. Teresa had seen these items, always overlooked by the rich foreigners in her care, as fair payment for a grey life. She buried the trinkets in a tin out by the well, and she would visit them sometimes, never actually putting them on her own body, only holding the emeralds to the sun, watching them wink in green complicity. She loved them so much that she felt no guilt.

It was the German family who had caught and dismissed her. Isaac had gone to talk to them, explaining that she had mental problems – which was a lie, but was better than letting the Frau report her to the Civil Guard. He'd returned everything to them, but she kept quiet about the Banetti box, the emerald necklace hidden in their garden. It was her little private escape.

'Tere,' Isaac said more softly, bringing her back into the room, the sound of the rabbit innards slick on the blade. 'Olive can't be your friend, you know.'

'You should take your own advice.'

'I know it must be lonely for you when I'm in Malaga. But she's some rich kid drifting around after her parents and before you know it, she'll be gone again. I don't want you to—'

'I'm not lonely. And I'm not a child. You don't need to be so patronizing. I don't want to be her friend.'

'Good.' He began to dismantle the rabbit's leg. 'Come and help.' She slunk from the table and stood next to him. 'You can't tell me what to do, either, Tere,' he said.

'I can try.'

He laughed, and she did too. 'Haven't I always looked after you?' he asked.

'Yes, Isa. But I never needed you to.'

Harold had not seemed to notice his wife and daughter's absence particularly. He seemed distracted, sitting at his desk in the middle of his study, marooned on the Moroccan tapestries he'd bought from a rug trader in Malaga, elbows digging into the fraying leather top, barely acknowledging Teresa as she dusted round him, or left him a glass of fino at his side. He looked like the captain of a drowning vessel who had found a piece of driftwood and was clinging on for dear life.

On the day the women were having their last painting session, and Teresa was in the finca preparing a stew, the telephone rang. She waited, but Harold was nowhere to be seen. 'Señor?' she called. The house was silent, except for the telephone ringing and ringing. She tiptoed along the corridor towards the study, listening through the door before she went in, making her way across the rugs. As she hefted the Bakelite handle to her ear, she knew she'd made a mistake.

'*Harold, bist du es?*' It was a woman's voice. Teresa remained silent, listening to the caught pocket of air as the woman inhaled sharply and the line went dead. She looked up; Harold was standing at the door, in his coat, holding his hunting rifle.

'What are you doing?' he said. 'Teresa, what the hell are you doing?'

Teresa looked dumbly at the receiver, wishing in that moment that she'd never come to this finca, that she'd found work elsewhere. It had not been enough for her to move only between the tissue layers of the Schlosses' lives – she had wanted to be closer, to the scars and the spots and the hot red mass of their hearts. But now she remembered the danger of knowing other people's secrets.

Harold came towards her as she slammed the receiver down. He put his hand on top of hers, and she was surprised by how warm it was. 'Teresa,' he said, smiling, his hand exerting the minimum of pressure. 'Who could you possibly be wanting to call?'

She looked at him in confusion, and then she understood, rearranging her face into humility, still hearing the echo of the woman's hopeful voice, her panicked breath when she realized Harold wasn't on the other end.

'I am sorry, señor,' she said. 'I wanted to speak to my aunt in Madrid.'

They fixed their eyes upon each other and Harold released her hand. He walked round and sat in his chair, opening the breech of the rifle. 'All you had to do was ask, Teresa.'

'I am sorry, señor,' she repeated. 'It will not happen again.'

'Good. All right. Off you go.'

She was at the door when he spoke again. 'Where is my wife?' he asked her, and Teresa turned back to face him, fear bursting in her stomach.

'She is at the market, señor.'

'At six in the evening?' Harold locked the rifle and pushed back his chair.

'Yes. But she wanted to visit the church after.'

'The church?'

'Yes. *La iglesia de Santa Rufina.*'

He laughed. 'You know Mrs Schloss is not well, Teresa. If she keeps wandering off like this, you must tell me. Keep an eye out for her.'

'*An eye out?*'

'Keep watch for her. Wait here until she comes back. And when she does, tell her I've got work in Malaga. She'll understand.'

'*Sí, señor.*'

'Is Olive with her, at the church?'

'Yes.'

'I'm glad they're spending time together.' He laid the rifle on his desk. 'Teresa, I want your opinion.'

'Yes, señor?'

'Do you think the villagers would like us to hold a party?'

Teresa imagined that a party held by the Schlosses would be the most glamorous thing any of the villagers had ever seen – and she would be in the centre, organizing it. They wouldn't mock her after that – no more gypsy slurs or bastard comments. The power of Harold and Sarah Schloss would reflect in glorious technicolour – on her. 'I think it would be wonderful, señor,' she said.

She hurried back to the kitchen to see to the stew, and heard Harold pacing in his bedroom, the stop-start of his feet as he moved back and forth from his closet to try on several outfits. He reappeared in a beautiful wheat-coloured suit, with a blue shirt underneath, which set against his dark hair and made him look incredibly refined.

His motor car revved and when he was gone, Teresa felt heavy again, burdened by *Harold, bist du es?*, by the secret they both knew he had entrusted her to keep. He had left a trail of cologne. An ambery echo of dark leather chairs and darker corners.

When she returned to the cottage, Isaac was packing away his paint materials in his bedroom. In the kitchen, a sheet was over the painting, as he would not allow anyone to see it before it was completed. Sarah had left, but Olive lingered at the table. She looked tired, and Teresa watched out of the corner of her eye how her hands moved constantly. Teresa could not marry this urchinous twitcher with the stately, confident artist up in her attic. She wondered if Olive had painted anything new, and whether she'd be permitted to see it.

'Your father asked where you were,' Teresa said. 'I told him you had gone to the church of Santa Rufina with your mother.'

'Where's that?'

'In the village square.'

'My mother doesn't know about this.' Olive rose to her feet. 'I'll have to get to her before Daddy does.'

'He's gone out,' Teresa said.

Olive's face fell. 'Of course he has.' She sat back down.

'Are you enjoying being painted?' Teresa asked.

'I don't think I make a very good subject. My mother loves it, of course.'

'Your father will be very happy to see it.'

'Maybe. If it's any good. Isaac won't let me look.'

'Your father – he tells me he is going to have a party.'

Olive groaned. 'Is that what he said?'

'Do you not want a party, señorita?'

'You haven't been to one of my parents' parties. I think I'd rather visit the church.'

She was in an irritable mood, and Teresa wondered quite how badly the portrait session had gone between Olive and her mother. All Teresa could conclude was that whilst Sarah was born to be watched, Olive was more of a watcher.

She walked to the counter, fetched an onion and a knife, and began to chop. 'Do you know the story of Santa Rufina?' she asked, hoping to distract Olive from her gloom.

Olive gazed towards the darkness of the corridor, where Isaac was moving around in his room. 'No.'

'It is a story about two sisters. They were Christians. They lived in Seville, in . . . *la época romana?*'

'Roman times,' said Olive.

'Yes. They made pots and bowls. The Romans wanted them to make pots for a party. A pagan party. But the sisters said, *"No, no we won't. Our pots are our own."* And they broke the mask of the goddess Venus.'

'Goodness me.'

'They were arrested. They threw Justa down a well. And Rufina – they made her fight a lion.'

Teresa noted with pleasure how Olive had stilled, listening to her story, as the shadows threw black dancers up the walls and the onion sweated in the pan.

'A big lion,' she went on. 'A hungry lion. *En el anfiteatro.* All the people watching. But the lion did not want to fight. He sat, he did not move. He would not touch her.'

'What then?' whispered Olive.

'They cut off her head.'

'*No.*'

'And they threw it down the well to meet her sister.'

Olive shivered. 'That's awful.'

Teresa shrugged. 'I like the lion.' Her eye was caught by Isaac standing at the door. 'He knows the value of peace. He keeps his place.'

'Maybe he didn't like the taste of bony girl,' Isaac said. Olive turned to him. He folded his arms and fixed Teresa with a look. 'Telling stories again, Tere?'

'She's a good storyteller,' said Olive. 'Imagine waiting down in the darkness whilst your sister faced a lion. Imagine holding her head in your hands; the rest of her, disappeared. What happened to Justa?'

'She died of the shock,' said Teresa.

'So would I,' said Olive.

'You don't know that, señorita,' said Isaac. 'You might be strong.'

'Oh, no. I'd definitely faint.' Olive looked thoughtful. 'Do you know, I might visit that church.'

'Señorita?'

'Why not?' said Olive. 'At least then we could say that one of our lies was actually a truth.'

PART II

Belonging

AUGUST 1967

7

*L*awrie and I made it to the cinema for our first date. In the end, we went for *You Only Live Twice*. There was so much bare flesh and sadism in it, I was embarrassed for making the suggestion. No romance, just gadgets and Sean Connery's chest that looked borrowed from an ape. I think, on reflection, I would have preferred to watch Catherine Deneuve, but I was happy simply to sit with Lawrie, to catch his lovely scent, the dense warmth of his body, this person who in turn had chosen me.

Over the next two weeks, we saw each other nearly every single day. It was a fabulous sickness. We went to the Wallace Collection and the National Gallery, to see if we could spot any more paintings with the initials I.R. (no success). We went to the theatre, and I still have the ticket stub. It was called *Play* by Samuel Beckett, and I had never seen anything like it. I remember my delighted shock as the curtain went up, the three actors revealed – one man and two women, playing his mistress and his wife – stoppered to the neck in giant grey funeral urns, unable to move, gabbling incoherently before they began interspersing their stories to the audience, remaining oblivious of one another.

We went to Soho restaurants and bars – All Nighters, the Flamingo – and discovered that we danced together very well. I didn't like having to shout to be heard over the noise and it got very smoky past eleven. We saw gangsters and their girls there: slick hair, gold rings, a shimmer of malevolence. But the important thing was the live music. It was wonderful – ska, calypso, jazz and blues.

I didn't know it, but a bond had been sealed, and who'd suggested what, who'd wanted what – that strange dance of allusion and manners that distinguishes the first time for anything – had faded. We were dependent on each other without really knowing each other, in that way the young can be when they have never been burned or hurt or discarded, when they share everything, making the mistake that the other person is the answer to their confusing sum. He was lonely and I was lost – or was it the other way round? We hadn't slept together; it hadn't got to that yet. It was very innocent, in its way.

Since our exchange in the rain on Piccadilly Circus, I'd hardly seen Quick. Only Pamela and I – and a couple of the academics, who normally kept to the basement with the archives – seemed to come in dutifully every day. Quick seemed to be absent more than you would consider acceptable, often only coming in for a couple of hours. We were attached to the research part of the building, not the gallery round the front on Jermyn Street, so it was always quiet. I missed Quick's attention.

In her absence, Pamela invited me to eat my sandwiches with her in the courtyard, leaving the reception desk unattended. I'd hesitated, firstly because I was still finishing my Muriel Spark book, a collection of short stories and radio plays she'd had published six years before. The second reason was that I did not really want to hear more about 'people like you' – a phrase that Pamela occasionally slipped into our conversations – but my lack of contact with Cynthia, and the absence of Quick, was making me miss female company. And thirdly: I really thought someone should be manning reception.

Pamela's lunchtime questions about life in Trinidad were a lesson to me in how little her school days, and all the days after, had taught her of the Empire's reaches. But she also had a genuine curiosity – the weather and what humidity and heat did to books, to clothes, and how they shaped the food your mother once made you, the music you listened to, the people you knew – Pamela's questions made me realize how far away from it I really was. It conjured Cynth, our long journey together, and then it reminded me of our stupid stand-off, and I thought I might cry, so instead I pushed Pamela to talk. She told me about her mother the seamstress, and how her father portered meat at Smithfield. She had five brothers – and a sister, she said, who'd died when Pamela was eight.

'I've got to ask, Odelle – you got a feller?' she said. 'You been looking sort of dopey these last few weeks.'

I hesitated. I so wanted to talk about Lawrie, about love – what it might feel like, and whether I was in it. 'No,' I said, instead. 'I haven't.'

Pamela narrowed her eyes. 'All right. You keep your secrets. *I've* got a boyfriend. Billy. He works behind the scenes at All Nighters, but I wouldn't expect you'd go there.'

'Why?' I said.

She laughed. ' 'Cos you're too sensible to waste your youth dancing in clubs.'

I laughed back, intuiting true flattery in her comment, that for the first time, she was imbuing me with some sort of sophistication and status. But I could still picture how Lawrie and I had danced in that very club, the sweat running down our backs. It did feel like a different me.

Pamela wore Billy like a medal, but thinking of the men I'd seen there, I wondered if he was more of a bronze than a gold. As the days wore on, and our sandwich lunches continued, my book of Spark stories still unfinished, I found myself surprised to feel sorry for Pamela, whose company I was coming to enjoy. 'Billy's got big dreams,' she'd say, but never elaborated about what exactly, and I had the feeling they didn't really include her.

REEDE HAD TELEPHONED LAWRIE, SAYING he'd had an 'inordinate piece of luck' with the Prado gallery in Madrid, and could Lawrie come as soon as possible. On the morning he was due at the Skelton, he was already waiting for me on a bench in the middle of the square.

'Hel-lo,' I said, sitting down next to him. 'Excited for news of the lion girls?'

He smiled. 'A bit.' As he leaned over to kiss me, a man walking past tutted loudly. I couldn't be sure, but I thought I heard the word '*disgusting*'. We ignored him; I was never going to say anything, however much I might have liked to, but I did wonder if Lawrie might speak up.

'Come on,' I said, when it was clear that either Lawrie hadn't noticed, never assuming such a comment might be directed at him – or that he didn't consider it worthy of attention. 'You'll miss your appointment with Mr Big Shot. But you go in first, I'll follow.'

'Why?'

'I don't want Pamela to know about us.'

'Are you embarrassed about me?' he said.

I laughed. 'Of course I'm not. It's just – well, if she finds out about you, I'll never hear the end.'

Sitting at my desk, having safely outwitted Pamela, I couldn't stop thinking about what was going on in Reede's office above me. I was very curious about Lawrie's painting. And although my mother always said that if you listen at doors you deserve every burned ear you get, I knew Reede wasn't going to tell me a thing. Quick was away that day, and Lawrie couldn't be trusted to relay every particular.

I took the back stairs to the next floor and hesitated before putting my eye to the keyhole. I could feel my pulse beating hard, fearful that one of them inside would turn, and hear me. Lawrie's painting was propped up on the easel by the desk. It was a perfect rectangle, filled with vibrant colours; vermilion, lavender, indigo, terracotta, livid greens. And to my complete surprise, sitting in one of Reede's low-slung leather armchairs, was Quick. Once upon a time, the Skelton had been a domestic house – most of the panelling was original – and I imagined Georgian ladies sitting where Quick was now, playing with a spree of little dogs and wondering what syllabub to feed their guests.

What was Quick doing here? She was staring into the empty grate, her arms wrapped around her body. She looked nauseous, as if she was waiting for an explosion. She reached down into her handbag and brought out her cigarettes, busying herself with lighting one.

'So. Isaac Robles,' Reede was saying, pulling out a photograph from a buff folder on his desk. 'Ever heard of him?'

'No,' said Lawrie.

'The Prado in Madrid sent me this. They think it's him, in Malaga, around 1935 or -6. We don't know who the woman is, but the photo was most likely taken in his studio, and she's probably a model he used. It matches up to other images of him in Madrid earlier in the thirties. He was just beginning to enjoy a bit of fame when this photograph was taken. But of course, what has excited me most is that the painting in progress on Robles's easel looks *exactly* like it could be yours.'

There was a silence. Lawrie had his back to me, so I couldn't see his expression through the keyhole, but he was very still, as if he'd been stunned.

'What?' Lawrie said, quietly. 'Is that possible?'

Reede smiled. 'Thought you'd like that. He's only started on the lion by the looks of it in the photograph, but it's fairly emblematic, wouldn't you say?'

Lawrie took the photograph from Reede's outstretched hand. His shoulders were hunched, head bent in concentration. Quick remained seated, watching him, dragging deeply on her cigarette.

'Where did the Prado get this?' Lawrie asked.

'They don't know for sure. Their records from the thirties are not complete, for obvious reasons. Robles might have left it with someone to keep it safe when war broke out. They might not have known what to do with it, so gave it to the Prado. Isaac Robles wasn't very popular with the authorities, and his work wasn't really to their taste. You didn't want to be caught with evidence that you were friends or acquaintances with undesirables.'

' *"Undesirables"?'*

'From what we know, Robles moved in quite left-wing circles. That meant he could have been a political agitator. They probably accepted this photograph and slipped it in their files. Robles didn't survive to match Miró or Picasso in output and trajectory. But what he *did* make is superlative. One theory for his small output, other than an early death, is that he destroyed a lot of his work. That sort of practice always makes a painter more special – it's his rarity. Now, to the point. I believe this painting of yours is what we call a sleeper.'

'A sleeper?'

'Yes, it's been lying in wait for us, overlooked for years. We're looking at 1936, perhaps,' Reede continued. 'The fact there is no frame is unfortunate. You can learn a lot from a frame's quality. I assume Robles wouldn't have had access to many, if he was back and working in the south of Spain. But if this *is* by Robles, and I think it is, then it was painted as he reached the cusp of his powers before war came. Look at the colours, the surreal narrative, the playfulness. It's highly unusual. I see why he was so prized at the time.'

'What happened to him?' Lawrie asked.

'War happened, Mr Scott. There are several theories. One is that he went north to join forces with other Republicans as Franco's troops inched up from the south. They never found a grave, but at that time, it wasn't uncommon. He was from the south, Andalusia, and he lived and worked in Malaga for a time, fairly unsuccessfully. He travelled to Madrid and Barcelona – there are a couple of his lithographs there, fairly minor.'

'I see.'

'But at the time *this* photograph was taken, Robles wouldn't have been so worried about war. He was working well. He'd abandoned his idealistic, figurative aesthetic once he was back home, and it appears that he started to paint quite differently. A few months before Spain cracked apart, he painted a work that caused a real stir. It's called *Women in the Wheatfield*. Have you heard of it?'

'No.'

Reede turned towards the door, and I swore he looked at the keyhole. I froze.

'It's not particularly famous, but it's a special painting,' said Quick, and Reede turned back to her. Gradually, I edged my heart back down my throat.

'Why is it so special?' asked Lawrie.

'I've done a little investigating,' Reede went on before Quick could say anything more. 'We know that Robles sold *Women in the Wheatfield* in Paris, around the time this photo was taken. A man called Harold Schloss sold it.'

'I see,' said Lawrie. Even through the keyhole, I could see that he was uncomfortable.

'It went to New York for a while, and now hangs in Peggy Guggenheim's house in Venice. I've seen *Women in the Wheatfield* myself,' Reede went on, 'and it has similar qualities to yours. Extraordinary in the flesh.' He touched the edge of Lawrie's painting. 'Sometimes, I think he would have been a genius, had he carried on.'

'Why?'

'That's not always easy to define. But you see, with most artists, you have one thing or the other – the visionary with sub-standard technical skills, or a short time frame of astonishing output that diminishes in quality, for one reason or another. These fellows have no training in composition, and most of them can't therefore subvert it. Or, you have the excellent trained draftsman with no imagination, who will never paint the world anew. It's actually quite hard to find someone who has it all. Picasso has it – you should see his early works. It's subjective, of course, but I think Robles had it too. And I think your painting demonstrates his skills to a higher level than *Women in the Wheatfield*. Some say his scant works are political; others find them to be escapist *tours de force*. That is the quality they have – perpetually interpreted, yet always standing up to every iteration. Robles has lasted. You don't get bored. You see new things. Moreover, on a basic aesthetic level, they wash gorgeously over the eye whilst never being twee.'

'But you can't prove this is a Robles,' Quick said.

Reede narrowed his eyes at her. 'Right at the moment, I can't, Marjorie. But there are avenues. He painted other pictures. It's a case of tracking them down and lining this up with them. Your mother is – recently deceased, I understand, Mr Scott?'

'That's right.'

'I wonder – do you think she kept receipts?'

'Receipts?'

'Yes, of things she bought. Paintings, for example.'

'She wasn't the sort of woman who kept receipts, Mr Reede.'

'Pity.' Reede looked thoughtfully at the painting. 'Anything you have regarding the purchase would be very useful. I ask about the provenance, not just in the instance of your wishing to sell the picture, or us perhaps to exhibit—'

'Exhibit?' Quick said.

Reede blinked at her. 'That's right. I ask, Mr Scott, because this painting may be a legal matter.'

'What do you mean?' said Lawrie, the panic palpable in his voice.

Quick stubbed out her cigarette. 'Perhaps there's no need to get into that now, Mr Reede. It's not really the Skelton's approach, an exhibition for a single painting—'

'You're probably aware of what happened in the thirties in Europe to valued works of art, Mr Scott,' Reede interrupted. 'A lot of them disappeared. The Nazis took them off gallery walls, removed them from private homes—'

'This painting wasn't stolen,' Lawrie said.

'You sound so sure.'

'I am. My mother wouldn't have stolen anything.'

'I'm not suggesting she did. But she could easily have purchased a stolen item. Robles was Spanish, working solely in Spain, as far as we know, although his paintings sold in Paris. Did your mother have any connection to Spain?'

'Not that I know of.'

'Well. Here's one theory. Artworks moved around Europe quite freely in those days. Harold Schloss was a well-known Viennese art dealer specializing in early twentieth-century modern art. If he sold *Women in the Wheatfield*, he might have sold more of Robles's work. Schloss had a Paris gallery, so it's possible your painting was there around the same time.'

'This painting went from Spain to Paris?'

'Possibly. By this point Robles was back in Malaga, so maybe Harold Schloss visited him down there. Dealers will go anywhere to sniff out talent.'

'This is all just conjecture, Mr Scott,' Quick murmured. 'Just an avenue—'

'Many of the gallerists in Paris were Jewish,' Reede went on. 'I don't know about Schloss's history, we'd have to find that out – but in '42, when the Nazis had occupied Paris for a year, they closed a lot of the businesses down and sent the owners to be interned before they went onwards to – well, to the camps. Many paintings were never recovered. Others were hidden away, only to turn up in the strangest of places. Junk shops, for example. Suitcases. Old train tunnels. Flea markets.'

There was a silence. On the other side of the door, I was barely breathing.

'Jesus Christ,' said Lawrie.

'After the war, the Nazis who were captured claimed they'd burned the lot. Poppycock, of course. They stole too many to have destroyed them all. And they knew what they were doing. They knew that what they were taking was valuable, even as they claimed it didn't fit the new aesthetic of the Reich.'

'What do you think happened to Harold Schloss?' Lawrie said.

Reede looked annoyed. 'I'll be investigating that, as I said.'

'This painting wasn't stolen,' Lawrie repeated.

'There's no way to be certain – at least at the moment. The first half of this century was a mess for the art market, and we're still picking up the pieces. Art has always been used for purposes other than pleasure, be it for political leverage or a loaf of bread.'

'All right.' Lawrie ran his fingers through his hair.

'I'm speaking to a representative at the Guggenheim foundation, who is being a great help in investigating what – if anything – they have on Isaac Robles, which may shed more light on this painting here.'

Lawrie exhaled slowly. 'Thank you – I think,' he said. He went to take the painting off the easel, but Reede stretched out his arm.

'Don't you think, Mr Scott – all things considered – that it might continue to be safer here? We have a night watch and an alarm system. I fear that in Surrey—'

'The crime capital of the world?'

Quick intervened. 'Your mother's death – was it announced in the papers?'

'It was.'

This surprised me – what sort of people had their deaths announced in the papers?

'That is the kind of thing that attracts art thieves,' said Reede. 'People who get death notices in papers usually have things worth nicking,' he went on. Reede's use of the word *nicking* pinged out to me; it was the sort of word Pamela would use. 'I know it sounds preposterous, Mr Scott, but even so. Allow us to look after it for you. It will be safer.'

Reede was a slick act; polite, pressurizing, authoritative, conciliatory all at once. 'All right,' said Lawrie. 'A little longer.'

'Thank you. Sincerely. I'll be in touch as soon as I have news. This is very exciting, Mr Scott. I can only thank you for choosing the Skelton as your base of investigation—'

'Can I keep this photo?' Lawrie said, holding up the battered square.

Reede looked puzzled. 'Keep it?'

'Until we meet again. Just to have a closer look.'

'Marjorie will get Rudge or Bastien to make a Xerox copy for you.'

I tingled at the sound of my name, terrified Reede would discover me hiding here, but I was unable to drag myself away. 'I'm convinced that photo's an original, Mr Scott,' Reede said, 'and I can't let it go. Marjorie – are you all right?'

Quick jumped. 'What?'

'I *said*, will you get one of the girls to make Mr Scott a Xerox copy of this photograph.'

Quick gathered herself and took the photograph from Lawrie. She carried it by the tips of her fingers, not even looking at it. I backed away from the keyhole and moved as fast as I could down the corridor.

I wasn't fast enough.

'Odelle?' Quick's voice was low and quiet. I stopped and turned, relieved to see she had closed the door behind her. 'Come here,' she said.

I walked towards her, shamefaced. 'You were listening,' she said. Given the faint glint of amusement in her eyes, I saw no point in lying; I'd been caught creeping down an otherwise empty corridor.

'I'm sorry,' I said. 'Please, don't—'

'Apparently, we're not supposed to look through keyholes.'

'I know.'

She looked down at the photograph in her hands and went still. 'Think he's got a talent?' she said.

'I do. Do you believe that's a genuine Isaac Robles in there?'

She pushed the photograph into my hands. 'If Reede says so. He's the one that knows. And it looks like it matches the one in this image. But what do *you* make of it?'

'I'm not an expert.'

'I don't want a bloody expert, Odelle. I just want to know if you like it. It's not a test.' She looked exhausted, and I noticed her hands were trembling slightly.

'It unnerves me.'

She leaned against the wall. 'Me too.'

'But it's very beautiful.'

'The subject matter is insidious.'

'What do you mean?'

'It's as if there's an extra layer to the painting we're not privy to. You can't get at it, but it's there.'

I looked closely at the photograph. It was bent, splodged, with a liquid stain in the bottom left corner. It was in black and white, and looked as if it had been through the wars. And yet the image was clear enough – a man and a woman, standing in front of a large, half-finished canvas. They were in a workshop of some sort. The man alleged to be Robles was without a jacket, his sleeves rolled up, a cigarette dangling from his mouth. He was unsmiling, staring straight at the photographer. He had thick, slightly wavy hair, and dark brows, a slender face, nice cheekbones, compact body – and even in this locked-away moment in time, his eyes were attractive, his glance determined. He was holding a large palette covered in many paints, and his body was turned all the way to the camera. He seemed defiant.

The woman on his right looked happy. She had an open face – she couldn't have been much more than a teenager really, but in those old photos, girls always look like women before their time. She was really laughing; her eyes were almost invisible, they were so creased. She had that cheery unselfconsciousness that always makes a person beautiful, however unremarkable their face. Her hairstyle was half-crimped, close to her head in the thirties style, but flyaway, as if she didn't care. She was pointing to the painting, and in her hand she held a brush.

'Who's the woman?' I said.

Quick closed her eyes. 'His muse, probably. Or just a model.'

'He's an Italian Paul Newman,' I said, and Quick laughed.

The photo jarred something in me. It was so potent, so full of a story. I flipped it over, and amidst the marks of time, at the bottom left, I read the handwritten caption, *O and I.*

'Did you see this, Quick – who are O and I?' I asked. 'Is it *I* for Isaac?'

But Quick was no longer in the mood for speculation. 'Don't stand there gawping, Miss Bastien,' she said. 'We haven't much time. Go and copy that for Mr Scott, will you? Off you go.'

8

Three days later, Quick invited me to her house. I had mentioned in passing that my birthday was coming up, and I found a small card, left on my desk, asking me to lunch on the Saturday. I was thrilled. It was not normal for employers and employees to mix like this, but my curiosity overrode any reservations I might have had. I told no one I was going.

My shoes clipped the pavement and my sense of adventure rose. It was the very last of summer; London was a motor-car fume, a cigarette stub on the paving, a cirrus sky. By now, I was a fully-fledged observer of the uneven spurts and scars of London housing. The postcodes, the brick, the rose bush absent or present, the foot scraper, the height of your front steps or the lack thereof was a language I had learned to speak. You couldn't live here and not notice the difference where roads reigned in peace or chaos, a mangy dog lolling by the gutter, ragged kids, a neat box hedge, the flicking net curtain. In London, there were many different ways to live, but few to change the life you had.

The bombings of the war had left odd patterns in so many streets, and Quick's long road was a familiar mongrel, starting with a handful of stately Victorian survivors, a slew of Edwardian terraces, a sudden and squat apartment block that had been erected in the fifties, with wide white balconies, concrete walls

and a midget ivy that someone had planted in an attempt at greenery, but which barely reached the first-floor window. Then, further
along, was where she lived, on the edge of Wimbledon Common.

I stood before Quick's house. It was a low-slung, pale-blue-
coloured Georgian cottage. You but half closed your eyes, and a
woman with a muslin dress and bonnet could so easily just have
slipped within. *Why the woman working if she have a place like
this?* I wondered. I thought Cynth would love to see this cottage,
and how unlikely it was she ever would. I used the knocker, an
old copper handle specked with verdigris, and waited. There was
no reply. Honeysuckle spilled everywhere around me, framing the
door. From within I could hear the strains of a classical piece, the
simple steps of a piano, complicating itself as the stanzas went on.

I wondered if the burn on my back was indeed eyes watching
me, or just my worried imagination. I hadn't been into a white
person's house, not even Lawrie's. This was, shall we say, a very
white street. The bolt slammed back, the door pulled open and in
a rectangle of gloom, Quick was before me. That silvery short hair,
those liquid pupils shrinking in the sunlight. She looked smaller
than at work. 'You came,' she said. I had never entertained the
thought that I might not. The piano was much louder now, playing
through the house like a theatrical opener to our pas de deux.

She gestured for me to step inside. It was a deep house, set back,
and the floor stretched down a corridor, on towards a glimpse of
garden, where leaves moved in a light breeze and the silhouette
of a solitary cat was shaped like a waiting vase. 'Garden?' Quick
asked, but it was not a question really, for she was already walking
towards it. She was taking delicate steps as if she didn't quite trust
her own feet. I swivelled my eyes to the left where the front room
opened out, and saw a brief glance of polished floorboards, wide
rugs, pot plants and an upright piano. Wherever I looked, the front
room, the corridor – the whitewashed walls were bare of pictures.

It looked decidedly un-English, no heavy Victorian tiles underfoot, no raised flock wallpaper, no cornicing, no heavy wood.
There were bookshelves though, and I longed to pry. To the right,

a flight of stairs began; I doubted I would ever see where they led. Another room opened off to the left as we carried on down the corridor, towards the square of light. It had a desk in it, and wind-up gramophone from where the dying notes of the classical recording was emanating. I thought it was quite old fashioned of her to have a gramophone.

When we reached the kitchen and the open garden door, Quick stopped. The cat skittered out into the undergrowth, where it settled, a pair of pale yellow eyes regarding me between the leaves. 'Lunch,' Quick announced. A large tray waited on the table. On it were bread rolls in a basket, a brash yellow cheese, some cold chicken legs, a pork pie and small red tomatoes, jewels of condensation running plumply off their sides. It all looked good, and I said as much.

'It's very simple,' Quick said. I offered to carry the tray into the garden. 'Not at all,' she said, batting me away, before conceding, 'but perhaps you can take those.' She indicated a large earthenware jug of water and two glasses, and I took them outside, following her stiff gait. 'Something stronger?' she asked over her shoulder, and this time it was a question. I declined.

Her garden was not large, but it was full of trees and bushes, and pink hollyhocks, more honeysuckle, the drone of accompanying bees, a little wilderness at the end. A church bell rang in the distance, a sombre line of twelve dongs to hold the time before it slipped away once more.

The garden moved in the breeze. Quick put the tray down on a stone table and a car revved in the road. 'Pull up a pew,' she said, gesturing to one of the three sun chairs. Two were old and saggy and had clearly seen much use. I obeyed, compelled by her authority. Lowering herself down gingerly into one of the older chairs, she slowly extended one leg after the other upon the grass. Kicking off velvet slippers, she revealed petite bare feet, browned by exposure. Looking at Quick's ten toes, I felt trussed in my winkle-pickers, my wedged pill-box hat, my plain green dress. She pushed a pair of sunglasses down onto her face and I lost sight of her expression.

'There are days like this,' she said, 'that I wish could go on for ever.' She poured us each a glass of water, struggling a little with the weight of the unwieldy jug. She glugged her glass and smacked her lips. 'Please eat,' she said. In her own habitat, she seemed much more relaxed. Gone was the haunted expression in Reede's office, even the debonair diffidence she sometimes employed for me and Pamela. I took up a quarter of the pork pie and began to eat it with a piece of bread roll. It was a good pie; the pastry melting away, the cool of the jelly, the rich shock of pig.

'I hope we're not giving you too much to do at the office?' she asked.

'Oh, no,' I said. 'It's all manageable.'

'Good.'

'How's your married friend?'

I looked at Quick, worried she was a mind-reader. 'Fine, thank you. She and her husband have moved to Queen's Park.'

'You're not lonely?'

'No.'

'Writing anything?'

'A little.'

'Can I read it?'

'*Read* it?'

'Well, that's what people usually do with writing, isn't it?' She looked amused.

'I don't—'

'I'd be honoured if you showed me.'

'It's not very good,' I said.

She pulled a face. 'Does it matter whether you think it's any good?'

'Of course.'

'Why?'

'Well – because – because I have to be critical of it, to make it better.'

'Well, that's a given. But isn't writing something as natural to you as breathing?'

'In some ways. But I have to work at what I write,' I said, my voice rising. 'Every writer does.'

'But you pick up a pen and write without much preamble.'

'I suppose.'

'And are you proud of breathing? Do you *revere* your ability to breathe?'

'It's who I am. So if it's not any good, then neither am I.'

She stared at me. 'Do you mean as a person?'

'Yes.'

'Oh, no. Don't be *moral* about this, Odelle. You're not walking around with a golden halo beaming out of you depending on the power of your paragraph. *You* don't come into it, once someone else is reading. It stands apart from you. Don't let your ability drag you down, don't hang it round your neck like an albatross.' She lit another cigarette. 'When something is considered "*good*", it draws people in, often resulting with the eventual destruction of the creator. I've seen it happen. So whether you think it's "*good*" or not should be entirely irrelevant, if you want to carry on. It's tough, but there it is. And of course, whether *I* think it's good should also be neither here nor there. Even more so, in fact. I think you're worrying too much.'

I was silent. I felt like I'd been shot.

'Do you want to publish your work, Odelle?' she went on, as if we were talking about nothing so substantial as a train timetable.

I dug my shoes into the grass and studied the tips intently. 'Yes.'

Surprisingly, my honesty created a companionable silence, a moment of reprieve. To publish my work was what I wanted; it was the only goal I'd really ever had.

'And do you hope to marry one day?' she asked. 'Have children?'

This was a swerve, but I had grown used to her staccato, jumping thoughts. Often with Quick you got the sense there was a whole other conversation going on underneath her words, one that only she could hear. The idea of being a wife was vaguely odd to me; the thought of being a mother, completely alien. Even so, the mind is elastic, so I thought of Lawrie and leapfrogged prematurely into the future. 'Maybe one day,' I said.

'The only problem is, children grow up. Or maybe that's a good thing, in your case. They can look after themselves, you can look after the words.'

'Can't I look after both?'

'I couldn't tell you. I've never tried.' I considered the house behind us; Quick had no sign of a family, children or otherwise. I tried to imagine Quick as a child, and I couldn't do it. She was too sophisticated and strange to ever have been such a rudimentary being.

Quick placed her cigarette in the ashtray. She readjusted her glasses, and forked a tomato with such expert precision that not a seed escaped. She plunged it into her mouth, and swallowed it. 'Mr Scott brought his painting to the Skelton because of you,' she said. 'Didn't he?'

My stomach flipped. 'I – what? – I—'

'Don't worry, Odelle. You haven't done anything wrong.'

'He didn't – it wasn't me, it was the Skelton's reputation – he—'

'Odelle,' she said firmly. 'I saw you kissing in the reception.'

'I'm sorry. We shouldn't have – I don't want—'

'Oh, don't worry about that. Are you happy?'

I thought about this. 'Yes.'

'Just be careful of him.'

I sat back in my chair, overwhelmed. 'Do you – know him?'

Quick lit another cigarette, her fist gripped so tightly round the lighter that her knuckles had turned white. She breathed out the bluish smoke. 'No, I don't know him. I'm only looking after you. That's my job. I recruited you, and I value you, and I want you to be all right. Men are not always – well – just make sure you don't do anything you don't want to do.'

I realized then, that Quick was not a person to make herself vulnerable. That in fact, she would do anything to avoid such a predicament. 'I won't,' I said. It felt like Quick was admonishing me; this flash of a harsh demeanour had curdled the garden's lovely atmosphere, where even the bees seemed to fall silent. 'He's not like that.'

She sighed. My bones felt like lead. But I could have got up, I could have thanked her for the pork-pie quarter and the bit of bread which was all I'd managed to eat, and walked through the cool bare corridor, back out to life and Lawrie and Cynth and the future, and never have talked to Quick personally again. Things might have been easier if I had.

'Has he told you anything about the painting?' she went on.

'Only that he's pleased it might be an Isaac Robles,' I said, dully.

'But he'd never heard of Isaac Robles before this?'

'No.'

She looked thoughtful. 'Why do you think he wanted a copy of that photograph?'

'I don't know,' I said, trying my best to hide my irritation. 'To look at it more closely, I suppose. To put the pieces together.'

'Odelle, does Mr Scott understand that Mr Reede would like to make this painting a big splash – not just for the Skelton, but for himself? He spoke of the possibility of an exhibition. Is that what Mr Scott wants?'

'I don't know what he wants. But surely an exhibition can only be a good thing.'

'Men like Edmund Reede are circus masters. They will spin a reputation from thin air. They will wrap it up and increase its wonder, just so what they possess increases in value. What I mean is, Odelle – be careful to remind Mr Scott what he's actually *looking* at. Don't let Reede take what he has away from him.'

'But I thought you agreed with Mr Reede that the Skelton should keep his painting safe.'

'Only until Mr Scott has made his decision.' She took a long drag on her cigarette and stared into the hollyhocks. 'If I was Mr Scott, I would keep it. I would keep it and enjoy it. His mother clearly did, and so should he.'

'But if it is an important painting, he could sell it, he could use the money. He's stuck, you see.'

She turned to me. 'So he *does* want to sell it. He's worried about money.'

'I don't know the ins and outs. But the painting could be useful. If there was an exhibition of it – a long-lost painting come to light, that sort of thing – I'm sure that would be popular. Lawrie could be involved. He could help with organizing. He's very clever. Enthusiastic. People like him.'

'You're not his mother.'

'And you're not mine.'

The words came out before I could stop them. Quick winced; I was horrified. 'I'm sorry,' I said. 'I'm very sorry—'

'No – you're right,' she said. 'You're quite right. You must think I'm interfering.'

'I didn't mean – I'm only trying to help him.'

'Mr Scott isn't stuck,' Quick said. 'I'm sure he could do many things. His existence doesn't hinge on that painting. He should just take it home and enjoy it for what it is. A very good painting – an *excellent* painting, designed for private pleasure.'

'But isn't it better that more than one person can see it?' I asked. 'Isn't that the ethos of a place like the Skelton – shouldn't it be shared?'

'That's fair. But like Reede said, we don't know enough about the painting yet. We need to go slowly. You don't just *happen* upon a painting like that, Odelle. People always have something to hide. Listen to the words Mr Scott isn't saying.'

'Lawrie is an honest person,' I said, my voice rising again.

'Of course,' Quick said, her own words tightening with emotion. 'Of course he is. But you can still be honest at the same time as having something to hide. And if there is something to hide, then the Skelton could look very foolish indeed.'

She levered herself out of the chair and walked slowly into the cottage. I sat, stupefied, unable to think properly. What was going on here? The bees appeared to drone again, looping from flower to flower. Above, the sky was now cloudless. Suddenly everything seemed so very alive, vibrating, the green leaves turning slightly gold, moving in a psychedelic pattern as the sunshine rippled.

For a mad moment I imagined Quick might be fetching a revolver, that she was going to point it at me and demand answers that I couldn't give. Something had switched rapidly over the brief course of our picnic, a change of energy like the light through the leaves, impossible to catch. But when Quick came back, she was holding a beautiful octavo leather notebook. 'I bought this for you,' she said, holding it out.

I could almost laugh, thinking about this scene now – no, it was not a firearm, but Quick knew full well it was still a weapon.

'For me?' I said.

'Just a small present, to say thank you for doing such a wonderful job. I'm very glad we found you, Odelle. Or you found us, more to the point. Happy Birthday.'

I took the notebook from her. It was handmade, thick calfskin leather with a matte green finish. The pages were the colour of cream. It was a Stradivarius of notebooks, compared to the flimsy numbers I bought in Woolworth's. 'Thank you,' I said. 'It's so kind.'

From somewhere over the fences, a lawn mower ground itself up to a mechanical whine, and a child shrieked. 'Well,' said Quick peaceably. 'Don't they always say? You never know when inspiration is going to strike.'

9

*O*n Sunday, I sat on my bed with my new notebook from Quick, and thought about what she'd said in the garden. Like most artists, everything I produced was connected to who I was – and so I suffered according to how my work was received. The idea that anyone might be able to detach their personal value from their public output was revolutionary. I didn't know if it was possible, even desirable. Surely it would affect the quality of the work?

Still, I knew I'd gone too far in the opposite direction, and something had to change. Ever since I could pick up a pen, other people's pleasure was how I'd garnered attention and defined success. When I began receiving public acknowledgement for a private act, something was essentially lost. My writing became the axis upon which all my identity and happiness hinged. It was now outward-looking, a self-conscious performance. I was asked to repeat the pleasure for people, again and again, until the facsimile of my act became the act itself.

Cynth's wedding poem was to me a perfect example of how I felt my writing to be bound up with obligation. I'd been writing for so long for the particular purpose of being approved that I'd forgotten the genesis of my impulse; unbothered, pure creation, existing outside the parameters of success and failure. And somewhere along the line, this being 'good' had come to paralyse my belief that I could write at all.

So admitting to Quick that I wanted to be published was no small step. It communicated, to a certain degree, that I believed I should be taken seriously. And here she was, telling me, *Well, maybe you're not that special, maybe you are – but that doesn't actually mean anything, and it certainly doesn't have any bearing on whether you can write. So stop worrying, and do it.*

She had told me that the approval of other people should never be my goal; she had released me in a way I hadn't been able to myself. She trusted me. Quick had encouraged me to lay myself bare, and it had not been that difficult at all.

I ran my fingers over the leather of the notebook and remembered. I first started writing as a little girl because I liked imagining parallel possibilities. That was all it was. That Sunday, I picked up my pen for the first time in a long time, and began to write.

At the end of the day on Monday – my actual birthday – I left a short story typed up on Quick's desk. I wasn't completely bullish – the top-grade schoolgirl dies hard – I did not creep into her office without a feeling of trepidation. I put no note on the top; she'd know who it was from.

I appreciated the irony that just like at school, at university, I was delivering a story for someone else to approve, but I had been too long inculcated with the act of writing for an audience. This time, however, I wasn't going to hinge everything on my audience's response. If Quick didn't like it, maybe that was a good thing. It was now out of my control.

Pamela stopped me as I was leaving. 'You can't hide it any longer, you know,' she said.

'Sorry?'

'Oh come on. You're going round like Cupid smacked you in the chops. You forgot to put stamps on these envelopes. That ain't like you.'

I winced; Pamela was more observant than perhaps I'd given her credit for. 'I don't know what you mean,' I said.

'Odelle, I'm only gonna keep askin'. Gonna be your Scotland Yard. It's you and that feller, isn't it? There was barely five minutes between you when he turned up.'

I weighed up my options. Don't tell Pamela, and suffer her interminable hypotheses, which, knowing her, would become more outlandish and indefatigable – or just tell her, and be done. 'Maybe,' I said.

'Lawrie Scott, eh. Bit posh, ain't he?'

'How do you know his first name?'

She looked pleased with herself. 'It's *right* here, in the appointment book. Written by your own fair hand. Shall I draw a heart round it for you?'

'Shut up.'

'Does Quick know?'

'Quick knows.'

'How?'

'Saw us kissing in the reception.'

'Hoo-ee!' Pamela whooped with laughter and I couldn't help a smile; it was a thrilling admission. 'Bloody *hell*, Odelle, I didn't know you had it in you. She must like you, 'cos most girls woulda been out on their ear.'

'Pamela, shut *up*.'

'Ahh, you *like* him.'

'Don't be an idiot.'

'All right, all right.' Pamela put up her hands, and her ringed fingers glinted in the light. 'I was like that when I first met Billy,' she said. I suspected no two men were more different than Lawrie and Billy, but I let it pass. 'It's like you can't *breathe*,' she said.

'I can breathe perfectly well.'

She laughed. 'Miss High and Mighty. Honestly, Odelle, are you sure you ain't a secret African queen?'

'I'm from Trinidad.'

'Keep your knickers on. Or maybe *not*.'

'*Pamela*.'

'Come on,' she whispered. 'Have you done it yet?'

'Mind your own business.'

She smirked. 'That'll be a no then. Get on with it, Odelle. You don't know what you're missing.' She fished under the reception counter and placed a brown-paper bag before me. 'Happy birthday,' she beamed, mischief dancing in her black-kohled eyes.

I eyed it suspiciously. 'What's inside?'

'Take a look, Miss Bastien.'

I lifted the edge of the paper. Inside were two strips of pills. 'Are these—'

'Yep. Got some spare. I thought you might want them.' Pamela looked at the expression on my face, and her confidence faltered. 'You don't have to take them—'

'No, thank you. I'll take them.'

Pamela grinned. It was funny to me, the different gifts people gave to show their friendship – with Quick it was a notebook, with Pamela, the contraceptive Pill. I'd spent weeks pressing novels onto Pamela, which in many ways says all you need to know about me. Pamela's offering was a reflection of her utilitarian sensuality; a pragmatic approach to the pursuit of pleasure. It was no small thing for an unmarried girl to get hold of the Pill in those days; no doctor would prescribe it.

'How did you get these?' I asked.

She winked. 'Rubbed a lamp, didn't I.'

'Come on, how?'

'Brook Advisory,' she relented. 'Gold dust.'

I shoved them into my handbag. 'Thank you, *Rudge*,' I said, skipping down the Skelton steps before Pamela could ruin the moment with a salacious addendum. Still – she was a woman of the new world, giving me a slice of freedom. I should have been more grateful.

FOR MY BIRTHDAY, LAWRIE WAS taking me to the house in Surrey. Gerry was away, he said, and he wanted to show me the place. In the near six years I'd been in England, I'd not seen that bucolic heaven peddled to us in Trinidad. I was ready for hedgerows, crumbling Eleanor crosses covered in yellow lichen, the dip of autumn trees overburdened by their fruit, village shops selling eggs in boxes by the step. In fact, when I saw Lawrie's house, this wasn't actually far off, which made me think that perhaps the only truth my colonial educators had told me was the one about the English countryside.

Lawrie's family lived near a place called Baldock's Ridge, in a detached red-brick Victorian farmhouse. In a childlike simplicity, it was called The Red House. It had a mature orchard of apple trees in the front, and peeling paintwork on its windows. It was enchanting. Inside, however, there wasn't much evidence of feminine life, despite how recently his mother had died. I wanted ball gowns hanging up in dignified tatters, tobacco-infused dining chairs, chocolate-box paintings on the wall, the smell of dog hair on old picnic rugs. But there was nothing like that. Either she'd lived as a spartan, or Bastard Gerry had cleared his dead wife out.

I sat in the kitchen, and closed my eyes as Lawrie made the tea. *Just be careful of him. You don't just* happen *upon a painting like that, Odelle.* I pushed Quick's words away with a flash of anger. Did she want to ruin this for me?

'Here we are,' said Lawrie, handing me a chipped blue cup. 'It's still lovely and warm out. Shall we sit in the garden?'

I followed him, my hands wrapped round the cup, padding along the rugless hallway.

THE BACK GARDEN WAS A bit of a mess in a Hodgson Burnett way; overgrown bushes and gnarled plum trees, broken terracotta pots sprouting mint, wild pansies faring perfectly. There was a greenhouse at the end of the long lawn, its windows streaked with dried mud and rain so it was impossible to see inside. Who had tended this place? Perhaps Lawrie had, once upon a time, up and down the furrows.

'How long have you lived here?' I asked.

'On and off all my life. We had a flat in London, too, but my mother stopped liking the city. She preferred it here.'

'I can see why. It's beautiful.'

He sighed. 'It has its moments.'

We sat in silence for a while, listening to the blackbirds in the dusk. 'Are you excited for what Reede might discover next?' I asked.

He stared out at the orchard. 'What if it *was* stolen?'

'It wouldn't be your fault – or your mother's.'

'Well – no. No, I suppose not. Imagine if it's worth a fortune. God, the look on Gerry's face. The only thing she left me and it's worth a bomb.'

'If you sold it, you wouldn't have anything of your mother left.'

He turned to me, a shrewd expression in his eyes. 'Don't you go soft. My mother was the least sentimental person I knew.'

'I think it is quite sentimental, leaving you a single painting in her will.'

'You didn't know her,' he said. 'It's more likely a loaded gun.'

'What do you mean?'

Lawrie cast his eye over the wilderness before us, sipping on his tea. 'She always attracted trouble. I think she would have liked you very much.'

'Why? I never attract trouble.'

'And she could be a pain in the arse as well.'

'*Hey.*'

He said he had made a shepherd's pie; I was impressed that he could cook. I wondered when Lawrie had learned, and had the suspicion he had spent quite a lot of his life looking after himself. He said he'd lay the table, I was the birthday girl – so whilst he was doing all that, heating up the oven and looking for forks, I took the opportunity to go upstairs.

I WENT INTO ONE OF the large back rooms, evening sunbeams slanting through its windows, a shade of deep whisky, dust motes swirling in the shafts. Again, no rugs or carpets on the floor, no paintings on the wall, just the bed frame and a wardrobe, empty save for a percussive clutch of wire hangers when I opened its door. Upturned bluebottles were scattered against the skirting.

There were piles of documents and boxes of paper everywhere, curled and faded with time.

I tried to imagine Lawrie's mother in this house; what she looked like, her marriage to Gerry, what she'd done in her life after her husband died in the war. There were no photos of her anywhere, but there was the faintest trace of perfume in the air; sophisticated, woody, alluring. I sat gently on the edge of the metal bed frame, wondering whether another family would fill this place again with life, with second chances, hopes and failures. I felt a pang of anxiety that Cynth would never speak to me again. *You must telephone*, I thought. *It's gone on too long. Or write, at least.*

I rose from the bed and approached the window to view the rolling Surrey hills in this extraordinary light. I rested my elbows on yet another pile of old papers, and Quick's caution over Lawrie entered my thoughts again. What was it that bothered her so much? It was none of her business, but I couldn't budge her comments from my mind.

Absently, I sifted through a pile of papers on the windowsill. They were receipts mainly, one for a butcher's delivery back in 1958, a Guildford shopping centre parking ticket, electricity bills, an order of service for the Baldock's Ridge Carol Concert, 1949. Here was someone who didn't throw things away, yet Lawrie had said his mother was not the type who kept receipts.

Underneath the carol service sheet was a tissue-thin pamphlet for an exhibition of young British artists, from 1955. I opened it. It had been held in the London Gallery on Cork Street, and whoever had attended had put a line through the names of the artists and their works one by one with a pencil. *No Sign*, they had written at the bottom. No sign of what? I wondered. The frustration of whoever had written this was evident in the pressure of lead upon the paper.

I folded the pamphlet in two, slid it in my pocket and went downstairs, telling myself that in that mess of papers up there, no one would miss it.

LAWRIE HAD LIT CANDLES, WEDGING them into empty wine bottles and a burnished, sinuous candelabra that had more than a hint of murder weapon about it. We sat in the kitchen, the day now faded, eating his shepherd's pie, drinking cider that the neighbour had made from the orchard. 'Happy birthday, Odelle,' he said, and raised his glass.

'Thank you. I feel like we're hiding from the world out here.'

'Sounds good to me.'

'It doesn't seem obvious that Gerry lives here. Upstairs is a bit of a mess.'

'That was my mother, more than him. I expect Gerry will sell the house.'

'How long were they married?'

Lawrie poured more cider into our glasses. 'Let's see. I was fourteen – so that's sixteen years.'

'How did she die?'

Lawrie visibly prickled. I saw his closed expression, sensed his self-protection. I regretted the question immediately, feeling like a blunderer.

He placed the bottle down gently. 'It's hard to explain.'

'You don't have to. I shouldn't have asked. I'm sorry.' Now I was interfering, just like Quick.

'My mother killed herself,' Lawrie said, and the words weighed down the air between us, the kitchen's atmosphere thickening to a soup. Looking at Lawrie, I saw how a ghost could suck the air from your throat.

'I'm sorry,' I said. 'I'm so sorry—'

'It's all right. No, really, it's all right. I would have told you eventually. Don't apologize. I mean, don't feel bad about it. In all honesty, it wasn't that much of a surprise.'

I tried desperately to think of something to fill the silence, but the admission seemed to open something in him: 'We tried to help. We were always trying. And now I can't even look at bloody Gerry, because every time we look at each other I know he's thinking,

What if you'd done more?, and I'm thinking exactly the same. But it's not his fault. It's just a horrible game of blame.'

'I can't imagine it.'

'Well, neither can I, and I was her son.'

He was very still, his voice very quiet, and I wanted to get up and give him a hug. But in the soupy air I felt unable to move, and I wasn't sure he wanted one anyway. I thought of the kitchen at Cynth's wedding, how Lawrie must have been reeling from his past two weeks – and me, mocking my own mother, rude when he tried to be nice about my poem—

'Anyway, that's that,' he said. 'But she *was* spirited, and she did a lot of things, and enjoyed herself a great deal, and that's really why she reminds me of you. And now there's her painting.'

'Yes.'

'So.' He exhaled brusquely. 'I've told you *that*. Jesus. I promise you that's the worst. Now you tell me something.'

'I don't have anything.'

'Everyone has at least one thing, Delly.'

I stayed quiet. He leaned back in his chair, fishing around in the dresser drawer behind him. 'A-ha. Gerry always leaves a few lying around.' He brandished a box of slim cigars. 'Care to join?'

WE WENT TO THE BACK room and Lawrie pushed open the French windows. The night was still fragrant with the smell of damp grass and wood smoke, bats dipping in and out of the garden.

'It's like paradise,' I said, even enjoying the smothering scent of Lawrie's cigar. I sat on the sofa and watched him, propping himself against the window frame.

'I don't know about that,' Lawrie replied. 'But one thing is – you can't hear the road. When I was little, my favourite book was *Peter Pan*. I used to pretend this garden was Neverland.'

'And was Gerry Captain Hook?'

'Ha, no, this was before Gerry. It was just me and Mum at that point.'

'I was just with my mother too.'

He turned to me. 'What happened to your dad in the war?'

Given what Lawrie had told me about his mother's suicide, I felt I had to dredge it up, although I really didn't want to. 'Well,' I said. 'My dad sold his bicycle and trumpet to pay for his passage to England in '41. He walked to the Air Ministry, passed the medical, and got himself twelve weeks' basic training. He served as an air gunner in the RAF. Then three years later, my mother found his name chalked on the death board in Port of Spain.'

He came over, and put his hand on my shoulder; it was warm, and I focused on it with particular concentration. 'I'm sorry, Odelle,' he said.

'Thank you. I don't remember him, but I know what it was like not to have him. My mother took it bad.'

He sat beside me. 'What was it like, on the island, in the war?'

'People were terrified what would happen if Hitler won. We've got one of the largest oil refineries in Trinidad. U-boats were already torpedoing British ships off our coastline.'

'I didn't know that.'

'We knew what Hitler wanted; the plan for a master race. We were always going to want to fight. My dad was no exception.' I sipped on my cider. 'England wasn't too keen on the colonies helping out at first, but as things turned bad they wanted the help.'

'Do you think you'll go back?'

I hesitated. Most English people I'd met would ask me questions about the island with the expectation that I should fit the complexity of Trinidad into my single body for their benefit. None of them had ever been there, so to them we were specimens of curiosity, realities risen from a tropical petri dish that until very recently sat under a British flag. Most of the time, as with Pamela, the Englishers' interest was not malicious (except when it was) – but their questioning always served to make me feel *different*, when I'd been brought up to feel perfectly understanding of British ways, because I was a child of empire too.

In the time I'd known him, Lawrie hadn't asked me a thing about Trinidad. I didn't know whether he was being polite, or whether he was genuinely uninterested – but either way, I was mainly glad of his failure to highlight our differences in life experience. I'd learned Latin and read Dickens, but I'd also seen the lighter-skinned girls get more of the boys' attention, in a way the boys probably didn't even understand themselves. Most of our 'differences' had been created by the white skin of the English. And yet, by the shores of the Thames, the complexity of our island life was reduced to one phenotype: *black*.

Practically every Englishman, even the enlightened ones, believed we would have more in common with a Sudanese than with them. But what did I know of the Sahara, of a camel or a Bedouin? My ideal of beauty and glamour for my entire childhood was Princess Margaret. With Lawrie, I'd talked about James Bond films, or my strange boss, or the painting, or Gerry the Bastard, dead parents. Stuff that bound us together as a duo, that didn't make me a representative of a whole island that I hadn't seen for five years. When Lawrie didn't ask me about Trinidad, I felt more of an individual again.

'Odelle?'

'Let me tell you about London,' I said.

'OK.'

'When I first got here,' I went on, 'I could not believe the cold.' Lawrie laughed. 'I'm serious, Lawrie. It was like the Arctic. Cynth and I arrived in *January*.'

'Of all the months.'

'I know. When I was a little girl, I was Autumn in a school play about the seasons. I didn't even know what autumn *was*, let alone winter.'

I was quiet for a minute, remembering my smaller self, in her little boater and English pinafore, telling her mother she needed 'russet leaves' pinned to a leotard – and my mother, who had no idea either what frost on the tips of grass might look like, what a conker was, how it felt to inhale London's November air and feel a sliver of ice in your lung – doing her darnedest to make this English costume in the humid Caribbean.

'I remember,' I went on, warming to this reminiscence, feeling that I could do this with Lawrie, that I was safe – 'an early day I was here – a feller saying to me in the shoe shop, "Your English is very good." My *English*! I told him, "English is a West Indian language, sir." '

'And what did he say?' Lawrie asked, laughing. I realized that never in Lawrie's life would anyone say to him what that man had said to me.

'He thought I was simple. I nearly lost my job. Cynth was furious. It's true though – I'd be quite at home with Queen Elizabeth and that tall Greek husband of hers, drinking a cup of tea and petting those funny midget dogs she loves so much. Quite at home. "Your English is not as good as mine," I should have said. "It does not have the length and the breadth, the meat and the smoke. Come at me with my Creole, with its Congo and its Spanish and its Hindi, French and Ibo, English and Bhojpuri, Yoruba and Manding." '

Lawrie laughed again. 'Oh, to see his face,' I carried on, draining my cider glass. 'With his Anglesaxon—'

'Angle what?'

'Two-up, two-down, a window with a view people never truly look at, because they think they know every shrub and flower, the bark of every tree and the mood of every cloud. But we made room for their patois too—'

'Odelle,' Lawrie said. 'I would be happy with you for the rest of my life.'

'Eh?'

'You have this light, and when it switches on I don't think you even realize what it does.'

'What light? I was talking about—'

'I love you, Odelle.' His face was hopeful. 'You inspire me.'

We sat in silence. 'You tell it to all the girls,' I said desperately, unsure what to say.

'What?'

'You're not serious.'

He stared at me. 'I *am* serious. I feel like time's tricked me, as if I've known you from before. Like we passed each other in our prams. Like it's been a waiting game to meet with you again. I love you.'

I said nothing, unable to respond. He looked down at the carpet.

No one had ever told me they loved me before. Why did he have to ruin our evening with talk of love and . . . *prams*? I felt panicked. Quick's warnings flashed again through my mind – and I cursed her inside. Why should I be careful – and yet why could I not bear to hear Lawrie's words?

I got off the sofa and walked to the windows. 'You probably want me to go,' I said.

He sat, motionless, looking at me with incredulity. 'Why would I want you to go, after what I've just said?'

'I don't know! I – look, I'm not—'

'It's fine,' he said. 'I'm sorry. It's fine. I shouldn't have—'

'No – it's just, I was – and then you—'

'Forget I said anything. I – please, forget it. If that's what you want, then I'll drive you home.'

SO LAWRIE DROVE US BACK in silence up the deserted A3. I clasped my handbag tight to my body, feeling utterly miserable, my fingers clenched around the pamphlet I had stolen, and the pills Pamela had handed me only hours before. How could I explain to Lawrie that this was terrifying for me, and that I couldn't exactly say why? We'd only just started, he barely knew me. I felt like he'd hoisted me onto a pedestal and left me with my legs dangling, and of course I'd managed to turn it into a trauma for the pair of us. Being alone was always so much easier.

I glanced only once at him, his profile coming in and out of the orange light as the car moved under the street lamps. His eyes were on the road, his jaw set. I didn't know which of us felt more humiliated.

When we reached my flat, he pulled in. 'I left your present in Surrey,' he said, the engine still running.

'Oh – I—'

'Anyway. I'd better go.' I got out, he revved the car and was off. I stood in the road, until the noise of his engine was replaced in my head by the sound of a silent scream.

I LAY IN BED AWAKE, my bedside light still on past three. In my chest, my stomach, in my aching head, I felt pain for us both. That Lawrie loved me, I could not easily believe. Though he had never made me feel like an outsider, I couldn't help worrying that he only liked me because I looked different to all the other girls in that gang he'd turned up with at Cynth's wedding.

Lawrie had rushed in with his declaration of love – but did he really *see* me? I couldn't imagine being someone who dived in for another like that; the sense that one's molecules were being recalibrated; the sheer, multi-layered joy of being seen and adored, and adoring in return, the cycle of shyness to confidence as each new step was taken. To seek your beloved in a crowd, to lock your eyes and feel you have no truer place – it seemed impossible to me. I was – both by circumstance and nature – a migrant in this world, and my lived experience had long become a state of mind.

I didn't know if I loved him, and that was also frightening – not to know, to be sure. *Just be careful of him. You don't just* happen *upon a painting like that, Odelle.* I had tried so hard to shut Quick's voice away. I wondered if she was the reason I could not drop my anchor with him as confidently as he'd declared his love. I leaned over, switching off the light, hoping in the dark for sleep. As I lay there, I couldn't tell which fears were mine, now Quick had slipped her own inside my head.

FEBRUARY 1936

VII

The painting Olive had finished was propped against the wall. She was more proud of it than even *The Orchard*, and felt that she was creeping ever closer to that shining citadel. The new piece was a surreal composition, colourful, disjointed to the gaze. It was a diptych; Santa Justa before her arrest and after, set against a dark indigo sky and a shining field. Olive had decided to call it *Santa Justa in the Well*.

The left half of the painting was lush and glowing. Olive had used ordinary oils, but had also experimented with gold leaf, which glinted in the light as she held the painting up. She'd always thought of gold leaf as an alchemist's dream, a contained ray of sun. It was the colour of queens, of wise men, of shimmering land in high summer. It reminded her of the Russian Orthodox icons she had always wanted to touch as a little girl, when her father took her to the Kunsthistorisches Museum.

In the middle of the healthy land on this left-hand side stood a woman, her hair the colour of the crop. She was carrying a heavy pot with deer and rabbits painted on it, and in its centre was the face of the goddess Venus. Both the faces of the woman and Venus looked proud, staring out at the viewer.

On the right half of the painting, the crop was deadened and limp. The woman appeared again, except this time she was curled inside a circle, hovering over the crop. This circle was filled with an internal perspective to make it look as if it had depth, as if the woman was lying at the bottom of a well. Her hair was now severed and dull, her pot had smashed around her, a puzzle impossible for anyone to piece together. Around the rim of the well, full-sized deer and rabbits peered down, as if set free from the broken crockery. Venus had vanished.

Olive could hear soft knocking at the attic door, and she sat up. 'Who is it?' she asked, her voice half-strangled with hope that it might be him.

'It is Teresa.'

'Oh.'

'The party is in a few hours, señorita. Can I come in?'

Olive leapt up and hid the painting under the bed. 'Yes,' she said.

Recently, Teresa had begun to help Olive keep her room in order. It was an unspoken agreement. Olive had not invited it, but she liked it; the attention, the paint brushes laid out for another day's work. Her clothes were always neatly folded on her chair or hanging in her cupboard, her unfinished canvases were turned to face the wall, the way she liked it when it was time for bed. Olive would turn them back in the morning, and work up there unbothered.

Teresa stood at the doorway, her satchel across her chest. 'Is there anything I can do?'

Olive lay back on the bed. 'I want to look like Garbo,' she said languorously, stretching herself out, running her fingers through her hair. 'Tere, how good are you at making waves?'

The girls set up a chair in front of the oval mirror, which Teresa had found in a spare room and nailed to the wall. The glass was foxed and misty round the edges, but the centre was clear enough. They were using a series of illustrations from one of Sarah's *Vogues* in an attempt to recreate Greta Garbo's look. Teresa lit candles around the room as the light outside faded.

'I've never been able to have finger waves anyway,' Olive said. 'My hair's too thick. But we should be able to do these curls.'

They remained in companionable silence for a good five minutes, Olive enjoying Teresa's calming administrations through her hair; a repetitive, smoothing motion that made her sleepy. 'I suppose it's good news about the election, but I keep thinking about that poor boy Isaac knew,' she said finally.

Teresa kept her eyes down, working at the nape of Olive's neck. 'One day, left, next day, right. The government changes the street names more than I change my bed. And at the end of it, señorita, I never see the difference.'

'Well, thank goodness there are men like your brother who *do* care.'

Teresa was silent.

'Do you like your father, Tere?' Olive said.

Teresa frowned at the back of Olive's head. 'I do not like the stories.'

Olive opened her eyes. 'What stories?'

Teresa wrapped small portions of Olive's sizeable mass of hair round and round her finger, before securing it tightly with the pins sequestered out of Sarah's bedroom. 'They say that once he cut a man's thing off and nailed it to a door.'

Olive swivelled her head round, and the hair sprang from its curl, the pin skittering across the floorboards. 'What? To a *door*?'

'He was his enemy.'

They looked at each other, then burst out laughing, high on the night to come and the violence they believed was safely avoided, because it had gone before their time, because neither of them had a *thing*, and because they were safe up here.

'Teresa, that's disgusting! Why would he *do* that?'

'It's just a rumour,' Teresa said, picking up the pin.

'But no man would drop his trousers to prove it.'

'And yet Don Alfonso never denies it.'

'Jesus, Teresa. And I thought I had problems with my father.'

Teresa looked up. 'What problems?'

Olive sighed. 'Oh, nothing really. I just . . . I feel a bit invisible, that's all. He never takes me seriously. I never know how to *make* him take me seriously. The only things he thinks about are his business and whether my mother has taken her pills. And she's never really taken the time to understand me either. When I have children, I am never going to be like her. I wish I was free of my parents. I suppose I *could* be free of them, if I put my mind to it.'

'If you had gone to the art school, you would be free.'

'You can't be sure. And painting here makes me feel freer.' Olive looked serious. 'Although I'm learning something else out here.'

'What is that?'

'That if you really want to see your work to completion, you have to desire it more than you'd believe. You have to fight it, fight yourself. It's not easy.'

Teresa smiled, working through the mass of Olive's hair with a level of attention that Olive wanted to bask in for ever. She had never had a friend like this, in her private room, combing her hair, listening to her, talking about silly nonsense and the uselessness of one's parents; how the future was perfect, because they hadn't lived it yet.

'I always find that the time *before* a party is happiest,' Olive said. 'Nothing's had the chance to go wrong.' Teresa lifted her hands away from Olive's head. 'Why have you stopped?' she asked, as Teresa walked over to her satchel.

Teresa removed a small, square package wrapped in tissue paper. She held it out, nervously. 'For you,' she said.

Olive took it. 'For *me*? My goodness. Shall I open it now?'

Teresa nodded, and Olive gasped when she saw the green flash through the paper, emerald strung on emerald, emerging like a stone snake, a necklace of such beauty and intensity she had never seen before. 'My God. Where did you get this?'

'It was my mother's,' Teresa said. 'Now for you.'

Olive sat frozen on the chair, the necklace swinging from her fist. No one had ever in her life given her such a present. This was everything Teresa possibly had of her mother; to take it would be a selfish act. 'No,' she said. 'I couldn't—'

'It's for you.'

'Teresa, this is too much—'

In the end, it was Teresa who made the decision for her, scooping the necklace out of Olive's grasp, laying it round her neck and fixing the clasp. 'It is for *you*,' Teresa said. 'For my friend.'

Olive turned to the mirror. The emeralds looked like green leaves, shining upon her pale skin, enlarging in size towards her clavicle. Stones from Brazil, green as the ocean, green as the forest her father had promised they would find in the south of Spain. These were not jewels, they were eyes, winking at her in the candlelight, watching the girls who watched themselves.

VIII

By the evening, Harold had returned from Malaga with supplies for the party. He was loping around the house, a cigar clamped between his teeth, calling for more gramophone records. Isaac was helping carry extra chairs and tables loaned by the villagers.

'Olive,' he said to her. 'The painting is finished.'

'Oh,' she said.

'You are not pleased? I did not think you liked being painted.'

She didn't know what to say; Isaac's finished painting just meant less opportunity to see him.

Sarah emerged, dressed in a long plum-coloured gown. In London, when they had parties, she would often come in fancy dress – the Little Mermaid, or Snow White – and one memorable year as Rapunzel, when her entire false plait went up in flames and they'd put her out with champagne. But tonight was a Schiaparelli number, *truly sophis*, as the girls at school might have said – with two women's faces embroidered on the back in sequins, their red lips glittering from the hundreds of candles Harold had brought back from the city, and which Teresa had been instructed to light. The dress was one of Olive's favourites; she had always been mesmerized by the Janus-like embroidery.

Sarah's eyes were drawn to the emeralds around her daughter's neck. 'Who gave you those?' she demanded, as Harold popped a bottle of Veuve Clicquot.

Olive realized that she had heard the sound of glasses clinking over trauma all her life. Annoyed that her mother had not even noticed her new hair, she tipped her chin and stroked the green stones. 'Isaac,' she replied.

IT WAS A RECKLESS EVENING. The guests began to arrive up the finca path at around eight o'clock, and Olive and her parents stood at the door to greet them. One of the first to appear was a man in an expensive-looking cream suit with a large cravat, as if it was cocktail hour on an ocean liner. His large black moustache had been oiled at the tips. Behind him, two younger men followed in neat suits. Olive wondered who they were – his children, perhaps? They seemed more like his hired guards than anything else.

The man proffered his hand. 'Señor Schloss,' he said. 'Don Alfonso Robles Hernández. I have been away on business for the duchess.'

'Don Alfonso,' said Harold, putting out his own hand. 'We meet at last.'

He spoke good English, and Olive saw echoes of Isaac in the man's face – but there was something inherently theatrical about the Don that his son did not share. Despite his flashiness, there was an intelligence in Alfonso's small eyes; calculation and black humour. She thought of the story Teresa had told about him, and tried to quell her anxiety.

'Gregorio, give Señora Schloss our offerings.' One of the boys hopped forward. 'Almond cake and a bottle of good port,' said Alfonso.

Sarah took the presents. 'Thank you,' she said.

'Are you settled in well?'

'Very well.'

Alfonso peered past Harold into the darkness of the hallway. '*Díos mio*, the kitten has grown into a cat,' he said, knocking one heel to the other in a cod-military gesture. The clipping heels of his boots and the creak of patent raised the hairs on Olive's skin. She looked back to see Teresa scowling in the dark.

'Still so scared of me, Tere?' Alfonso said, in Spanish. 'I don't know why. I've heard about your claws.' The younger men laughed. 'She's not giving you trouble, I hope?'

Harold glanced at Teresa, who stared at him with round black eyes. 'None at all,' he said.

'Well, let me know if she is.' Alfonso looked up at the finca's many windows, every one illuminated with tiny, flickering flames. 'Señor Schloss, I hope we are not going to be burned alive. I thought this house was blessed with electricity?'

'We wanted a little atmosphere tonight, Don Alfonso. Please come in.'

'I brought Gregorio and Jorge – you don't mind if they come too?'

'Not at all. Everyone is welcome.'

The three men moved past Olive and her mother, Jorge's gaze lingering a little too long on Sarah.

'Is that brother of yours here?' Jorge asked Teresa.

'Maybe. But he won't be talking to you,' she said.

IN TOTAL, SIXTY-SEVEN RESIDENTS OF Arazuelo came to the party. The presence of this small family from London and Vienna imbued the locals with a carnival, topsy-turvy feeling. There was a permissiveness in the air, as if a taboo had broken apart, and its scent was going to drown them all. Don Alfonso stayed in a corner of one room – a few people came up to him, but generally he was left alone.

The guests wrote their names in a book that Harold produced. Some inscribed their signatures eagerly, happy to be included in this cosmopolitan event, with its dancing lights and jazz music, and the smell of oleanders in every room. They jotted short messages of approval or goodwill – *buen vino* or *Dios bendiga*. Others were more cautious, looking worried about being permanently embedded in this foreign book, as if it might be a politically controversial gesture. Olive remembered Adrián, the murdered boy from Malaga, Isaac's concerns about what was going to happen to the country, and wondered if they had a point. Nevertheless, she wrote down her own name, directly underneath those of Teresa and Isaac.

Having drunk three glasses of champagne, Olive sensed the ghost of the boy moving through the rooms. She sat back in her wicker chair, and saw his bloodied body drag itself between the guests. She imagined there was a determination to their drinking, their dancing, their shouts and claps, as if they were pushing him back to the land of the dead, to reclaim this house for the living.

A woman wore a long satin dress the colour of a dawn mushroom. The candle flames sparked a glint in a brass cufflink, lifted with a crystal glass of moonshine. Teresa scurried hither and thither, always with a tray of drinks, or some meats and cheeses, or slices of cake. She was studiedly avoiding her father. The room was full of voices, the music pulsed from the gramophone in the corner – and there was Sarah, in her double-faced purple dress, flitting between the groups. She laid her hand on Isaac's arm, and made him laugh. People turned to her as they might to a beacon of light.

Olive watched Isaac wherever he went, feeling her attraction sing up to the wooden beams above her head, down to the slosh of champagne in her glass. Her curls had begun to droop and she tugged them nervously, worried she was walking around with a half-hairstyle. Now he was deep in conversation with the local doctor, looking sombre at something the man had said. He too had not spoken to his father. He was wearing that perfect pair of dark-blue trousers, cut close to the line of his body; a dark linen jacket, a blue shirt. She imagined what colour his skin was underneath. When was he going to turn round and notice her? She touched the emeralds around her neck and downed a fourth champagne. The fumbling child she'd been all her life was soon to be a spectre; one more glass would flush that kid away.

Two of the guests had brought guitars, and from their fingers cascaded a confident duet, note after perfect note, up and down the fretboards. People cheered when they heard it, and someone lifted the needle off the gramophone, scratching the record. There was a moment's worried hush, but Harold, very drunk by now, roared with approval and shouted, 'Let them play! I want to hear this magic! ¡Quiero oír el duende!'

At this, the party seemed to surge as one. The father and son who'd brought the guitars knew flamenco songs as well as the popular *canciones*, and they played a couple, a wide ring of people around them, before a woman in her sixties stepped forward, and began to sing, opening her mouth to let forth a soaring sound of pain and freedom. For a second time that night Olive felt the hairs on her neck rise up. The woman had the room under complete control. She sang, clapping her hands in a fast, percussive rhythm, and there were shouts around the room of '¡Vamos!', people stamping their feet and crying out in admiration.

Gregorio whirled two little girls around the room, and they screamed with delight as the guitars and the singing grew ever more fevered. The woman's voice was like an ancient sound come to life, and Olive stood up, drinking down a fifth glass of fizz – except no, this wasn't champagne, this was a spirit of some sort, a firewater that set her insides burning. The woman's voice was rough and plaintive and perfect, and outside the night deepened, and moths flickered to die amongst the lanterns. In this room of strangers, Olive had never felt more at home.

HER FATHER WAS CALLING THAT it was time for the fireworks. '*Fuegos artificiales!*' he bellowed in a terrible accent, and Olive's eyes roved the room for Isaac. She spied him slipping through the door. The crowd began to move into the back of the house, out onto the veranda to watch the fireworks exploding over the orchard. Olive stopped, dazed by the flow of people in the corridor. Then she saw him going in the other direction, crossing the hallway and out of the front door. She was mystified – why was he running away from the centre of the world?

She began to follow him, stumbling onwards, away from the light of the house and into the pitch dark of the February night.

Above her, the sky was soaked with stars. The moon was high but she lost sight of him, and her blood was quickly cooling, but on she went, out of the rusted main gates onto the dirt path towards the village, stumbling on stones, cursing that she had been idiotic enough to come out in heels.

A hand clamped on her mouth. An arm locked round her neck and dragged her to the side of the path. She wriggled and kicked, but whoever had her pinned had a strong grip. Olive brought up her hands and began tugging; she opened her mouth to bite hard on the fingers that wouldn't let her breathe.

'*Mierda!*' said a voice, and Olive was released.

'Isaac?'

They stood, panting, both bent over in disbelief.

'Señorita – I thought someone was following me.'

'Well, they were. *Me.* Jesus bloody Christ!'

'Are you hurt?'

'I'm fine. How about you?'

'Please, do not tell your father—'

Olive rubbed her neck. 'Why would I tell him? Do you make a habit of jumping out at people like that?'

'Go back to the party. Please.'

Olive could tell he was agitated. 'Where are you going?' she asked.

'Nowhere.'

'That's a lie.'

'Go *back*. It's dangerous for you.'

'I'm not scared, Isaac. I want to help. Where are you going?'

She couldn't make out his expression in the dark, but she sensed his hesitation, and her heart began to pound harder.

'I am going to church,' he said.

She laughed. 'To confess your sins?'

'Something like that.'

She put out her hand and reached in the darkness for his. 'Lead the way,' she said.

LATER, WHEN OLIVE WAS LYING awake and going over everything back in her bedroom, she supposed it was the alcohol that did it. When Isaac was painting her, she couldn't stand it. She didn't feel enough of a satisfying subject, and she couldn't match her mother. But here, she and Isaac were equals, not watcher and watched. In the dark she could be her real self, a woman who took men by the hand and forced them onwards, down the path.

'YOU MUST BE COLD,' HE said, and she could hear that he was quite drunk too. When he took off his jacket and put it round her shoulders, Olive's skin sang, her whole body almost dipped in pleasure at his solicitousness and concern.

In ten minutes, they reached the church of Santa Rufina, which abutted the main square of Arazuelo. The place was deserted, as most of the village were up on the hillside, revelling in the music and the manzanilla they had rolled up in barrels as a gift to their host. Olive and Isaac turned back to see the fireworks which had begun to explode in the sky; red and green and orange, gigantic sea urchins, falling fountains. Isaac forced the door of the church and slunk in, and Olive followed – frightened now, choked by the smell of stale incense. The moonlight came through the window, touching the beeswaxed pews, the baleful saints, set into the wall. She felt Isaac's hand slip from hers, and heard his footsteps padding away up the nave.

'Isaac—'

The gunshot rang out beyond the pews from where she stood, and then another, then another. Olive was too terrified to scream. Beyond the walls of the church, the fireworks continued. She was rooted to the spot, cowering in terror. Suddenly, Isaac was next to her, his hand on her arm.

'*Now*,' he said. 'We have to go.'

He took her hand and they fled. 'What have you done?' she hissed. 'Was the priest – Isaac, what the hell have you done?'

They ran all the way back to the finca. Olive had to kick off her shoes and go bare-footed, the skin on her feet tearing on the occasional stone. At the gates, they stopped, breathless. The fireworks were still exploding, and she could smell the sulphuric tang of gunpowder.

She collapsed against the gate. 'Am I an accessory to murder?' she whispered. 'Jesus, I'm not even joking.'

Isaac put his hand on her face. 'For Adrián,' he said.

'What do you mean?'

He began to kiss her, cupping her face with his hands, scooping her by the waist. Olive felt the pride he had in her in the way he was clasping her hair, running his lips along the side of her neck, down on to her chest, under the emeralds which had heated with her skin. She'd proved herself to him, at last.

Isaac ran his fingers over the stones. 'Where did you get these?'

'A friend.' She kissed him on the mouth to stop him asking more. She'd never known her body could feel this way, or that she could inspire a man to do such things to her.

He kissed her again, and Olive parted her lips and put her hands through his hair, the rusted railings hard against her back. They pushed into each other, kissing, kissing, kissing, as the old woman in the finca resumed her plaintive music, and a figure watched them, silhouetted at the door.

IX

*O*live tried to sit up, but a lightning bolt of agony split her brain. Her mouth was a desert, her neck was lead. Lying in the mussed sheets, guts addled, scalp stinking of a thousand cigarettes, her hands flew to her body. She wasn't wearing any clothes. Jesus, where were her clothes? She winced to her left. Someone had folded her dress neatly over a chair; her stockings laddered and bloodstained on the soles, her fox stole swinging off the arm. It looked like a hunter's trophy, skinned and broached overnight, a dead glass eye in the head, those awful glued teeth. She touched her neck. The emerald necklace was still there, a snake upon her collarbone.

She heard the gunshot again – the church, the darkness, the fireworks, a rusting gate – had it been a dream? So much, all in one day. Far off, she could hear the telephone ringing. What if the civil guard were waiting outside, ready to take her away?

Isaac. The kiss – how was it possible she had endured life until now without that kiss – how had she lived? He'd dragged her through the darkness to let a pistol off inside a church, and then he'd kissed her. She wanted another kiss from Isaac more than she wanted to breathe.

SHE FELT AUGMENTED, AS IF a door, long hidden inside her, had been opened, revealing a sinuous corridor, and she herself was running through it. Since the moment she met him, this man had clung to her imagination. He had made her feelings enormous, the depths of her horizons doubling. For once in her life, Olive had been made to feel monumental. The nervousness of what might come next went hand in hand with a desire for him so extreme that she wondered whether even being possessed by Isaac would assuage it.

SHE HADN'T NOTICED TERESA, AT the end of the bed, scanning the peaks and hollows of the sheets. 'I have made you a bath,' Teresa said, looking quickly away in the face of Olive's nakedness.

'Who was that on the telephone?'

'No one.'

'No one?'

Olive saw Teresa hesitate. 'I do not know.'

'Are the police here?'

'No, señorita.'

'I'm never drinking again.'

'There is a glass of milk by your head.'

'I can't.'

'There is a bucket by your side.'

Olive leaned over and looked into the bucket. Bits of soil from the garden were scattered in the bottom. She retched into it, wanting to expel the sick feeling, her eyeballs hard as rocks.

'Señorita,' Teresa said, 'my brother is going to show his painting today.'

'What?' Olive groaned, collapsing back onto the bed. 'Tere – was there – has there – been any news today, from the village?'

'Someone broke into the church last night. They shot the statue of the Virgin Mary.'

'What?'

'Padre Lorenzo is crazy,' Teresa went on. 'He has taken her into the centre of the main square and he's shouting.'

Olive tried to speed up her thoughts. 'Taken who?'

'*La Virgen*,' Teresa repeated, in Spanish. 'She was very old wood, very expensive. She was shot three times. They took her to the office of Doctor Morales. As if he could bring her back to life,' Teresa added, with a slight sneer. 'Do you know what the men are asking, señorita? They are asking, who is the kind of man who puts a bullet through the tit of the Madonna?'

Olive said nothing, and closed her eyes. 'My brother looks more sick than you today,' Teresa said.

'Well, it was a good party.'

'I know. I have been cleaning for four hours. Come, get into the bathroom before the water is cold.' Teresa stood at the side of the bed and opened out a huge bath sheet. Olive obeyed; Teresa wrapped her up and shuffled her from the room.

Outside, Teresa's seeds were growing well; tiny leaves emerging from the fertilized furrows, where back in January she and Olive had marched up and down. The cork oaks and sweet chestnuts had turned a deeper green, and the sun was a few degrees warmer. Although the flowers were not in bloom, and the air was still thin, Teresa could smell the departure of winter, the inexplicable awareness the body has of the change to the most hopeful of seasons.

Sitting on the tatty green sofa in the front east room, she could hear Olive upstairs, draining her bath. She thought of Adrián, how it was inconceivable someone so young should be dead. She thought of the Schlosses' mad party, of Isaac's anger, their surly father, the shot Madonna. Everything was so uncertain. And yet, with regards to today's unveiling, Teresa had never felt so sure. She'd asked her brother whether he would miss painting Sarah and Olive, but he'd ignored her, trudging off down the hill to fetch the table and chairs that Doctor Morales said they could borrow for the party.

This morning in the cottage, Teresa put her head round Isaac's door and told him that if he wanted she would take the portrait over and prepare it for a grand unveiling. 'I'll put it on an easel in the front east room,' she said.

Isaac, flannel on face, lying in the dark of his bedroom, lifted it once, peered at her and said, 'Fine. I'm glad it's done. But wait until I get there before you show them.'

TERESA HAD CHILLED ONE OF the remaining bottles of Clicquot, leaving it out on the veranda overnight. All the windows had been thrown open to let fresh air into the corners where cigarette smoke clung. Stubborn patches of spilled sherry attracted columns of ants. Teresa crushed them with her foot, arranged the sofa and the other chairs in a semicircle around the easel, and draped a white sheet over the artwork. She put the champagne in a metal cooler and went to the kitchen. She had never felt so clear-headed, nor had she ever felt a greater sense of purpose than today. The excitement for it almost made her feel sick.

THIRTY MINUTES LATER, EVERYONE WAS gathered. Harold, the best recovered of the family, was in an impeccable suit. Sarah looked frail, a tremor in her fingers as she passed a champagne flute to her daughter, who looked green at the sight of it. Isaac was perched on the edge of the sofa, dragging deep on a ciga-rette, his foot jigging. This was his moment to shine – here, in the presence of the great dealer, Harold Schloss. Teresa saw his eyes meet Olive's, and the girl's smile was an open beam of pleasure. Harold was looking in puzzlement at his wife, as to what this was all about.

Teresa wondered whether he had answered the telephone this morning, for she had vowed never to pick it up again.

Sarah rose to her feet. 'Darling Harold,' she said. 'Well done from all of us, for *such* a wonderful party. It seems, even down here at the end of civilization, you haven't lost your touch.'

Everyone laughed, and Harold raised his glass. 'Now, as you know, things have been a little up and down of late,' Sarah said.

'But we like it here, don't we, darling? And we're doing well. And I – well, *we* – wanted to give you a little present to say thank you. It's Liv and me, darling,' she said, pulling the sheet off the painting. 'Mr Robles painted us – for you.'

Teresa swallowed the champagne she'd been offered, and a sick, irresistible tide of fear flushed through her, the bubbles filling her mouth, the metallic fizz agitating her blood. Isaac ran his fingers through his hair. As the sheet cascaded to the tiles, Olive's knuckles turned white on the arms of her chair. There was a small collective gasp.

OLIVE WAS IN DEEP DISLOCATION. She couldn't understand what she was seeing. The painting was two-thirds drenched in indigo blue, there was a glint of golden wheat, and two women, one holding her pot aloft in a shining field, and the other, curled in semi-defeat, surrounded by her broken shards.

It was her painting. It was *Santa Justa in the Well*. She turned to Isaac; he, too, was staring in confusion. What was it doing down here – why wasn't it upstairs, hidden in her room? Olive looked at Teresa; the grim triumph on her face.

There was a sound of clapping. Her father was looking at her painting. Her father was *applauding*. 'Bravo, Isaac,' he was saying. 'Bravo. What you've *done*!'

Sarah frowned, hands on hips. 'Well, it isn't quite – what I was expecting. But I like it. Which of us is which, Mr Robles? Do you like it, Harold?'

'I've not seen something like this in a very long time. Liv, you look like you've seen a ghost,' her father said. 'You're not upset that Mr Robles hasn't done you a society turn?'

Olive couldn't speak. All she could do was look at her own painting, her father pacing around it. 'This is *wonderful*,' he went on. 'I *knew* you had something in you, Robles. Lithography, my eye.'

Harold's voice was intense and warm; it was like this whenever a new painting was speaking to him. It was a silent conversation; the painting slowly heating him up, running round his mind – and Harold was working on it like a child might a boiled sweet, sampling its flavours, softening its corners, edging inexorably towards its core.

Olive felt as if she too was being honed away, soon to snap and disappear. 'This is real. Oh, this is good,' her father was saying, and it felt like she was hearing him from the bottom of a well. 'Look at the pot – and the deer. Oh, this is *good*! This is excellent.'

Isaac was staring at the painting. His eyes began to dart around it, as if the colours, the composition, the line might speak to him too. Was he angry? Olive couldn't tell. Like her, he wasn't saying a thing. She wondered where Isaac's painting was, whether he was going to speak up. She turned to see Teresa staring at her, her look of triumph now replaced with one of urgency.

'Mr Robles, you're a star,' said Sarah, placing her hand on his arm. 'Well *done*.'

Teresa nodded at Olive, her eyes wide – and in that moment, Olive understood. She knew, then, what Teresa wanted her to say – *That's mine. I did that. There's been a mistake* – although she could not understand Teresa's desire. She felt her mouth open, the words almost there, but then her father spoke.

'We should take this to Paris,' Harold said. 'I think this might be something a few collectors over there would be interested in. I'd like to act for you, Isaac. I'll get you a better fee.'

'*Paris?*' said Olive, and then she closed her mouth.

'What's it called?' Harold asked.

'It has no title,' said Isaac.

Harold stared at the painting. 'I think we should avoid any mention of Liv and Sarah in it, given that I might be selling it. How about *Girls in the Wheatfield*?'

'Harold,' said Sarah. 'This was a present for you. You can't just sell it.'

But Harold wasn't listening. 'Perhaps *Women in the Wheatfield* is better.'

'Poor Liv, painted curled in a ball like that,' said Sarah, draining her glass of champagne, and pouring herself another. 'Mr Robles, you really are terrible.'

Isaac stared at Olive and Teresa. 'Yes,' he said. 'I am.'

He got to his feet. The painting had caused an almost alchemical transformation in him. The new Isaac was solidifying, like smoke into gold, before their very eyes. He was a real artist, something about him they could all sense but not quite touch – however much they wished to.

'Teresa,' Isaac said, and Olive could hear the shake in his voice as he uncharacteristically stumbled over his English. 'Come and help me in the kitchen. I brought the turnip you wanted for that soup.'

X

'What the *fuck* have you done?' Isaac hissed. He pushed his sister inside the kitchen, jabbing his hand between her shoulder blades.

'I haven't done anything,' Teresa hissed back. 'I can't believe you said that thing about a turnip—'

'Shut up. I had to think of something.' He closed the door. 'Whose painting is that?'

Teresa stuck her chin in the air. 'It's Olive's,' she said. 'It's Olive's, and it's better than yours.'

'*Olive's?*'

'She paints every day. She got a place at art school and stayed here instead. You didn't ask her that, did you, when you had your tongue rammed down her throat.'

Isaac slumped at the kitchen table and put his head in his hands. 'Oh, Jesus. She put her own painting up there.'

Teresa flushed. 'No, she didn't. I did.'

'*You* did? Why?'

'You're going to break her heart.'

'Oh, Jesus. This is about me kissing her?'

'You sneaked in here—'

'And what else did you do but creep through the orchard with your chicken as an offering, like a bloody Indian to Columbus—'

'I help them, every day. They'd be lost without me.'

'You could be anyone, Teresa. You're just the maid.'

'And you just cause trouble.'

'Sarah Schloss *asked* me to paint her, so I did. And you might as well know. Alfonso has stopped my money.'

'What?'

'You heard – he doesn't like the "taste of my politics". And so the money from Sarah Schloss was supposed to keep us going. I wanted to keep this professional, Teresa—'

'And you expect me to believe that?'

'I've got more important things to worry about than some rich *guiri* with a taste for big parties—'

'What, like shooting your pistol in the church and lifting Olive's dress?'

'You're just a spy. A stirrer.' He stood up, his voice low and vicious. 'You came to these people, Tere, because you knew how your life was going. You've been doing it since you were little. With a dad like ours and your gypsy mother – don't pretend to me you're some saint. Don't think I don't know where Olive's necklace came from. I know all about your little box in the garden. And now what? What are we supposed to do?'

'You're going to admit it isn't your painting,' Teresa said, pinch-faced and shaken, 'and give Olive the credit she's due.'

'No, he isn't,' said a voice from the doorway. 'He isn't going to do that at all.'

OLIVE HAD OPENED THE KITCHEN door quietly, and had been listening at the threshold. Her expression was not easy to read. She looked incandescent – but with rage, or sorrow, or excitement, neither Isaac nor Teresa could easily tell. They froze, waiting for her to speak again. Olive moved inside the kitchen and shut the door.

'Why did you do it?' she asked Teresa.

Tears sprang into Teresa's eyes. 'I wanted to—'

'She wanted to punish me. She saw us at the gate last night,' said Isaac. 'This little trick is Teresa's revenge.'

'No! It is not revenge, señorita,' Teresa pleaded. 'Your father should see how brilliant you are, how—'

'That's not your responsibility,' said Olive. 'Tere, I trusted you. I thought we were friends.'

'You can trust me.'

'How?'

'I am sorry, I did not—'

'It's too late,' Olive sighed. 'We can't all just stand here like some mothers' meeting. They'll be wondering what's going on.'

'I will tell them it isn't mine, señorita,' said Isaac. 'It is not fair Teresa should trick your parents. They have been good to her. And my own painting is ready. Teresa brought it over this morning.'

Olive looked thoughtful. 'Where is Isaac's painting, Teresa? Fetch it.'

Teresa went into the pantry. They heard her dragging barrels across the tiles, and she came tottering out with the large canvas, propping it up against the wall before she pulled away the protective cloth.

Olive stared in silence. She and her mother were recognizable, but their eyes had been made gauzy, their lips had a generic redness. Behind their heads were strange nimbuses of light, and beyond that, a plain green background. There was no humour, no spirit or power, no exciting use of colour or line, no originality, no intangible magic. No hint of secrets, no play, no story. It wasn't terrible. It was two women on the front of a Christmas card.

Olive glanced at Isaac. He was looking at his own work, arms folded, a frown of concentration as he assessed his effort. What was he thinking? Was he pleased – did he think this was *good*? There was nothing wrong with the kind of art that Isaac had replicated – after all, why should everything be an intellectual gauntlet? It was easy on the eye, but it was juvenile. Her father would hate it.

She realized, in that moment, that despite her discomfort of sitting for a portrait, part of her had wanted Isaac to be really good. It would have been easier than him having no gift at all. Perhaps she was more her parents' daughter than she thought. It was always easier to admire someone with a talent, and pity was the path to indifference. Olive closed her eyes, resisting the potential damage to her heart that this painting, or Isaac's lack, might cause. She told herself that Isaac didn't deserve to face her father's disdain. When she opened her eyes, Isaac was looking at her, and she gave him a bright smile.

'Isaac, you heard what my father said. He wants to take the painting to Paris. He wants to sell it.'

'You see, señorita,' said Teresa. 'I know you said you did not care for the recognition of the world – but look at what has happened. I am glad I took the risk for you—'

Olive turned to her. 'I didn't want you to.'

Teresa set her jaw. 'Are you sure about that?'

'Tere, enough,' said Isaac.

'But – we must tell him, now,' said Teresa.

'My father thinks Isaac painted *Santa Justa in the Well*, or *Women in the Wheatfield*. He wants to take Isaac's painting to Paris, not mine.'

'But all you need to do is tell him that you painted it.'

'But would it be the same painting?' Olive asked.

Teresa frowned. 'I do not understand.'

The exclamations and murmurs from the front room could be heard through the kitchen door. 'I don't think my father would have quite the same enthusiasm if he knew I'd painted it,' said Olive.

'No,' said Isaac. 'That is not true.'

'How can you be so sure?' she said. 'I want my father to go to Paris, you see. I want him to take it. It might be fun. I simply want to see.'

'This is not right,' Teresa pleaded. 'Your father, when you tell him – he will be surprised, yes – but then he will see your other paintings—'

'No.'

Olive held up her hand for silence, but Teresa ignored her. 'You do not see your father. He will—'

'Oh, I see my father, thank you very much.' Olive's voice was hard. 'And my mother too. They believe it's Isaac's painting, and that's all that matters, isn't it? What people believe. It doesn't matter what's the truth; what people believe becomes the truth. Isaac could have painted it – why couldn't he have painted it?'

'He could never have painted it,' said Teresa, and she stamped her foot.

Olive made a sound of frustration. 'You're to blame for this. So you'd better be quiet.'

'But I did not want for you to—'

'This is madness,' Isaac said. 'This is *una locura*. My painting is here.'

'Isaac, it's just a bit of fun.'

'This is not a game,' said Isaac. I have my painting here—'

'Please, Isaac. Look, he might not sell *Women in the Wheatfield*. So it stays in the family after all. This will be forgotten. Then you can give him your one.'

'But what if he sells yours? What if he sells an Isaac Robles that has not been painted by Isaac Robles?'

'If it sells – well, I don't want the money, and you *need* the money. I heard what you said about your father. If *my* father sells the painting, you could spend the money any way you wanted. New schoolbooks, trips out, food, equipment for your students, the workers.' Olive paused. ' *"What do you want in this life?"* Isn't that what you asked me, Isa? Well, I want to be useful.'

'Art is not useful.'

'I don't agree. It can make a difference. It can help your cause.'

'I cannot do this.'

'Isaac. Claim the painting in the other room. It means nothing to me.'

'I don't believe that, Olive.'

'Let me do something useful. Let me be needed. I've never done anything useful in my life.'

'But—'

'I'm not going to admit that the painting in the front room is mine, Isaac. Not to my father, at least – and in this case, he is the only person who matters.'

'But he has *praised* it. Teresa is right. I do not understand—'

Olive drew herself up, her face pale. 'Listen. I cannot tell you how rarely my father has this reaction. Let's not risk damaging that. Be the Isaac Robles that's out there now. Just one painting.'

Isaac said nothing for a minute. He had a look of misery, his mouth downcast. Next to him, Teresa was pulling nervously at her cardigan. 'But it is not *his*,' she whispered.

'It is, if I give it to him,' said Olive.

'You will be invisible, señorita. You are giving yourself away—'

'I'm doing the absolute opposite of giving myself away. As far as I'm concerned, I'll be completely visible. If the painting sells, I'll be in Paris, hanging on a wall. If anything, I'm being selfish. It's perfect; all the freedom of creation, with none of the fuss.'

Isaac looked between his own painting and the kitchen door – beyond which, down the corridor, *Women in the Wheatfield* was waiting on the easel, and Harold's exclamations could still be heard. The bottle of champagne Teresa had prepared popped, and Sarah laughed. Back and forth Isaac's eyes went, between two possible selves.

'Do not do this, Isaac,' Teresa whispered. 'Señorita, go in there and tell them that it is yours.'

'Isaac, this could be our chance to do something extraordinary.'

Isaac pushed through the door and lumbered along the corridor. When he'd disappeared, Olive turned to Teresa, her eyes alight.

'Take this upstairs for me. And don't sulk. It's all going to be fine. Hide it under the bed.' She studied Isaac's poorly rendered version of her face. 'Is that what he thinks of me?'

'I do not know,' said Teresa. 'It is just a painting.'

'I know you don't really think that,' Olive said, with a smile.

If the smile was supposed to be a gesture of forgiveness for what Teresa had done, it did not lift her spirits. She watched as Olive skipped down the corridor, following Isaac's path. The door of the front room opened again. Alone in the kitchen, Teresa heard laughter, and the repetitive clinking of glass.

XI

Isaac walked back to the cottage in a daze. He was so tired, so hungover. Harold had got some woman on the telephone about the painting; she'd expressed interest, and he was off to Paris in the morning. The Schlosses had implored Isaac to stay for a celebratory dinner, but he couldn't bear it. He felt like half a man. He almost hoped the thing wouldn't sell, that Olive's vendetta against her parents was a delayed adolescent whim soon to be forgotten, something she would look back on in years to come and laugh. The *people*. She wanted to help *the people*. She wanted to help herself, and Isaac knew he had made it possible.

He patted his pockets for his cigarettes, lit one, inhaled deeply and breathed out the smoke on a sigh. What was he doing? As he began the ascent to the cottage, the kites circled above him. He pushed open the door and thought again about the party, that kiss against the finca gate. It seemed half a year had passed since then. Olive's insistence on coming to the church had showed a spontaneity and rebelliousness that he'd admired. He just didn't realize quite how deep that spirit went.

He should simply have kept away from the finca from the very beginning. He should have said no to the commission, he should have told Teresa to find work elsewhere, he shouldn't have stopped

Olive in the dark, in her evening gown, hair flying everywhere. He should have marched into the front east room, bearing his own painting. He wasn't up to pretending, and he didn't want it.

The sound of feet on the gravel made him turn. It was Olive, running up the hill after him. She stopped to catch her breath, and he waited, immediately wary.

'I just wanted to say, don't worry. It's going to be all right, I promise. If he sells it, the money's yours. That's it. The end.'

'It's done now.'

'I promise you, Isaac. Just the one painting.'

'Fine.' He began to turn away.

'And was it just the one kiss?' she asked. He turned back to her, and she came closer, stopping just beyond his reach. They surveyed one another.

Isaac was done with her words, and tired of himself. He took her by the waist and pulled her towards him, kissing her hard on the mouth. Beneath him, Olive sprang to life, and he felt the power of her body responding as she kissed him back. He forced himself to pull away.

'I've wanted this,' Olive said. 'Since the day we met.'

He gave a harsh laugh. 'Wanted what?'

She stepped back. 'You've allowed me this chance, Isaac. And I wondered why – and I thought – well, I thought—'

'I did not allow you this chance. You took it.'

'I think both of us can see this pretty clearly.'

'Are you sure? What we have just done is exactly what a child would do. The three of us, whispering like children in the kitchen. It is make-believe. Only my sister tried to inject a bit of honesty into it.'

'I wasn't talking about the painting, Isaac.' He was silent. A look of fear flickered over her face. 'You don't want me, then,' she said.

Isaac felt something collapse inside himself. He turned towards the cottage and could hear Olive following him. 'I just – I want it to be you,' she said. He carried on walking, and could hear her steps.

He closed the door, and they stood facing each other. The light was dim, but he watched as Olive reached up and undid the top button of her blouse. She carried on, methodical as a sergeant major, button after button, letting the blouse fall off her shoulders, no brassiere beneath.

She stood before him, and her torso was perfect, her skirt a fabric stillness over the shape of her thighs. She must have thought Isaac was thinking of her, but he was not. He was thinking of that long-lost woman, Laetitia, twenty-seven years old and him, fifteen – and how grateful he was for her generosity to him that morning, how she'd never laughed, how she'd treated him like the man he'd been so desperate to become.

Isaac stepped forward and wrapped his hands around Olive's waist. She gasped as he lifted her onto the table, her feet just touching the floor. She sat rigid as he drew a single finger all the way from her neck, between her breasts, down to the top of her skirt. She shivered and arched her back, lifting her hips and Isaac thought then, *Why not, why not*, and he brought his mouth to her breasts, kissing and kissing her, hearing her sharp inhalation as his finger stroked up the side of her leg and slid inside her knickers. Her legs tensed. 'More?' he murmured.

There was a pause. 'More,' she said.

He ruched Olive's skirt up around her waist, dropped to his knees and prised apart her thighs. When he ran his tongue down the fabric of her knickers, Olive gasped again. He stopped.

'More?' he asked. 'Yes,' she said, so he pushed the fabric aside and dipped in his tongue, dipping and lapping, opening his mouth onto her.

'Is this a real thing?' Olive whispered, and then her words were lost.

He carried on, and soon Olive was pushing her hips hard into him, her moans turning upwards into a huge sigh. She shuddered onto the table, her arms thrown back on the wide, gnarled wood. Isaac stood up and surveyed her, his hands holding the sides of

Olive's legs, how her arched spine now lay flat, how her face was turned away, closed to everything except her smile, her undeniable triumph and bliss.

'More?' Isaac asked.

Olive opened her eyes, widened her legs, and looked at him. '*More*,' came her reply.

PART III

The Lion Girls

OCTOBER 1967

10

*T*he first story I ever published in England appears on pages seventy-four to seventy-seven of the *London Review* of October 1967. It was called 'The Toeless Woman', and they even paid someone to draw an accompanying illustration. They missed the *e* off the end of my first name, so it looks like my father wrote it. I still have two copies of that particular edition – the one that I'd purchased myself, and the other I'd posted to my mother in Port of Spain, and which was returned to me years later, after her death.

My mother had annotated her copy with the words *'My girl!'* and to my amusement, added the missing *e* in biro. Years later, at her funeral, my second cousin Louisa told me that Mrs Bastien had passed that *Review* round all her friends like a one-woman lending library, strictly insisting that they could only have an evening with it each. I think more people in Port of Spain read that story than in the literate sections of London town. What they made of it, I'll never know.

It was Quick, of course, who was to blame – or thank – for the story finding its way to the editor. I think she relished the symmetry of it – how, after my leaving the raw thing on her desk, she was able to leave a copy of the magazine containing it on mine. I thought it was odd, how she had sat in her garden and exhorted me to disregard the opinions of others, only to go and submit my work for mass approval.

'Find page seventy-four,' she commanded, scratching aggressively at the base of her neck. I obeyed her, sitting in that viewless room in the Skelton, wishing she would go away, so that I could be in private to study this vision of my almost-name on the page. But Quick did not leave, and I had to hold in the tsunami of sound I wanted to unleash across the square, a cry of satisfaction so loud it would have travelled over the rooftops to the coast of Kent. My father's name, *Odell Bastien*, his daughter's writing underneath. Next time, I swore there would be no missing *e*. But for now, it would do. The words, at least, were mine.

Quick smiled, and the effect on her gaunt face was transformative: gleeful, youthful, briefly illuminated with pleasure. She was dressed that day in a dark green pair of trousers, slightly flared, and a pussy-bow silk blouse with a seasonal repeating pattern of brown leaves. I noticed the slight sag of the material on her thighs; she was definitely thinner. 'It was an excellent story,' she said, 'so I sent it in. I even got you a fee. Thirty pounds.'

'Thirty *pounds*?'

'I hope that was all right. You don't mind I went ahead?'

'I don't know how to thank you. Thank you.'

She laughed, sitting down opposite me, fumbling in her trouser pocket, lighting a cigarette and taking a deep drag. 'Don't thank me,' she said. 'It was a fantastic read. Did you base it on something that happened at Dolcis?'

'Sort of.'

She gazed at me. 'How does it feel, to be a published writer?'

I looked back down at the page; the ink that couldn't be rubbed away, the deceptive permanence of the paper. I felt exalted, my mind a cathedral, with an actual congregation who wished to visit my altar. 'Incredible,' I said.

'You'd better write some more,' she replied. 'Keep going at it. It seems to work.'

'I will. Thank you, thank you again.'

She went to the window, cigarette in hand, and looked down at the alley where the smokers gathered. I couldn't imagine her mixing with them, a bird of paradise amongst the canaries. 'Would you have let me look at it,' she asked, 'if you'd known what I might do?'

'I don't know,' I said. It was a good question.

'I wondered. Anyway, you've got a terrible view here. Did Pamela choose this room? We can get you a nicer one.'

'I'm fine, thank you. A nice view would probably distract me from my work.'

She raised an eyebrow. 'How puritanical.'

Quick could tease me as much as she wanted; I didn't care. I was published. She remained at the window, her back to me again. 'How about Reede's news on Mr Scott's painting, eh? He's looking very pleased with himself. Looks like we are going to have an exhibition. He wants to call it "The Swallowed Century". But we cannot exhibit only one painting.' I could hear the disdain in her voice. Her body was slightly curled over, as if she was shielding a ball of pain.

'I didn't know,' I said.

She turned. 'No? Is everything all right between you and Mr Scott?'

'Yes. No. Just a misunderstanding.'

'I see.' She straightened up, leaning against the wall. 'Want to talk about it?'

'There's nothing much to say.' Quick fixed her gaze on me, so reluctantly, I went on. 'I went to his mother's house, in Surrey.'

'Nice?'

'Nice. We had dinner. And then afterwards, he told me he loved me. And I didn't say it back. And it all went wrong from there. I haven't spoken to him for three weeks.'

Quick inhaled thoughtfully on her cigarette. 'No harm done. I saw the way he looked at you. You've got him in the palm of your hand.'

'I don't think so. I wasn't very polite.'

'Odelle, you don't have to say, or do, anything you don't want to. I don't suppose he loves you for your politeness.'

'But he hasn't called. I haven't seen him.'

'Does that bother you?'

I was astonished at the tears pricking my eyes. 'Yes.'

'Then it'll work itself out. Don't go flailing back in. Never helps, in my experience. Did you stay long in the house?'

'A few hours.'

'Big place?'

'Fairly. I didn't see much.'

I considered telling Quick about the pamphlet I'd smuggled out in my handbag, but something stopped me. Maybe it was my reluctance to look like a thief, but there was also something about the way Quick constantly hovered over the issue of Lawrie and the painting that made me wary. Given her attitude towards Lawrie, she might jump on anything to use against him – although what a long-forgotten pamphlet might mean in all this was anyone's guess. Lawrie and I may not have been quite on speaking terms, but I didn't want Quick to make him even more defenceless in the face of any attack.

'Come and have dinner with me tonight,' she said. 'Let's have champagne.'

'Champagne?'

'I'm feeling victorious. I've got a couple of lamb chops that need eating. And someone needs to give you a pat on the back.'

I hesitated. Being alone with Marjorie Quick was always a very intense experience, and after the last time in her garden, I didn't know if I was up to it. But then I thought about another night in the empty flat, with only the crackle of the radio and my overly read books for company, and suddenly I didn't want to be alone. 'Thank you,' I said. 'Shall we ask Pamela?'

'She wouldn't want to come. Besides, I've only got two chops.'

I felt I couldn't insist, because it wasn't my house, my dinner, my champagne. But I do remember thinking it would be no problem at all to pop to a butcher and buy Pamela an extra chop. Quick seemed keen to have me there alone.

'Good,' she said, taking my silence for assent. 'That's settled. See you later, Odelle. We can take a taxi home together. And well done again. I'm very proud.'

11

When I went to find Quick in her office at the end of the day, her door was closed. Voices were coming through the wood – hers, and that of Edmund Reede, more angry than I'd ever heard.

'We should use these discrepancies as opportunities,' he was saying. 'Why are you undermining me, Marjorie?'

'Edmund—' she began, but he interrupted.

'I've tolerated a great deal from you in the past, but your doggedness over this is ridiculous.' There was a silence. Reede sighed. 'You've seen the accounts, Marjorie. You've seen what's happening to us. I just cannot fathom your reluctance. It's a stunning painting. It has a story. It has a handsome young man on the end of it. Two, in fact, if you put owner and painter together. We'll have a crowd; we might even have a sale. The Guggenheim are going to send me what they have, but there's already so much here. The mystery of Robles – how did he die? Who ordered his death, and why?'

'That's got nothing to do with the painting, Edmund,' Quick said.

'I disagree. His personal tale reflects the international stage. It prefigures by less than a decade the vanishing of hundreds of artworks under Nazi rule, and, in many cases, their creators and families.'

'But the art first, eh, Edmund?'

He ignored this reproof. 'Robles is universal. When we tell the tale of this artist, we tell the tale of war.'

I heard the flick of Quick's lighter. 'I'm surprised you of all people want to tell the tale of war,' she said. 'I don't see this painting as political at all.'

'Look here, Marjorie, what's the problem? We've always been frank with each other.'

'Have we?'

'Oh, come on. As frank as it was possible to be.'

Quick was silent for what seemed a long time. 'There is no problem,' she said. 'It just isn't political in the way you think it is. It's not about war in the way you see it, Edmund. It's not about the artist as a man. It's about the canvas. Two girls facing down a lion.'

I was astonished at the way they were talking to each other, so fluid and intimate. Pamela said they had known each other for years, and it showed. It was almost fraternal, and he was talking to her much as he might talk to one of his friends at the club.

'We'll agree to disagree, Marjorie,' Reede said. 'As we have done for longer than I care to remember.'

I could hear Reede moving towards the door, so I ran back along the corridor to my own desk, waiting instead for Quick to come and find me. It seemed that Quick had capitulated – to what exactly, I was not sure. She was resistant to the idea of an exhibition – but the true focus of her reluctance, this wavering derision and fear, was still not clear to me. It seemed that she was placing herself in opposition to whatever Reede thought philosophically about the painting, more than she was against the idea of actually exhibiting it.

QUICK INDEED TURNED UP AT my desk shortly after, looking drawn and upset. 'Ready?' she said. 'There's a taxi downstairs.'

We walked past the reception desk together. I glanced at Pamela, and saw the confusion in her face. I was surprised to feel that I was betraying her, going off with Quick like this, when Pamela worked just as hard as me and had been here longer. But I couldn't turn back. I was too drawn to Quick's enigma, too determined to find out what was really going on.

After our dinner, Quick invited me into the sitting room at the front of the house. She lowered herself into a sleek grey armchair, its wooden arms carved like the strings of a harp. Everything she owned, apart from the gramophone, seemed stylish and modern. 'Keeping an old woman company,' she said. 'I feel guilty.'

'Hardly old,' I replied. 'I was very happy to come.'

We hadn't talked of much over dinner; a little about Pamela, Reede and the donors he had to court, how he hated flirting with old marchionesses holed up in damp castles, where God knows what treasures were rotting in the lofts. 'You've known Reede a long time?' I asked.

'A long time. He's a good man,' she added, as if I'd said otherwise.

We were drinking brandies, a quiet piano concerto floating through from the gramophone in the other room. Quick closed her eyes, and she was so still, neither of us speaking, that I thought she'd dropped to sleep, the glow from the electric table-light beside her turning her face orange. She didn't strike me as the kind of person to invite a guest over and then fall asleep in the middle of a conversation. She was in her fifties, not her nineties, but it was peaceful to watch her in repose and I didn't wish to disturb. I wondered why she was so interested in me – placing my story in the magazine, the invitations to lunch, the solicitous questions over Lawrie and my future.

The electric fire was switched on, although it was a mild October. Quick even had on a shawl. I felt the brandy overheating my body and thought maybe I should leave, and I was on the point of rising from my chair when Quick said, her eyes still closed – 'Did you ever talk to Lawrie Scott about his mother?'

I sat back down. 'His mother?'

Her eyes snapped open and I saw their leonine intent. 'Yes. His mother.'

I thought about the suicide, and realized that it might have taken place in one of the very rooms I'd wandered through. I suddenly missed Lawrie. I wanted us to start again – a trip to the cinema, a walk in the park – but I had no idea how on earth to make it possible. I couldn't let him float adrift as well as Cynth.

'He didn't talk about her at all,' I lied.

'Then he must be thinking about her an awful lot. I'd lay money on it, if I were a betting man. Grief's a pressure cooker if you don't deal with it. One day, you simply explode.'

'Do you?'

She drained her brandy glass. 'Things crumble. Bit by bit. They shift, you don't notice. Then you notice. Jesus Christ, my legs are broken but I never moved my feet. And all the time, it's been coming towards you, Odelle – orchestrated in the hearts of strangers, or a God you'll never meet. Then one day, a stone is hurled – and by accident or design, that stone hits the car window of a powerful idiot who wants revenge, or who wants to impress his mistress, and – whoosh – the foot soldiers move in. The next day, your village is burning down, and because of stupidity, because of sex, there's a coffin for your bed.'

I couldn't think how to reply to this. Sex, death, coffins – how many brandies had she had? I didn't see what this had to do with Lawrie at all. I stared into the electric bars.

Quick leaned forward, and the arms of her chair creaked. 'Odelle, do you trust me?'

'Trust you with what?'

She leaned back again, visibly frustrated. 'You don't, then. If you did, you would have just said yes.'

'I'm a cautious person. That's all.'

'I trust *you*, you know. I know you're someone I can trust.'

I think I was supposed to be grateful, but instead I felt a simmering unease. The bars of the fire were making me hotter and hotter, and I was tired, and she was in a strange mood.

Quick sighed. 'It's my fault. For all my conversations with you, I'm probably even more guarded than you are.'

I couldn't disagree with this, so I didn't try and persuade her otherwise.

'I'm not well,' she said. 'I'm not very well at all.'

IT WAS CANCER, SHE SAID. Late stage, pancreatic cancer with an inevitable outcome. My own body ached at these words, which was selfish, but entirely predictable. I assumed that the outrageous fact of her cancer had made Quick want someone at home with her – a desire which had possibly surprised her and made her even more brusque. Quick, who had been alone with her secrets for so many years, no longer wished to be alone. Perhaps submitting my story, and therefore making me obliged to her, was a baroque plan to satisfy her simple need for company? When life is running out, such decisions may not seem so invasive or dramatic, and you willingly commit. This was why she spoke to Edmund Reede with no fear of reprisal; she knew she was soon to be reprised entirely.

I do think, looking back, that Quick perhaps regarded me as the child she never had, as someone who would perpetuate her essence after death. She told me at our first meeting that I reminded her of someone she once knew. I suspect that person was the closest companion she ever had. I'll never be sure of this, and she never mentioned a name, but her expression when she said those words makes me think that it was so. She looked at me tenderly, mingled with terror, as if to come too close would lose whatever she'd lost all over again.

Sitting in that overheated front room, I realized quite how thin she was, how tired. And although I probably thought it unfair that someone should suffer something like that alone, I don't imagine I cried in front of her. Quick was not someone you would sob in front of unless you absolutely had to, and when it was a question of her own pain and loss, you might feel a monstrous booby to cry when she herself was dry-eyed, dragging on the cigarettes that were helping to kill her. She was a curio, out of her time, not given to standard emotion – and in her presence, you did what Quick did.

'Well, say something,' she said.

'Does Mr Reede know?' I asked.

Quick snorted. 'God, no. And he's not to.'

'Does anyone else know?'

'No one else, but don't worry, I haven't told you because I want you to be my nursemaid.'

'Why have you told me?'

Quick reached for the brandy bottle and refilled her glass. 'Do you know, I got my diagnosis the day you started at the Skelton?'

'Goodness me,' I said. I remembered Quick coming up to my desk that first day; her flushed face, the way she batted away the porter's questions over her absence from work.

'Indeed,' she said. 'A day of ups and downs. Death imminent, followed by Odelle Bastien.'

'I can't imagine I was much of a tonic.'

She lit a cigarette, the last of the packet. 'You have no idea.'

I couldn't help wondering how long she had left, but I didn't want to ask if she knew, nor enquire about medications, or anything practical. It seemed too brutal, as if I was asking about her expiration date. She was still here, still vital, still mercurial.

IN THE SILENCE BETWEEN US, I reached into my handbag and handed over the art gallery pamphlet. I still wonder why I did it, even though it felt like a betrayal of Lawrie. I think it was the pride I felt, from knowing that Quick had confided in me. It was my consolation offering in return, even though I didn't know if it was something she'd find useful.

She took it, almost as if she was expecting it. 'This was in Lawrie's house,' she said.

'How on earth did you know?'

'You've been looking like you wanted to tell me something since the moment I mentioned your visit there.'

'I didn't know I was so obvious,' I said.

She smiled. 'You're not that obvious. I've had lots of practice.' She opened the pamphlet and placed it gently on her knees, her finger tracing the pencilled message, *No Sign*. 'Was there anything else with it?' she asked.

'No. Just odds and ends on a window sill. Butcher's bills, church service sheets.'

'Church service sheets?' she repeated, her eyebrow raised.

'A carol concert, actually.'

'I see.'

'What do you think it means – where someone's written *No Sign*? The name of a painting?'

'I imagine it's simpler than that. Someone was looking for something, and they didn't find it.'

'You know what they were looking for, don't you, Quick?'

She looked up at me, the electric fire turning her irises hazel. 'I do?'

'Well,' I said. 'It's just – you're very interested in Lawrie's mother. And Lawrie's painting.'

' "Interested" is not the word I would use.'

Obsessed? Frightened? I thought. *As if I would say those words to you.* 'Well,' I faltered, sensing her stiffen, 'you seem averse to the idea of exhibiting it.'

'I'm not averse to the exhibition of that painting. I think everybody should see it.'

'All right,' I said. 'But that's not what you said last time. You said Lawrie should take it home.'

She took in a deep breath. 'Well. I'm not entirely happy with how Reede is planning to use it. Until we get more information from the Guggenheim institution, my doubts remain.'

'What doubts are those?'

Quick's face took on a haunted expression. I'd seen it before, through the keyhole at the Skelton, when Lawrie had returned to continue his discussions with Reede. Her eyes darted back and forth on the rug between us. She kept breathing in as if to speak, and not speaking. It was frustrating, but I knew that to speak myself might ruin the slim chance she would finally say something.

'Isaac Robles didn't paint that picture, Odelle,' Quick said, her fingers tightening on the pamphlet.

My heart began to thump harder. 'But he's standing in front of it, in that photograph.'

'So? I could go and stand in front of any number of artworks and be photographed. It doesn't mean I made them.'

'It was taken in his studio—'

'Odelle, it's not that I don't believe he painted it. I know he didn't.'

Her last four words sang through the air between us, and hit me in the stomach. Something shivered over me, and my skin turned to gooseflesh, the way it does when someone tells you the truth and you hear it with your body.

I must have looked dumb. 'He didn't paint it, Odelle,' she repeated. Her shoulders sagged. 'It wasn't him.'

'Then – who was it?'

My question ruined everything. Quick looked stricken, aged, weird. Looking at her, I felt a bit sick and scared myself, because she seemed terrified. 'Are you all right?' I said. 'Should I call a doctor?'

'No. It's late. I'm fine.' But I could hear that she was out of breath. 'You should call a taxi. I have a number, out in the hallway. Don't worry, I'll pay.'

I rose, stumbling over the threshold of the front room into the cool darkness of the hall, where I switched on the light standing on the telephone table. There was no number to be seen. The house behind me was silent. I sensed a presence in the shadows, and my back prickled. I turned around and something was on the stairs, moving towards me. I gripped the edge of the table, as Quick's cat emerged into the pool of yellow light, and sat very still before me, turning his green eyes. We regarded one another, only the faintest movement from his ribs dissuading me that he was stuffed.

'Look in the drawer,' Quick called in a ragged voice, and I jumped. 'There's an address book in the drawer. *T* for Taxi.' I turned back to the lamplight, feeling foolish, praying that nothing else was waiting for me in the shadows beyond the cat.

I STILL DON'T KNOW WHETHER what happened next was another of Quick's plans – her, leading me deeper into the wood – or whether in her illness, under strong medication, she just hadn't realized what I'd find.

I pulled her address book out of the drawer, where it lay amongst old maps and balls of string and unopened mousetraps. I flipped to find *T* for Taxi, and saw two things. The first; under *S*, in Quick's flowing black nib, were written the words:

Scott – The Red House
Baldock's Ridge
Surrey HAS-6735

And secondly, a small white letter, folded in two, and pressed between these pages.

'Everything all right out there?' Quick called.

'Fine!' My voice quivered. 'Just getting it now.'

I looked at the Scott address in confusion. This entry might be a recent addition, of course – Quick undertaking some investigating of her own into Lawrie and the painting – and God knows it would not have surprised me. It was unbelievable that Quick might actually know the Scott family. And Lawrie didn't seem to have recognized her, did he? He was far too convincingly bemused by Quick to be hiding the fact that he actually *knew* her. And yet, here was his family's address. None of it made sense.

I opened the letter quickly, knowing I didn't have much time. A thin slip of paper fell out from the fold and fluttered to the floor. I knelt to pick it up and read it, hunched in the semi-darkness, Quick's cat still watching. It was a telegram, and my eyes bulged on the words. "DARLING SCHLOSS STOP," it read: "VERY EXCITING PHOTOGRAPH STOP WE MUST BRING R TO PARIS-LONDON-NYC STOP LOVE PEG." It was dated: "PARIS – MALAGA 2nd JULY 1936."

I can see myself even now, kneeling like a sinner in Quick's hallway, skin tingling with the twitch of connecting threads, a knowledge just beyond my reach. Schloss. *Harold* Schloss? It was the dealer Reede had mentioned. What the hell was this telegram doing here, in Wimbledon, in Quick's telephone book? Quick was in her living room, steps away from me, but there could have been a thousand miles between us.

I sat back on my heels, hoping time would stand still in order for me to think. *Peg* could be Peggy Guggenheim, *R* could be Robles; the date fitted, and it was sent to Malaga, where Reede said Robles resided. If this was real – and it looked real – then this was a piece of correspondence Reede might kill for. And here it was, out of Quick's drawer and in my hands.

'Odelle?' she called, and I heard the note of panic in her voice. 'Are you summoning that taxi in Morse code?'

'The line's engaged. I'm just waiting,' I called back. I placed the telegram on the table and picked up the letter. The date was 27 December 1935. I inhaled the scent of the old, thin paper. There was something familiar about it; but I couldn't place it. It was addressed to a person called Miss Olive Schloss, at a flat in Curzon Street. It ran:

Further to your application to the Slade School of Fine Art, it is our pleasure to invite you to undertake the Fine Art degree course, commencing 14th September, next year.

The tutors were highly impressed by the rich imagination and novelty on display in your paintings and studies. We should be happy to have a pupil such as you, continuing the rigorous yet progressive tradition of the school –

'Odelle.' Quick was calling very sharply now.

'Coming,' I said. 'There's no answer.'

I began to refold the letter in haste, placing the telegram back inside it. I was on the point of reaching for the discarded telephone book, open on the Scott entry, when Quick came into the hall. I froze, the letter still in my hand. My face must have been a vision of guilt. The living-room light shone through the fabric of her blouse. She seemed so small, the outline of her ribcage far too narrow.

She looked at me – stared, actually – deep into my eyes. She reached out, took the letter and the telegram from my mesmerized grip, placed them in the telephone book and closed it. And then my realization came, and I saw in Quick's face a younger woman smiling, a woman in a photograph, a moment of happiness as she clutched a brush. *O and I. O*, a full circle. *O*, for Olive Schloss.

'You knew him,' I whispered. She closed her eyes. 'You knew Isaac Robles.'

The cat brushed against my legs. 'I'd murder a cigarette,' Quick said.

I pointed at the telephone book. 'Who's Olive Schloss?'

'Odelle, would you go and fetch me some cigarettes?'

'You were there, weren't you?'

'I've run out, Odelle, would you mind?' She fumbled inelegantly in her pocket, and thrust out a pound note.

'Quick—'

'Go,' she said. 'There's a shop just round the corner. *Go.*'

SO I LEFT, TO FETCH her cigarettes. Numb, I floated into Wimbledon Village to buy her a packet, and I floated back. And when I returned, the house was in complete darkness, the curtains drawn. The pamphlet I'd taken from the Scott house was on the step, weighted down with a stone. I put it back in my handbag and knocked and knocked, and called her name quietly through the letterbox.

'Quick. Quick, let me in,' I said. 'You said you trusted me. What's happened? Quick, who is Olive Schloss?'

There was only silence.

Eventually, I had to push the cigarettes through the door, and they landed lightly onto the mat on the other side. I pushed through her change also, as if I was throwing money down a wishing well that would never grant me any wish. Still there was no movement. I sat on the other side of that door for a good half an hour, my limbs going stiff. I waited for the sound of her footsteps, sure that Quick would give in to the craving of her nicotine and come for the cigarettes.

What was true, and what was I already beginning to concoct? It mattered greatly to me as to whether Quick had intended for me to find the clues in her telephone book, or whether it was a mistake. It seemed as if she had been deliberate about it – why else invite me here, and grill me about Lawrie, and the painting? Why else tell me to look up *T* for Taxi? Or perhaps it had been a genuine mistake, and I had stumbled across her secrets – and now my punishment was this silent, locked door.

Outside, I could hear car doors closing arrhythmically, and see the street lamps flickering to life. I didn't want a policeman to catch me sitting there, so I got up, and walked away to the village high street to wait for a bus.

Whatever the truth was, Quick was now fragmented to me. The illusion of her perfect wholeness and easy glamour had been shattered by tonight. Despite her confession about her ill health, I realized I knew so little about her. I wanted to put her back together, to return her to the pedestal on which I'd placed her, but our encounter tonight would make that impossible. Now, when I thought about Quick, I couldn't stop thinking about Olive Schloss.

My imagination was extravagant, and I believed that Olive Schloss was a ghost I might control. But had I turned back that night, and looked up at Quick's window, I would have seen a silhouette, orchestrating my retreat.

APRIL 1936

XII

omen in the Wheatfield did sell, and it was a woman who bought it. Harold had sent a telegram to the post office in Arazuelo three days after his departure to Paris, and Olive went to fetch it. The buyer was called Peggy Guggenheim, and according to Harold, she was a rich friend of Marcel Duchamp and was thinking of dabbling in the art market.

'So not a real collector,' said Isaac.

'Well, she's got the money,' Olive retorted.

Guggenheim purchased Isaac Robles's painting at a fairly high rate for an unknown; four hundred French francs. To Olive, the sale of the painting was glorious, hilarious: it made no sense, and yet it did. It was as if *Women in the Wheatfield* was a completely separate painting from *Santa Justa in the Well*, whilst remaining exactly the same thing. The image was identical, it just had a different title and had been made by a different artist. She was free of identity, yet what came from her was valued. She could create purely, and also bear witness to the muddier yet heady side; the selling of her art.

Having had her father unwittingly sell one of her paintings, Olive could admit to herself that part of her plan to attend the Slade had been solely to spite Harold, to show him what he had overlooked.

But the Guggenheim purchase had eclipsed this desire; it was both a grander personal validation, and a much more wonderful joke.

Soon after Harold's telegram arrived with the news, Teresa began to have a dream that was strange for someone who had always lived in such a dry part of the land. It was dusk, and she was on the veranda, and the body of the murdered boy, Adrián, was lying out in the orchard. She couldn't see much beyond the small lamps she'd laid out along the ground, only the eerie glow of his body. In his tatters of flesh, he began to rise up and move towards her – and yet Teresa couldn't, or wouldn't, flee, despite knowing that to stay would be her end.

Beyond the boy's body she sensed an ocean, wide and black and churning, and she noticed what he did not – that a huge wave was coming, a looming wall of water, ready to lay waste to his life for a second time, and to wash hers away with a biblical magnitude. She could almost taste the salt in the air. Olive was screaming somewhere, and Teresa called out to her, '*Tienes miedo?*' *Are you scared?* And Olive's voice came floating back over the trees: 'I'm not scared. I just don't like rats.'

Teresa would wake at this point, just as the wave took Adrián's body away. She'd had the dream three times, and it disturbed her not only because of the content, but because she never normally remembered her dreams, and this one was so easy to recall. Once, she would have told Isaac about it, in order to laugh with him at her imagination, but she didn't much feel like sharing with him these days.

Throughout the end of February and into March, Harold remained in Paris on business, and so the women were alone in the house. Teresa began to long for Harold to come back, if only to fill the place with noise, his heavy English, even his whispered German. Too much was happening elsewhere, out of Teresa's control. It felt as if she and Olive were orbiting each other, like opposing moons. Olive would go upstairs, claiming a migraine, or women's pains. Teresa hoped she would be painting, but often Olive was nowhere to be found, at hours that normally coincided with Isaac's return from his job in Malaga.

If Sarah wondered about her daughter's sudden ill-health, these domestic absences, she wasn't saying anything. But Teresa could sense a change in the other girl; how she had become more sure of herself since the sale of the painting. Olive was crackling with energy, and the effect was remarkable. The idea that she was suffering headaches was idiotic. Teresa would watch Olive, leaning up to inhale the burgeoning jacaranda, the honeysuckle, the roses come in an early spring, her finger gripping the stems so hard that Teresa worried they were going to snap. Olive, for her part, looked through Teresa as if she was a ghost.

As far as Teresa saw it, Olive was pouring herself away into Isaac. She wondered if Olive believed that she was drawing power from pretending to be him. Teresa wanted to shake her and say, '*Wake up, what are you doing?*' But it was Teresa, not Olive, who suffered the bad dreams and painful days. She began to regret ever swapping the painting. She'd made a gamble and failed, sacrificing the only friendship she'd ever had.

Teresa had never missed a person before. It revealed a dependency within herself which outraged her. Olive's diverted attention was a pulsing wound, a peculiar type of torture; the loneliness hard to quantify when the source of it was before her, walking up and down the staircase, or round the orchard, out of the front door and away. Teresa never knew when the next pang of it was going to hit. And when it did, it was as if the floor had fallen away and her heart sprang into her mouth, stoppering her breath – and there was no one to catch her as she stumbled to a hidden corner of the finca to cry. What had happened to her?

Alone in the cottage at night, Teresa would sit up in bed and move through the pages of the old *Vogue* like a child with a storybook, savouring each image and paragraph, underlining with her nail the words she didn't understand. She ran her finger down the side of the model's face, before lifting her pillow and slipping the magazine under, a perpetual love note to no one but herself.

SINCE THE SALE OF THE painting, Sarah was gloomy, too. She would lie on her bed, not speaking, watching the blue smoke of her husband's cigarettes disappear towards the ceiling. The telephone would ring and ring, and she would never answer it, and she wouldn't let Teresa pick it up either. Teresa thought it odd that Sarah would not lift the receiver, to see if it was her husband. She wondered then if Sarah knew full well it would be a different voice entirely; a woman's voice, whispering in timid German.

Teresa could now see Sarah's faultlines – the telephone left ringing, the champagne bottles empty by three in the afternoon, the uncracked spines of discarded books, the dark roots growing from her blonde head. She stopped dismissing them as a rich women's problems, and to her surprise, in her own pitiful state, began to feel pity. Life was a series of opportunities to survive, and in order to survive you had to lie, constantly – to each other, and to yourself. Harold had the motor car, the business, the contacts, the cities and spaces he inhabited, manifold and varied. Sarah, despite her obvious wealth, had just this one bedroom and her beauty, a rigid mask that was setting her into an existential rot.

'I WAS THE ONE WHO discovered him,' Sarah said to Teresa. It was a late night, and Olive was upstairs. They could hear her, pacing back and forth. Despite everything, Teresa longed to go up there, to knock and be admitted, to see what Olive was painting. Forcing herself to stay put, she picked another camisole from off the floor.

'I was the one who suggested Isaac painted for us in the first place,' Sarah went on. 'And I get no thanks. Harold as usual takes the reins, riding off into the sunset. I don't even get to keep the painting, because of course he has to go and sell it. He said,

"Why would we keep it here, where only the chickens will see it?" Because it was a painting of *me*, for *him*, for Christ's sake.'

Outside, the cicadas had started to rasp in concert, so aggressively that it sounded as if the grass was vibrating. Teresa marvelled that Sarah had managed to see herself in the images of *Santa Justa in the Well*. Couldn't they all see that Olive's painting was of the same woman, repeated twice, once in her glory and again in her despair? Perhaps, Teresa supposed, if you were determined to see yourself in a certain way, you would – however much the evidence presented otherwise.

'It should have stayed with us,' Sarah said. 'It's wonderful for your brother, of course, but it's the principle of the thing. It was something he did for us. And Harold just hands it over to the highest bidder.'

'Did Isaac accept your money, señora?'

'No,' said Sarah. 'I did try. I hope he's happy with Peggy Guggenheim's, that's all I can say.'

Teresa knew that Isaac had travelled to Malaga to pick up the money wired from Paris, and gone straight to the Workers' General Union headquarters, donating two-thirds of it to pay for agitating pamphlets, clothes, an emergency fund for those laid off, and food. In some ways, you had to admire the efficacy of Olive's plan, turning her painting into a political cause with her father the unwitting middleman. Isaac had kept the last third of the money, a fact which incensed Teresa. She'd told her brother to give it back to Olive, but he'd said that Olive wanted him to have it. 'I have to eat,' he'd said. '*We* have to eat. Or do you fancy eating rats this year?'

Rats. Was that why she'd been dreaming about rats?

'Teresa, are you listening to me?'

'Yes, señora,' Teresa said, folding up the last of Sarah's camisoles and placing them in the wardrobe drawer.

'I was his inspiration.'

'I am sure he is very grateful.'

'Do you think so? Oh, Teresa. I wish something would *happen*. I'm really beginning to miss London.'

Teresa plunged her hands into Sarah's drawer of satins and gripped her fists out of her mistress's sight. *Then go, and take me with you*, she screamed silently, even though she knew this was an impossibility. For all the pity she showed Sarah Schloss, the woman would never do such a thing in return.

XIII

Her father's absence made it easier for Olive to see Isaac, and they met several times a week, usually in the cottage when Teresa was in the finca working and Sarah was taking her afternoon rest. For days afterwards, Olive could almost physically summon the memory of their meetings, how it felt when Isaac entered her – the indescribable sensation of making space for him as he pushed deeper, and what she believed was his utter bliss, mirrored by that of hers.

And yet, she never felt sated. Her appetite was unstoppable, a revelation; and she felt so happy that here was something she could summon whenever she wanted, but which never ran out. She felt that he improved her, he made her the woman she was meant to be. And afterwards, at night, she would lock herself in her attic, and paint. She was growing ever more confident, and saw Isaac as her key. This was not something Teresa would ever be able to understand – Isaac as essential to her development as an artist. Olive couldn't bear to look at Teresa's mournful face, her little scowl. It was an energy the opposite of him.

The olive trees, lined in serried swoops on the hillsides, were greening. Along the road, oranges were coming into fruit, and Olive scratched her nails on the hard skin, and made a scar on the early citrus. It was fresh, it was perfect, the world was fresh and perfect.

What next to paint? What next to do? Everything was possible. She was now the Olive Schloss she was always supposed to be.

When she reached the cottage, Isaac was reading a letter by the wood burner in the kitchen. She walked towards him to give him a kiss, but Isaac held the letter out and stopped her path.

'What is it? What's wrong?'

'This is from Miss Peggy Guggenheim. Read it for yourself.'

Disconcerted, Olive took the letter, sat at the table, and read.

> Dear Mr Robles,
>
> Harold Schloss gave me your address. Forgive my forwardness, but I do believe that in these matters, honesty of expression is invaluable. I hope that you, as an artist relatively new to these transactions, would agree. For I have no wish to be a faceless 'purchaser' – your work has enlivened my wall, and I am enthralled.

Olive looked up at Isaac, her mind racing. 'Oh, Isaac. How wonderful—'

'Read on,' he said.

> When Schloss said he had something special to show me, I was dubious. Art dealers say this a lot to me, and I am quickly learning to develop a "sang froid" when it comes to such declarations. But Schloss was adamant; even coming to Paris specifically to show it to me. He said you were from the land of the Moors and the endless starlit skies, of Arabic palaces and Catholic forts, where blood is in the soil and the sun beats the sierra. Your dealer may sound a theatrical Viennese, Mr Robles, but I have come to entirely trust his opinion.
>
> I am so delighted I agreed to meet. The enriching effects of your painting change by the day for me. My friends, who know better than me, call it a chimaera, a chameleon, an aesthetic pleasure and a metaphysical

joy. I would rather say that *Women in the Wheatfield*
is not an easy painting to categorize, and that this
is a good thing. Whilst I admire your figurative
stubbornness in a time of abstract shapes, this is not
to say I think you are part of a reactionary, regressive
force – far from it. You are up to something new.

The colors – where to start with your colors? I joked
to Herr Schloss, "perhaps if we cut Mr Robles open,
we will find a rainbow hiding inside?" But guard your
hands, Mr Robles – I know we will only find out this
rainbow through the process of more paintings.

The overall spirit of *Wheatfield* to me feels mythical
and unbridled. Yet there is something fastidious in
your animals, as if their lines have been rendered by
a Renaissance master with a realist's touch – and the
fact you have painted oil onto wood compounds this
sense of tradition. It is both dream and nightmare,
irreligious yet striving for some faith. Yet the colors of
the women – their expressions, the sweep of the sky –
they seem derived from a somewhat more modern
soul.

This is just what I take from it, of course. You must
do as other great artists do, and ignore all "opinion".
Anyway, Mr Robles: I love it; take or discard that as
you will.

Schloss probably told you that I am planning to
establish a gallery in London next year, and I have
your painting intended for the opening exhibition. I
do not know if I shall be able to part with it for public
consumption – I do not want to share it and for now, it
hangs on my bedroom wall. There is a call to intimacy
within it, a personal struggle and defiance that seems
so essentially human – dare I say, so essentially *female*
– which has come to beat inside me like an extra heart.

But I want to be a good collector, you see – and good

collectors always share. I would love for you to see it on the public wall.

I will never make an artist explain himself to me, unless he himself chooses to do so – so I ask here no questions of impulses, process, your wishes for what may come. But here is my one request. Schloss has assured me that there will be opportunities to see more work, and all I ask is that you consider me a supporter. To wit: when it comes to showing you to the wider world, I would love to be your first port of call. The first of anything is so often the most indefatigable.

Yours, in admiration,

Peggy Guggenheim

Olive started to laugh, giddy laughter – the laughter of someone whose lottery ticket has just come through; her winner's mind already racing over the transformations of her life to come. 'Oh, Isaac,' she said. 'You've made a new friend. She *loves* it.'

'She is not my friend.'

'Come on, Isa. There's nothing to worry about.'

He went very still. 'Is it true that your father has told her I have more paintings?'

Olive placed the letter slowly on the table. 'I don't know. That's the honest truth. But it's inevitable he would – he's a dealer. It's half his job. He got Guggenheim – hook, line and sinker – and he wasn't going to let her go again without a little bait.'

He ran a hand over his face. 'Did you know this would happen, Olive?'

'No.'

'Did you *suppose* it would happen?'

'I didn't think about it.'

'You didn't think about it.'

'I – just knew I couldn't tell my father that it was mine.'

'But why not?' He pressed his finger on the letter and she

watched the skin turn white. 'Would it not be easier than all this?'

'Teresa put me on the spot. She interfered—'

'Mr Robles does not have any more paintings,' Isaac said, folding his arms. 'That was the one painting he had. And now it's sold. And now there are no more.'

'Yes, but—'

'So I am going to tell your father, the *dealer*, that I do not have time to paint. My work in Malaga does not give me the time for it.'

'Peggy Guggenheim bought you, Isaac. Her uncle—'

He made a sound of disgust. 'Listen to yourself. Peggy bought *you*.'

'Peggy bought *us*. Don't you see? We're together in this. Your name, your face: my work.'

'Olive. This is very serious. There is no balance.'

'Just one more painting. One more.'

'I have not enjoyed this. I said yes, like a fool. I was tired, I was stupid. And now you are like a drunk, searching for the hidden bottle.'

'Blame your sister, not me. I never wanted this situation, but here it is.'

'You could have stopped it. You didn't want to.'

'Did you give the money to the workers?'

'I did.'

'And didn't that feel like you were doing something? Aren't we all supposed to make sacrifices – isn't that half your credo that you've been telling me since the day we met?'

'And what sacrifice are you making, Olive? As far as I can see, for you this is a big joke.'

'It's not a joke,' Olive snapped, pushing her chair back and facing him square-on.

'You have been behaving as if it is.'

'Why do you and your sister think I'm so stupid? Do you know how many artists my father sells? Twenty-six, last time I counted. Do you know how many of them are women, Isaac? None. Not one. Women can't *do* it, you see. They haven't got the *vision*, although last time I checked they had eyes, and hands, and hearts and souls. I'd have lost before I'd even had a chance.'

'But you *made* that painting—'

'So what? My father would never have got on a plane to Paris with a painting he thought was mine. I've lived with that realization for years, Isaac. Years and years, before you and I met. When I came down here, I didn't know what I was going to do with my life; I was lost. And then I met you. And then your sister – your interfering little sister, who perhaps did me the greatest favour anyone's ever done, even though the truth of it is killing her – came along and changed everything. And I like it, Isaac, and I don't want it to stop. One day I might tell him – just to see the look on his face. Maybe that will be a joke. But not now. It's too late.'

'Too late – for what? And please do not say it is because you want to carry on helping the Spanish working man. I do not think I can tolerate it.'

'You were happy enough to take my money.'

'Peggy Guggenheim's money—'

'Which was probably double your annual salary. Do you think I truly don't care about what's happening down here?'

'You may care. But it is superficial. You do not understand it at the heart.'

'But *I'm* the one who can actually pump proper money into it, not you. And who says you're the expert?' She threw up her hands. 'All right, Isaac, I'll tell you why I want to carry on – it *is* for me. But I can help some people along the way, at least. I want my paintings to be so valuable and so important that no one can pull them off the market and hide them away because – heaven forfend – they were painted by a *woman*. And it's not just that. I've seen what success does to people, Isaac – how it separates them from their creative impulse, how it paralyses them. They can't make anything that isn't a horrible replica of what came before, because everybody has opinions on who they are and how they should be.'

'I am glad you are being honest. But it would still have been the same painting if your name was on it,' Isaac said. 'You could have changed things.'

'Oh, God, I could wring your neck. You're so naive – it wouldn't have worked out the same way at all. There'd be no flirty letter from Peggy Guggenheim, no exhibition in her new gallery on the basis of one painting, nothing like it. And it would take all my energy "changing things" as you put it, with none left over to paint – which is the whole bloody point of everything. The energy a man might use on – oh, I don't know, making good work – you want me to use on "changing things". You don't understand, because you've lived your life as an individual, Isaac. And yet everything you do as a man is universal. So enjoy the glory, enjoy the money, and do it for me, because I certainly wouldn't have been allowed.'

'A cheque from Peggy Guggenheim isn't going to change the political situation round here,' he said. 'You are the naive one.'

'Well I'd rather be naive than boring. What's wrong with the pair of you? I've given you this! You and Teresa are as bad as each other.'

'My sister is angry with me,' he said. 'She's right.'

'Well she's angry with me too. We're hardly friends. It's a mess. But let's face it, when is Teresa not angry?'

This was a brief moment of unity, of levity, as they thought of Teresa and her scowling, her defiance, her sense of what was right, and her unorthodox ways of going about it. 'I don't think she considered any of this when she put my painting on the easel,' Olive said. 'She doesn't know me at all.'

Isaac leant back in his chair and exhaled the moment of truce. 'No. It did not go according to her plan. But she still idolizes you. And I think she knows you better than you know yourself.'

'What's that supposed to mean?'

'That maybe, Olive, you didn't want your painting to be so secret after all.'

She stared at him. '*What?*'

'You let her into your bedroom. You showed her your paintings.

Did you never wonder that my sister might skip ahead of you a few steps?'

'I showed her my paintings as a *friend*.'

'Teresa did not do this to you maliciously. Stop pretending that she has done you a harm.'

Olive slumped onto the table. 'If you're so worried about your sister's feelings you should never have touched me in the first place. That's what's really bothering her. I don't know why.'

'Olive, you came to me – you wanted . . . All right. How about we stop this, now?'

Olive lifted her head. 'What do you want to stop?'

'This . . . *lie*. I feel I am deceiving your father—'

'It doesn't matter about him. He's happy. He's delighted. He's sold a piece of art and he's cultivating the reputation of a very promising artist—'

'Who doesn't exist.'

'But the Isaac Robles we created – *he* exists.'

'We are going round in circles.'

'Just one more painting. *One* more.'

'You are so bossy, Olive. So careless with other people's feelings.'

'Am I? What about you? You didn't even want to kiss me when I turned up.' They faced each other in silence. 'Please, Isa. I know it's a lot. But I've got a painting called *The Orchard*. We could give Peggy Guggenheim that.'

'The more we play, the more dangerous this gets.'

'Nothing bad is going to happen.' Olive knelt down by Isaac's side, her fists locked together in supplication, resting on his knee. 'No one will ever know. Please, Isa. *Please*.'

He ran his hands nervously over his head. 'What if Peggy Guggenheim wants to meet me?'

'She's not going to want to come down here.'

'What if she invites me to Paris? She has already mentioned London.'

'Then say no. Play the elusive artist.'

Isaac narrowed his eyes. 'Now is not the time for English irony.'

'No, I mean it. Isaac, *please.*'

'What will you do for me?'

'Anything you want.'

Isaac closed his eyes and drew his hand down his face, as if he was washing away his thoughts. He lifted her from the floor and rose from the table, leading her across the kitchen towards his bedroom door. 'One painting, Olive,' he said. 'And then – no more.'

XIV

Isaac demanded to see *The Orchard* before it was shipped to Harold's office in Paris, 'so at least I know what I am putting my name to.' Teresa suggested that perhaps Sarah should view it too, because it would be useful for her to see Isaac with *The Orchard*. This would reinforce the general belief that the painting was his, should Sarah ever mention seeing it to her husband.

Olive was surprised at Teresa's suggestion. 'I suppose it's a good idea,' she said to her. 'But I thought you didn't want anything to do with this?'

Teresa merely shrugged.

'OH, IT'S WONDERFUL,' SAID SARAH, standing in front of the painting that afternoon in the front east room. Olive scuttled away from it – rather like a crab, it seemed to Teresa – running from a great wave, unable to put her head out of her shell. Her confident attitude had evaporated, and she sat herself in her father's armchair to watch her mother. Teresa took in the vision of Sarah's red woollen trousers, the deep blood shade against her creamy skin; Sarah had clearly rallied herself. 'It's so like *our* orchard,' she said. 'But . . . different.'

'Thank you, señora,' said Isaac, in visible discomfort.

'Isn't it good, Liv?'

'Yes,' said Olive, unable to meet Isaac's eye.

Sarah insisted that Teresa fetch Isaac tea and *polvorones*. 'We're so glad to have Teresa,' she said. 'It would all be such a palaver without her. And I'm so proud of finding you, Mr Robles,' she said to him, leaning against the back of the sofa where he was sitting. She was warm, conciliatory. 'How does it feel, to be the toast of Paris?' she asked.

'What is *toast*?'

'It means you're everyone's new favourite. He'll be champing at the bit when he sees this.' She waved her hand in the direction of *The Orchard*. 'Honestly, Mr Robles, I'm so glad I commissioned you in the first place, although it's hard to share you. It's just a shame my painting is hanging on another woman's wall.'

'Yes,' he said.

'Well,' she sighed, and it sounded like twenty words in one. 'My husband will be home soon.' The marital noun made it sound as if Isaac would have no idea who Harold was.

'It will be good to see him,' said Isaac.

Sarah smiled and left the room, and Teresa felt as if the wattage of the day had dimmed as they listened to her moving back up the main staircase. Olive stepped quickly to the door and shut it. 'Well, Isa?' she asked, whirling round. 'Do you like it?'

They all stared at the painting, the undulating patchwork of fields, the surreal intensity of colour, the white house which once was his to roam and now the home of someone else. 'Does it matter whether I like it?' he asked.

Olive looked uncomfortable. 'You don't like it.'

'I can see its merit, but it is not what I myself would paint,' he said.

'He does not like it,' said Teresa.

'It is not that simple,' Isaac snapped.

Olive stood before the painting. 'I think it is that simple, really. What don't you like about it?'

'My God!' he cried. 'Why do I have to *like* it? Is it not bad enough I am pretending I have made it?'

'Do keep your voice down,' she said.

'You have even painted my initials.'

'A necessary touch.'

He stood up. 'I hate it,' he said. 'I hope your father does too.'

'Isaac—'

'Good day, señoritas.'

Olive looked as if he had slapped her in the face. When he left the room, Olive ran to the window, watching his figure disappearing down the slope to the rusting gates. He pushed them open roughly, not looking back once.

'Do not be upset,' said Teresa, stepping forward. 'What does it matter if he doesn't like it?'

Olive made a sound of frustration. 'He can hate what I create, but I can't *create* if he's angry with me. I just can't.'

'But why not? You painted before you knew him.'

Olive gestured at *The Orchard*. 'Not like this, not like this!' She pressed her forehead against the peeling wooden shutter. 'And if he doesn't like it, how can we be sure he'll ship it to my father? It has to go soon. We'll lose momentum with the Guggenheim woman.'

'I am sure she will wait for genius.'

Olive wrinkled her nose. 'That's a word that gets bandied about too much. I'm not a genius. I just work hard.'

'Well, she will wait. And if my brother will not do it, I can take it to the port myself.'

'You?'

'You can trust me.'

Olive kept her face hidden, still leaning her forehead on the shutter. 'You broke my trust when you put that painting on the easel. I never know if you're my friend or not.'

Teresa was silent for a moment. She couldn't hide her pain. Sometimes Olive was as coquettish as her mother, for all her determination to be different. 'You cannot see? You can trust me with your life.'

Olive lifted her head. 'Never mind about my life, Tere. Do you mean it about the painting? You'll take it to the port?'

'Yes.'

Olive peered down the slope towards the gate, through which Isaac had long disappeared. 'I've never had a true friend.'

'Neither have I.'

'Have you ever been in love? Have you ever been with a man?'

'I have not.'

'Been with a man – or been in love?'

'Been with a man.'

Olive turned to her. 'But you've been in love.'

Teresa felt her cheeks flame. 'No. I do not think so. I do not know.'

THAT NIGHT, TERESA DID NOT go back to the cottage. She was permitted to install herself in the corner of Olive's attic, sorting the artist's brushes and her clothes, a heady bliss that followed truce. Olive revealed that she had been painting a portrait of Isaac. It had been a long time coming, Teresa thought – given the speed with which the girl could usually work, the sketchbooks overflowing with the pencilled planes of his face.

Glancing over at Olive by the easel, Isaac's features developing on the wood before her, Teresa could see it was an astonishing beginning. He had greenish skin, and a consumptive, claustrophobic look in his eye. But his head seemed on fire, sweeps of dandelion and canary yellows up to the top of the painting, where red flecks were being spattered like the wake of murderous thoughts. It was a livid rendering, and Olive looked to be as if in a trance. Teresa knew that the balance between her brother and this girl wasn't right, but she doubted Olive was aware of these layers of infatuation and fear, manifesting by her very own hand.

OLIVE FINISHED HER FIRST GO at Isaac in the small hours. At three in the morning, exhausted, she lay back on her mattress, staring at the roof beams and flaking ceiling plaster, its rough, raised corners illuminated by the weak glow from her bedside candle. A wolf howled, distant in the mountains.

'Come and sleep here,' she said to Teresa. Teresa, who'd been reading one of Olive's books in the corner, put it down and obeyed, climbing onto the old mattress, lying rigidly next to Olive under the dusky pink coverlet, unable to move for fear that to do so might expel her from this magic kingdom.

They lay side by side, staring at the ceiling together as the atmosphere lightened in the room, the energy of Olive's work and concentration dissipating into the air, until all that was left was the glowing green face of Isaac on the easel. Beyond the window, into the land, no rooster or dog or human cry broke their silence as they fell asleep, fully clothed.

Two days later, Olive decided to go with Teresa to Malaga, 'to make a day of it,' she said, 'and why not?'

'But how long are you going to be?' asked Sarah. Teresa supposed she was agitated, because for the first time in months she was going to be alone.

'We're going to the shipping office for Mr Robles, and then I thought we'd have a lemonade in Calle Larios,' said Olive.

'Well, make sure you get that farmer fellow to bring you back before nightfall.'

'I promise.'

'He isn't a red, is he?'

'*Mother.*'

The Orchard was a large painting, and it took both girls to carry it down the finca path, as if it was a stretcher missing a body. Teresa looked back up at the house and saw Sarah watching, staying at the window right until they were down in the valley and she disappeared from their sight. The mule man was waiting for them in the town square. Teresa tried to ignore the uneasy feeling in her gut when she imagined Sarah on her own. She couldn't pinpoint the worry, so she focused instead on the pleasure of a day trip. She was in her best blue dress; she'd washed her hair and doused herself with the distilled orange blossom Rosa Morales, the doctor's daughter, sold out of her kitchen. It could almost be *feria* time, for the sense of holiday Teresa felt.

As she sat with the wrapped parcel of *The Orchard* propped beside her, on the back of a mule cart thirty kilometres along the Malaga road, Teresa was surprised at how bulky the package was under the string and paper. She did not question it, simply because she was now deliciously in Olive's good books again. She would do as she was bid. Olive's hair was flying in the wind, and her white-framed sunglasses made her as glamorous as her mother. Why would you want to ruin such a blue-sky day?

The mule pulled along the white-dust road, and Olive pointed out more red ribbons that had been tied around the girths of the cork oaks. The vision was vaguely unsettling, like shining lines of blood fluttering in the breeze. 'What are they?' she asked in Spanish.

The mule driver turned over his shoulder and said, 'They're trouble.'

Teresa saw them as an omen for what violence might come to this land, as it had so many times in centuries before. No one ever saw who tied these ribbons – Adrián had been one of them, apparently – but the fact that there were people determined to adorn the trees suggested an undercurrent of defiance, a desire to turn things on their head. Teresa didn't want anything turned on its head. She had only just managed to achieve this day.

Full of self-importance and happiness, they reached the shipping office and arranged with the mule man when and where he should come back to fetch them. They made the post office just before it closed for siesta, sending off the parcel for today's shipment to France. *The Orchard* was off to the Galerie Schloss on Paris's Rue de la Paix.

Afterwards, they walked the wide boulevards, admiring the wrought-iron lamp-posts adorned with hanging baskets, trailing petunias and geraniums in hot pinks and scarlets. They looked through shop windows, pointing out to each other the best-dressed of Malaga's high society. They went inwards to the narrower, cobbled streets, all shutters closed against the midday heat. It was metropolitan, so different to their rural hideaway on the slopes of Arazuelo. Teresa was pleased to see how impressed Olive was with her native city. It might not be London, but it was by turns stately and timeless, as the sun beat down on the stone, or reflected off the polished vitrines and ornate wooden frames of department stores and pharmacists.

They walked down to the harbour and sat to enjoy a lemonade, wondering which of the enormous ships that pulled in and out with such constant frequency would be taking away their duplicitous cargo.

'Isaac knew the painting would go,' Olive said. 'He just didn't want to be the one who sent it. Do you think I'm being fair to him?'

'What you mean to ask is – will my brother carry on doing this for ever.'

Olive looked at her in surprise. 'Yes, I suppose I do.'

Teresa gazed out to sea. 'The money will never be a good reason for him.'

She was telling the truth; it had never been enough for either of them. Even though he had kept some aside from the sale of *Women in the Wheatfield*, they had both always wanted things that money couldn't buy; legitimacy, love. Teresa did think that Olive was being thoughtless, that her use of Isaac's name as a front for her own work was not something he would continue to tolerate. As for herself, as long as Olive wanted it, she was happy to oblige.

Olive frowned. 'That sounded like a threat.'

'No, no,' said Teresa. 'But – he is a man, you know.'

'What do you mean?'

Teresa couldn't answer with the precision she wanted in English. And although she worried that Olive's actions were bringing her closer to some undefined, simmering danger that was coming, which Teresa couldn't name but could almost taste – she was so happy to be here, by the sea, the lemonade, that she didn't want Olive's thoughtlessness to stop.

'My brother can speak for himself,' she said obliquely, and Olive, not wishing to go any deeper into the sourer elements of this plot of theirs, turned away to look at the gigantic liners moving out to sea.

THEY RETURNED TO THE FINCA at dusk, tired and happy. 'Teresa,' Olive said, as they reached the front door.

'Yes?'

'I won't let anything happen to you. You can trust me, I promise.'

Teresa smiled, amazed to hear her own words being spoken back to her, the second half of the same spell. When they went inside, Sarah was nowhere to be seen.

'Where is she?' said Olive, and the panic in her voice was so childlike, so easily accessed.

'She has probably gone out for a walk,' Teresa said.

'My mother doesn't go for walks.' Olive ran out into the orchard, and on the pretext of searching for Sarah in the upper rooms, Teresa took the opportunity to slip into the attic and confirm her suspicions. It was as she thought. The green-faced portrait of Isaac was nowhere to be seen. By now, it was deep in the bowels of a liner, on its way to Peggy Guggenheim.

XV

$\mathcal{S}$arah began frequent walks out of the finca estate, an unprecedented gesture for someone usually more inclined to smoke on a sofa. She began to pull the ready vegetation from the rented land, piling it up in a wide wicker basket, the earth-encrusted roots still attached. She would announce her trip to the village to buy artichokes, and soon there was a molehill of them in the kitchen. The vases of wildflowers had multiplied so considerably that Teresa was running out of receptacles.

Ten days after their trip to Malaga, a telegram from Harold arrived. Teresa went down to pick it up, and ran all the way back to the finca, handing it to Olive, who was shelling peas with her mother at the kitchen table.

'GREEN FACE GENIUS GOES TO GUG STOP ALSO BOUGHT MAGNIFICENT ORCHARD STOP BACK END OF WEEK STOP,' Olive read aloud. 'Peggy Guggenheim bought them both,' she breathed. 'Isaac will be pleased.'

'I wasn't aware there were two,' said Sarah, one fingernail flashing down an open seed-pod. The lacquer, Teresa noted, had chipped, and her mistress had done nothing to remedy it.

'There was *The Orchard*, but Isaac had another painting. A self-portrait.'

'You saw it?' asked Sarah.

'Briefly. It looks like Daddy's coming back.'

'Just when that telephone finally stopped ringing,' Sarah sighed.

Teresa went to the sink to busy herself with the washing up. Sarah laid down her empty pea pod. 'Darling,' she said. 'Do you like it here?'

'I've got used to it. I like it very much now. Don't you?'

Sarah looked through the kitchen window. The garden and the orchard beyond it were now abundant with fruit and flowers, honeysuckle, *dama-de-noche* and all the oranges and olives Harold had promised his wife and daughter back in January, when, cold, bedraggled and shaking off the after-effects of one of Sarah's storm clouds, they had arrived here, knowing no one.

'I don't know if *like* is the word I'd use. I feel I've lived here about ten years. It sort of . . . saturates you, a place like this. As if it's the living embodiment of Isaac's painted fields.' She turned to her daughter. 'It's extraordinary – how he captured it, isn't it?'

'Yes.'

'How do you think he does it?'

'How would I know?'

'He's a genius.'

Olive sighed. 'Nobody's a genius, Mother. That's lazy thinking. It's practice.'

'Ah, practice. I could practise for ever and not produce anything as good as that.'

'You seem better, Mummy,' said Olive.

'I do feel a lot stronger. Daddy got me that last round of pills from Malaga and I haven't touched them.'

'Really? Is that a good idea? You gave me and Tere a real fright when we got back from Malaga and you weren't here. I was worried you'd—'

'I wouldn't do that, Livvi. It's not like it was.'

They continued shelling peas in silence. Her mother had caught the sun, and she seemed peaceful; self-contained. It was once again painful to Olive how attractive her mother was, and how Sarah barely registered this fact – her hair a bit of a mess, her sundress crumpled as if she'd just pulled it out of a trunk. Her roots had now grown out considerably, and she didn't seem to care. Her natural dark blonde was a stark, yet oddly pleasurable visual contrast to the peroxide ends. Olive had the itch to paint her, to capture this ease, in the hope that she too could have some of it for herself.

'Summer's nearly here,' Sarah said, breaking Olive's thoughts. 'It's going to be so hot.'

'You were complaining when it was cold.'

Sarah laughed at herself. This too, was rare. 'It wasn't a terrible idea of your father's to come here. Not a terrible idea at all.' She reached over and squeezed her daughter's hand. 'I do love you, you know, Liv. Very much.'

'Goodness. What's wrong with you?'

'Nothing. Nothing. I just think you should know.'

SARAH WENT OUT ONTO THE veranda with her packet of cigarettes and the latest Christie shipped over from a friend in London, and Teresa began to mop the flagstones in the hall. Olive followed her, standing on the dry patch Teresa hadn't yet reached.

'Teresa, will you sit for my next painting?' she asked, her voice quiet. 'I'd love to use you as a model.'

Teresa's spine stiffened, her fists tightening round the mop handle. 'You didn't tell me about the second painting we took to Malaga,' she said.

'I didn't want to get you into any more trouble.'

'Trouble?'

'Look, I know you think this whole undertaking demeans me as an artist.'

'*Demeans?*'

'Makes less of me. You think Isaac gets more importance round here than he deserves. But it's what I want. I want the freedom. You're my friend, Tere. Let me give this to you.'

Teresa straightened, meditatively plunging the head of the mop into her bucket of filthy water. She knew, in a way, that she had wanted this moment ever since she saw Isaac in the sketchbook. And the decision to help Olive in her deceptions – taking the paintings into Malaga, making sure Sarah still believed they were by Isaac, keeping the attic clean – had all been leading to this less than noble truth; that Teresa wanted to be painted. She wanted Olive to want her as a painting.

As Teresa walked behind Olive upwards to the attic, she knew she had departed from her place in the script. She turned back once to view the floor, half-agleam, the mop resting, accusatory. She was no longer the servant who rid the house of stains; she was going to make a mark so permanent no one would ever forget it.

IT WAS TO BE A painting of Rufina, Olive told her, locking the attic door. 'I've done Justa in the Well, and you'll be my Rufina. It was you who told me the story, after all. I've been wondering what part of it to tell.'

Teresa nodded, not daring to speak. What would Isaac say, when he found out Olive had painted his face green and sent it as a self-portrait to Peggy Guggenheim? When would he realize that painting after painting would come out of this girl? Olive believed Isaac was the source of her inspiration, but Teresa thought that nothing he could do now – no tantrum, no withholding of affection – would stop the flow.

'Rufina with her pots, Rufina with the lion, or Rufina, beheaded, with her sister?' said Olive, mainly to herself. 'The last one's grim, but it is the apogee, even though she's down a well.'

Teresa heard the unusual word, and thought Olive had said *apology*. 'There is nothing to be sorry for,' she said.

Olive smiled. 'I'm glad you think so, Tere.'

She had decided to abandon the diptych format that she'd used for *Women in the Wheatfield*, and paint just one scene. In the end, she wanted all the stages of the story involved. So Rufina would be there in her full body, but she would also be carrying her own head.

'You could put your face in it, too,' said Teresa, then immediately wished she hadn't, for she was probably overstepping herself.

Olive bit her lip, considering the idea. 'Well, let's paint yours first,' she said. 'I'll decide later whether to add mine. It is supposed to be one person, after all. But I'm definitely going to lay gold leaf on the lion's mane. He'll be tame as a pussycat.'

Olive placed her on the chair she usually sat in when Teresa brushed her hair. There was a surety to Olive's touch, she was operating in her space of confidence and possibility. 'Such solemn eyes,' Olive told her, as she put her paintbrush to the treated panel. 'So dark and watchful above your little snub nose. You and Isaac have become as engraved in my mind as a woodcut.'

Her expression grew distracted as she began to draw away from the outer elements of the room and closer to her artistic vision. Teresa was locked out of it, and yet she felt the source of it. She willingly sank into this phantom role, where she could disappear and be anything Olive wanted. She had never felt so invisible, and yet so seen.

XVI

*J*n the end, Harold returned the first week of June, driving himself back from Malaga airfield. 'Where is he?' he called, as soon as he'd parked up the Packard. 'Where's my prodigy?'

The women stood on the front step, shielding their eyes from the sun. Harold's wave was breezy. *He's been with her*, Teresa thought, surveying him as he neared the front door. He looked sated, well fed, and yet his grin was a little fixed. He seemed to have the air of a man rolling away from vice and back into the straits of virtue. *Maybe he sent her a ticket to Paris.* The anonymous woman's timid German, which had grown fainter in Teresa's memory, now returned. *Harold, bist du es?*

Teresa glanced over to Sarah. She had a self-contained look, as if she was conserving her energies, girding herself. *Does she know?* Teresa thought. *She knows.*

'Hallo, darling,' Sarah said. 'Isaac doesn't live here, you know.'

Harold stalked forward, depositing two kisses either side of his wife's face. 'It's Isaac now, is it?' He turned to Olive. 'You look well, Liv. In fact, you look glorious.'

Olive smiled. 'Thank you, Papi. So do you.'

Teresa cast down her eyes, hoping Harold wouldn't see her thoughts. *'Buenos días*, Teresa,' he said. She looked; the journey had left him with a day's stubble. She discerned the smell of travel, the possibility of someone else's perfume mingled on his skin.

'*Buenos días, señor.*'

'Fetch my suitcase, will you.'

She descended the step, feeling folded inside the Schlosses' life with such cloying intensity that she could hardly breathe.

THAT NIGHT, TERESA WAITED FOR Isaac outside their cottage, as the shadows lengthened and the cicadas began to build their rasping wall of sound. He appeared at the base of the hill at about seven o'clock, and she was struck by how tired he looked, burdened down by an invisible weight as he moved towards her.

'He's back,' she said, by way of greeting.

Isaac dropped his knapsack on the grass, where it clunked.

'What's in there?' she asked.

'You'll see.' He sank to the earth and lay on his back, his hands enlaced beneath his head.

'There's something you should know,' she said, irritated by this evasion. 'Olive didn't tell you, but she sent an extra painting to Paris. Don't be angry. He's sold it. I wanted to tell you before Harold did.' Isaac remained prostrate, and he nodded, patting his jacket pocket, pulling out a box of battered cigarettes. 'Are you angry, Isa?'

'No.'

'I thought you would be. Why aren't you?'

'Do you want me to be angry? What's the point? She's done it. And it doesn't surprise me.'

'More money for the cause, I suppose.'

'Always that.'

'Isa. I know what's going on.'

He looked up at her, sharply. 'What do you mean?'

'I know what you two do. Apart from the painting stuff. That she's in love with you.'

A look of relief passed across his face as he lit a cigarette. 'Olive,' he said.

'Are you in love with her?'

Isaac sat up and dragged on his cigarette, hunching his knees as he looked down over the sierra. It was dusk by now, and the bats had started to appear out of the copses at the foot of the valley. The air was warm, the earth still giving off its heat. 'They'll leave,' he said. 'They won't last here. They belong in the city. In the salon.'

'Sarah, yes. Harold, maybe. Not Olive.'

'She's turned you into a romantic.'

'The opposite. I understand her, that's all. She won't leave you. She'll follow wherever you go.'

'What makes you so sure of that?'

'She says she can't paint without you.'

He laughed. 'True in one way, perhaps. Well, if she does love me, that doesn't make any of this all right.'

'I don't think she needs you at all.'

'And that doesn't surprise me either, Teresa.'

PARIS HAD BEEN A TRIUMPH, Harold said; Isaac Robles was now the pole star in the firmament of Galerie Schloss Paris. The next afternoon, Harold, legs stretched out in the front east room, drinking a glass of fino, told them in no uncertain terms that thanks to *Women in the Wheatfield*, *The Orchard*, and *Self-Portrait in Green*, he and his partners were enjoying a renaissance.

'People heard through Duchamp that Peggy wants to buy art,' he said. 'But I got there first. She's incredibly excited about the next one, your companion piece to *Women in the Wheatfield*. She wants a photograph of it in progress, though, if that's possible. Is it possible, Isaac?'

Olive slugged back another fingerful of sherry. 'The "companion piece"?' said Isaac.

'Am I rushing you?' said Harold. 'Tell me if so. We don't have to send her a photograph if you don't want that. It's what's best for you. You have a great gift, Isa. Truly. I cannot wait to see your future.'

'It will not be what any of us expects,' Isaac replied. 'Mr Schloss, I have brought something for you.'

Olive put the sherry glass down and began to rise from her chair, but Isaac reached into his knapsack and withdrew a pistol, the barrel made of shining steel. No one spoke as he weighed it in the flat of his hand.

'Is that real?' Sarah asked.

'Real, señora.'

'Why on earth have you brought us a gun?' said Harold, laughing. 'Bring me a painting, for Christ's sake.'

Olive sat back, the relief visible on her face. 'Do you shoot, señor?' Isaac said.

'I can. I have.'

'Can the women shoot?'

'Of course we can't,' said Sarah. 'Why do you ask? This is terribly dramatic.'

ISAAC HUNG AN OLD FLOUR sack, packed with earth, upon a protruding branch of a cork oak at the end of the garden. One word covered the rough sacking, H A R I N A, and they agreed that the makeshift bullseye was the space between the 'R' and the 'I'. They all trooped past the empty stone fountain and lined up to have a go, and there was almost a carnival atmosphere to their endeavour; the silly swinging sack, the birds scattering out of the oak at the crack of Isaac's pistol.

Harold hit the last *A*. Sarah shot into the bark and handed the pistol back to Isaac, saying she would never touch it again. She went to lie on her back in the grass, staring at the sky, her hands resting on her stomach. Isaac shot the middle of the *N*, and looked sheepish. He handed the pistol to Olive, and Teresa watched the intertwining of their hands.

Olive lumbered over to the shooting spot and raised the pistol. She squinted, and pulled on the trigger, releasing the bullet with a gasped shock as the pistol recoiled in her hand.

'Liv,' cried her father.

'I'm fine.'

'No, you nearly shot the centre.'

Olive looked in surprise towards the sack. 'Did I?'

Teresa thought it natural that Olive should have such a good eye, a steady hand. 'Do that again,' Harold said.

'No. It was a fluke.'

Sarah lifted her head up to look at the bullet-riddled sack. 'Liv, you've got a hidden talent. Maybe we should enter you in competitions.'

Teresa hurried over to take the pistol from Olive, and Isaac came to check she was reloading it correctly. Teresa brushed him off, setting the pistol perfectly on her own. 'You bought this with her money, didn't you?' she whispered to him.

'It won't be the last. It's a Soviet T33,' he replied, with a note of admiration.

'Are you giving this gun to them?'

'They might need it.'

'Why? Are you trying to protect them, or put them in danger?'

'Keep your eye on the target, Tere. And your voice down.'

Teresa wondered where Isaac was finding the means to source Soviet weapons, but part of her didn't want to know. She concentrated on raising the pistol, her legs apart, her other hand supporting her wrist. Her body was taut, every muscle tensed on her spare frame, the set of her jaw fixed as hard as the stone satyr in the fountain. She inhaled deeply and pulled the trigger. *You're not the only one who shoots rabbits*, she thought. The pistol went off and the bullet sailed through the air, hitting precisely through the knot attaching the sack to the branch. To Isaac's cry of frustration, the entire thing tumbled to the grass. The packed earth spilled everywhere, and the game was ruined.

Late that afternoon, Harold said he was driving to Malaga. He wanted to visit a bodega, pick up some new supplies of sherry. Sarah announced that she would accompany him. 'I need a chemist,' she said. 'Then I'd like a coffee on Calle Larios and a walk along the sea.'

Teresa saw Harold's hesitation, but he said, 'That's a good idea, get some air into your lungs. Isaac, would you join us? A man with local knowledge might help when it comes to the sherry.' But Isaac, who Teresa knew would once have craved a drive in such a powerful car, who had to content himself with a bicycle, did not wish to join them at all. He demurred, politely. 'Of course,' said Harold. 'You've got work you want to do.'

Outside the finca, Olive and Isaac waved her parents off. 'We could take the photograph for Peggy Guggenheim now,' she said, as their car disappeared. 'Daddy has a camera in his study.' Isaac was silent, staring at the swinging gate, gaping open on the path towards the village. 'What is it?' she asked.

'I was foolish,' he said.

'You're weren't.'

'I thought your confidence, your happiness, was out of love for me.'

'It was. It is.'

'I do not think so. I think this has always been inside you, waiting to come out. I just happened to be there, at that particular time, in order for you to use me as your canvas.'

'I love you, Isaac,' she said. The words landed short between them.

'Your love is not with me. It is for the walls of the Guggenheim house. How is this going to end, Olive?' he said. 'Because it is going to end.'

Olive turned to him, placing a hand on his arm, but he brushed it off. 'I've made you angry,' she said. 'But I do love you—'

'You say one more painting. But then there is one another. A green face, one more, one more, one more.'

'I'm sorry. I'm so sorry. This will be the last. I promise, I swear. I swear on my life.'

He turned to face her squarely. 'Did you and my sister plan all this from the very beginning?'

'Of course not.'

'She seems very comfortable with the situation now. She sounds like you. Always, she has a plan.'

'No, there was never a plan, Isaac. This just happened.'

'Teresa is a survivor. She was the one who put you on the easel, but don't think she will always put you first.'

'What are you talking about?'

He laughed, without humour. 'I am famous in Paris, a city I have never even seen. I paint portraits of my own face I have never even seen. You are stealing me, Olive. I feel like I am becoming invisible, the more visible I become.' The breath had got stuck in his throat, and he looked embarrassed, his words breaking up. 'And after all this, you expect me to believe you love me.'

'I don't expect anything, Isaac. I never wanted you to feel like this. I do love you. I never expected you to love *me*. I've got carried away, I know that. But I – we've – been so successful, I never thought it could be so easy—'

'It is not easy, Olive. It has never been easy. I cannot, I will not do this any more. And if you send that Guggenheim woman one more picture, then I cannot promise my actions.'

'What does that mean? Isaac, you're frightening me.'

'The painting you are working on – you must destroy it.'

She looked horrified. 'But I can't.'

'Why not?'

'Because it's the best thing I've ever done. Because they're waiting for it in Paris.'

'Then you cannot expect me to have anything to do with it.'

'Isaac, please. *Please—*'

'You promised me, Olive. You went behind my back.'

'And you haven't touched me for four weeks. Is that the price

you're forcing me to pay, for once in my life doing something brilliant?'

'And what about the price you are forcing me to pay? No man
would put up with a woman who asks so much. A man needs a
woman who understands him, who supports him—'

'Who puts him first?'

'My absence from you is an exchange you seem more than willing to make, as long as Miss Guggenheim continues to sing your
praises.'

'That's not true. I miss you.'

'You do not miss me, Olive. You miss the next chance to send a
painting over.'

'I do miss you. Just come upstairs and see it,' she pleaded. 'And
then tell me if you still feel the same.'

THE PAINTING WAS THE SAME size as *Women in the Wheatfield*,
and yet it felt bigger. Up in the attic, Isaac stood before it, staggered by its sensuality and power. Even though it was still
unfinished, the lion already looked possessed by the sight of the
double-headed Rufina. This piece was breathtaking, sinister,
revolutionary.

'Is that you?' he asked. He pointed at the disembodied head.
'And is that Tere?'

'Yes, and yes,' said Olive. 'But it's supposed to be the same person. It's called *Rufina and the Lion*. That's Rufina, before and after
the authorities got hold of her.'

Isaac stared at the painting, the riot of colours and gold leaf, the
curiously level gazes of Rufina carrying her head; the lion, waiting
to take action.

'Do you like it?' she asked.

'It's wonderful.'

She smiled. 'It happens sometimes. My hand guides my head
without much pause to worry or think.'

In that moment, all she wanted was for Isaac to see her as talented and confident – and to love her for it. 'We've done a wonder-

ful thing, Isa,' she said. 'The paintings are going to be famous.' But Isaac kept his focus on *Rufina and the Lion*. 'Let's use the camera,' she said with a bright voice. 'Peggy wanted snaps.'

'*Snaps?*'

'Photographs. Of the painting. Isa,' she said gently, 'do you really want me to destroy it?'

He looked at the floor, and Olive knew in that moment that she had won this battle, if not the war. 'You could fight a lion too, Isaac – if you had to. I know it.'

'And a lion would run away from you. Do you know how to use the camera?' he asked.

'Of course,' she replied, unnerved, unable to pinpoint what was happening between them. 'But – I was hoping Teresa would take a photograph of the two of us, together.'

Isaac closed his eyes, as if in pain. 'Let's get it done,' he said. 'Call her.'

'I'M A LION,' TERESA ROARED, putting her free hand up, a pantomime paw as she hovered her finger over the camera button. She'd been taking rather formal pictures for the last half-hour – of the painting, of Isaac next to it, but in this moment, Olive threw back her head in laughter, eyes slightly closed, whilst next to her, Isaac, impervious to his sister's humour, gazed straight down the lens with a look of such possession on his face that Teresa forgot she was the king of the jungle at all.

Teresa knew then, as she pressed that button and captured them in these poses, that something had broken in this room. And she understood, for the first time, that they could never go back.

WHEN ISAAC WENT TO PICK up the developed film in Malaga a week later, he discovered that in some of the pictures, Teresa had put Olive in the centre of the image, and the painting itself was half-obscured. He thought he looked funereal in every single one. Olive, because she had been moving so much – jumpy in the face of his acute reluctance that afternoon – was slightly blurred, her mouth ajar, her lips making a silent *O* of pleasure. The sight of her – her expression of freedom and joy – made his conscience flicker briefly before dying away.

When Harold was shown a photograph of the painting on its own, cropped closely so you couldn't tell its location, he asked Isaac, 'Why is the girl carrying a head?'

'In my mind, it stands for duplicity,' Isaac replied. 'Because we are surrounded by lies.'

XVII

*O*live continued to paint *Rufina and the Lion* throughout the rest of June and into July. Harold's telephone began to ring again in his study, every two or three days, and he would close the door on them in order to answer it, his voice hushed and incomprehensible. When he'd been in Paris, he said, the news from Vienna had not been good. Businesses were closing, crimes going unpunished; but not even smashed shop windows were as frightening as the political rhetoric being hurled from one side to the other. Jews were coming in from Germany for shelter, but he wondered how long their luck would last.

He told his family that he would focus on the Paris gallery, trying to work out the logistics of getting his artworks out of Vienna before the business suffered. Peggy Guggenheim was going to open her gallery in London, and he was hoping he might be able to transfer some of his stock to her there. In Vienna, he told them, Jewish friends were selling their art for knock-down prices to raise capital to pay for train fares, lodgings, food, new lives beyond the borders of Austria. People who had prided themselves on varied, intelligent and abundant collections of old masters and new were forced to accept prices they would have baulked at twelve months earlier.

Harold was unsurprisingly gloomy, only perking up when there was talk of the next work by Isaac Robles. Isaac Robles had become his raison d'être, two fingers to the nationalistic narrowness peddled in every paper; his colourful child, his man with a vision, his delight and defiance. 'Paint, Isa,' he said one night, drunk. 'God knows we need you to paint.'

It was odd to think such tempests were happening all around Europe, for Arazuelo seemed relatively peaceful. Sarah continued with her walks out; by now there was a mountain of artichokes in the kitchen. They would never be able to consume them against the pace that Sarah was coming home with them, and Teresa regarded them with a sense of foreboding. She noticed how freckles had appeared over the bridge of Sarah's nose, from the punishing July sunshine; she had lost some of her brittle elegance, and seemed somewhat more grounded in her surroundings. At night, Teresa could hear the Packard's engine as Harold trundled it down the slope and through the gates towards Malaga. Sarah seemed serene about Harold's leave-taking. She slept in, and complained of headaches, rising late enough for her husband to have made his way back home in the dawn, as if he'd never left.

Olive no longer commented on her father's disappearing acts. Teresa wondered whether she was using it as a spur, duping her father as he was duping her. Perhaps Olive's pursuit was not one of success, but of an enemy's humiliation? Teresa wasn't exactly sure. Olive simply seemed most herself when painting, day and night, to finish *Rufina and the Lion*.

JULY WAS A GOOD MONTH in Arazuelo. The smell of sage fields and rosemary, lizards making their way like small secrets out of the walls, jerky and neurotic in motion, ever wary of predators in the sky. But when they stilled themselves to bask, how poised they were, such pragmatists of nature, soaking up the heat of the sun.

It was a time of long evening shadows, the raw rasp of crickets filling the hot night. The fields were now shades of parsley, lime and apple. Wildflowers; spattered reds and royal purples, canary-yellow petals moving in the breeze. And when the wind got up, salt tasted on the air. No sound of the sea – but listen, and you could hear the articulated joints of a beetle, trundling through the corn root.

From the hills came the dull music of bells as the goats overtook these smaller sounds descending the scree through the gauze of heat. Bees, drowsing on the fat flower heads, farmers' voices calling, birdsong arpeggios spritzing from trees. A summer's day will make so many sounds, when you yourself remain completely silent.

They didn't see it coming. Of course they didn't. Who wants to look for trouble, every single day? You turn away, as long as you can. Even the government didn't see it coming. Perhaps later, when the locals recalled how no one had ever been brought to justice over Adrián the factory boy, or when they considered those red ribbons tied to the trees, or the shot statue of the Madonna, they would turn to each other, and say, *Ah yes; the writing was on the wall.*

The Schlosses were too wrapped up in their own internal battles to realize what was going on north in Madrid, what was going to surge up towards them from Morocco. They were not paying attention when on the twelfth of July in Madrid four Falangists shot dead the socialist lieutenant of the Republican Assault Guard. In retaliation, his friends assassinated the country's monarchist deputy, a prominent right-winger. Life in Spain, and life in the finca, was on the cusp of being broken apart, letting in a flood of recriminations, ambitions and long-buried resentments. But at the same time, in those early days, it didn't seem that war was on its way at all.

Sarah and Olive heard it on the radio first. On the eighteenth of July, four generals, out of the eighteen that ran the national army, rebelled against their left-wing government and took over their garrisons. The Prime Minister, frightened of revolution and mass unrest, ordered all civil governors not to distribute arms to the workers' organizations, who would inevitably want to resist potential armed rule. He then resigned that night.

Isaac came racing up to the finca. Harold was out – in Malaga, of course. 'Get the pistol,' he was calling, and on hearing him, the women had spilled out of the house.

Later, Teresa would think about the Schloss women's conflicting expressions. Olive looked relieved. Perhaps she still believed that Issac still cared about her – so much so that he had run all the way because some soldiers were throwing their weight around. Teresa remembered Sarah's smile of pleasure, her steady hand as she poured him a glass of water.

Seville was the nearest city to Arazuelo to fall to the army rebels. Its conquering general was a man called Queipo de Llano, who used the radio at ten o'clock that night to broadcast his intentions. Isaac and the three women sat listening in Harold's study, the fear they felt mirrored in each other's faces as Queipo de Llano's haranguing crackled through the speaker:

'People of Seville: to arms!' he bellowed. *'The Fatherland is in danger and in order to save it a few men of courage, a few generals, have assumed the responsibility of placing ourselves at the forefront of a Movement of National Salvation that is triumphing everywhere. The Army of Africa hastens to cross to Spain to join in the task of crushing that unworthy Government that had taken upon itself to destroy Spain in order to convert it into a colony of Moscow.'*

'A colony of Moscow?' said Sarah. 'What the hell is he talking about?'

'Shut up!' hissed Olive.

'All the troops of Andalusia, with whom I have communicated by telephone, obey my orders and are now in the streets . . . all the authorities of Seville, and all who sympathize with them and with the so-called Government in Madrid, are under arrest and at my disposal.'

'Isaac,' Olive whispered. 'He's talking about you. Isaac, you have to run.'

He looked up at her, and she saw the hollows under his eyes. 'Run? I am not going to run,' he said. 'You think I am going to hide from a man like him? You think because Queipo de Llano has telephoned some people, they will do as he says? We have already mobilized. We will fight back. They did not succeed in Madrid or Barcelona, and they will not succeed here.'

'*People of Seville!*' the general bawled on. '*The die is cast and decided in our favour, and it is useless for the rabble to resist and produce that racket of shouts and gunshots you hear everywhere. Troops of Legionnaires and Moroccans are now en route to Seville, and as soon as they arrive, those troublemakers will be hunted down like vermin. Long live Spain!*'

'Isaac,' Olive said, her voice rising in panic. 'They've got troops. Weapons. Trained soldiers. What would men like that do to you?'

They could hear the sound of Harold's motor, fast and loud, crashing up the hill. The car door slammed. 'Are you there, are you there? Have you heard?' he shouted through the hallway.

Teresa veered away from the desk, stumbling along the unlit corridor, bashing into the walls as she fought her way through the kitchen and onto the veranda, as far away as possible from everybody else. She ran down into the darkness of the orchard and felt the bile come, her body retching the words she could not find to spell out the terror inside – that this was it, the wave was here, the land ripped, her brother taken, and Olive – Olive would leave. She kept shaking her head, willing herself to get a grip, that she'd got this far – but in her heart she could hear the soldiers. Stomping jackboots along dark routes, *thump thump thump*, butt of a gun, split head; no place to hide.

'Tere? Tere!' It was Olive, calling for her. 'Tere, don't be scared. Where are you?'

But this was how she would end, Teresa knew. Here, on her knees, in the dark, in the company of those Spanish wolves.

PART IV

The Swallowed Century

NOVEMBER 1967

12

When the telephone rang in the hallway two days after I was locked out of Quick's house, I ran downstairs, still in my dressing gown, to pick it up. When I heard the person on the line say, 'Wha' happen now, Delly?' I was so glad, I nearly cried. It wasn't Quick I wanted, nor Lawrie. Her voice was permission to live.

'Cynth!'

'You still alive, girl?'

'Just about.'

'Ah – Ah free today. You want to meet up?'

IT HAD BEEN JUST OVER two months. I saw her before she saw me. Cynthia was immaculate as ever, leaning on one of the lions in Trafalgar Square, wearing a thick sheepskin coat which I'd never seen before, and a new pair of denim flared trousers. She looked . . . cool. She'd let her hair out of its French plait, and it was cut in a new shape; the beginning of a rounded Afro. I felt frumpy in comparison, in my thick tights and sensible heels, my woollen scarf and hat clamped round my ears like something out of a Blyton book. But still. A cold November morning in London; you do not mess.

My heart surged at how wonderful Cynth was. The realization of how far I'd travelled alone swamped me, as I saw her face, my friend, my oldest friend. Cynth caught my eye as I moved towards her, her arms wide open like a flightless bird trying to flap her wings.

'Ah sorry, Cynth,' I said. 'So sorry. Ah was dotish, Ah was mess up—'

'Hey, Delly,' she said. 'Ah marry and lef' you. Ah sorry too. What I was thinking?' But there was a twinkle in her eye. 'Ah miss you real bad, girl.'

'Me too. Me too. Me too.'

Her face broke open in a smile, and we turned shy. My emotion left me embarrassed – how I, a grown woman, could be so childish, so effervescent. My heart thumped in my ribs to be near her; I was giddy with her, my giddiness exacerbated by the fact she seemed to feel the same. We walked down under Admiralty Arch and into St James's Park, finding a bench to sit. 'Sherbets,' Cynth said, opening her handbag, proffering me a paper sack of sweets. 'You thin, Delly. What goin' on?'

'Ah pining for you,' I said, mocking myself, trying to show I still had grit. When she laughed aloud, the sound almost hurt. How good it always was to make her laugh.

'Nah, come now,' she said.

SO I TOLD CYNTH EVERYTHING – about meeting Lawrie after the wedding, and our dates after that – the mother he lost and the painting she left – and how Quick's attraction to the artwork seemed mingled with repulsion. I told her how the name 'Isaac Robles' came up, Edmund Reede convinced that this was a long-lost artwork by a forgotten genius, and how Quick was more doubtful about this, until her declaration last night that actually, the painting was nothing to do with Isaac Robles at all.

Cynth was much more interested in Lawrie, how it was going, and was it serious – but I tried to keep the focus on the conundrum of Quick, rather than of my own heart. 'The worse of it, Cynth,' I said, 'is that she dyin'.'

'Dyin'?'

'Cancer. She tell me is in a late stage. They didn't catch it early. Pancreatic.'

'Poor woman,' said Cynth. 'She sound scared about it, invitin' you round. Why she worrying about paintings when she goin' to dead?'

'This is what bothering me. Because listen to this; she running out of time on something, I sure of it.'

'What you sayin'?'

'Reede find out that the person who first sell Lawrie's painting in 1936 is an art dealer called Harold Schloss,' I said. 'The thing is, I find a letter in Quick's house addressed to *Olive* Schloss, inviting her to study at the Slade School of Art.'

'Delly, you snoopin' round a dyin' woman house?'

I tutted. 'No! It there in her telephone book she *tell* me to fetch. But listen – Quick also have telegram address to Harold Schloss, date of July of 1936.'

'What, just lyin' there in her telephone book, thirty year later?'

'I know. I know. But – is like Quick want me to find it. Is like she lef' it out, because she dyin' and don't want the truth to die with her.'

'Delly . . .'

'Quick too interested in where Lawrie get the painting from. And then she tell me last night is not Isaac Robles who paint it. Olive Schloss is key to this, Ah sure.'

'But who is this Olive Schloss?'

I exhaled, and my breath made condensation in the air. 'That is the question, Cynthia. That is *it*. Clearly a body who could paint, otherwise they wouldn't have been offered the Slade. Someone probably relate to Harold Schloss.'

'His wife?'

'Maybe. But if you going to art school, you usually younger, a student.'

'His daughter, then?'

'That's what I think. Olive Schloss was Harold Schloss's daughter. And at the Skelton, it have an old photograph of a man and

woman standing by Lawrie's painting. On the back someone write
"*O and I.*" That stands for Olive and Isaac. Quick say that Isaac
Robles didn't paint the pictures. Then who did it, and how she
know? I don't think Quick who she say she is.'

'Delly . . .'

'It always bother me, how she never have any painting on her
wall. Why's that? And the thing is, Quick went funny when I ask
her about Olive Schloss. She shut the door on me, lock me out. Is
like she *want* me to know, to get closer to the truth of it, and at the
same time – she cyan bear it.'

Cynthia appeared to be thinking, staring at the ducks gliding
across the pond before us. Beyond the trees, the spindly brown
turrets of Westminster poked up into the air. 'I always thought
Marjorie Quick was a funny name,' she said.

We sat in silence for a moment. I loved my friend for believing, for not saying I was mad, for accompanying me as I moved
to and fro over my narrative. It gave me permission to entertain seriously the possibility that Quick might once have gone
by another name, lived another life, a life she was desperately
trying to remember – and to tell me – before it was too late. I
couldn't imagine the pain of seeing someone else take credit
for your work, whilst you languished unnoticed, uncelebrated,
knowing death was so near.

'The English mad yes,' said Cynth. 'So you goin' to ask her about
all this commesse?'

'But what Ah goin' to say?' One couldn't exactly confront Quick,
and I wasn't sure if I wanted the woman I knew to vanish further under scrutiny. I felt that if I could show her my support, this
might coax her out of the corner, but I wasn't sure of the best way
to go about it. 'Ah think she keeping secrets for a reason,' I added.

'Shoe shop was never like this,' Cynth sighed. 'You put a shoe on
woman foot and that is it.'

We laughed. 'No, that is true,' I said. 'But you know what else?
Quick help me publish a short story, so I in her debt.'

Cynth only heard the bit she wanted to hear, and her eyes lit up. 'Oh now, published! Oh, that is *good*. What it called?'

' "The Toeless Woman". Remember that woman who come in and have those blocks of feet?'

'Oh, my God. Yes. I have to read this.'

Tingling with pleasure at her excitement, I told her it was in October's *London Review*, but that if she liked I could send her a copy, I could send her ten. I told her how it had all unfolded, Quick sending the story personally to the magazine.

'I think she like me,' I said. 'I think she trust me. I just don't know exactly what she trustin' me with.'

Cynth nudged me. 'It take some white lady to get you to do it, eh, not me?' I started to protest that I'd had no idea what Quick was planning, but Cynth put her hands up. 'I jokin', I jokin',' she said. 'I just glad. Is about time.'

'How's Sam?' I asked, wanting to change the subject away from me, suddenly nervous that Cynth was going to read the dramatization of our joint life in that story about the toeless woman.

'He good. He very good.' She looked shy. 'It have somethin' I want to tell you, Dell. I want to tell you first. Ah havin' a baby.'

She looked very nervous about telling me this, which was a shame. But then again – consider how well I'd handled her getting married and leaving me alone in the flat. But this time, I was not going to get it wrong. I was genuinely excited for her. How could you not be, when you saw her pleasure and fear and wonder – that right now, there was this little thing in there, such a good thing, such a good mother to meet it when it finally showed its face.

'Oh, Cynthia. Cynthia,' I said, and to my shock tears filled my eyes. 'I sitting here talking about mysterious women and you the greatest mystery of all.'

'Delly, you sound like a poet even when you chokin' up.'

'Come here. I proud of you.'

We embraced, I held her tight and she held me, breathing out relief and crying a bit, because my happy reaction just made her happier still.

She was due at the beginning of April. She was terrified but excited, and worried they were not going to have enough money for it. 'You'll manage,' I said, thinking how much Cynth's life was going to transform, whilst mine was going to stay exactly the same. 'Sam have a good job. An you too.'

'So, Lawrie,' she said, dabbing her eyes with tissue. 'Don't wriggle. You had a fight.'

I was unable to hide my surprise. 'How you know?'

'Because I know you, Delly. I also know that if things were harmony, you would da be seein' him today, but you at some long loose end and see your boring ol' friend instead. Let me guess. He tell you he love you and you run a mile.'

'Is not like that.'

She laughed. 'He is miserable, Delly. Mis-er-ab-le. He the one who pining.'

'What? Come on, how you really know?'

'I hear it from Patrick, who hear it from Barbara, who see the feller mopin' around like someone chop off his arm. He lost. And he's a good one, Dell. Don't be dotish. He say he love you and you push him off a cliff.' Even though it was an admonishment, Cynth wheezed with laughter.

'But what if Ah don't love him? Why I have to love him?'

'You don't have to do anything, Delly. You don't have to rush. But you could give the feller explanation. If only to give his friends a break.'

'Lawrie the type of man to push a rhino down a rabbit hole. It won't work.'

'You a rhino though, Delly, so it would be amusing at least.'

We laughed, me from relief at being able to talk about it, and Cynth because it refreshed her to tease me, to be her younger self, to pull on the old ties and discover they were still intact. I still didn't know what I wanted, but it was sad to know Lawrie was going around feeling like someone had severed a limb.

After another hour or so, we embraced outside the Tube station, Cynth descending north on the Bakerloo to her new life in Queen's Park. We promised to see each other before Christmas, and I thought how bittersweet it was, how once upon a time, we'd have made sure we were catching up within the week.

I watched Cynth move down the steps carefully, thinking that surely she had no need to be so ginger. She stopped and turned back. 'One thing, Dell. If you do speak to Lawrie again, maybe keep this Olive Schloss story to yourself.'

'Why? If it true—'

'Well, yes. But you don't know it true for a fact, do you?'

'Not yet, but—'

'And he want to sell that painting, if I hear it right through Barbara. His stepfather selling the house and that painting is all he have. You goin' around sayin' that what he have is not an Isaac Robles – it goin' to knock his ship right out of the water. Don't make trouble where it don't have any, Delly. Think of your heart for once, not that clever head.'

I watched her go, knowing that there was sense in what she said, but also aware that Quick's behaviour wasn't something I was going to let lie.

I called Lawrie that night, but Gerry the Bastard answered. It was a shock to have him pick up.

'Who's this, calling on a Sunday?' he said.

Immediately, I put on my BBC tones. You couldn't help it – you heard an Englishman like Gerry, you just tried to make your voice sound the same as his. 'This is Odelle Bastien,' I said. 'Is Lawrie there, please?'

'Lawrence!' he yelled. Gerry must have put down the receiver because I could hear him move away.

'Who is it?' said Lawrie.

'Couldn't catch the name. But it sounds like the calypso's here.'

There was a wait, and then finally Lawrie put his mouth to the receiver. 'Odelle? Is that you?'

The sound of relief, mingled with wariness in his voice, was painful to hear. 'It's me,' I said. 'How are you, Lawrie?'

'Fine, thanks. You?'

'Fine,' I lied. 'I got a story published.'

'You called to tell me that?'

'No – I – it's just. It's what's happened, that's all. Was that Gerry I spoke to?'

'Yes. Sorry about that. Well done on the story.'

We were silent for a moment. Ironically, I didn't know how to shape these particular words, how to tell him that I missed him, that strange things were happening with Quick, that my best friend was having a baby and I felt like a teenager out of my depth.

'I'm coming to the gallery tomorrow, as it happens,' he said, his voice more hushed. 'Is that why you've called?'

'No. I didn't know.'

'Reede's had more information from a fellow who works at Peggy Guggenheim's palazzo in Venice. A couple of interesting things, apparently.'

'I see.'

'So why did you call? I thought you didn't want anything to do with me.'

'No – that's not – I do. I do. I spoke to Cynthia. She said you've been miserable.'

There was quiet on the line. 'I was miserable.'

'You're not miserable any more?'

He was silent again. 'I shouldn't have rushed in like that,' he said.

'No, it's fine – I mean—'

'I won't ever say what I said to you again.'

'I see.'

'Not if you don't want me to.'

'I don't really know what I want you to say, or not say,' I admitted. 'I just know that when I heard you were miserable, that made me sad. And I realized I'd been miserable too. And I was wondering whether it might be a bit easier – if we were miserable together.'

Quiet on the line again. 'Are you – asking me on a date, Odelle?'

I didn't – couldn't – say anything. 'Well, there's a first time for everything,' Lawrie went on. 'Thank you. Let me just check my diary – oh, no need. I'm free.'

A pleasurable warmth spread through my stomach and I couldn't hide the smile in my voice. 'Convenient,' I said.

'Isn't it?' he replied. 'Now, where would you like to meet?'

13

We met early the next morning, as early as we could, in the middle of Skelton Square, before I started work and Lawrie went in to see Reede. He was clutching a bottle of champagne. 'For your first published story,' he said, handing it over. 'That's vintage, you know. Sorry about the dust. Nicked it from the house.'

'Gosh, thank you.'

'Actually . . . I knew about the *London Review*.'

'What?'

'We do take modern periodicals in Surrey, you know. I read it.' He looked down at his shoes. 'It was just brilliant.'

'Shut up.' I took the bottle, my head about to explode with pleasure. I read the label: *Veuve Clicquot*. 'Lawrie, can we start again?' I said.

He sighed. 'I don't know if that's possible.'

I sat down on the bench, trying to bat away my despondence. I was so sure he'd say yes. He was here, wasn't he? 'I suppose not,' I said, looking up at him.

'You could hit me over the head with that champagne bottle,' he suggested.

'What?'

'Knock the memories out of me. But then I'd lose the first time

I saw you, reading that poem. Or the first time I spoke to you; those yellow rubber gloves. Or the way you pretended to like the Bond film, your nose all wrinkled up. Or when you out-danced me at the Flamingo and the manager offered you a job, or when you told me about that idiot in the shoe shop. Or when we had that shepherd's pie, and I messed everything up. It's all part of it, Odelle. It's not going to be perfect. Personally, I don't want it to be. I'd go through that horrible drive up the A3 again, just for the sweetness of hearing your voice after so long. I wouldn't change any of it. I don't want to start again, because that would make me lose memories of you.'

I couldn't say anything for a moment. Lawrie sat down next to me and I felt the warm solidity of his body. I took a deep breath. 'I – get scared,' I said. 'I don't know how else to explain it. I get feelings that I'm lost, that I'm no good, that if someone likes me there must be something wrong with them.'

'But why?'

'Well, if I knew that, Lawrie . . . and when I met you, I told you things I'd never told anyone. Then you swept in with your declaration that you loved me, and – well – it felt that like you were filling out a form, obeying some pattern.'

'A pattern?'

'Of what people do, what they think they're supposed to say.'

'No one tells me what to say.'

'But I also realized I didn't want you *not* to say it. I just wanted you to say it – when I wanted to hear it.'

He laughed. 'You really are a writer, aren't you? All right. How about, whenever I feel that I might be about to say I've fallen in love with you, or that I love you, or that you're wonderful, we agree on a sign that such a declaration is coming – and you recognize the sign, and give me the go ahead or not as to whether I can say it.'

'You make me sound mad.'

'I'm joking. I'm sorry. Whatever you need. I just want to see you, Odelle. Is that OK?'

'Yes,' I said. I hesitated. 'More than OK.'

'Good. Right,' he said. 'Let's go and hear what the venerable Mr Reede has to say.'

'Good morning, Odelle,' Quick said, stopping smoothly at my door. Lawrie had been with Reede for about thirty minutes. Quick looked tired, a little apprehensive. Her appearance was a world away from my first week, when she had breezed up to my type-writer and suggested a light lunch – in order to pick my brains – for what exactly, I still wasn't sure.

'Good morning, Quick.'

She froze, her eyes on the champagne bottle standing on the desk. 'Where did you get that?' she asked.

I swallowed, intimidated by the look on her face. 'Lawrie gave it to me.'

She turned her gaze to me. 'Friends again?'

'Yes. He's here. He's talking to Reede,' I said. 'I think they're discussing the exhibition.'

'I know they are. I scheduled the meeting.' Quick came in, clos-ing the door. To my surprise, she walked over and sat down oppo-site me, taking the bottle in her lap. 'Lawrie gave this to you?'

'To say well done for getting "The Toeless Woman" published. Is there something wrong with it?'

She ran her thumb across the neck, leaving a clean smear through the dust. 'It's vintage,' she said.

'I know that. Quick—'

'Odelle, what happened on Friday night—'

I sat up straighter. 'Yes?'

'It shouldn't have happened. I broke a professional barrier when I told you about my illness. I've compromised you. I've compro-mised myself. I don't want the attention.'

'You've done rather a good job of getting mine, though.'

She looked at me, sharply, but I refused to shrink away. 'I want you to know – that whatever happens – your job is completely safe.'

'Safe?'

Quick seemed to suffer a spasm of pain, and the bottle sagged heavily in her lap. 'They've got me on rather strong painkillers,' she said. 'No choice but to take them now. I'm hallucinating. I can't sleep.'

'What are you hallucinating?' I said. 'What is it that you see?'

I waited, barely able to breathe, my fingers drawing away from the typewriter and resting in my lap.

She didn't answer, and we sat in silence for a few moments, the clock on the wall syncopating my heartbeat. I took the risk. 'On Friday night, you said that Isaac Robles didn't paint the picture. Do you remember that, Quick?'

Quick sat, staring at her hands. She was swallowing hard, her throat constricted.

'Did he paint *any* of the pictures, Quick – the ones in the Guggenheim?'

Still, Quick remained silent.

'If he didn't paint those pictures, who did—'

'All I wanted,' she said, abruptly, in clear distress. 'I just wanted to see.'

'What, what was it that you wanted to see?'

I watched in horror as Quick fanned her fingers open on the neck of the bottle, and the entire thing slid between her legs and cracked against the floor. The base smashed clean off and the champagne gushed between us, fizzing and pooling everywhere. She jumped up crookedly, staggering from the mess before us. 'I'm sorry,' she mumbled. 'I'm so sorry.'

'It was an accident,' I said. I stared at Lawrie's ruined bottle, lying on the floorboards in a puddle of champagne. The green glass was so dark it was almost black, winking as the overhead lights caught its jagged edges. I'd never even got a taste. I swallowed hard and looked at Quick.

She was drained of colour. I knew the conversation was over, that I would get no further now. Would she really go so far as to sabotage my present from Lawrie? I ushered her to her own office, and she leaned on me, snaking her arm through mine. I could feel her bones so easily through the skin. Now I knew about the cancer, I could see how ill Quick was. But it wasn't just the cancer in her body. I was also witnessing her psychological recalibration.

I wouldn't say Quick's mind was diminishing, despite her protests of hallucinations and insomnia. It was almost the opposite to her body; an augmentation, her imagination inhabiting more than just the present. Somewhere inside her memory, a drawbridge had been lowered, and the foot soldiers of her past were pushing through. She wanted to talk; but couldn't. She didn't have the words.

'Please lock the door,' she said, beginning to rally a little. 'Odelle, I'm so sorry about your bottle.'

'It's all right.'

'I'll make it up to you in my will.'

Her black eyes glimmered with gallows humour. 'Got a cellar in Wimbledon, have you?' I said in kind, trying to chivvy her spirits.

'Something like that. Fetch my handbag, would you? I need the pills.' She moved slowly to the drinks table. 'Gin?'

'No thanks.'

I watched her pour one, breathing deeply, corralling herself as the clear liquid glugged into the tumbler. 'Those are bloody strong,' she said as I handed her the pills. 'I fucking hate them.'

The expletive, the bitterness in her voice, shocked me. I forced myself to sit, reminding myself I was a junior employee, and must be mute and mild. Pushing Quick to tell me things I wanted to know was clearly not going to work. I'd suspected that it wouldn't, after the night with the telephone book, and now I had one smashed champagne bottle as confirmation. As frustrating as I found it, I had to be her blank canvas. Patience was never my strong suit, but as long as it kept her talking, it was better than silence.

'There's a fellow called Barozzi in Venice,' she said, lowering herself into her leather chair and reaching for her cigarettes. 'Works for Guggenheim. Around the time Mr Scott's painting was being made, Peggy Guggenheim was attempting to open a gallery in London.' Quick stilled herself for a minute, before finding the strength to continue. 'She succeeded. The place was on Cork Street, before the war turned it on its head and it closed.'

'I see.'

'You don't. The point is, she – or others at her gallery – are good with keeping paperwork. Barozzi found some rather interesting correspondence in her archives, sent it to Reede, and he's beside himself.'

Cork Street. I knew the name – it was the street that the pamphlet came from. My skin began to tingle.

'He now has evidence that Mr Scott's painting was a commission for Peggy Guggenheim, as a twin to *Women in the Wheatfield.*'

'A twin?'

'He's found a telegram addressed to Isaac Robles, which for some reason was never sent. It was destined for Malaga in Spain, dated September '36, enquiring how much longer she will need to wait for the "companion piece" to *Wheatfield*, which Robles had called *Rufina and the Lion*. Barozzi has acknowledged that no deposit was actually given Robles for the Rufina piece, otherwise Mr Scott could have found himself in a lot of trouble, given that he's apparently got no proof of purchase. The Guggenheim could have tried to claim it as theirs.'

I marvelled that Quick could talk about another discovered telegram, as if the one hidden in her own house wasn't inextricably tied up with all this too. Not only was she acting as if the smashed champagne bottle was not deliberate sabotage, she was now pretending that our evening with the telephone book had never happened.

'*Rufina and the Lion*,' I repeated. 'That's what Lawrie's painting is called?'

'That's what Reede believes. Ever heard of Saint Rufina?'

'No.'

Quick sipped her gin. 'The image of Mr Scott's painting fits the story perfectly. Rufina lived in Seville in the second century. She was a Christian potter, who wouldn't kow-tow to the authorities' rules when they told her to make pagan icons, so they chucked her in an arena with a lion. The lion wouldn't touch her, so they cut off her head. And with this mention of a "companion piece", Reede believes he's found a connection between Mr Scott's painting and the more famous *Women in the Wheatfield*, which might change the way we look at Robles entirely.'

I gazed at her, feeling determined, ready to enter into a battle of wills. 'But you told me that Isaac Robles didn't paint it.'

Quick slugged back another painkiller. 'And yet, we have a certified telegram from a world-class art collector, stating that it was intended as a companion piece to one of the most important paintings to come out of Spain this century, currently in the Guggenheim collection in Venice.'

'Yes, but there was someone else in that photograph too. A young woman.'

I waited for Quick to speak, but she did not, so I carried on. 'I think she was called Olive Schloss. In that letter at your house, it appears she won a place at the Slade School of Art around the time that Isaac Robles was painting. I think she painted *Women in the Wheatfield*.'

'I see.' Quick's face was impassive, and my frustration grew.

'Did you think she made it, Quick?'

'Made what?' Her expression turned hard.

'Do you think Olive ever made it to the Slade?'

Quick closed her eyes. Her shoulders sagged, and I waited for her to reveal herself, to release the truth that had been broiling in her ever since seeing Lawrie's painting in the hallway of the Skelton. Here it came, the moment of confession – why she was in possession of the telegram from Peggy Guggenheim and the letter from the Slade – how it was her own father who had bought Isaac Robles's painting, a piece of art she had created herself.

Quick was so still in her chair, I thought that she'd expired. She flicked her eyes open. 'I'm going to hear what Mr Reede is saying,' she said. 'I think you should come too.'

I followed her down the corridor, disappointed. But I was getting nearer, I was sure.

WE KNOCKED ON REEDE'S DOOR and were told to come in. Lawrie and he were sitting facing each other in the armchairs. 'Can I help you?' Reede said.

'Miss Bastien and I will be the ones on the front line once this exhibition gets underway,' said Quick. I saw how tightly she was gripping the door frame. She was torturing herself. 'It might be wise if we were to sit and take notes, to understand what you're proposing.'

'Very well,' said Reede. 'You can sit over there, ladies.'

We looked to where he was gesturing; two hard wooden chairs in the corner. Either Quick was being punished, or Reede was blind to how frail she was. Lawrie caught my eye as I sat down; he looked excited, alive with the possibilities of his painting. *Rufina and the Lion* was propped up on the mantelpiece, and I was no less overwhelmed by its power than the first time I saw it, by how much that girl and the severed head she held in her hands had already changed my life. If Lawrie hadn't used it to try and take me on a date, would any of us even be sitting here today – would Quick be unravelling like this, despite her insistence on blaming the cancer and its painkillers?

Directly above Reede's head sat the lion, imperial and implacable as so many painted lions are. Yet today, it looked so curiously tamed. I gazed at the white house in the distant hills; its painted red windows, how tiny it was compared to the vast, multicoloured patchwork of fields which surrounded it. Rufina and her second head stood looking back at me, at all of us. Thirty years ago, Isaac Robles and a girl I was sure was Olive Schloss stood before this very picture, for a photograph. What had Isaac and Olive been to one another?

Inevitably, I looked to Quick. She seemed to have gathered herself from her earlier distress; sitting straight now, notebook on her lap, eyes on the painting. Whatever the truth was, it seemed to me that she was going to let this exhibition go ahead with no sabotage on her part, and I felt confounded by her capitulation.

'As I was saying, Mr Scott,' Reede went on, 'three years ago, Peggy Guggenheim's entire Venetian collection came to the Tate on temporary loan. Whilst *Women in the Wheatfield* was here on the Tate's public walls, your own Robles painting was hiding in the shadows. It's extraordinary to think we could have matched them then, had we known. There was so much to-ing and fro-ing over that exhibition, between the British government and the Italian authorities,' he said. 'Tax issues, mainly. But that was for a hundred and eighty-odd pieces, and I've only asked for three. So the good news is, they're letting us borrow their Isaac Robles pieces.'

'That is good news,' said Lawrie.

'It's wonderful. It'll really bolster the exhibition. I hope the news pages will give us coverage as well as the arts sections. We're getting *Women in the Wheatfield*, a landscape called *The Orchard*, and rather brilliantly, something I wasn't aware of – his *Self-Portrait in Green*. And what will be exciting about the reunion of *Women in the Wheatfield* with *Rufina and the Lion* is that it could change the way we view Isaac Robles generally.'

'Why?'

'Rufina was one of a pair of sisters,' Reede said. 'Justa was the name of the other.'

'Justa?'

'The story goes that Justa was thrown down a well to starve. I believe that *Women in the Wheatfield* is actually the story of Saint Justa – and that there's only one girl in it, not two. We see Justa before and after her punishment, once in happiness, and then in torment. The smashed pots around her back up this idea. It's the mask of the goddess Venus, broken in half, and that appears in the myth.'

'I see,' said Lawrie.

'There have been different interpretations of the circle that the woman lies in over the wheatfield. Some art historians say it is one of Dante's circles, others says it's the moon – and some identify it as the rotundity of planet earth, particularly with those woodland animals around it. But I believe she's actually lying at the bottom of a well, as per the myth. Here,' he said, handing Lawrie four pieces of paper, which had copies of paintings on them. 'Robles wasn't the only Spaniard to paint Rufina and Justa. Velázquez, Zurburán, Murillo and Goya, all four great Spanish painters, painted those sisters. I'm trying to get a loan of at least one of these paintings to complement the exhibition.'

'Do you think you'll get them?' asked Lawrie.

Reede rose to his feet, and rubbed his hands together. 'Maybe. Maybe. I really do hope for it.' He smiled. 'It would be something extraordinary. The chances are Robles was well aware of these other works. I've told the galleries who have these pieces that I want to examine the particular Hispanic pathology around the myth of Justa and Rufina.'

'The Spaniards have always been incredibly subversive artists,' said Quick.

'Yes,' said Reede, looking at her more warmly, one arm propped up on the mantelpiece. 'Creative rebellion against the status quo. Just look at the Goya. He would be the one to put in a lion, kissing her toe. And can you imagine what Dalí would do with it?'

'But why is the Guggenheim Robles called *Women in the Wheatfield*, with no reference to Saint Justa, if mine's called *Rufina and the Lion*?' Lawrie asked.

'Harold Schloss might have called it *Women in the Wheatfield*, not Isaac Robles,' said Reede. 'Robles might have easily called it *Saint Justa*, for example. We'll never know. He may not have given it a name at all.'

At the mention of Harold Schloss, I glanced over again at Quick. Her head was bowed, and she was massaging her temple. I wondered if she needed another painkiller. She seemed determined to get as close to Reede's plans as possible, despite the visible trauma it was causing.

'The salesman in Schloss,' Reede went on, beginning to pace around us, 'probably wanted to make the painting more attractive for Guggenheim's purchasing sallies. She hadn't bought much before this; he didn't want to scare her off. It's the same sort of thing as Picasso wanting *Les Demoiselles d'Avignon* to be called *The Brothel of Avignon*, and his exhibitors changing the name, apparently to make it more appealing. And Schloss may not have known that a companion piece to Justa and her well was on its way. Somewhere along the line, I believe that what Isaac Robles wished to communicate in these paintings was lost.'

'And what did he want to communicate?' said Lawrie.

I looked at Quick again; she was gazing up now at Reede, with a blank expression on her face.

'I think Robles was very interested in this myth,' Reede said. 'And discovering this connection between the Guggenheim Robles and the Surrey Robles allows us a new window on to his artistic process, to reinterpret his preoccupations – to reinvent him, if you like. This exhibition may be "The Swallowed Century", but we are still trying to digest it, so to speak.'

'Reinvent him?'

'Succeeding generations do it all the time, Mr Scott. Don't be alarmed. We can never bear to think we haven't thought of something new. And tastes change; we have to be ahead of them. We are resurrecting an artist at the same time as enacting his retrospective. My approach will allow us to describe Robles's awareness of a glorious national historical tradition – Velázquez and the rest – whilst being something of a contemporary international star, cut down in his prime.'

'You've really got it all planned, haven't you.'

'That's my job, Mr Scott. I can't tell you yet what exactly he was trying to communicate, but I want to take a political slant with your painting in particular. Rufina, the defiant worker saint, facing down the lion of fascism. Have a look at this,' he said, handing over yet another document for Lawrie to read. 'I was sent that from Barozzi at the Guggenheim foundation. Harold Schloss wrote it to Peggy Guggenheim when he was in Paris again, and she had returned to New York.'

'Mr Scott,' said Quick, and the men jumped. 'Could you read it out loud? Neither Miss Bastien nor I are furnished with a copy.'

Lawrie obliged.

'*Dear Peggy,*

Forgive me for not making my presence known to you in time before you left Paris. Everything, since my departure from Spain to my arrival back in this city, has been very difficult. I tried to bring Rufina with me, but have failed. I know how much you were looking forward to it, and I am deeply sorry.

I have a couple of early Klees you may like to look at instead – I myself will not travel to Vienna, but am organizing them to be sent to London – or perhaps, if you're staying in New York for some time tying up matters, and are interested, I may send them straight there?

My best to you, as ever,

Harold Schloss.'

Lawrie looked up at Reede. 'He doesn't mention Robles at all.'

'I think we can do something with that. I'd like to blow this letter up large, and have it on one side of the gallery wall. We could speculate on what happened to Robles.'

'What do you mean?'

'I don't think he made it through the war. We would surely have heard about him if he had. There was a lot of bombing in the south of Spain in those days. Say the rest of Robles' paintings went up in flames. We could consider how the immolation of Robles' body of work reflects the disappearance of the artist himself.'

Reede began to pace again, his hands behind his back, lost to us as he expounded his vision. 'We could extend the metaphor, into the conflagration of the Iberian corpus, and the world war to come. The man is a symbol, as much as an individual. He was a vision of Spain's future, which was annihilated.'

Lawrie crossed his legs, his voice hard. 'But you don't know his works went up in flames. You can't build an exhibition on a rumour. They'll laugh at me.'

'They won't laugh. People love a rumour, Mr Scott. You can do more with rumour than you can with fact. And the fact is, we have a limited supply of paintings. Another fact: Harold Schloss did not have *Rufina and the Lion* when he went back to Paris. Where was it? That's where you come in.'

'Me?' said Lawrie. Something in his tone of voice made me turn. I looked to Quick; she had clearly thought the same as Reede, for her eyes were on Lawrie, concentrating hard.

Reede came to sit opposite Lawrie, and spoke more gently. 'I think that Harold Schloss realized it was untenable to remain in Spain, and in fleeing, the painting fell out of his possession, either through theft or carelessness. It is unusual for a dealer to confess so openly a loss, as he does in that letter. Normally they're glib, smooth talkers. I think Harold Schloss came back to Paris with his feathers ruffled.'

'And you think the painting was left behind in Spain?' said Lawrie.

'Well, Schloss doesn't seem to have it. He's got no reason to lie to his best collector. But I don't know, Mr Scott. The next person to be attached to it was your mother. And apparently, we have no idea how she got hold of it.'

Lawrie gazed up at the painting, and down again, into the empty grate. 'It's always been on her walls,' he said quietly. 'I don't remember a time it wasn't there.'

'So you say,' Reede sighed. 'Well, we can play with the question mark. I don't think we have a choice. The survival of an artwork through the Spanish Civil War and a world war to a house in Surrey is not without its romantic possibilities.'

'What do you think happened to Isaac Robles, in the end?' asked Lawrie.

'Mr Reede,' said Quick, her voice hard and clear across the room. 'What is the timescale for this? When are you planning to open this exhibition?'

Reede turned to her. 'A delegation from the Guggenheim is coming in two weeks with the paintings. And two weeks after that, I believe we can open.'

Quick looked down at her diary. 'Four weeks from now? That's ridiculous. That's no time at all.'

'I know, Marjorie. But it's what I want.'

I watched as Quick marked the day of November 28th in her diary, a slight tremor in her hand, the pen drawing across the page in a thick black cross.

14

*T*hat evening, Lawrie and I took the commuter train to Surrey. He told me that he'd already sold the MG. 'I just didn't use it much,' he said, but he sounded wistful. I considered that perhaps there was more pressure than I initially imagined to sell his mother's painting.

As we pulled out of Waterloo, me with the Xeroxes from Reede on my lap, I looked at the four paintings of Rufina and Justa by the older Spanish artists. I loved the passive lion in the Goya, but my favourite overall was the Velázquez; a young girl with dark hair and an inscrutable gaze, holding two little bowls and a plate in one upturned palm, and a huge plume in the other. Velázquez, like Robles, had painted Rufina on her own too. I moved on to the copy of Harold Schloss's letter. Schloss had written by hand, and had started it neatly enough, but in places it became barely legible. His rounded arcs and sweeping curves descended into crossings-out and ink blots everywhere. I did not think it was the letter of a happy man.

'We're here,' said Lawrie.

We were not normal passengers getting off at Baldock's Ridge; the normal passengers were men in their late forties, paunch incoming, signet ring, *Telegraph* under their arm, an embossed briefcase. Women, country-tweeded, middle-aged with distant faces, thoughts buried deep within their handbags, coming back from a day in town.

'After you left the meeting, Reede said he could try and sell the painting for me,' Lawrie said as he opened the door and helped me down. 'For a commission.'

'How much does he think it will fetch?'

'It's hard to say. *"Art doesn't always behave itself like other things you might put up for sale, Mr Scott"*,' Lawrie said, parroting the pomposity Reede could stray into when on home turf. 'He said it isn't like a late Van Gogh coming onto the market.'

'What does that mean?'

'Well, apparently everyone would want one of those. But *Rufina and the Lion* is unique in a different way. Reede said he doesn't want to underplay it, but neither does he want to over-egg the pudding. He said selling always has its risks.'

'But he's so enthusiastic about it.'

'As a historian, maybe. As a personal preference, yes. But perhaps as an auctioneer he wants to manage my expectations. Not everyone's going to like Isaac Robles.'

'You could always donate it to a public institution.'

Lawrie laughed. 'Odelle, I haven't got any money.'

QUICK AND I HAD NOT had a chance to talk for the rest of the day. She had gone home shortly after the meeting with Lawrie and Reede was finished. She claimed a headache, but I knew of course it was more. I felt torn; I wanted to be with Lawrie, to revel in the rush and headiness of making up, of realizing how much a person means to you, the thrill of having nearly lost them only to be reunited. But at the same time, I was the only person who knew something was very wrong with Quick, that her pain seemed to be worsening, and yet I had no idea how to help her manage it.

'Are you all right?' said Lawrie.

'Just thinking about Quick,' I said. 'She's – not very well.'

'She didn't *look* very well.'

Lawrie leaned in to kiss my cheek as we walked down the

station path. There was an intake of breath behind us. I turned; one of the tweed women, trying to look as if she hadn't made the noise at all.

'Come on,' said Lawrie quietly. 'Let me take you out of the eighteenth century.'

Except it wasn't the eighteenth century, was it, Lawrie? It was late October, in 1967, in Baldock's Ridge in Surrey, and you weren't allowed to kiss me without comment. Or perhaps, more accurately, I was not allowed to be kissed.

WHEN WE GOT TO THE house, the lights were on. 'Oh, Jesus,' he said. I turned; Lawrie looked genuinely frightened.

'What is it?' I asked.

'I thought Gerry wouldn't be here. We should go.'

'I don't want to go,' I said.

'Odelle, Gerry isn't – I don't think he— I just want to warn you.'

'Let me guess. I'm one of the natives.'

'Oh, God, this is going to be a disaster. He's – very old-fashioned.'

'We should get along perfectly, then.'

'You won't. You shouldn't have to—'

'*Lawrie*. I don't want you to protect me. Let me be the judge of Gerry. Just as no doubt he'll be the judge of me.'

How to describe Gerry? Gerry the Bastard, Gerry the Merry. As soon as he clapped eyes on me, his face lit up. 'I thought Lawrence was a queer!' The tone with which he said it made me think that Gerry was possibly inclined that way himself. I have never met a man like him since; that particular strain of upper-class English – so camp and Wodehousian, a madness at which no one bats an eye. Anything that was inappropriate to say, Gerry would say it. He was overweight, and handsome, but he looked like a man closing down on himself. I could smell the grief; six months down the line, you'd find him a puddle of skin on the floor.

'I understand you work at an art gallery, Miss Baschin?' he said, pouring yet another whisky.

Lawrie winced at Gerry's mispronouncing my name, and I could see he was about to correct his step-father. 'That's right,' I said quickly. 'As a typist.'

'Set up home here, then?'

'Yes, sir. Nearly six years now.'

'Odelle's father was in the RAF,' said Lawrie. I could hear the desperation in his voice, and it annoyed me. I knew what Lawrie was trying to do, of course – repackaging me in a context the man might understand. But I did not feel I needed my father's military record as any introduction; I felt, in a strange way, that Gerry was accepting me regardless. By some weird alchemy – perhaps because I was inside his house – Gerry seemed to exempt me from the unconscious hierarchy of colour he also inadvertently revealed now and then. Perhaps he was whitewashing my skin? Perhaps he rather liked the thrill, his colonial days coming back to him? Or perhaps he just liked me. Whatever it was, I felt invited in.

WE ATE A JUMPY DINNER – well, Lawrie was the jumpy one; Gerry and I fumbled our way through. At least he didn't mention calypsos again – or bongos, or the miracle of my excellent English.

'We went to the Caribbean once,' Gerry said, as Lawrie cleared the plates. He drained his tumbler of whisky, and stared at it.

'Did you like it?' I asked.

Gerry didn't appear to hear me. 'Worked in India after I left Oxford.' I looked at Lawrie's expression: thunderbolts at the tablecloth. 'Was there for years. I think the travel bug was in my blood from then on – probably got bitten by something. Beautiful place, India. Difficult though. Incredibly hot.'

'Which islands did you go to, in the Caribbean?' I asked.

'Feels like a lifetime ago now. I suppose it is.'

'Odelle asked you a question,' said Lawrie.

'It's all right,' I said.

'Jamaica,' the man replied, with a sharp look at his step-son. 'I'm not senile, Lawrence. I heard her.'

'I've not been to Jamaica,' I said.

Gerry laughed. 'How extraordinary. I thought you all just hopped between the islands?'

'No, sir. I have been to Tobago, and Grenada, and Barbados. I do not know the other islands. I know London better than I know Jamaica.'

Gerry reached for the whisky. 'It wasn't my choice to go there,' he said. 'But Sarah said everyone went to Jamaica. She loved heat, needed it. So off we went. I'm glad we did. The sand was so soft.'

Lawrie snatched the whisky bottle. 'Let's go and listen to that record we bought,' he said.

'Who's Sarah?' I asked.

Gerry looked at me through bloodshot eyes. 'Lawrence didn't even tell you her name?'

'Whose name?'

'His mother,' Gerry said, sighing when Lawrie turned away. 'My beautiful wife.'

15

*L*awrie lunged up the stairs, three at a time.

'What's wrong with you?' I said. 'He just misses her. He wants to talk about her.'

Lawrie stopped on the landing and whirled round at me. 'Don't think he's some sort of saint,' he said.

'I don't, Lawrie.'

Lawrie seemed to be battling with a particular thought. He looked half fearful, half furious. 'When my dad died,' I went on, trying to sound soothing, 'my mum used to hear his voice in the radio. Saw his face in every man she met. You've got to be patient.'

'She was my mother.'

'Of course.'

'I was the one who found her. In that room down there.'

'Oh, Lawrie.'

I turned to the darkness where he was pointing, and felt a preternatural repulsion, an overwhelming desire to walk in the opposite direction. But I didn't move; I didn't want him to see me scared. 'Gerry's held together with whisky and sticking plasters,' I said. 'You should be kind to him.'

'And what about me?'

'I'll be kind to you,' I replied, taking his hand.

WE LAY SIDE BY SIDE on Lawrie's eiderdown, hearing Gerry shuffling beneath us, until a door closed and the house fell silent. 'You shouldn't live here,' I said.

'I know.' He turned on his side to face me, propping himself on his elbow. 'But it's all I have. This place, Gerry and a painting.'

'And me,' I said. 'You've got me.'

Gently, he ran his hand down the side of my face. The window was still open, and I heard a blackbird, so musical and effortless, singing in a tree like it was dawn. 'Come on, Writer. What's your favourite word?' he asked.

I could see he wanted to change the subject, so I obliged. 'You're asking me to pick? All right. *Lodgings.*'

He laughed. 'You had it ready – I knew you would. That's so stodgy, Odelle.'

'Is not. It's cosy. *"My lodgings were clean and comfortable."* You?'

'*Cloud.*'

'Such a cliché,' I said, inching towards him and giving him a squeeze.

We talked on – for now, mothers and step-fathers and paintings forgotten, or pushed away at least, banishing them to the outer edges of our memories as much as we could. We talked about how beautiful the English language could be, in the right hands – how varied and nuanced and illogical. *Hamper* and *hamper*, and words like *turn*, that seemed boring at first but were deceptive in their depths. We discussed our favourite onomatopoeia: *frizz* and *sludge* and *glide* and *bumblebee*. I'd never been so happy alone with another person.

Because of the blackbird singing in the tree, we ended up drifting into a game of bird-tennis, our intertwined hands the raised-up net, and a kiss for each bird that we exchanged. *Plover* to *lapwing*, *honey-creep*, *lark*. *Coquette* and *falcon*, *manakin*, *hawk*. His hands upon my skin, *curlew*, *oriole*, and mine upon his. *Jacamar*, *wren*. Then the birds flew away, their names turned to kisses, a silence to spell a new world.

The next morning, I woke very early. Lawrie was in a deep sleep, his expression peaceful. I considered the astonishing moment he'd pushed inside me, how that was never going to happen for the first time again. I put on my knickers, his shirt and woolly jumper, slid out of the bed and tiptoed along the corridor to the bathroom. Had Gerry known I'd stayed? How mortifying it would be to cross him now.

I went to the toilet and felt between my legs; a little dried blood, but the more obvious symptom was the stomach pain I could feel, slight, low-seated, a dull ache, a sense of having been opened up and bruised. I had never even been naked with a man, had never been touched like that before; it was strange that one might feel pain over something that had been so pleasurable.

We had broken through a frontier, and I had told him, very quietly, that I loved him, and Lawrie had pressed his ear to my mouth, saying, *You might have to repeat that one, Odelle, because I'm getting on and these days I don't hear so well.* And so I said it again, slightly louder, and he kissed me in return.

I LOOKED AT MY WRISTWATCH; five-thirty. Below me, I could hear Gerry's snores. What a place to be, I thought; urinating in a clapped-out Victorian toilet in deepest Surrey over a man called Gerry's head. I would not have predicted it; and I was glad of the lack of forewarning. Had I known such things were going to be promised me, I would have been too intimidated by their weirdness and they probably wouldn't have happened.

I finished, washed my hands and face and used a little soap on my upper thighs. I felt the sudden desire to tell Pamela that this had happened, to give her the gift of my gossip, to make her birthday present worth it after all.

I came out of the bathroom and was about to head back to Lawrie's room, when I hesitated. I turned to my right, looking down the long corridor. There would be no other time, I knew; with Lawrie awake it was unlikely he would lead an expedition down here. And for me, the curiosity was too great.

The door was slightly ajar. It was her bedroom, Sarah's bedroom; you could tell. There were still lipsticks on the dressing table, a silver powder compact in the shape of a shell; paperback novels and old magazines. Along the sill were china and glass ornaments, vases of flowers, now dried out. The curtains were open, but the sun was not yet up. The silhouettes of naked trees were crooked against a lavender sky.

I looked at the bed. Had it happened here? There was no sense of the scene, for which I was grateful. I felt deeply sorry for both these men, clearly lost without her – or confused, at least. Gerry was right – Lawrie had been so evasive about his mother. Gerry, far from being a heartless bastard, appeared to want to discuss her. It was Lawrie who wouldn't. Only now, being in the house with him and his step-father together, could I see how deeply Lawrie had been affected by Sarah, by this second marriage, by the manner of her death.

In the corner of the room was a large wardrobe. I opened it, and a cloud of camphor hit the back of my throat. Hanging inside was a solitary pair of delicate red trousers, and I pulled them out and held them against my body. If these were Sarah's, and I assumed they were, she had been tiny. They barely cut the middle of my shins. They were made of scarlet wool, which in many places had been attacked by moth, most unfortunately at the groin. Yet you could tell that these trousers had been particularly stylish. They made me think of Quick. She'd have liked these, holey groin or not.

'They won't fit, you know,' said a voice. 'But I couldn't bear to throw them away.'

I jumped. At the door was Gerry; scant, sandy hair on end, large body wrapped in a deep blue dressing gown, his hairy legs and bare feet sticking out at the bottom. Embarrassed, I stammered something incomprehensible as I moved to put the trousers back. I felt terrible for thinking that Gerry had just cleared away his wife without a second thought. This place was like his little shrine. He probably visited it every morning, and I was an intruder. I was beyond mortified. I'd stayed over; I was just wearing a man's shirt and jumper. I'd had sex under his roof. Thank God Lawrie was much taller than me, in terms of my modesty, but I might as well have had the word SEX emblazoned on my forehead, I felt it was so obvious.

But Gerry seemed uninterested in the morals of his step-son and girlfriend. Perhaps he was more modern than I gave him credit for. That, or he was too mired or hungover in his grief to care. He waved his hand as he padded in. 'Don't worry,' he said, sitting heavily on the end of the bed. I was still holding the trousers. 'You can have a look around. She was a mystery to me too, in many ways.'

With his glum expression and rotund stomach, Gerry reminded me of the morose Humpty Dumpty from Lewis Carroll's *Looking-Glass*. And I felt like Alice – being riddled and challenged in every direction I turned.

'I'm sorry,' I said. 'I shouldn't be in here.'

'Don't be. Lawrie really doesn't talk about her, does he?'

'Not much. Mr Scott, can I ask—'

'I'm not Scott,' said Gerry. 'That was Sarah's maiden name.'

'Oh.'

'Lawrence chose to keep her name rather than mine,' Gerry said, shaking his head. 'Still, he was sixteen by then, and you can't tell a sixteen-year-old what to do. Never really understood him.'

'He didn't take his father's name?'

Gerry looked at me shrewdly. 'Not a very good idea to call yourself Schloss in the school playground in the forties.'

I stood, frozen to the spot, the red trousers hanging limply in my grasp. 'Schloss?' I repeated. 'Lawrie's father was Schloss?'

Gerry looked up at me, interested by the energy in my voice. 'Well, strictly speaking, yes. Sarah gave him the surname Scott from the moment he was born, but in terms of his father, it's Schloss. Her first husband was an Austrian of all things, just before the Great War.'

'Austrian?'

Gerry looked amused. 'You seem a little perturbed by all this. Is everything all right?'

'Oh, I'm fine,' I said, trying to look as casual as I could, in Lawrie's oversized woollen jumper, clutching his dead mother's trousers, as if this news about Lawrie's father meant nothing to me at all.

'When she came back to England and had Lawrie, she thought it prudent to give him her own name. Nobody trusted a German name in those days.'

'What was her husband's first name?'

'Harold. Poor bastard. God, when I think what happened. Sarah never talked about it, but I think perhaps she should have, now I look at Lawrence. The man is so pathological when it comes to his parents.'

I tried to recall how Lawrie had behaved, on the occasions that Reede had mentioned the name Harold Schloss. I didn't remember any particular show of emotion, or moment of recognition. But he had asked if Reede knew what had happened to him – I did remember that.

'What happened to his father?' I asked.

Gerry bared his teeth in a grim smile, revealing long incisors. 'He doesn't tell you much, does he? Well, it's a sensitive subject.'

'Clearly.'

'Perhaps you two don't have time spare for talking. I was the same, once.'

I tried to turn my blush into a weak smile, half wanting to flee, half wanting to find out from this man more than Lawrie would ever tell me. 'He has a point, not talking about it,' Gerry said. 'It's useless for a man to rake over things he can't even remember. Lawrie never even met the fellow.' He ran his hand over his head and fixed me with a look. 'Hitler happened to Harold Schloss, that's what. Like he happened to us all.'

I went to speak, but Gerry rose to his feet, yellow-nailed against the dark wood floorboards. 'It's very early to be talking about all this,' he said. 'I'm going for a walk to clear my head. I suggest that you go back to bed.'

16

I returned to Lawrie's room. He stirred and opened his eyes with a smile, throwing his arms up to let me into the warm, crumpled sheets. I stood at the side of the bed. 'What is it?' he said, the smile fading. 'What's wrong?'

'You're Lawrie Schloss,' I said. 'Your father sold *Rufina and the Lion*. That's how you have the painting.'

I admit, there might have been a better way to approach the situation – *your father* this and *your father* that – talking of a dead man Lawrie had never met, at six fifteen in the morning. I think it was because I had always thought of Lawrie as fundamentally honest; had even defended him to Quick when she was raising her doubts. And I realized now, that time and again, Lawrie had evaded the question not just of his mother, but of how she might have come into possessing such an artwork.

Lawrie lowered his arms and surveyed me. 'I'm Lawrie *Scott*,' he said. He closed his eyes. 'You've been talking to Gerry.'

'You lied,' I said.

He opened his eyes again, and propped himself on an elbow. 'I didn't bloody lie. I just never told you the whole truth.'

'But why? What does it matter who your father was?' He said nothing. 'Lawrie, have you really sold your car?'

He rubbed his eyes, frowning as if trying to slot his thoughts

into place. 'Yes, I have really sold my car. Gerry's definitely planning to sell this house. And then what will I do?'

'He'll never sell it. There's a room along this corridor devoted
to your mother. It's even got her clothes and make-up still inside.'

There was confusion in his eyes. 'How d'you know about that?'

I sat down slowly on the side of the bed. 'It's where I just bumped
into Gerry.'

'You were snooping?'

I looked away, embarrassed. 'He told me about your mother
giving you her maiden name when the war was on. When Reede
mentioned Harold Schloss – why didn't you just say something?'

He fell back against his pillow. 'It would have made things too
complicated.'

'It would have simplified them. That's how you have the painting in your possession. Provenance and all that.'

'It might simplify things for Reede, but not for me.' He clasped
his hands together into one fist. 'Look, we never, ever talked about
him, Odelle. My family doesn't *talk* about things. And if you've
spent your whole life never talking about something, do you think
you're suddenly going to be able to discuss it – just like that – to
some stranger who's after your painting?'

'But why—'

'I don't have the words for it, Odelle. I don't have the words for
something that happened when I wasn't even alive.'

'But surely your mother talked about him? He was your *father*.'

'I knew his name, that's it. I knew my mother changed hers
when she came back to England. It was her and me for sixteen
years, and then Gerry came along. I wasn't going to claim a dead
man just to satisfy Edmund Reede's little genealogy.'

'All right. I'm sorry.'

'There's nothing to be sorry for.'

'I just . . .' I thought of Quick. 'I'm just trying to make sense of
the painting, that's all.'

He sat up. 'My mother never told me how she got that painting,

Odelle. I wasn't lying. My only guess is, my father never managed to get it to this Peggy Guggenheim – and then in the chaos that followed leaving Spain, my mother took it with her and brought it to England.'

'What happened to their marriage, if he was in Paris and she was in England?'

Lawrie sighed. 'I don't know. She came to London; he stayed there. And then the Germans occupied Paris. My mother never even wore a wedding ring before Gerry.'

'And you never asked her about it?'

'I asked,' he said, his voice tight. 'She didn't like it, but she told me he died in the war being brave, and that now it was just the two of us. I heard that line at three years old, at ten, at thirteen – and you hear something like that over and over again, it just becomes the way things are.'

'Perhaps she wanted to spare you the grief of it,' I said.

Lawrie looked grim. 'I don't think my mother ever really thought about sparing me anything. My guess is, either he walked out and chose not to have contact with her, or she was the one who severed ties. It was a nice idea, her and me, against the world, but it got a little claustrophobic. She was very over-protective. Said I was her second chance.'

'And that's all she said?'

'You don't know what she was like. It just wasn't something you talked about to her. And lots of people had missing dads, you know. It was after the war, lots of widows. You don't pick at some-one else's grief.'

'Of course.' I knew it was time for me to stop. I wanted to ask if Sarah had ever talked to him about Olive; how she might fit into all this. As I'd discussed with Cynth, a young woman with that surname could easily be Harold Schloss's daughter – but Lawrie had never mentioned a sister, however much older than him she would have been. And if Lawrie knew as little about Harold as he was claiming to, this hardly came as a surprise. I looked at him, trying to see echoes in his face of Quick's. I couldn't imagine how I'd broach the subject that he and Marjorie Quick were possibly related.

Lawrie sighed. 'I should have told you about it. But things were up and down between you and me, and it wasn't on my mind. I'm sorry you had to bump into Gerry. I hope he was wearing his dressing gown, at least.'

'Yes.'

'Small mercies.'

'Can I get in?'

He lifted up the blankets and I snuggled under. We lay in silence for a while, and I wondered if Lawrie would ever have told me about his father, if I hadn't pushed it. When it came to our blossoming relationship, I had to consider whether it mattered, either way. Lawrie was still Lawrie to me, surely, regardless of who his father was. But it did sting a little, the amount I didn't know about him, what he'd chosen to hold back. I suppose I was holding things back, too. 'We sat looking at Harold's writing on the train,' I murmured into his shoulder.

'I know.'

'Did you feel anything, looking at it?'

'Not in the way you probably want me to. I was a little sad, I suppose. The way life works out.'

'Yes,' I said, and thought again of Marjorie Quick. 'You never quite know how it's going to end.'

17

*Q*uick telephoned in sick on Monday, and was still not back by Wednesday, and I was too tied up working with Pamela to get everything ready for the opening night of the exhibition to go and see her. Reede was amassing an impressively eclectic list of attendees for 'The Swallowed Century', and had placed Pamela and me in charge of organizing the invitations. Reede wanted coverage, relevance, attention – for the Skelton Institute to be cool and viable, a place where money flowed – and *Rufina and the Lion* was going to help him. Mixing high culture with pop, there was even a rumour that a Cabinet minister might turn up. And it had to be said, *Rufina and the Lion*, as both an intellectual challenge and an aesthetic offering, more than stood up to it. Reede had commissioned a frame for the painting, the first it had probably ever had. He had good taste; it was a dark mahogany, and it radiated Rufina's colours even more.

Julie Christie had confirmed she was coming, as had Robert Fraser, the art dealer. Quentin Crisp, Roald Dahl and Mick Jagger had all been invited. I thought the Jagger invitation an unusual choice, but Pamela pointed out that earlier in the year, when the Rolling Stone had been put in custody on a drug charge, the papers reported that he'd taken with him forty cigarettes, a bar of chocolate, a jigsaw puzzle, and two books. Pamela knew everything about the Stones. Mick's first book was about Tibet, she told me. The second was on art.

The newspapers picked up the story of the exhibition, as Reede had hoped they would. The *Daily Telegraph* ran a headline on page 5: *The Spanish Saint and the English Lion: How One Art Expert Rescued an Iberian Gem*. According to the journalist, *An extraordinary, long-lost painting by the disappeared Spanish artist Isaac Robles has been discovered in an English house, and will be brought to public recognition by Edmund Reede, art historian and Director of the Skelton Institute.* I wondered what Lawrie might make of this last sentence – or indeed, Quick – for both of them, in very different ways, were helping Reede achieve his aims. It annoyed me, but it did not surprise me.

In *The Times*, the art correspondent, Gregory Herbert, wrote a long essay focusing on rediscovered artists like Isaac Robles – and how paintings such as *Rufina and the Lion* both reflected and extended our understanding of the turbulence of the first half of the twentieth century. Herbert was invited for a private view, and he told us, as he stood before the painting, that he'd fought in the International Brigades in 1937, before the Spanish government had sent the volunteers home.

In Auschwitz and at Hiroshima, Herbert wrote, *the toll has been written in ledgers and carved on sepulchres. In Spain, the Republican dead can be tallied only in the heart. There are few marked graves for those who lost that war. In the name of survival, the damage was internalized, a psychic scar on toxic land. Murderers still live near their victims' families, and between neighbour and neighbour twenty ghosts trudge the village road. Sorrow has seeped into the soil, and the trauma of survivors is revealed only by their acts of concealment.*

Even today, Pablo Picasso still stays away from the Andalusian city of Malaga, despite being its most famous son. When Spain broke apart, many artists escaped the cracks, fleeing to France or America rather than endure isolation, imprisonment and possible death. Life in its variety was cauterized, and so was art. For the poet Federico García Lorca, it was too late to escape. One can only surmise that his fellow Andalusian, the painter Isaac Robles, may have met a similar fate.

Spain's past is a cut of meat turning green on the butcher's slab. When the war ended, people were forbidden to look back and see the circling flies. Soon they found themselves unable to turn their heads, discovering that there was no language permitted for their pain. But the paintings, at least, remain: Guernica, *the works of Dalí and Miró – and now* Rufina and the Lion, *an allegory of Spain, a testament to a beautiful country at war with itself, carrying its own head in its arms, doomed for ever to be hunted by lions.*

By the end of Herbert's essay, you would imagine that Isaac Robles was well on his way to becoming highly collectible, enjoying a second renaissance of prices the likes of which the humble painter himself would never have dreamed. Herbert sounded so sure that he knew what the painting was about, that Isaac Robles had intended a political commentary on the state of his country. But I thought the painting, combined with the images of Justa in *Women in the Wheatfield*, seemed more personal – sexual, even.

By Thursday, when Barozzi and the other Guggenheim people from Venice arrived with their paintings – an ambassadorial art entourage, with better presents and suits – Quick was still not back, and Reede was furious.

'She's not well,' I said. Quick wasn't answering her telephone. The nearer the exhibition had drawn to opening night, the further she had shrunk away from it. Even though I feared the pressure of the impending opening was crushing her, I almost hoped it would crack her open whatever the consequence, so the secret she was hiding from me would be forced into the light.

'I don't care if she's on her death-bed,' Reede raged, and I shuddered at his macabre accuracy. 'This is the most important visit to happen to the Skelton in all my twenty years and she can't even be bothered to show up?'

He was in an extremely bad temper, for he had failed in his bid to get the Prado museum in Madrid to loan him the Goya. 'Then who's the person I can speak to in the convent with the Murillo?' I had heard him saying through his open door one afternoon.

In Quick's absence, Reede had directed the hanging of the paintings himself, ordering Pamela and me to oversee the tea-making and the clearing up of boxes, packing crates and twine. The Venetians were very friendly, I recall, and slightly disturbed by the freezing London winter. 'Have you ever been to Venice?' one of them asked me.

'No,' I said.

'Go. It is like the theatre has been turned onto the street.'

The photograph of Isaac Robles and the unnamed woman had been blown up to cover four enormous boards. Two archivists were trying to affix it to the end of the gallery wall. No one dared point out that the camera was clearly centred on the slightly blurred face of the smiling young woman, holding the brush. 'It's the only photograph we have of him,' Reede said, 'so it's going in.'

The Venetians pulled their own Isaac Robles out of a crate and a gasp went up from Pamela.

'Oh, Dell,' she said. 'Look.'

The Orchard was indeed worth gasping at. It was stunning, far larger than I was expecting, at least five foot long and four high. The colours had lasted well over the past thirty years – it was so vibrant and modern in its sensibility, it could have been painted yesterday. There were echoes in the patchwork fields of *Rufina and the Lion*, but the detailing was almost hyper-real, diligent on the ground, giving way to a symphony of brushstrokes in the sky.

'It is my favourite,' admitted one of the Venetians.

'It's beautiful.'

'Where does Signor Reede want it?'

I looked at the plan. Reede wanted *Rufina and the Lion* to share a wall only with *Women in the Wheatfield*, which was still in its crate. *The Orchard*, because of its size, was unlikely to share wall space. 'Put it here for now,' I said, indicating that the Venetians could park it safely in a corner of the gallery.

Although it was very exciting to be in that space that day –
opening the wooden crates, like Christmas on a grand scale; saw-
dust and nails everywhere, and a magical sense of occasion – I
had a deep feeling of unease. Yes, there was the momentousness
of this being Isaac Robles' first ever London exhibition – but the
one snag was that Quick didn't think Isaac Robles painted these
paintings at all.

I wandered down the gallery to take another look at the photograph, and stood before the woman I was so sure was Olive Schloss,
Rufina and the Lion half-finished behind her. It felt imperative that
I understand this photograph, that it was the key to unlocking the
truth about that painting, and what was happening to Quick. I
sought in that girl's slightly blurred face a younger Quick, full of
hope and passion. And although Quick had become gaunt over the
past months, I believed I could see in this bounteous, full visage,
the girl she once had been. But I could not be sure of it. Over the
last months, Quick had given me so much, in a way – and yet at the
same time, so little. My desire for answers had supplied me with
my own, and although they were attractive to me, they were not
necessarily true. Looking again at this life-size photograph, and
with no time left, I knew what I had to do.

In my lunch break, I sneaked up to Quick's office and took some
Skelton headed paper from her supplies, hurriedly practising
Reede's signature several times on a notepad. I typed up a brief
letter of introduction and explanation, with regards to enhanc-
ing the contents of *The Swallowed Century*, before taking a deep
breath and faking Reede's squiggle at the bottom. With the letter
in my handbag, I walked over to the main office of the Slade School
of Art on Gower Street, and asked to check their alumni records.
They barely glanced at the letter, and I spent the whole hour looking through 1935 to 1945.

No Olive Schloss had ever been registered. It felt like one of
the last remaining threads had snapped, but I refused to believe
that Olive had truly disappeared. She was in the Skelton, on those

walls, surrounded by her work – she was in Wimbledon right now, a person I was determined to pin down. I found a phone box and dialled Quick's number, praying that she would answer.

'Hello?'

'You never made it, did you?' I said.

'Odelle, is that you?' The words came out oddly, her voice slurring. She sounded frail, and my relief at finally hearing her voice soon gave way to fear.

'Quick, I've been to the Slade.'

There was silence on the other end. I went on, frustrated and desperate, my face getting hot, my heart beginning to thump. 'No Olive Schloss ever registered at the Slade. But you knew that, didn't you? Just tell me the truth.'

'The Slade?' she repeated. 'The Slade . . . why were you at the Slade?'

'Quick, the exhibition opens tomorrow. Isaac Robles is going to get your glory. I don't think you should be alone.'

'I'm not alone.' She stopped, wheezing for breath. 'I'm never alone.'

I peered through the phone box's grimy squares of glass, Londoners rushing back and forth in front of me. I felt as if I were underwater, and their bodies were not really bodies, just smudges of colour, moving across my sight.

'I'm coming to see you,' I said, surprised at how adamant I sounded, more than I'd ever dared to sound before.

I could hear Quick hesitate, thinking, the catch of breath as she stopped resisting. 'What about your work?' she said. 'They need you for the exhibition.'

Her protest was weak, and her words were everything I needed to hear. Quick needed me; she knew she did. '*You* are my work, Quick,' I said. 'Can't you see?'

'I'm not in a good way.'

'I know.'

'No – you don't understand. I'm scared. They're coming. I never meant to hurt her.'

Suddenly I felt very claustrophobic in this phone box; I wanted to get out. 'Who didn't you want to hurt?'

'I can hear them—'

'No one's coming,' I soothed, but she was unnerving me. I needed air, and her voice was so desperate. 'Don't be scared,' I said. 'Quick, are you still there? You can trust me, I promise.'

'What did you say?'

'Listen, Quick. I'll be there soon. Quick?'

The line had gone dead. Feeling sick, I pushed my way out of the phone box, and hurried to the nearest Tube.

SEPTEMBER 1936

XVIII

$\mathcal{J}$t was still warm by late September, the air in Arazuelo heavy with honeysuckle, the earth reddened and cracked. Lying beneath this beauteous landscape was sour matter, but it didn't feel like war; not how the Schlosses thought war was supposed to be. It was something worse, a localized, persistent terror. Italian and German bombers would fly overhead, shooting at stationary planes on airfields, at Malaga port, at petrol tanks. But there was a strange sense of limbo, an intermittent hope that all this would be tied up soon, that the Republican government would sort a resistance against these nationalist rebels and their foreign allies, who were stretching their reach across the country.

The nationalists had gained control of Old Castile, Leon, Oviedo, Alava, Navarre, Galicia, Zaragoza, the Canaries and all the Balearics, except Menorca. In the south, they had seized Cadiz, Seville, Cordoba, Granada and Huelva. Malaga was still in the Republican zone – as was Arazuelo – but nevertheless, the rebels felt very near.

Harold would drive into Malaga in order to bring back supplies. He said some shops and bars would be open, whilst others were closed, and the trains and buses would mysteriously cease and resume their timetables with no warning. Nothing was stable. No one was even wearing neckties any more, for such flourishes were taken as a sign of bourgeois tendency and might make you a target for the reds. Harold hoped the worst the Anarchists might do was steal his car, vehicles requisitioned 'for the cause', petrol siphoned off for trucks, elegant motors left to rust.

The days were bearable; the worst was the nights. The family lay awake in the finca as gunshots peppered the fields, ever nearer. Each side of the growing battle saw the other as a faceless, viral mass contaminating the body politic, requiring excision from society. Right-wing and left-wing gangs were taking the law into their own hands, removing opponents from their homes, leaving them in unmarked graves amongst the hills and groves.

In many instances, politics was the cover for personal vendetta and family feud. Most of the right-wing terror was directed against those who had influenced the violence against the priests and the factory owners back in 1934 – union leaders, prominent anti-clericals, several Republican mayors. And yet – mechanics, butchers, doctors, builders, labourers, barbers – they too were 'taken for a walk', as the phrase came to be known. And it wasn't just men. Certain women who had become teachers under the Republic were removed, as were known anarchists' wives. None of it was legal, of course, but there seemed no means of stopping it, when hate and power were in play.

As for the rogue elements on the left – despite the posters Harold had seen plastered around Malaga, imploring them to stop shaming their political and trade organizations and to cease their brutalities – they went for retired civil guards, Catholic sympathizers, people they knew to be rich, people they *believed* to be rich. Houses were looted, their property damaged – and it was this fear that often struck first into the imagination of the middle classes, rather than the chance they would be shot.

The Schlosses did not fear for themselves. They thought no one would touch them, as foreigners. They were nothing to do with all this. Death was taking place beyond their village, outside municipal authority and the sight of the people. The violence in the country – against both the body of a village and a villager's bullet-riddled corpse – was concealed, although everyone knew it was there. Because you couldn't see it, you carried on. It was odd, Olive thought, how you could live alongside this; how you could know all this was happening, and still not want to leave.

She had long ago abandoned trying to listen to the BBC to seek the facts, for it offered little more than an improbable-sounding hybrid of information from Madrid and Seville, adding it together and dividing it by London. Yet the Republican government stations were one long barrage of victory speeches and claims of triumph, which were rather undermined by actual events. Granada's frequency always crackled, not a word could be heard – and the same applied to the northern cities, whose radio waves could not penetrate the southern mountains.

The city of Malaga, however, was constantly broadcasting denials, rumours and myths; Republican calls to arms, meeting times and orders to build a new Spain, free of fascists. And on the other side, the alarming nationalist invective was a frequency in Seville. In the daytime, it would play music and personal announcements, as if there was no conflict going on at all. But by night, the insurgents would broadcast, and although there was still much bombast and warmongering in it, Olive used it to deduce the changing state of her adopted country's fortunes. She listened as Queipo de Llano, the general who had first broadcast from Seville, maintained his unrelenting bloodthirstiness, crying out that there was a cancer in Spain, a body of infidels that only death would remove.

IT WAS UNNERVING, ALL OF it; and yet there were heartening stories of people refusing to do exactly what the generals wanted. Teresa reported how a priest in the neighbouring village prevented a Falangist gang from shooting the atheists in his parish. She had also heard rumours of leftists reprimanding Anarchists for trying to burn down the local church, even hiding right-wing neighbours in their bread ovens, protecting them from certain death when the radicals turned up.

Olive, listening to these tales, could see how most people were massed in the middle. They wanted no disturbance, desperate just to live their lives away from these demonstrations of power, talks of purge, of brutality sprayed in blood against a whitewashed wall. But their desire couldn't change the truth of Arazuelo's atmosphere. She would walk into the village and see people's pinched faces, worrying who was going to defend whom when Arazuelo's day of reckoning finally came.

ISAAC PURCHASED A RIFLE IN Malaga from a trade-union contact, who was fond of poaching his boss's boar. He reinforced the bolt across the cottage door, but he knew this would mean nothing to someone determined to get him. More 'people of interest' to the nationalist rebels had left their villages to hide out in the countryside, or join the militias run by the Communist party in Malaga. But this wasn't far enough for Teresa. She wanted him to leave.

'I think you should go north,' she said. 'You've made too many enemies here. You don't fit. The left won't trust you because of our father, and the right don't trust you for not being his legitimate son.'

Isaac regarded his sister, the new severity in her face. 'You don't fit here either, Tere,' he said.

'But you're the one who put a bullet through the Madonna. *You're* the one who's spent his life teaching peasants their rights. You're the one—'

'All right. But you think they're only going for men? You'd have to come with me.'

'I won't leave.'

'Jesus, you're as stubborn as the Schlosses.'

'Well, we all know why they won't leave. Because of you. If you think about it, Isa, you're endangering them too.'

The British Consulate in Malaga had sent letters out to any of His Majesty's registered subjects it knew of in the region. Wide-eyed, Teresa handed over the consul's letter, which was addressed to Sarah. After a thin breakfast, bread being scarcer and the goat milk drying up, the Schlosses discussed whether they should stay or go.

The letter informed them that warships were waiting to take them off Spanish soil into Gibraltar – and on, if they wished, to England. The threat, it said, was not from these nationalist insurgents and their foreign troops, but from those on the Spanish far left, the reds – who might soon loot these British-rented fincas, and confiscate any private property.

Olive was determined that they should stay. 'We can't just leave when it doesn't suit us. What sort of example is that?'

'*Liebling*,' said Harold. 'It's dangerous.'

'You're the one still driving into Malaga. We're foreigners. They won't come for us.'

'That's exactly why they *will* come for us,' said Harold, pointing at the letter. 'That's what the consul said.'

'Liv's right,' said Sarah. 'I don't think we should leave.'

Harold looked at his two womenfolk in bemusement. 'You *both* want to stay?'

Sarah got up and walked to the window. 'London is over for us.'

'I'm confused,' said Harold. 'Only two months ago, you were clamouring to leave.' Sarah ignored him. '*I* think,' he said, 'that we should leave if it gets any worse, but invite Isaac to come with us.'

The women turned to look at him. 'It's my duty,' said Harold. 'He's too valuable.'

'Isaac won't leave,' said Sarah. 'He'll fight.'

'What would you know about it?'

'It's obvious. He feels great loyalty to this place.'

'As do I,' said Olive, still on the sofa, reaching over to light one of their dwindling supply of cigarettes. Her parents did not stop her. 'Mr Robles isn't a coward,' she said, exhaling deeply, surveying them both. 'But if you're planning to take him, then quite frankly, you should take Teresa too.'

'Has he nearly finished this *Rufina* painting?' asked Harold. 'I keep dangling the bait for Peggy, but have not been given any news.'

'I do not know, señor,' said Teresa.

'You normally know everything, Teresa,' Sarah said.

'He's nearly finished,' said Olive. 'It won't be long.'

'When you next go to Malaga, darling,' Sarah said to Harold, 'buy a Union Jack.'

'What?'

'I want to hoist the Union Jack. So whatever bastard comes along to shoot us up, they know that we are neutral.'

'We're hardly *neutral*, Mother,' said Olive. 'Have you even looked at the newspapers?'

'You know I don't like the newspapers, Olive.'

'Unless you're in them.'

'*Liv*,' said her father, a warning in his voice.

'Well, she lives in a bubble. Our government has refused to get involved. So have the French. They're saying that defending the Spanish Republic is tantamount to a defence of Bolshevism.'

'They're worried, *liebling*,' said Harold. 'They fear revolution, that the situation here will spread to France, up and up across the Channel, into Regent Street, along the Strand and the Pennine Way.'

'Baldwin's so scared of Hitler, he won't do anything.'

'I don't think he is,' said Harold. 'The Prime Minister is buying *time* rather than German favour.'

'Either way – where does that leave you, Mr Vienna?' said Sarah. 'Better for you – for all of us – if we stay in Spain.'

Rufina and the Lion was in fact completed, and Olive hadn't painted anything since. She'd never experienced this lack of willingness to approach a canvas, and she didn't like it at all – feeling useless, and frightened by her lack of confidence. She didn't want to connect it directly to Isaac's lack of interest in her – she wanted to work independently of him, of any factor outside her own creative impulse – but it was proving impossible. She had begged Isaac to present *Rufina and the Lion* to Harold, but he wouldn't do it. 'I've got more important things to worry about,' he'd said.

'But you could just hand it over. My father's waiting. Peggy Guggenheim's waiting.'

'I do not care if the Pope is waiting,' he snapped.

Olive started to feel that *Rufina* was clogging up her mind. Its power over her had become a reflection, not just of her relationships with Isaac and Teresa, but of the political situation that was swirling around them. Fear was stoppering her. She had painted it as a purge; now she needed it gone. When Isaac wouldn't take it, Olive suggested that Teresa take the panel down to the pantry, out of her sight.

Teresa refused. 'It is too cold in there, señorita,' she said. 'It might be damaged.'

'But I can't paint anything now.'

'*Tranquila, señorita*,' said Teresa. 'It will come and go.'

'Well, it's never gone anywhere before. What if that's *it*? What if it's just been these paintings, and that's it?'

ONE EVENING IN EARLY OCTOBER, the Schlosses invited Isaac for dinner. He was quiet throughout, and afterwards Olive caught him alone, staring into the darkness of the orchard. She slipped her hand in his, but he did not take hers, his own resting there like a dead man's. She tried to cajole him again, saying that surely he could do with more money for the Republican side, and that giving Harold *Rufina and the Lion* would be the ideal way.

'The Soviets have promised us arms,' he said. 'We may lose Malaga. We may lose Madrid and half of Catalonia, but we will win the war.'

She leaned over to plant a kiss on his cheek. 'You're so brave,' she said.

He seemed not to notice her kiss at all, as he ground the cigarette under his heel, ash smearing black on the veranda. 'Teresa thinks I should go north. Our father is becoming more and more . . . loud, about those on the left. I represent something that holds him back. He's ambitious. Ambitious men do well in times like these.'

'Will he hurt you, Isa?'

'He will not get his hands dirty. Those days are over. But some-one else might.'

'Isaac, no.'

'They're bombing Malaga again. You should leave, Olive. You all should go.'

'But we *live* here.'

'Imagine if you stayed. You might never paint again, all because you wanted to be brave.'

'If I was dead, I don't suppose I'd much care. Besides, I haven't painted a thing since finishing *Rufina*.'

He turned to her in surprise. 'Is that true?'

'Yes, that's why I keep asking. I know it's selfish, Isa, I know.' She could feel a cry coming, but she swallowed it down. 'Without you I'm stuck.' He did not respond, and she turned away to the blackness of the orchard.

'You don't need me, Olive,' he said, eventually. 'You just need to pick up your brush. Why do you insist so much on involving us? Is it so that you can blame us if it goes wrong?'

'No.'

'If I had half your skill, I wouldn't care who loved me.'

She gave a dry laugh. 'That's what I thought too. But I'd rather be happy.'

'Being allowed to paint is what makes you happy. I know that about you at least.' She smiled. 'I like you, Olive,' Isaac went on. 'You are a very special girl. But you are so young to be thinking of for ever.'

Olive swallowed again, tears pricking at her eyes. 'I'm not young. You and me – why can't this be for ever?'

He waved his arm towards the darkness. 'War or no war, you were never going to stay here.'

'You don't *see*, do you?'

'What don't I see?'

'That I love you.'

'You love an idea of me.'

'It's the same thing.'

They were silent. 'I have been useful to you,' he said. 'That is all.'

'What is it, Isa? What's changed?'

He closed his eyes and shivered. 'Nothing's changed. It's always been the same.'

She pounded the veranda rail with her fist. 'You should *want* to be with me. You should—'

A muffled explosion from beyond the valley silenced them both. 'What the hell was that?' said Isaac, scanning the horizon.

'Teresa said they've started to bomb bridges again. Is it true your father is helping them?'

Isaac's eyes were so dark with anger, she moved back. 'I need to go to Malaga,' he said.

'At midnight? What use will you be now?'

'More useful than standing here.'

'So that's it, is it? Us?'

'Our ideas of what this is have always been different. You know that.'

'What am I supposed to do with that painting?'

'Give it to your father. I must deal with my own.'

'What do you mean? I won't give up on this—'

'You're mixing things up, Olive. You're frustrated you cannot paint—'

She grabbed his arms. 'I need you. I can't paint without you.'

'You painted before me.'

'Isaac, don't leave me – please.'

'Goodbye, Olive.'

'No!'

Isaac stepped down from the veranda and walked towards the orchard. He turned back to the house, his face half-illuminated by the moon. Behind her, Olive felt a presence at the kitchen door.

'Where's he going?' Sarah said.

'*Suerte*,' Isaac called over his shoulder, before slipping between the trees.

'What does that mean?' asked Sarah.

Olive could feel her tears coming, but she refused to let her mother see her cry. 'It doesn't matter.'

'Olive, tell me what he said.'

Olive turned to Sarah, struck by the expression of worry on her face. 'All it means, Mother,' she said, 'is good luck.'

XIX

A few hours after Isaac slipped away from the Schloss women and into the darkness, Don Alfonso's finca was attacked with fire and a second salvo was launched upon the church of Santa Rufina in the centre of Arazuelo. Later, people whispered that yes, they'd seen a disrobed Padre Lorenzo, running away from the flames into the village square, with a naked woman fast on his heels. Some said there hadn't been a woman at all, just the priest in a white smock, the bump of his private part visible under the cotton. Others swore on the Holy Bible there'd been a woman – a vision of Rufina herself, running from the godlessness behind her before she took flight into the air.

The only truth Arazuelo could attest to was that by dawn, the church was a shell and Don Alfonso's estate a blackened skeleton. Wood smoke hung over the air, smarting the eyes of those trying to go about their business, until the whole village fell into an uneasy stupor, knowing full well that retaliation for something like this would eventually come.

When Teresa came running through the grey dawn light, bashing on the front door of the finca, Olive knew something was very wrong.

'Isaac has done something stupid—'

'What's he done? Where is he?'

Teresa looked stricken. 'I don't know. The church is gone.'

'Gone – what do you mean, gone?'

'Fire. And my father's house also.'

'Dear God, Teresa. Come inside.'

AROUND TWO HOURS LATER, DON Alfonso appeared, his once-pristine suit now smeared with charcoal. He too banged on the finca door, and upstairs with Olive, Teresa cowered. 'It's going to be all right,' Olive whispered.

Teresa gripped her wrist. 'No, señorita. You do not understand.'

Harold let Don Alfonso in, and the man moved angrily through the hallway into the front east room. Olive crept down the stairs to peer through the crack in the door.

'You have heard what happened?' Don Alfonso said.

'I have.'

'News travels fast. It is an outrage. I could have been dead. My wife, my children – it is only because my daughter Clara is an insomniac that any of us are still here. Three of my stable grooms, an under-butler and a pot-washing boy had a part in it. I've found these men, Señor Schloss, and they are all in the jail, waiting their punishment. And do you know what they tell me? They tell me that Isaac Robles paid them for their help. Where did Isaac get the money to pay those men? It was certainly not from me. I cannot get the answers, because I cannot find my bastard son. Do you know where he is, señor?'

'No.'

'And yet you know my finca was set on fire.'

'Is he not at his cottage?'

'I sent Jorge and Gregorio there. All they found was *this*.' Don Alfonso held aloft an old copy of *Vogue*. 'Your wife's, I assume?'

A look of surprise passed over Harold's face, but he adjusted quickly back to an impression of calm. 'She gives them to Teresa.'

'My son set loose thirty of my thoroughbred horses, señor. He torched my stables. He burned down Lorenzo's church.'

'Sit down, Don Alfonso, please. These are severe accusations.'

'His own friends have turned him in. He is a devil, señor.'

'I beg to differ,' said Harold, clearly irritated now. 'Don Alfonso, your son does not have time for these games. Your son is a gifted man.'

It was Don Alfonso's turn to look surprised. 'Gifted?'

'Have you never seen his work?'

'What?'

Before Harold could explain further, Olive pushed into the room. Both men jumped and turned to her. 'Go upstairs,' said Harold in a tight voice.

'No.'

Behind Olive, Sarah appeared. 'What's going on?' she said. Her eye rested on the figure of Don Alfonso, and the colour drained from her face. 'Is he dead?' she whispered. 'Is Mr Robles dead?'

'Don't be ridiculous, Sarah,' said Harold, unable to mask the stress in his voice.

Don Alfonso inclined his head towards Sarah in a curt bow. 'Is Teresa here?' he asked her.

'Upstairs,' replied Sarah.

'*Mother*,' said Olive. 'No.'

'Please bring her to me,' said Alfonso.

'No,' said Olive. 'You can't have her.'

'Liv, don't be ridiculous,' said Harold. 'Be civilized.'

'*Civilized*?'

'Go and fetch Teresa.'

OLIVE WENT UPSTAIRS, BUT TERESA was nowhere to be seen. Olive waited, buying time, pretending to look for her, praying that Teresa had got herself somewhere safe. She moved back down with determined steps and returned to the front east room. Don Alfonso narrowed his eyes when he saw she was alone. 'Are you hiding her, señorita?' he said. 'I know you think you are her friend.'

'I'm not hiding anyone.'

He turned to Olive's parents. 'It won't be good for you, hiding them. Isaac is wanted for theft, arson, criminal damage, attempted murder—'

'For God's sake,' Harold interjected. 'We are not hiding your children.'

'They are no longer my children. You should leave here,' said Don Alfonso. 'You should go.'

'On the contrary,' replied Harold. 'I think we should protect those who do not enjoy your protection. I am beginning to understand you much better.'

Alfonso laughed. 'You foreigners, you're all the same. You think you are protecting Teresa and Isaac? They will be the ones who will have to protect you. And do you think they will? That you are under some magic shroud, that your maid and gardener love you?'

'Teresa is our maid, yes, and a bloody good one – but Isaac is not our gardener. You have no idea about what your son—'

'I know him better than you do. What will he use to defend you, señor – a saucepan? Those degenerates he consorts with are more likely to put a hoe through your heart and join up with the Reds.'

When Don Alfonso had disappeared in his motor car shortly after, Olive ran through the finca's rusty gates, down the path, into the village – by this time breathless and leg-sore – and out and up the hill again, to Isaac and Teresa's cottage. They were not there, but Jorge and Gregorio had turned the place over. God, this cottage was a spare place, sparer than Olive had remembered it to be. In her mind's eye, it had become a rustic haven, a place to think and breathe and paint. In truth, it was a place one might wish to escape.

Isaac's room contained nothing but his unmade bed and a jar of dying roses on the windowsill. Teresa's meagre belongings were scattered on her bedroom floor. Olive was surprised to see one of her old paint tubes – the grasshopper-green shade she'd used for *The Orchard*. There was a Veuve Clicquot champagne cork, and stranger things; a cut-out square of material that matched her father's pyjamas. There was a crushed packet of Harold's cigarettes, and when Olive went to shake it, several stubs had been saved inside, their ends covered in the unmistakeable rouge of her mother's lips. Lying around the floorboards were loose pages ripped from a notebook, with words and phrases written in English in a diligent, neat hand: *palaver – snaffled – crass – gosh – I'm starving – ghastly – selfish*. Alongside them were their Spanish meanings.

Olive's heart began to thump. Looking at this flotsam from her parents' lives, this notebook of the things they had probably said in careless passing – she had the chilly sensation that she didn't really know Teresa at all.

The front door banged; her skin turned to gooseflesh. No footsteps followed and she told herself it was the wind. The noise still unnerved her, and she imagined a wolf, sneaking in from the mountains. She was about to move out of Teresa's room, when she saw a photograph on the floor. It was a picture of herself and Isaac in front of *Rufina and the Lion*. Olive was smiling and Isaac, his eyebrows slightly raised, looked ready for his painter's pose. Olive had never seen this picture before, and without thinking, she rammed it deep into her pocket.

As she passed back down the corridor, she saw Isaac's original painting, propped against the wall. Teresa must have moved it back here, out of sight. The idealized faces of herself and her mother seemed to loom out, and Olive was struck again by their mannequin, monstrous blankness.

SHE WENT OUTSIDE TO LOOK at the hills. There was a wreathing pallor of smoke still in the air, the taste of the fire's aftermath. Isaac knew these hills well, better than Don Alfonso. He knew where to hide – but Teresa had not had as much time to escape. Something terrible was coming, Olive could feel it; and there was nothing she could do.

'Teresa?' she called to the land, and her own voice rebounded back. 'Teresa?' she shouted again, her panic rising. But all that Olive heard was the echo of Teresa's name, falling down the hills.

XX

Jt was Jorge who spotted her, disappearing into the forest on the outskirts of the village. He and Gregorio were on the hunt, but it was only by chance that Jorge had his head turned in that direction; the glimpse of a slim brown leg, the flash of a dark plait. What happened next changed Arazuelo for ever, the place that was always supposed to stay the same. The trauma of it rang out, long and ineradicable down the years to come, however hard those who witnessed it attempted silence.

Had he been any further away, Jorge would have lost her; for Teresa was swift-footed and he was much heavier. But together he and Gregorio stalked her through the trees. When Jorge shot his pistol into the air, she spun to face the direction of the sound, and Gregorio took the opportunity to grab her from behind.

She kicked and screamed, but Gregorio did not let go. 'Where is he?' Jorge shouted at her, lumbering through the bracken.

'What do you mean? Put me down.' Teresa felt as if her heart was inching its way up her body, weighing down her tongue.

'Where's your brother?'

'I don't *know.*' Jorge moved forward, pushing his face close to hers. She could smell the sour catch of old alcohol on his breath. 'Come on, Teresa, you know everything, little bird-eye. Little spy. Where's your fucking brother?'

'I don't know,' she repeated.

'Tie her to the tree,' Jorge said, but Gregorio hesitated. 'You heard me. Do it.' Gregorio didn't move.

'I don't know where he is, Jorge, I swear,' Teresa said, sensing a chance. 'You think he'd tell me? No one tells me anything—'

'Your brother set half the village on fire last night. When we catch him, he's a dead man. And you're going to help.'

He began to drag Teresa by her plait towards the tree. 'Isa's known you since you were schoolkids,' she said, gasping at the pain arcing across her skull. 'Twenty years your friend. How does your mother look you in the face?' she hissed.

'At least I've got a mother who does,' said Jorge.

'You're shaking, Gregorio,' Teresa went on at the softer man, out of her wits with fear, but scenting his discomfort.

'Jorge,' said Gregorio. 'We should take her to the station.'

'Shut it,' Jorge said.

'I mean it. I'm not tying her to this tree. Don Alfonso never said – let's put her in the truck.'

JORGE EVENTUALLY RELENTED, AND THEY put Teresa in a cell at the civil guard headquarters, and all night Teresa was silent. 'Check she hasn't done herself in,' Jorge spat. 'Like her mother before her.'

'What?' said Gregorio.

Jorge looked at his colleague. 'Don't tell me you never knew. Her mother drowned herself. Probably didn't want to hang around to bring up that piece of shit,' he added, directing his voice down the dank corridor, loud enough for Teresa to hear.

The next morning, Teresa had barely slept. She had not been wearing many clothes in the first place, and no one had offered her a blanket – but what hurt more, what made her skin palpably shiver, was that no one had come from the finca to speak for her. In the deep of the night, staring up through the bars, thinking of the cruel words Jorge had uttered, Teresa had convinced herself that any minute Olive would come, Olive would call her name, demanding that these brutish boys let her out. Teresa had to believe it, because if she didn't believe it, then the firing squad would come instead.

But Olive never came – and neither did Harold, even though he would have had more authority than his daughter. And as dawn broke, Teresa began to think, *Of course, of course, why would they come?* – and she was glad that no one could witness the pitiful embarrassment of hope.

Jorge and Gregorio came into her cell at eight o'clock in the morning, where she was sitting upright on the bed, every one of her vertebrae pressed up against the cold stone of the wall. 'Up,' said Jorge.

She stood, and he approached. 'For the last time, Teresa. Where is your brother?'

'I don't kn—'

He whacked her round the mouth and her head flew back, cracking against the wall.

'I said, where is he?'

Teresa began to scream, until Jorge punched her again and she heard Gregorio cry out before she fell unconscious. The next thing she knew, she was blindfolded, bumping up and down in the back of their truck again, the iron tang of blood and a loose tooth in her mouth.

She tried to turn her head to the open air to see if she could sense where they were going, but she was still disorientated. Her neck hurt, her skull throbbed. The blindfold had been tied so tight that it cut across her eye sockets. It smelled like sweat, someone else's blood. Was this it? Deep in her heart, in her dreams, she had feared this moment. She was going to be shot in the head, round the back of some hut, fifty kilometres away from her home. And who would miss her? Who would mourn her passing?

The truck stopped. Teresa heard the men jump out of the wagon and swing down the back flap of the truck.

'Don't shoot me. Don't shoot me,' she pleaded, hearing the crack of her own voice, surprised at this overwhelming passion to live, and how prepared she was to abase herself in order to do it. Anything, to live. 'Gregorio,' she said. 'Please. *Please*. Save me.'

But Gregorio did not speak. A hand took her arm and walked her a few steps, pushing her down onto a chair. Teresa heard footsteps moving away, crunching against what sounded like gravel. She had been placed in the direction of the sun, and she could feel it warming her face, orange and gold through the blindfold and the tender skin of her eyelids. *This is it*, she thought.

'Olive,' she whispered, 'Olive.' She kept saying the name, and the blindfold was lifted. There was silence, then the sound of a few birds as they flapped across the sky. Teresa squinted, blinking to adjust her vision to the light. To her surprise, she saw Olive standing to her right, her head haloed in gold, the buildings behind her squares of white.

'Am I dead?' Teresa said.

'No,' replied a man.

Teresa could see now that she was in the main square, on a chair placed directly in front of the charred frame of the church. The villagers had started to gather – shrinking away like a shoal of fish, as Teresa turned her head. She tried to rise from the chair towards Olive. Olive took a step towards her, her arm outstretched, but Gregorio pushed Teresa back down.

Jorge waved his pistol at the gathered villagers. 'Keep back!' he shouted, but Olive stayed forward.

'What are you going to do to her?' she shouted in Spanish. 'What are you going to do?'

'Shut up!' Jorge said, going over to the truck and pulling something from the passenger seat. He walked back to Teresa, hands on his hips, assessing her, pacing round her slowly before taking her plait in his hand, weighing it like he was a widow at market, turning his nose up at the produce. With his other hand, he lifted up a large pair of shears, the kind gardeners used to prune their plants and flowers.

'I'll be fair,' he said, his fist wrapped round the plait. 'Let's unravel it, bit by bit. I'm going to ask you one more time about your brother, and if you cooperate, you can keep your hair.'

TERESA HAD TURNED TO STONE, the only living thing her plait, coiled and twitching in Jorge's fist. Her gaze was distant; her body was there, but she was not. As Jorge undid her hair with an air of industry, she didn't flinch or cry out – she just sat, staring into nothingness. So still, so meditative, she looked almost complicit in the spectacle, until you noticed her bunched fists, the knuckles whitening through the skin.

'Don't do this,' Olive said to the men. 'She doesn't know where he is.'

Jorge swung round to face the other girl. 'That's what she says.'

Snip went the shears, a long tendril of black hair falling to the ground, where it lay in the dust like a snake. No one whispered, no one even seemed to breathe. 'Señorita,' Gregorio said to Olive. 'This is not your affair.'

'Don't hurt her,' said Olive. 'You'll regret it. Does her father know you're doing this—'

'If you don't shut up, you'll be next,' Jorge shouted, lifting the shears again. 'Where's your brother?' he asked Teresa, and still Teresa did not speak. Jorge began to hack the second handful of hair.

Just say something, Tere, Olive thought. *Anything, a lie.* But Teresa was mute, keeping her eyes on the burned-out church, and Olive could almost feel the whisker-touch of dark hair falling against her own neck. Teresa still did not flinch, but Olive could see fear glimmering in her eye, buried within that blank look.

'Where is he?' came the question, again and again. And still, Teresa was silent, so Jorge cut more of her hair, close to the line of the skull, emerging as a clumpy, patchy thing. 'You're a furry mushroom,' Jorge said, laughing. No one in the village joined him, but neither did they move to stop this spectacle.

'Teresa,' Olive called. 'I'm here.'

'For all the good you've done her,' said Gregorio.

Once the bulk of Teresa's hair was gone, Jorge produced a barbering razor from his pocket. 'What are you doing?' hissed Gregorio. 'She got the message.'

'I don't think so,' said Jorge, placing the blade on the top of Teresa's head. He began to shave the remaining patchy tufts until she was completely bald, the ancient humiliation, back to the Bible days, the days of blood.

'This is what happens,' said Jorge, holding the razor aloft, 'when you conceal information about a wanted criminal and fail to cooperate with the law.'

'The law?' said Olive.

The villagers remained immobile. Teresa's skull was covered with weeping nicks where he'd cut into her skin. Jorge pulled Teresa up out of the chair, and she moved with him like a puppet.

'Now take off your skirt and blouse,' he said.

'Stop!' shouted another woman next to Olive, and Jorge stalked towards her.

'You next, Rosita?' he said. 'You want to look like a mushroom too? Because I promise you can be next.' Rosita shrank away, shaking her head, fear distorting her face.

Slowly, Teresa peeled off her skirt and blouse, revealing her skinny legs, her underwear. Olive wanted to seize her, but she worried that darting forward and grabbing Teresa might now make things worse for her. Jorge seemed so pumped up, and even though Gregorio was less sure of himself, he could be equally dangerous.

From the truck, Gregorio fetched a smock-like dress that looked like it had been sewn in the sixteenth century, and a bottle, the contents of which Olive couldn't work out. He put the smock over Teresa's head, and helped her elbows and hands through the heavy sleeves. 'Take off your shoes, Teresa,' he said, like a parent to a child, and when Teresa obeyed him, it was absurdly painful.

Teresa's fingers fumbled over the knot in her shoelaces. Gregorio grew impatient and sliced them in two with his flick-knife. And it seemed to be this – more than the shaving, more than the stripping – that finally unleashed Teresa's rage. Her one pair of shoes, so neatly polished despite their age, were now unbound flaps of leather lying in the dust. She cried out and fell down.

'Get up!' Jorge screamed, but she didn't move. Jorge thrust the bottle at her. 'This is what we do to traitors,' he said.

'Who's the traitor?' Teresa replied, her voice a croak.

'Do you want me to pour it down your throat myself?'

Teresa stared up at him, still refusing. 'Gregorio,' Jorge said. 'You do it.'

Gregorio was upon her before Teresa could ready herself. He pinned back her arms and drove his knee into her lower back. Pallid and sweating, he grabbed her jaw and hinged it open. 'Drink it!' he screamed. The shock of Gregorio turning on her seemed to make Teresa numb with terror, and Jorge worked the neck of the bottle into her mouth with relative ease.

'Drink it,' Gregorio hissed. 'Drink the lot.'

Opening her eyes wide, Teresa turned her head so that Gregorio was forced to meet her gaze, and she kept them open as the contents were emptied down her throat. Some of the villagers ran away at this point, the spell of violence finally broken by this horror.

When the bottle was empty, the men let Teresa go. She gagged, strands of oil falling from the corners of her mouth, pooling into the dust.

'Who knew we lived next door to the Devil?' one man near Olive whispered.

'Go home now, Teresa,' Jorge said. 'And try not to shit yourself. If we haven't found him in the next few days, expect another visit.'

Teresa rose to her feet and stumbled, and Olive pushed past the men to take her by the arm. This time, they didn't stop her. Teresa sagged against Olive's side, and the two girls staggered out of the square, the remaining villagers parting to let through this gagging, bald creature, whose bowels might go at any minute, thanks to the dosage of an entire bottle of castor oil.

No one jeered her progress – not even half-heartedly, in the presence of Jorge and Gregorio. No one said a thing, slack-mouthed in horror. They watched the girls up the dusty path, out of the village towards the finca. They kept watching, until they couldn't see them any more.

Jorge and Gregorio stepped into the truck and revved away in the opposite direction. Gradually, the square fell empty except for the dark clumps of Teresa's hair, abandoned in the gravel.

XXI

*O*live bathed Teresa and burned the filthy smock. She dressed her in her own Aran jumper and a pair of blue silk trousers that Sarah donated. Perhaps the beauty of the blue silk was to distract Teresa, but all it did was make her look incongruous; the luxury compared to the woollen jumper and her bald head. By the time Harold came back late from Malaga, Teresa had been administered two of Sarah's sleeping pills, and she was upstairs in one of the first-floor bedrooms, fast asleep.

Before she could even tell him what had happened in the town square, Harold unburdened what he'd seen in the city. He was very shaken. The roads were terrible, he said. Since the two main bridges had been destroyed, isolating the centre, no one had done anything to fix them. He called it the perverse Buddhism of the Spaniards. Letting fate flow was all very well – but not at the expense of life. For how else could one explain not mending a bridge that might help feed citizens waiting in the city, let alone the troops?

He'd parked outside and walked in on foot, and when he'd finally made it to the centre, there wasn't much food to be had. No tins at all, no cheese – no cheese! – no cake. He'd managed to find a kilo of sugar and one of weak acorn coffee, a rationed amount of salted cod, some fresh sardines, a box of cigarettes and a feeble chorizo. He said the place was becoming unrecognizable – where once there were hanging baskets were now bombed buildings, the staring faces of the recent homeless, with nowhere to live and little to eat. Although the hotels were still standing – safe enough, for they were locked at night against marauding gangs – certain parts of the city were now nothing more than a smoking shell.

'The organization's hopeless,' he said. 'It's a fucking disaster,' he spat, and his wife and daughter flinched. What was bothering Harold so much – he, who was not from this place, who could leave any moment he wanted?

He told them that the ex-pats who were staying in the city were holed up in the Regina Hotel, but the vast majority of foreigners were leaving on the second wave of destroyers the British Consulate had sent news of. He saw them down at the dock, their passports in hand, travelling trunks scattered around like a game of dominoes. English, Americans, Argentines, Germans and Chileans, some wealthy-looking Spaniards. 'They're saying the red wave will strike them, but it's Mussolini's bombers overhead,' he said. 'The sea might be the only reliable way of sourcing food from now on. I don't see, with those bridges down, how it's all going to get in.'

'We're too far from the sea here for that to be of any comfort,' Sarah snapped, picking up the sardines and chorizo and disappearing with them into the pantry. 'Did you find the flag to purchase, like I asked?' she called.

'Don't you have a clue?' he shouted back. 'The air raids, the Italian warships bombing the port? You think I'll find a Union Jack in the middle of that?'

BUT DESPITE MALAGA'S TERRORS, OLIVE believed it was Teresa who really began to unnerve her parents. Her presence was like a dark mass in the first-floor bedroom, and an atmosphere of guilt pervaded the house. Sarah did not know what to do with her, puffing perfume around the girl, bringing all the *Vogues* and *Harper's* she might desire. On seeing these offerings, Teresa said nothing, fixing Sarah with a surly look. Sarah kept away after that, unwilling to be near such volatility. Harold lugged the gramophone up the stairs, but she played not one of his crackling jazz records.

By the third day in the finca, Teresa had contracted a fever. She lay in bed, muttering, *Bist du es? Bist du es?* over and over, as Olive dabbed her forehead and prayed a doctor might dare to come. Olive called for Sarah to help, but Sarah did not answer. Teresa's expression was fixed, her eyes clamped shut, face swollen with fatigue, her skin pale and clammy like a peeled egg.

There was no news of Isaac. Every night in the village, one of the bar owners would turn his wireless towards the hills, so that all those who might be hiding out there in the woods could keep up with the news. General Queipo de Llano, still broadcasting from Seville, told his listeners that he had fifty thousand Italian troops, three *banderas* of the Foreign Legion, and fifteen thousand North African tribesmen known as the Army of Africa, waiting to come in to Malaga. The report made Olive shiver, but she comforted herself with the idea that Isaac was somewhere near, listening too. She didn't want him to be in the north, she wanted him here.

Teresa's fever broke, and she lay on her back in silence for several more days. At night, listening to the whine of the distant bombers, Olive could hear Teresa moving up and down the corridors, a bare-footed catharsis of pacing – but what did she want? Was this a night-time vigil to call back her brother? Why, when he was the reason for her humiliation? Olive remembered Teresa's scream of rage in the town square, her look of impotence, her terror as Gregorio clutched her. She wondered if, after all this, Teresa really knew where Isaac was.

But Teresa was buried beneath the memory, by day curled up on the bed like a foetus, her face towards the wall. She called for no one. It was a trauma none of them knew how to handle. Olive would wake at dawn and stand in front of a blank canvas, unable to lift the brush. She could not escape the image of the chair in the village square, the smock stained with faeces, Teresa's head a dull white glow, her feet weaving up over the finca hallway. Fearing she might never paint a picture, nor see Isaac again, Olive was ashamed to realize that she couldn't tell which deprivation struck her deeper. *I have been useful to you*: Isaac's words resounded in her head.

As the days progressed, Olive waited for the crust of Teresa's silence to crack open. Silence like this was Harold's worst nightmare. He thought people should speak, voice their pain. He became all bluster, trying to force the issue of the prone girl lying up in one of his rooms. But Olive was sure it was coming; she could almost taste the power of Teresa's humiliation in the air, damming up the door of the spare bedroom, soon to break.

Harold said that as soon as Teresa was better and set up back in her cottage, they were going over the border into Gibraltar. As for Isaac, he had made his bed and was going to have to lie in it. Trying to sleep in her own bed in the attic, Olive could barely picture a proper pavement, a cultivated park, the slate roofs of Curzon Street and Berkeley Square wet with rain. To get to London meant leaping a metaphysical boundary as much as a country's border, and she didn't know if she could, if she even wanted to at all. London might be a different sort of suffocation. If she was truly honest with herself, Olive could admit that there was something life-affirming about living here, so close to the possibility of real death.

She began to feel responsible for Isaac's disappearance. He had been so angry when he departed through the orchard that night on the veranda, calling *good luck* before he left. How long ago it seemed now, arriving here under the thin January sun, Isaac laying his hands on that chicken. Olive remembered the provocation she felt in her own body as he broke its neck. He'd given her so much. Had she satisfied him in return? No, she did not think so. When she tried to summon the memory of his hands on her, she found that she could not.

'Do you think Isaac got away?' Sarah asked her one evening, when it was just her and Olive sitting in the front east room. Harold was in his study, Teresa still upstairs.

Olive rubbed her arms. The firewood was dwindling and they were rationing supplies. 'I don't know.'

'I'm sure he did,' Sarah said. 'I'm sure he caught a train.' Olive noted how well her mother looked, despite the meagre rations, and Teresa's trauma that was threatening to engulf them. It was as if the stressed situation had finally given Sarah a sense of purpose.

'Do you want to leave, Liv?' Sarah asked.

Olive pulled at a thread on the tatty sofa. Isaac had been right after all. They had come here and they would go again. 'No,' she said. 'This is home.'

Later that night, Olive heard a knock on her door. 'Who is it?'

Teresa shuffled forward, hovering on the threshold. She was thinner than ever, and her hair had grown a little bit, but mostly Olive was relieved to see the determined look in Teresa's eyes.

'Do you know what your father is saying?' Teresa asked.

Olive lay back on the bed. 'He says many things.'

'He talks about the fatalism of the Spaniards.'

'Ignore him.'

'What he says is not fair.'

'I know it isn't.'

'Does he think we are not trying to fight?'

'He doesn't think that. It's easy when you're an outsider to say these things.'

'It is not safe.'

'I know, Tere.'

'You should go.'

'I'm not leaving you.'

'You are not staying for me, señorita. I know why you are still here.' The girls looked at each other. 'He isn't coming back,' Teresa said.

Olive sat up in the bed. 'He might.'

Teresa laughed. It was a cracked, bitter sound. 'You of all people should open your eyes.'

'I should say they're pretty bloody open, thank you very much. More than most of the English back home.'

Teresa walked slowly into the room, running her hand over the top of *Rufina and the Lion*. 'My brother has done damage,' she said.

'To the village?'

'To this house.'

'What do you mean?'

'I would like to thank you,' Teresa said. 'For taking me away from Jorge and Gregorio.'

'I wouldn't have done anything else.'

'I have tried to fight.'

'I know.'

'But it is hard. It is like fighting yourself. And there are times I don't see why we should have to. Why should we have to fight?'

'I don't know the answer to that, Tere.'

'If you go, Olive – could I go too?'

Olive hesitated. Her father had no plans to take Teresa with them. 'Do you have papers?'

Teresa made an unconscious gesture with her hand, patting her head where the scabs were beginning to heal. 'No.'

There was a silence. 'Let me neaten that situation,' said Olive.

'What does it mean – "*neaten*"?'

Olive got off the bed and came towards her, putting her hands on the other girl's arms. 'You need a new notebook of words. Here, I won't hurt you. I'll be gentle.'

Placing Teresa on the edge of the bed, she used a razor taken from her father's dressing table, and slowly shaved away the remaining patches of hair on Teresa's head. She rubbed calamine over the cuts as Teresa sat motionless, looking out towards the window, listening to the far-off crumps of the guns in Malaga.

'This is my brother's fault,' Teresa said dully.

Olive held the razor above Teresa's head. 'Well, we've all been foolish. You could blame it on your father. And he'd blame it on the government. And they'd blame it on the last government. I don't think Isaac meant for this to happen to you.'

'Isaac thinks about the land, but forgets his doorstep,' Teresa said.

'Isaac is a good man.'

'You think so?'

'He has a conscience.'

Teresa laughed.

'You know where your brother is, don't you? I promise I won't tell anyone. I just need to know.'

Teresa turned again to the window, her shoulders sagging. 'It is better that you do not know.'

She heard a *snip*. Horrified, she turned to Olive and saw that the other girl had removed an enormous chunk of her own hair. 'What are you doing?' Teresa said, as Olive cut away another handful.

'You think I've just been playing a game down here, don't you?' Olive said.

'Stop with your hair. Stop it.'

Teresa went to grab for the razor, but Olive pointed it in her direction, as warning to keep back. She began to hack and hack at herself, tufts of her thick hazel-coloured hair floating to the floor. Teresa watched her, mesmerised. 'Now you shave my head,' Olive said.

'You are crazy.'

'No, I'm not. What do I have to do to make people take me seriously?'

'Having the same hair as me does not give you the same grief as me.'

'Teresa, just do it.'

As she delicately scraped away every last hair on Olive's head, Teresa tried to hide her tears. She could not remember the last time she had cried in front of someone. She thought about that first painting of Olive's she had swapped onto the easel, Saint Justa becoming a woman in a wheatfield. Isaac had been convinced she'd done it because of the kiss she'd witnessed against the rusty gate, that Teresa was punishing him out of jealousy, taking away his opportunity to shine. Teresa had to admit, seeing what happened between them had hurt her at the time, making her feel left out and ignored, although she couldn't exactly articulate why. But she also knew her impulse had always been something more deep-rooted, not really connected to Isaac. It was something else Teresa couldn't quite understand herself. The nearest way to describe it was as a bond she had made for herself, and Olive being rightfully rewarded.

'Tere, I'm going to ask you again. Do you know where he is?' Olive said.

Teresa almost felt the pressure of the question in her body. 'Forget Isaac,' she said. 'He does not love you in the way he should.'

'Oh, Teresa. What do you know about love?'

Teresa's brief time in the house with the Schlosses had taught her more about love and its problems than Olive could ever imagine. But she had also known, long before the arrival of the Schloss family and their overflowing hearts, that whilst everything has a consequence, nothing can simply be put down to fate. Teresa had always made her choice – to see, and stay silent. All her life before Olive, she had kept her own counsel.

But Olive, and her paintings, and her parents, had changed that stance. They had opened Teresa up, made her vulnerable to the worlds of other people. And once again, Olive was forcing her hand. Perhaps there was no good to be had in staying silent any longer. Perhaps it was time for Olive to truly see, and to free herself for ever.

'A shepherd's hut,' Teresa said.

'What?'

'Go and look for a shepherd's hut. You will find him there.'

Olive looked at her in astonishment. 'I don't believe you.'

'You'll find him. Ask my brother what it means to be in love.'

TERESA WATCHED HER DEPART, AND began to sweep away the other girl's severed hair with a mix of dread and elation. She wasn't sure exactly what Olive would find, but she had a fair idea. She noted the back of Olive's newly bared head with something bordering pride. When the reckoning came – and it was certainly going to come now – Teresa knew that they would question her character. At least they would see that she had not left a mark on her mistress. It was not possible to mend Olive's heart, but at least the girl's head was finally clear.

XXII

*T*he plane engines over Malaga had grown quieter as Olive pounded down the hill from the finca, in the direction of the cottage. No one seemed to notice as she tiptoed out of the house. It did not occur to her there might have been no one left in the house to hear.

At dusk Arazuelo was a ghost village. The main square was empty, the shutters of the bar on the corner were up; the church was its blackened shell; the butcher was closed; the school and the offices around it blanked of life. Olive patted her pockets, feeling in one the torch she'd grabbed from the kitchen, and in the other, the cold bulk of the pistol Isaac had left with them.

She could barely allow the hope that he might still be near. Teresa, it appeared, was a locked box of secrets, until you found the right combination. Whilst everything outside her seemed quiet, Olive's thoughts cascaded with a force she found hard to control. If she could find him and bring him back, everything would be all right. Panting, she tried to regain her breath as she scanned the woods beyond, the line of the trees inkier and inkier as the last natural light disappeared into a smoky sky.

INTO THE GROWING DARKNESS OLIVE ran, switching on the torch. *Don't use a torch*, Teresa had told her. *You don't know who else is out there.*

I'm not afraid, Olive had replied – but now, out in the hills, she couldn't see a thing without it, and her adrenalin was coursing. She barely knew where she was going, but she supposed it couldn't be far. Towards the foothills, she would find him; she would, she would. *You think he's gone north?* Teresa had said. *He hasn't gone north.*

If you hate him so much, why didn't you tell the civil guard all this? Olive had asked; but she knew the answer to that already. Teresa had revealed nothing about Isaac – not to protect her brother, but to keep Olive near.

I'll be waiting, Teresa had called out, as Olive fled the attic. No one had ever said such a thing to Olive before.

THE FIRST THING SHE SAW was the sardine tin, glinting in the grass. It had clearly blown from inside the hut, and now rested several metres from where Olive stood. She switched off the torch and watched the shepherd's hut. A faint light was showing between a hewn-out window hole and a piece of flapping oilskin. Olive crept nearer. She could hear a voice, a low murmur – Isaac's voice. Teresa had not been lying to her. Her heart rose with joy to know he was here, and she ran forward.

Then she heard a woman's laugh. She recognized it. She thought she was going to choke. Her throat tightened, her tongue felt too big at the back of her mouth.

A noise, a deep sigh, another and another from inside the shepherd's hut, and finally Olive understood what Teresa had meant, what she had squirmed to say, resisting the outright truth, sending her here so she could see it for herself. She understood it, even as she couldn't bear to. And there it came again – regular, deep, and unbearable; an expression of pure pleasure. As the universe above Olive's head deepened in its darkness, she fixed her fingers on the pistol and pushed open the door.

XXIII

Sarah screamed, pushing back against the wall. *'No dispares!'* shouted Isaac. *Don't shoot!*

Olive lifted the lantern that was on the floor. Isaac and her mother were both naked, their limbs still intertwined. Sarah twisted her body away in panic, and Olive saw the dome of her stomach clearly risen with a child.

'Olive,' said her mother, dumb with shock. 'What's happened to your hair?'

They stared at each other. Seconds passed that felt like hours. 'Does Daddy know?' Olive eventually said, her voice a husk, the sound robotic. 'Does Daddy know?'

Sarah scrambled to sit up, clutching Isaac's coat to her chest, reaching for her trousers. 'Liv. Livvi. Put the gun down.'

Olive kept the barrel up in the direction of her mother. 'Does he know?'

'He doesn't know,' said Sarah, gasping. 'Put that down, for Christ's sake.'

'Is it yours?' Olive asked Isaac. 'Is the baby yours?'

'It's not his,' Sarah interrupted. 'It's not.'

Isaac got to his feet. 'Olive,' he said gently. 'Put the gun down. No one needs to be hurt.'

Olive felt a roaring in her ears. 'Why?' she said. 'Why?' Her question soared into the night.

'Ssssh!' Isaac hissed. 'Keep quiet.'

'You hypocrite. All that talk about going north, fighting for your country, and you're less than a mile away, with her—' Olive put her hand on her mouth, fighting back a sob.

'Livvi,' said Sarah.

'Don't you *Livvi* me. Don't fool yourself it could ever be love with her, Isaac. Is it yours? Is that baby yours?'

The look that passed between Sarah and Isaac was almost worse to Olive than discovering them. The intimacy of it, the fluency; complicity.

'How long have you – when did it start? What was wrong with me? Why couldn't I—'

Isaac began to come towards her. 'Calm down, Olive. Please. I can explain—'

As he approached, Olive fired a shot through the thatch of the roof. '*Mierda!*' he shouted. 'Shit! Do you want to get us killed? Now every gang out there will know that someone is here.'

Sarah let out a low moan and began scrabbling around in the dark for the rest of her clothes. 'I have to go. I have to go,' she kept repeating. 'He'll be back.'

'You snake,' said Olive.

Sarah looked up at her. 'I'm no snake.'

'I'd say you are. I never want to speak to you again.'

'How did you know I was here?' asked Isaac.

'How else do you think?'

Sarah groaned. Olive closed her eyes to blot out the scene before her.

'How long has Teresa known about this?' whispered Sarah.

'I don't know,' said Olive, and it was the truth. Had Teresa's silence until now been out of protection, or something else – the power of knowing what Olive did not? Had they all been laughing at her, so in love with her Boris Mon-Amour? Better to have kept Isaac a figure in a book, a man in her imagination, than the monster she had created in real life. She could hear one of the last things Teresa had said to her, up in the attic: *Ask my brother what it means to be in love.*

'Olive,' said Sarah, more in control now that she was fully dressed. 'I know it's not always been easy—'

'Oh, God. No, I don't want to hear it.'

'I never meant to hurt you.'

'And yet you always do.'

Sarah got to her feet and faced her daughter. 'Do you think you're the only one who's lonely? The only one who suffers?'

'I don't care about your loneliness. You're married. To my father.'

'And do you think it's easy, being married to him?'

'Shut up. *Shut up.*'

Isaac was in the corner, hastily putting on his clothes, his face darting between the women with an expression of misery.

'Isaac isn't yours, Olive, no more than he's mine,' Sarah said.

'He is mine – we've – what are you going to tell Daddy? He won't take you back.'

Sarah laughed. 'I never knew you were so old-fashioned.'

'Old-fashioned?'

'You know his paintings don't pay for all this, Liv. The finca, our travel, our lives. It's not a question of "taking me back". One day, Olive, you'll understand what a mess everyone makes of their life. I don't know a single couple who hasn't had their problems. Marriage is *long*, you know—'

'Stop. I don't care. When did you first seduce Isaac?'

'Darling, it was the other way round. In fact, not long after Daddy bought Isaac's first painting.'

'Just get out,' said Olive.

SARAH STARTED TO WALK OUT of the hut with all the insouciance of leaving a Mayfair restaurant, but she faltered at the dark. 'I can't see anything,' she said.

'I'm sure you know the way by now. Watch out for wolves.'

'I'll go with you,' said Isaac.

'You're not going anywhere,' said Olive, lifting the pistol in his direction.

'Olive, you're being so bloody foolish,' said Sarah.

'Just *go*.'

'I'll see you soon,' Sarah said to Isaac. 'Olive, come back when you've calmed down.'

Isaac and Olive watched as she disappeared into the night. 'You shouldn't have let her go alone like that,' Isaac said.

'I wouldn't have shot her, you know. Or you.' Olive lowered the gun and switched on the torch. In the bright white light, he looked wary. 'For God's sake, Isaac. Have you any idea what happened to your sister?'

'What happened?'

'No, I don't suppose my mother bothered to tell you. How Teresa paid the price for your heroics.'

'Do not hide things, Olive. I do not like it.'

'That's rich, coming from you.'

'What have they done to her?'

The panic on his face was genuine, so she relented, telling him about Jorge and Gregorio, the hacking of Teresa's hair, the castor oil, the midnight wanderings through the finca corridors.

His face crumpled in pain. 'But why have you no hair?' he asked.

'To make her feel better. Less alone.'

Isaac looked beyond the torch's orbit, out into the darkness. 'So she told you I was here.'

'Yes.'

'Did she tell you about the child?'

'No. Just that you'd be here.'

'Did she mention Sarah?'

'No. I asked her what she knew about love, that's all.'

They were silent for a moment.

'She is the cause of so much trouble,' he said.

'Yes. But at least now I see you for what you are. I suppose that was her intention.'

'Do you truly think my sister has always had your best interests at heart?' Isaac said. 'She is a cat, always landing on her feet.'

'You overestimate her power. You haven't seen her. And anyway, she hasn't hurt me. You have.'

'Perhaps that's true. And I am sorry for it. But you just see an idea of me that suits you. You never stop trying to create me. Your mother – how do you say? Clear-sighted. She sees me as I am. She does not want me to change.'

'Yet. But probably she doesn't have the imagination. And she's ill.'

'Is boredom an illness? She is not ill. It just suits you to say she is. Even her'

'You took advantage.'

'I did? Olive, I never promised you anything. I never told you I loved you. You heard and saw what you wanted.'

'You slept with me, Isaac. Several times.'

'Yes. And I said yes to the paintings too. We all make mistakes.'

'What are you trying to say? The more I painted, the less you liked me?'

He looked away. 'I'm trying to say that your mother – it is a different thing. It is a separate thing.'

'It isn't separate, Isaac. Her behaviour affects us all, just as my father's does – and as mine does, I suppose. Did you stay here for her?'

He hesitated. Olive closed her eyes, as if in pain. 'You think you're the first,' she said. 'She only slept with you to punish me.'

He laughed, putting his hands up to his head. 'You really are an artist, aren't you? You think it's all about you, and you never stop looking for pain. It isn't about you, Olive. You have nothing to do with this.'

'I'm going. Good luck, isn't that what you said?'

Olive turned to the darkness, in the direction her mother had descended.

'What will you do?' he asked.

'I'll go back to England. You were right. I'll find somewhere to live. Leave my parents to it. See if the art school will take me.'

'That is a good plan.'

'We'll see. Here.' Olive handed the pistol to Isaac. 'You might need this more than me.'

'And Tere?' he asked, tucking it into the back of his belt. 'Will you take her with you?'

Olive sighed. 'I don't know, Isaac. She doesn't have any papers.'

'She has had a hard time.'

'A minute ago you were saying how much trouble she was.'

'She is only sixteen.'

Olive couldn't hide her surprise. 'She said she was eighteen.'

'Well, there you are. But if Jorge decides – if my father—'

'You don't need to tell me. I was there when it happened. When you were up here.'

He put out his hand. Olive looked down at it. 'You know,' she said, 'I'm glad I painted you with a green face.'

SHE HAD MEANT IT AS a joke; she had not really meant that he was naive, or sick. It was just an assertion that she was the artist, that she would paint him in the colours that she saw fit. She wanted Isaac to see that she was grown up enough to deal with this, even though she did not feel it. He would always be the man who had changed her life. But as she had gone to take his hand and hold it, and tell him this, Isaac crumpled at her feet.

It seemed unreal to her at first, as she stared down in horror, her torch darting over the blood that was gushing out of Isaac's head, the red cascading into his eyes. And then she heard what she'd missed the first time; the muted pop of a gun firing in their direction. Two more shots ricocheted around the hills, their reports cracking the air, thinning to nothingness above the woods. She started to run.

Jorge, who had heard Olive's pistol being fired half an hour earlier, had come up to the hills to see if he could find its source, and had been watching them from a distance. He couldn't believe his luck; Isaac Robles in hiding, and his bald sister, handing him over another firearm. And the stupid girl had kept her torch on, so after shooting Isaac, he could follow her easily enough, the torchlight juddering all over the place as she stumbled down the hill.

Jorge fired three more times, watching as the torch tumbled, coming to rest like a small white moon upon the ground. He waited. Nothing moved. So close was the quality of silence that followed, so sickening that mute after-note of execution, that it seemed as if the fields were turning in on themselves, and the earth was giving way.

PART V

Rufina and the Lion

NOVEMBER 1967

18

The lifts at Goodge Street station were broken, and when I finally caught a Tube in the direction of Waterloo, it kept stopping in tunnels. In total, it took me an hour and a half to reach Quick's house after leaving the phone box outside the Slade. The front lights of her house, both upstairs and down, were blazing. She had not drawn the curtains, and I could see in the top room a white, cracked ceiling with a naked bulb, which seemed at odds with her usual cultivated aesthetic. A sharp pool of light haloed across the cornicing, a decayed grandeur to the fissures she had not sought to fill in.

Feeling deeply uneasy, I knocked on the front door and waited, and there was no answer. 'Hello?' I called through the letterbox, but the house remained silent. I deliberated – I could stop this, go home back to Clapham and my equally silent flat. But guilt kept me there; and curiosity, a need to see this through.

It was very dark as I slipped along the side fence, the last of the fallen autumn leaves crisping under my shoes. Even the lights through the side windows shone out – an electric conflagration, every light bulb burning, giving me the distinct feeling of being exposed. It was like a film set – a giant rig of dazzling sodium illumination – a wattage to attract and drown.

When I reached the garden and looked into its darkness, my

eyes could not cope with the loss of light. Every time I blinked, orange orbs slunk across my sight, fading to smaller planets which danced around the outlines of the trees. The clock tower struck eight. I was in a fable again.

What I saw when I turned back to the house, I shall never forget. Quick was sitting in the kitchen, upright on a chair. The curtains here were also drawn back, the whole place lit up. I thought I might cry out in shock. Quick had no hair. There was nothing on her head but a few dull tufts, a patched map with no coordinates. She was looking at me, and I raised my hand in greeting, but she did not react, and then I realized with horror that she was not looking at me at all – but at someone – or something – beyond me, waiting in the garden.

I heard a twig snap and my throat closed in fear as I turned to face the darkness she'd lured me to, ready to fight, ready to yell. I was sure there was a presence beyond the shrubbery, concealed behind the hanging branches of the wilderness, but nothing showed.

I whirled back to the house, ran to the kitchen door and forced my way in, desperate to get away from whatever was waiting in the garden. I was in front of her now. She was still upright, still in the chair. There was a macabre perfection to her pale skull, a look of beatitude and finality on her serene face. Her wig lay on the floor like the pelt of an animal. I had no idea she'd ever worn one.

'Quick?' I said, the horror churning in my throat.

But of course Quick did not reply, because Quick was dead.

I called the police before thinking about how this looked – the house locked, but me inside it, the kitchen door still open, my foot marks in the grass. It wasn't until the post-mortem revealed the estimated time of Quick's death, and that her bloodstream contained ten times the amount of painkillers she had been prescribed, and the coroner learned of her cancer, that the suspicion was removed from my head and it was declared an accidental death. It made me so angry, I can't tell you. That I, the only person she had come to trust, might ever be suspected of breaking into her house and killing her. I was the only one who'd ever been willing to find out Quick's true story.

AFTER CALLING THE POLICE I came back to the kitchen, and knelt down beside her, touching her body. It was still warm. Perhaps I had missed her by a matter of minutes. She had not strictly invited me that night; it was me determined that she should not be alone. But had she wanted this end? I told her I was coming over – she would know I would be the first to find her. Maybe she had wanted to be saved. I'll never know.

I looked around. The bottle of pills was in front of her, and half a bottle of gin. This didn't necessarily mean anything; she loved drinking, and she had been in pain. I could not countenance that what she'd done was deliberate.

'Police,' said a voice. I jumped, and went to the front door.

THERE WERE TWO POLICEMEN, AND they'd also brought an ambulance. I was in shock – their energy was so different as they came into the house; officious yet weary, seen-it-all-before. I was jumpy, new-born with the fear and shock. 'Who's her next of kin?' asked one of them, and I said I didn't know, but Edmund Reede was her boss – and perhaps they should call him.

Reede was still at work, the exhibition due to open the next day, and he was working to the nail. I couldn't hear his response as the policeman stood in Quick's hall, telling him what had been discovered. The call was brief. I sat in the front room, and a policeman came and placed himself opposite me. The clock ticked. He eyed me, and then I realized what he might be thinking, and I envisaged my incarceration, the Carib murderess – the outrage it might cause, the inevitability of it, of people like me.

Reede seemed to appear within minutes. He'd hared down over Waterloo Bridge in his car, and burst through the front door, *What the hell's happened, where the hell is she, what the* . . . and the words died on his mouth as he watched the paramedics carrying Quick out. She looked so tiny and frail, and I saw the shock on Reede's face, a pain that for once he had no means to control.

It was actually thanks to Reede that the police didn't arrest me there and then. They were intimidated by him. He gathered himself quickly, exuding power and authority, and their uniforms meant as little to him as they meant everything to me. He became angry when he got the whiff of their questions and attitude, and he told them that if they wanted to accuse me of anything, they could bloody well go through him. 'She was with me in the office until an hour ago,' I remember him saying.

I have to admit, I was surprised. I never thought the day would come when I would feel in debt to Edmund Reede, and I didn't really like it, because I didn't know what I would be able to give in return. We left the house together; him giving me a lift back to my flat in Clapham.

'How did she sound when you called her?' he asked, as we zoomed along Clapham Common.

'Weak.' I went to say something more, but I stopped.

He looked at me. 'What is it?'

'She was ill, Mr Reede.'

'Ill?'

'Very ill. I don't think she – had long left.'

He looked back to the road. 'Jesus Christ. She always was too good at keeping secrets. And so are you, apparently. No wonder she liked you.'

We sat in silence. I felt completely drained. I couldn't believe she'd gone, with so many of my questions left to answer.

'Mr Reede – did you know her long?' I asked eventually.

'Since she was practically a girl.'

'I'm sorry.'

I wondered what he was thinking – was he hurt that Quick hadn't told him how ill she was, or was he simply in shock and sadness that she was dead?

'I'd like you and Miss Rudge to organize the funeral,' he said.

'Of course. Does she have any family I should tell?' I asked.

'None that I know of. But you'll have a bit of time. The police won't release her body yet.'

'Why won't they? What do they think I've done?'

'Don't worry, Miss Bastien. It will all be fine.'

But I didn't see how it would be. 'Will the exhibition still go ahead?' I asked.

'Don't see we have much choice. And it's what she would have wanted.'

But half the problem, I thought, kicking off my shoes and sinking on to my bed still in my clothes, as Reede's car revved off up the road, was that none of us had ever really known what Marjorie Quick had wanted.

19

*T*he next evening, the exhibition opened, with Quick's body still lying cold in the police morgue. I couldn't marry these two facts easily; she, dead and alone, and here, so much noise and colour, milling bodies, excitement brewing at the discovery of the new Isaac Robles.

Julie Christie walked past me, her face too good to be true. The gallery was full. I recognized her, but who were these other people? Actors, critics, lords and bankers, gold buttons forged not from battles, but casts of power. Wine being drunk like it came from their own cellars. Jagger wasn't there, much to Pamela's chagrin. Rotund cabinet ministers talked to haggard-looking old men of art as some optimist put on a blues record, the trumpet's scattered notes whirling towards the ceiling. At the unleashed sound, two men in blazers swapped glances of disdain. Where were their deft van Dycks, their easy Gainsboroughs, their plump majestic Stubbesian horses? All they had here were modernist streaks of colour, women, holding heads, women, curled amidst their shattered pots, a poised lion, third wheel in a tragic game of Renaissance saints.

A snare drum snuck into the blues, a syncopation that only just nipped my bud of bitterness. I felt utterly disorientated without Quick. She should have been there; she was going to tell me the truth. At the end of the room, the photograph of Isaac Robles and

Olive Schloss loomed, black and white and granular, the girl's face locked in what I now felt was a misplaced expression of hope. It was almost an insult that the photograph was up there. I wanted the blues to be louder, for a pair of these wine-flushed stuffed shirts to break into a jive, whirling one old tanty round till she false teeth fly.

With an inward sigh, I moved on, my wine glass a weapon. Shuffling past the growing crowd, I neared *Rufina and the Lion*, protected now by a scarlet rope, two guards flanking its sides. Reede clearly knew the special touches to make things seem official.

I noticed a thin, grey-haired man in a suit, leaning over the rope to peer at one of the painting's corners. He was very close, his nose inches from the minuscule crests of paint on the girl's severed head. He was incredibly curious; he couldn't stop looking. The left guard's feet shifted, sensible shoes of menace. I felt a surging anxiety that something bad was going to happen; but then again, the worst already had.

'It's ghoulish, Frederick,' said a woman, coming to join the man. 'It's painful.'

Behind me, the noise in the gallery lifted. As the temperature rose and the crowd grew, guests began looking through each other like open doors. A woman laughed above the swell, and it sounded like a cry for help. Why were these people here? They didn't care about Isaac Robles. They didn't care about Quick.

I felt a tug at my elbow; Pamela. 'You all right?' she said. 'Look like you've seen a ghost.'

'I think I have.'

Pamela frowned. I hadn't told her about Quick; Reede had said he wanted a lid on it until the exhibition was on its feet.

'You read too much, Dell,' Pamela said. 'Ain't no such thing as ghosts. Listen.' She looked pained. 'I broke up with Billy.'

'Oh, Pamela. I'm sorry.'

A cloud passed across her face. 'Turned out he didn't want to marry me. I gave notice on my room and everything, and then the bugger broke it off. And another girl's moving in.'

I wondered if she meant on Billy, or into her old room. I didn't ask. Instead, I said the words I never thought I'd say. 'Would you like to share with me?'

Her face opened into a smile. 'That'd be good. That'd be really good.'

'I'd like it too.'

Pamela went pink, giving me a hug before she turned away and melted into the crowd.

I FOUND LAWRIE, AND STOOD close beside him. 'My mother would never believe all this,' he said, drawing his arm in an arc across the gallery. 'She'd love it though. What a snowball. It's just got bigger and bigger.'

'Lawrie,' I whispered. 'I have to tell you. Quick's – she's dead.'

He turned to me. 'What?'

'I found her. Last night.'

'Oh, Delly. I'm so sorry. Are you all right?'

'Not really.'

'What happened?'

'I'll tell you later,' I said – for how to explain, at the launch of his exhibition, that I didn't think the paintings around this room were by Isaac Robles at all, that the real painter behind these works had died with her secret intact? Cynth had warned me to keep all my ideas about Olive Schloss and Marjorie Quick to myself, if I wanted harmony in my love life. But if this entire exhibition was predicated on a lie, that sat uneasily with my sense of creative integrity. I was struggling to work out which was more important – Lawrie's feelings, or Quick's artistic restitution. If it was me who'd painted these pictures, I'd bloody well want everyone to know.

Lawrie took my hand. 'I know she meant a lot to you.'

I hadn't thought of mine and Quick's connection in that way before – in terms of affection, or quality. Nor did I think I'd ever communicated such a sentiment. Until now, I'd treated Quick as an interesting conundrum, a diversion, both a source of inspiration and an obstacle. But Lawrie was right. She did mean a lot to me. Despite her mercurial manner, Quick had welcomed me, helped me. I liked her. And it was too late to tell her so. There was still, at the back of my mind, some niggling thought that she had wanted me for something, but that now it was too late.

'Dell, do you want to leave?'

'No, of course not. I'll be fine.'

'All right. Listen, Gerry wants you to come over for dinner. He's here, you know.'

'Really? That's good he's out and about.'

'Yes it is, I suppose. You don't have to come if you don't want to. But he's always asking after you. When he read your story in the *London Review*, he boasted to his friends he knew a writer. I think you've got a fan.'

'I'm not a writer.'

'Of course, I forgot. You're a typist.' The exasperation in his voice made me turn. 'Well really, Odelle,' he said. 'Are you going to keep on like this? Do you know how many people would give their eye-teeth to be in the *London Review*? I wouldn't waste it.'

'I'm not going to waste it,' I said. I was tired, unable to keep the hurt out of my voice. 'And it's not up to you to tell me what I should or shouldn't call myself.'

He up put his hands in surrender. 'All right. I just – you must keep writing, you know.'

I rolled my eyes. 'You sound like Cynthia. You sound like Quick. Everyone wants me to write, but they never try it themselves. If they tried it themselves they might shut up.'

He shrugged. 'Quick did you an enormous favour. And I bet if she knew you were dragging your heels—'

The last few hours finally caught up with me. 'I'm *not* dragging – don't use her – she *dead*, Lawrie. She dead. I don't – I can't – we don't all have paintings we can sell, you know. I have to do other work.'

'You're right. Of course. But sometimes I do think you need reminding how good you are.'

We stood in silence for a few minutes. I knew it was true that I had stalled again on my writing. For once, I was too caught up with actually living my life to stop and turn it into words. People like Lawrie – who never wrote a single line of prose, as far as I knew – seemed to want those who *did* to walk around with a pad and pencil hanging round their neck, jotting down the whole thing, turning it into a book for their own pleasure.

As if he knew he'd trod on tender ground, Lawrie changed the subject. 'It looks like there's a couple of people interested in buying *Rufina*,' he said.

'That's good.' I saw his rueful grin. 'Isn't it?'

'Grass greener for Rufina. Told you I was a poet. Thing is, now there's a chance I'm not going to have it any more, I'm rather reluctant.'

'Well, it's not any old painting.'

Lawrie looked across the gallery, where the colours of *Rufina and the Lion* glowed, the people crossing back and forth, intermittently obscuring our view. 'It certainly isn't. But what am I going to do with it, Dell? I don't have any money and it isn't going to feed me.'

As we looked at the painting, vanishing and reappearing again and again behind people's heads, I knew that Lawrie and I were looking at different things. In its uniqueness, I read multiple stories. Through its technical brush-strokes, I experienced metaphysical sensations. It was a one-off I should do my utmost to protect and keep in public view. I could guess at the impulses behind the artist's decisions, I could meditate on how the painting made me feel, but I understood that I would never know its truth.

But Lawrie saw something else. The new frame Reede had commissioned was a window, and the painting within was a curtain he was pushing aside. He claimed he was reluctant to sell it, but he hadn't seen the cheque yet. He didn't really want to keep hold of *Rufina* – although it was his mother's, he seemed unbound by the memories it clearly had evoked for her. And why else had he come to the Skelton in the first place? He said it was to find me, but maybe I was a bonus. For him, the painting was a thing for sale, a transitional object that would take him places. He saw in it opportunity, a chance to start again.

Reede tapped his wine glass and began to address the crowd. He stood in front of *Rufina and the Lion*, starting by taking us through the skeleton story of Isaac Robles; his importance in the early journey of art in the twentieth century, his gift cut short. He thanked the Guggenheim foundation in Venice, and built on the particular mystery of the discovery, pointing out Lawrie in the crowd, who blushed and raised his glass to appreciative applause at his good fortune for having such a painting concealed in his house, and his generosity in deciding to show it.

When Reede spoke of how Robles' work was a meditation on adversity, the people in the Skelton gallery probably thought he was talking about war and dictatorship, and the struggles many of them were old enough to have lived through and remember on a visceral level. But I just thought what Quick had said about it: *It's the subject that overwhelms. As if there's an extra layer to the painting we're not privy to, that you just can't get at.*

Rufina and the Lion moved me that night in a transcendental way; it was the conduit through which I channelled my sense of loss, of accepting I might never know the truth, but that that was the secret of art. And perhaps I wasn't alone. Because after Reede had finished speaking, I noticed how people – even the old buffers in club blazers – began to look at *Rufina* with a little more respect.

The reviews for the opening night of 'The Swallowed Century' were mixed. Some were veritably lukewarm. *'The painting is a tableau that summons death, and it is wrong to ignore it,'* was as praising as the journalist in the *Telegraph* went the next morning, before going on to speculate how much money it might fetch – *'Edmund Reede confirmed at the end of the night that* Rufina and the Lion *was going to auction.'* In *The Times*, there was an article on the star-studded event, with very little information on the artist himself. I smiled; Quick would have seen the irony in that. And when the journalist referred to the *'express symbolism'* in the paintings,

I disagreed. He was dismissing the painting as obvious, but I think there was another language in those paintings, and the only person who knew how to speak it was gone.

The *Daily Mail* asked whether the whole thing was an elaborate practical joke, that Isaac Robles should have been left where he was found, and that if this was the state of modern art, what fresh hells would we be forced to look at in the 1970s. The *Observer*, however, went in the opposite direction, congratulating Reede on refusing to rest on his laurels when it came to '*art history revisionism, forgotten painters and colour.*' It made me laugh, to think all these men had been looking at the same painting.

I felt Quick's absence through the corridors, knowing that never again would the lunch summons come, never again would the restaurant next door send up a cold bottle of their best Sancerre. Reede was not in; I wondered if he'd seen the papers, and how we would deal with it. Pamela, who'd been informed about Quick, had been sniffling in the loos, and even the empty rooms felt as if they were in mourning. I wondered whether, had Quick been there, the reviews might have taken a more praising timbre; Quick cajoling the critics, forcing them to put their egos aside and see what was in front of their noses.

And yet, if anything, the *Mail*'s diatribe helped us. There were queues forming to come in and see *Rufina*, to see if it was really a joke. But for me, it only made things worse. Why hadn't Quick spoken up? Why was she so determined to keep her life a secret?

I began to meditate on what Lawrie had said about Quick doing me an enormous favour when she sent 'The Toeless Woman' to the *London Review*, and that I shouldn't waste it. My green notebook had lain untouched for several weeks; but I just didn't know what I wanted to write about. I don't think Quick ever wanted me to feel in her debt; she had facilitated something, and was happy to do so. Nevertheless, I began to think about how I might thank her for what she'd done, in a way I hadn't managed when she was alive. The funeral was scheduled for the following week, and I decided I would use the intervening time to write her eulogy. After all, Reede had left it to me and Pamela to organize, and no one else had volunteered.

The first post came late that day; Pamela was outside dragging dolefully on a cigarette and I was covering reception. It seemed strange to me to receive post at the Skelton, but there it was; an envelope with my name on it.

If the first letter Quick had sent me was a touchstone of transformation, then this was in another realm. Although I have received many extraordinary letters since that time, the one sent to me at the Skelton still beats them all.

A law firm called Parr & Co., whose offices were in Bread Lane in the City of London, were requesting my presence on Thursday – and would I please bring my passport and some proof of address? I recall how terrified I was. If you are made to feel, repeatedly, that you do not belong in a country, despite previous assurances to the contrary, then a letter telling you to bring your identity papers will freeze your blood.

I tried to imagine how Quick would deal with this. I felt lost without her assurance, the shelter of her steel wing. If I'd called Lawrie and told him, he wouldn't understand, because he belonged. He was wrapped in a web of invisible yet unbreakable tissue, layer upon layer of it, that had begun to spin for him before he was even born, binding him in safety, giving him such a sense of security that no letter from a City lawyer would ever have scared him. His possible amusement at my nerves would only confirm my worry.

I decided to show it to Pamela instead. 'What do you think it is?' I said.

'God knows, Odelle. But it ain't nothing to worry about. If they wanted to arrest you for something, they'd just do it here.'

Pamela had a point, as ever, and so that Thursday I went. Would I have been less terrified or more had I known that I was going to hear the final will and testament of Miss Marjorie Quick? I cannot say. The choice was made; there was only ever one path, and just as in life, Quick kept me on it from beyond the grave.

PART VI

The Sticking Place

XXIV

They buried her under an olive tree in the orchard. Teresa didn't remember much about it, but she could always remember the sound of the earth being flung on top of the casket, the same earth they'd once dug together, the rainbow through the falling drops. Padre Lorenzo had left the village, so Doctor Morales led a makeshift service. Harold and Teresa stood by and watched, virtually propping each other up, and Sarah was sedated upstairs.

The doctor would not look Teresa in the eye. Did he truly believe the rumour that she'd been the one to pull the trigger? She knew what was happening in the village. Jorge, probably in a preemptive strike against any guilt falling on his own head, had been going around saying that he'd bet a month's wages it was Teresa who'd shot Isaac and Olive up on the hill. She'd probably wanted to punish her brother. Teresa was sure Jorge was responsible for the shootings, but had no evidence to prove it. And in times like these, the truth was no barrier to men like Jorge. She did not sleep at night, wondering what would happen to her when people started to take Jorge at his word.

And in some ways, Teresa believed that what Jorge was saying was true. She had wanted some punishment for her brother. She had been responsible for sending Olive out, so that Olive might learn the truth about the man she considered the key to her success. Teresa came to believe that Olive had died because of her, and at night, she howled the guilt into her pillow. That Harold might hear of Jorge's rumour was both Teresa's greatest worry and her dearest wish. Harold might kill her in his grief – but at least it would end her misery.

IN THE DAYS AFTER OLIVE was buried, Harold, Sarah and Teresa moved around as if underwater. Teresa felt she was choking for the lack of air. Marbella and Alhama fell to the rebels, and still the Schlosses did not move. It was not until a 500-kilo bomb killed fifty-two people in one building in Malaga, and at the Regina Hotel a girl lost both her legs on the eve of her wedding day, that the family shook the stupor off their grief.

The naval bombardment was stepping up, as were the aerial attacks. There were five warships in the waters round Fuengirola. In Malaga, they reported, there was no longer anyone in control, nobody in authority. No public services, no organization whatsoever. The militia were half-crazed, there was no electricity, no trams, no police. Madrid looked like a picnic after its air attacks, they said, compared to Malaga.

'We must leave,' Teresa told Harold. 'Please. Isaac is dead, and half of the village already think that I am guilty – how will I ever live?'

'You'll survive,' he said.

'Please, señor, I have worked hard. I am innocent.'

He looked at her. 'Are you?'

Teresa held his gaze. 'Señor. I have always kept your secret.'

She watched the comprehension dawning on Harold's face, keeping her own expression neutral, although her heart was thumping. She had no choice. 'Señor,' she went on, 'would your wife keep you in money if she knew about the German?'

'WE'RE TAKING TERESA OUT OF Spain,' Harold said to his wife, the very next day. 'It is the least we can do. She will go on Olive's papers.'

'Fine,' Sarah said, unwilling to catch Teresa's eye. Teresa knew full well that Sarah had her own good reasons to wish her far away, but Teresa held Sarah's secret too, and so the Englishwoman said nothing.

It was a cold afternoon when they left. They were a strange reconfiguration, the most fractured trio on that ship – and that was saying something. There was no glamour in departure to echo the way that they'd arrived; the sky a sheet of changing greys, the sea beyond unending. The noise of the rusty chains loosening from the quay at Malaga caused in Teresa a monstrous sort of happiness. For under her sense of relief that she was leaving, she felt already the pulse of guilt. She had paid her escape with Olive's blood.

Her own expression was mirrored in the faces of the other passengers, as the land began to diminish and thin. It was a bitter miracle. They'd done it; they'd got away, but at the same time they hadn't, of course they hadn't. Teresa knew that part of her would never be able to leave.

SHE HAD NEVER BEEN ON a ship; she'd only ever known the land. Harold said the vessel was called a *destroyer*. Teresa thought of her ruined notebook, of how blackly apt an English noun could be. She gripped the rail, resisting the desire to jump, to plunge into the churning waters. It was so many colours, the sea; mud and milk, slate and leaf, and bronze when the light caught the crest of a wave – and at times, where it was still settled beyond, where the bows had not carved through it, a purer blue. Teresa realized that over the months, she'd come to understand how many colours there were that she had never noticed. She wanted the wind to whip her face, to sting and numb her, but it wasn't happening. No force of nature could erase her.

SHE THOUGHT AGAIN ABOUT THE morning they found Olive. Harold still didn't know why Olive had gone out into the darkness the night before. In his grief to flee, to get out of this hellhole, his daughter dead, he didn't stop to wonder why Olive might have been out there in the first place. He didn't consider that other members of his family might also be looking for love, for some purpose or salvation in another person. But when that morning had dawned, and Olive didn't come down to breakfast, Sarah and Teresa looked at one another, and assumed between them that silence on this matter would be better. So it remained.

The initial, mild discomfort of that morning had turned to horror, as Harold, realizing his daughter was missing, had taken the car out and found her body on the hillside. An hour later the women heard his motor again, the clang of the gate as he clipped it with the car, Olive's body lolling on the back seat. Harold staggered towards the women, his daughter in his arms. *I'm taking her with us*, he'd said, his voice oddly dull, as if he were miles away, speaking down the tunnel of his own body. At the sight of her dead child, Sarah had broken down.

Now, trying to recall all this, forcing herself to face it in order to carry on – Teresa could only remember fragments of these moments. It was the physical that stuck with her; the thud of her knees sinking to the ground, the taste of the cheap acorn coffee coming up her throat as she vomited onto the flagstones. The touch of Olive's body. White-skinned but bluish, stiff and bloodstained, three gunshot wounds visible through her jumper.

'She called this place home,' Sarah had said, slurring, hours later, the three of them sitting in the front east room. Harold was drunk, Sarah was on some pill or other. It was a living nightmare. They had placed Olive's body in the kitchen, the coldest part of the house, at the back. 'We must bury her here,' Sarah whispered, haggard with grief.

'What happened to my brother?' Teresa asked. Sarah covered her face with her hands.

'Jorge came for him,' said Harold. 'I only carried Olive.'

'*Jorge?*' said Teresa. 'Where did he take him?'

'I don't know.'

When both Sarah and Harold had passed out – Sarah on the sofa and Harold upright in the armchair, his whisky tumbler beginning to slip – Teresa set the glass on the floor and tiptoed down the corridor. She imagined Jorge, slinging her brother's body somewhere in the woods, a shallow grave perhaps, no means of ever finding him again. She had to lean against the wall, ramming her hand into her mouth to stop herself from screaming.

OLIVE DIDN'T LOOK LIKE OLIVE any more. Mottled, eyes closed, mouth slightly ajar. Her teeth were visible, which made her look even more vulnerable. Teresa reached out to touch Olive's arm, feeling how solid it was, now the blood no longer flowed. She touched Olive's head, and felt dead herself – a dead person living, a ghost with flesh on her bones. She saw something sticking from the pocket of Olive's skirt. It was the photograph from Isaac's set; Olive and Isaac standing in front of *Rufina and the Lion* in the attic.

I promise you on my life, she said to Olive in Spanish, putting the photograph in her own pocket, *I will not let this go unpunished*.

But even as she spoke, a quiet voice within Teresa told her already how hard it would be to avenge their deaths. How can you battle with a shadow in your own village square? This was the worst of it; that in the face of this senseless waste, Teresa was powerless. There was nothing she could do to bring them back. The only thing she could keep alive was memory.

THE NEXT DAY, SARAH HAD come up to the attic as Teresa was finishing her packing. All Olive's paints and sketchbooks were stowed away. All that was left was *Rufina and the Lion*, propped against the wall.

'Is that it?' Sarah had asked. 'The next one?'

'Yes.'

Sarah stood in front of it, saying nothing, drinking it in. Then she turned to Teresa, fixed her eyes on her, and said, 'Teresa, what's Isaac's painting doing up here?'

'Olive – was looking after it.'

'Why?'

'I don't know.'

Sarah turned back to the painting. 'I see.' She walked towards it and placed her hand on its edge. 'Well I'll be damned if that Guggenheim woman gets it,' she said, her voice breaking. 'This is for me.'

'No, no, señora, it must go to the Guggenheim gallery.'

Sarah whirled on her. 'Are you telling me what to do? This is the last thing I have—'

'Señora,' Teresa pleaded.

Sarah narrowed her eyes. 'What's that in your hand?'

'Nothing,' said Teresa, putting the photograph behind her back. 'Show me.'

Sarah grabbed the photograph. On seeing Isaac and her daughter, captured in what looked like a moment of happiness, she put a hand to her mouth and turned away, dragging *Rufina and the Lion* with her along the floor.

Teresa called down the stairs. 'I think Isaac's body is in the wood. Will you help me bury it—'

'Shut up,' said Sarah. She stopped, but did not turn round. Her hand came up and touched her straggly curls, and Teresa saw that she was trembling. 'I can't,' she whispered. 'I can't help.' She stumbled down the stairs.

To see the painting disappear with Sarah felt to Teresa as if her own strength was leaking away. But she could hardly wrench Olive's painting out of Sarah's hands. If she wanted to leave for England, for now at least there was nothing she could do.

TERESA TRIED TO PUSH THESE memories away, placing her chin on the handrail as the ship gained speed through the water. She wondered what Sarah was going to do with the painting and the photograph. The painting was in the hull, right now. Idly, she considered sneaking down and putting it into her own trunk. But it was too risky; she had to keep a low profile. The photograph would be easier to lift with light fingers – it was probably in Sarah's purse. Was it that Sarah had wanted an image of Isaac, or of Olive? It was hard to tell, but either way, Sarah had clutched that photograph like a talisman. She was vaguely aware of other passengers behind her on deck, taking a walk before night fell.

'Hello,' said a man, breaking into her thoughts.

Teresa flinched, her gaze fixed on the horizon as she tugged the woollen hat she was using to cover her short fuzz of hair. She didn't want to talk.

'Bloody shame, isn't it,' he went on.

He was English; young and upright. Teresa saw his fingers on the rail; black hairs sprouting on each one. 'Not good at all,' he said. 'I should have stayed, but I couldn't. We had to close the consulate.'

Teresa turned: he had blue eyes and a stern face. He looked like something out of an adventure book. He was frowning, almost talking to himself. She noticed the shadows of sleeplessness on his face, but he was the one to ask her if she was quite well.

'I am, yes, thank you,' Teresa replied, in her best English. She looked over her shoulder. Harold and Sarah had not emerged from their berths. She didn't want them to see her talking to anyone, but she wondered if they would by this point even care. Sarah had been insistent on going back to London, but Harold wanted to pick up the thread with Peggy Guggenheim in Paris. They were going to separate; Teresa could see it, even if they couldn't. Olive was a shadow between them, a touchstone of guilt, recrimination and pain.

'Why couldn't you stay?' she asked him.

'The bombs. That, and other parts of Europe requiring our attention. But still.' He cleared his throat. 'Don't think it's right.'

'No.'

'What's your name?' he asked.

She said nothing, and there was amusement on his tired face. 'I see,' he went on. 'Like that, is it? I detect an accent though. Do you speak Spanish?'

'Yes.'

Teresa could tell he was intrigued by her. In the satchel she had not let go of since leaving the finca, she had Olive's admission letter from the Slade, and a telegram from Peggy Guggenheim expressing her impatience for the next Isaac Robles. Given that Harold had kept hold of her identity documents, these flimsy bits of paper were all Teresa had left. She touched the satchel, her guard down with tiredness, her mind hopping too quickly to hold her nerve. Picturing being thrown off the side of the boat for her failed impersonation, she gripped the rail harder.

'Any other languages I should know about?' the man asked, passing her his hip-flask, which she drank from, hesitantly. She told him she knew a bit of German and at this, he became even more intrigued. 'Where are you going?' he asked.

'England.'

'Nowhere more specific?'

'London. Curzon Street.'

'Very nice. Family there?'

'Parents.'

'I see,' he said, but he did not look convinced, and Teresa felt herself collapsing within. 'And what are you going to do when you get there?' he pushed.

Teresa suspected that Harold and Sarah, for their separate reasons, would be glad to see the back of her. They'd done enough, bringing her out of Spain to protect their respective secrets, using their daughter's name to do so. Teresa knew she was already a nuisance they'd rather forget. She wasn't sure how far she'd be able to push her luck.

'I don't know what I am going to do next,' she said to the man, thinking there was no harm in fusing a true statement in the middle of her evasions.

'I might be able to help you. If you're willing to help me.'

'How?' she asked. Behind his head, the coast of Spain had by now completely disappeared.

'Come to this address,' he said. 'Whenever you can. A Monday is best.'

Teresa took the small card he was proffering, and read the words *Foreign Office, Whitehall, London*. She didn't know what that was, or how to get there, but she worried that if she confessed to this man, he would take his offer away. She tried to assess him; was it her body he wanted? It didn't seem so, but then, she knew by now how false the English could be, how good they were at saying the opposite of what they really meant.

He picked up on her hesitation. 'I promise, it's quite all right.'

Teresa turned back to watch the horizon. She pictured Olive's *Rufina*, the girl and her severed head and her lion, buried deep in the ship. *A girl has died*, she thought, *because I tried to save her*. She looked down at the water, remembering the promise she had whispered to Olive's body. 'Whitehall,' she repeated to the man. 'Best on a Monday.'

He smiled again. 'Excellent. I hope to see you there.'

Teresa heard his footsteps receding. She ran her fingers over the card. It was cream-coloured, and it had weight to it, a touch of authority. She flipped it over. There was nothing on it but a name: *Edmund Reede*. She repeated the strange words under her breath, before slipping the offering into her satchel. While she could not envisage what this Whitehall was, nor what Mr Edmund Reede might do for her, she knew that there was nothing left behind that would make her turn back.

The other passengers had retired. It was very cold by now. The sun began to disappear, but Teresa stayed on deck. Even when she could no longer feel her limbs, even after the night had claimed the horizon, she waited. She watched the blackness, watched the stars, as the destroyer carved its passage to England's shores.

Afterword

20

I recognized Quick's lawyer immediately. He was the thin man in the suit I'd seen at the gallery on the opening night of 'The Swallowed Century', staring closely at *Rufina and the Lion*. He was called Frederick Parr, and without much ado, he welcomed me into his office and handed me a thick folder, tied at the side with a red ribbon. My hand shook slightly; the breath was tight in my throat. I wanted to ask him how he'd come to be in the gallery that night – whether it was Quick who had invited him, and why, but I was too intimidated, and the weight of the folder in my hands seemed to keep my mouth closed.

'It was Miss Quick's request that no one read that but you,' Parr said.

'Thank you.' I fumbled the folder into my bag and began to exit the office, relieved that our transaction was over.

'That's not the only reason you're here,' he went on. 'Please, come and sit down, Miss Bastien.'

I obliged, walking across his dark green carpet, lowering myself into the large wooden chair in front of his desk. Parr stalked round this wide piece of furniture before settling himself opposite me. The air between us thickened. I saw why Quick might have employed him for such disbursements, for he remained unmoved by my obvious nerves. Parr suited her purposes entirely. He was a sphinx; his job to execute her wishes and nothing else. He looked down at the document on his desk. 'Miss Bastien,' he said, pressing his spindly fingers together to make a temple. 'Marjorie named you in her will.'

I heard these words, and although I understood them, I could not grasp their implication. 'I'm sorry?'

Parr blinked, impassive as a lizard. Outside, below us, the city traffic honked and beeped. 'She had a cottage, in Wimbledon,' he said.

'Yes.'

'She bequeathed it to you. In perpetuity.'

I MUST, AT SOME POINT, have left the offices in Bread Street and walked back to St Paul's Tube station. I imagine the walk was slow, that my heart felt odd. Quick had left me her cottage. I had signed some papers. It was overwhelming. When, *when* had she made such a decision? And why me? It was an inheritance the like of which I would never have imagined.

I must have clutched her folder tight. At least here was a solid thing – a gesture embodied in paper that I might better understand. Perhaps the answers to all my questions were in here. I was probably terrified that I might be mugged, and I must have sat on the train all the way to Clapham Common, refusing to open it in public. It burned my lap, but I needed to be alone, in quiet, when I finally read it.

I managed to get off at my stop, and was barely up the stairs and through the flat door before I tore the ribbon and began to read. *Dear Odelle, This is a long story*, it began, and I sat up till midnight reading it. I forgot to eat, my neck was stiff, but I didn't care. Here was everything Quick had ever wanted me to know, but couldn't find the words to tell me to my face. People, places, evenings spent under the vast Andalusian skies. Her story was bigger and brighter than anything my own imagination would have pictured. And as I finished it, my eyes red and shrunken with tiredness, my head pounding, I realized something else. Here, also, was everything that Olive Schloss had never wanted the world to know.

This folder was the evidence of Quick's perpetual, honourable silence over *Rufina and the Lion*, which conflicted with her anxiety to pass on the story of Olive Schloss before it was too late. For most of the time I knew Quick, she had been in crisis. Her centre could no longer hold. It must have been an astounding trigger to see that photograph of Olive and her brother, and the painting of *Rufina*, all those years later, to understand better than anyone what it represented – and to watch it be commodified, re-moulded, attributed to Isaac, yet again.

As Teresa Robles, she knew Olive had wanted to remain anonymous. As Quick, she felt the injustice in that. Nothing had been resolved between these two selves. This pressure, and the memory of what happened in those last days in Spain, coupled with the powerful pain relief she was on, no doubt exacerbated Quick's hallucinatory states and her general inability to put it all to rest. What she left for me to read in the folder explained why her behaviour had wheeled between solicitous and elusive. Teresa had cracked open; the reappearance of the painting had proved too much.

I still do not know if her death was accidental. Most of the time, I believe that it was not. She realized she would never find the words to speak the trauma of Olive's last days. And one might argue, that in the face of such aggressive cancer she saw that she could at least control her end, leaving the folder for me to find through her lawyer. I think often of Teresa's notebook of English; discarded by Jorge, discovered again by Olive, and then, in that folder, by me. It seems that she – like myself – always found the written word an easier means through which to understand the world.

She left no specific instructions with Parr as to what I was supposed to do with this folder. So for years, I did nothing. In fact, until now, I never told anyone what I read, that cold November night under my bedsheets. I didn't even speak to Reede about it, although I wish I had.

In the folder, Quick didn't detail exactly what happened when she arrived in England, but she must have taken up Reede's offer to meet him in Whitehall. I imagine that with her languages, and

Reede's connections in the Foreign Office, she would have been useful to Britain as the world groaned its way to war. There were quite a few Nazis in Spain by the early '40s. And in its way, I'm sure that Britain – and Reede – was useful to her too. Gratitude comes in strange shapes. A beautiful cottage on Wimbledon common, for example.

I BECAME AS GOOD AS Teresa at keeping people's secrets. I never told Lawrie that Quick was possibly his aunt, an aunt he'd met several times without realizing their true connection. I didn't want to set something in motion that I could never conclusively prove, I suppose, and besides, Quick was dead. It might have made it worse for him, knowing there had been family left behind, but everything being too late. In the folder, Quick mentioned Sarah's *affair* with Isaac, but not a pregnancy. *I* knew Sarah Schloss was Lawrie's mother, that she was pregnant when she came back to England, because Lawrie told me that himself. But it is arguable – given the time frame – that Teresa, and therefore Quick, had not known that Sarah was pregnant when she was having her affair with Isaac. Quick would not necessarily have made the connection between Lawrie and her brother.

This leaves unexplained, of course, why Quick had the Scotts' address in her telephone book, and her interest in the question of Lawrie's mother. It could have been due to her own investigations over Lawrie's possession of the painting, before the cancer was too much. But sometimes, I wonder. Did Quick look at Lawrie and see her brother's face, echoed there? Or did she see Harold Schloss's features imprinted in his son? Or did she think nothing of it at all? Whatever it was, she always seemed unenthusiastic that Lawrie was my boyfriend.

One only need look again at the photo of Isaac Robles to see similarities between him and Lawrie – but Harold had dark hair too. Lawrie's paternity remained a question mark. I do sometimes wonder if Lawrie knew this, too – given how vague his mother always was to him about his father. And yet, I will always remember how he requested from Reede a copy of that photograph of Isaac Robles.

SOME PEOPLE WILL THINK THAT my silence all these years was wrong. After all, the rare times that an Isaac Robles comes onto the market, it sells for astronomical sums. Olive Schloss deserved her artist's triumph, Lawrie deserved to know the whole story – but is there ever such a thing as a whole story, or an artist's triumph, a right way to look through the glass? It all depends where the light falls. Teresa Robles witnessed the benefits of working anonymously, and as I read Olive's story, so did I. As far as I can tell, she certainly enjoyed the pseudonym. The work, for her, was everything.

Rufina now hangs, of all places, in the National Gallery in Trafalgar Square, beyond those huge lions where once I saw Cynth waiting, dressed in her new sheepskin coat. After several years in a private collection, it went back into auction, and was purchased by the nation as part of the gallery's drive to acquire more twentieth-century art. There was fierce competition from the Prado in Madrid, and I expect Reede was grimly satisfied that they didn't get it. He never forgot the time they wouldn't lend him that Goya. The photograph was returned to the Prado. How it got there in the first place is a mystery; I can only suppose that Sarah returned it to Spain's national gallery, in a mistaken attempt to keep their interest in Isaac Robles alive.

IT WAS A STRANGE TIME, after Quick died. The exhibition was considered a success by the Skelton, and Reede was pleased with the attention and income it generated. Gerry did sell Sarah's house, so Lawrie lost his home, just as I found mine. The sale of *Rufina and the Lion* severed Lawrie's ties to his mother's past, to Gerry; all of it. Or at least, he probably hoped it did, for art rarely obeys human desire. I expect such a painting left its imprint, even when he couldn't see it. With *Rufina* sold, Lawrie used some of the funds to go on a trip to

America. He invited me, but I stayed in London, because I wanted to be in Quick's house, to keep working at the Skelton.

In the end, Lawrie didn't come back.

I'd like to say that the elasticity of youth meant the skin stretched easy. He would call from New York every week, to tell me he missed me, why didn't I come over – but I was where I wanted to be, and the fact was, I did not miss Lawrie as much as I might have missed my work. He had told me to keep writing, so I did. I would have preferred not to have to choose between writing and loving; because for me, they were often the same thing.

It was a time of new experiences, without the benefit of the old to mitigate the after-effects. My life was a beanstalk and I was Jack, and the foliage was shooting up and up, abundant, impressive, at such speed that I could barely cling on. I loved and I lost love; I found new creativity and a sense of belonging. And something deeper happened, something darker, which we have all gone through – and if we have not, it is waiting for us – the indelible moment when we realize we are alone.

Perhaps I didn't have to choose. Perhaps that was a dichotomy I set up myself. Regardless; the phone calls became more sporadic, and then they stopped.

ON THE DAY I WENT to Quick's cottage with the keys, I took both Cynth and Pamela with me. The place was much as it had been that night the ambulance men carried Quick out on the stretcher. There was the faint smell of her Eau Sauvage in the air. It was cold. The heating had been off and it was nearly December. I expected the face of her cat to appear at the kitchen door, but he had fled.

We went from room to room. It is not a large cottage. There are four rooms upstairs – three bedrooms, and a bathroom that freezes your skin in the winter months due to the inappropriately huge single-glazed window and tiles everywhere. Quick didn't have much. Simple beds, attractive rugs, cracked ceilings. In the room I assumed was hers, she had a small table wedged under the window, which overlooked her garden. On the table was a typewriter, the same she had used to write the contents of the folder. I stared down at the machine. It felt like it was staring back at me.

Every day since, I have tried to put that typewriter to good use.

ON THE OCCASIONS I AM asked to look back and reflect on my own books, I realize it has been my lifetime's purpose to try and understand what happened when I started working with Marjorie Quick. It started with me writing her eulogy, and has gone on from there. The preoccupations, the timbre, the shape of my writing have hinged on that short period of my life. My writing is the constant reconfiguration of how I myself was once reconfigured.

I often visited the gallery, specifically to see *Rufina and the Lion*, to stand with the public and admire its enduring power. What Teresa intended all those years ago, had, in its own way, come true. And yet more recently, as I have watched the sisters, I know that behind those eyes and underneath those brushstrokes there is another story, a story that is now partly mine. One woman, her body buried by the roots of an olive tree. Another, fleeing and facing unknown waters. Then me.

The rediscovery of *Rufina and the Lion* in 1967 was bound up with my own awakenings: my understanding of Quick, Cynth and her baby, my affair with Lawrie, a growing confidence in my own writing. That painting set delayed time bombs, which carried on exploding – sometimes gently, sometimes with perturbing force – as the decades rolled on.

And last year, a question began to press inside me, as persistent as a lion who sets his sight upon you and will not let you go. For years I had enjoyed the girls' hidden truth, this extra privilege, this miraculous secret of a nineteen-year-old, painting in the attic of her father's rented house in Spain. And I wondered: might someone look at Rufina, at me, and believe such things? A new curiosity, rather than my hard-earned confidence, became the fuel to write.

Although any collective answer to my question remains to be seen, personally I feel quite certain of it. Because if there's one thing I've learned, it's this: in the end, a piece of art only succeeds when its creator – to paraphrase Olive Schloss – possesses the belief that brings it into being.

Odelle Bastien

Wimbledon, 2002

BIBLIOGRAPHY

ART

Berger, John – *About Looking* (Writers' and Readers' Publishing Co-op, 1980)

Bernier, Rosamond – *Matisse, Picasso, Miró – As I Knew Them* (Sinclair Stevenson, 1991)

Bernier, Rosamond – *Some of My Lives* (Farrar, Straus & Giroux, 2011)

Chadwick, Whitney – *Women, Art and Society* (Thames & Hudson, Fifth Edition 2012)

Guggenheim, Peggy – *Out of This Century: Confessions of An Art Addict* (Deutsch, 1980)

Hook, Philip – *Breakfast at Sotheby's* (Penguin, 2013)

Mancoff, Debra N. – *Danger! Women Artists At Work* (Merrell, 2012)

LONDON

Reed, Jane – *Girl About Town: How to Live in London – And Love It!* (Tandem, 1965)

SPAIN AND THE SPANISH CIVIL WAR

Barker, Richard – *Skeletons in the Closet, Skeletons in the Ground: Repression, Victimization and Humiliation in a Small Andalusian Town – The Human Consequences of the Spanish Civil War* (Sussex Academic Press, 2012)

Buckley, Henry – *The Life and Death of the Spanish Republic: A Witness to the Spanish Civil War* (I.B. Tauris, 2014)

Casanova, Julián – *A Short History of the Spanish Civil War* (I.B. Tauris, 2012)

García Lorca, Federico – *Romancero Gitano* (1928)

Graham, Helen – *The War and Its Shadow: Spain's Civil War in Europe's Long Twentieth Century* (Sussex Academic Press, 2012)

Koestler, Arthur – *Dialogue with Death* (1942)

Lee, Laurie – *A Moment of War* (Viking, 1991)

Lee, Laurie – *As I Walked Out One Midsummer Morning* (1969)

Preston, Paul – *The Spanish Holocaust* (HarperPress, 2011)

Woolsey, Gamel – *Death's Other Kingdom* (1939)

TRINIDAD AND THE CARIBBEAN EXPERIENCE IN BRITAIN

Braithwaite, Lloyd – *Colonial West Indian Students in Britain* (UWI Press, 2001)

Chamberlain, Mary – *Narratives of Exile and Return* (St Martin's Press, 1997)

Dathorne, O.R. – *Dumplings in the Soup* (Cassell, 1963)

Hinds, Donald – *Journey to an Illusion: The West Indian in Britain* (Heinemann, 1966)

James, C.L.R. – *Black Jacobins* (Martin, Secker & Warburg, 1938)

Lamming, George – *The Pleasures of Exile* (Michael Joseph, 1960)

Miller, Kei (ed.) – *New Caribbean Poetry; An Anthology* (Carcanet, 2007)

Mittelholzer, Edgar – *With A Carib Eye* (Secker & Warburg, 1958)

Naipaul, V.S. – *Miguel Street* (Deutsch, 1959)

Schwarz, Bill – *West Indian Intellectuals in Britain* (MUP, 2003)

Selvon, Sam – *The Lonely Londoners* (Alan Wingate, 1956)

Stuart, Andrea – *Sugar in the Blood* (Portobello, 2012)

Tajfel, Henri and John Dawson – *Disappointed Guests* (OUP, 1965)

Radio

Radio 4 (2015): *Raising the Bar: 100 Years of Black British Theatre and Screen*, presented by Lenny Henry – particularly episode 2, *Caribbean Voices* – writers and actors from the Caribbean coming to work in London

Film

The Stuart Hall Project (dir. John Akomfrah, 2013) – Key domestic and international historical events feature West Indian migration to the UK, the Suez Crisis, the Hungarian Uprising, the birth of youth counterculture, the Civil Rights movement and the Vietnam War, and Hall's mixed experiences with 'Britishness' as a post-war immigrant

London – The Modern Babylon (dir. Julien Temple, 2012)

Fighting for King and Empire: Britain's Caribbean Heroes (BBC4 documentary, producers: Marc Wadsworth and Deborah Hobson of The-Latest.com, first aired May 2015, based on the documentary, *Divided By Race, United By War And Peace*, also made by The-Latest.Com)

ACKNOWLEDGMENTS

*T*hank you to:

Francesca Main, Megan Lynch and Jennifer Lambert, who
made this possible

Juliet Mushens, who saw me through

Sasha Raskin and Sarah Manning, who brought up the rear

Professor Mary Chamberlain, who gave her time and opened my
eyes a bit wider

Colin McKenzie, who lent his erudition on matters of art

Professor Patricia Mohammed at the University of the West
Indies, Trinidad, who generously advised on Odelle and Cynthia's
language

Gail Bradley, who diligently scoured the script

Any inaccuricies in these matters are, of course, my own.

Also to:

Alice O'Reilly, Teasel Scott and my family; in less obvious, but
equally important ways, you helped me write this novel

and

Pip Carter, for everything

ABOUT THE AUTHOR

Jessie Burton studied at Oxford University and now lives in southeast London. She is the author of the international bestseller *The Miniaturist*.

THE FOOL'S TALE

_WM_

WILLIAM MORROW

An Imprint of HarperCollins _Publishers_

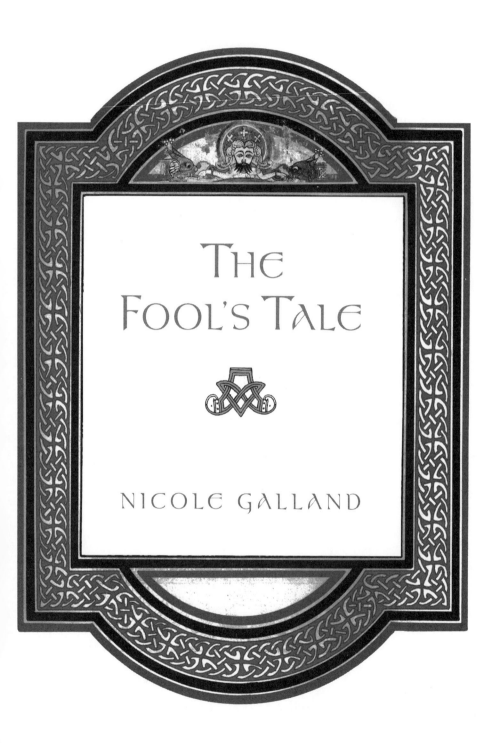

THE
FOOL'S TALE

NICOLE GALLAND

FIRST EDITION

Designed by Judith Stagnitto Abbate/Abbate Design
Map by Steve Lewis, the famous fourth-grade teacher

Printed on acid-free paper

Library of Congress Cataloging-in-Publication Data has been applied for.

ISBN 0-06-072150-2

05 06 07 08 09 WBC/QWF 10 9 8 7 6 5 4 3 2 1

FOR LOTHLÓRIEN HOMET

CONTENTS

Acknowledgments

The completion of this story in itself makes quite a story, and perhaps someday I'll write it. Until then, it must suffice that I acknowledge and thank the featured characters.

Above all, I salaam my personal holy trinity: Marc Glick, who gives attorneys a good name, and thank God knows how to spot a diamond in the rough; Jess Taylor for brilliant editorial assistance and hilariously helpful sarcasm along the way; and Liz Darhansoff, agent extraordinaire and superwoman. Steve Breimer and Jon Karas round out an exceptional teulu that I feel blessed to have on my side.

Jennifer Brehl, my editor at Morrow, has the amazing ability to help me actually *enjoy* performing surgery on my firstborn child.

Alan and Maureen Crumpler were so generous that folks assume I'm exaggerating when I describe them. They had barely met me when they invited me into their home to finish the manuscript, providing the best writer's retreat I could ever ask for—as well as fonts

of knowledge on nearly every topic, and delightful dinner conversations to boot.

Ray Thomas—innkeeper of The Lion, raconteur, and native son—brought Radnorshire (Maelienydd) to life for me far beyond mere bookish scholarship. He also afforded me the chance to see the land from horseback (and J.S. the horse helped me to examine the bracken at very, very close proximity). The next time you're in Wales, stay at The Lion in Llanbister.

On the home front, Steve Lewis offered extraordinary support, belief, patience, love, food, and computer help throughout the first draft. The second draft would have been so much harder to complete without the assistance of my father, Leo Galland, in getting to Wales; the third draft likewise was abetted by my grandparents Rachel and Hans William Galland.

Brian Caspe and Eowyn Mader were my first readers and critics; their enthusiasm gave me the enthusiasm to go on to a second draft.

Beryl and David Vaughan, like the song says, made me a pallet on their floor when I had no place to go; Robert (Jippity) Sicular has done likewise through the years, as have my parents Mike and Karen Colaneri. Laurence Bouvard was and is a font of linguistic insight, hospitality, and camaraderie in London. Alene Sibley and Bonnie Corso offered spiritual sanity, and Paul Hyman all the other sanities. Julian Lopez-Morillas provided some eleventh-hour reality checks, and Bonnie Akimoto offered end-of-the-haul enthusiasm. And Lorien, praise be, both listened and *insisted*.

Sion Davies set me straight on history and tried valiantly to keep me honest. I am responsible for any failings, deliberate or otherwise, therein.

Paul Remfry's writings on the castles of Radorshire grounded my imagination in reality. I'm also indebted to the work of John Davies (*A History of Wales*), Thomas Peter Ellis (*Welsh Tribal Law and Customs in the Middle Ages*), H. W. Howse (*Radnorshire*), and editor Thomas Charles-Edwards (*The Welsh King and His Court*). The full list of source material is far too long to include here, but for those interested in primary sources, Gerald of Wales (see chapter 4) is very

readable and can be unintentionally hilarious. There is also the *Law of Hywel Dda* and *The Chronicle of the Princes.*

I also want to thank the many people who contributed in smaller but still deeply appreciated ways. This includes Carys-Hedd of the Mid-Wales Film Commission, and other helpful souls, who know more than I ever will, at the British Library, the National Library of Wales, and St. Fagins; it includes also Mary Remnant, the patron saint of early music, and Gail Tipton, my intrepid fellow wanderer on my first two trips to Wales. I often relied on the kindness of strangers, especially in Cymru. Sundry passing navigators at each crossroad that I came to helped me in all sorts of ways. There are too many to keep track of, but they include: the entire village of Llanbister, Rhian Davies Wooldridge and Glynn Davies, my grandmother's ghost (for telling me to take the tart), Kalimata, David Hatcher, Cadw, and all the folks who played traditional music for me. *Diolch yn fawr.*

Finally, a special thanks to each genuine, rare Fool it has been my pleasure, pain, and privilege to know—and you know who you are.

PRONUNCIATION GUIDE AND GLOSSARY

PLACES

CYMARON: Cum-AAR-on (sounds like "Aaron"), the castle
MAELIENYDD: Mile-ee-EN-ith, the kingdom
GWYNEDD: GWIN-eth, a kingdom to the far north
POWYS: POW-iss, a kingdom to the immediate north and west
DEHEUBARTH: De-HI-barth, a kingdom to the south and west

PEOPLE

MAELGWYN: MILE-gwin, ruler of Maelienydd
CADWALLON: Cad-WA-thlon, ruler of Maelienydd
GWIRION: Gwir-EE-on
TEULU: TIE-lee, a lord's bodyguard and personal warband
PENTEULU: Pen-TIE-lee, the title for the captain of the teulu forces
GWILYM: GWI-lim, the castle steward
MARGED: MARE-ged, the castle cook
DAFYDD: DA-vith (Welsh David), Marged's grandson
EFAN: pronounced "Evan," the king's penteulu
HAFAIDD: HAV-eye-th, the castle usher
GORONWY: Gor-ON-wee, the royal judge
GWALLTER: GWATHL-ter, the king's chamberlain
HYWEL: pronounced "Howell," the king's bard
CADWGAN: Cad-OO-gan, the castle marshal

EDNYFED: Ed-NUV-ed, the marshal's son

ANGHARAD: Ang-HAIR-ad, the queen's woman

GENERYS: Gen-ER-is (hard *g*), the queen's woman

MADRUN: MAD-rin, the queen's woman

LLWYD: pronounced similarly to "Floyd," the queen's doorkeeper

HUW: pronounced "Hugh," a baron of Maelienydd

OWAIN: OW-in, a baron of Maelienydd

HUMFFRI: HIM-free, a baron of Maelienydd

LLEWELYN: Thlew-EL-in, prince of Gwynedd

CYNAN: CUN-an, a baron of Gwynedd

RHYS: Rh-ees, the deceased ruler of Deheubarth

NOTES

1. A "dd" is pronounced as "th" (as in *leather*); "th" written as "th" is pronounced as in *smith.*
2. The Welsh double "l": an aspirated "l"; the nearest description for someone unfamiliar with Welsh is "thl."

WALES AT THE CLOSE OF
THE TWELFTH CENTURY
Maelienydd under
Maelgwyn ap Cadwallon

GWYNEDD

POWYS

England

River Severn

Newtown

Owain's Manor

Cymaron

Rhaeadr •

MAELIENYDD

• Wigmore

Mortimer's
Lands

to Gloucester ➔

deBraose's
Lands

River Wye

DEHEUBARTH

• St. David's

Scale in English Miles
5 10   20   30   40   50   60

Cardiff

The Fool's Tale

Prologue

Late September, 1179

he prince was fully a head higher than his friend, but Gwirion was cleverer; Maelgwyn won all their fistfights and Gwirion all their arguments. They were a contrast in temperament as well: Maelgwyn already had unnerving poise for one so young while Gwirion was an unruly imp. Some council members had fretted to Cadwallon that the dark-haired foundling needed reining in, that he was old enough now to realize his constant playmate was also his future sovereign and needed to be treated with some deference. The king doubted Gwirion was capable of grasping that sentiment—and anyway, he almost envied his son for having such an unself-conscious friendship. He had a soft spot for Gwirion, in part for the youngster's musical gifts (he had leave to practice on the king's own harp), and in part for the unfettered playfulness that made him disregard the tense sobriety of court. He was at the moment, for example, trying to practice equestrian acrobats: He perched behind the prince's saddle,

clutching Maelgwyn's blond hair for balance as they rode. Maelgwyn as always calmly ignored the mild indignity.

The riding party was returning home from King Henry's court in Gloucester, and this foggy afternoon found them on a road rising over a valley of harvested farmland. They were ten in all: King Cadwallon, Prince Maelgwyn, Gwirion, and some of the king's personal warband, the teulu. It was both boys' first time in England and they were delighted by it, especially Gwirion, who loved exploring and had announced that he would chart the length and breadth of all Britain as soon as he was old enough to travel without a chaperone.

"If these are Mortimer's lands, won't he try to kill us?" Maelgwyn asked his father hopefully, a cocky nine-year-old's reaction to romanticized danger. He knew all about the Mortimer clan, powerful English barons whose properties served as a buffer between Wales and England. He knew, for example, that they had murdered most of his family, that they had tried for a century to conquer his small Welsh kingdom of Maelienydd. He knew that they had on occasion been successful, that the very castle he lived in had been built years ago by Hugh Mortimer during an Occupation. But he also knew that his father, with the help of their cousin Lord Rhys, had always driven Mortimer away again.

Gwirion looked alarmed by Maelgwyn's question, and Cadwallon smiled reassuringly. "It is Mortimer's land, but there's no danger to us. We're traveling under Henry's writ of safe passage. Hugh Mortimer is Henry's subject and that means he must let us pass through without harm." As if that were the cue for a macabre joke, an arrow flew past his arm and struck one of his teulu in the shoulder. Both boys screamed.

The second arrow hit the king in the chest. He slumped in the saddle with a grunt, groped toward the shrieking children on the palfrey beside him; ignoring his son, he grabbed Gwirion from his precarious perch to haul him closer. They slid to the ground between the two mounts and landed in a heap on the hard dirt road as shouts and horses' screams broke out around them. For one moment

in the midst of panic and confusion, Gwirion thought he was being singled out to help the wounded monarch. Then he realized he was a decoy.

The furious stamping of hooves around their heads made him wince even as he shrieked, but Cadwallon's unridered stallion galloped off and they were left exposed to their attackers, which was worse. An arrow passed so close before Gwirion's face he could nearly have bitten it. Terrified, he looked back up toward the palfrey but Maelgwyn was already gone, spirited away by one of the teulu. Four more of the soldiers leapt from their horses and ringed their fallen sovereign, shields facing out, from the boy's perspective towering yards over them; the attackers, who seemed to come from all directions at once, shot at the soldiers' shins, barely above the level of Gwirion's head, and when the men tried to avoid the arrows, a second spate was already on the fly toward the breaks in their defense. All four were pierced through their leather armor and staggered out of Gwirion's view. The horses were fleeing; the indifferent grey sky above seemed full of arrows and the air was shredded by the sound of their flight. Out of the corner of his eye Gwirion saw two more of Cadwallon's men fall near the bracken. Then he heard the triumphant attackers riding toward them, whooping.

"Sire," Gwirion begged, near hysteria, turning to the large man beside him. His mantle was trapped beneath Cadwallon's heavy arm. "Sire, what shall I do?"

Cadwallon's face was ashen. He just managed to turn his head toward Gwirion and breathed, "Protect your king."

Gwirion desperately tugged the cloak out from under Cadwallon's arm, and tried to climb onto his body to cover it with his own. He gagged when he realized that the warm dampness his fingers sank into was the king's bloody tunic. "Not me," Cadwallon coughed, lacking the strength to push him away. "Protect Maelgwyn, or we fall to Mortimer."

"Hugh Mortimer?" Gwirion cried. "But you—"

He stopped as Cadwallon's glance moved past him. Safely beyond the skirmish and watching it with satisfaction, a young man

dressed in blue and gold was reining in a large grey destrier. Gwirion recognized him: It was not Hugh Mortimer, but Roger his son, whom they had met at Henry's court just two days before, a youth already known for his rash ambition. The king whispered something weakly but his words were inaudible under a chilling new sound: The attackers were plunging their swords into the wounded riders' guts. Cadwallon took a final breath. "I go to God," he murmured with angry resignation, then closed his eyes and did not move again.

Gwirion tensed and waited for him to go to God, but nothing happened. The soul was not material, but he was sure there must be some evidence of its departure or else how would Father Idnerth know to speak of it? Hywel the bard said even an oat stalk had a soul, although he never spoke of it going to God. Gwirion waited without moving for a long time, fearfully breathing in the odor of sweat, blood, and earth, his focus desperately and entirely on the corpse beside him. Nothing changed. The king's body was unnaturally still.

Shouts had dulled to weak moans, and even these were fading. He raised his head carefully and looked around, suddenly shivering with cold. The dirt road was trampled nearly to mud all around him, and every one of the soldiers who had been riding with them was dead or dying. The horses had all fled, he hoped back home to Castell Cymaron where their presence would summon an alarm. The six attackers had dismounted and were gathering less than a dozen paces away from where he lay, giving each other congratulatory slaps on the shoulder in greeting. He couldn't believe there were only six, for all the arrows and all the damage done. He didn't dare look at their faces, but their strange foreign gibberish sounded rougher, harsher, than the foreign gibberish in the English king's court. Two of them stopped at a fallen guard close to Gwirion and he held his breath as they leaned over the inert body, frisking it. They found nothing of worth, and spat on the corpse in annoyance. Then one of them saw a sealed parchment rolled up in the dead man's belt, and pulled it out. He unrolled it, glanced at it, and held it out to his companion, who laughed.

Gwirion recognized it: King Henry's writ of safe passage. The man tore off the seal as a keepsake, crumpled the rest of the writ, and ground it under his heel.

They noticed Gwirion at the same moment and he didn't know if he had shut his eyes fast enough to fool them. One of his legs was twisted uncomfortably under him; he was afraid it would begin to shake and they would notice. But they gave him only a cursory look, assuming from the blood and the awkward posture of his body that his soul was wherever Cadwallon's might be.

Roger Mortimer had dismounted and joined the huddle. Gwirion lacked the French to understand what they were saying, but Mortimer was displeased about something and kept repeating a word Gwirion thought he recognized, from eavesdropping on the prince's language lessons, as "boy." He rested his head against Cadwallon's stiffened arm and watched Roger through lowered lashes.

They were obviously looking for the prince. The bracken on these hills was high enough to hide a child, but three of the marauders had tracked some broken fronds and were heading into the dying, waist-high greenery with purpose. There was nowhere else Maelgwyn could have been; if he'd fled, they would have seen him on the unsheltered hillside. Panicking, Gwirion glanced at the dead man beside him. Protect the king. He tried to think clearly: If he leapt up they would know it was a deliberate distraction and they might ignore him, so he would have to get their attention but make it seem accidental. That was as far as his foresight went. He never considered what would happen if he succeeded.

He rolled his head back onto the ground and moaned slightly, moved one arm limply, then was still again. It worked: The men all turned at once away from the bracken and ran toward him, shouting with excitement. Looking dazed, he pulled his twisted leg from under him and struggled shakily to rise. From the corner of his practiced eye, he saw a few fronds rustle slightly and knew Maelgwyn was moving out of danger. Gwirion was not yet to his knees when a violently strong hand grabbed the front of his tunic and hoisted him

roughly. He found himself staring at the blue-and-gold tunic, and as he was released and felt his feet touch the ground, he looked up into the enemy's face.

Roger Mortimer was giving him an eerie, almost dreamy smile. With a monotone accent like King Henry's, he announced in Welsh, "You are not the prince." Gwirion said nothing. "But I remember you—you're his bosom friend. Almost as valuable."

The king was valuable and the king was dead. He didn't want to be valuable. "I'm just a peasant, sir."

"A peasant? Dressed like that?" He poked the shoulder of Gwirion's worn but finely woven tunic—like all his clothes, a castoff of Maelgwyn's.

"We dress our peasants well in Maelienydd," he said in a voice of utter innocence. The situation now lacked all sense of reality, and therefore danger. "Especially our royal servants."

"A real servant would not have phrased it like that. I saw you at the court, boy, you never left the prince's side. You're much more than a servant."

Gwirion's nimble imagination failed him. "The prince is blind, sir," he said, trying to sound earnest. "I'm his guide, I can't stray more than a few inches away or he might hurt himself. I'm not his friend, he never even says my name right."

Mortimer laughed briefly. "The lie is feeble, but I commend your excellent delivery."

"It's not a lie," Gwirion insisted. "Didn't you see me standing on the horse when you attacked? I had to steer, but Cadwallon doesn't want—"

"Cadwallon *didn't* want. Cadwallon is past tense." He grabbed Gwirion's collar and pivoted him around to face the corpse. "He's dead. *Your king is dead.*" He was annoyed that this failed to break the boy, although he felt him shudder. "They are all dead except you and the prince, and you'll be dead too if you don't cooperate. Are you truly nothing but a Welsh peasant?"

"I'd sooner be a Welsh peasant than a filthy English lord."

Mortimer ignored the comment, bored by the finer points of ethnicity. He calmly pulled a large knife from his belt and pressed the tip into Gwirion's throat near his ear. The boy blanched and almost pissed himself. "Where is your prince?" Gwirion pursed his lips closed and Mortimer pressed harder. "You know where he's hiding," he said in a soft, almost hypnotic voice. "And this blade is hurting you. All you have to do is tell me where he is and I'll stop hurting you. It's a very simple game."

"I don't know where he is. You were the one interested in him, not I."

"You're not being very helpful," Roger Mortimer observed quietly, and whisked the blade up to Gwirion's head, nicking the skin at the temple. The boy cried out in startled pain and clamped his hand over the cut. "There'll be more of that if you don't tell me where your prince is. I don't want to kill him, I want to speak with him."

"Attend his coronation, then," Gwirion suggested through clenched teeth, both hands now pressed to the wound. "He's sure to give you a seat of honor, since you've helped get him there so early."

Mortimer looked grudgingly impressed by the boy's pluck. He lowered the knife but did not return it to his belt, and spoke in French to his men, who exchanged looks that made the bottom of Gwirion's stomach drop out. Mortimer addressed him again in Welsh. "As entertaining as you are to chat with, I have better things to do with my time," he explained in the same false dulcet tone. "I'd kill you for your cheek, but you're the prince's friend. So you will be our bait."

The first blow, across his face, sent him spinning into the damp roadway spitting blood. He heard loud, hooting laughter that seemed to come from all sides at once as Mortimer reached down and hoisted him to his feet again. "That won't work," Gwirion managed to protest thickly, trying to feel his tongue. "Told you . . . just a servant . . . I'm nothing to him."

"I'm a betting man, and I bet that's a lie," Mortimer replied and added, pleasantly, "But if we kill you and he does nothing, you've won the bet."

HE knew his father was dead and he knew he would soon be distraught, but he wasn't now. Now he thought of nothing but survival, horribly aware of how immensely more important his existence had just become, furious that such awareness required him to stay hidden in the damp bracken. He had a dagger, a recent gift from his father, and he had fantasized about having cause to use it; it was grotesquely ironic that the best way to preserve himself now was to refrain from action.

He'd seen Gwirion distract the men and could tell it was deliberate. He wanted both to throw his arms around his friend in gratitude and to scream at him for his idiotic and misplaced selflessness: *I could have taken care of myself,* he thought. Usually it was he who looked out for Gwirion, whose size and heedlessness made him the victim of harassment from the teulu and other castle youths. The prince had often needed to go to his defense.

Mortimer did not actually think Maelgwyn would come leaping out of the bushes like an avenging devil, but he was certain he could get the prince to give himself away. He assigned three of the men to study the bracken for movement, especially where the likeliest trail began. There was no wind. Maelgwyn did not allow himself to move, tried not even to breathe too hard. Hard eyes scoured the bracken fronds near him—and one pair locked onto his and stayed there. He tensed, and tightened his hand around the dagger hilt, ready to spring. But the eyes did not actually see him, they moved on and after a moment he made himself relax his grip. He would have given anything for a bow and arrow—he knew he could hit Mortimer and was sure the others would flee if he did. He was ashamed to realize he was trembling.

Maelgwyn saw Mortimer strike Gwirion once, then he closed his eyes and cupped his hands over his ears, his heartbeat amplified and filling his head, his throat a knot of tears. He could hear the Norman's hollered offer that they would release Gwirion if the prince revealed himself—not to surrender, simply to talk. He knew it was a trap and

prayed Gwirion knew that too, so he would understand why Maelgwyn couldn't act on it. He dimly heard his friend's voice crying out in fear and pain and outrage, and the offers gradually turned more sinister: The boy would be taken hostage and subjected to continual torture if the prince did not come out; he would be killed; he would be skinned alive; he would be skinned alive right now, in front of the prince's eyes. Gwirion's cries grew louder and Maelgwyn wondered, with the dispassion that comes from shock, if either of them would survive the afternoon. Three times, unbidden, his eyes flickered open and then shut again—and then he kept them shut to keep from shrieking.

After a very long time, there was quiet and the prince hesitantly lowered his hands from his ears, fearing the worst. He heard voices and opened his eyes to look.

They had released Gwirion, literally dropped him onto the road, three of the disheveled thugs breathing hard and grinning at their handiwork. Mortimer, who had stepped back to watch the scene with dispassion, was leaning over Gwirion and speaking to him loudly. He was asking Gwirion to help them find the prince, in exchange for a reprieve. Gwirion stubbornly said nothing.

After a long beat of silence, Mortimer stepped back and gestured for one of the men to resume, when Gwirion stammered, in a thin voice of defeat that Maelgwyn could hardly make out, "All right, then, I'll tell you where the prince is." Maelgwyn tightened his hand on the hilt of the dagger, his pulse racing.

Mortimer signaled his man to retreat and leaned over Gwirion again. "Yes?" he said.

For a moment, Gwirion stared at him, glassy-eyed, his face pressed against the road and his mouth half full of dirt. He spat the dirt out weakly. "I shoved him up my arse," he muttered. "I dare you to look for him—he's waiting for you with a naked blade."

After an astonished pause, Mortimer burst out laughing. "I don't know if I should kill you or *adopt* you," he declared admiringly, and drew his sword. "I've never been so sorry to reduce the Welsh population." Before Gwirion could answer, a distant cacophony of hunting horns sounded over the valley floor, a celebratory stutter of

notes, and church bells began chiming far down the valley. Mortimer looked delighted by the interruption. "*Alors,* good news of some sort," he announced to his men. "Anna's time was upon her when I rode out this morning—I want to get back to Wigmore to hear if I'm become an uncle." He sheathed the sword and made a dismissive gesture toward the battered child lying at their feet. "That's enough. The little whoreson's gone. You accomplished a fair amount today; I'll call it a good day's work." In Welsh he said very clearly to the boy, "Your friend left you here for us to torture you. The friend you risked your life for doesn't care a whit for you. You Welsh are all alike." Gwirion did not rouse himself for a response. He lay limp on the cold earth; his fevered mind wondered randomly if Cadwallon's soul had finally gone to God. Mortimer crossed to him and stood directly over him, his feet in front of Gwirion's bruised and muddied face. With a final smile of satisfaction at the royal corpse, and a passing glance at the other dead surrounding it, he mounted, gestured to his men to mount as well, and led them away down the valley.

When he knew for certain they were gone, Maelgwyn crept out of the bracken and ran on stiffened legs to his friend, sobbing angrily. Gwirion lay like a doll tossed aside by a truculent child. Maelgwyn ripped off his cloak and wrapped it around Gwirion's trembling body. The two boys looked at each other. Each almost began to speak and then each stopped abruptly.

"I'll carry you, I'll take you back to Gloucester," the prince finally ventured hoarsely.

Gwirion's eyes widened in fear. "No!" he whispered. "Take me out of here! I'm going straight home to the castle."

"We're much closer to Henry's court than we are to Cymaron—"

"I don't care," Gwirion interrupted. "Take me out of England." Wincing, he picked up a corner of the cloak and brought it to his lips, then pressed it ceremoniously to his friend's chest and added, with pained reverence, "Please, Your Majesty."

HONORING tradition, Cadwallon's murder was at once added to every Welsh bard's repertoire of lamentation. Gwirion's ordeal was not. They both knew they were forever marked by this, and for nearly twenty years they never spoke about the horrors of that day.

ENEMIES

May Day, 1198

SABEL WAS OLD for a bride, nearly twenty, and orphaned with little dowry beyond her bloodline. She was considered a great beauty in her own country—small and boyish in build, with an intelligent, squarish face and a high, graceful forehead—and supremely desirable for her education, skills, and absolute lack of feminine triviality. But she had always known she'd be married for politics. It never bothered her; until she'd heard Chrétien de Troyes's romances of Lancelot and the Round Table, at the age of thirteen, it had never even occurred to her that there could be other reasons to bind herself to a man. She remembered Adèle chasing away the minstrel reciting them, then chastising Isabel for corrupting her own wits and sense. So she had never dwelt on the possibility of romantic love. But she'd assumed a match would at least be within her own race, and she had been taken aback when her uncle Roger had revealed her suitor's identity: not only a Welsh prince, but the only prince still referred to by the English chroniclers as "Rex"—*King.* A small kingdom, and a poor one, but

she would be a queen. And the king, when she'd met him, was so disarming and handsome and his accent so melodious that it had made her knees weak, although she was hardly the sort to get weak knees. When the date was set and the terms agreed upon, she had spent a fortnight smiling to herself.

But that smile waned on the journey to a land that was far too alien, considering it began almost at her childhood doorstep.

They had left the homey fields of England for windy Welsh hillsides, hillsides carpeted by dead bracken that looked like russet snow, and nothing else for miles at a stretch but grass and prickly gorse—not a tree, not a house, not even a rocky outcrop to vary the landscape. Nothing but herds of white sheep and black cattle being driven upland for what passed as summer. The songbirds had been cacophonous, magpies and curlews, red kites and buzzards perched on the skeletons of sheep that had not survived the winter. In England there had been farmers, already sowing, bowing respectfully as they passed; here they'd found undernourished peasants digging up peat under the damp grey sky and pointedly ignoring them. Isabel tried not to be disheartened by this; she hoped she could eventually make these people understand that not all Normans were butchers. Below them, the valleys and lower hillsides were impassable bogs shadowed by dense groves of scrub oak (considered by the natives sacred and haunted), so the ancient Roman roads had kept them high on the slopes, windblown, chilly and exposed. She had known it would be highland, and she'd thought that meant mountains, which would have at least been *interesting*. The first few hills had been promising, with lovely sweeping views of river valleys, but by the time they were well into the kingdom, the entire country was high, with decidedly undramatic undulations from valley to hilltop—there were no peaks to speak of anywhere. It looked, her brother Thomas had muttered, like the English moors flung over a gigantic bowl of lumpy porridge. Wigmore Castle was only a day's ride off but in that day she had been transported farther away than her pilgrimage to Santiago de Compostela had taken her.

GWIRION had been incensed when he'd learned the wedding was set for May Day, and the Spring Rites canceled because of it. ("Usurped," he'd protested, "by a *Mortimer*, by a bitch of an English virgin.") When the king warned him not to use this public gathering as a chance to make sport of anybody, Gwirion had rebutted that he would never condescend to dignify the occasion by immortalizing it with a prank of any sort. And so the entire castle population knew there would be trouble.

It was May Day at last. Boughs of birch twigs hung over windows and everyone wore brilliant colors—even the usually bedraggled dwarf Corr wore green hose under his linen tunic. The one exception was Gwirion, who had donned sackcloth to mourn the end of the king's finest years as a bachelor. He insisted the day was too splendid to waste on a wedding, particularly one involving Mortimers, and would have avoided it altogether if Corr had not begged him otherwise.

"You know how ladies react when they see me for the first time," he lamented, his colorless lashes blinking almost spastically in the sunlight. "If you're beside me I can pretend to myself it's partly your hideous mug."

Gwirion grinned at this and then a thoughtful gleam warmed his eyes. It was a look Corr was all too familiar with.

"Whatever you are thinking of thinking," he said, "don't think it."

"It seems to me," Gwirion mused, ignoring the request, "that we've never fully exploited that particular aspect of your appearance."

"I doubt she'll give us much satisfaction that way. I've heard she has a sensible head on her shoulders."

Gwirion considered this. "But what has she got on the *rest* of her?" he asked. Rhetorically.

Corr sighed in capitulation. "And how severe a whipping will this be bringing us?"

Gwirion lowered his voice even though they were yards above the

crowd. "This wedding is an invasion. She'll try to coerce us to join her Norman civilization." A loaded pause, and then he grinned. "If we're expected to become like her, why don't we just become her?"

The two of them stood atop the king's tower, watching people mill about in anticipatory disarray around the ashes of the Beltane bonfires in the courtyard below. They descended the wooden stairs that hugged the stone curtain wall, bickering over the details of their plot, and began to scout for the bride's brother. He was a younger brother, named Thomas, and he was hardly in whiskers. Gwirion discovered him by the stables. He was standing near a cluster of dangerous-looking youths not much his senior—the infamously rowdy teulu, the king's resident warband. Their massive leader, Efan the penteulu, was showing off his horse's battle scars. Thomas, a doughy-faced boy with light brown hair, was looking very short and very young, and embarrassed about it. The teulu glanced toward Gwirion, realized who his target was, and returned to their boasting.

"Thomas Mortimer, isn't it? Your presence is required above," Gwirion whispered in his ear. The boy didn't recognize the oddly dressed man, but he was so grateful to be taken seriously by somebody that he went along, unquestioning. He failed to notice the looks of the young men he walked away from.

Gwirion led him past the pipers trying quietly to tune, past the large stone well, and up the wooden stairway to the top of the curtain wall. The garderobe up here, intended for the king's use, was not as foul as the one below—Gwirion was willing to incur only so much wrath for his prank. Thomas was too bewildered to understand what was happening; even after Gwirion had chained his makeshift gate fast across the open doorway, and the boy was penned into the toilet, he continued to ask innocently where his sister was.

"I'll just get her for you," Gwirion said cheerfully, and departed with no intention of returning for hours.

At least three hundred people were crowded around the large courtyard. Most were landowners of Maelienydd, handsome, sturdy Welshmen, many claiming distant kinship to the king. There were a

few visiting dignitaries from England, but Roger Mortimer, Lord of Wigmore, baron of the March, was not among them. To pass the time until Corr was in place, Gwirion thought to seek the presence of Hywel, the old court bard who would bless the ceremony for real after the queen's priest performed his doddering church ritual. But he was arrested by better entertainment: His Majesty the bridegroom was forcing himself to chat with a cousin they both detested. Anarawd, the man next in line to the throne, obviously did not like this match. Besides the fact that he would soon be supplanted as heir, his father, like the king's, had been ambushed and killed by Roger Mortimer. He was a violent man himself—he'd blinded his own brothers and taken their inheritance—and he'd raged against this latest treaty with the Marcher baron, but today he was trying very hard to appear respectful and resigned because he knew the teulu would have been all too pleased to disembowel him. King Maelgwyn smiled politely as they spoke, visualizing just such sport.

He had no personal interest in his wedding or his bride. This union was only to seal an uneasy truce. Over the course of two decades he'd thrice thwarted Mortimer's attempts to conquer Maelienydd, but earlier this year, when the king's powerful comrade-in-arms Lord Rhys had died, Mortimer had redoubled the effort in a raid that had severely taxed both sides. With this wedding that would all be—theoretically—behind them now. There were several benefits to such a match: Although he could have made any son his heir, even a bastard, a child of this marriage would be half English— Norman English, the ruling class—and would be safe no matter which side ultimately prevailed.

The king was dressed magnificently in green and gold and he truly looked heroic, if not especially Welsh. Fair-haired and tall with fierce blue eyes revealing a sliver of Viking ancestry, he was as ever poised and effortlessly charismatic, and Gwirion conceded silently that the king deserved in earnest the title he had once given him in affectionate mockery: Maelgwyn Urddol, Maelgwyn the Noble. In their adolescence, this private joke—inspired by a summer of sexual exploits of questionable virtue—had spread throughout the castle

and out to the surrounding countryside, the irony replaced immediately by earnest images of an able and handsome young ruler, and for years now he'd been referred to admiringly among his people, and by Gwirion, mostly by this sobriquet.

Noble excused himself from Anarawd, only to be immediately overtaken by Lord Ralf, one of the queen's maternal uncles, who was no improvement. "Your Majesty!" he trumpeted, a sharp-featured bearded man with hawkish eyes. He loudly began an inventory of his niece's many qualities as if Noble and the populace at large still had to be convinced of the match. "I'm sure you know that she was her brother's regent until this year—very unusual situation," he announced, with a smugness that suggested it reflected well on him somehow. "Excellent administrator. Did you know she's multilingual?"

"French, Latin, Welsh, and a little of the Saxon tongue," Noble recited sardonically. He'd been told this near a dozen times.

"Yes! And an able horsewoman."

"I intend to speak to her only in Welsh and I do not expect her to ride into battle with me," Noble said, smiling dryly. "But I do appreciate the match's value. And I assure you all my subjects do as well." *With one exception,* he thought, watching Gwirion slip through the crowded courtyard.

Gwirion had finally spotted Corr, his white hair gleaming as he whispered to the quartet of young women huddled near the dovecote. These creatures had been brought in from around the kingdom to become the new queen's officers and attendants, and Gwirion had already established that they were the silliest women he had ever met. They were bending over Corr now. Two of them looked confused, but the little redhead managed a smile and the tallest one even giggled. A grim, sharp-eyed old woman dressed incongruously in silk, who must have been Adèle, the queen's English attendant, had been inside the chapel with the as-yet-unseen bride, and stuck her head out to examine the crowd at a most inopportune moment: She caught Corr whispering to the girls and marched toward him with a frown.

Gwirion was afraid Corr would falter and tell her everything. He had to prevent them from speaking. He had to create a distraction.

"Friends!" he yelled with a piercing bray into the droning hubbub. He scrambled up onto a stack of upright mead barrels for nuptial celebrations, which made him high enough to command instant attention. The sight of the slight, wild-haired man who looked like Pan in sackcloth startled everyone and the yard fell quiet. He saw the king, just outside the chapel door, turn toward him and purse his lips. He had been listening to one of the bearded foreigners, but now he absently motioned the man to shush. "Friends!" Gwirion repeated. "Before we begin today's solemnities, we must introduce the new faces you see here today. I trust you shall receive them graciously." Adèle ignored him, continuing toward Corr. Gauging the distance to the ground, Gwirion leapt high off the cask, somersaulting in the air as people scrambled to get out of his way. He landed hard on his feet on the stone paving, as the crowd scattered from him, then he shook his head once to clear it and ran toward where Adèle was just about to accost Corr. Before the old woman could entirely register Gwirion's presence, he had crawled between her legs and stood again, hoisting her brittle frame up on his shoulders and gathering her skirt behind his head. She let out a short, undignified squawk, which delighted the crowd.

"Behold Adèle," he intoned, grabbing her ankles to keep her secured. "Lifelong companion to our new queen. This is the closest she's ever come to having a man between her thighs, and we owe her a debt of gratitude for raising her ladyship to be the chaste and lovely creature that she is. Salute her!"

Most of the assembly burst into good-natured applause and cheers. Adèle looked livid. But she restrained herself to a dull scowl and once he had set her on her feet, she glared at him then slunk away, forgetting about the dwarf, just as Gwirion had intended. Corr nodded to him and slipped quietly behind the king, toward the chapel door.

Noble could barely maintain his composure when Gwirion

hoisted the old woman. He wanted to let him go on, to test his shamelessness, but the bride's uncle was standing gaping right beside him and he couldn't risk it. "Gwirion!" he snapped. "Stop that nonsense at once or I'll have your head."

"But I have two heads, sire. Shall I give one to you and one to your fair bride? The inferior one would probably be of more interest to her, don't you think?" He pointed broadly with both hands at his groin, an exquisitely grotesque grin on his face. "I'm quite sure it's superior to anything you can offer her!"

The Norman uncles exchanged looks of shocked disgust across the yard, and the crowd in general hesitated, especially those who saw the ladies in the retinue blush purple. A disappointing response, Gwirion thought—the locals would have laughed. The king gestured sharply to Efan the penteulu to remove Gwirion from the yard. Tiring of the prank, he ignored the fact that Corr was in place and relying on him; he went with uncharacteristic cooperation, and waited patiently in the kitchen for people to get drunk enough to appreciate him.

THE queen apparent, hidden behind the chapel door until the moment the ceremony began just outside it, missed the entire episode. She'd been in here since dawn, when she had celebrated mass for the first time with her future husband, and despite the high-arched windows the room was starting to feel very claustrophobic. She was trying gamely to keep in good humor, but she hated the gown Adèle had insisted on lacing her into, an excessively tight kirtle with an equally suffocating surcoat over it, and under the elaborate gold circlet on her head, cascades of silk that distracted her like a swarm of flies. For the years Isabel had stewarded her brother's estate, she'd worn only the loosest-fitting kirtles she could convince her seamstress to fashion for her. "I'll be tied up tight enough when I'm married," she had reasoned to Adèle. "Let me breathe a little until then." Adèle's rebuttal—which she now saw the truth of—was that

when she was finally tied up tight it would be far more uncomfortable than if her body had developed into womanhood already constrained. This outfit, which any other female her age and build might have been comfortable in, took her to the point of fainting. This was the first time she was wearing a wimple, which made her feel like an aging abbess, and the thought that her glossy, rosewater-scented coil, the sole thing she was prideful of, the source of so many admiring stares, would now be forever hidden from the world depressed her. Her heart was beating faster than she wanted to admit; for the thousandth time she repeated to herself she would someday be at home here—more than that, she would enhance the well-being of those who now probably considered her kin to the devil himself.

She was aware of the crowd noises, but hardly noticed what they were. At one point she did hear the king's raised baritone, and assumed he was gathering people to congregate just outside the door. That meant Thomas would be stepping into the chapel for a final embrace, then escorting her to the priest, who would give her to the king.

But the person who entered wasn't Thomas.

It was an albino dwarf. Being startled by a stranger—and particularly this stranger—made her take a sharp breath in, and the dress was so tight that she nearly swooned before he even began his patter.

"Your brother is detained, milady," he said by way of greeting, polite and expressionless.

"Detained?" On reflex she reached for her belt, for the rosary and precious crucifix holding the saint's relic.

"A bad flux of the bowels. He can't leave the garderobe just now. The priest asked me to escort you outside in his place."

She stared at him, dumbfounded, the ringing in her ears getting worse. He held out his cocked arm for her to take. She tried to back away, straining to keep her composure. "Why are you doing this to me?" She spoke so softly that Corr felt ashamed. But Gwirion was relying on him; he had to see it through.

"Doing what, milady?" he said innocently, and reached for the furred hem of her sleeve. Instinctively she released her rosary to grab

her eating knife, then remembered that the wedding outfit had none. Corr took her slender hand in his knubbly, callused one and—as Gwirion had instructed—sloppily licked her palm with an expression of deadpan reverence on his face. She made a strange, unpleasant sound, and fainted.

*Y*OU'RE the one who fouled it up," Corr snapped. "Where *were* you? You were supposed to come in through the side door!"

"I told you, he sent me to the kitchen. Apparently I overstepped my bounds."

"And what did *I* do, then?" demanded the dwarf. "I only nearly gave the bride a concussion!"

Gwirion said nothing.

They sat glumly in the castle prison, a dank, clammy cage dug into the basement floor of the barbican. Despite Noble's frequent threats, neither of them had actually been locked in here before and they were both unnerved. They were hungry and sober, which neither of them had expected to be by this hour of the king's wedding day, and it did not help their mood.

"He's coming," Gwirion suddenly said into the tense blackness, and grabbed the bars. The cell was half a level lower than the rest of the basement. Gwirion could look out—or could have looked out, if there had been any light—but Corr was too short.

Moments later, a torch glimmered above them, and Corr heard feet on the stone floor. The king appeared in his long green-and-gold wedding tunic and his heaviest ceremonial crown, dazzlingly overdressed for his surroundings. He had brought the unsociable-looking porter Einion and a guard, both holding torches, and three other men. No . . . two other men and Thomas. They all crowded into the tiny antechamber outside the cell and the visitors' extremely annoyed

faces peered down to inspect them. The strangers wore Norman beards, and clothes similar to Thomas's in cut and color. Gwirion and Corr knew what this meant: They were not about to be released, they were about to be humiliated.

"Let me handle this," Gwirion whispered.

The dwarf made a derisive sound.

Noble crossed his arms and glared down at Gwirion. Gwirion mimicked him. For a long moment they stood there glowering at each other, until finally the king let out a sigh of disgust. "I hope," he said, "that you're both ashamed of yourselves."

"I certainly am," Gwirion said. "I've never botched anything so thoroughly. I say I should be whipped for incompetence."

"Yes, you should," Corr muttered, as one of the strangers demanded, with an atrocious accent, "Are you saying you did not intend for that to happen?"

"Of course not," said Gwirion. "I never should have got myself thrown out of the yard, that was thoughtless on my part, I lost interest in the whole affair, and that was irresponsible, because it left Corr to fend for himself, and it was a two-man affair. There's really no way he could have managed it on his own."

"What are you saying?" the stranger pressed him, not looking pleased.

"Well, when she fainted—we were nearly certain she would faint—I was planning to—"

"You *intended* for my niece to faint?" The man's sharp face looked menacing, and Corr wished he could hide.

"Of course we did, that was the whole *point* to it. I was right, you see," he added in a conversational aside to Corr. "About the kirtle."

"What about the kirtle?" the uncle demanded.

"Wedding gowns are always tight—it's the bride's last chance to show off her wares, isn't it? And she was probably nervous, probably not breathing right. They swoon very easily when they're not breathing right. But we didn't want her to hit the floor that way. I was supposed to be there to catch her. To keep the gown from getting dirty.

Because the laundress has been ill and I couldn't bear to give her any more work than she already has. But then—"

"Hang him," said the stranger, straightening, and left with one of the torches.

After a startled pause, Gwirion asked, "And who was that?"

"He's my uncle Ralf and he's important," said Thomas, trying in vain not to sound like a whining child. "His approval is worth more than a parasitic—"

"That's enough," Noble said brusquely. "When you're wise enough to not follow strangers into strange dark rooms, you may insult him all you wish."

Demoralized, Thomas shut his mouth.

"But don't you want to hear how it was *supposed* to happen?" Gwirion said to Noble with a cherubic smile.

"No, I don't. Idiot." He turned to the other Norman, the tallest and gravest of the three, and said something in French beginning with "Walter." Walter said nothing, merely stared in disgust at them. After a moment, he signaled to Thomas and the guard. They lit a wall sconce for the king and the porter, and exited.

For a long time, Noble stared at Gwirion, until the prankster, who had nearly convinced himself he had done nothing wrong, had to look away.

"Have you any idea how stupid that was?" Noble demanded in a quiet, dangerous voice. "This marriage is to secure their loyalty. The ceremony today was to show them how civilized and respectable we can be. The English mock us and belittle us. We finally had a chance to show them we're to be taken seriously, and you ruined it."

"I didn't want to, sire, it was his idea," Corr said miserably.

"Spineless," Gwirion spat at him. "I didn't have to hold a knife to your throat for it." Beaming boyishly, he insisted, "It truly was clever, sire, subtle and sophisticated—we even worked the 'Norman usurpation' theme into it."

"Stop it, Gwirion," Noble said shortly. "Do you understand me?"

"You're telling me I must behave myself until they leave,"

Gwirion said, sighing. "And if I don't, half of England will attack us." He smiled with satisfaction. "I had no idea I was so dangerous."

"I'm not of a mind to jest now, Gwirion," the king continued evenly. "There's only one way to make certain you're not either. You're staying down here until they're gone."

Gwirion was shocked. *"Sire?"*

"You heard me. Both of you. Until they're gone."

"Oh, sire, for the love of God—" Corr began.

"That's final," Noble said. "When I let you out, you'll pretend you've been whipped within an inch of your lives. And you'll be decent to my wife."

Gwirion, as if stung, jerked away from the door. He curled up against the cell wall, and tried to sweep the meager straw into a pillow. Noble peered down at him for a moment, then turned to Einion. "Bring them blankets. And food. See if anything's left from the feast, but don't say it's for them. And send your boy down here to watch the door—Gwirion can pick locks."

The porter nodded gruffly, separated some burning rushes out of the wall sconce, and departed, leaving the king completely alone with the prisoners.

Noble turned back to the cell. "Well?" he said after a pause.

Gwirion said nothing. Finally Corr very hesitantly asked, "Well what, sire?"

"How was this subtle and sophisticated prank supposed to work?"

Corr glanced at his cell mate. There was a moment of stillness. Then Gwirion, without quite uncurling himself, looked over his shoulder at the king. "If she was completely out, I would take her veil and Corr would walk me out of the chapel and hand me to you in front of the priest. If she came to, I would carry her in my arms out the door, and then run past you and through the gate as if I were abducting her."

Noble's face betrayed the faintest tic of amusement. "Christ in heaven, I'm grateful you botched it, then."

"You have a strange way of showing it," Gwirion said, and turned his head away.

THE bridegroom was gentle with the bride that night, even gentler than he had assumed he would need to be, because of the afternoon's misadventure. He disappointed the revelers by canceling the traditional bedding ritual, refusing to allow the carousing guests to come with them into the wedding chamber. When they were finally alone together for the first time he was surprised, but not displeased, by her absolute stubbornness: She would not let him touch her until he swore to send at least one of the offenders away. He relented, refusing to provide details, then caught both of her hands in one of his and reached for her wimple, and she looked down, blushing, and became at once obedient.

She was far from his ideal. He liked trollops, he liked wild dark hair and curvy flesh and the fluid peasant accents of his mother tongue. She offered nothing coy or feverish. Her hair was the color of hay, and hung heavily, with startling flatness, nearly to her knees. Her eyes were such pale brown they looked feline, entirely too calm for him. And naturally there was some part of him that saw her flesh only as a piece of Mortimer's. Here it was, literally in his grasp, under his weight, crushable and trusting—a limb of the animal that had murdered his father and damaged his friend. It was his. The flesh that had wronged him was finally in his hands, spiritually obliged now to bend to his will, and he found this so thrilling that it almost made him dizzy.

But he did nothing untoward. His better side won no internal moral victory, nor did he remember that he had entered into this marriage in service to his people's need for stability, not his own need for vengeance. Her safety was secured by something far more elemental: He loved the female form too much. He could not have forced his hands to touch her for any purpose but pleasure.

IT was neither as tremendous nor as terrible as she'd thought it would be, their first night together. From almost the moment he touched her, Isabel felt safe. But the part of her that knew it wouldn't be terrible had expected it would actually be marvelous. That there was a mystical secret she was to be let in on. That they would be joined soul to soul afterward, and that did not happen.

Still there was great pleasure in it. Vague urges that her body had felt for years overwhelmed her, and he knew just where to touch and what to do. She assumed some older woman must have instructed him in these arts, and she was grateful for his education. He was patient with her bumbling shyness, and promised her that the physical union itself was all he required for satisfaction, a polite fiction he would rectify when she was ready for it. It did not hurt the second time, and without the pain, she shivered with the pleasure that he brought her. Adèle had never even hinted that the burden of womanhood could be so agreeable.

GWIRION picked the lock their first night of confinement when the porter's boy fell asleep. Corr wouldn't go with him, terrified that they should further anger anybody. So Gwirion went alone, slipping silently through the dark of the porthouse, out of the barbican and into the bailey.

The daily life at Cymaron took place around this bailey, a large walled courtyard with corner towers and several freestanding buildings within. Across a steep trench to the south was a smaller but much higher earthen motte, which housed the looming keep tower used for protection during sieges. The moon was only a few nights past full and shining defiantly through a cloud cover that had slunk in from the north, and Gwirion knew there was a watch on the roof

of the keep, so he didn't dare walk straight through the courtyard to his destination. To circle the yard to the left would take him past the great hall and then the kitchen, both full of lightly sleeping servants trained to wake at the slightest sound. Instead, he took the long way around, skirting silently along the curtain wall to the right, past the chapel, the dovecote, and the steward's corner tower with its snoring court officials; along the western wall where the kitchen garden and council chamber stood; past another corner tower and then along the southern wall—past the kiln house where the unkempt chief hunts-man slept, the kennels where an early litter whined for its absent mother, the stables housing Cadwgan the marshal and his grooms. The large D-shaped tower in that southeast corner held the king's bedchamber; Gwirion had learned long ago to scale the wall, despite the sleek external whitewash that made the castle look carved from a single piece of stone.

He climbed up past the room of the sleeping judge and cham-berlain—the fattest and thinnest men in the council, respectively—to the top floor, where he peeked into the room through a window whose shutter had been left open in the cool spring night. What he saw nearly made him laugh aloud.

The new queen's most impressive addition to the castle, a source of fascinated and suspicious gossip, had been a wedding bed—a large canopied, curtained feather mattress far softer than any self-respecting Welshman should ever sleep on, Gwirion had scoffed. The bed curtain facing the open window was pulled aside. He had never laid eyes on the queen until now, when she was splayed naked under her husband. Not really interested in her, Gwirion noticed only that she was very slender and small, and therefore would be of no lasting interest to the king. What was of interest, and amusement, was how she moved beneath him: She looked excessively virginal. Over the course of years, Gwirion had seen the king with women of all sorts, and this was sending him back to the nursery. He must have been so bored, Gwirion thought sympathetically. And of course he wouldn't tell her that, so he was in the unusual position of having to be bored

and polite about it. That was what had made Gwirion want to laugh. When looked at from such a perspective, he decided, this marriage could be exactly what Maelienydd needed after all: The king might develop a working sense of diplomacy.

G UIRION and Corr were ecstatic to be out in the air again, especially after Noble made them sit through a sermon by the chaplain on their moral perdition. They danced about the fog-dampened courtyard drunk with rowdy laughter, and no one could quiet them for half an hour.

"So did you even meet her?" Enid asked when Gwirion finally stopped for breath by the herb garden to steal a sprig of mint. Enid was a pretty, dark-haired kitchen girl brought to the castle for the Spring Rites four years earlier, and had been the king's favorite ever since.

He shook his head and grinned. "Caught a glimpse of her, though—certainly no threat to you."

"What about a threat to you?" she teased.

H IS glee was shattered an hour later when the king announced he would—eventually—be sending Corr away. "It's my fault—I even admitted it!" Gwirion protested angrily in Noble's private receiving chamber, pounding his fist against the mantel stone. "And I think the valor required of me to admit that should cancel out all blame against both of us." Noble, slouching in his leather chair, responded with a droll expression that showed he disagreed. "Then at least send *me* away!" Gwirion shouted.

Noble gave him one of those slow stares of his, the hypnotic

gaze that Gwirion thought must explain his sway over the entire court. "You know you're not going anywhere."

"The mischief was my brainchild, I bullied him into it," Gwirion insisted. Corr stood quietly by the door, cleaning his fingernails, fretting as he always did when he was made the center of attention.

"He was the one caught in the act," Noble said, shrugging.

"I locked the boy in the garderobe!" Gwirion stamped his booted foot in exasperation. "Half the teulu saw me take him there!"

"The teulu will never testify against you, Gwirion, you know that. You're the only entertainment they've had since I made them stop vandalizing the abbey."

"Noble," Gwirion said sharply, shedding the feigned adolescent tantrum. "You know I'm the one to be punished."

Noble folded his arms and pretended to consider this. "You're right," he said at last. "You should be punished. Your punishment is to remain at Cymaron and learn to tolerate the Mortimer-born queen consort. Corr will be spared this dreadful fate by retiring to someplace far away, once I have found him a suitable guardian."

"That's not amusing!" Gwirion said through clenched jaws.

"I find it hilarious," Noble said in a humorless voice that ended the discussion. "Let's have a song. What key is your harp in?"

Gwirion scowled and with annoyance ran his hand through his unkempt black hair. "I invented a new tuning in honor of your wife," he answered, with a mocking bow. "Every string is tuned to the same pitch. I call it 'the Anglo-Norman Drone.'"

·2·

Decorum

Approaching Midsummer, 1198

OBODY AT CASTELL Cymaron knew what to make of the new queen, of her brocade Norman kirtles, bewimpled head and foreign manners. They'd all heard that English women were trodden on by their men, and had vaguely expected her to be submissive, but Isabel never was. Awkward or socially shy occasionally, high strung not infrequently, but submissive never.

She was out of place, however, and she knew it. Her accent alone set her apart: The murmuring monotone of Norman French lacked all the punchy singsong of the Welsh. Assuming he would in time control the whole of what he coveted, Roger Mortimer had insisted that his extended household learn to speak Welsh; even Adèle was fluent. But Isabel, although technically proficient, had found little occasion to practice, and it dazed her to face a castle full of talkative characters who spoke nothing else. She felt lost in this new home, further lost in this new culture, a world that seemed at first simply a

primitive version of her native England but was at second glance alien in a hundred subtle ways.

She had been master and mistress of a large estate—unheard of for a young woman in her circumstances—and had anticipated certain sovereign privileges as the consort of a Welsh king. But she found herself instead an outsider in a tight household that already had a master and had functioned smoothly without a mistress since the queen mother died years earlier. She would have no political power, and because she was socially superior to the court, court officers claimed even the domestic duties she had assumed would be hers. The tall understated man named Gwilym, the steward, ran the household and oversaw the use of the great hall, the nexus of castle life; Marged, the cook's rotund, aging widow who had ascended to her husband's station, was not only the overseer of all provisions, but the spiritual mother of Cymaron. Everyone was unfailingly respectful to their queen, but she could tell that they considered her superfluous; they certainly would not interrupt their comfortable routines merely to accommodate her. She suspected that if she had been a military strategist, a horse breaker, or a smith, there would be much to occupy her here on the harried fringe of civilization, but she was not. The hardest thing for her was to feel useless; beyond her political worth as queen consort and mother of the heir, she would be almost useless here.

She had say only over her attendants. She did not know them, and their collective intellect was not quite equal to a rabbit's (which Isabel doubted was common of Welsh women), but she took them in hand to make the best of it, since they were a privilege she had petitioned for. The royal court was rigidly structured and the officers she was entitled to were of tradition male. She'd accepted many of these: her doorkeeper, her groom, and others. But for the offices more intimate to daily life, positions nearer an English noblewoman's retinue, she had requested female attendants—and she was beginning to wish she hadn't. The only things they knew how to do were the distaff chores she had always loathed: spinning, weaving, and sewing. It be-

came clear, too clear, that these were also the only things that would be expected of her. And in this backward land, even the local technology of weaving seemed primitive to her.

After mass on the morning that she and Noble came out of their connubial seclusion, she had first entered her new solar—a painfully ironic term considering how little sun there was to warm it. As well as the second curtained bed she'd brought, this chamber had been outfitted with spindles, two upright looms, and Adèle's sole valuable and exotic possession: the spindle wheel. Isabel's spirit sank at the sight of it all. Her sovereignty, the steward Gwilym explained with a kindly voice and an awkward bow, would be limited to this room.

It was a room, he added tactfully, that she was fortunate to be housed in. The great hall had been built snug into the courtyard corner by this tower; her solar opened directly onto a balcony with stairs leading down to the hall floor. The apartments in the other towers, even His Majesty's, required their occupants to cross either through the courtyard or up along the wall walk to reach the hall. This one bedchamber had the luxury of internal hall access, which would make all the difference when winter came. With a forced smile, she told Gwilym she appreciated it.

This was to be her world, then: a round, whitewashed stone room some ten paces across hung with bright tapestries, with one large fireplace and windows looking out over the undulating, grass-crowned hills of Maelienydd. Even now, at the height of spring, it was a watery grey light that filled the room; here it was even cloudier than England, and there was a constant subtle clamminess that she could only hope to grow inured to. During the day, she and her women would be joined by any female servant with a passing free moment. They were all entertained on occasion by Hywel, the old bard, with his muted hair-strung harp on his lap. He knew a stream of stories, poems, elegies, and sagas, but for all his vast impressive repertoire, his was a humorless sentiment and his voice was not what it had been, so everything sounded like a dirge. The entire arrangement depressed her, although she knew that most women would be honored, even ec-

static, to begin married life with all of these amenities. Her husband, or Gwilym, or whoever furnished the solar, no doubt meant to please her. And she was never one to brood, so she pushed her despair into that corner of her heart reserved for such indulgent emotions, and concerned herself solely with mastering each day.

There were four girls, differentiated almost exclusively by looks: Angharad (blond and delicate), Generys (brunette and sturdy), Madrun (a petite redhead, the youngest), and Gwen (tall and curving, with a wild dark mane). Like all Welsh women, they had cut their hair fetchingly short across their brows, and covered their braids with a simple white veil. Isabel wanted to imitate the style—it must certainly be more comfortable than the wimpled headdress Adèle wrapped her into every morning—but Adèle insisted she maintain her native grooming as a silent reminder of her intrinsic superiority. They were poised, could all read and write, but to her mind they were disturbingly unlearned and superstitious, although Noble had chosen them out of highborn families from the four most far-flung corners of his realm. Two of the girls excelled at general sewing, and the other two were very fast weavers. Adèle jealously guarded the spindle wheel, which dazzled them all with its newfangled efficiency, and the spindles and teasels for carding the wool were usually shunted between servants over the course of the day. This left Isabel at a loss. She took up some embroidery, but she realized within a week that she would go mad if she spent her life like that, and begged Adèle to let her take on the spinning.

"It will callus your fingers," said the old woman without pausing from her work.

"My fingers were callused before. My hands need useful work."

"The king won't want you if you have callused fingers."

"That is absurd," she answered. "Let me at the wheel."

When Isabel had the wheel up to speed, she was surprised by how relaxing it was. The monotony was soothing. She remembered the feeling of Noble inside her, and a pleasing chill ran down her spine. If only they could have spent a few more days doing nothing but that—the pleasure of his closeness, his skin rich with a warm

smell that made her want to leap up from the wheel and run through the castle to find him. It was the only thing in this new life that helped her feel alive.

THE recent death of old Lord Rhys, ruler of Deheubarth, Noble's powerful cousin and long a companion-at-arms (when they weren't fighting each other) had made all of Wales uneasy. Rhys had been both stabilizer and protector, always ready to assist his fellow princes with the Marcher lords. For decades he'd been Maelienydd's staunch supporter in her defensive campaigns against Mortimer, without once suggesting that Maelienydd's king was in any way his vassal, even when that king was a boy of ten. Upon Rhys's death his own kingdom had been thrown into near anarchy, torn apart by his inept, ambitious offspring; Powys, directly to the north, had suffered similar internal intrigues and been splintered in two, with terrible bloodshed.

And yet even knowing how fruitless warfare had been for all the kingdoms, the council was (respectfully) leery of Noble's declaration that sustained diplomacy might be a true alternative. "This is an experiment," he repeated calmly, "to see how far Mortimer can be trusted. Now that we have the English border stabilized by this marriage, we don't need so many troops on the Marches there. If Roger gives us any reason to mistrust him, we can call them back there within days, and remind him that we have his niece. Otherwise I want to redeploy those men; we need them near the deBraose lands. In fact we might even be able to coax our new English allies into sending some of their men to strengthen our southeast border. Somebody find out who's in charge of the troops that are potentially accountable to my wife—surely not that idiot boy Gwirion locked in the garderobe?"

"Do you mean your brother-in-law, sire?" Gwilym ventured dryly.

Noble responded with a dismissive wave. "Don't refer to him

that way in my hearing. But it's not him, is it? We need to find out if it's Mortimer or those two boors who were at the wedding." He smiled bitterly. "That would be ironic, Mortimer securing our borders at his own expense."

The burly red-haired marshal Cadwgan offered to make inquiries, and a courier was sent ahead to inform the idiot boy that he would be receiving an emissary from the King of Maelienydd. They reviewed the status of the northern and western borders, and agreed that, for a change, nobody in Powys was behaving in any way alarmingly.

When council was adjourned, Noble told Gwirion he wished to have a nap. This was flatly unimaginative code for an afternoon assignation in his private receiving room, usually with Enid. Gwirion looked for her in the kitchen, but was told she had gone up to help in the queen's solar. He made a face and mounted the steps.

ONLY Enid could have charmed Adèle into letting her try the precious wheel; only Enid was that thoroughly disarming. She looked so delighted by the privilege that Isabel was almost ashamed of her own grudging attitude toward the work. The coordination of it was beyond the girl, so Adèle turned the wheel for her and Enid's brown eyes danced when the wool was nearly torn through her fingers as she drew it away from the spindle. "We should have one of these for each of us!" she announced.

"And where would they fit?" asked Generys as she finished weighting the warp of the larger loom. "There's hardly room to sleep all of us now."

"Especially when His Majesty visits," whispered Madrun, the petite one, mischievously. The four attendants exchanged looks and guilty grins. Isabel turned crimson and lowered her face, sticking the iron needle so hard into the linen she was embroidering that she stuck herself.

Enid alone laughed. "He takes the five of you at once?" When Adèle scowled at her she grinned in response. "Oh, pardon me,

Adèle, I didn't mean to slight you—it's all six of you, then, is it?"
Even the queen smiled at the absurdity of that and felt slightly less
embarrassed. But Adèle stopped the wheel abruptly. "That's
enough," she grumbled, and gestured for Enid to yield the stool.

There was a single rap on the door, which swung slowly open as
the girl stood, and everyone in the room stiffened when Gwirion
stepped halfway through the crack. Ignoring the eyes upon him, he
gave Enid a look that she read at once. "Where are you going?"
Adèle demanded as Enid, looking down, headed for the door.

"She's wanted," Gwirion said coolly, and ducked back out of the
room and onto the shadowed balcony. Isabel swallowed her indignation: He had not even acknowledged the queen's presence, had ignored her just as thoroughly as he did on every rare occasion they
were near each other.

Enid met him outside on the balcony looking over the hall. She
whispered, "Couldn't you tell him it's my—"

"I tried that last time," Gwirion said, anticipating her. "It excited him."

She saw that he was struggling not to turn back to the queen's
door, and she knew him well enough to almost read his thoughts: He
wanted the newcomers to know where Enid was going; he wanted
them to understand that the king preferred a Welsh peasant girl to a
Norman gentlewoman. Her hand moved nearly in unison with his as
he reached again for the door latch, and she slapped his knuckles.
"Don't do anything stupid," she said.

"Or you neither," Gwirion retorted, but stepped away from the
door. "He's a married man now, remember."

She chuckled. "Oh, that makes a difference, does it?"

Gwirion followed her down the steps. After seeing her to the
door of the king's receiving chamber, he wandered into the kitchen
and eyed the supper preparations. Marged was severing rabbit meat
from its skeleton while her grandson helped the baker, a smiling,
silent man, prepare barley quick bread for supper.

"Where is Enid?" demanded Adèle, from behind him in the
doorway.

Marged and the others suddenly found their work vastly more preoccupying. Gwirion smirked but did not turn around. "I told you, she was wanted."

"She works here."

"She works here, but she was wanted elsewhere." Adèle sighed and exited again, ignored by all of them. "Here, lad, let me do that," Gwirion said grandly, nudging the boy out of the way. "You help your grandma with the rabbit."

"He's too young for that knife, now," Marged objected, but Gwirion smiled at her.

"I'll keep an eye on him. I want to make the loaf for the high table tonight." He winked at her. "A special little treat for Their Majesties."

AT supper that night, the loaf laid before the center of the high table was shaped like a pair of buttocks, and decorated: On each cheek, outlined by sprigs of herbs, was a decorated shield. It was somewhat warped and blurred from baking but it took little imagination to delineate the geometric pattern that was the Mortimer coat of arms. Noble found it hilarious; Isabel was outraged. Gwirion's name was never mentioned. It went without saying.

"Please," she begged as they undressed for bed later in Noble's chamber. "Muzzle him somehow."

"He can't be muzzled," he replied in an indulgent tone. She wasn't sure if the indulgence was for Gwirion or for herself, but that seemed to end it for Noble. He kissed the top of her head as she sat undressing, and smiled down at her. His face, Isabel had decided in an uncharacteristic flight of romantic fancy, was the human equivalent of a lion's: handsome, calmly arrogant, cool and yet unflappably paternal. "I'm growing fonder of you," he said. As her face warmed to return the smile he added, "How can you possibly be a Mortimer?"

She stiffened. "Is it absolutely necessary to insult my family?"

· "Absolutely? I suppose not," he admitted. "But it's certainly a pleasure."

"Not for me."

He grinned and slid his hand down to the small of her back. "Well, now that I've had my pleasure, let's attend to yours."

SOMETHING about that evening affected her in a way Isabel had not expected. If asked, she might have said she had fallen in love—a common mistake, to confuse love with the more advanced mechanics of fornication—and the next morning, she awoke with a new delight in her married life. She reached for Noble in the bed, and was disappointed to find him gone. Then she remembered that he'd suggested riding out beyond the village gates in the morning and dining together on the hillside across the Aron. She smiled and got out of bed.

It was not sunny—she hadn't seen the sun since her wedding—but the diffused early-morning light felt more silver than grey today, and seemed to promise better weather later. Dressed and freshened, she made her way out of the king's chamber, down the wooden stairs and through the already bustling courtyard. In the great hall, Enid was placing cups of ale at the high table as other servants set up trestles for breakfast. She was the only one who bothered to smile at Isabel, so the queen headed toward her.

"Good morning," she said as the girl dropped into a curtsy. "Where is my husband?"

"Gwirion begged him to ride out alone together this morning, Your Majesty," Enid replied.

"Gwirion?"

"That's what I was told, Your Majesty."

"They're already gone? Before mass even?" Enid nodded. "When will they be back?"

"I'm not sure, milady, but they took their dinner with them." Seeing some squelched emotion on the queen's face, she asked gingerly, "I trust this news is not disturbing to you, milady?"

Isabel cleared her throat, hating how stuffy this made her sound, and said with a feeble pretense of offhandedness, "My husband had asked me to join him for a ride this morning."

Enid silently cursed both men for putting her in this position. "That's an unfortunate complication," she said vaguely. "I'm afraid Gwirion's infamous for those. Is there something I might do for you?"

"No. Thank you. I . . . would like some breakfast." She had paled almost imperceptibly.

"Shall I bring it up to your solar, then, milady?" Enid asked. "You look like you may be wanting to rest for a bit."

"No," she said shortly, then reconsidered. This girl was the only person other than Adèle who had expressed the slightest solicitousness toward her. That was not something to shrug off. "Actually, yes, in my solar. Thank you." She walked stiffly toward the stairs to her room.

WHEN Enid entered, with wimberries and oat bread, Isabel was standing with her arms folded tightly before her, vainly willing herself to calm, determined not to let a servant perceive how furious she was. Enid seemed to consider something briefly. She placed the platter on the bed, curtsied, and quietly announced, "You should understand, milady, that no one comes before Gwirion."

"I beg your pardon?" the queen said, playing with the tassel on her belt to feign indifference.

"Gwirion, milady. He'll always come first."

Isabel stared at her. "Gwirion is just an entertainment."

Enid hesitated, but she knew it would be said eventually and at least she, perhaps, could soften it. "No, milady. *You're* just an entertainment."

Before Isabel knew what she was doing she had smacked the girl, hard. Enid recoiled and Isabel, shocked, stared at her own hand as though it were possessed. "*Mon dieu*, did I do that?" she gasped, and gave Enid a troubled look. "Did I really do that?" Stammering, she switched to Welsh. "Forgive me, please forgive me. Are you hurt?"

"No, milady," Enid said, but stayed several paces away. "I'm sorry, I didn't mean to be impertinent. It's just that you're still a stranger here and perhaps you don't know our ways."

After a pause, Isabel sat down again and asked, warily, "What do I need to know, then?"

"I wouldn't presume to have all the answers to that," Enid began carefully. "I only know that you're here for the king, but Gwirion is also here for the king, and he's been here longer."

"But I'm the king's *wife*," Isabel snapped back. "I'm his political ally and his social consort and his bedfellow, and I'll be the mother of his children. Gwirion is merely *diverting*, he's not *significant*, he isn't *useful*—"

"Your Majesty," Enid interrupted gently, "Gwirion is necessary." She said this with such simple conviction that Isabel, without understanding the words, suddenly knew better than to contradict them.

But she wanted to make sense of them. "Why?" she demanded. "What does he *do*?"

Enid looked at once surprised and awkward, both rarities for her. "It's what he *did*," she said delicately. "Your Majesty doesn't know? He saved the king's life when they were children."

Isabel frowned. "Really? When?"

Enid blinked. She did not want this responsibility. "I wasn't quite born yet," she replied evasively. "But everybody knows about it." Although she'd never heard him even mention it, she cautiously suggested, "Perhaps if you asked Gwirion for the story, it might afford you a chance of civil conversation from him."

The queen laughed humorlessly. "Yes, I'm sure he'd love the opportunity to gloat about his preciousness to Noble."

Enid pursed her lips a moment then said, almost furtively, "Don't envy that attachment, milady." The queen gave her a bemused

look, but hurriedly she added, "I hope you'll eat now, Your Majesty," and withdrew.

WHY did you ask me to ride with you this morning, sire?"
"You suggested it," Noble informed him.
"No I didn't. When do I ever ask to leave the castle?"

This was a rarity for the king: a pleasure ride near the royal hunting area across the River Aron, a hillside almost overgrown with bracken. He was riding the large grey-spotted Spanish charger he'd claimed as booty from an English raid three years earlier; Gwirion rode an aging, native Welsh hill pony, a mare that the king had jokingly gifted him long ago. The mare was strong and fast, but her legs were very short; she always had to trot to keep pace, and the charger, used to her, allowed itself to be reined in more readily than otherwise. Two of the teulu, carrying spears and the royal dinner, had followed at a respectful distance; otherwise, the men were alone. They'd turned off the road, which was barely visible on the wide, bare hilltop, and settled in a shallow dip on the slope to dine.

The youths had laid brychan and board for them, then retreated a hundred paces. Now Noble and Gwirion were stretched out comfortably on the brychan, sharing the wine flagon and eating by hand from the same hardened trencher loaf. Gwirion swallowed a final mouthful of lamb, and rolled over onto his back to contemplate the sky. It was still grey, but the clouds seemed farther away now. He watched two red kites circle lazily on a rising column of warm air. He was edgy: Open hillsides always felt exposing. "I never ask to leave the castle," he repeated, a distracted murmur.

Noble gave him a significant look. "You suggested it. It was just a whim you had. I indulged it."

"So you won't tell me the reason."

"I don't need a reason."

Gwirion laughed. "Now I *know* you're up to something."

Noble gave him the sardonic stare that Gwirion knew so well. "Was there something better you had intended for your morning?"

"Endless fornication," Gwirion replied cheerfully, shifting his back on the blanket to avoid a pebble. "Not with you, if you'll excuse the insult, but perhaps with those charmingly articulate attendants of your wife."

Noble pursed his lips thoughtfully. "I don't know how successful you'd have been. You can't offer position or wealth—the usual aphrodisiacs."

"What are you saying?" Gwirion protested. "I can be any lord that a lady wishes me to be—I've studied the rutting vocalizations of every man in court, I can imitate them all."

Noble was delighted with this news. "Really? Show me one."

Gwirion laughed briefly. "I was lying."

"It's a splendid idea, though. Improvise." Gwirion made a face. "Go on, show me someone. Einion the porter."

Gwirion sighed. "When he's with a woman or a sheep?"

Noble grinned. "Can you do the sheep as well?"

"With pleasure." Gwirion pulled himself up, then balanced on his haunches and mimed bending over a stout body. A hundred yards away, one of the teulu nudged the other and they turned to watch: Like any males old enough to shave but not to marry, the teulu adored Gwirion's libidinous humor.

Thrusting his pelvis back and forth, he rolled his eyes up and stared slack jawed into the recesses of his skull. The king snorted with amusement, and after a few moments, Gwirion went on to the moans. "Oh, lovely. Lovely," he droned earnestly with each thrust. "Yes, lovely, *bah*—lovely—ugh—lovely—ugh—ugh—*bah*—lovely, *lovely!*" His whole body began moving with the thrusts, and the slack look on his face tightened into anguish. The soldiers inched toward them as Noble bellowed with laughter. "Yes—yes—oh, lovely, *baaaah,* lovely!" Gwirion cried, and finally, after several moments of increasing hysteria, screeched out, *"Lambikins!"* and collapsed.

Noble applauded. "That was marvelous," he announced. Gwirion sat up and rubbed his neck. "We'll do it at the next feast."

"Sire?" Gwirion looked at him, ignoring their guards' whooping approval.

"You'll work your way right through the court." Seeing Gwirion's alarm, he placated, "Or just a few of them. We'll use a lottery to select the victims."

Hoping to avoid this assignment, Gwirion insisted, "It's not a bachelor household any longer. The queen and her women wouldn't care for it."

"Pff," the king said, dismissively. "You have no sense of Isabel at all, Gwirion. She's quite a little tomboy, really."

"Ah. I see. Being a tomboy allows her to appreciate grotesqueries."

"It wasn't grotesque, there was something charming about it. Wasn't there, lads?" he called out to the teulu. They cheered.

Gwirion looked at them in disbelief. "You have the sensibilities of rodents in heat!" he shouted at them.

The king smiled broadly. "That explains their passion on the field," he said.

THEY returned in the early afternoon, and Noble stayed at the stables to summon the rest of the teulu for a mock skirmish in the tangled woods of the lower hills, despite the light rain that had begun. Gwirion at once made his way through the dampening yard to the kitchen in search of Corr, who was still waiting anxiously for further word of his banishment—Noble refused to send the little fellow away until he knew there was a good home waiting for him.

Nobody was in the kitchen but Enid, minding some leek-and-cabbage stew in a huge cauldron hung over the fire.

"Oh, you're finally back," she said, sullen.

"And what's up your nose?"

"Nothing." He waited, refusing to play along. Finally she explained, airily, "It's just that His Majesty had told Her Majesty

they'd be spending the morning out riding together, and she wasn't pleased to learn he'd gone with you instead."

Gwirion stared at her. "You're not serious."

"I am."

"Who told you?"

"*She* told me. We had a right good talk. And afterward she invited me to serve her at dinner." She smiled coyly. "I think there's a promotion coming."

"Oh, good, you can sit in that cage of a room and listen to cackling dullwits all day."

"I might *replace* those cackling dullwits." Enid beamed. "She seems to prefer me to them, even the grouchy one she brought with her."

"Why? Gave her some hints for tickling the king, did you?"

"Certainly not! I wouldn't tell her that, it'd break her heart."

Gwirion was genuinely surprised. "She doesn't know?"

"She doesn't know about any of his women—and don't you even *think* of telling her. You've disturbed her enough as it is."

He was astonished. "This is a pretty change of tune. When did you defect to the French side?"

"Gwirion, Christ," she sighed, and returned her attention to the stew. "It isn't a matter of sides. We all have to live here." She glanced over her shoulder at him. "It's a small place, suddenly. It's different. It can never go back to what it was."

"It's just a few more girls shoved into one of the towers."

"It's not that simple—"

"Yes it is!" he snapped, with such anger that she stopped fussing with the pot and turned fully around. He was self-conscious for a moment, but then continued. "It's not as if we've been invaded or there's some sort of plague. He's got another belly to jump on, and a consort for feasts. That's all it is. For the love of God, Enid, she's a *Mortimer*, it's not as if he'll ever *like* her."

Enid looked at him for a moment. When she finally spoke, she was almost as cross as he was. "Do you know how stupid it is for you to be scared of that poor lady? She's not here to replace you."

"I know that!" Gwirion snapped back scornfully. "That's what

I'm trying to say! D'you—d'y'think I'd have been invited to ride along with him today if *she* had any say over it? So there!"

"Christ, you're such an ass!" Enid threw the wooden ladle at him. He leapt at it and caught it between his teeth—one of her favorite tricks, but she ignored it now. "Don't you understand *anything*? He set up the whole thing."

"Whuh?" Gwirion asked, the ladle in his mouth.

"He told her he would be riding with *her* today, and then he went out with you instead."

Gwirion took the ladle out of his mouth. "So?" He shrugged. "He's entitled to change his mind."

"He *didn't* change his mind. He made plans with her with the *intention* of breaking them. He told everyone the ride was your idea. He said he was—"

"—indulging a whim," Gwirion said in unison with her, startled.

"You see? But it wasn't even your whim. He set up the entire thing just to show her—"

Gwirion nodded, understanding her point. "He wants her to see that he'll throw her over if I want his attention. He wants her to know I matter more."

They stood silently for a moment in the empty kitchen, looking at each other across the chopping table. Enid could almost see the thoughts crowding his brain as he considered the responsibility this placed upon his shoulders. The king had raised his status without telling him, but now that he realized his position, Enid doubted it was enviable. How could one face a friendless woman, armed with the power to make her loneliness even more absolute?

Gwirion moved closer to her, and Enid realized he was handing back the ladle. "Well," he said. "Thank you for telling me. Do you know what this means?"

"Of course I do. What matters is do *you* know what it means?"

"Of course." He gave her a most solemn gaze, and then suddenly threw his arms around her and burst into delighted laughter. "It means I've won!"

Knowing that he spoke more from fear than malice, she could not bear to chastise him.

ADÈLE was too irascible to offer good company, and her women's chatter was, as ever, substantial as milk bubbles, but with Enid's deliberate and distracting attentions Isabel had weathered the day, and was trying hard not to brood now. To show Noble the insignificance of the slight. The effort was not lost on him when he found her in his chamber late that afternoon.

He entered in the sweaty leather corselet and red linen tunic that he always wore with the teulu, and his dusty blond hair still had tiny wet twigs clinging to it. The mock battle had been, as usual, deep in the recesses of wooded slopes: groups of young men armed with blunted spears and arrows, trying as much to outwit as to outfight each other in the confusion of scrubby overgrowth and treacherous footing, an imitation of traditional Welsh warfare. His team had won the skirmish. His team almost always won. And as so often in the aftermath of such brute exhilaration, he wanted a woman. Any woman, even his wife with her small breasts and lack of ingenuity in bed.

Isabel pretended to have been working on some embroidery that she'd actually borrowed from one of the bevy in her room. "Did you have a good ride this morning, milord?"

"Yes, and thank you," Noble said with a smile. "Gwirion wanted to visit one of our childhood haunts."

Isabel, petulant despite herself, ventured, "Forgive me for saying so, but he really is the most indulged fool I've ever seen."

"Gwirion's no fool," Noble said sharply. "You'll gain no ground with me by insulting him."

Pretending to focus on the embroidery, she said, in a tone that implied it should have been self-evident, "I didn't mean I think he's feebleminded. I meant an *allowed* fool." Noticing his blank look, she

added, with tentative condescension, "As they have on the continent?" and returned to her sewing.

Noble shook his head. "What are you talking about?"

She set the embroidery frame aside on the bed. It was pleasing, under the circumstances, to feel worldlier than he was. "Fools are the latest rage in the continental courts. You haven't heard of this? The princes and barons take in eccentric ragtag confidants, as pets almost. They have license to do whatever they want—they make a lot of mischief and everybody thinks it's very witty."

Noble looked delightedly intrigued. "Are there really that many impish foundlings in the world? I must tell Gwirion he has a brotherhood."

Isabel made a dismissive gesture. "They're not foundlings. They're usually just clever vagabonds out to make an easy living by the entertaining shock of saying things other people dare not even think. They earn their keep entirely by personality, not usefulness. Roger finds them repulsive, and so do I." She returned her attention to the embroidery pattern.

Noble's face lit up. "Well, that settles it," he said congenially. "If Roger Mortimer dislikes them, there must clearly be value to them! I take back my chastisement—the term applied to Gwirion is highly complimentary."

She looked mildly exasperated. "I only even said it because I assumed you'd hired Gwirion to play that role."

Noble shook his head, looking superior. "Gwirion's no vagabond, and he's certainly not *hired* to the task. So I suppose with him it's more of a . . . spontaneous vocation." He smiled, nodded his head a little, tickled. "I rather like that. Gwirion: my Fool."

"I stand by my observation that your fool is very much indulged."

A pause, as he crossed to her and lifted her chin to face him. "He's feeling a bit threatened by your arrival."

"I don't see why. My presence has no effect on him. We've never even spoken to each other."

"I know, but I had to reassure him." He smiled at her then

turned away, shrugging out of the corselet and pulling the tunic over his head.

"I might like such occasional reassurance myself," Isabel suggested, pretending to struggle with a snarl in the embroidery thread.

"I can hardly imagine why you'd require it, milady." He looked at her meaningfully as he brushed the twigs from his hair, and she knew that if she let it, the conversation could end right here, with her complaint unheard but her dignity intact—and her subordination to Gwirion cemented. She'd known that to accept any man's hand was to subject herself to certain elemental insults, but being bested by a parasite was not among them.

He was waiting to see if she would pursue it.

"I was hurt to hear you'd forgotten about our ride this morning," she announced, almost defiantly, and tossed the embroidery frame to the ground.

"I see." He sat beside her and caught her off guard by running his tongue under the edge of her wimple, along the side of her face. He knew they had to have this conversation—he had planned it— but now he was really only interested in removing her clothes. "Surely you're not jealous of Gwirion?"

She jerked her face away from him. "I am trying not to be."

"But, madam, that's a waste of your time," he insisted, taking off her circlet and laying it near the bed. He tugged at her veil with a playful grin; she tried to maintain a dignified expression and ignored him. "You can't replace him, and he can't replace you." He ripped the wimple from her head, exposing her chin and neck and the great coiled whorls of her braids. Isabel bristled but otherwise wouldn't acknowledge the action.

"Envy isn't jealousy. I don't envy him. But I trust I will occasionally be the one whom you will choose when there's a clash of interests."

"No," he said casually, "that will quite certainly never happen."

She looked so annoyed by the declaration that he barely had the patience to go on. He was pleased she understood that this was a lesson, but he didn't want to take up time with an argument just to lay

the ground rules. So he reached down to the silver belt at her hips, and began to unfasten it as he spoke. She did not move. "But don't fret about it. It's unlikely your requests for my time and attention will conflict very often. Gwirion has a habit I quite approve of and strongly recommend." He tossed the belt on the floor and picked up the hem of her long silk kirtle. "He befriends everyone. He doesn't sit on his *posterior* waiting to see if I'll pay attention to him." As he said the word, he shoved the back of her kirtle up under her buttocks while she sat stubbornly immobile on the bed. He reached up the front of the skirt, and rested one hand on each of her thighs, high up her lap, and his splayed fingers pulled at the flesh of each leg, parting them. She flushed and her body lurched toward him despite herself. "Do you have an argument with the attention I pay you? I thought you enjoyed it." His fingers crept inward. "If you don't, I'll withdraw it." And he began to pull away. Almost not knowing she did it, she clapped her hands down hard over his to keep them where they were. This was the one thing Gwirion could never threaten. She released his hands, returned his smile, and drew up the hem of her skirt.

THE next morning, Gwirion was playing harp in the hall in the rapid Celtic style Isabel still found amazing. The horsehair strings gave the harp a clearer sound than the gut-strung instruments she was used to, and every little grace note stood out clearly. It was a soft, mellifluous effect; it did not, in her opinion, fit Gwirion at all. Nor did his pleasant composure this morning as he relaxed beside the fire, chatting with Noble, with a comfortable familiarity she had yet to attain. He looked like a well-bred young musician, perhaps a bard in training; the gleefully vicious adolescent lurking within showed no signs of striking out, although he still refused to address the queen directly.

Resisting the entrancing tease of the music, she retired early to her solar from breakfast while the sewing bevy and Adèle were still

eating in the lower end of the hall. Stout maternal Marged, amused by the notion that one of her kitchen girls might end up in service—legitimate service—upstairs, had released Enid from morning duties to give her time at spindles with Her Majesty. The two young women found themselves alone in the queen's chamber and Isabel was about to sit at the wheel when she noticed a small silk bag lying on her bed. Curious, she opened it and looked in.

There was a large handful of Welsh-minted coins in the bag. "What is this for?" she wondered aloud, and Enid, with permission, peered over her shoulder.

"Oh," she said offhandedly. "That's your *cowyll*, milady. Hadn't he paid it yet?" She returned to her stool and picked up a spindle.

"My what?"

"*Cowyll?*" Obviously the term meant nothing to the queen. "I don't know what they call it in Norman," Enid said. "Maiden fee? What he owes you for your virginity?"

Isabel stared at her, then at the bag, shocked. "I'm not accepting this," she said.

"Isn't it enough?" asked Enid, standing again to reexamine the kines in the bag. It was a lot—more than she or any girl she knew had received, more money than she'd ever seen together in her life. "Perhaps, no offense, milady, but perhaps it's less for your being a foreigner? I thought foreign women got nothing at all, to be honest, but then it is very bad luck to deprive a woman of—"

"It has nothing to do with the amount," the queen said impatiently. "I just can't accept it."

Enid's eyes widened and she gave the queen a conspiratorial grin. "Weren't you a maiden, then, milady?"

"Of course I was!" the queen snapped. "But I did not *sell* my body to him, I'm not a—" She couldn't recall the Welsh for prostitute, but Enid understood. She laughed without malice at the confusion and returned to spinning.

"Oh, no, milady, it's not like that. The man always pays it to the woman, doesn't matter who. You don't have a maiden fee where you come from?"

"*No*," Isabel said shortly.

"Isn't your virginity valuable to you?"

"This is an extraordinary conversation," the queen announced, shaking her head, and moved to the window seat that looked out over the river.

But Enid's curiosity was piqued now. "Pardon, milady, but do you mean where you're from, they just give it away? They're that eager for it?" She laughed approvingly. "I certainly hadn't heard that about the Saxon women!"

"I am Norman," the queen corrected.

"It's the same thing, though, isn't it, milady?" Said without intended offense, it was more statement than question, and it wasn't the first time here that her lineage had been so casually insulted. Saxon, Norman, English, French—the terms were used almost interchangeably to describe anybody, of any background, who came from beyond the border to the east, although Saxon, which was the greatest insult to Norman aristocracy, was the commonest. Frustrated, Isabel pressed her hands against her forehead and leaned back in the felt-covered cushions of the window seat.

"I need an interpreter. Speaking the language does not begin to suffice for comprehending anything here."

Pleased by how fortune was smiling on her today, Enid put aside the spindle and stood up. "If Your Majesty wouldn't be offended by a villein's daughter from the kitchen . . ." She let it trail off as the queen looked up with obvious interest. But before she could actually speak, the door opened and Adèle's wimpled head popped into view.

"What's going on here?" she demanded, stepping fully into the room.

"Do you know what that is, Adèle?" the queen responded, pointing to the bag on the bed. She looked resignedly amused now, the first flicker Enid had ever seen of a possible sense of humor in the woman. Adèle glanced at the sack and used a finger to draw it open.

"It's that Welsh money, kines, isn't it?"

"It's a bit more complicated than that, and we would both have made fools of ourselves wandering around the bailey asking people

why it was lying on my bed this morning. Enid is going to ensure that we do *not* make fools of ourselves. With that or anything else."

"Why Enid?" Adèle asked at once, leveling her eyes on the girl. Enid looked entirely untroubled by the scrutiny.

"Because I *like* her, Adèle," said the queen with patient amusement. "Enid, what is the legal procedure to have you added to my retinue?"

Adèle glanced at Isabel and said something in the dull nasally language Enid could not understand. There was a brief exchange between them without apparent emotion—neither of these women was very expressive, which Enid knew the entire castle found unattractive. She wondered if that should be on the list of things to explain to them.

"Excuse us, Enid, that was rude," the queen said in Welsh. "Adèle is concerned about the dynamics of raising a villein to court level."

"Oh, I doubt it's even allowable, I'm not freeborn," Enid said comfortably. "But the cook will let me go whenever you need me to explain something for you." She smiled and politely excused herself, knowing there were certain things that would never be explained, and glad she had control of them.

SUCH bright colors," Enid said admiringly some days later, looking at a red-and-yellow kerchief that Adèle had left on the sill after wiping off the rain. "It's rare to see a linen take the dye so well."

"It's from France, they're more advanced with textiles," the queen said offhandedly, squelching the impulse to add that they were actually more advanced with everything. She smiled as Enid's pretty eyes grew round. The sewing bevy exchanged looks: They were tired of both the queen's trumpeting her foreign identity and the servant girl's fascination with it. The woman was *here* now. She should try to be *Welsh*. They had already weathered a disagreement between the royal

couple over this room's decoration: Isabel had started to wainscot it in the French style, until her husband, leaning languidly against the door frame, began reciting worthier uses for both the wood and the laborers. Everybody knew this was not the real issue, but it accomplished what he wanted: She had called off the work herself.

"May I hold it?" Enid asked, her hand hovering near the kerchief.

Isabel looked up and considered Enid for a moment. The peasant's occasional cheekiness was worth the cheer she added to the solar. "You may keep it," the queen said, smiling, and returned to her sewing.

The Welsh women at once exchanged expressions usually reserved for gossip. Enid blinked. "Your Majesty, are you sure?"

"Yes, of course," Isabel answered, a little confused by the group reaction.

The women once again swapped glances, quickly, and then deliberately busied themselves in their sewing. Enid pressed the kerchief to the good-luck amulet she wore tied around her neck, then tucked it into her belt. "Thank you, milady," she said. "May I be excused to the kitchen, then?" She lowered her voice. "I'd like to show Marged."

This seemed a dramatic reaction to receiving what was practically a rag, but the queen nodded, and Enid scampered off. Again there was a quick exchange of glances among the women and then they busied themselves in their work again.

"What is going on?" Adèle demanded.

"Nothing," Gwen said quickly.

"Somebody explain what is wrong with Her Majesty giving Enid a gift," she insisted. They stared at her blankly.

"Is it favoritism?" the queen asked, knowing that of course it was. The eyes all swiveled from Adèle to Isabel. "Is it wrong to have given her a gift without giving the four of you one? I didn't mean to insult anybody; it's just a trifle."

Again the exchange of glances. "You didn't insult *us*, milady," stout Generys hummed.

"Then whom did I insult?"

And yet again the exchange of looks, as if they were clairvoyantly

discussing who should next speak for the group. "Nobody, yet, mi-lady," Gwen finally answered, the only one who seemed amused. "But wait until Enid opens her mouth."

Frustrated, Isabel dropped the discussion. It was always like pulling teeth, trying to speak to these four; if it would not have been a diplomatic disaster, she'd happily send all of them home to their parents. She returned to her embroidery.

B Y the time Isabel went down to supper, the entire castle knew that she had given Enid a used linen kerchief. The queen was aware of cold eyes on her in hall, especially from the officers and par-ticularly from Gwilym the steward, who was a man of great dignity and usually most civil. Enid, and only Enid, looked content, al-though people were eyeing her as much as they were Isabel. Enid didn't seem to care.

There was a flurry of bows around the room as the king and Gwirion entered from the courtyard, their hair and long tunics damp from the dense evening fog. Noble was laughing at a story Gwirion was telling with the aid of obscene gestures, but he stopped himself and elbowed his friend when he saw Enid standing near the kitchen screens. "It's the kerchief that brought down Cymaron! I *knew* it was a French conspiracy," the queen heard Gwirion declaim, grinning, as he went to get his harp from its chest. Noble began walking toward Enid. Concerned that she had gotten the girl into trouble, Isabel watched him. As Gwilym and Hafaidd, the wiry court usher, helped people into their seats for the meal, the queen moved toward her own chair, her eyes still on her husband. Enid curtsied deeply, and when Noble spoke to her, she proudly presented the kerchief. He swiveled so that his broad shoulders and back blocked both of them from general view, and they fell into quiet conversation. Isabel noticed Gwirion watching them too, as he set his harp on its back a few yards from the hearth. He still sported a derisive grin. What was going on?

When she turned her eyes back toward the conversing pair, Enid had vanished into the kitchen and Noble held the kerchief. He presented it to his wife with a small ironic flourish when he reached his seat.

"You can't do that," he said quietly, and gestured to the chamberlain to pour his ale.

"Why not?" she whispered.

"Not here," he muttered back. He turned to Hafaidd. "Ask Father Idnerth to begin the blessing."

W OULD you like me to explain your blunder, then?" Noble said after the chandler had left them with a blazing hearth that evening.

"*Please.*"

"We have a custom here of handing down used clothing through the ranks."

"We do that in England too, especially at Christmas." Isabel began to unfasten her wimple, readying for bed.

"I think we must do it differently here, at least when it comes to livery." He stretched out on the bed and crossed his booted feet, clasping his hands comfortably behind his head. "It's a very structured system. To step outside the bounds of it . . . discomfits our charges. It makes a bit of a statement."

Isabel sighed. "And what statement did I make?"

"Well . . ." he said, with wry amusement. "You realize that red and gold happen to be my colors. Considering the queen gives the gift of linen livery to court officers by rank, and Enid was the only one who received any from you, you effectively raised her status above everyone else's, even Gwilym and my penteulu Efan. And Father Idnerth. And Justice Goronwy. And Cadwgan the marshal. Shall I go on?" He glanced up at her as if they were sharing a private joke.

She scowled in frustration as she unplaited one of her braids. "I gave her a used piece of cloth."

"Used by you," Noble corrected. "That only makes it more valuable; it is imbued with the essence of royalty. Father Idnerth receives an entire outfit of my used clothes for Lent each year—I give him the rattiest thing in my chests, to be honest, and he responds as if it's manna from heaven. It's rather endearing. But when it comes to the queen and linen, it's very strictly regulated. If you'd given her a silk gown, there would have been less fuss."

"She wasn't interested in a silk gown—she liked the kerchief! This is absurd."

"Structure is proof of an advanced society," Noble said complacently.

"*Success* is proof of an advanced society," Isabel shot back, too aggravated to be prudent.

His humor vanished; he sat up snapping, "And what is that supposed to mean?"

"Nothing." She hesitated. "I just mean there's no sense in having all these rituals and beliefs and traditions if they don't help you to thrive. And, Noble"—she paused again, but decided she had to say it—"Maelienydd is not thriving."

He looked at once disappointed and relieved, and threw himself back down into a comfortable slouch. "Yes, and it's entirely because I won't let you give Enid a rag. Regicide and genocide and treachery have absolutely nothing to do with the state of my kingdom." He gave her a withering glance. "I didn't ask to spend all of my resources fighting off Norman persecution, you know."

Isabel let the loose hair fall so that it blocked her face from him. Very quietly she said, "It doesn't have to be persecution."

He froze, and then looked genuinely alarmed. "What does that mean?"

She hesitated again, but decided to press on. This was her belief and it would out eventually. She could not conceive of speaking to a man of her own race this way, but surely as a Welsh queen of Norman blood she was entitled. She pushed her hair away from her face and looked at him directly. "If you let the Norman influence in. It would take so much burden from your shoulders and your people

could embrace modern civilization—trade and scholarship and statecraft—that they have no access to now because your minds are all as guarded as your borders."

He gaped at her, furious and horrified, and stood up. "Is that why your uncle sent you here, to lull me into this most singular reasoning?" he whispered, then grabbed her roughly by the wrist, jerking her toward him. *"Answer me!"*

"Of course not," she stammered. "I'm sorry, that's not what I—" She silenced herself as he released her arm and shoved her roughly down onto the bed. She had misjudged, she had gone too far even as queen consort, and she steeled herself for punishment.

But Noble, his quicksilver temper instantly reined in, only looked at her curiously. "Why are you cowering?" he demanded. "You look like you expect me to strike you." She said nothing, and he took a step away to view the whole of her posture. He had never seen her like this. "You do expect me to strike you, don't you?" he concluded, the harsh amusement she was already too familiar with creeping into his voice. "Why?" She said nothing. He nodded, the derision growing. "Is that what an Englishman would do in my position? Strike you for no good reason? Strike you for having an articulate opinion that happens to oppose his?" She glanced at him awkwardly and then away again, and slowly straightened up. Her behavior only offered him greater entertainment. "One of your own would have struck you for that, is that it?" He laughed. "And *we're* the barbarians, are we? Is this a part of the enlightened Norman influence you think I should introduce to my primitive people—telling the men they can slap their women around just for challenging their authority? How extraordinary."

"Then I may safely challenge your authority?" Isabel ventured, collecting herself.

"If you ever speak again of 'letting in the Norman influence,' your king will deal with you very harshly," he assured her. "But you may challenge your husband. That doesn't mean he'll acquiesce, but he certainly won't *beat* you for it." He seemed almost tickled by the image.

"Then I'm challenging your authority," she said calmly. "I am giving the kerchief back to Enid."

"No you're not," he said firmly, serious again. "Your king doesn't allow it."

"Then your wife shall withhold her affection from you."

"If you insist on punishing yourself," he said agreeably, and opened his door. Gethin the doorkeeper took a step toward him.

"Sire?"

"The queen is feeling poorly this evening and would like to retire to her own chamber early. See she gets there safely." He handed her off to Gethin, her hair uncovered and half unbraided, and then, without another glance in her direction, he began to undress for bed.

SOME called it Midsummer and some St. John's Day. Mostly, for them, it was the day to celebrate the end of sheep shearing, and weather permitting it called for a great supper to be taken in the courtyard under the latest twilight of the year.

Noble knew, as had his forefathers, that a land of shepherds and poets would not happily yield up their traditional solstice celebrations, so the emphasis around Castell Cymaron was not especially Christian. The evening before, lintels and sills had been festooned with St. John's wort, dangerously large bonfires lit in the courtyard and village, and birch poles raised to dance around. The chaplain and the village priest grudgingly acknowledged the nature of the day in mass, but few rose in time to attend mass this morning anyhow. Egged on by Gwirion from the castle walls, some of the local peasant youths rolled blazing wooden wheels down the steep castle mound and into the Aron, crowing that they were Llew the sun god incarnate.

The war began that evening after supper.

Despite damp from the intermittent morning rain, the evening feast was held outside. The courtyard easily had room for the

hundred-odd souls who, in addition to Noble's teulu, made up the population of the village, as well as dozens of families within two hours' walk of the castle, and a few of the nobility within an hour's ride. The high table was on a small dais beside the steps to the hall, and trestle tables ran lengthwise from it to the kitchen garden at the far end. Servants circled the tables with fronds of bracken to keep the evening midges at bay. Castell Cymaron was brilliantly sited for domestic comfort—Isabel's own ancestors, not Noble's, could take credit for that. It was on an elevated spot within the valley, warmer than the surrounding hillsides: high enough to be out of the river mist and valley bogs, but low enough also to be sheltered from the wind. Although the stone was far inferior to anything in England, the bailey afforded one of the most pleasant courtyards Isabel could think of, somehow both spacious and cozy. Her grandfather had built this place—she chose not to think about why—as a literal home away from home, not simply a military outpost.

With Enid's assistance, the queen was finally adjusting to Welsh dining habits. These people were as clean and fastidious as the Norman English, perhaps more so, but the stilted patterns of etiquette she had been raised with were almost unknown here ("here in the wilderness," Adèle muttered in French). And it was supper rather than dinner that constituted the largest meal of the day. From what Isabel could tell, the wild-eyed young teulu, who lived in the village but ate at the castle, did not even stop for a midday meal, and entertainment was nearly always reserved for the cooler evening hours. It had taken her a while to develop any taste for the food at all. Even in the castle, they seemed to live on meat, oats, and vast quantities of cheese; wheat bread was entirely missing and barley was a sour substitute. There were no vegetables but leeks and cabbage, and there was such a narrow range of culinary herbs that Isabel sometimes wondered what the kitchen garden was really used for.

But there was a stranger thing about the Welsh at board. At any well-mannered English table, people sat in pairs, with a cup, platter, and trencher loaf between them. Here, they shared these things among three people, which led to a louder, messier, but more con-

vivial mealtime. She and Noble were exempt from this, partaking only with each other; Gwirion and the yet-to-be-exiled Corr, who sat not at board but behind the king's left shoulder, had nothing except their laps with which to share their portion. Their meals were the most convivial of all.

Isabel was happy, especially to be in an official capacity at her husband's side tonight. After weathering their first real argument, she actually felt closer to him. And there was, for the populace, still a vague aura of romance to her presence—it was pleasant to feel admired for a change, even if they still considered her an outsider. It was almost a relief to have the villagers and farmholders present. For all the aromas they brought with them there was also a freshness and vigor compared to the stilted atmosphere of her solar, which she was beginning to hate. Only Enid's sunny company, a presence she had called upon often these past few weeks, made that room bearable to her. At her insistence, and to the usher's perturbation, Enid had been temporarily promoted to queen's cupbearer, and rather than joining the other servants at the lower tables, she was attending to the queen's mead, displacing Generys of the sewing bevy. This had caused some friction in the solar—although not as much as the kerchief had. Isabel didn't care; by her reasoning, honors ought to be bestowed by merit, not exclusively by birth. She had given the kerchief back to Enid in secret and the girl kept it tucked into her belt, underneath her apron. She understood it did not signify the outrageous honor she had thought at first, but it was still a favor and she cherished it.

The evening wore on while the sun lingered, as if suspended in hazy indecision, just enough silver cloud cloaking it to spare their eyes as they sat facing into it. The old bard Hywel lugubriously recited the adventures of the hero Pryderi and of Arthur, the gigantic, terrifying warrior-ruler of the ancient Britons. Council members and freemen made speeches to the queen, the king, and the two of them together. Bawdy toasts regarding the number of their offspring were offered throughout the meal; she had blushed at first, but by the time the tables were being cleared and villagers were unwrapping musical instruments, she'd grown immune to it, and understood that they

were meant to be flattering. The Welsh of Maelienydd were surely an earthier lot than her own people, but there was something welcoming about them that warmed her.

The only dark spot of the evening was upon them now. She'd known that Gwirion would perform beyond his traditional opening song, but what he was doing—at Noble's insistence, which made it worse—was disgusting. And the commons' delight with it dampened her joy of their presence.

It was entertainment that would never have been allowed at Wigmore. Gwirion stood on each of the five long tables in turn. At each table he would roll a small ball from one end toward the other, and people would grab for it. Whoever caught it was invited to name any one of the landlords or appointed officials who lived in or near the castle, and Gwirion would do a crude imitation of that man in sexual congress. Noble justified this rancid debauchery as "entertainment befitting the heat of the day," but she was certain Gwirion was itching for any excuse to do it. He was very specific and very lewd, and the crowd adored him. The sewing bevy had faces so red their eyes were nearly bloodshot; Adèle, appalled, had retreated to the far end of the courtyard. Each subject of imitation turned even more crimson than the queen's ladies, but Cadwgan the marshal was good-humored enough to laugh at his caricature, and the subsequent victims felt it only manly to follow suit. Noble had announced that if Gwirion failed to perform to the ball catcher's satisfaction, the ball catcher could whip him, which put a certain forced enthusiasm into his act.

Finally, as the air was turning periwinkle under a cloudy, moonless sky and the silent chandler had begun to light the torches, Gwirion stood on the final table. By now everyone was exceptionally drunk and anything resembling manners or decorum was forgotten. Mothers from the village had gathered up their younger children and departed, but the crowd was still large. As the ball bounded down the length of the table, a very tall man reached out with an enormous paw and almost caught it—but a wizened arm elbowed past him and someone else had claimed it. The tall man sat back, drunk beyond

caring. Noble, Isabel, and Gwirion were all surprised to see Adèle's bony hand clenching the ball.

"Show us the king," she challenged.

The crowd lost itself for a moment in a collective, drunken mumble, trying to decide whether this was riotously funny or offensive to the point of corporal punishment. *What are you doing?* Isabel thought. Adèle's behavior lately had bordered on eccentric.

"I don't believe the king is on the list," Gwirion called back to her.

"You said any lord or official. His Majesty is both. Of course, you could do the proper thing and refuse." She smiled up at him with rheumy eyes. "I won't whip you too hard."

Their audience exploded with laughter and began to pound on the table boards. Hating his life, Gwirion in the dusk turned to look at Noble. Noble stared back at him, his face unreadable. Gwirion looked then at the queen, who was giving Adèle an expression of alarm. He saw Enid scowling at him from the foot of the dais; remembering her lecture in the kitchen, he grudgingly squashed his first instinct, which was to portray the king nodding off from boredom while mounting his wife.

He looked once more at Noble. The courtyard grew silent with tense expectation. The king, who enjoyed this sort of spectacle, sat back in his chair savoring the crowd's collective bated breath. He offered an innocent shrug in his friend's direction, leaving it to Gwirion.

But then he smiled slightly, to encourage him.

"His Majesty will certainly excuse me from a whipping if I fail to comply?"

"Of course not," Noble replied pleasantly. "I can't break my own rules—what sort of ruler would that make me?" The crowd cheered him, then settled back into their edgy anticipation.

Finally Gwirion looked back down at Adèle. "Well then, madam," he said, sounding more nervous than he'd realized he was. "I always try to think of the ladies' best interests, and I don't want you to jeopardize your health by beating me just for the king's amusement."

"It would be for my own amusement," Adèle assured him, and everyone laughed.

"I'm sorry to disappoint you, then," he said, shifting his attention to the yard at large. "Ladies and gentlemen—and all the rest of you as well—with tremendous reverence and respect, I give you His Royal Majesty in the heat of rutting."

Everyone wanted to clap and no one did; instead they all looked up at the dais. "Oh, God," Isabel whispered, and reached out instinctively for her husband's arm. "Make him stop. Nobody should be allowed to be so disrespectful."

Seeing her distress he promised, "I'll stop him in a moment, I just want to see him squirm a bit." He gave her hand a reassuring kiss, which the audience responded to loudly, taking it to mean the royal couple was amused to see themselves caricatured. He gestured to the chandler, and a torch was held up near where Gwirion stood.

On the near end of the table, Gwirion had already begun his performance. "Good evening, love," he purred, with an overdone affectation of the king's velvet baritone. "Don't you like my beautiful blue eyes? I'm delighted to meet you—now come over here at once and take your clothes off." The crowd guffawed.

"Get to the good part!" an anonymous drunk called out from the back.

"Watch yourself, you're next," Gwirion hissed, and willed his attention back to his lamentable situation. Adèle, apparently, had vanished. He hoped the queen would give her a good beating for setting up this unfortunate scenario.

He couldn't be humorous without getting into trouble. The previous caricatures had been easy: His marshal was more interested in cleaning tack than the fellatio he was receiving; his horny young penteulu got stuck in a series of contorted positions trying to prove his ruggedness; his deadpan steward suffered satyriasis; and his chaplain was a marvelously subversive study of equating guilt and pleasure. But the king would not take kindly to an unflattering portrait, so Gwirion opted for a routine of generic mimed humping, punctuated with occasional interjections of lust. There was nothing clever to it,

but the simple fact that he was depicting *the king* made it electric to his audience, king included. Every now and then he would pause in his acrobatics to announce with withering suavity, "Don't worry, then, you marvelous creature, I've barely started here." The crowd loved this, and so did Noble, so Gwirion decided to keep the routine going for as long as he could. He was pleased with himself for saving the situation and hoped that old bat Adèle was watching, wherever she was.

Isabel was surprised. She was certain Gwirion would have tried to humiliate her, but this was almost flattering. She and Noble exchanged looks and grinned, although her cheeks felt hot in the torchlight. He kissed the palm of her hand, which made her shudder pleasantly and added fuel to the crowd's rising heat. Gwirion's imitation of Noble's voice in the midst of abandon was almost unnerving. As a performer—even of such a perverse entertainment—he had surprising charisma. She could see his satisfaction at owning the crowd's collective mood: He knew exactly how far he could take this before they became bored, and although she found the idea unsettling, he must indeed have seen his master in the act once. She blushed more deeply, hoping it wasn't with her.

"Oh, Lord, yes, oh, God—" Gwirion groaned. "Oh . . . oh . . . oh . . . oh yes . . ." He swiveled suddenly so that his upturned face was turned straight to the king and queen, and as loudly as he could he finished off with an ecstatic cry of "I'm coming, Enid!" Then he leapt nimbly off the table to sprint past them, up the steps and into the hall.

Pandemonium broke out instantly. The crowd bellowed, some with hilarity, others with indignation that the queen had been so publicly embarrassed. She snapped her head toward her husband and saw Enid, between them, pale to the color of cold ashes and run from the dais out of sight. Isabel leapt up, half determined to quiet the yard with her own wrath, but the pained amusement on her husband's face humiliated her beyond words, and she stalked off the dais and toward the stairs without a word. Adèle, seething with an enraged thrill from the back of the crowd, went after her.

Meanwhile, across the tables, those who found Gwirion clever (mostly the teulu) were scolded by those who found him rude (everybody else), and inevitably drunken brawls broke out. It took the castle garrison the better part of an hour to clear the yard.

SHE won't see you, sire," Adèle said coldly. They were standing on the balcony outside the queen's solar. Irritated, he grabbed her by the shoulder and pushed her aside, snatching the torch from the chandler's grasp.

Isabel was alone in the darkened room, fuming. She turned her head slightly when the door opened, but recognizing his step turned away again. "I'm not going to look you in the face, I don't want to be bewitched by those beautiful eyes you use on kitchen sluts."

He drew his breath in sharply, but stopped himself from speaking on impulse. "Isabel," he ventured after a calming pause, and placed the torch in a wall brace. "It was a performance. It was not meant to be taken seriously."

"Are you saying you've never been with Enid?"

"No, I'm not," he answered. "I had a life before you arrived, you know."

"So did I," she replied. "I did not bring mine with me into this marriage."

"Of course you did," he corrected. "I'd have gained nothing by marrying you otherwise."

"Are you in love with her?" she blurted out, and instantly regretted it.

But he only laughed, relieved by the absurdity of the question. "I had no idea you were such a child! I barely know the girl, I never bother about friendships with women. If I falter as a partner, it's because I lack experience that way. In fact, that's part of what upsets Gwirion about you. He prefers knowing my women are only—"

"Your *women?*" she repeated, and despite herself turned to glare at him. "Would you please explain that phrase?"

"Don't do this," he said in a tired voice. "I was warned that this is what wives do. You're an intelligent woman, I thought you were exempt. Please don't prove me wrong now."

"What are you talking about?" she demanded.

"The oration on fidelity." He closed his eyes and rubbed his temple. "I'm sorry Gwirion did that, but if his intention was to hurt you and humiliate you, remember that you're just letting him win if you get upset. Come to bed now. Or would you rather sleep in here?" He opened his bleary eyes again.

Isabel was standing directly in front of him, shaking with anger. For a moment he was simply amused by her exaggerated expression, but then he realized the anger was directed at him, and he'd have to deal with it before being allowed to retire. He looked at her ruefully. "Give me the speech, then, if that will offer you relief. But be quick, I'm likely to fall asleep standing up."

"*Get out!*" she hissed, and slapped him hard across the face.

Like a serpent springing, he grabbed both her hands and pinned them fast in one of his. "That is not allowed," he said as if speaking to a willful child, and held her chin. "You will not strike your sovereign lord. Ever. Do you understand?"

"Bastard!"

He slapped her. Unlike hers, it was controlled and deliberate, intended not to hurt but to startle. "Don't become hysterical or I won't talk to you. Do you understand?" After a sullen moment of resistance, she glanced down and nodded. He released her hands. "Then you're free to speak."

She looked up at him with angry eyes. "I want to know what you meant by your 'women.'"

He considered this. She probably did not really want the truth, she simply wanted something that would mend her pride.

"What do you want to know?"

"I want to know what you meant," she insisted.

"I meant women I have nonconjugal fornication with." It was an effort not to laugh at himself for sounding so formal.

"In the present tense?"

He wished Gwirion were here, there was probably a pun in there crying out to be discovered, but he couldn't get his mind around it. His delay upset her.

"In the present tense?" she demanded.

"Of course in the present tense," he said impatiently. "Go on with the pontificating, just be quick about it."

She looked up at him for a moment. "No," she said sadly. "If this marriage is a sham, no pontificating is going to change that."

Again he laughed at her naiveté. "It's not a sham, what an absurd thing to say. It's a political contract. I have no personal obligations to you." This was, in fact, a lie, but she with her stubborn adherence to foreign custom wouldn't know that, and he was content to keep it that way for as long as he could. "You think like all the other wives, don't you? That's a disappointment, but I'll get over it." He surprised her by kissing her affectionately on the forehead. "I hope you'll come to me tonight. But if you don't, I'll see you at morning mass."

He left, taking the torch with him.

H E stepped into his own chamber to find a candelabra blazing on the floor by the unlit hearth. Sitting beside it was a familiar dark-haired figure, his sharp features strangely shadowed in the candlelight.

"And what are *you* doing in here?" Noble asked.

Gwirion looked over his shoulder at him. "It's the one place I was certain she wouldn't come tonight."

Noble sat on a chest near him and leaned back against a wool tapestry. "There was no need to be so cruel, you know."

"There would have been no *chance* to be cruel if you hadn't *insisted* upon that absurd game."

Noble shook his head. "That's a specious defense. I never suggested that the game include humiliating my wife."

"I was trying to get back at the old lady."

"You didn't upset the old lady nearly so much as the young lady."

"It's ridiculous for her to be upset about your romps," Gwirion protested, fidgeting with the tuning key he kept tied by a string to his belt. "I can't believe she didn't know about them until tonight."

"I was a little surprised by that myself," Noble admitted. "But even if she had known, Gwirion, it was a nasty thing to do. It's one thing to face it—it's another to face it in front of half the kingdom."

The smaller man sat up very straight and looked at him with hard dark eyes. "I'm not saying it was kind of me," he admitted. "But honestly, what's really upsetting her now? That I embarrassed her? Or that you have a healthy appetite?"

"That's not the issue—"

"No, that *is* the issue. She'd be upset no matter how she heard the news. She's upset with you, Noble, not with me."

"She's upset with both of us."

"She'll recover," Gwirion said with a deliberate yawn. "I'm glad we had this little chat, but I'll be off to sleep now."

He rose with angular, feline grace and took a step toward the door, which suddenly opened as the queen stepped into the room. Seeing Gwirion, she stopped. Seeing her, Gwirion stopped. The king rose. There was an awkward moment of silence.

"I don't believe the two of you have been formally introduced," Noble finally said. This seemed extraordinary given that she'd been there over a month, but Gwirion had managed to avoid it. "Gwirion, this is your queen. Pay your respects to her." Gwirion looked at him, incredulous. *"Now."*

With the enthusiasm of a punished boy apologizing under duress to some smaller child he has tormented, Gwirion approached her and presented himself with a deep but grudging bow. "Milady," he muttered, not looking at her. Still bent over, he glanced at Noble. "Shall I kiss the hem of her train?" he asked sarcastically.

"No," she said firmly. "I don't want it soiled." She heard Noble

chuckle at this, which pleased her. Gwirion stood up abruptly, black eyes sparking, but her satisfaction waned when she saw that he was not the least insulted.

"Perhaps she has promise after all," he said to the king, and walked out of the room without further acknowledging her.

"I'm glad you came," Noble said quietly after a moment.

"I couldn't bear the thought that you would bring another woman in here tonight."

Noble laughed harshly. "What do you think I am? Under the circumstances, that would be cretinous."

"Oh? Then how does it work? Do *you* go to *them*?" she asked, angry with herself for caring.

"Isabel—"

"Or perhaps you do it in the stables with the other beasts."

"For the love of Christ," he muttered, irritated. "I won't discuss this." He gestured. "Undress now, and come to bed."

She pulled away from him and left.

Once he knew she was safely gone, he opened his door a crack to speak to his doorkeeper. "Enid," he said.

But he was relieved when Gethin returned with the message that Enid had refused to come.

· 3 ·

USES OF ADULTERY

High Summer, 1198

HAT SUMMER, Noble's greatest headaches were domestic, but he could not ignore the forces at his borders. The late Lord Rhys's kingdom of Deheubarth was close to anarchy as his sons squabbled over it; north of Maelienydd lay the divided and increasingly unstable Powys, half its forces slaughtered in a recent misguided uprising against the English.

A bigger concern for Noble, however, lay farther to the north, in Gwynedd. Llewelyn ap Iorwerth, an upstart would-be prince just a few years his junior, was fighting and strategizing his way toward a united crown of Gwynedd on a wave of public adoration. An able warrior and charismatic leader, he promised to be unreliable as an ally—he did want stability, and wanted all of Wales to throw off the Norman yoke, but to Noble's mind, he wanted the ultimate glory in this achievement to be reserved only for himself. Even if he proved to be, in power, the next Lord Rhys, Llewelyn did not seem the sort to encourage a true confederacy of fellow rulers. He made no aggres-

sive gestures; he was still working on uniting Gwynedd, and anyway, a thick slab of Powys served as a buffer between them. But Noble didn't trust him, and was determined to glean what his intentions were toward the English—and particularly toward King Richard's brother John, who watched Wales in his brother's absence, and who might succeed the bellicose monarch once he killed himself on a continental battlefield. Richard's reign had not been good for Wales; the Marcher barons had run wild with frontier ambition during his perennial absence from England. But John might strike his own bargain with the Marcher lords. He had been one of them, and he was not averse to guile. This thought, in turn, reminded Noble of the worst of his worries.

"Damn Roger Mortimer," he grumbled, his head on Enid's lap, reclining nude beneath a sheet in his receiving room. Their afternoon dalliance had been intended to get his mind off politics. It hadn't worked. Nothing worked.

Gwirion had been called in to play for them and he was helping Enid, wearing only her shift, to tie her veil back on. It was the first time since the Midsummer feast that she was civil to him; she'd refused to even speak to him until he had admitted, in front of Noble, that he'd been a malicious ass to the queen. "*Now* what has our beloved Roger done?" Gwirion asked.

"Nothing yet," Noble muttered. "Literally nothing—my scouts have all vanished into the ether. I send new scouts to find the old ones and they vanish as well."

"And which one is Mortimer, again, sire?" Enid asked playfully.

"Trade lives with me, won't you?" Noble pleaded, reaching up to tweak her nose. "I want your ignorance."

"I am not ignorant, Your Majesty!" Enid replied with cheerful indignation, and swatted his hand away. "But which is Mortimer? All those Norman names sound the same to me."

"I believe," Gwirion said, reading a small gesture from Noble and moving toward the door, "that I'll depart and let the king"—he waggled his eyebrows—"fill you in."

Enid laughed. "Your subtlety is deafening, Gwirion."

Noble sat up, stretching densely muscled arms as the sheet rolled off him. "Where's my wife?" he asked, and for a fleeting moment Enid shifted uncomfortably. Gwirion looked bored and pointed at the ceiling to the queen's solar above them. Noble rolled his blue eyes slowly toward Enid and gave her a seductive smile. "Just the very thought of Mortimer's exhausted me. I need another nap."

She grinned as he reached for her again. Gwirion, grateful not to be held in attendance for a second round, opened the door—and found himself face-to-face with the queen, who carried a heavy book under her arm. "Your Majesty!" he said with genuine alarm, and behind him heard the king curse under his breath. Gwirion reflexively raised the harp to his chest and wrapped his other arm protectively around it, as if she might injure it. "I was just looking for you, milady. I was wondering if you could give me lessons in that beguiling language of yours." He loosened the grip on the instrument and took her arm, trying to back her out of the doorway. "If you could—"

With a glare, she pulled her arm free and pressed past him, holding out the book. "I need to speak to my husband about a matter of Welsh law that—" She stopped.

It was impossible to hide what was happening. Enid had the sheet wrapped around her and was huddled facing away from the door. Noble sat in profile to his wife, splendid and naked, not looking at her but not deliberately avoiding her either. For a long moment she stood staring silently at one, then the other, her face unreadable. Finally, Noble, as much out of boredom as charity, took a breath to say something, and as if that were her cue, she turned sharply away and walked out of the room. After an awkward beat, Gwirion closed the door.

"Pardon me," he said, "but was I the only one who found that amusing?"

"Gwirion!" Enid snapped.

"At least she had some warning!" Gwirion insisted. "Imagine if I hadn't given her a hint."

"Shut up," Noble muttered, getting to his feet and reaching for his drawers. With a long-suffering sigh he started to pull them on.

"Mortimer had better behave himself for all this," he said under his breath.

NOBLE, like most Welsh rulers, kept his barons committed to him by personal loyalty. Several times a year, he made a circuit of the kingdom, spending weeks in transit visiting his lords, giving gifts, hearing local cases with Goronwy his judge, checking the training progress of the barons' own youthful teulu forces, taking time to speak even with the villeins along the route. It reassured him politically, but he also loved the fuss people made. Even the humblest servants and villagers around Castell Cymaron grew used to him eventually; on the road, amidst the far-flung collections of his subjects, he was a permanent celebrity. Tournaments were held for him by the local teulu, feasts were thrown, and he and Goronwy dispensed their royal justice to plaintiffs. The plaintiffs were often charmingly sycophantic.

His absence allowed his servants to have something like a holiday. Nearly all the court officers went with him, and those of the teulu who didn't serve as bodyguards went off on a circuit of their own to keep them out of trouble, so there were few officials in the castle to cater to. This year it was to be a short tour; he was too concerned about the general political climate to be away from Cymaron for very long.

He avoided the east and his English border, where his scouts were still mysteriously silent and invisible. It was a feint: If Mortimer was up to something, Noble wanted him to proceed as carelessly as possible and thus give himself away, which was less likely if he knew the king was traveling nearby. So he sent Efan, his own penteulu, east to keep a subtle eye on Roger, but he himself moved much more ostentatiously along the southwest border, an area that he and Lord Rhys had tussled over more than once. Custom decreed that at this time the queen go on a circuit of her own, but she had not yet estab-

lished diplomatic ties with any of his people, so he had brought her with him hoping she'd develop some. This meant dragging her through the wind-beaten, heather-crowned hills of one of the bleakest parts of his kingdom, but it also meant that they would have hours a day on horseback with little to distract them from coming to a personal understanding.

Isabel had been stone-cold to him at first and turned away from his touch in bed. Against his native inclination, he persisted with patience and indulgence, allowed Adèle to travel beside them instead of at the back of the train with the rest of the queen's officers, indulged his wife's peculiar newfound fascination with Welsh justice and permitted her to bring the codex of the *Law of Wales* with her. He gave her not one moment to suspect he was straying. She gradually softened, and one afternoon on their trek between manors, their bodyguards began unsentimentally to place bets on the king's chances of riding his wife that night.

They were in the far west, heading north from the village of Rhaeadr on a hillside blazing yellow with gorse, in that awesome quadrant of the kingdom boasting dramatic cliffs and precipices. Isabel conceded a growing fondness for the landscape: As with the castle courtyard, there was somehow both a coziness and spaciousness about it. The royal couple had spent a genuinely pleasant morning together under clouds that looked, as usual, almost close enough to touch. They raised their voices over the slow, damp gusts that cooled the hilltop roads, discussing safely neutral topics like Roman ruins and folk beliefs about the spirits of the local flora. The casual ease between them, as companions, seemed secure enough that even Adèle stopped hovering obsessively, and warily slid back into her assigned place in the procession.

Isabel noticed a small stone pillar high atop a hill on the far side of the valley to the north. She asked her husband if it might not be the remnants of one of the Roman hill forts he'd described. He glanced to where she pointed, and stiffened. "No," he said. "That's a monument." After a pause, he added, "To mark where your uncle killed my uncle." Caught short, she drew a sharp breath. "*One* of my

uncles," he went on, gratuitously. "I believe the final tally was approximately three uncles and one father, limited of course to the one generation. Would you like to go across for a better look?"

She closed her eyes against his icy sarcasm. "Your grievances are starting to resemble boasting, sire. Have you never killed a man? Have the men you killed had no families?"

"I've never killed a man in ambush days after celebrating Christmas with him," said Noble caustically.

She snapped her head around to glare at him. "Roger would never have done such a thing," she declared.

"I'm glad to hear it," he said. "While you're rewriting history, please expunge my father's murder too."

"There must have been some provocation, then."

"Oh, great provocation. Cousin Rhys hosted a Christmas festival at Aberteifi, to celebrate the unprecedented state of nobody being at war with anybody else for more than a week, and my uncle Einion Clud's team bested your uncle Mortimer's in a tournament there. Clearly murder was the only possible response to such an insult, so Roger ambushed him on the ride home. Or perhaps that was just a convenient excuse to take up his father's hobby—the obliteration of my line. Two years later he killed my father and tried to kill me too."

She'd known about Cadwallon, but never having heard the bardic laments, details were unknown to her. "You were *there?*" she gasped, louder than she meant to.

He snorted with contempt that this was news to her. "Don't your minstrels crow triumphantly about it?"

Suddenly she felt very tired. "I'm appalled that he did that, but it's not my duty to atone for him."

He swung around in the saddle to glare at her. "Yes it is," he growled. "That and more. Doesn't it strike you how few men in the prime of life there are about Cymaron? That most of my officers are approaching old age except for Efan, who's barely a grown man?" He spoke rapidly, a recitation too familiar to dwell on: "Gwilym and Hafaidd lost their sons, each about to have ascended to his father's post, less than a year ago in Roger's last attack. Efan's father, who to be

honest had not quite prepared his son to take over my personal teulu, let alone my entire army, was killed the same day. Marged, in the kitchen, has lost a husband, half a dozen sons, and four grandsons over the past ten years. Cadwgan the marshal lost a son, Einion the porter a brother, Father Idnerth and Hywel several nephews each. And many women were lost as well but I'll spare you the particular details. The only native soul in Cymaron who has not lost close family to your uncle within the last decade is Gwirion, because he has no family to lose. Even your women, your doorkeeper, your groom. These people see your Norman face at the king's table every meal eating the food they worked to put there. Don't expect them to stomach that if you offer no atonement." He began to urge his horse ahead of hers.

She grabbed his arm and when he looked back at her, she tried not to sound imploring. "You resent me for my heritage but you don't help me at all to embrace yours. I'm no use to you unless I belong to both and you know that, that's why you chose me."

His laughter was harsh. "Oh, it's my fault, is it? I must convince my people to embrace you although I know you won't embrace them back—what you want is to soften them to the man who killed—"

Fed up, she almost spat at him: "Have you atoned for the sins of *your* people, Noble? I'm not entirely ignorant of your family." She felt her throat tighten; if they'd been in private, she would have shouted at him. She had been taught a recitation too, less personally bitter but still damning, and keeping her voice low and her face neutral in case anyone was watching them, she hissed it all at him in French. "One of your cousins killed his own brother, another *blinded* both of his brothers, and your own sainted father sold his brother as a hostage. That's what your family does *to its own*, not to its rivals. You are *dazzlingly* sanctimonious." She let go of his sleeve, took a deep, satisfied breath and looked away. That had felt wonderful.

He stared at her so hard she felt it as a physical force, and reluctantly found herself looking back at him again. "Yes, my family did all that. After your family had distressed them beyond reason," Noble said quietly, all trace of humor, even sarcasm, vanished. "We must both of us atone for the sins of our families. Anarawd, who

blinded his brothers, is my legal heir, and the only way to save the kingdom from his hubris is for me to have a son. Do you think I've spent the last two weeks coddling you because I'm sorry you were upset about Enid? Listen to me!" he snapped. She had looked away, and he grabbed her palfrey's rein to force her toward him, which brought the palfrey to a jerking halt. The train behind them awkwardly pulled up. Noble was angry now, and the entire entourage could see it, but he lowered his voice for her hearing alone. "Caring what we think of each other is not a luxury allowed to us. I'd prefer not to force myself on you, but you're bordering on treason if you would put your own petty pride ahead of giving me a child, when you know that if I die without issue, this kingdom will fall into such hands. Would you do that to your own people?" She looked stung, and he tried to speak in gentler tones. "When you've reconsidered the consequences of your selfishness, I will be ready for you." He released her horse's rein and spurred his own mount on ahead.

THE king never brought Gwirion with him on circuit. Gwirion hated leaving Cymaron, and anyway, His Majesty claimed, he was far too unpredictable. When Noble was away, Gwirion tended to slip into lackadaisical ennui. This had not always been true; in earlier years, he had made it a habit to steal the great seal, which was kept in the royal coffers, and use it on a variety of interesting proclamations. One year he demanded the arrest of all fleas, another time he issued a warrant outlawing the issuing of warrants, and once he officially declared that on the first of June all goods in the village could be paid for by the sound of money in lieu of actual currency. When following a bad harvest he managed to send out, to the entire kingdom, an edict that all land-use fees for the year could be paid in human excrement, Gwilym the steward—never losing his calm demeanor—seized the seal and kept it with him at all times until the king returned. He had ever since maintained a vigil over it

whenever Noble left Cymaron. On only one occasion in over a decade had Gwirion managed to spirit the seal away from him, and used it to stamp an order that made dying a capital offense. The steward's vigil had tightened after that, and Gwirion resigned himself to boredom in Noble's absence. It was still better than being out on the open road.

When the watch on the keep roof called down that the royal party was in sight of home, the announcement set village and castle into a frenzy of activity. The mayor oversaw the village and Gwilym the castle, organizing the populace as they raised the images of Noble's gold lion, *rampant regardant*, on a field of crimson. The porter's deputy ran down to the village and offered the children a halfpenny an armload for flowers to strew along the hamlet's single thoroughfare. In the castle, everyone assembled outside on the steps leading up to the hall, in formation according to their status—this meant Gwilym, followed by the smith in his black conical hat, followed by officials' wives, followed by everybody else. Except Gwirion. True to the ambiguity of his rank, the man who was not even given a place at table stood in front of everyone else to welcome his monarch home.

Enid hesitated to join the welcome party. The queen had stumbled upon them a second time before the circuit started, under even more compromising circumstances, and had forbade Enid entering her solar or even straying unnecessarily into her view; the girl was debating whether anybody could really hold a grudge for weeks. "Look at you," Gwirion said, shaking his head at her uncertainty. "Further evidence of the damage that Saxoness is doing all of us. It takes a potent dose of poison to dull your pretty smile." She scowled at him, which to him only proved his point. "You'll be out there to greet *him*, not her," he insisted. "What has he done to you for you to disrespect him?" Ten minutes later, she was standing with the kitchen crew watching the gates draw open.

There was a small vanguard of teulu and then the king himself entered on his Castilian charger, in his red-and-gold traveling uniform, looking as ever casually bedazzling. The queen was behind him in similar colors, small and demure, looking and feeling almost invis-

ible. Grooms stepped forward to take the horses' heads and the couple dismounted while behind them the rest of the retinue continued to ride into the bailey. Following Gwirion's lead, the assembly on the hall steps bowed in unison to their sovereign, and Noble, followed by his wife, formally bowed in response. "Now get you back to work, you lazy scoundrels!" Gwirion cried out playfully, turning around. "Haven't you anything better to do than stand here and gape at the king's consort? It's the same woman he had when he left . . . well, *that's* novel, anyhow," he admitted, intending no real malice. To his mind it was even a compliment. He turned back around toward the king, and saw the queen walking past him briskly, her expression unreadable behind the linen veil that had shielded her face from the road dust. She made such a show of ignoring him as she passed that for a minute he actually pitied her ineptness, and very nearly offered to show her how to snub somebody more effectively. Instead, he took a step down to join the king, who was watching her go with a look of exasperation on his face. Gwirion was about to offer him sympathy when he realized the exasperation was aimed at himself.

"It took some hard words, but I had her feathers smoothed before you started in," Noble said. "Thank you."

"My pleasure," Gwirion said brightly, not sure how else to respond. "Are you in need of a nap?"

"No, Gwirion," Noble said with tired patience. "I am in need of domestic serenity."

"Ah." Gwirion considered, briefly. "I don't think I can help you much with that."

Noble looked at him. "That is more than abundantly clear. Make yourself useful somewhere, would you please?" He passed by him and up the steps.

THE queen took supper in her room that night, citing travel exhaustion. Adèle was in the village arguing with the tanner

about a belt for her mistress, so taking the platter up to the queen was left to Marged's discretion.

Ever since Noble's rebuke above Rhaeadr, Isabel had been troubled and meditative. There was a large chasm in her mind between her initial awed thrill at the title "queen," the notion of all the useful Christian work that such a role might offer her . . . and the sole obligation to bear a son who would exist only to rule bogs, hillsides and shepherds. She was seeking solutions to her internal dissonance when there was a knock on the door and her doorkeeper Llwyd stuck his head in. "Your food, Majesty," he said in his soft, somnolent tone. She put down the enormous law book she had been reading in the last stretch of daylight, and got up from the window seat. When she turned her attention back into the room, she was shocked to see Enid laying the platter on the bed. "Here you are, Majesty," she hummed, curtsying and sounding chipper. The queen did not acknowledge her. "Would you like company while you're eating?"

"Not yours," Isabel said shortly. "Thank you for bringing my supper, but please have somebody else come for the platter." She sat again and pointedly looked out the window.

Enid sighed and straightened up from arranging things nicely on the tray. Her impulse was to roundly scold Her Majesty, arms akimbo, but instead she clasped her hands sedately before her. "Milady," she said, "it will not be possible for me to hide from you for the rest of my life. If I may be presumptuous enough—"

"You've already been more than presumptuous, Enid."

She paused, and tried again. "You have forgiven him, milady, and his crime against you is worse than mine."

"Is it?" Isabel asked in an ironic voice, looking at her.

"It's his body you engage with, milady, not mine."

"Your crime is not your body," Isabel scoffed. "It's encouraging my intimacy on false pretenses. You knew the significance of what you were hiding from me and you hid it so that you could worm your way into my affections." She spoke with bitterness. "You were being duplicitous."

"I thought I was being discreet, milady," Enid answered quietly.

"How long did you expect that to last? What were you planning to say to me when I finally found out? What could you possibly have said that would preserve amity between us?"

"Preserving amity with you was not my first concern, Your Majesty," Enid said. "You seem to think we are talking about a man, milady, but we are talking about the king, and my duty to the king comes first. I'm sorry for deceiving you, but my presence here does not diminish who you are. You are the queen. Doesn't that satisfy you?"

Isabel stood up from the window seat. "You may not presume to tell me what I should be satisfied with!"

"Exactly—because you're the queen and I'm not. Good evening, milady, and as you asked I will send somebody else up for the platter." Enid was unused to the frustrated anger the conversation evoked in her; she had to get out of there before she said something she'd regret. She began to wonder if Gwirion was right about the queen's universally poisonous effect. But it saddened her too. She liked the young woman and had even fancied there was something of herself in there, some happy spirit begging for release.

WHILE the queen was preoccupied with Welsh law, Corr was preoccupied with confirmation of his banishment.

"It's not banishment. It's retirement! How many parasites ever manage to retire? With full corrodies—lodging, food, clothing, everything! What a luxury," Gwirion insisted, forcing cheer. Humffri ap Madoc, a baron to the north and the last stop on the king's circuit, had volunteered to take the dwarf into his care, offering to give him a minor position in his own kitchen. Corr, who had always yearned for the pride of actually earning his own keep, almost wept with gratitude, and began counting the hours to his departure with happiness instead of distress.

The night before he left, with filial affection, Gwirion organized

a farewell party for him. Adèle bristled when she learned of it: Corr was supposed to be leaving in shame as punishment for distressing the bride on her wedding day, but this was a near heroic send-off. Isabel did not bother sharing Adèle's indignation; she had ensconced herself in her room, contemplating the various paths the *Law of Wales* might allow her. Nobody at the court paid her enough heed to wonder at her sudden interest in legal matters.

Noble composed Corr's traveling party the next morning to his own advantage. Besides two members of the teulu, one of them about to leave to take holy orders at Cwm-hir, he ordered Gwirion and Enid to go along. This was a peace offering to his wife: Now the people she least wanted to see would be out of sight for a day, and perhaps he could coax her back out of her shell. Besides, although Gwirion usually refused to leave the village walls without the king, he was anxious to see where Corr would be spending his greying years, and Enid had long desired to visit her parents, who lived a few hours north of the castle. She would ride behind Gwirion on the mare, stopping on the way, and they would pick her up on their return.

The dwarf on his own tiny hill pony looked like a swaddled infant, wrapped protectively against the white-hot sun that would damage his fair skin so easily. The trip out was uneventful, but leaving Corr was far more distressing than Gwirion was prepared for. His usual endless chatter grew still, and he was a morose traveling companion as they headed back south. He rode very slowly through the dense yellow gorse, claiming it was his mount's discomfort in the summer humidity; whatever the cause, they didn't reach Enid until nearly sundown.

Enid's parents, who were so aggressively dull that they left the source of their daughter's buoyancy and beauty a mystery, breathlessly offered to host the royal party in their shoddy hovel on the edge of a hamlet. When Gwirion realized this meant they were planning to go without supper and sleep on the ground outside, giving their food and bedsheets to their guests, he refused. To the soldiers' annoyance but Enid's profound gratitude, he declared his intention of

making it back to the castle by midnight; once they were safely out of sight of the hut, of course, they stopped again to make camp. They were at least off the main highway, he pointed out, far enough down the hillside to be out of the wind, but shielded from the cold valley mist by an oak grove below them.

The teulu mounts were always outfitted with travel gear: a small tartan brychan, flint, a water skin, and a miserly ration of cured meat behind each saddle. Once Gwirion volunteered to poach fallen branches from the oak grove—Enid and the guards were too super-stitious to enter any grove of sacred trees—they were able to make a fire and a woefully thin meat broth to share, but there was an awk-ward moment about the sleeping arrangements. Enid had ridden be-hind Gwirion on the pony, so there were only two horses and therefore two blankets. Two blankets, and four people. It would be common enough to share a brychan, but these were cut too small for two men, even if one of them was slender Gwirion.

Since one guard would always be awake on watch, only three blankets would ever be needed, but that was still more than they had. Gwirion was about to offer Enid the second brychan when Caradoc—the stocky young soldier who was clearly *not* about to en-ter the brotherhood—asked Enid to share his with him. She laughed.

"I'm not for general consumption," she said.

"His Majesty need never know," Caradoc offered, and gave his cohort a meaningful glance. The monk looked disgusted and went to tether the horses away from the poisonous bracken. Ignoring Gwirion's presence, the wooer turned his gaze back to Enid who, de-spite her youth, was probably older than he was. "Come on, then. You're a fine girl and I'm not so bad, am I? We could have some fun, no harm done, and none's the wiser." He licked his lower lip. "I've fancied you for months."

"Jesu, that's enough," Gwirion interrupted. "Enid, you take the second brychan. I'll sleep in the bracken." He began to walk toward the monk's saddle.

"No," said Caradoc in a menacing voice, moving toward Enid with ogling deliberation. "She's mine."

Enid stared at him, suddenly very aware of how large he was. Alarmed, she glanced at Gwirion, who changed course and immediately put himself between the two of them, glowering up at Caradoc, arms crossed. "No she's not, Caradoc, she's under my protection."

The younger man laughed derisively and patted his sword hilt. "Your protection? Is that meant to intimidate me?"

"Think on who I am, you idiot," Gwirion said in a calm voice, trembling in the darkness.

Caradoc considered him with an angry frown, then snorted with resignation and turned away, making a dismissive gesture. Gwirion barely managed to hide how relieved he was, but decided not to leave Enid's side for the rest of the evening. He announced that she would sleep on the near side of the fire in the second brychan, and he would sit guarding her. The soldiers would split the night into two shifts, one of them sleeping at the far side of the fire, the other keeping the watch from near the top of a sheltering incline.

The monk had soothed Caradoc's frustrated intentions by miraculously producing fermented liquid rye, and plied him with it until Caradoc fell asleep. Gwirion sat cross-legged at the corner of Enid's blanket. "You look so maternal," she teased, as she lay down on the tartan. He smiled, uncomfortable. He had seen Enid naked on the king's bed and other places on plenty of occasions, but there was an unsettling intimacy to her snuggling down for something as innocent as sleep right in front of him. "You know," she added, "we're both small, we could probably share the brychan."

He caught his breath. "Oh, no, that's all right, I'm fine. I've got to keep my eye on Caradoc."

"Caradoc's asleep," Enid whispered.

"Well . . . the young monk, then."

She gave him a savvy look. "Gwirion, do you really think he's going to try anything? Get some rest." She moved over on the blanket and patted the empty space.

"Mmm—no. Many thanks." He nodded almost spastically. "I'll be fine."

"Gwirion! Are you trying to insult me?"

"No," he said in a voice tenor with tension. "I just want to be honorable. And see that you sleep unmolested."

A coquettish and purposeful grin spread across her face. "Are you saying you'd molest me if you slept beside me?"

"Oh, no, I didn't mean—that's not . . ." His breathing grew shallow and quick and he looked pained. Delighted, she sat up, grabbed him by the shoulders, and pulled him back down on top of herself. "What . . . what's this about?" he asked in the same boyish treble.

"I have a present for you," she whispered into his ear. "To thank you for protecting me."

He swallowed hard and tried to sit up, but she clasped him close above herself. "I'm very flattered but—"

"The king need never know," Enid whispered, imitating Caradoc's blustering diction. "We could have some fun, no harm done, none's the wiser." She smiled invitingly at him. "Anyhow, you know he has no jealousy of me."

He stared at her, bemused and almost unhappy, for a long moment. Then he firmly removed her arms from around him and sat up. "Why are you doing this?" he asked quietly.

She sat up too, to stay near him. "Because I like you, Gwirion. I think you're sad right now about Corr, and I want to take your mind off it."

"I've known you since you were a girl," he said softly. "Since nearly before you had *breasts*."

"Is it the breasts you don't like?"

"Lord, no, you have beautiful breasts. Fit for a king," he said sheepishly.

"If you don't object to the breasts, what is it you object to?" she pressed.

He blushed. "I just don't . . . it's been a long time since I—"

"Well, let's make sure everything's still functioning, then," she purred.

He stopped resisting. Trembling, he watched her reach up under the short skirt of his linen tunic to loosen his drawers and tug them down below his bony knees. He stared at her stupidly, hardly breath-

ing, afraid even to touch her. His eyes jerked nervously toward Caradoc across the fire, but the guard was sleeping soundly, turned away from them. A wriggling movement beneath him snapped his gaze back to Enid. She was lifting her skirt. Her eyes flickered up to meet his, and she smiled.

"I can't," he whispered hoarsely.

"Why not?"

He couldn't answer that. To hear she was like a little sister to him would only make her laugh, and he had been present at her intimacies with Noble too often for a claim of modesty to ring true. "It's just conditioning," he said at last. "I see you with that look on your face and my fingers start itching for a harp."

"I think we can find a better way to scratch that itch. Close your eyes if you need to. I'm not going to, though." She grinned. "Half the fun in this is that it's *you*."

"Oh," he said stupidly, not sure what she meant, and then bit his lip to keep from crying out as she reached up under his tunic and closed her hand around him. She guided him down on top of her and, with nearly maternal affection and attention, shifted her hips to give him access to her. He almost passed out before collapsing against her, trying to choke back sobs that were a confused mixture of pleasure, gratitude, and shame.

Across the fire from them, Caradoc slept soundly.

THEY returned to Cymaron by midmorning, crossing paths just outside the village gates with a departing emissary from Llewelyn, the upstart prince in Gwynedd. When they reached the stable, Enid skipped at once through the yard and into the kitchen to see if Marged needed her. Things were nearly prepared for dinner, which was always a simple meal, and after minding the stew for a short while, she headed into the hall to help the steward's workers set up the trestle tables.

Too late, she realized the queen was standing in her path, reviewing a saint's-day calendar with Father Idnerth and Gwilym. Not wanting to draw attention to herself, Enid hesitated, and overheard enough of the conversation to sober her. The queen, her face as inexpressive as ever framed by the dark red wimple, was being informed of what would take place on each of the feast days. She was not dispensing orders herself; the officers were not asking her opinion on anything, or even seeking her approval. They were, as always, respectful, even kindly, but aloof. There was an easy camaraderie between the two men that had nothing to do with rank—Enid knew even she would have been welcomed into it but the queen was absolutely excluded. She wished she had a reason to interrupt; she wasn't fooled by the patient resignation plastered on Her Majesty's face. She knew what was under it.

"Excuse me, milady," she said on impulse, stepping into the triangle and nearly shrugging the frail old chaplain aside. All three of them stared at her, astonished by her impertinence. "May I speak with you for a moment?"

The queen's face registered polite disinterest. "Certainly. Excuse us, gentlemen." The tone was of dismissal, not departure, and after a pause they understood, drawing away with slight, stiff bows. She considered Enid for a moment—confusing Enid because, far from its usual coolness, the queen's face suddenly seemed bordering on conspiratorial amusement. "What do you want?" she finally asked.

Enid scrambled for an excuse. "Lady Humffri sends her warmest regards."

The queen gave her a droll look. "I was not aware you met with Lady Humffri."

"No, that's true, she gave the message to Gwirion but I thought I would spare you the displeasure of being approached by him."

"I've been learning about Welsh law," Isabel said abruptly. Her voice was low, eager and confiding, and for a moment Enid almost believed the queen had been awaiting her return to Cymaron just to share this with her. "Do you know much about Welsh law? There is no love lost between myself and the elements of this hill country,

and I would welcome an excuse to leave, politics be damned. If I catch the two of you a third time, I'll have that excuse—I can divorce him. But if I do, Enid, however content *I* might be with that, the 'Saxons' you all sneer at will have killed him and overrun the kingdom within a month. Apparently Welsh law *is* more progressive than Norman—where I come from, a kitchen servant fucking the king could never wreak that kind of havoc."

Enid gasped to hear such language from the queen's mouth, but before she could reply, her eye caught sight over the queen's shoulder of the king. There was something about his posture that made her look twice; for a flash she was more aware of him as a burdened human being than as a ruler or even as a bedmate. She remembered the messenger they'd passed outside the gates; whatever was distressing His Majesty must have something to do with Llewelyn. He walked slowly from the door of his receiving chamber to the hall hearth, stared into it for a moment, then lifted his head, looked around—and fixed his hypnotic gaze on Enid. Seeing her in civil conversation with his wife, his eyes widened briefly, then he shook his head and began walking toward them. Enid knew the expression: He wanted her, alone.

"Did you hear me?" the queen demanded. "I have been discussing Welsh law with Judge Goronwy. I know what my rights are."

"It's not for me to say anything, milady," she stammered.

"Yes it is," Isabel retorted sweetly. "Jealousy is not the issue, Enid—I would *like* to catch you in the act again, I could be home in England by harvesttime. One more time, let me surprise you just once more." She lowered her voice to an intimate whisper. "Give me that, Enid, as atonement for your sins against me. Wigmore is so lovely in the autumn," she sighed, then turned officious. "But you must be willing. He can't force you. Do you have any idea what it would cost him if you accused him of rape? I read that part of the law as well."

"Did you read the part that says the king is, under all circumstances, exempt from punishment?" demanded her husband behind her, quietly. She started and turned to face him, but he switched his

blue gaze to Enid. "I could take this adorable harlot by force if I chose to, but happily that's never necessary with her. And while we're on that subject, Enid," he went on, in a suggestive tone, "go to my receiving room immediately."

"I'm coming too," Isabel announced. She glanced triumphantly at Enid but veiled her excitement from her husband lest he understand it.

"Very well," he said, not looking at her. "You are, as ever, utterly transparent. I'm not going to alter my plans, but you're welcome to watch."

"Sire," Enid said nervously, "Marged requires my presence—"

"I require it more," he said with calm authority, and turned to head back to the audience chamber. "Come along or I'll have to carry you, and that will make quite a scene."

When both women had stepped inside, Isabel nearly humming with perverse anticipation, Noble shut the door with a small flourish and turned to Enid. "I was just speaking with that young would-be Cistercian. He brought distressing news about something that happened last night."

"It was nothing, sire," she insisted.

"He said the other guard made an unwelcome advance on you."

"Caradoc. It was nothing. Gwirion stared him down."

"That was honorable of him."

"Yes it was. He's an honorable fellow," Enid said, and added for the queen's benefit, "in his own strange way."

"I'm also told that after Caradoc turned in, you and Gwirion were intimate with each other."

This caught her completely by surprise and she blushed for perhaps the first time in her life. Isabel involuntarily recoiled. "Well," Enid stammered. "Yes, sire. That's true."

"Who initiated it?"

She hesitated. "I did."

Noble took a breath that almost sounded like satisfaction, but his response, incongruously, was, "I'm not pleased about that, Enid." He looked at his wife. "You're welcome to stay but this topic is the

sum of my interest in her today. This particular liaison will afford you no grounds for divorce and I'm sure there are more satisfying ways for you to spend your time."

Isabel was so unprepared for the direction in which the encounter was going that it took her a moment to answer. "Yes, there are," she agreed, and opened the door to leave.

But when she'd pulled it shut behind her, her curiosity kept her there. She lingered for a few moments, tempted to go back inside, and she had just convinced herself not to, had nearly taken a step up the stairs toward her solar, when the door was suddenly flung open and the two of them came out in a rush. Noble was angry and Enid looked shocked, almost dazed. He had her by the back of the neck, pulling her along beside him as he walked quickly toward the main door to the hall, with his captive scrambling not to lose her footing. "Sire, please——" she heard Enid say, sounding frightened, and she rushed to intercept them.

"Noble, leave her alone!" she insisted, stepping directly in front of them. He stopped short but did not release his grip on Enid's neck. "You don't own her."

"I do, actually, but that's beside the point—and you have no idea what the point is, so stand aside."

"Where are you taking her?"

"Away from mischief," he announced, and elbowed his wife aside to continue the harsh promenade to the hall doorway.

AFTER seeing his mare safely to the stable, Gwirion retreated into the tiny closet off the kitchen that had long ago been designated his sleeping quarters. He fell asleep effortlessly, grateful to be back under his own blanket and enjoying that rare privilege of privacy. He was surprised to be awakened by Marged's grandson with the news that the king wanted to see him at once. It was after supper. He had slept more than eight hours.

"Can't he entertain himself for once?" he grumbled, but he went along obediently.

Noble sat alone in the audience chamber. This was Gwirion's favorite room in the castle, small but brightly whitewashed, and carpeted with pale pelt rugs. Although wall paintings and tapestries throughout the castle offered color and cheer, there was something almost celestial in the simplicity of this space. The king's elegant leather chair faced a padded settle across a low table—actually an ornate chest—and there was a cushion at his feet where Gwirion sat sometimes. Otherwise the room was empty. It had only the one door opening into the great hall, and no window but a high-up slit of an air vent, too small even to shoot an arrow from, that opened away from the yard. But the glazed white walls, broad hearth, and generous array of sconces kept it from ever seeming dark or stuffy. Gwirion performed what passed as a bow and at Noble's gesture, sank down on the cushion with his harp beside him.

"This is formal," he commented. Noble looked tired and careworn; probably from being left alone with his wife for a day and a half, Gwirion decided. Then common sense intervened: He knew the source of the king's distress. "We passed a courier by the gate this morning—was he wearing the colors of Gwynedd?"

"Yes," Noble sighed. "The upstart prince Llewelyn has requested an official diplomatic relationship—not as an upstart but as a prince. As a peer." He did not sound pleased about it, but his tone hardly explained how grim he looked. "That's not why I called you in here, Gwirion. I know about what happened last night."

"It wasn't a problem, sire," Gwirion waved it off. "Caradoc—"

"Not that. I already have a full confession from Enid. I know she pushed you into it. I don't hold you responsible." Gwirion's face reddened and he uttered a sound that wasn't quite a word. "What's the matter, didn't you enjoy it? Your monk friend seemed to think you enjoyed it quite a lot."

"I wasn't planning, I mean, I had no intention—"

"I know that."

"And I'll never let such a situation hap—"

"No, *I'll* never let such a situation happen again," Noble snapped. He sat up very straight and stared down at Gwirion with an alarming expression. "It was such a *trespass* for her to do that. I couldn't let such wanton use of power go unpunished."

Gwirion leapt unsteadily to his feet. He hoped he misunderstood. "Sire? What do you mean?"

Seeing Gwirion's face, Noble couldn't help a short, harsh laugh. "Calm down, I haven't killed her." Gwirion relaxed. "I've just had her sent away."

The alarm sprang back to Gwirion's eyes. "What?"

"I didn't hurt her. Just had them shave her head a bit before they drove her out."

"Drove her *out*?" Gwirion echoed. "Why?"

Noble gave him a long, slow stare. Then he abruptly changed his expression and said, lightly, "The queen was troubled by her presence. It's just as well she's gone."

Gwirion frowned. "You threw her out because the queen was upset that you had her, or because you were upset that I had her?"

"Neither," said the king. "I was upset that *she* had *you*." Gwirion gave him a bemused look. "It's a matter of ethics, Gwirion, so you probably wouldn't understand: you mustn't take other people's things." Gwirion started at what this implied and tried to protest, but impatiently the king added, "Actually, Isabel was waiting to catch me with her a third time to sue for divorce, so now I've removed the temptation. That's all. I just wanted to tell you what had happened." Gwirion stood openmouthed before him. "What?"

Disoriented and not knowing which explanation was the truer, or what to make of either one, Gwirion managed to stammer, lamely, "Won't you miss her?"

"Probably, but I'll find someone else. I might even give monogamy a try—my wife really is plotting to divorce me otherwise." He laughed. "In fact, I think I'll take her right to bed. The least she can do is give me a son."

HE felt no stronger affection for her but his need to make his cousin Anarawd irrelevant compelled him to take her frequently, until it became almost a chore for both of them. Although a private skeptic, he even consulted his physician and his bard to see if there were any astrological considerations, amulets, or spells that might assist; the suspicious silence from his border with Mortimer and the too eager whispered rumors of Llewelyn's rising star made him desperate for an heir.

He did at least take steps against Gwirion to keep things comfortable for the queen. Gwirion rebelled as much as he dared, and protested ferociously that after robbing him of his only two companions, Noble had no right to make his life even more miserable by muzzling him. The king stood firm. So Gwirion was called upon to play the harp in the evenings after the bard had finished his more respectable performance, but he was not allowed to speak publicly in hall. His position had always been peculiar and his status a source of perennial dissent—in a world of strictly established court positions, he conformed to nothing. Noble had despaired of passing him off as the chief of song, because the office required things that were beyond him. He should, for example, have begun each evening's entertainment with a song of religious praise, but he was already perceived as such a rascal that on the few occasions he'd tried to do it, it had sounded like a parody.

So Gwirion lived in an odd limbo. He was allowed to play the gilded willow harp with the carved lion's head, loaned to him by King Cadwallon years ago—the most valuable object in the castle outside the relics of St. Cynllo in the chapel—and he played nearly every evening, but only after the official bardic entertainment had finished. He maintained his stool just behind the king's chair at board, and they often whispered together, snickering, when there was no other conversation, but Noble was aware of his wife's eyes on him and would be careful to give her equal, if dispassionate, attention.

Robbed of his usual outlets for both anger and amusement, Gwirion turned his attention to writing letters to Corr. He did not have a pretty script, and he was nearly positive Corr could not, in fact, read. But he needed to express his indignation to somebody and no one else would listen. The consensus of the court was that this was simply how things would be from now on—less entertaining but more civil—and it was Gwirion's problem if he could not adjust.

I T'S a hopeless situation, my friend," he scribbled. "It's the most ill-starred marriage since Adam and Eve. It's just as well Noble won't let me mock her, I wouldn't even know what to say, she gives me nothing to play with. It's very frustrating.

"He is truly restraining from all entertainment outside the marriage bed, the poor bored lad. She seems to take this as her due, as if it were to be expected. She has no idea what a monumental, even heroic, effort it is on his behalf—not only to restrict himself to one woman, but for that woman to be her! She should be kissing the hem of his robe, and instead she struts around smugly as if she were entitled to the preferential treatment! She seems to think it will always be this way. I tell you, Corr, she'll be disappointed. And probably soon."

T H E betrayal took place on her own bed. She had been vaguely aware that Gwen, her tallest attendant, resembled not only Enid, but nearly every woman who caught Noble's eye: wild dark hair, impossible to tame even braided under a veil, glistening dark eyes and most of all, extraordinary curves. "You could fit the queen's buttocks into that girl's cleavage and there'd still be room left over," Gwirion had made the point of saying loudly in hall one afternoon. Noble, grinning, had lined the two of them up as if measuring them

for the accuracy of this assessment, and Isabel had assumed that his public playfulness meant he would go no further in private. She was wrong.

Gwirion entertained that evening after Hywel the bard retired to the village. He was very solicitous toward the queen, asking what she would like to hear and playing with extraordinary grace. Somewhere he had found a set of gut strings and restrung the harp with them; that simple, subtle change in tone, to the more resonant flavor she was familiar with, made the music even more distracting. He was an excellent harpist, which annoyed her: It seemed unfair that such a cretinous soul should have that talent.

Her suspicion of his motives began when he apologized profusely, almost self-flagellating, for being ignorant of the excellent and varied Norman repertoire. Then she realized that the king, who had excused himself to the garderobe, had been gone nearly half an hour. When Gwirion finished "Rhiannon's Tears" for the second time—his signature tune, which she was unwilling to tell him was also a favorite of hers—she thanked him for the recital and excused herself to bed.

"Bed?" Gwirion echoed with a blink. "You mean the king's bed, surely. He'll be wanting you there." This was true: Noble had given Gwirion orders to distract the queen as long as possible before sending her directly to his room, to keep her out of her own, where Gwen was finishing a weaving project.

"I assumed my husband had already retired for the evening," she said, acutely aware of the entire court, officers and servants, ogling their interaction. It was rare for these two to acknowledge each other directly.

"Oh, no, milady," Gwirion said with slightly too much insistence. "He expressly asked me to tell you to retire to *his* chamber." He had the gift of telling the truth as if it were a lie, and she thought she was catching him in a falsehood. Just as he had counted on.

"Is he in his chamber now?" she asked.

"He'll be there," Gwirion said, nodding his head earnestly.

"Where is he now?" she pressed.

"He'll be in his room soon, Your Majesty. That's where he wants you to go."

Isabel rose from her seat. She didn't know what was going on, but anything to do with Gwirion made her uncomfortable, and that, in turn, made her want to withdraw. "I am retiring to my own chamber," she informed him, unaware he'd neatly shepherded her to this decision. "When you see the king, please invite him to send for me when he's ready to retire."

"If you insist, milady," he answered, and remained expressionless until she had mounted the steps. Then he grinned hugely, tickled by the prospect of approaching chaos.

Adèle was near the kitchen screens and saw his glee. She thought she understood it, and raced across the width of the hall after her mistress, hoping she could intercept her.

She couldn't. She slipped on some wet rushes, and as she recovered and scrambled up the stairs to the queen's solar, it was clear from the sounds within what had happened: The queen had found her husband undressing dark-haired Gwen.

She glared at them in silence, but her appearance and expression so frightened Gwen that the girl shrieked in alarm, and it carried clearly down into the hall, where Gwirion fell off his stool from laughing. Noble tried to assuage his wife, who was almost too furious to speak. When she found her voice, she was barely coherent and switched between Welsh and French without realizing it. "You're finished!" she whispered furiously at the traumatized, confused Gwen in a language the girl didn't understand. "You will be out of this castle tomorrow and I never want to see you again." Gwen, trying to get back into her tunic, looked at the king in confusion. Adèle shut the door behind her to keep them from continuing to entertain Gwirion, and very brusquely started to help Gwen into her surcoat.

"She's throwing you out," Adèle explained shortly, and escorted her to the far side of the room, beyond the tapestry that closed off the attendants' sleeping area, so that she could finish adjusting her clothes.

Isabel's anger transformed into vengeful ecstasy as she turned her full attention to her husband. "That's the third time I've caught you, Noble! I can do it now. Even as a king you have no right to stop me." She pointed triumphantly to the heavy law book beside her bed. "I," she announced, looking radiant, "am suing for divorce."

Noble crossed his arms and gave her the overly patient look of a tired parent. "And what will you be going home to, madam?"

· 4 ·

FALSE DISPATCHES

Around Lammas, 1198

 HE DID NOT sue for divorce, but her increasing malaise began to infest Cymaron. All day the solar was a silent, humid, dreary cage; at night she regularly refused her husband's summons to his room. Determined for an heir, he began coming to her bed, and for the first time in a decade found himself lying with a wholly unreceptive woman, which only reaffirmed for him how much he liked his wantons. Had he not so despised and distrusted the cousin who was next in line to the throne, he would almost have preferred not bothering with issue. His wife understood him well enough now to know how to play against him: She acted bored by his attention, unimpressed when he tried to arouse her. That was not a game his pride would indulge, and one night he spent half an hour coaxing a physical response from her—but even then she was so doggedly still and silent that he would hardly have known she'd climaxed if he hadn't been inside her. "An interesting skill," he mused sarcastically, hovering over her. "Not es-

pecially useful, but interesting." She blinked away humiliated tears and would not look at him.

Adèle, desperate to see her mistress's spirit restored, begged a private audience with the king to offer a solution. The Cistercian abbey of Cwm-hir was less than three hours' ride to the west; Cadwallon had founded the retreat in the serenest, most beautiful valley in the kingdom and the holy brothers were in the process of building an enormous church there. Noble regularly gave them money in his father's honor, but he was their official patron and he'd been remiss in patronizing them. The queen, Adèle proposed, might go in his stead. The church would be under construction for years—as royal overseer of the project, it would keep her occupied for a very long time, doing something genuinely useful. Adèle suggested the idea because it was a religious house and therefore civilized; Noble approved it because it was Cistercian and therefore not English. He was impressed that the increasingly truculent old woman had presented a constructive idea. A lay brother was summoned from the abbey early one morning to show the queen simple hand signals should she need to communicate with the silent monks. Then the royal couple, Adèle, and a small van of bodyguards followed him back to the holy valley so that the king could officially introduce the abbey to its new patroness. He ruefully suspected she would not receive a warm reception.

But he hardly recognized the woman he rode out beside. Despite the dull white sky, Isabel's mood obviously lifted once the riding party was out of sight of the castle. She cooed over the gentle open countryside as if she had never encountered such beauty. Noble hid his surprise, watching her smile with a warmth he'd never seen, at the smallest things, bumbling lambs and mewling calves, children playing with their grandfather on the edge of a village, even a cavorting couple they surprised in the sea of green bracken. He shot a glance at Adèle and read from her giddy expression that she had anticipated this—which meant, amazingly, that there must be some precedent for it.

They arrived at Cwm-hir in time for dinner, and the queen disarmed the wary, white-robed congregation of the complex—none of whom had ever seen a woman so elegantly dressed—by insisting

upon leaving her husband's party to join them in their simple, silent meal. They were all flummoxed but cautiously accepted, afraid to insult either royalty or Normans. Noble felt Adèle scrutinizing him, and granted her the satisfaction of looking pleasantly impressed. He took no meal at all: Intrigued by the alteration in his wife, he watched her from behind as she broke bread with the monks. She refused a better portion or preferential treatment, communicating entirely with the sign language she'd practiced with the lay brother as they rode.

After dinner the royal couple met with the abbot, who showed them plans for the church. Isabel examined them quickly then made several astute suggestions; Noble's wonderment increased and he was afraid Adèle might explode from too much gloating when a tour of the construction revealed that the queen knew more about church architecture than the abbot did himself.

They stayed for nones at Isabel's insistence, and she left a gift from her own coffers in honor of Maelienydd's patron, St. Cynllo, whose feast day it was—something the native-born King of Maelienydd himself had not thought to do. By the time they headed home in the late afternoon, Noble was almost speechless with admiration and determined to keep Isabel in this spirit indefinitely. Adèle was all pleasure and relief to see her mistress once again behaving like herself. This was the girl she knew; this was the pluck with which to win over Cymaron. This was a strength that neither Gwirion nor the king could sap.

THE king returned from the abbey in an unusually genial mood, and Gwirion found himself entertaining informally in the hall for hours after supper had been cleared away. Nearly everyone played an instrument, but nobody played as well as Gwirion and he was always in demand. There had been many nights like this before the queen arrived and he was happy for a return to normal—and even *she*, returned from Cwm-hir, was behaving like a pleasant human being tonight. Noble stretched out with her on what would later be

bedding for the unmarried servants, drinking wine; farther away from the fire, Gwilym, Hafaidd, Efan, Marged, and (remoter yet) a few of the kitchen workers were settled on the floor with beer. The servants whose bedding Noble had commandeered were gathered in the lower end of the hall, quietly gossiping or playing dice, while couples and families sought slumber behind curtains in the side sections of the great room. Gwirion performed the simple, often bawdy songs that were forbidden at board or when court was even marginally in session, those that no bard had in his repertoire. Those, in other words, that most people privately preferred to hear.

As he was loosening a string to go into his favorite key—"the drunkard's tuning"—he unexpectedly addressed the queen; it was a civil gesture to acknowledge (grudgingly) her civil mood, although he was suspicious of the royal couple's sudden easy amity together. "And so, Your Majesty, what do you think of our little Abbey Cwm-hir?"

"Little?" she said, almost stammering in her surprise that he'd addressed her without sarcasm. "That church is going to be the size of a cathedral. You have excellent stonemasons." Feeling generous, she added the highest compliment she could think of: "It will be quite as grand as any church on the continent."

"With all respect to Your Majesty's weakness for Frenchiness," Gwirion commented, keeping his attention focused on the harp peg, "nobody here has been to the continent, so we can't appreciate how profoundly you must be flattering us."

"My husband has been there," she corrected him complacently.

"I have?" her husband said, taken aback.

She frowned up at him. "You went on Crusade."

He was even more astonished. "I *what?*"

She faltered. "Years ago. I thought—"

"Where did you hear that?" He looked amused, as if it were a preposterous suggestion. She felt foolish and wished she hadn't started the conversation in front of others. But surely Noble wouldn't brush her off or bruise her dignity, not now that he had seen how desirable a companion she could be for him when she was treated fairly.

"In a book," she muttered, trying to sound offhand.

"In a *book?*" Gwirion echoed, and looked at Noble. The king straightened, staring down at his wife. "What book?" Gwirion asked. "What else did it say about him?"

"It was just the one reference," she replied quickly in the same quiet voice, feeling the heat rising to her cheeks.

"And . . . ?" Noble prompted when she said nothing else.

"It was only a private manuscript one of the Benedictine brothers wrote. Uncle Roger loaned it to me before I came here. It mentioned all the Welsh princes, and naturally I read about the man I was about to—"

Gwirion could not contain himself. "This is brilliant!" He affected grave fascination. "Tell me, then, Your Majesty, is this typical of French scholarship in general?"

"Who wrote it?" Noble demanded. "What did they say about me?" He did not share Gwirion's amusement.

She should never have mentioned it. She glanced at Adèle, a ubiquitous shadow near the kitchen screens, and knew the old woman was thinking the same thing. Her recent stiff self-consciousness came crashing down upon her, erasing the ease of the day. "Archbishop Baldwin made a tour through Wales," she began awkwardly. "To enlist men for the Crusade, and he brought a Welsh brother named de Barri who—"

Noble almost choked on his relieved, dismissive laughter, and relaxed back onto the blanket. *"Gerald?* It's my cousin's cousin, for the love of God. Gerald de Barri—a spy for Canterbury, eh? Who would have thought it?"

"I remember that visit!" Gwirion announced, his face lighting up. "We all drank like fish! Don't you remember it, Noble?" he asked the king, forgetting to use an honorific in front of members of the court. "Gerald kissing Baldwin's buttocks all night? That man is a predicant phenomenon," he told the queen. "His head is bigger than Noble's and his mouth is bigger than mine."

"Good God," she said without thinking, sounding horrified, but Gwirion only laughed and asked, now with genuine interest, "What did he write, then?"

"He kept a journal of the trip, and published it. Noble met them at some fort—"

"It was Eryr, Crug Eryr," Gwirion said, grinning at the recollection. "Noble nearly had to drug me to get me to go with him. What did our little Gerald write?"

She hesitated. "He wrote that Noble took the cross. That he swore to go on Crusade—"

"Yes!" Gwirion crowed, remembering the detail, and erupted again into laughter, turning to the king. "Your mother was *furious*. Cadwallon left you with an abbey full of Welsh Cistercians to support and there you were offering your soul to the Archbishop of Canterbury. She didn't want to let us back in when we came home. Now *that* queen," he said with a nostalgic chuckle, "was a queen to *worship*."

Noble finally recalled it too. "Oh, yes," he said dismissively, amused. "That was just political farce—nobody intended to go to Jerusalem."

"That's shameful," Isabel chastised.

"No, it's not," her husband said, sobering a little. "The Crusade was a front. Baldwin wanted to remind us that Canterbury controlled the Welsh church."

"I'm surprised you agreed with him," she said, trying not to sound sarcastic, trying to reclaim some sense of their earlier rapport.

He shook his head. "Like everything else, love, it's tit for tat. Once you take the cross, you're a soldier of God and woe to any man who wrongs you. We sold our souls to Canterbury so that Canterbury would forbid the English barons to attack our lands. The barons attacked anyway, and more than once. And your esteemed archbishop did nothing. When the shepherd stands idly by as the wolf wounds his flock, the flock does not feel much indebted to the shepherd."

"But the wolf does," Gwirion said dryly, plucking out a dissonant chord.

"Anyhow, they were boors," Noble went on, lightening the mood again. "Even without the politics, we'd have agreed just to shut them up and make them go away. And we're all clever fellows, we'd have each found plausible reasons not to follow through."

"Rhys said his wife wouldn't let him go," Gwirion chortled. "The Lord Prince Justice of all South Wales, henpecked out of going on Crusade! And Gerald, that sanctimonious woman hater—Gerald fell for it!" He and Noble starting laughing convulsively, remembering.

As they quieted, Noble affected nostalgia. "Ah, Cousin Gerald."

"Ah, good Queen Efa," Gwirion said in exactly the same tone. With all apparent friendliness he told the queen, "I do wish you could have met her, Majesty. She might have helped you find your feet more easily."

She was completely taken aback by the tone—and so was everyone else. There was riveted silence as she asked, tentatively, "How?"

Never losing the guileless, helpful look, Gwirion explained, "She didn't want Noble learning about women from the teulu, so when he was thirteen she sent her attendant to his room for a nocturnal education. A very practical lady, that one. She could have set you straight about the monogamy problem right away and it would have saved us all a hell of a lot of grief—we might have had so many lovely evenings like this one."

"Gwirion," Noble chastised wearily, his smile vanishing. "That was uncalled for."

"It was also accurate," Gwirion said pleasantly, and began to play "Rhiannon's Tears." Isabel was already standing, and without addressing any of them she began walking toward the stairs to her room. Gwirion watched her go, looking disappointed. "She might have stayed and fought a little," he sighed. "The Saxoness has no play in her at all." He heard a rustle in the shadows and looked over to see Adèle glaring at him as she headed after her mistress.

THERE was another courtyard feast in early August. It marked the start of harvest, and caused Adèle apoplexy because it did not even try to hide its heathen roots: It was proclaimed even by the chaplain as a day of homage to the pagan god Llew, and the populace

celebrated it like all the other feast days. Isabel ignored Gwirion's jubilant afternoon rhetoric in the sweltering courtyard, claiming that
Llew, as god of both the sun and harvest, offered manifest proof that
even an oat stalk was animated by a divine spark. Except for the sac-
rilegiousness of it, it seemed utterly out of character for Gwirion to
turn his attention to anything divine, but he was as casual about it as
if he were explaining why the rain falls. His audience—villagers, castle workers, and some landed gentry arrived early for the feast—listened to him with the same placid interest with which they had
earlier listened to his tales of the last dragon in Wales, asleep in Rad-
nor Forest. It was off-putting to Isabel, but fascinating, how matter-
of-fact these people were about even their most fanciful and
superstitious beliefs. Sorcery was not a sin to them, but simply a
power that could be used for good or ill; dead kings seemed closer to
a second coming than even Christ himself. Especially when the bards
got hold of them.

For the feast itself that evening, Gwirion was not asked to entertain, but by the end of the evening Isabel almost wished he had been,
for she found it excruciating to sit through the alternative. The aging
bard Hywel donned his long blue ceremonial robe and spent the entire evening reciting elegies to fallen heroes. They were exceptionally
wordy and filled with linguistic tricks; this in itself she would have
found merely tiresome, although she enjoyed watching how intensely
emotional everyone—landowners, villeins, teulu, castle servants, and
even her own husband—became over the stories. But the finale,
which took up almost half the evening, was an epic poem about the
valor of the kings of Maelienydd through the years, and the theme
became tedious. For years the princes and their retainers lived out of
saddlebags, battling to win control of Maelienydd back from the evil
Mortimers. Finally, after more than a decade of battle and intrigues
that followed the assassination (by the evil Mortimers) of good King
Madoc, his surviving son Cadwallon reclaimed Castell Cymaron
(from the evil Mortimers). For more than three decades, there was
glorious stability, and every attempted invasion (led, usually, by some
evil Mortimer) was valiantly rebuffed. The fair-haired Prince Mael-

gwyn was born to the incomparably beautiful and righteous Queen Efa and all was well in the kingdom of Cadwallon, who was referred to as "the holiest flame of all humanity" and a few other things Isabel considered just a bit excessive . . . and then, moaned the bard, came the day that changed everything. In late September of '79, Cadwallon was summoned to Gloucester to meet with Henry of England. It was a large party that rode to the high king and a large party that began the return . . . but only the young prince and his companion made it back alive. At this point the evil assassin's name was so obvious it did not have to be mentioned, but of course it was anyhow, at least five times. Gwirion was absent for the recitation and she wished she had been too.

"I assume you are aware of how humiliating that was," she said later in the king's solar, in a cadence intended to be calm but instead sounding standoffish.

"It could only be humiliating if you think yourself a Mortimer," Noble retorted. "Call yourself the Lady of Maelienydd and I think you'll feel quite different."

IT was very warm the next day, despite the silver barricade of clouds that blocked the sun from view, and at Noble's request, he and Goronwy held court outside. The queen was not welcome to participate, but he did not begrudge her watching, although the cases were almost always very dull. They were not, however, as dull as sewing. Her presence at the abbey, although welcomed, was not useful more than once a week, and she was desperate for distractions from the distaff life. She knew Noble was finding other women again, and she resented it, but not enough to estrange herself from the entire castle by being peevish—that was Adèle's pastime. So she made it a habit to insert herself, however silently, into court life as often as she could. This was not the manner of Welsh queens, not even the incomparably beautiful and righteous Queen Efa, but the

king's benign neglect of her behavior afforded nobody the chance to challenge it.

When Hafaidd brought her chair out for her to sit behind Noble, the first case of the morning had already begun, and this one showed signs of intrigue. A young woman, hardly more than a girl and dressed very demurely in a worn-looking long tunic with a high collar, was standing before Goronwy's chair tearfully murmuring her version of whatever the argument was. Behind her, looking agitated and resentful, was a rough-looking man dressed all in leather, nearly old enough to be her father. They were not from the castle village; they must have come from several valleys away. The chubby, pink-faced judge, sitting on a lower level to Noble's right, listened attentively and occasionally murmured asthmatically to his assistant, who took notes. When the girl was finished, she curtsied and backed away from the low dais.

The man glared at her and moved closer to Noble and Goronwy. "She's lying if she says I touched her. She's claiming she was virgin when I took her—well then, she's virgin yet. I swear that on the holy book, and it's all I have to say."

King and judge exchanged meaningful glances, sharing some unspoken knowledge that seemed to burden the justice but tickled Noble's sense of humor. "Where's your heir?" Goronwy asked, which struck Isabel as a remarkable non sequitor.

Noble shook his head. "My beloved cousin is a day's ride away and I don't care to have him near me anyhow. I'll appoint a worthy substitute." Then he grinned, and Goronwy sighed with resignation.

"Sire, it's a delicate matter, by the rule of law it ought to be your heir—"

"I can appoint someone else my heir for the next hour," Noble said reasonably.

Without waiting for the king to say the name, the judge phlegmatically dispatched Hafaidd to find Gwirion, and Noble relaxed against the back of his tall wooden chair looking pleased with himself.

Gwirion was in the kitchen with his harp, in a silk brocade tunic

that had once belonged to Noble, too old now for its color to be clearly discernable. He was entertaining Marged's workers with improvised, outrageous divinations. Absolutely straight-faced, his right hand fluttering dramatically over the lower strings of the harp, he claimed that the bard Taliesin's prophecies (which had never been wrong in over six hundred years) predicted that the world would end the following Thursday unless they all rose in revolt against the king and replaced him with whoever in the castle could drink the most cheap ale without passing out—so they should all start imbibing immediately, for the good of humanity. Hafaidd caught him in the midst of this exhortation, ignored the treasonous commentary that would have hanged anybody else, and briskly escorted him out to the yard.

Arms crossed, blinking his dark eyes in the harshly hazy daylight, Gwirion considered the two suppliants warily and then looked at the king. "Why am I here, then?" he asked.

Noble folded his hands together, made a steeple of his forefingers and tapped it against his lips, a lifelong habit Gwirion knew meant he was trying not to laugh. "This young woman," he said matter-of-factly, "claims this man forced her to yield him her virginity, and he denies it. To begin examining the case, therefore, according to the rule of law, we must first examine her to see if she's intact." He allowed himself the slightest indulgent smile. "That's going to be your job."

"*What?*" It came in stereo, from both the queen and Gwirion at once. "Noble, are you *mad?* Have a woman do it! Or at least the physician," the queen insisted. Gwirion was too shocked to say anything else. Even the two suppliants were astonished; the girl looked outright alarmed.

"It's not my place to change the law," Noble said with mock humility. "I confess it sounds peculiar, but who am I to challenge Hywel the Good?" He smiled beatifically. "It has been the law in rape trials for centuries. The notary of maidenhead is supposed to be my heir, but he's too far away, so I'm appointing Gwirion as substitute. Go on, Gwirion."

"Not in public," Isabel announced firmly, standing. "That's *barbarous.*"

He shrugged agreeably. "Very well, in private, then, but you'd best go along as my representative to keep an eye on him."

For one disorienting moment, the queen and Gwirion were united against him, as Gwirion made generic sounds of protest and the queen declared, "*I'll* examine her, don't subject her to a man."

"You?" Noble crossed his arms and looked at her, his sarcastic smile twitching the corners of his mouth. "I didn't realize you were experienced with women's private parts."

There was squelched laughter from onlookers and the queen shot back, "I didn't realize Gwirion was either." This earned a bigger reaction and for a moment she was pleased, until she realized that she had just cemented the situation, for now Gwirion would be goaded by them into proving her wrong.

Gwirion stood in the middle of a circle of teasing spectators who were all ignoring the usher's stern requests for silence. For a moment he stared at Noble, his face unreadable. Then he turned to the nervous girl and said in a tone of resignation, "Let's go in here," gesturing to the ground-floor room of the nearest corner tower. He turned toward the queen without quite looking at her. "Are you coming, milady?"

Childishly, she wished that Adèle would miraculously appear from the solar and deal with the situation. With a heavy breath, which she hoped made her appear disdainful, she nodded and followed. "Remember, she's there to keep you honest," Noble reminded him cheerfully as they entered. "There's a very hefty fine at stake here."

This room, below the steward's well-appointed chamber, housed several of the lower officers. Their beds were mats of brychan-shrouded heather and the room, ill ventilated, had a heavy, sweet aroma to it. The wiry Hafaidd escorted them in and crossed at once to swing open the shutter of the only window, letting in some light and air.

When the door was closed behind them, Gwirion turned at once to the girl, who looked traumatized. "Are you devout?" he asked. She glanced down shyly and nodded, and Gwirion held his hand out to the queen. "Your rosary, milady, if I may."

Isabel hesitated. She didn't trust him and the piece was precious to her—Adèle had fashioned the beads by hand from the pulp of crushed roses, and the crucifix held a lock of hair from the head of St. Milburga, at whose abbey she'd been baptized.

"I'll be careful with it," he promised impatiently, understanding her expression. She gave it to him, frowning, and he pressed it into the girl's cold hand, bending over her. "Will you swear on Her Majesty's cross to be truthful?" Her eyes flickered up to his, then down again. She pursed her lips together and nodded. "Are you still a maiden?" he asked quietly. Her face crumpled and she nodded again, close to sobbing, but his calm reaction reassured her and she kept herself in check. "Why are you doing this, then? Who put you up to it?" She shook her head, pursing her lips again, and he sighed. "You'd better tell me or you're in a lot of trouble." The girl shifted her eyes pleadingly to the queen, hoping for feminine sympathy.

She found none. The queen was waiting for her to speak; her expression was far less lenient than Gwirion's, and framed by her wine-red wimple it looked especially severe. "My brother," the girl finally said, whispering miserably, then blurted it all out at once. "That man killed our sister when she refused him years ago and he made it look like an accident, like a drowning; I saw it but I was only six then and they wouldn't take my testimony in court, so he was acquitted but I saw him do it and he never paid the blood fine for it and we need money terribly so Iorweth thought to get it by accusing him of something else we could fine him for."

Isabel wanted to be sympathetic but she couldn't let this pass. Anticipating Gwirion's thoughts, she warned, "Even if you play along with her and say she's been deflowered, he can claim it was by someone else's hand."

"We don't use *hands* for that here. You English are a weird lot,

aren't you?" Gwirion retorted, and was relieved to see the shadow of a grin on the girl's face. He patted her shoulder. "What's your reputation where you come from?"

She sobered instantly, looked guilty. "It never occurred to anybody in the village to question me when I said it, and anyway he's known for taking anyone he pleases."

Gwirion looked up at the queen with an expression of satisfaction. "I think it's very obvious what to do here."

"I can't let you," she said with sympathetic firmness.

"Oh, for the love of God, milady!"

"First of all, you don't even know that a thing she says is true, and anyway, I won't let you lie to the court, it makes a mockery of justice."

"Letting a murderer go free *isn't* making a mockery of justice?" he demanded and then, before she could reply, he gave her an ironic look of comprehension. "Ah! How could I forget, milady, you're a Mortimer, your sort does that all the time."

She wanted to hit him. "I believe in the rule of law," she said through clenched jaws. "Perhaps you haven't heard of that here." She turned to the girl. "We can try to exonerate you from this scheme, but you're taking justice into your own hands and I can't condone that." Seeing the look on Gwirion's face she added, "I'm representing the king, Gwirion, you know I have to do this."

He stared at her for a moment. "Allow me to treat you precisely as I would the king on this occasion, then," he said, and walked to the exit, grabbed the latch, and threw the door open.

Twenty paces away sat Noble and Goronwy, on the far edge of a ring of waiting onlookers, most of them starting to perspire in the summer-morning haze. All eyes were immediately on Gwirion.

"And how was the anatomy lesson?" Noble called out.

Gwirion ignored him and crossed to the accused man, standing alone in the middle of the circle, idly picking at a scab on his elbow. Barely moving his lips, in a voice too low to carry beyond the two of them, Gwirion muttered ominously, "I know about the sister and I have the proof to hang you if you don't confess to this instead." The

man's alarmed reaction, although quickly buried, was cognizant enough to satisfy him. He turned to Noble and the judge. "This man is guilty," he said loudly, with finality, and marched back to the tower.

The queen was at the threshold, on her way out, as Gwirion returned. To a collective gasp from the onlookers, he grabbed her arm and pushed her back inside, hesitating for a moment in the doorway until he heard the man start to confess the rape. Then he slammed the door closed.

"Let go of me!" Isabel ordered.

He released her but kept his hand leaning on the door. "Milady, if you call this girl's bluff now, that whoreson will go free, unpunished—"

"For something he didn't do!" she snapped.

"And also for something he *did* do!" he insisted. "And the family, who has been wronged, and by that man, never gets any reparation. I would never let Noble do that and I won't let you do it either."

"You think you're above the law?"

"Oh, no, milady, very much below it," he said comfortably.

"I'd say so," she muttered. "Even your charity is underhanded."

If it was meant to insult him, it failed. Looking pleased with himself, he collected the rosary from the shaken girl and held it out to the queen. She snatched it up from his open palm and headed at once toward the door.

"He just confessed to the lesser charge, milady. If you tell them all the truth now you'll be doing nobody a favor, except perhaps God, but in that case I must say that God is a twisted bastard."

She winced at his impiety. "The law is not for doing people favors, Gwirion, it's for *justice*. Nobody's being punished or rewarded according to their just desserts and that's an affront to the rule of law itself—*and* to the king who executes it."

He considered this briefly, then shrugged. "Well then, tell the king to sue me for it." He walked past her to the door, exited the tower, and walked through the court, straight back to the kitchen, his harp, and his audience.

A mockery of justice?" Noble echoed her in disbelief that night. He was in bed, waiting—very patiently, he thought—for her to calm down and join him for her wifely duties.

Isabel was pacing his chamber in her shift and his bedrobe, which was far too big for her. With her long braids swaying and the robe dragging behind her she looked like a child playing at being an angry adult. "Gwirion mocked the law today—because you decided to *entertain* yourself by giving him authority you shouldn't have given him."

"I don't exist to serve the rule of law, Isabel—the rule of law exists to serve me."

"It exists to serve the *kingdom!*" she insisted hotly.

"I am the kingdom," he said, quite cool.

She began pacing more excitedly. "That is the most hubristic, self-centered definition of kingship I have ever—"

"No, it's not, Isabel," he said with an exaggeratedly tired sigh. "In fact, it's absolutely self-*less*, but it's too late for political philosophy, as charming as it is to find that you are so inflamed by the subject. Come to bed now."

"How does appointing Gwirion in that way serve the kingdom?" she demanded, her pacing bringing her no closer to the bed.

"You would rather I'd called Anarawd over from Elfael to molest her? Just because that would be the legal thing to do, you'd subject that poor child to him? Come to bed."

"No, I wouldn't want Anarawd either," she said impatiently. "But if you were reassigning the job, you should not have given it to a rascal like Gwirion. If you're going to manipulate the law, do it *responsibly*, do it with *sense*," she insisted, slapping the back of one hand upon the other palm for emphasis. "Just because you're the king doesn't mean you can reorder the universe to suit your whim."

He raised his head off the cushion and gave her a look of amazement, almost choking as he laughed at her. "My *whim?* I've never done

anything in court to suit my whim! Short of picking the women I bed for pleasure I don't think I've ever done *anything* to suit my whim."

"Assigning Gwirion to that position was a whim."

He shook his head. "I knew the girl was virgin, I could tell by the way she *walked*, let alone that she was a truly incompetent liar. Gwirion was the best choice to resolve the situation, never mind why. Come to bed, Isabel, that's an order."

"You treated it as if it were a whim," she insisted.

"Of course I did," he said in exasperation, relaxing his head on the cushion again. "Half Gwirion's value is that nobody, including Gwirion, takes him seriously except for me. It's part of that fool mystique I'm so charmed you introduced me to. If you don't come here at once, I shall summon someone else to take your place, and I'll be glad of the replacement."

Her anger suddenly refocused, she spun around to glare at him. "It *is* possible for you to philander without insulting my station that blatantly," she informed him.

"Yes, it is. But it is not possible for me to procreate without a willing partner. I have a genocidal Norman baron, an upstart Welsh prince, and a criminally-minded cousin to ward off with the fruit of my loins. Where would you prefer that fruit to ripen?"

Looking sickened, she forced herself to join him.

H AI I knew the monogamy experiment would never last," Gwirion wrote gleefully to Corr, some two weeks later. "He's returned to his natural ways with a vengeance. It's refreshing. I myself think he should try to seduce that addle-pated Adèle, just on principle.

"Our Saxoness queen consort is showing a little more mettle now, which I actually admire although it's not nearly as entertain-

ing. But her entire life revolves around where he shoves his cock, and she's being incredibly backward about it. After raising such a fuss about Enid, she could have divorced him over Gwen, but she didn't—apparently in England that would make her 'damaged wares,' and I understand that's even worse than having a virile husband. And now that she's put up with him for more than three episodes, of course, she's even lost her right to ask for reparations, so we are all doomed to listen to her rant and rave when any reasonable woman would have dealt with the thing by now." This was a fiction of Gwirion's; the queen's reactions were as always icy, not volcanic. "At least I finally have something to make fun of. But he won't let me *use* it.

"And Adèle is becoming a nuisance. Is it *my* fault that the queen is always within earshot when I'm practicing a new verse about the king's latest conquests?"

An hour after handing this last letter to the increasingly fidgety messenger, Gwirion was in the kitchen showing Marged's grandson Dafydd some sleight-of-hand tricks with a kerchief. The kitchen workers were taking a short break outside, soaking in a rare moment of genuinely bright, dry sunshine and blue sky. Marged, relaxing on a sack of oats that was only marginally wider than she was, nursed a mug of ale before starting in on supper, watching these two with a contented grin. She remembered when Gwirion was that age. She even remembered when Corr was that age.

The peace was shattered by Adèle storming into the kitchen from the hall, her face nearly purple, murder in her eyes. She rushed up to Gwirion and without warning or explanation slapped him across the face as hard as she could. Astonished, he stood up and glared down at her. "What in hell was that for?" he demanded, as the boy leapt away and Marged scrambled to her feet.

Adèle, almost too outraged to speak, shook a handful of documents in his face. It took him a moment to recognize that they were the letters, *every* letter, he had written to Corr. They had never left the castle. "That's private correspondence," he cried. "You had no right—"

"I have the right to do anything in defense of my mistress," she shrieked. "You heartless bastard!"

"That's just me sounding off to a friend who can't even read!" Gwirion shot back. "I'm not planning anything against her, there's no malfeasance—"

"You sent her to find the king with that whore in her room," the woman shouted, shaking the packet under his nose.

"No I didn't!" Gwirion shouted back. "She found them on her own! You silly, ranting—"

She slapped him again. "Get out of this castle," she ordered. "Get out of my lady's life. You're good for nothing here, you're nothing but a parasite."

Gwirion laughed bitterly. "Do you think I don't know that? You convince the king to get rid of me, and I will readily go wherever he sends me. But he'll never do it."

"Then go on your own," Adèle said. "You're obviously miserable here. Go someplace where they'll let you unleash your vicious humor. Just walk out of here and go somewhere they'll appreciate you. If there is such a place."

Gwirion shrugged. "I can't," he said. As if that settled it, he resumed his seat and gestured for the boy to join him again with the kerchief. Adèle pushed between them and chucked the letters under the cauldron, into the flames of the gaping fireplace.

"What are you doing?" Gwirion yelled, trying to grab them back. He salvaged only half of one burned page, puckering his nose against the smell of burning parchment. "Those are mine! You have no right!"

"Sully her name one more time," Adèle threatened, "and even if nobody reads it, I swear on all I hold sacred, I will make you suffer. And I'll make the king suffer for keeping you."

She looked alarmingly serious, but Gwirion calmed at once and gave her an appraising, almost approving look. "Very well, I'll take that dare," he said. "You're *far* more satisfying to bait than she is—I wish you'd've let me know that sooner! As soon as I've taught my little friend this trick, I'll get a fresh quill."

A DÈLE decided she would have to get rid of him. It became her monomania; she made it her business to learn everything she could about his background, certain there would be grounds for an accusation of unchristian ways, but she was disappointed. Father Idnerth was helpful with the start of the story, which was disappointingly mundane. Gwirion had been a foundling; the holy man had wanted him christened and when nobody else expressed an interest in naming him, the priest himself had chosen Gwion, the birth name of the legendary bard Taliesin, who had also been a foundling of sorts. When Prince Maelgwyn as a toddler, stumbling over his expanding vocabulary, called him "gwirion"—not a name, just a word meaning both innocent and foolish—the entire court had humorously taken up the misnomer until the orphan thought it was his real name. Maelgwyn and Gwion, the chaplain pointed out with parental and slightly senile affection, had rechristened each other.

Marged—not yet the cook then, but the cook's wife—was Gwirion's wet-nurse, and he slept with Corr in the little closet off the kitchen, which was unorthodox since private sleeping quarters, even modest ones, were unheard of for anyone but royalty. Because he was of an age with the prince they were sometimes left together, and Marged noticed almost at once that Gwirion was the only one whose presence calmed the infant prince's tantrums. This elevated his potential from domestic drudge to royal companion, and when the prince began his studies Gwirion was not officially tutored, but he was invited to learn on the periphery. So he learned to ride, but not to lance; to fight, but not with sword or arrow or spear, only with fists. He never studied politics, but he learned to read and write faster than the prince, and when he took an interest in and had an aptitude for Hywel's harp, Cadwallon invested in training him to music.

There was one detail that challenged credulity: Older castle resi-

dents insisted that Gwirion, although never respectful of authority, had been the sweetest-tempered child until the murder of Cadwallon. Again and again she heard the chorus that Gwirion had saved young Maelgwyn's life that day, although nobody seemed to know or care about the details. In fact, nobody seemed to care about much of anything about Gwirion's past, including Gwirion himself. Adèle realized she would have to look to the present or worse, the future, to find a way to deal with him.

And then the queen presented her with an unexpected opportunity.

NOBLE was surprised that the tentative knock at the door that wet September evening was his wife's. He had asked for one of the steward's girls, but she must have seen her mistress on the way and wisely dropped back. Thanks to Gwirion, the queen's tantrums were legendary, despite the fact that she had never thrown one.

"Milady," he said, and stood up, straightening the tunic and drawers that he slept in, glad he hadn't yet removed them. "I wasn't expecting you tonight."

"Do you want me to leave?" she asked quickly, hesitating to take off her cape, already soaked from the short walk across the bailey. She was in a strange mood, tense and yet distracted. Usually when she was upset about something she had the focus of a hawk. Now her attention was turned inward.

"No," he said, placating her. "I ... perhaps I just misread the moon, but I assumed—"

"You did misread," Isabel said. "My flux should have been upon me nearly two weeks ago. Nothing has come." She didn't know where to look. This was why they had married, after all, it should have been an announcement of extraordinary joy, but she had sobbed in Adèle's arms for most of the afternoon.

Noble took a breath and found his hand at his chest. He pushed the cape off her and had his arms tight around her, his lips pressing her brow. "This is wonderful!" he announced, almost trembling.

She managed to give him a weak smile. Her hands were cold.

SINCE he now understood exactly who his audience was, Gwirion obligingly tailored his wit. "To my revered correspondent," he scribbled onto a pilfered piece of the king's best paper, sitting by Marged's hearth, and paused. He wanted to provide material worthy of Adèle's awesome wrath. "The queen is suddenly no longer allowed to ride out to the abbey. No one is saying why, but I'm sure she's with child. Why must they all be so *precious* about it? Why can't someone just say, 'Ah, he finally ploughed her deep enough,' or words to that effect, and be done with it?

"My personal theory is that his other women enjoy him so much that they don't want to lose his favor by becoming fat with pregnancy, and they take precautions, so he's never sired a bastard. I'm glad they know to do that; she'll be so swollen and crabby soon that he won't want to touch her, but you know as well as I do that he can't go more than a few days without activity. I suspect he'll be riding the entire female population of the castle by Advent. Perhaps he'll even make her watch, so that she might finally learn a little of what really pleases him.

"Or perhaps, once there's an heir, he'll dispose of his marriage altogether. I don't think Mortimer is behaving himself anyhow, so she's essentially useless. The gaggle of girls who do nothing all day but play with balls of yarn and giggle at each other's stupid jokes have been displaced from her solar and are spending their time in a corner of the great hall, where they get in the way of the people who have real business to attend to. Only Adèle spends any time with the queen now. How could anyone possibly have a healthy pregnancy with such a humorless, mad old shrew hovering about? Half the time

she won't even let the king in to speak to his own wife! Well, she's such a frail little thing, she'll probably die in childbirth, and then we won't have her to deal with anymore. Then he can find himself a nice Welsh wife and restore Cymaron's dignity. We all pray for such a time—and if he has any sense, he prays so too."

He found Adèle by the hall fire. "Here you are," he said angelically, handing her the letter. "Do let me know when you're ready to begin the persecution." He bowed extravagantly and went back into the kitchen. She pursued him with her eyes.

"I'm ready now," she gloated.

· 5 ·

So Shall Ye Reap

Harvest Festival, 1198

INALLY, AFTER FAR too many hours, the audience-chamber door was opened to let in the cool air of the September afternoon. The king, beginning to recover from being shut up with Gwilym the steward and Gwallter the chamberlain settling the state accounts of the past year, had been interrupted by a runner from the English border with disturbing news of Mortimer—after all these months, at last, concrete news of Mortimer, and astonishingly damning too. After receiving it in brooding silence and dictating several sharp responses to send back east at once, Noble could do nothing further for the moment, and he was trying to push it from his mind. Now he just wanted to be down on the tourney field with his men but there were other domestic duties to attend to first.

He did, however, indulge himself in a few moments of Gwirion's prattling.

The prattling had sunk to this level: "Think of all the furrows you've ploughed, and never a seedling or even a weed reported yet.

You haven't the power to spawn. It's God's punishment upon you for seducing that darling bride of Christ when we were young."

"She hadn't yet taken the veil," Noble insisted mildly, nostalgia pulling at the corner of his mouth.

Gwirion was already back to the present. "Face the truth, sire," he said with a mischievous grin, knowing there was no danger he would be taken seriously. "Your wife is obviously having an affair. It's another man's son."

Noble laughed a little, stretching across the leather chair back with leonine indolence. "Even for a fool, that's dangerous territory."

Gwirion rose to his knees on the cushion and leaned against the king's shin. "She's so distraught when she learns of your indiscretions. A little upset would be one thing, that would be her being a woman. But she becomes hysterical," he insisted, although he knew she didn't. Working within the inconvenient confines of reality was Noble's burden, not his. He lowered his voice conspiratorially. "The one who cries 'Foul' the loudest is usually guilty of the very sin he denounces. That's an ageless truth. I warn you, she's been carrying on with another man."

Noble, grateful for any trivial distraction, played it out. "And whom do you suspect?" he asked with all apparent seriousness.

"Well, sire," Gwirion answered, equally straight-faced, "she's very religious. Do you think it might be Father Idnerth? I think it might be Idnerth, sire."

"He's old enough to be her grandfather."

Gwirion gave him a knowing look. "Some women prefer older men for their experience."

"Of which Idnerth must have untold thimblefuls." Noble laughed and stood up. "Thank you for bringing it to my attention. Go make mischief elsewhere. I must visit with my wife, assuming her living chastity belt will let me through the gates."

"There's no one left for me to make mischief with." Gwirion frowned, also rising. "You've disposed of everyone who made good company."

"*I'm* still here," the king said expansively, affronted.

"I said everyone who made *good* company," Gwirion corrected, and Noble, grinning, made an obscene gesture at him.

"Then go harass someone," he said, picking up the Mortimer scroll from the arm of his chair. Turning toward the door, he was surprised to see Adèle standing at the threshold, in a dusty shaft of sunlight from a hall window. "There you are, Gwirion, practice on that." He walked past the old woman without a greeting, and disappeared into the hum of the great hall.

Gwirion and Adèle stood for a moment staring at each other, two wiry bright-eyed creatures in their masters' castoffs, aflame with mutual defiance. Suddenly Gwirion smiled and said heartily, without sarcasm, "I appreciate that you hate me as much as I hate you. It takes a certain courage for anyone, especially a mad old woman whom nobody likes, to be that genuine. But weren't you going to persecute me? After that delicious fodder I provided? I almost offended my own sensibilities," he said, confidingly.

"What has my poor girl ever done to you," Adèle demanded, "that you would try to convince the king she's been unfaithful to him?"

"He didn't believe me."

"Of course he didn't, but you were in earnest."

"I was not!" Gwirion said, laughing.

"That's blood lust," she insisted with intensity, as if she hadn't heard him. "You're a sick creature, and a demeaning influence on His Majesty." She turned to walk away.

"Wait a moment, then!" Gwirion cried. "Why don't you ever fret about His Majesty being a demeaning influence on *me*? Do you think I was *born* to be this way?"

She paused, looked back into the room, and for a flicker of a moment seemed on the verge of lowering her armor. "Do you think *I* was born to be this way?" she asked, quite earnestly.

"Of course," he answered at once. "That face was never beautiful. You're not going to be her midwife, are you? You'll scare the wee one half to death, one look and he'll try to climb back into the

womb. Then he'll rupture her spleen in the effort and she'll die and it will all be your fault. There truly are such things as killing looks!"

THERE was a slightly awkward formality between them, and he would have to be the one to overcome it: He knew her pride was wounded that he now no longer sent for her, that both he and Gwirion were so casually blatant in setting up his trysts. It did not inflame her righteous indignation as it did Adèle's, thank God, but it took a toll on her already rattled spirits.

"You are well?" he asked at last.

Isabel was having a difficult time of it, but she only nodded and adjusted her wimple in the mirror. The silver threads caught the fading daylight from the window and glittered prettily about her wide face, but they were stiff and confining and she would happily have traded the whole thing for a simple Welsh veil. Adèle still insisted on the wimple. "There is only the nausea, and Adèle has concoctions for that. I've invited Thomas for a visit."

"You've what?"

"When I wrote my family, I invited Thomas for a visit."

A cold hand closed over his heart when he heard this and he gripped the scroll harder. With effort, he kept himself calm and asked, "Are you sure it was wise to tell them?"

She frowned. "Why wouldn't it be?"

"Your status has changed," he said. "You'd make a far more attractive hostage now, carrying my child."

Her eyes widened and she turned from the mirror to face him. "Noble, don't be ridiculous. They're my family, not my enemies."

"No, I'm your family and they're *my* enemies," he said.

"You married me because you aren't enemies anymore," she said with some exasperation.

"Then why is your uncle acting like one?" Noble snapped.

She hesitated. "What do you mean?"

He threw the scroll down onto her bed, almost as if he were expecting a confession. "Mortimer tried to buy the loyalty of our eastern and southeastern guard," he announced. "He's been working on them for months. My men have been playing along with him to see what he's up to—"

"Southeast?" she said, confused. "Your southeast border touches the deBraose lands, not Roger's."

"Yes," he said, annoyed. "*Our* southeast border does. Either Roger is trying to hire my men as mercenaries to attack deBraose, which I would consider ungentlemanly but forgivable, or he's trying to use deBraose as a shield to plan something against us. Which do you think is more likely?" She was too shocked to speak. "I'm sending more men to the area and I've already written deBraose and Prince John. This will be resolved quickly now. But nothing is what it seems at the moment, Isabel. I won't stand any hostile elements having access to you."

"You consider my own brother a hostile element?"

"Not Thomas," Noble said impatiently, "Roger. Roger will see this child only as a prince of Maelienydd—a new target to dispatch."

"All of that is over now," she said firmly, with a frustrated sigh. "And justice was served, after all, he paid for his crime *years* ago."

"No he didn't," Noble snorted.

"Yes he did," she corrected. "Henry imprisoned him for two entire years. Do you know how extraordinary that is? For the English king to imprison an English lord for killing a *Welshman*?"

"For two years!" Noble flared. "Two years! What kind of punishment is that for regicide? Anyway, it *wasn't* for regicide, it was for disregarding the writ of safe passage—it's a debt Mortimer paid Henry Plantagenet of England. It has nothing to do with the debt he owes Maelgwyn ap Cadwallon of Maelienydd."

She shook her head. "What are you talking about?"

"He owes me a blood fine."

"What, an eye for an eye?"

"No," he scoffed. "How pathetically English of you. It's to *prevent*

an eye for an eye. It's the law of Wales—I thought you studied that this summer with my pudgy little judge; didn't you bother with anything that wasn't to do with my cock? The killer pays a fine—a galanas—to the victim's family. And *then* it's over."

She tried, and failed, to imagine her uncle acquiescing to this. "And if it's never paid?"

"Then we devolve to the barbaric customs of your own beloved nation," he said dryly, "and it does become an eye for an eye. But it need not be Roger's. Any Mortimer suffices."

"Is that a threat?" she demanded sharply.

He had meant it merely as a barb, but her response made him think. "Only if you consider yourself a Mortimer."

"Don't play games about this, Noble—of course I'm a Mortimer. If I'm *not* a Mortimer, why did you marry me?"

"If you *are* a Mortimer, why did *you* marry *me*?" She blinked at him, and he nodded. "You understand, I hope, that I require an answer before I can allow you to see your kin again." He left, pulling the door closed behind him, as the severity of this sentence sunk in.

She rushed after him and threw the door open again. "Noble!" He paused on the first step, his back to her, his broad shoulders silhouetted against the light from the hall below. "What exactly did you mean by that?" she demanded.

Without turning to look at her he said firmly, "I mean that I will not allow fraternizing between a Mortimer who is in physical possession of my heir and Mortimers who would like to dispossess my heir."

"But I'm not a Mortimer, I'm the Lady of Maelienydd," she said, trying not to sound desperate.

After a pause, he turned and with a cocked eyebrow appraised her. "Is that so?" She nodded. "I'm glad to hear it. The Lady of Maelienydd has no earthly reason for wanting to spend time with those wretched Mortimers, so obviously the issue of doing so, or even writing them, will simply never arise. Until the child is safely delivered and can stay in my custody should you make the questionable choice of discoursing with Mortimers, you shall not be dis-

coursing with any Mortimers at all." He gave her a politely triumphant smile and descended the staircase, not noticing Adèle in the shadows of the balcony. The old woman gave him a murderous look as he passed by her.

THE harvest feast that night, the feast of Michelmas, would include the official announcement of the queen's condition, as well as a celebration of her birthday, but it was mostly a festival of thanksgiving for a successful harvest and an acknowledgment of the leaner months to come. It was the time of year when masses of Noble's subjects migrated with their herds and flocks from summer farms in the hills to the winter dwellings closer in to the villages. The valley of Cymaron saw its population increase by nearly a third this month.

The hall had been swept, the floor covered with dried rushes and aromatic meadowsweet, and the heavier winter tapestries hung upon the walls. Some of these were new, brought by the queen from England and mostly religious in theme. Gwirion had stood in front of each of them in turn, caricaturing Christ and paraphrasing scripture—obscenely—with an exaggerated French accent, until the chaplain arthritically swatted him away. The other hangings, although not as colorful as the English ones, were old favorites of heroes, battles, and hunting scenes. Above the main door hung an elaborately braided ribbon of what looked like hay: the very last tuft of grain harvested that day in the king's fields, brought into the court earlier amidst laughter and ceremony that Isabel could not begin to comprehend. Adèle assured her, bristling, that it was not Christian.

For the feast, hundreds of oaten threshing cakes with thyme and savory had been prepared; rook cakes with thyme and savory were baking; gallons of rabbit stew with thyme and savory had been seasoning for days. This year there would be an additional and exotic treat, wholly novel to the Welsh palette: a ginger dish, with neither

thyme nor savory, that the queen's woman had brought from beyond the border. Adèle was given a corner of the kitchen and enough eggs and milk to make jance sauce for several hundred—a chore even for her industrious hands. Marged the cook, proprietary and motivated as much by suspicion as curiosity, loomed over Adèle as she worked and insisted on sampling it before allowing it to be served to the king. With an unpleasantly surprised expression she spat it out, but having recovered, she demanded to sample it again and then, after another involuntary grimace, a third time. Gwirion, chuckling, pronounced it a success, reminded Adèle with a hopeful grin that he was waiting to be persecuted, and returned to the bustling hall to wrestle with his harp. Noble had bought him wire strings from Ireland, which he was having a calamitous time experimenting with. The bright, almost harsh sounds they made as he tried to tune the instrument reverberated off the rafters, and half his notes, it seemed, were swallowed up by the echo. "Crazy Irish!" he spat at last, and changed back to gentler horsehair.

IT was unthinkable to Noble to apologize for anything, but when he saw his wife approach the high table as the feast began, her face so grim within the pale wimple, he regretted what he'd said to her and drew her to him to whisper that she was free to welcome Thomas for a visit. She relaxed into his embrace, grateful and appeased; there was something more vital than mere affection binding them together now and her respect for that was visceral. But she couldn't bring herself to reciprocate any show of affection, feeling Adèle's eyes on the two of them: In Adèle's very black-and-white world, the king was very black, and tonight Isabel lacked the energy to fend off her chastisements for weakening to him. Even she was getting weary of Adèle's venom, although the old woman only ever deployed it in service to her mistress.

Hafaidd called out sharply for silence so that Father Idnerth

might deliver his blessing. It was in Latin, which meant nothing to most of them, and almost at once he was competing with a dozen whispered conversations round the hall about more important things, such as who was joining in the peat-stacking party this year, or whose ailments had been healed magically by the old wise woman in the hazel grove. When Idnerth had said amen, the smith was given, as he always was at feasts, the first drink of the evening. "That's because," Gwirion called out approvingly, "a sod like you needs an early start to get at all inebriated!"

When the meal was over (Adèle's jance sauce having been admiringly discussed but not much eaten), servants cleared away the board and trestles, and the guests gathered around an open space in front of the dais to dance and play games. Gwirion was in his element here, and despite her general resentment, Isabel finally saw a side of him that was not entirely repugnant to her. He was by instinct a common entertainer, and harvest was a time for common revels. Almost everyone had brought instruments of some sort—crwth, pipes, and harps of a dozen strings at most—and when Gwirion began a tune they all joined in, those without instruments singing. It was a raucous but innocent and truly joyful din and Gwirion, Isabel realized with grudging appreciation, was its natural conductor.

But when the third or fourth tune was in full swing, just as she was willing to concede that he might even have a winsome touch, the common entertainer in him once again appalled her. Carefully he laid his harp down on its back, then leapt up from his stool and in rapid succession grabbed a young woman and some half-dozen men out of the torchlit crowd. He steered them nimbly through a short, bizarre ritual in which the girl and one man were tossed into the air together by the other men, her skirts flying and their legs tangling together while everybody roared with approving laughter. Isabel had no idea what they were doing, but it seemed obscene, the leavings of some pagan fertility ritual of which Gwirion was a perverted form of minister, and at the end of it she was dismayed that the entire hall, even children, burst into deafening applause and cheering. She caught Adèle's eye; the older woman shook her head. "Godless heathens all,"

she mouthed in French, and exited calmly to the kitchen to prepare for Gwirion's death.

AFTER about an hour the general hilarity of the crowd was softened by the ready flow of ale, and the guests' instruments, at Hafaidd's urging, were finally put away. Now there would be gentler entertainment in honor of the queen.

Gwirion (under orders he resented) began this too, leading a pack of village men through a Christian hymn in stunning close harmony, with more parts to it than a full English choir. Hywel the bard, his voice growing ragged from years of overuse, told a story of King Arthur's heroic exploits that startled Isabel with its violence. Poets and musicians attached to the households of visiting lords contributed songs and stories, including one praising Noble's maternal family line, which went back to Rhodri the Great and the legendary Elystan Glodrydd. There was a rash of obsequious toasts, and then the messengered greetings were read aloud; even Anarawd, the cousin who would no longer be the heir, sent warm regards that sounded plausible. The only moment that displeased the king all evening was a last-minute delivery on horseback: the proclamation of congratulations sent from Llewelyn of Gwynedd—a patently political move, nothing more than an excuse to have his status as Noble's supposed peer trumpeted in front of Noble's subjects.

Adèle hovered in the kitchen by the screens to the hall, watching the bustle of servants going in and out, waiting for one of the sewing bevy to pass through. Fortune favored her and Madrun, the most trusting and naive of the trio, entered through the screens, carrying an empty pitcher. She deposited it on the central table and was headed back toward the hall when Adèle called out to her and she turned back.

"Run an errand for me, the cook's instructions," she ordered the girl with brusque offhandedness. She held out a wooden cup.

AS Isabel sat envying a silken-voiced songstress with a harp, she felt a tug on her sleeve and glanced back. Madrun stood in the shadow behind the throne, her wild red hair a demure auburn in the low light. With an innocent smile, she presented a wooden chalice. "Your Majesty's medicine?" she offered.

The queen looked at it in confusion, then rose and slipped back with Madrun to the shadows behind her throne. She reached for the cup and glanced at the contents, no more than a mouthful. "What is this?" she asked.

"From the kitchen," Madrun said, as she had been instructed to. "To settle your stomach."

Isabel sniffed it. Adèle had exhausted her own knowledge of the herbs but Marged was still gamely experimenting, and sometimes something helped a little. The oily liquid smelled like ginger and nutmeg, but there was a hint of other things she could not recognize. Ginger sometimes helped the nausea, so, desperate for relief and suspecting it would taste foul, she brought it to her lips and downed it in a single swallow.

It choked her. Juice of raw ginger made her eyes and nose smart fiercely and her throat constricted in pain—but it was only masking some other taste, something oily, alien and bitter. It burned her all the way down to the lining of her stomach. She grabbed the girl's arm in alarm, gasping for breath. "What was that?" she demanded, not quite in a whisper. *"What did I just drink?"*

"It's fine, milady, please don't distress yourself," Madrun said assuagingly. "The cook said it would go down very harshly, but it does marvels when it starts to work." Noble was glancing back over his shoulder at them, frowning and looking concerned. Isabel raised a hand dismissively to tell him not to worry himself. Madrun, her task not quite completed, returned to the kitchen.

Noble gave his wife a passing smile as she rejoined him, then re-

turned his attention to the female musician who was performing. She was not a pretty woman to his eyes—too small in build, too placid in demeanor—but she sang like an angel, and played a better harp even than Gwirion. Her master was staying overnight as a guest, so a proposition would be easy. He glanced at his wife, glad for both their sakes she couldn't read his mind.

Something about her complexion made him look again. She was very pale and a fine sweat had broken out over her face. "Isabel," he whispered, frowning, "are you unwell? Should you be lying down?"

"No, no, I'm fine," she said hoarsely, and reached out to touch his hand. He was surprised and pleased by the gesture, and held her hand in his, stroking it. She smiled gratefully, which was the best moment of the night for him. He smiled back.

"Do you need anything?" he pressed. The song had ended; the herald introduced another singer into the performing space.

"No, I'm all right, really. It's only that the mead tastes off to me."

"Gwilym tested it. That's the best in the kingdom, it's been waiting some eight years for a celebration like tonight. And so have I." He lowered his head toward her, pressed his lips against her fingers, and then, more intimately, against her palm. The throng, watching them, cheered. King and queen smiled tentatively at each other.

"When they do that, it almost feels as if they're our children," she whispered.

He nodded, and then winked at her. "If this one goes well enough, we might start work on a brood that size."

She blushed despite herself. "Noble," she murmured, confused by her own pleasure at these words, "that's hubris."

"A king should be allowed a little hubris," he said, and then shifted his attention to the crowd. "We thank you for your spirit, people. The singer may begin now."

Half an hour later they were nearing the end of the night's entertainment, and Isabel felt far worse than she had before she had drunk Madrun's offering. It was not nausea now; it was something more acute, as if a hole had been drilled through her stomach and her

muscles were clenching around it. Concerned, she was about to excuse herself to the kitchen to ask Marged about the concoction, when she found Madrun standing demurely at her elbow again, trying to stay hidden behind the thrones. "Excuse me, milady," she whispered in the queen's ear. She spoke hesitantly, bemused by the instructions that this message required delivery at just this moment and no sooner. "But now I am to tell you it was not Marged who made up the potion you drank earlier. It was Adèle."

A DÈLE in her grey wimple, ignoring and ignored by the harried workers cleaning in the kitchen, had moved nearer the doorway leading out into the courtyard, fidgeting with a piece of paper and awaiting the familiar footsteps. She looked up calmly when she heard them.

Isabel stopped beside her, pale, frightened—and furious. In a slow, threatening whisper she demanded, *"What have you done?"*

"Come with me," Adèle said quietly, and went outside. She closed the door behind the queen and stayed on the steps overlooking the yard, their privacy assured and the torch offering the fire she needed.

"Adèle, you *must* tell me what you've done."

"You know what I've done," Adèle said. "And you know why." She hoped she had timed this to accommodate her mistress's wrath.

Isabel slammed the back of her hand to her mouth to stifle a horrified cry. "I'll vomit it out," she announced, furious.

"It's already in your blood," said Adèle complacently. "But go on, feel free to try if it will ease your conscience." She gestured to the far side of the stairs, where it was dark enough that nobody in the yard could see anything. Immediately Isabel crouched in the shadows and frantically took herself to a state of pained gagging that brought nothing up. After a long, shuddering dry heave, she

gave up and collapsed, gripping the cold stone steps for balance. Adèle waited.

At last the queen rose and returned to her, lashes wet, contained but more enraged than Adèle had ever seen her. "I won't do this, Adèle!" she whispered, fuming. "Give me an antidote."

"There is none."

Isabel spun away and slammed her foot hard on the stone step in a childish, impotent explosion of rage. She took a few ragged breaths and then turned back to Adèle, demanding, "Was it oil of pennyroyal?"

"And other things. If you're thinking of asking Marged for help, don't bother. There's a lot of ginger in it and Marged never saw ginger before this week, she knows nothing about its properties and won't dare interfere with a mix she doesn't know, for fear of complications. And it's too late now anyhow."

"Dammit!" Isabel hissed, her throat constricting again, barely controlling the urge to throttle Adèle. *I should have seen such madness coming*, she thought with a wave of panic. "I'm telling Noble this minute—" She began to push past her for the door. Adèle stopped her by holding out the paper.

"Read this first."

"Later—"

"*Now*," Adèle said in a voice from Isabel's childhood, and Isabel stopped at once.

But she didn't take the scroll. "This is *treason*," she whispered, glaring at the old woman and starting to tremble. "And anyhow, how could you do this? It's *my child*, Adèle, you had no right—"

"It's not your child, it's his heir," Adèle said harshly.

"That makes it worse!" she insisted. "I'll tell Noble, perhaps I can convince him it was a mistake and—"

"You can always make another one. I'm doing this for you, don't muck it up."

She shook her head, incredulous, and stared at Adèle as if she'd never seen her before. "I don't want this! Have you lost your senses?"

"Don't become hysterical," Adèle said without quite meeting her eyes. "You're a practical girl and you'll see in time the value of this action. There's nothing you can do to prevent it now, so your choices are to tell the king at once and gain nothing by it but my execution, or to help me use this to the best advantage." She waved the scroll. Isabel shook her head, hugging herself and shaking from the cold and the drug, her face starting to crumple into tears. She released one arm and began to cross herself repeatedly. "Be despondent later," Adèle ordered fiercely. "Pay attention now or this really will be for nothing."

The queen blinked back the tears and stopped crossing herself. Feeling ill, she slowly took the scroll and hesitantly unrolled it. " 'To my revered correspondent'—Who is this intended for?"

"Does it matter?" Adèle replied serenely. "I intercepted it. Read what it says and then tell me if you'll work with me."

Isabel looked down and squinted to read it in the torchlight. She was trembling so badly now that Adèle had to hold the paper for her. "The queen is suddenly no longer allowed to ride out to the abbey. No one is saying why, but I'm sure she's with child." She looked up. "Who wrote this?" Adèle gestured for her to keep reading. "Why must they all be so precious about it? Why can't someone just say, 'Ah, he finally ploughed her deep enough,' or words to that effect, and be done with it?" She closed her eyes a moment, knowing who the author had to be, then resumed reading in silence. She grew paler as she read and chewed her lip ferociously to keep her bitterness in check.

" 'She's such a frail little thing,' " Adèle recited with righteous disgust when she saw Isabel reach the words, " 'she'll probably die in childbirth, and then we won't have her to deal with anymore. Then he can find himself a nice Welsh wife and restore Cymaron's dignity. We all pray for such a time—and if he has any sense, he prays so too.' "

Isabel closed her eyes again when she had finished, light-headed now, and Adèle reached up and fed the scroll into the torch fire. "An

unborn child is easily replaced. That villain, thank God, is not. Will you work with me?" she asked.

WHEN the final guest performer had graciously dipped his head to acknowledge the applause, Gwirion stepped out away from the shadow of the dais and moved into the empty space. Noble, after playfully grilling Isabel on the finer points of continental foolery, had ordered him to change his outfit to a deliberately clownish one for the evening, with ass's ears attached to a cap on his head, and the audience hooted at him now. He tried to ignore them and begin his dancing prattle, but he couldn't. "So you think this is ridiculous?" he demanded.

"Hell, yes!" several drunken voices chorused in reply, accompanied by muted chuckles. He glanced down at himself.

"Well," he said. "You're right. I look absurd. Of course, many say I *am* absurd, so that's all well and good. But I worry about those who look absurd when they're not supposed to. The king, for instance," he offered, and headed up the steps of the dais. Noble theatrically rolled his eyes, and people in the front laughed.

The queen shrank back as Gwirion approached them. The moment she'd seen him as she was returning to her seat, sanity returned and she'd determined to sabotage Adèle's ludicrous, murderous scheme, but by now she was having a hard time thinking clearly. Still she managed to keep a small smile plastered to her lips.

"Stand up, sire," Gwirion was saying loudly. "I want to show the crowd that your attire is also absurd."

Misreading his wife's discomfort, Noble reluctantly shook his head. "No, Gwirion, none of that tonight."

"It's fortunate you never say that to the queen or we might not be celebrating this happy occasion," Gwirion chortled. He turned his face but not his attention toward her, not noticing her jaundiced

flush. "Now here's another absurdity," he announced to the crowd, gesturing to her silk kirtle and pelisse. "Here we have the expectant mother dressed in silver and the palest of flowery hues. She looks veritably *virginal.* But we're here tonight in testimony that she's certainly no virgin!"

The room was spinning; she was about to lose consciousness. This was the moment Adèle had told her to act but she was sickened with guilt for even considering it. Confused, fighting an encroaching fog, she could remember only that his proximity was what endangered him, that she was to get as near to him as possible, so that Adèle, stationed in the crowd, could convince the drunken revelers that they had seen him lay hands upon the queen. She cowered away from him, and disoriented by the drug that was making her belly clench, shouted what she meant to whisper, desperate and unhinged: "Move away, for God's sake, Gwirion, move *away* from me!" She flailed her arms at him and he worriedly shot a look at Noble. Noble made a gesture to carry on as he leaned in toward his wife and put a reassuring arm around her, gently hushing her and checking her forehead for a fever. As if it were a delirious litany, she continued pleading for Gwirion to keep away from her.

Unnerved, Gwirion jumped down to the open space on the floor and tried to continue his patter. "Is this some peculiar Norman custom? If anyone can explain to me why we should celebrate proof of her fecundity by dressing her as if she were a little girl—"

He was interrupted by a scream of pain. He spun around to look, and fell victim to the general panic that swept the hall.

There was a growing streak of blood across the skirt he'd just mocked, and the queen, vomiting blood onto the dais, had turned a disturbing yellow. For one shocked moment, nobody was capable of movement but the queen herself, as she stood then convulsed violently and doubled over, clutching her abdomen. The last word from her mouth, still pleading and barely audible, was "Gwirion." She began to tumble down the dais steps, but Noble leapt from his seat and caught her. He lifted her in his arms as she fainted, her body still convulsing, blood seeping from her nostrils and the cor-

ners of her mouth. Women screamed as the blood continued to splatter the steps, some people pressing forward, others frantic to back away.

Gwirion tried to run back up to the dais, but the guards had stepped in to push the mob back, and within seconds many people—starting with a woman's voice that was distinctly accented—began to cry out his name accusingly and claw at him, murder in their eyes. Suddenly terrified, he changed direction and began struggling to get away from the guards and out of the hall, but his costume made him easy to identify. He felt a tug on his leg, and as he pulled away his cap was torn off. People grabbed at him from all sides as he ducked, pushed, scrambled, and climbed out of the crowd, his heart rippling in his throat.

NOBLE refused to leave her side. Too distracted to heed Adèle's hints that she needed to be alone with Isabel, he sat by her bed and would not release her hand. Finally Adèle gave him a damp rag and told him to make himself useful by keeping his wife's brow cool. Her priest hovered near her other shoulder muttering something ominous in Latin, the sewing bevy rushed to fetch rags and poultices to stem the flow of blood; Angharad asked to drape a cord of sheep gut on her as a talisman but the priest shrilly denounced the idea. With his approval, though, Adèle placed the handmade rosary housing the relic of St. Milburga around her neck. There was much more blood than Adèle had expected, and she was frightened for a while. Isabel was pale and sickly yellow and unconscious for over an hour. By that time, the women had cut her out of her bloodied silks, sponged her clean, wrapped her in a warm mantle, and placed her under the blankets.

Noble, hovering anxiously by her head, was the first to hear her speak. He couldn't make out what she was saying over the priest's endless intonations and the women's talking, and he held up his

hand. At once there was silence and all attention in the room was on the bed.

"Adèle," she moaned softly, her eyes still closed. "Adèle, what's happening?" She spoke in French.

Adèle sat across from the king, on the bed. She placed her cool, weathered hand on Isabel's damp cheek, kissed her forehead, and answered in their mother tongue.

"You're safe now, child, you're safe and back with us. You're beyond harm."

She opened her eyes, and blinked in the muted candlelight. Her eyes glanced at Adèle, at Noble, and quickly back at Adèle.

"You lost the child," Adèle whispered in Welsh. No one had actually said the words aloud and when he heard it, Noble grunted and gripped his wife's hand harder. Isabel erupted into furious, impotent tears. "The parasite had just come up uninvited onto the dais and was very close to you, in fact I think he was touching you—"

"That's enough," Noble interrupted in a low, threatening voice.

"Sire, you can't deny—"

"I can and I do," he said, keeping his voice quiet for his wife's sake. "She was feeling ill well before that. If you try to turn this against Gwirion, Adèle, I warn you, you'll regret it."

"Where is he, then, Your Majesty?" Adèle asked, defiantly. "If he were innocent, you'd think he'd make some gesture of sympathy toward his sovereign lady."

Noble let go of Isabel's hand and turned his full attention on Adèle, his blue eyes blazing angrily but his voice controlled. "Gwirion is hiding somewhere right now because you convinced four hundred superstitious people that Isabel was accusing him."

"I?" the old woman said, defiant and incredulous.

He gave her a knowing look. "However backward you think my people are, none of them would have made that inane association on their own. I heard your voice, Adèle."

"You're mistaken, sire, but he's certainly an evil influence in this court, and this was a sign from God that he should no longer blight these walls."

"That's nonsense."

"With all respect, sire—" the priest began from the across the room.

"This is beginning to sound like a conspiracy," the king said, in a warning tone that silenced them. Now the only sound was Isabel's bitter weeping. Noble stood up. "Look to my wife; I'm going to find Gwirion."

GWIRION was not to be found. Anywhere. The castle denizens had gone through the bailey and keep several times throughout the night, finding nothing even with the help of sunrise. A hue and cry was raised, and by early morning scouting parties formed and were sweeping the countryside, beating through heather, gorse, and bracken, hacking through the dense undergrowth of the valley floors. Noble had immediately sent messengers conveying his proclamation that he, the king, personally guaranteed Gwirion's innocence, but it had little effect. Seeing the royal scouts work their way across the hills only incited rural imagination, and soon illicit well-armed posses were also beating through the bracken. It made the people feel important to think they were on a holy crusade against the demon who had robbed them of their baby prince.

Noble was finishing a belated hasty breakfast before returning to his wife when Gwilym approached him hesitantly, his calm demeanor shaken. "Sire." It took him a moment to continue. "There's a rumor of a reward for bringing Gwirion's head into court."

Noble sighed heavily. "As if there weren't enough nonsense to deal with. Do what you can to dampen it. Cadwgan, Goronwy, get their help." He began walking toward the stairs to the queen's solar.

Gwilym looked pained. "Someone is here to *claim* the reward, sire."

Noble froze. He jerked around and stared at the steward, wide-eyed. "No," he said quietly, and for a flash Gwilym remembered the

child Maelgwyn after his father's murder. The two men turned together to march quickly in long, matching strides to the door toward the barbican.

From the hall steps, the barbican was within spitting distance, and Noble, blinking fast in the sudden brightness, saw a man with a peculiar package, standing at the open gate arguing with Einion the porter. A step closer and the thing became identifiable: It was a dark-haired human head stained with fresh blood, and the man grasped it by a set of ass's ears sewn into a cap tied under the chin. The king stopped in midstride and blanched. He closed his eyes briefly to collect himself, then nodded curtly to Gwilym and they continued to the gate.

"This man is a criminal," the porter growled to the steward. Then he saw who Gwilym's companion was and quickly bowed. "Sire. He's committed butchery—"

"Let me see it," Noble commanded sternly, pushing past him. He braced himself and examined the monstrosity.

Blood had seeped everywhere from the ass's ears; they were from a donkey that must have been alive an hour earlier. The head itself was from a half-rotting corpse, unearthed for the occasion. Noble let out a breath, almost laughed. He turned to the perpetrator, who did not realize the game was over and grinned at the king expectantly as he bowed.

Noble replied to the grin with a look of contemptuous disgust and tersely ordered Gwilym to have the man publicly flogged. "And make sure people hear about it," he growled before walking away.

MIDMORNING, despite the priest's insistence that the queen was still too weak for conversation, Noble pushed his way past the sewing bevy and into her chamber. She was sitting up in bed; her women had bathed her, clothed her, braided and coiled her

hair. Adèle had nursed her with nettle juice to cleanse her blood, and some color had returned to her face, but she was still exhausted and unnaturally yellow. The look she gave him—grief and apology and tentative affection all mixed together—wrenched his heart. "Isabel," he said gently, sitting beside her pillow. "Tell me how you are."

She leaned her head against his arm. "I'm alive and grateful for it."

"The physician saw you?"

"Your physician said he knows nothing of women's ailments, Noble. There were only my ladies and my priest to attend to me."

"They don't know the cause?"

She hesitated and lowered her eyes, suddenly transfixed by the embroidered stitching on the border of her blanket. "You heard what Adèle—"

"*Don't,*" he said in an iron voice. He looked around the room. Adèle was asleep on a cushion by the hearth. She awoke at once when he called her name, and didn't want to leave the room, but the king gave her one of his stares and she finally obeyed.

When he was alone with his wife, he took her hands in his and kissed them. "I don't mean to scare you," he said. "But Gwirion's life hangs on this issue now. Wherever he is, he won't be safe until his name is cleared."

"I almost died last night. You lost your child. But what matters to you most is clearing a parasite's good name?" Her tone was tired but not peevish.

Reflexively furious, he pulled away from her for a moment, but then with a resigned sigh moved back and took her hand again. "Of course I'm grieved for our loss. And concerned for your health too. But there will be more loss to mourn if I don't get this situation under control."

"I don't feel well, Noble, I need to sleep."

"I'll let you sleep in a moment, as soon as you tell me what happened."

She pretended again to be absorbed in the bedding's embroidered edge. "I've already told Adèle everything, why don't you ask her."

"I want to hear it from you, I don't trust her," he replied. "Please." He waited for her to make brief eye contact, then pushed on. "You were unwell while the woman was singing, weren't you? I noticed you were in a sweat while she was still singing. When did you first feel ill?"

She couldn't look at him. "It's hard to say, I have morning sickness so often—"

"This was different. You turned a strange color and seemed to have trouble breathing. When did that start?"

"I don't remember, Noble, I'm sorry."

He pressed her. "Your redhead gave you something to drink. Could that have done it? What's her family background—might her people be in with Anarawd?"

Horrified that she had put the girl in danger, she looked up and said with absolute sincerity, "It wasn't Madrun's fault, Noble, don't suspect her." Then she looked harder at his eyes and realized she'd given too much away.

"I didn't suspect her, actually," he said, his tone triumphantly flinty. "But if *that* is your reaction to mistaken accusations, I am intrigued by some of your other responses." He kept staring at her and she looked down, fidgeting with the blanket. "Adèle prepared that draught for you, didn't she?"

"Noble, please, I'm dizzy, I need to rest—"

"This is *important*," he insisted, taking her little chin in his broad hand and forcing her to look into his face. "Did Adèle mix that potion?"

She nodded reluctantly. "But I was already feeling ill when Madrun gave it to me."

"It clearly didn't help. It might have made it worse. What was it?"

She couldn't move her head from his grip, but she lowered her eyes again. "I don't know. You might ask Adèle."

"She said it was ginger water, but I don't know what that is. Why did she have Madrun give you the drink? I don't remember you asking for anything."

She knew she should look up at him to seem sufficiently defiant, but she couldn't. "Are you suggesting Adèle would try to harm me?" she asked, willing her lips not to quiver.

He let go of her head, his attitude softening. "Look at me, Isabel," he whispered, very gently, his baritone voice fatherly and soft as velvet. "Please look at me."

It was Adèle's undoing: Isabel met his gaze and started sobbing. "I didn't know what it was," she blurted out. "I didn't know, and then there was nothing I could do."

He swallowed a wave of nausea, stunned by the revelation although he had suspected it, and clutched her tightly, rocking her against his chest. He would have held her that way for hours, even days, but she forced herself to almost instant recovery, angry at her own lapse as her mind raced in fruitless panic trying to concoct anything to save Adèle.

He helped her lie back against the mound of felt cushions and they looked at each other for a moment in pained silence. "This makes her a criminal," Noble finally said.

"I don't think she meant for it to happen—"

"Of course she did. She planned it exactly." Suddenly it was so obvious, he was angry for not realizing right away. "Is she mad to think such a thing would work? She drugged you. She timed it to affect you at the end of the evening, when Gwirion would be performing and you—" He cut himself off and sharply pulled away from her, eyeing her as if she were something poisonous. She chose to become fascinated once again with the embroidered border of the sheet, picking at the stitches. After a moment, forcing himself to calm, he continued. "Was she the one who told you to wear light colors? It wouldn't have been nearly so dramatic if you'd been wearing your usual colors, your reds and maroons. You trust her like a mother—she knew you would drink whatever she gave you." He stood, agitated. "That's what happened. She killed my child for the sake of trying to kill him." He ran to the door, hurled it wide, grabbed Adèle by the arm from out of the small waiting huddle on the balcony, and pulled her roughly into the

room, slamming the door closed again. He pushed her down to the wooden floor hard enough to knock the wind out of her.

"Noble!" Isabel begged.

"Be quiet," he snapped, and turned all his fury on Adèle. He hauled her up, smashed her hard across the face, punched her furiously in the ribs. Something cracked and she gasped, clutching her torso and convulsing in pain. He shoved her to the floor again and slammed his boot into her over and over, forcing her slowly across the floor with the impact of each blow.

"Stop, sire, please, sire, I'll explain," she begged between kicks, grabbing her ribs and shuddering.

"*Noble, stop!*" the queen screamed, sitting up in bed, but he didn't stop. She cried out wildly for help, and two of the teulu came through the door at once, bearing knives. When they saw that the king was the attacker, they hesitated.

"Stop him!" she yelled at them. "He's killing her! Stop him, *stop him!*"

The two of them, barely more than boys, looked at each other in confusion. No one had told them what to do in such a situation, and they were too stunned to try anything on their own. "Stop it, Noble!" Isabel screamed again, and pulled herself out of bed. She could barely stand, but she stumbled toward her husband, collapsed against him, and tried to pound against his back. He shoved her away with a wave of his arm and continued his attack on Adèle.

She landed on the floor with a cry, and the cry won his attention. He left Adèle in a trembling heap, and turned at once, breathing hard, to pick up his wife and place her back on the bed. He handled her gently—but he glowered at her.

In the sudden quiet, the door opened again and the priest stumbled in, followed cautiously by the others. Noble followed their gaze to the old woman's softly moaning form. "She did it," he said, sounding disgusted and exhausted. "Adèle did it. Someone fetch the physician."

"He's in the village," one of the teulu said, heading back out the door. "I'll go."

"Who else can heal?" Noble asked.

"Adèle," said the priest. "Marged."

"You"—this was to the other of the teulu—"take her down to the kitchens and see what Marged can do for her. But stay with her—she's a condemned woman, I don't want her trying to escape."

Isabel made a wordless sound of protest from the bed. The priest begged for an explanation but Noble impatiently sent everyone back out of the room, Adèle voicing agony with each forced, assisted movement. Alone with his wife, the king crossed his arms; unspeaking, he pierced her with a scrutinizing stare that made her skin crawl. He leaned back against the wall as if waiting for something.

"Noble, she's very old," she said nervously, to fill the icy silence. "I think she's senile. I can't believe she set out to endanger me or the child."

"Then what was she up to?"

"I don't know. Perhaps she just wanted me to faint."

"Why?"

She had no answer.

"She has to hang."

"*What?*"

"Public hanging. She brought it on herself."

"Noble—"

"It's treason. I have to obey the rule of law."

"But you can't prove it!" she said desperately. "Even I couldn't swear that she did it—I really don't know what was in the drink."

"That can be traced. Goronwy will have no choice in the matter."

"You can pardon her—you're the king, for the love of God, you can pardon anyone for anything," she implored.

"I will not exercise the privilege of pardon unless you can explain to me how that benefits Maelienydd. And even if I were to pardon her killing my child and nearly killing my wife—which I'm not inclined to do—there is still the other matter to consider." His voice was suddenly harder, flatter.

She shuddered without knowing why. "What other matter?"

"The matter of your singling out Gwirion before you fainted,"

he said coldly. "I'll pose the question that I hope to God you have an answer for, but to be honest I can't imagine what it is. Can you explain your behavior in a way that does not implicate you in this catastrophe?"

She took a breath, silently exhorting herself to face the moment calmly.

But another voice preempted her reply. "*I certainly can't!*" It was anxious, muffled. The king jumped and put his hand to his belt, forgetting he had no sword. They both looked around in alarm, but there was no one else there. Then Noble's eyes widened. He dropped to his knees and reached deep under the bed. With no resistance, he pulled out a very dirty creature wearing the tattered remains of a jester's costume. He hoisted him to his feet and looked him over: Only once before could he remember Gwirion ever looking so pathetic. "I commend your choice of hideout," he finally said with a small smile, feeling far more than he was willing to show either of them. Isabel sighed hugely with relief.

Gwirion backed away against the wall farthest from the door, looking leery of the queen. His face and arms were stained from the dust under the bed that had caked itself to his sweat. He had soiled himself and one cheek had three small parallel scabs across it, the scratches of a sharp-nailed hand reaching out to grab at him.

"Have you been here the whole time?" asked Noble.

"I'd just slipped under the bed when you brought her in last night," he stammered. "I didn't think anyone would look for me here, and here I'd know when it was safe to come out."

"You look dreadful."

"I feel dreadful." He jutted his sharp chin toward the queen. "She didn't answer you."

Noble sighed. "No, she didn't." He turned back to her. "I believe we were on the threshold of confession."

She grimaced nervously. "By then, yes, by then I knew. I was actually trying to *protect* him, though, not accuse him. I was trying to put distance between us, I wasn't thinking clearly—and I swear I didn't know what was in that cup when I drank it."

"But you drank it knowing what it would do?" He sat by her again with a dangerous heat in his eyes.

"No!" she insisted.

"Prove it," he demanded, grabbing her wrist hard. "Now."

"Ask Madrun," she gasped. "Madrun will tell you I was unaware, I thought Marged had mixed it up for my nausea."

"Why did you do nothing when you realized?"

"I did! I tried to vomit it up, but it had already started working. Adèle claimed there was no antidote and that if I asked Marged to help she must refuse for not knowing the properties of an ingredient."

"This was certainly staged to assure you could exonerate yourself," Noble said sarcastically. He released her wrist and stood again, looking agitated.

"I'm not pretending I deserve an unconditional pardon," she admitted, rubbing the freed wrist nervously. "I was drugged, I was confused, and I changed my mind at once, but I had one moment of intending to act against him, and that robs me of true innocence, I confess that." She took another breath to calm herself. "But, Noble, guilt rests in the *act*, not in the impulse, and my actions on the dais were a confused attempt to *protect* him."

"If in the span of half an hour your impulse and then your actions both endangered him, it's mere semantics to suggest the two have no connection." He looked at her with disgust. "I should charge you with conspiracy to murder."

"Sire," Gwirion interjected quietly. "I believe her."

"Thank you," Isabel whispered.

"It doesn't matter what you believe, Gwirion, only what I know," the king announced flatly. He took a step toward the bed and looked down at her threateningly. "I hold her accountable for a long chain of events, and justice will be served accordingly—as it just was to Adèle."

Isabel stifled a squeal of fear and curled up defensively under the blankets. But his expression changed, and he flashed a peculiar, brittle smile. "Indeed," he said tightly. "And considering the net effect you've had on Gwirion's well-being, I have no choice but to exonerate you."

They both stared at him. The queen cautiously half uncurled.

"Sire?" Gwirion questioned. "I am not asking you to punish the queen, but what inspires you to say that?"

Noble looked between them for a moment, weighing something. Abruptly, he turned his gaze to the window and the hills beyond, and after a silence said, "She saved your life." There was pained amusement in his voice.

They exchanged bewildered looks. "How?" Gwirion finally demanded.

"By being born."

Gwirion at once felt as if he was both airborne and under water. He staggered to his knees near the fire, holding out his hand to grasp at a tapestry for balance. "The hunting horns?" he asked faintly. "The horns and the bells?"

"Announced her birth, yes. I sat in the bushes with a naked blade, and I could do nothing—*because* I was the king, I could do nothing," he emphasized bitterly. "Mortimer wanted to go back to Wigmore to see if the child had come. You don't understand French, so you couldn't have known that. But that was the reason he let you go. Bask a moment," he suggested, finally looking back into the room, "in the poignant irony of that thought."

"What are you talking about?" Isabel asked.

Noble turned to his wife. "You haven't heard the famous tale of Gwirion saving my life? He was with us when your uncle ambushed us, and Roger was about to kill him. These past two decades would have been unbearable without . . ." He looked at Gwirion, who appeared the least likely of worthies in his torn and dirtied clothes. Noble made a sound that was both mocking and affectionate, and gestured grandly toward his friend. "Without *that*," he said, laughing. Gwirion was dazed, still in the past. "He manages both to distract me from reality and to make me face it clearly without the warping camouflage of court etiquette. He is the only luxury I am allowed in life, and he would be dead nineteen years by now if you had not been born. The bargaining chit that saves you today is that you were the agent by which he was restored to me. I thank you for that."

He gave her a small smile and the tension in the room relaxed. For a moment there was peaceful silence.

Then his smile devolved into a severe look of warning. "But Isabel, that chit is spent now. If you ever again become the agent by which I might lose him, I will make an example of you as I just did of Adèle."

Gwirion, recovering, saw alarm on the queen's face and protested with a nervous, forced laugh, "You've already beaten one defenseless Saxoness to death this lifetime, isn't that enough?"

"Don't speak that way," Isabel said crossly. "She didn't die, she didn't even swoon."

He shook his head. "I'm sorry, Your Majesty. I saw the light go out of her eyes."

"She was still breathing when they carried her out of here," the queen corrected him.

Gwirion shook his head. "She was letting go. She's gone by now. I'm sorry."

"Noble," she said firmly. "He's wrong. Tell him he's wrong."

The king held up his hand for quiet and went to the door to ask after Adèle.

The priest was already waiting on the balcony with a leaden face, and stepped into the room at once. "We did not even get her to the kitchen, sire." Isabel gave a cry of shock and buried her face in the embroidered sheet. "I just gave her last rites, and called some men up from the yard, but I don't know where you want us to place her."

Noble sank heavily on the bed. "Oh, Christ," he said slowly. "Father, I don't know where she should be. Leave her where she is—"

"She's lying at the foot of the stairs."

"Take her to the chapel," the queen said in a broken voice, without looking up.

"I'm sorry, Your Majesty, I can't allow that," said her priest awkwardly. "She's accused of a mortal sin."

"No she's not," Gwirion piped up. The priest saw him and did a double take. Gwirion coughed, trying to look dignified in his torn, befouled clothes. "She did nothing wrong. The miscarriage was an

act of God. But . . ." He scrambled mentally. There was no plausible way around this, so with typical Gwirion instinct he simply let each phrase tumble from his mouth without knowing what would follow it. "The queen thought I was responsible—that was a mistake—and God was displeased with the queen for putting my innocent life in danger, and Adèle, Adèle is such a God-fearing woman that when she realized her mistress had erred she asked God if she could take the queen's sin on herself and God afflicted her for the queen's failing by sending her into an epileptic fit, and she beat herself to death against the walls in here." He laughed nervously, patting the curved wall, which was plastered over and padded almost everywhere with tapestries. "So she's exonerated her mistress's mistake and proved her own worth, and she should be taken to the, uh, to—" He looked at the queen. "The chapel?"

"Yes," Isabel said quietly, teary and astonished.

"The chapel. God has forgiven them both—especially our revered queen—and Adèle deserves an honorable burial."

No one spoke for a long moment.

"I think we can all live with that chronicle of events," Noble finally said.

"Thank God the *rule of law* is not for doing people favors—it's only for *justice, n'est-ce pas,* Your Majesty?" Gwirion, recovered, muttered quietly—but not very quietly—to the queen. She pressed the fingertips of one hand against her closed eyes, too overwhelmed to manage a response.

"Father, you heard him," Noble said heavily. "Adèle should rest in the chapel until burial arrangements can be made. I'm going there with you. I need to go to shrift."

Alone, Isabel and Gwirion looked at each other in self-conscious silence.

"Thank you," he said tentatively, almost as a question.

"Please," she said with a teary sigh. "Please, Gwirion, I haven't the energy for sarcasm."

"I'm not being sarcastic," he assured her, awkward. He looked like a wreck, but the dark eyes considered her with a deference she'd

never seen before. "I'm forced to contemplate the fact that as well as being the source of all my woes, you're also the reason I'm alive."

She shrugged, not knowing how to answer. "I owe you thanks as well," she said, barely above a whisper. "However absurd that explanation was, she'll rest in hallowed ground for what you said."

"I had as much to gain as you did," he replied.

"No," she said. "You could have saved yourself without saving her."

"I didn't save her, Majesty. She's dead. I'm alive. For that, you are not actually grateful." His gaze, cold again, turned away from her, and bowing, he left the room.

THE funeral was modest but respectable, and Isabel went into seclusion for a week, spending her waking hours in chapel. Her rosary was almost always in her hands, her fingers touching the home-made beads as affectionately as if they were Adèle herself. Gwirion, still wary of the general public, was afraid to leave the castle, and spent much of his time in the receiving room failing to distract the abruptly brooding king.

Adèle's violent dispatch in front of his wife had been unavoidable when he considered it strategically, but he hated having the need for it. Although it had made Isabel understand at once the power and position of the king, it had made her demonize the nature of the man, and Noble couldn't blame her.

It rained unceasingly for days, the first severe rain of autumn; it added a pallor to the world. Even the sconces that the small audience chamber depended on seemed to shed a watery light. Gwirion played for hours at a stretch without speaking, the harp in its sad tuning, the music melancholy.

"How is she recovering?" he asked after three days.

"She's a little stronger, and trying to forgive me. We've reached certain . . . understandings."

"Such as? You're not being yoked into monogamy again, are you?"

Noble shook his head. "That romantic bubble has burst, thank God, but we have an agreement now that I'll be more discreet."

"And which testicle did you have to cut off in exchange for this?"

Noble gently cuffed Gwirion's head. "Neither. All she wants is dignity, and Lord knows Adèle's the only one who ever really gave her that. She'll have a little more say over the household, but you know how Gwilym is, he won't yield pride of place. And she doesn't have to sew anymore. Apparently she doesn't like it."

"That's it? And what's the catch?"

"No catch. No, that's not quite true." He gave Gwirion a pained, wry smile. "Anglo-Saxon law has finally insinuated its way into our court. Do you remember we pressed King Henry for the blood fine from Mortimer when he killed my father?"

"Of course."

"She considers it paid."

Gwirion frowned. "How? You've never received anything from Mortimer."

"We believe in restitution—the English believe in revenge. As far as she's concerned, it's an eye for an eye. Adèle's life for my father's, and now the score is settled."

Gwirion laughed in scorn. "A serving woman's death avenges a *king's*?"

"Adèle was like a mother to her. A mother's death avenges a father's."

Gwirion shook his head. "You can't expect someone who's never had parents to begin to understand that." They sat in silence for another moment and then Gwirion ventured, tentatively, "Of course, there's a true poetic irony—"

"I know that, Gwirion," Noble said in a voice that forbade further comment. Adèle had died on her mistress's birthday, the anniversary of Cadwallon's murder.

DAY OF THE DOGS

All Hallows' Eve, 1198

S THE DAYS shortened and the wind grew sharp, Isabel tried to turn away from her losses to help to prepare the castle household for the winter. Between the queen and Gwirion there was a kind of truce. They had nothing to talk about, but with Adèle as agitator replaced by a shared remembrance of her death, they were finally at least tolerant of each other.

The rising star, that upstart Prince Llewelyn of Gwynedd, continued to make his presence known at Cymaron, sending first a flowery message of condolence and later an offer to fill Adèle's office with the spinster sister of a minor official in Llewelyn's court. Noble, after spending weeks convincing his wife he was not really a monster, allowed her to respond to this herself. She graciously declined the offer. With equal graciousness, Noble himself declined Llewelyn's suggestion that they consult toward forming a confederacy of Welsh princes—which Llewelyn, as prince of the once and future greatest kingdom in all of Wales, would naturally lead.

Something had derailed Mortimer's ambitions to the southeast with the deBraose family. There was much dissension about it in the council—Gwilym and Efan, who differed in philosophy even more than in temperament or age—were clearly annoyed with each other for some reason, but the issue was never discussed openly outside the council room and Isabel sensed that nothing good would come of her prying for more information. As long as Roger's mischief didn't reflect poorly on her own character, she decided she could not waste the time in thinking much about him anymore. Her brother's struggle to run his estate as well as she once had, a challenge frequently bewailed in his letters, was the only piece of her family's fortune she indulged herself to care about.

It was the last day of October now, the beginning of winter and the end of red-deer season, and the king was preparing to ride on the annual first hunt. On this daylong outing, the youngest hounds were taken into the hills without their elders, to gauge their general competence and maturity for hunting winter game. This year, it was particularly significant, since fate and illness had conspired to kill many of the older dogs. The first hunt would let the huntsman know what sort of pack he had to see him through the winter. This in turn affected much of the rest of the castle: November was the month to slaughter livestock and today would give the butcher a sense of how much stock would have to be killed, which would in turn alert Marged and Gwilym to how much brining salt would be needed to cure the meat, which would in turn determine how Cadwgan would go about securing it.

Gwirion, generally reluctant to leave the castle in any event, had been wary of even an unescorted walk down to the village since the night of Adèle's death, and he had never been one to enjoy a hunting day. But he made it very clear that he wanted to go this time, and the chief huntsman warily welcomed him. He wrapped an extra mantle around himself and went on his pony beside Noble and the other riders, out the main gate and down over the River Aron, through grey fog as thick as fleece at an hour he would not normally consider decent.

IN the dark of the morning, an early mass had been held to bless the dogs and the hunters. They were gone, lost in the heather of the higher hills, by the time the castle as a whole had risen, and they weren't expected back until well after dinner. They were not missed; that evening would be the sober festival of All Hallows' Eve and those in charge of preparing for it were glad to have fewer extra people underfoot all day. There were the common feast foods to ready—geese, pork, lamb, vegetable stews, white barley bread, and mounds of cheeses—as well as whatever the hunt would bring in. But today people also had to prepare food for the dead, tiny loaves made of barley, water, and so much salt they were inedible to any sentient tongue. The village children would collect these soul cakes later—and, of course, demand payment for seeing to it that the dead received their nourishment. There were similar customs in England although they were confined to the lower Saxon classes. But the queen, still grieving for Adèle, went to the kitchen early on in her somber surcoat, gown, and wimple to make a dozen soul cakes with her own hands. Her presence caused a wordless stir and she was awkwardly avoided by everyone but Marged, who enjoyed watching the foreign woman trying to conform to their ways.

Outside, once the mist burned off, all of the men who were not on the first hunt were helping the fueler collect enough wood for the evening's bonfire. In a land devoted to celebratory flames, this would be the biggest blaze of the year. The entire castle would spend most of the night around the fire playing games, feasting on apples and nuts, and indulging in divination—something Gwirion was particularly called upon to do because he could improvise nonsense and deliver it with such convincing, deadpan earnestness. As with every other feast day she had spent in Maelienydd, when Isabel heard of these festivities she shook her head at how much more cheerful, loud, and outright pagan the formal observations were here compared to her native Wigmore Castle.

There was a feeling of morning levity around the bailey. For the

first time in months, the sky was completely cloudless, and brilliant blue above the crisp autumn air. Most court functions had been suspended for the hunt, and the officers who remained behind, led by grinning Maredudd the brewer, collected together in the wide courtyard. As they helped assemble the bonfire on the middle of the courtyard paving stones, the men sang rowdy tunes accompanied by teulu members on the bowed crwth and the pipes. Some of the older teulu (all of one and twenty years) dragged a few of the hall maids out into the yard for an impromptu dance. The kitchen servants began preparations for curing the meat that the hunt would bring in, doing as much of it as possible outside the kitchen scullery to enjoy the weather and the music. Even when Marged sat down with Gwilym to finesse details for the supper feast, they sat on the hall steps watching the dancing and marveling at the warmth in the air. It was an afterthought, but Gwilym politely invited the queen to join them, and so only the sewing bevy remained inside, within the queen's solar, working on a couple of twill weaving projects and staring out over the river at the gentle swell of hillside, watching for the hunting party.

When the meeting was over and the spontaneous carousing in the yard had quieted, the queen helped Marged in the kitchen until there was no room for her unskilled hands in the growing crowd of workers, and finally, brushing oat flour off her skirt and feeling happily involved with something other than distaff chores, she retired toward her chamber. It was barely midmorning. On the balcony outside the door, she heard the three young women murmuring together with a growing urgency. "Milady, look!" they said nearly in unison as she entered, and they gestured out the window together.

The glorious blue still dominated the sky, but huge white clouds in exotic shapes were rising over the northern hills. Standing out in sharp relief against the clouds was the hunting party, returning early, two dozen men on foot and horseback meandering their way slowly down the grassy slope, skirting gorse bushes and green-and-russet swaths of dying bracken. The marshal led a pony in full tack that had

no rider in the saddle, and the huntsman, his scowl visible even from a distance, led a sumpter horse that had something thrown over it. Something like an animal but far too large for winter game.

"Who is that?" Isabel asked, squinting and moving toward the window.

"We think it's Gwirion," Angharad replied. "Isn't that his mare?"

"What's happened? They shouldn't be home for half a day yet."

"*He* must have done something," announced Madrun, wide-eyed, but Angharad shook her delicate blond head.

"He looks hurt, I think someone did something *to* him."

"And where are the dogs?" asked Generys. "The dogs aren't with them."

"They sent the runner ahead this way," said Angharad.

"Stay here," the queen instructed. "I'm going down to meet them at the gate."

She rushed back down the stairs and crossed the hall to the crowded, noisy kitchen. "Has there been a messenger from the hunt?" she demanded above the din.

A score of voices called, "No, Majesty," and she headed out of the kitchen and into the yard. A long-legged boy in Noble's livery was approaching her from the barbican gate, out of breath. In this high country, footing everywhere was treacherous, so swift travel on horseback was impossible; runners were the preferred couriers.

"Your Majesty," the boy gasped, and bowed. "I have a message from the king."

"Rise and speak."

"I am to give the message to the steward."

The steward, of course the steward, not the queen. Peeved, she gave him leave to find the man. "I'll be in the king's receiving room," she said, "should Gwilym condescend to share the news with me."

Gwilym and the runner arrived at the round white room just moments after she had. The boy was not recovered from his final sprint, but he couldn't wait to give his important news, so he blurted it out between breaths. "His Majesty is bringing a criminal home

and wants the prison cell prepared to receive him. He'll hang him tomorrow at dawn in the village, and in the meantime, there is no game meat for tonight's supper and the feast of All Hallows' is canceled."

"Who's the criminal?" she asked, perversely thrilled. Based on what she'd seen, the crime was obvious: Somebody had hurt Noble's darling Gwirion.

"The criminal is Gwirion. His crime is sorcery," the boy announced.

They gaped at him. "Sorcery?" stammered Gwilym, barely maintaining his unflappable demeanor.

"Yes, sir. He bewitched the dogs and made them afeared of the animals they were supposed to hunt."

Queen and steward exchanged amazed looks. "You can't mean that, boy," Gwilym insisted.

"Milord, I wouldn't believe it if I hadn't seen it with these eyes. We put them on the scent, and they yelped and whined like someone had stepped on their paws. They put their tails between their legs and tried to hide behind the horses. It was the most unnatural thing I've ever seen."

"How did the king stop them?"

"He couldn't stop them, Majesty. Nor the chief huntsman. They told Gwirion to take the spell off; he laughed and laughed and said he couldn't, it was no spell, it's how they were. His Majesty thought it was funny at first, but not when Gwirion said he couldn't fix it. They even put the whip on him to make him undo it, but he wouldn't."

"My God, he's so perverse," the queen said under her breath.

"I wouldn't know anything about that, Majesty," the boy said, looking briefly embarrassed. "He thought it was right funny, though. He laughed up until they started whipping him."

She winced. "I saw him slung over the packhorse."

"Yes, Majesty. He's not laughing anymore. I think he's scared now."

"Disaster always follows when Gwirion gets scared," the queen muttered. She turned to the steward, who looked to be in shock. "Gwilym, take the news to the kitchen, and ask them to put it around

the court. I'm going to meet the hunting party at the gate." She'd never given Gwilym an order before and despite the upset of the moment, she was pleased with herself. He bowed his head with dignified coolness and she hurried out of the room, wondering what was really going on. Obviously Noble could not mean to do it.

As she reached the steps of the hall, the riders entered the bailey, and the solemnity of the procession made her stop short. Gwirion still lay facedown over the sumpter horse, strapped by his wrists and ankles. He was whimpering and he looked too miserable to be alive. His face was a shocking greyish-green, his belt was gone, his faded tunic and shirt were both shredded along the back from the whip, and angry welts were storming up where it had dug into the skin.

Noble, by contrast, was furious but elegant and collected. His broad, grandly handsome face was as stony as a statue, his brown hunting outfit was unsullied by an actual hunt, and his horse was barely exercised. He dismounted, handed the reins to his groom, and gestured toward Gwirion without actually looking at him. "Have Einion put him in the cellar," he said, between clenched teeth. "Waste no food on the wretch for dinner or supper." Head bowed, he began walking toward the tower that contained his bedchamber, his fists clenching and unclenching.

"Noble, wait!" the queen cried out after him, rushing down the steps to catch up with him near the well. He stopped and turned back to face her, and she went down on one knee, her silk skirt pressing into the sandy mud.

"Oh, for God's sake don't do that," he said impatiently, and pulled her up with unusual roughness. For a moment their faces were very close and she saw something in his eyes that frightened her— beneath the cool exterior he looked crazed. By now the entire hunting party, a number of the teulu, and many of the kitchen staff were watching, and he addressed the whole yard, looking annoyed that he was expected to speak. "There is no game today. At all. And there'll be no meat for the rest of the winter, unless we slaughter *all* the livestock, and even then some of you will probably starve. He did some-

thing to the dogs, they wouldn't hunt. That's not a prank, it's not the license of a fool, it's treason. He's put the court in danger."

"Where are the dogs?" Isabel asked.

"The dogs are dead," he said harshly, and turned the crazed glance back to her as if daring her to criticize him. "I had the archers shoot them all. He'd ruined them."

"Sire, as I tried to point out—" stammered the agitated chief huntsman, whom Noble was not fond of under the best of circumstances.

"I am not interested in anything you have to say on the matter," Noble cut him off angrily. "The dogs would not hunt, they were *afraid* of the scent."

"Ask the barons for dogs as part of their tribute for the year," the queen said. Noble stared at her.

"I intend to," he replied. "That's not the issue here." He turned and continued toward the wooden staircase outside his tower. She moved with him, lowering her voice. "Noble," she whispered, their backs to the yard, "I agree he should be punished for this, but a death sentence is absurd." He glared at her and began walking faster, balling one hand into a fist and closing the other one around it. She forced herself to continue, straining to keep her voice too low to be heard. "Noble, stop. You're angry right now, and you're right to be angry, but please don't act out of anger." They were at the bottom of the stairs now, and he took the first step up, cutting her off from following. "You regretted it with Adèle—you will never forgive yourself if you hurt Gwirion. He's your closest friend. You don't know what that loss is like. I do." She took his hand, which was still a fist, and tried to meet his eyes; he wouldn't look at her. He turned on his heel and walked slowly up the wood steps toward his room, signaling the porter before disappearing from sight.

She wrapped her arms around herself, suddenly aware of a chill. She'd slipped off her surcoat while she sat listening to Marged and Gwilym and wore only a thin kirtle now. Several people approached her offering her their mantles and cloaks, but she brushed them all

aside. "I'm fine," she announced. "Someone make certain Gwirion is fed."

"Your Majesty," said Gwilym quietly. "The king said there will be no food wasted on—"

"Give him my portion," she ordered.

She stood there, unmoving, and listened to the buzz behind her slowly fade. She heard Gwirion lifted off the horse, moaning as he was carried to the barbican and down into the holding cell. She heard the horses led past her to the stables, and the hushed gossip of teulu and castle workers fade away. The playfulness of the morning was harshly extinguished.

By now the sky was definitely clouding over. She wished her husband were superstitious enough to take this as an omen that he was making a mistake. Certainly she had never liked Gwirion, but she'd never truly wished him dead. Only Adèle had made that mistake. How could Noble possibly exterminate the only person in the world he loved?

With a gasp of insight, she ran up the stairs, into the tower and Noble's chamber. "Sire," she called from the anteroom, pounding on the door, choking back relieved laughter now. "Noble, I know what you're up to, and you've won your point. You don't have to go through with it."

There was a moment of silence and then he pulled the door open so fast that she jumped. "And what do you think I'm up to?" he demanded, glowering down at her with the furious gleam still in his eyes.

She was taken aback by his intensity, but made herself smile up at him. "You want to make me beg for his life. You want me to come to his defense so I'll appreciate him. And I do, I do appreciate him, so you're very clever and devious and it worked brilliantly, but please, *please* don't continue this nonsense." She sank to her knees and looked up at him. "I am officially begging for Gwirion's life."

He was condescending and disgusted. "I wouldn't threaten Gwirion's life just to make you 'appreciate' him. But by your reaction,

I *could* be doing it—although I'm not—to test the theory that you *always* oppose me, no matter what the circumstance."

"Noble," she protested, getting to her feet. "That's nonsense."

"You defend a man you despise rather than support me," he said. "You beg clemency for a man whom you yourself *conspired to kill* little more than a month ago, just to contradict me—trust me, madam, I won't forget that." She tried to interrupt but he silenced her with a furious glare. "And for Gwirion, this will be an actual execution, and he brought it upon himself, with no assistance from you. What we saw today frightened my bravest men. It truly felt ungodly. It has nothing to do with my personal feelings." His voice caught and he looked away from her angrily. "Cutting off my own arm would be less painful—but were it gangrenous, I'd cut it off."

"I don't understand how you can do this," she protested.

He touched his slender crown of gold and garnet, and then her slighter circlet. "That is because I wear this and you wear only that," he said coldly, and slammed the door on her.

GWIRION was in the same cell he had shared with Corr less than six months earlier, but the internment was infinitely more traumatic this time. Despite the cooling unguents Marged had slathered on his wounds, he was in throbbing pain, and lay curled on his side on the damp floor. He knew the king's step and it was not the king who was approaching. It was a woman. But not Marged coming back. Not Enid, even if it could have been Enid. He had never bothered to learn the queen's step. This could have been her, but there was no reason for her to come down here. Except perhaps to gloat. In her position, Gwirion admitted to himself, he probably would have.

Einion stood straighter, and awkwardly bowed his head toward the approaching person. Without uncurling, Gwirion stretched his neck slightly up toward the bars of the door to see.

"Your Majesty," he said, still confused, when he realized it was the queen kneeling down to see him. "Pardon me but I'm not getting up."

"It wasn't really sorcery, was it?" she asked. She felt ridiculous. "Why don't you tell him what really happened?"

"I *did.*" This was a piss-poor time for the woman to decide to play the good Samaritan, he thought. What feminine self-indulgence. "I told him what I did and he refused to believe me. Even the huntsman backed my claim, and he hardly knows how to open his mouth."

"What did you do?"

"I switched the dogs," he said, and laid his pounding head back down on the cool stone floor. "Last spring, Corr and I saved a litter of runts from drowning, and I hid them with a farming family near the village. The son Ithel smuggles them into the woods by the tourney field and we've been training them this whole time to go against their instincts and act frightened when they smell their prey. They were so good at it!" He sounded almost fatherly.

"And you switched the runts with the castle dogs?"

"Yes. Of course the huntsman could tell right away, but I begged him not to reveal it, and he likes me, so he kept mum. Then when we found the scent . . ." He chuckled painfully. "It was extraordinary. You've never seen so many bewildered men in your life." He sobered. "And the king killed all of them. All of my pups. Right in front of me—they were like *children* to me."

"He thought you'd bewitched the real dogs."

"But the huntsman *told* him. As soon as he saw what I was up to, as soon as he saw that I'd be in trouble for it, he told the king these weren't the castle hounds, and the king would not believe him."

"Why not?"

"I think you refused to spread your thighs for him again unless he got rid of me."

"Gwirion," she said sharply, and moved away from the bars. She had been leaning into them, hanging on his words, without realizing it.

"He was willing to *entertain* the notion that they were changelings, but I couldn't prove it," Gwirion explained, too ex-

hausted to go into detail. "We were near the farmstead, and he sent Efan, the penteulu, there to find the boy and the real hounds, but he came back saying the farm was deserted. I don't understand that part—Ithel was supposed to be waiting there with the real pups to return them." He sighed. "Please let me sleep. I'm in a lot of pain right now."

"Of course you are, I'm sorry," she said, and stood to leave. "Is there anything I can do for you?"

There was a pause, and then a slight rustle, as if he was trying to move. She couldn't see clearly enough, and anyhow he grunted and stopped abruptly. "Tell him I'm sorry for offending him," he said. He sounded bitter. "But I'm flattered he found my prank so . . . significant." A pause. "And tell him I hope he has a long and joyful marriage, and many healthy sons."

"Thank you," she said awkwardly.

"I didn't say with *you*."

He grinned despite his pain, listening to her irritated departure.

AFTER letting the chandler in to light the fire, the king refused to speak with anybody for the rest of the day, with the brief exceptions of the court justice and the chaplain. Goronwy appeared at His Majesty's door, wheezing slightly from the effort of lifting his weight an entire flight of steps but insisting it was his duty to intercede: Only a judge might mete out punishment. The king welcomed him into his chamber long enough to point out that the judge meted out punishment according to the *Law of Wales*, which did not recognize sorcery, and the case was therefore out of his jurisdiction. The meeting lasted less than a minute. An hour later, Noble summoned knobby-knuckled, liver-spotted Father Idnerth to his chamber to write out the official condemnation, to be read the next morning on the gallows.

After Idnerth was free, Gwilym as steward called an urgent meeting in the council chamber, even remembering to invite the queen, but it came to nothing beyond frustrated, baffled conjecture. The chaplain and judge both testified from their brief encounters with him that the king was deeply distressed but absolutely inflexible about his decision. The huntsman swore they had not been his dogs, but he couldn't find his own anywhere to prove otherwise; Efan had said they hadn't been where Gwirion claimed they would be. The penteulu himself was absent, leading his charges in some solemn All Hallows' Eve tradition—which probably had something to do with scaring young women out of their skirts, Gwilym observed sardonically.

SHE did not go to her husband's chamber that night. But he, claiming lonely wretchedness, came to hers.

She refused him.

"Are you frightened of me now?" he demanded, impatiently. He looked terrifying, his expression one of the fevered intensity of a man who had strayed from reason.

"Of course not," she lied, pulling away as he tried to push her down onto the bed. "Noble, stop it!" Always uncomfortable when he came to her room, she fidgeted with the tapestry that provided the only privacy from the sewing bevy. "I don't want his death on my conscience."

"There's no reason it should be." He sat on the bed and gestured for her to come to him. She ignored the gesture.

"He thinks I won't lie with you unless you kill him."

"No he doesn't," Noble said contemptuously. "He's playing with you."

"I need to know in my own heart that that's not the reason," she insisted, suddenly grateful that her women were in the room, and the

doorkeeper outside was within easy earshot. "The only way I can do that is to refuse you unless you agree to pardon him."

"And yet a new way to oppose me," he said, irked. "You will espouse *any* philosophy, grab *any* opportunity that lets you thwart me from an heir. Condemn Gwirion, defend Gwirion—whatever will forestall my fathering living issue. Who are you in league with? My cousin? Your uncle? Perhaps Llewelyn? Does Adèle manipulate you still, even from beyond the grave?"

Her eyes widened. "Noble, you don't mean any of that. That's ranting."

"No it's not, madam," he said in a low, lethal voice. "Strategy does not become you. If you're determined not to have my child, just say so, don't muddy the issue with Gwirion's fate."

She almost laughed from frustration. "Gwirion's fate is the only issue!" At a loss, she untied her robe at the throat and waist and pulled it off, tossing it to the bed. The cold air bit into her skin and she tensed, but she began to pull off her shift as well. "Bed me, then," she said. "If that's what it would take to convince you I am only after saving a man's life, bed me. I will do and be whatever you request if you will just call off this nonsense."

Noble made a face. "Put your shift back on, your Norman blood can't take this cold so early in the season. I don't want to lie with you tonight anyway, it's not a night to indulge in any form of pleasure. *That wretched fool,*" he added under his breath, miserably, and left the room too quickly for her even to try to hold him back.

She redressed quickly and went after him. Although the usual games and gatherings were canceled, the courtyard was brilliantly lit by the bonfire, but even so, she lost track of him. He wasn't in his room. She found him finally in the chapel on his knees, in a pose so mournfully and deeply meditative that he did not hear her approach. His hands were clutched together tightly, his knuckles white. After a few moments, she touched his arm. He opened his eyes and looked at her blankly, with a frightening glint as if he were quite mad. He would not speak, and when she tried to speak to him, he signaled her own priest to remove her.

I N the middle of the night, Gwirion was awakened by Einion prodding at him from above with a stick from between the bars of the cell.

"Get up, you," the porter said in a muffled tone. "Show some respect for Her Majesty, now." He thrust a rush light into a brazier by the door.

"Oh, Christ," Gwirion groaned, and didn't move. "And what is it this time?"

This was not the reception she'd hoped for. "Gwirion, I want you to know that I did everything I could to talk Noble out of this."

There was a pause.

Then his voice, reedy and weak: "I'm still in here, so I assume you failed."

"I'm sorry, but I want you to know I tried."

"That makes a hell of a difference."

"You could at least appreciate the effort," she huffed, and instantly regretted her pettiness.

With a grunt of pain, he raised his head a little to look straight up at her. His face was pale in the rush light and the large eyes were bloodshot, but without his comical grimace, she could hardly recognize her tormentor lying in the straw; indeed, in Noble's castoffs, he almost looked like an imperiled aristocrat. "I'm sorry, I hurt the lass's feelings. You're such a good lass. Doesn't matter that you've spent the last six months trying to estrange me from him, no, all that matters is that at the last hour when it was obvious you could do nothing, you decided to wake me up from my last night of earthly repose just to tell me you could do nothing. Thank you. Thank you! That makes you a good girl, so of course I'm obliged to absolve you from all those sinful months of wishing I was dead." He tired of the rant suddenly, but she was too shocked to speak. "Milady," he said in a kinder voice, "you're doing this because you feel guilty for hating me. You're not doing it because you crave my continued existence or

even my gratitude. It's the guilty conscience of past days. That's all it is. Good for you for wrestling with your conscience and letting it win. But let me sleep now."

She wanted to rip out his tongue. She opened her mouth for a stinging response, but he was quicker.

"The angrier you are, the more what I've said is true. And you're a smart lass, after all, you know I'm right."

She forgot her retort, but he didn't expect a reply.

IT was raining slightly, and still dark, when the tiny village green at the foot of the castle mound filled with well-wrapped and bundled-up onlookers: The entire population had come to watch. News that Gwirion was in trouble for a prank would not have made an impression on anyone; even news of his impending execution would have been dismissed as another crazy rumor about him. But the feast of All Hallows' being canceled affected everyone directly, and gave an unpleasant, heavy credence to the gallows being erected that night. Sudden piety ran rampant. Father Idnerth had offered to hold midnight mass in the village—the king insisted on having the castle chapel to himself—and there was a bigger turnout in the cramped church than anyone could remember. The bard Hywel joined him and in an unprecedented meeting of old and new traditions, half of the evening was given over to the recitation of the bard's oldest and most sacred poems lamenting dead heroes. This was the day when the veil between the worlds was most transparent, and people were troubled enough about the dead impinging upon the realm of the living; Gwirion's execution at dawn would reverse the flow in a way that was even more disturbing.

No one in the castle had slept well—except for Gwirion, at last. The superstitious porter had drugged him to keep his powers at low ebb. He would have been grateful if he had known.

While it was still dark, he was roughly woken and hauled out of

his cell. In place of regular garrison guards, a dozen armed teulu were to escort him to his hanging. He was told this was a great honor, and responded with a tired, sarcastic laugh. Gwilym silently delivered to him a special outfit of black brocaded silk, and the youngest of the teulu—a boy of fourteen, the only one who didn't look hungover—helped him to change in the darkness of the porthouse, since his muscles were too cramped and sore, and the skin on his back too raw, for him to manage on his own. The clothes felt strange, only in part because he'd never worn anything so new before. He lived in Noble's oversize castoffs, but somebody had troubled themselves enough to take in the tunic, the drawers, and even the hose, and he faced the last morning of his existence with the novel experience of wearing clothes that fit properly. With his hands manacled before him, he let the boy escort him out into the courtyard. He was surrounded by the teulu and marched down into the village, squinting against the spattering of raindrops.

He squawked in amazement when he saw the crowd in the cold, grey light creeping over the hills. "All of these people want to watch me die?" he whispered to the little soldier who had helped him dress.

"I wouldn't take it personally, sir," the boy replied uncomfortably. "Everyone's fond of you. But a hanging is a hanging, it's an event."

Gwirion looked at him angrily. "Thank you for putting it in perspective," he said sarcastically, and wouldn't look at the abashed young man again.

It wasn't, in the end, to be a hanging. An hour earlier, as the crowd was gathering in the wet, Noble had conferred wearily with the butcher, who doubled as executioner, and decided a beheading was a better idea. It was a more honorable way to die, and Gwirion deserved at least that much. So the low scaffold remained, but the gallows were struck and an executioner's block was waiting for them. The king in sackcloth, a growing look of madness on his face and his hair as unkempt as the convict's usually was, sat with his irate wife who clutched her rosary, on a temporary covered dais that had been erected to the side of the green.

In the cold, ashy dawn, one of the teulu nudged Gwirion toward the rough wooden step to the scaffold with the butt of a spear. He raised his foot onto the first step.

Another nudge. The next step.

Another nudge. The next step. It was the slowest climb up a flight of stairs Gwirion had ever made.

His insides felt full of mud. If he could somehow wash the mud away, the insanity would stop and Noble would restore him to grace. When he reached the top step and saw the executioner's block rather than the gallows, he froze.

"It's a token of honor," the king called out.

Without taking his eyes off the block, Gwirion called back, "I don't want honor, I want life."

The crowd collectively made a strange sound, as if it had expected to hear a quip, was already prepared to laugh at it, and then realized it wasn't one. It was unnerving to see the antic fellow dressed not in his usual ragtag garments, but in a neat black silk tunic and hose. Someone had combed his hair and even tamed his cowlick—a rare event—and rubbed water across his face. He looked presentable. He almost looked handsome, his sharp, wily features suddenly seeming chiseled. Worst of all, he looked *normal*, no less and no more eccentric than anyone else in the square. There was nothing there but a frightened man who couldn't take his eyes off the executioner's block.

"Someone offer him water," the king said in a tight voice, clearing his throat, and his hands clenched briefly into fists. The executioner's young son, dressed and masked like his father, stepped forward with a bucket of water and a wooden ladle. He offered it to Gwirion, who wanted to refuse it but couldn't. Despite the rain his lips were dry and cracked, and he was hungry. He could hardly swallow, but the boy held the ladle steady for him and he awkwardly sipped some.

"Thank you, lad," he said. The boy put the ladle aside and wouldn't look at him. Gwirion studied the boy's mouth, set in a tight

grimace, and his nervous, fidgety body language. He remembered when he'd taught this boy to juggle.

At an anxious nod from the king, the teulu fell into formation around and behind Gwirion holding up their spears, and moved closer to the block. He hesitated but then moved with them. A trumpet sounded. Father Idnerth's assistant, as herald, unrolled the parchment scroll that the king had dictated the night before. "Gwion called Gwirion of Maelienydd, you have been sentenced by Maelgwyn ap Cadwallon ap Madoc ap Idnerth ap Cadwgan to die," he read loudly and unsteadily. Noble shifted his weight in his chair, looking burdened by the recitation of his formal name. "Insofar as you bewitched the royal hounds to turn them off the scent, you have rendered the castle incapable of self-sufficiency and placed the lives of His Majesty and members of the royal court and all their servants in dire jeopardy. You are therefore doubly condemned, for sorcery and for treason." He lowered the scroll because it was getting rained on, but continued to recite, without looking at Gwirion. "What are your last words, sir?"

Gwirion couldn't think of anything to say. Something cutting and witty would have been best, but anything at all would have served. His mind was blank. He opened his mouth relying as he often did on intuition, and realized he had lost his voice. Finally, in a hoarse whisper that couldn't be heard beyond the scaffold, he managed to sound out the words, "Don't you want to know where the real hounds are?"

It was repeated by one of the teulu so that the king could hear it. He frowned and made a desperate, impatient sound, caught between annoyance and pain. "No, Gwirion, I'm not playing that game. This is unbearable. Get on with it," he ordered, his voice on the edge of breaking. He looked away, and at his gruff but shaky signal the penteulu shoved Gwirion down onto his knees before the block.

"Noble!" Gwirion suddenly screamed across the green. "Don't do this! These people know our friendship—if you cast me off like this, they'll know you for an irrational tyrant and they'll rise up in arms!"

"Noble, please—" Isabel said at once, turning in desperation toward him as the crowd began a distraught mutter.

"Enough!" Noble thundered, his eyes flashing. He pointed to the executioner and demanded in a quavering voice, "*Do it.*"

Efan tied a rag around Gwirion's eyes and then with a jerk lowered his forehead onto the damp block. The crowd froze. Gwirion trembled violently but made no sound. Isabel turned her head away. "Watch," Noble commanded, grabbing her shoulder in his trembling grasp. There was a bitter intensity on his face, almost a brutality, that terrified her.

The executioner cleared his throat, and lifted the axe to his shoulder. Behind him, Idnerth began chanting quietly in Latin, although he had not formally given Gwirion last rites or even offered a final shrift. He knew the fellow would not have accepted.

The executioner lifted the axe over his head, and looked at the king.

The king nodded, looking wretched.

The executioner glanced at his son.

The son dumped the bucket of water over Gwirion's head. Gwirion yelled in shock and fell over.

A mass of confused faces turned toward Noble, who opened his mouth wide and roared with laughter. A nervous chuckle of relief circled around the green, but the hundreds of onlookers combined did not drown out his hilarity.

The executioner had put down his axe at once, and had already unshackled Gwirion's hands and removed his blindfold. "Here you go, then," he said gently, and tried to help Gwirion to his feet. But Gwirion could barely sit up. He glared at the king like a frenzied bantam cock. The expression, familiar in its ferociousness, reassured the crowd and they laughed.

Isabel did not laugh. She rose and marched down from the covered dais, and on foot made her way through the rain, back up toward the castle, appalled and unescorted. Noble didn't notice her leave.

"I convinced you, didn't I?" he howled. Gwirion glared at him. "I convinced the lot of you!" He slapped his hands on his knees. "A

round for the executioner and his son!" He began applauding them and the crowd obediently followed. The two masked figures nodded sheepishly and looked as if they wanted to hide.

AFTER inviting the assembled crowd to join him in the great hall for ale, which rendered them even more appreciative of his handiwork, Noble went in search of Gwirion.

He made straight for the kitchen, knowing that Marged would be mothering him after the shock. His Majesty seldom came in here and the kitchen workers were flustered, but he waved them aside.

"Where is he?" he asked, grinning, and they parted for him nervously.

Marged had settled Gwirion on her only comfortable stool, by the fire, and wrapped him in a brychan snatched from his bed. He was holding a cup of something steaming hot, but he was trembling so much he spilled a bit every time he brought it to his lips. The king slapped him chummily on the arm, and the cup crashed to the floor.

"Oh, dear." Noble laughed. "Someone get him another." Nobody moved, but the king didn't notice. "That was brilliant, wasn't it?" he chuckled. "I bet you can't top it."

"You should be whipped," Gwirion said. Noble laughed and the assembly tittered nervously. "I'm serious. You really should be whipped."

"Can't you swallow your own medicine?" Noble teased.

"What medicine? I've never pretended I was going to kill anyone!" Gwirion squealed. "That wasn't amusing. Embarrassment is amusing. Comeuppance is amusing. *Terror* is not amusing."

"You don't think that was inspired? I gave a consummate performance—nobody understood me, but *nobody* thought I was faking." He was too pleased with himself to stop smiling.

With a deliberate grunt of righteous annoyance, Marged picked up the spilled cup and signaled Dafydd to get a fresh one.

Gwirion continued to stare at the king. His relief at being alive was almost entirely negated by his fury. "Dignity can be trifled with. Not mortality."

Noble was abruptly sober. "You're absolutely right," he said pedantically. "Which is why I had to punish you for making thirty men believe they'd starve this winter."

"If you hadn't meddled, they'd only have thought that for a moment!" Gwirion snapped. "I stared my mortality in the face for the whole of a day and a night!"

"I was visiting upon you the collected fear those thirty felt both for themselves and for their families." He smiled, softening. "With a little interest, perhaps, just to raise the stakes and prove that I can beat you at your own game."

Gwirion grabbed hold of a hearthstone and pulled himself up. His green pallor deepened into a very unattractive purple and he hurled himself at the king, screaming. There were no teulu here, no guards, no one but the kitchen servants, and they were all far too flustered to do anything besides gasp and yelp and wring their hands. But Noble was stronger than Gwirion and managed to fend off his friend's enraged attack. He held Gwirion almost like a poppet at arm's length, and shook him hard to get his attention—but the king was more startled than angered. "You're a terribly sore loser," he complained.

Gwirion sprang to life again, trying in vain to scratch at the king's face. "*Ogre!*" he screeched. "You bastard son of a whore devil, I'll rip your liver out with my teeth, you mud-sucking leprous swine!"

The crowd drew back with eyes widening and mouths closing into nervous little Os. Noble was hard-pressed to keep Gwirion under control; he finally shoved him back down on the stool, pulled a dagger from his belt, and pressed it against Gwirion's throat. Gwirion grunted and then sat back, panting, staring murderously up. "Go ahead, do it," he snapped. "Or better yet, pierce me enough to do some serious harm and then tell us all it was just a prank."

"There's been no serious harm, you fool," Noble said with condescending affection. "You're fine."

"I am not fine! You scourged me yesterday for no good reason, you whoreson!"

The dagger remained where it was to keep Gwirion seated; otherwise, Noble acted as if this were a friendly chat, enjoying his performance and his audience. "That was to make it believable," he said reasonably. "If I didn't seem absolutely incensed, someone—you, even—might have known it was all in play. My God, do you know how difficult it was? I didn't tell *anyone*—except Efan before I sent him out to find the farmstead, so he would know to say it was deserted, but otherwise not a *single soul*, until this morning when I met with the butcher. I had an elaborate plan for a false hanging, but he warned me something might stick and you'd get hurt, so we agreed on the bucket of water instead. It wasn't gratuitous violence against you. I did what was necessary for the trick to work, that's all. Trust me, if you really had done something to the dogs, you'd have been in for a far worse fate. The flogging was a mild one, Lord knows you've weathered worse. You'll be fine."

"I just faced my own death," Gwirion said.

"So did my entire court," Noble said sharply, but then he grinned and gave Gwirion a comradely nudge with his elbow. "You're taking this in the wrong spirit," he insisted. "Honestly, Gwirion, you disappoint me. I think of you as a master craftsman. Can't you appreciate somebody else's comic craftiness?"

"It would have been comical," Gwirion said, "only if I'd died of fright when the water hit me. That would have been comical."

"No it wouldn't!" Noble said, shocked. "That would have been horrible."

"And comical," Gwirion insisted. "Then at least there'd be irony."

"You don't think it's ironic as it stands?" demanded Noble. Gwirion ignored him.

Little Dafydd carefully handed Gwirion another cup of the

brew. There was a commanding silence as he wrapped his hands around it and shivered from the pleasure of the heat.

Noble finally put up his blade. "I am disappointed," he said. "I really did it to entertain *you.*"

Gwirion gave him a weary and withering glance. "I do a grand job of entertaining myself, sire—it's not something you're properly trained to do."

"The crowd liked it."

"How lovely for the crowd. How lovely for the chroniclers. You'll be remembered as the king who pretended he was going to kill his prankster—as a prank. Don't tell me you didn't think of that." He took a slow sip of the infusion. There was brandy in it, he noticed gratefully.

"It wasn't *just* as a prank, Gwirion. Besides." Noble smiled. "There are other things I hope to be remembered for."

"I meant things they can tell children about," Gwirion retorted. People laughed nervously. Noble looked at all of them, considering something.

"Leave us," he ordered.

He watched the servants scurry from the kitchen, and when he was alone with Gwirion, turned back to him. Gwirion would not look him in the face, just continued to sip his warm, inebriating medicine. There was an awkward silence.

"I did nothing wrong," Noble finally said. "But I am sorry this did not go over with you the way I thought it would." Gwirion said nothing. Noble cleared his throat. "And I am sorry you suffered such anguish, really I didn't think it would affect you so deeply. I was seeing myself in your situation—I would have responded differently, but that's how I was trained."

"Oh I see," Gwirion said with cold sarcasm. "I was supposed to see it through the eyes of a trained soldier. My mistake entirely, Your Majesty. I was seeing it through the eyes of a young boy who decided to throw himself to his king's assassins so as to distract them from murdering—who was it now? oh, yes—you, *Your Majesty.*"

Noble was silent for a moment. "I propose a truce. Assure me

you understand there must be limits to your mischief, and I will offer restitution for what I put you through."

"How? Let me get away with something that really is a hanging offense?"

"I've done that many times over the years, Gwirion," the king said patiently. "Perhaps something more immediate."

"Gold?" Gwirion asked at once. It was a long-lived joke between them that the king would provide Gwirion with anything but money. Gwirion, who could break into every coffer in the castle, didn't really mind.

"If that's what it would take. But anyone with means can give you gold. Ask me for something that only I might give you."

Gwirion nodded, and briefly glanced at his master. "That's tempting," he admitted. "I'll think about it."

"There isn't something that comes to mind right away?" Noble pressed, anxious for levity.

"I would ask you to get rid of the queen but she's the only one who was decent to me yesterday, even when I was a lout to her, so I suppose that maybe she can stay."

Noble grinned. "She is my wife, you know."

Gwirion gave him a questioning frown. "Meaning . . . ?"

The king winked.

"You're disgusting!" Gwirion cried. Then calming himself he immediately added, "You could at *least* offer me one of your mistresses." He made a face. "The queen. Yech. I said she could *stay*, I didn't say she was *attractive*. Jesu, Noble, but you're full of charm today, aren't you?"

S H E avoided him all day; he hardly noticed. He was enjoying being congratulated by everyone he could find for having staged such a clever prank. That night, he went again to her chamber, and in a rare instance of genuine naiveté, expected a warm response.

She refused him.

"You said you'd refuse me unless I spared his life. I did better than that—I never even meant to take it in the first place."

She calmly sidestepped away from his reach. "You are demented."

He pretended to pout. "If Gwirion had no problem with it, I don't see why you should."

"I heard about the row in the kitchen. Don't tell me Gwirion had no problem with it." She took the stool from the wall loom and placed it by her small dressing table, then began brushing her hair, that heavy mane that always disappointed him with its simple sleekness.

"You of all people ought to understand what I was demonstrating to him. I do not enjoy tormenting my best friend, but my duty is to protect my charges, and the situation required dramatic action."

That was Adèle's reasoning, she thought, and nearly said it aloud.

He relaxed onto her bed, watching her. "And I wanted to see what it felt like," he added, with a confiding smile.

"To kill someone for a thrill?"

"To be Gwirion."

She put the brush down and stared at him. "Which part of this conversation was I asleep for?"

"I wanted to spend a whole day getting attention for making mischief instead of order. It was wonderful. I wish I could do it more often. Gwirion has the best life of any man alive."

"Gwirion dresses in rags and isn't allowed to make eyes at a woman without your permission. And I can't believe those words are from the man who boasts of never abusing his authority to indulge his whims."

"It wasn't a whim, it was valuable research," Noble said with an impish smile. "To *continue* such a delightful practice might constitute a whim, but I shall selflessly refrain from doing so."

"Thank God for that much," she muttered under her breath. "You'd do less damage making Gwirion king for a day."

Noble sat up, beaming. "That's a wonderful idea!" He leapt playfully from the bed and wrapped his arms around her. She tried

to push him aside with the brush, but he spun her around to face him, kissing her forehead. "You are my little muse!"

"Be quiet, you'll wake my women," she hissed.

"That's exactly the way to make it up to him. I'll make him king for a day."

"*What?*"

He grinned at her. "Just for a day. Tit for tat. He's earned it and I can certainly undo whatever mischief he creates in one day." He hooted with laughter, ignoring her attempts to shush him, and got to his feet. He hovered over her to rifle through the random trinkets on her dressing table. "And especially with your family coming. That uncle of yours, what's his name, Ralf I think, the one who—what is it?"

She was staring up at him, astonished. "My family? My family is coming?"

"Didn't I mention it?" he said with false offhandedness and began pacing the room, peering into chests in search of something. "Your brother and your insufferable uncles. Not our beloved Mortimer, of course—just the old coots from the other side. You haven't got a quill in here by any chance, have you? I really must write this down or I'll forget it. King for a day." He chuckled softly to himself.

"When are they coming?" she demanded. She had not seen Thomas since the wedding.

"I expect them tomorrow, probably in the late afternoon. I sent a writ of safe conduct three days ago."

Her eyes rounded. "When were you planning to tell me this?"

He shrugged. "It's a working visit, it doesn't involve you. Do you really have nothing in here to take dictation with?"

"It's my *family.*"

"Meaning?"

"I want to see them! I can't believe I should even have to explain that to you."

"I didn't want to interrupt your sewing," he said mischievously, and leapt toward her to grab the brush away because she truly looked as if she was about to throw it at him. He added, placating, "Family

to me is so ubiquitous it's absolutely meaningless." He handed her back the brush like a peace offering. "You're the only family I have that counts," he said quietly, kissing her neck.

"I'm touched," she said. "But I don't believe you—what about Gwirion?"

He made a dismissive gesture. "That's so much more than family." He leaned toward her to peck her forehead again, but she pushed him away with a look of annoyance.

She turned back to her mirror, one of the few extravagances in her room, and continued to brush her hair. The thick, straight strands were silky and glistened in the rush light. This was a ritual she relied on whenever there was tension between them in private. She loved her hair, and she knew that he didn't. It was a perfect way for her to soothe herself without providing him any satisfaction.

"Why is Thomas coming?" she asked.

Noble abandoned his search for a stylus and threw himself sprawling back onto the bed, affecting ennui. He was glad there was an English-style bed in both their chambers; it was a luxury easy to grow used to. "It's nothing of import to you. Just a few new problems with the border."

She put down the brush and swiveled on her stool to look at him warily. He was never so casual about these issues. "How can that not be important to me? That's my land, those are my people."

The king raised his head slightly and craned his neck to meet her gaze. "You're a little slow about this, aren't you?" he said. He gestured around the room. "This is your land now. I am your people."

"You can't expect me to stop caring about them just because I'm no longer there. I tended to those people for years. I'd like to know what the problems are."

"I don't want you worrying about it." He grinned. "Women who worry lose their looks."

"I'm going to worry more if you don't tell me. Or I'll ask Thomas tomorrow and believe his version of it."

Amused, he relaxed his head back against the bed pillows. "Such

a stubborn little thing. I forget that sometimes." He rolled onto his side and propped up his head on a bent arm. "All right, then. Your dear innocent devoted brother has been plotting with Roger Mortimer to invade our kingdom."

She leapt to her feet, panicked. "That's a lie!" She rushed to the bed and grabbed his arm, trying to propel him up and off. "Get out! I won't speak to you if you say such rubbish."

He laughed and went limp, sprawling on his back again, ignoring her anger. "Be quiet, you'll wake your women," he teased. She was bending over him seeking the leverage to pry him into a sitting position, and their faces were close. He smiled at her, an expression that frustrated and perplexed her because it looked so genuine, so utterly without malice, even as he made this inflammatory accusation. "I just need to have a little chat with the boy about some rumors I've heard." He reached out and stroked her cheek. "Just rumors. I don't want to trouble you with it."

"Don't insult me by infantilizing me."

Impatience flickered in his blue eyes and he spoke more genuinely. "Actually, Isabel, I'm trying to protect you, not insult you."

"Protect me from what, the real world? You don't think that's insulting?"

He scrutinized her for a moment, then chuckled with affectionate sarcasm. "You really are enthrallingly artless. I'm trying to protect you from slander, dearest. Suspicion of all foreigners is high right now and you have not exactly distanced yourself from your Norman identity. Reminding any Welshman of your ties of love or blood to any Norman is not in your best interest." He looked at her more seriously. "My councilors aren't idiots, Isabel, they all have suspicions about what really happened when you lost the child. You're on very thin ice and it grows thinner every time you so much as glance out your solar window to the east. I'm manufacturing your indifference. Then if there is something nefarious going on with Thomas, you might be shielded from being associated with it."

One panic subsided in favor of another. "I'm sure there's a rea-

sonable explanation for whatever you think is happening," she insisted.

"There is no reasonable explanation for my brother-in-law signing a sworn oath promising to fight beside Mortimer in all circumstances."

"His allegiance is with you. You're holding his sister hostage."

Noble, still slouching, laughed. "Is that what I'm doing? Let's agree not to share that perception with our devoted subjects. And for the record, I seem to recall some sort of marriage ceremony last May that we both entered into of our own free will."

She pulled away from him with frustrated disgust. "What kind of free will? What would have happened to me if I'd refused?"

He propped himself up on his elbow, amused again. "Are you telling me you didn't want to be a queen?"

Some string inside her pulled so tight it broke. "Queen of what?" she spat, forcing herself to whisper. "I might as well be some minor baron's wife in England—at least then I'd be a member of civilization and run my own household. I have no sovereignty here at all. You won't let me oversee anything but an unfinished abbey in the middle of the wilderness! I have no political power or even domestic power, and really, what else is there?"

"Pardon me if I'm putting this too bluntly but there are supposed to be children." He had sat up on the edge of the bed, his humor replaced with a harsh matter-of-factness. "And I can't beget children if you won't let me have you, so if you really want something important to do, take off your clothes and lie down."

She instinctively clasped her hands over her chest in a protective gesture. "You are a brute."

Standing and taking a step toward her, he gestured to the bed. "I'm serious, I won't be refused." He pulled her to him and uncrossed her arms, cupping a hand over one of her breasts. He felt the familiar flicker of disappointment that she wasn't more buxom. He would have to find a replacement for Enid soon, someone he could reliably turn to without any of these exhausting complications. He would ask Gwirion to start looking in the morning.

He saw her jaw was twitching, and softened despite himself. Releasing her breast, he put his arms around her gently, a platonic gesture of comfort, kissing the top of her head, rubbing his cheek against her satiny hair. "Never mind, then, I won't trouble you tonight. I only hope your brother doesn't trouble us tomorrow."

COLLABORATORS

All Souls' Day, 1198

GWIRION DIDN'T KNOW the purpose of their visit, some diplomatic thing about the borders, no doubt. It was always the borders. He wished there were a huge wall built around the kingdom, like the walls around the castle and the village. He thought about suggesting this to Noble, but the king was in a foul mood, as he usually was on All Souls' Day because the land-use fees came in and it created havoc that took half the court half the day to control. Each village and farm in the kingdom owed the crown a portion of its worth, and most of it came due today—and never in anything as simple as coin. While the usher efficiently directed traffic and the chaplain noted down what came from where, it took the marshal, the steward, the falconer, the huntsman, the butler, the cook, the baker, and the brewer most of the day to send the sheep, cattle, pigs, vessels of butter and honey, vats of mead and ale and wine, and cartloads of oats and barley flour in the right directions for care and storage. Gwirion's assistance, it was universally agreed, was the last thing anyone needed.

Which suited him. He was still recovering from both the trauma and the pain of his mock execution, and anyway he remembered the glaring, speechless Lord Walter and the other uncle, the one who had demanded his death. He wasn't eager to cross their paths, nor did he particularly want to see Thomas, the poor boy he had so humiliated the day of the wedding. Gwirion grudgingly conceded a growing respect for the queen's character and found it hard to believe that Thomas had sprung from the same loins.

After sleeping for most of the day, he was in the kitchen having his welts dressed by an exhausted Marged and evaluating, in the weak rays coming in from the setting sun, a half-dozen oblivious kitchen girls as potential royal playthings. Noble flattered himself by not possessing any woman who wasn't eager: He never took one by force and was even known to decline, without penalty, those who were simply lackluster. One of Marged's helpers, a new girl Gwirion didn't know, had promise. She was hardly Enid, but there were curves and curly hair, and no indication of prudery. Gwirion wondered if he should try her out himself so that he could deliver a more thorough report, but dismissed the idea with irritation, knowing he would never actually take such initiative no matter how extravagantly he fantasized about it.

He glanced through the window into the courtyard, and saw the group from the Marches heading toward the council chamber, their vague shadows stretching long and misshapen behind them in the sunset. He was surprised to see the queen accompanying them. Perhaps they were planning a family dinner.

THE king glared across the table at them. "I consider it an act of war."

Thomas and his uncles were white-faced. The queen stood behind her husband, out of the circle at the table. He had told her she might attend but not speak, so she gave her uncles pointed looks,

silently begging them to make the obvious arguments that would protect her brother. Noble had posted as guards his most intimidating teulu—four of them in one small room—and armed them rather extravagantly with spears, swords, and daggers. Their presence alone made the visitors almost too cowed to speak.

"It's not an act of war," the queen said, quietly but firmly, feeling her pulse beating in her throat, and all the men in the room turned to stare at her.

"Madam," the king growled low, almost a whisper.

"You have no idea how complicated relationships are between the Marcher barons and the crown," she protested, speaking slowly because they were using French, and she wanted to make sure that Gwilym—the only senior councilor the king listened to—understood each word. "Uncle Roger needs reassurance about who his English allies would be against other Englishmen, not against you! Six weeks ago, when you suspected him of colluding with deBraose against you on the southeastern border, he was probably plotting somehow *against* deBraose in his own defense." The councilors all exchanged quick, impressed glances and she realized, with relief, that she had guessed right about that. She pressed on. "Everyone's afraid of him, but that means everyone wants to see him fall—"

"I'm not asking to see him fall," Noble said. "But I refuse to fall *to* him. That's the only issue here."

"No, it's not," she insisted. "Please try to see this in context—"

Noble leapt to his feet, turning on her, and she sank down onto a chest against the back wall. After a final harsh look, he turned again to Thomas. "If you swear allegiance to Mortimer, you must also swear it to me."

"You're married to my sister," Thomas said cautiously. "Isn't that enough?"

"You're a *blood relative* to Roger Mortimer. But *that* wasn't enough?"

Thomas fumbled for an argument as Father Idnerth quietly summarized a translation to Efan and the other officers who had no French. The penteulu looked expectantly at Thomas, as if waiting for

him to say the wrong thing so he'd have an excuse to pounce upon him. "It has nothing to do with the Welsh borders," the boy finally stammered. "It's an internal English issue."

"Good," Noble said briskly. "Then swearing amity toward me should not cause any conflict of interest for you. You'll be doing that before you leave here."

Thomas blanched and glanced at his uncles, who suddenly seemed to be sitting on something extremely uncomfortable. Clearing his throat and trying to sound like an adult, which he wasn't quite, he answered, "I'd like to hear your terms and discuss them with Roger first."

"Very well," Noble agreed. "My terms are that I'm holding you hostage until you swear amity to me." He switched to Welsh. "Escort the little Saxon to the cellar."

Everyone reacted at once. Isabel clamped her hands over her mouth to keep from shrieking; her uncles stood up spluttering in unison; Thomas fell back in his chair and nearly swooned as Hywel, Efan, and Gwilym leapt out of the way, anticipating the two larger guards who made straight for the boy and had raised him up and bound his arms behind him before he registered what was happening. The two remaining guards shadowed the uncles, discouraging any physical protest.

HIS cry of distress was not loud, but it carried. Gwirion heard it even in his little closet, where he was dressing gingerly after Marged's ministrations, and its plaintiveness brought him back to the kitchen window. He saw, across the dusky yard, two of the biggest teulu lugging a teenage boy out of the wood-frame council room.

"Oh my!" he chortled. "Marged, look at this! You too," he said specifically to the new girl. This turn of events suggested she would almost certainly be invited to Noble's room later that night. "Her

Royal Majesty's esteemed brother is being trundled around like a sack of barley!"

The two women came to the window, everyone else crowding in behind them craning to see. They watched in dumbfounded silence as Thomas, hands bound, was led roughly through the courtyard toward the porthouse by the barbican. His two uncles came chasing after him, but they were coaxed toward the guest quarters by their guards with the wordless efficiency of sheep dogs.

"Where are they taking him?" asked the girl.

Gwirion kept staring out into the yard. "The barbican. I'd say they're either throwing him out entirely or putting him in the dungeon."

"The dungeon!" she gasped.

Marged made a face. "It's not a dungeon, it's just a little holding pen. Don't frighten the lass."

Gwirion kept his gaze focused out the window, then finally turned away and moved through the kitchen, heading for the side entrance by the well. "This is simply too intriguing," he announced loudly.

"Hey, boyo!" Marged snapped, more maternal than chastising. "Stay out of it. You're not to be seen today, remember?"

"I won't be," he promised, and was gone.

THIS is a classic example of what we refer to as *irony*," Gwirion said to the youth, who was too distressed to register a word.

"What," he answered stupidly, as Gwirion settled down on a moldy pile of straw outside the cell.

"Irony," Gwirion repeated. He adjusted the rush light to give Thomas's new quarters better illumination. "The last time we saw each other was at this very spot, but we were on opposite sides of the bars."

Thomas registered at last his visitor's identity. He took in a dis-

gusted breath and made a face almost identical to one the queen often made—an expression which, for reasons he pretended not to fathom, Gwirion frequently inspired. "You were supposed to be hanged."

"You were supposed to stop getting yourself locked into dark rooms. What happened?"

"I will not discuss it with you."

"And what's wrong with me?"

Thomas gave him the look of an emperor disdaining the supplications of a beggar. "You are beneath contempt," he said slowly. "You're a nonentity."

"I'm the king's favorite nonentity," Gwirion warned him. "I don't know what you did to get in here, but unless Noble's attempting another stupid prank, you're in serious trouble right now, and it's only myself who can make him reconsider whatever he plans to do to you."

Thomas shook his head at him. "My sister's interceding for me. She'll take care of it."

Gwirion laughed. "You poor idiot, do you really believe that? Your sister has no power over the king at all, except perhaps at the exact moment of sexual climax, but even that's debatable—especially tonight when I know for a fact he's riding a pretty kitchen girl. No, no, lad, if you want help, you'd best tell Uncle Gwirion all about it." Thomas's flustered expression was irresistible and Gwirion felt compelled to make it worse. "What's the matter, laddie, does it embarrass you to think of your sister copulating? That's the only reason we brought her here, you know that, don't you? So that our king could plunge his great Welsh spear into her moist, submissive little Norman crevice."

Thomas was instantly crimson. "How dare you talk that way!" he shouted, smashing the heel of his hand against the iron door. "About my sister *or* your queen!"

Gwirion gestured calmly to their surroundings. "Do you see where you are? Do you see where I am? If I want to help you, I'll talk however I please."

Thomas glowered at him. "Why do you want to help me? You hate me and you hate my sister."

"Aha! And therefore, nobody would expect me to help you. Anything involving irony—there's that word again—that's my specialty." He winced as he shifted to lessen the pull of his tunic across his tender back, and added more seriously, "Plus the king is in need of severe comeuppance right now. I'm not wont to place a Mortimer's well-being above my monarch's but I'm perfectly willing to use you as a tool for my own retribution. Tell me what the problem is and perhaps we can assist each other."

"You'll want gold, I suppose," the boy sniffed, trying to maintain a disdainful and contemptuous facade as his insides wobbled.

"No, I don't want gold," Gwirion said impatiently, lying. "I just want gossip. Tell me what happened."

LONG after night had fallen outside, bringing sudden clouds and rain, Thomas finally finished explaining the situation to Gwirion. He had been surprised by the Welshman's quick understanding of subtle details, but frustrated by his obsession with going off on tangents, punning, or caricaturing the different people mentioned, most of whom he'd probably never met. He went on about Roger Mortimer for nearly twenty minutes with more gleeful venom than Thomas thought was deserved. What should have taken a few minutes of simple description took more than an hour, and half the time Thomas had no idea what Gwirion was talking about. Although Gwirion was clearly entertaining himself, the boy could see that he was also trying in some odd way to entertain him, and he grudgingly appreciated it. That was probably the fellow's only stock-in-trade, which explained his nearly frantic need to turn everything into the butt of a joke, usually sexual or worse. He wondered how his sister could bear the fellow's presence, and remembered with sorrow her letters lamenting that she couldn't.

"Well, knowing the king and knowing the history, I understand why he reacted as he did," Gwirion said. "I don't think what you did was intelligent, but I wouldn't call it an act of war."

"Will you help me?"

Gwirion gave this question much more thought than Thomas felt it required. He was finally about to speak when he was distracted by approaching footsteps, and Einion came toward them, someone in a damp cape following.

"The inmate has a visitor," he informed them tersely.

"We're busy," Gwirion informed him just as tersely in response and began to turn back toward the boy, when the figure cloaked in purple surprised him by stepping forward and revealing itself as the queen. "Milady," he said, sheepish at being found here. He chuckled awkwardly. "We're spending far too much time down here together. People will be saying things."

She spoke without shrillness or pleading. "If you have any human decency, Gwirion, you will not taunt my brother now."

He was annoyed for a moment, but realized there was no reason for her to think he was here for any reason but ill. "I'm actually here to perform an All Souls' mass for him," he said. "I know what pious Christians you Mortimers are and I didn't want to deprive him of an opportunity for monotony. You're welcome to join us, though." He pressed his palms together before his face and chanted in Gregorian tones: "*O nominae patrie. Nobilitae es jackassium. Gwirionius assistium Thomassium.*" She gave him a strange look and he lowered his hands. "Milady, he's told me of the situation and I'm trying to find a way to help him."

She blinked. "You are?" she asked, and when he nodded, demanded suspiciously, "*Why?*"

"Repaying the king's abuse of me by aiding a Mortimer—isn't that a *perfect* irony?" he asked blithely, and returned his attention to the boy. "Answer a few questions so I have the whole of it. Why can't you do as Noble wants? Why don't you simply swear an oath of amity?"

"Uncle Roger would react to that the way Maelgwyn is reacting

to this—he'd see it as double-dealing. I just want to explain the situation here to Roger before I make such a commitment to Maelgwyn."

"So then, why couldn't you have explained Mortimer's situation to Noble—Maelgwyn—before you made such a commitment to Mortimer?"

Thomas shrugged uncomfortably. "He's a long day's ride away in another country. Uncle Roger is breathing down the back of my neck. And he is my overlord after all. Your king isn't."

Gwirion took a new tack. "Well then, on the topic of kings, what does *your* king think of his barons plotting to attack each other?"

"*Our* king," Thomas corrected, then hesitated before conceding "... is not in England."

Gwirion gave him a sardonic look. "Is Richard off fighting infidels again? Never you mind, he'll get himself killed off any day now and then we'll all have brother John to play with, and—"

"And until that happens," the queen cut in, to preempt Gwirion's tangent, "the Marcher lords consider themselves accountable to no one. They're all but sovereigns unto themselves, and Roger sees himself as Noble's peer, perhaps even his superior."

Gwirion shook his head. "Noble will never concede that," he said.

"That's not *my* problem," Thomas said desperately.

"Gwirion is saying that it has *become* your problem," the queen said. "And I agree." Gwirion did a double take and then pretended to gape at her. She saw the look out of the corner of her eye and smiled wryly. "That's right, Gwirion, we're in complete accord on something. And the lion shall lie down with the lamb."

"What, the Second Coming? You're rushing things a bit, aren't you? We haven't even come once yet." He leaned toward her with a lecherous expression in his impish dark eyes. "Would you like to be the lion or the lamb?"

She made a disgusted face but then, despite herself, shook her head with grudging amusement.

THE next morning the castle was thrown into chaos with the news that the prisoner had escaped. It had been raining on and off for hours, and the lack of footprints in the mud around the barbican defeated even the marshal. Mass was canceled, a hue and cry was raised, and search parties were sent out through the downpour to comb the towers, the village, and the hillsides, with their dying bracken groves so thick a person could easily disappear in them. Messengers staggered through the mud to the nearest landowners to warn them against harboring the fugitive, and a search party in oiled cloaks was sent to the eastern border. The king, his council, the queen, and her uncles convened in the chilly wood-frame council chamber for what quickly devolved into a rabid, bilingual frenzy. Noble accused the uncles of spiriting Thomas away; the uncles accused Noble of murdering him. Efan threatened Ralf theatrically for making such an accusation; Gwilym threatened Efan subtly for being so theatrical. Einion the porter was called in to give his brief, unhelpful report for the seventh time in twenty minutes: He believed he had been drugged, had fallen into a deep sleep, and when he'd awakened, not only the prisoner but the prison key was missing. Outside help was presumed. Noble and Ralf growled at each other for nearly an hour, arguing loudly and angrily over who would have custody of the boy when he was found. The council was endlessly breaking down into side arguments, tangential conversations, brainstorming sessions, and name-callings, when the only person who could make things worse entered the room.

"Excuse me," Gwirion stammered, thrown by the disorder. He gave his soggy tartan mantle to the guard, shaking the rain from his hair. The only one who noticed him was Ralf. It took him a moment to place Gwirion's face, but it was clear the moment he did.

"You!" he snapped, turning all his attention to the smaller man. Gwirion recognized his rodent-bright eyes and reflexively took a step

backward. Enraged, Ralf spun back around toward the king and managed to cry out above the din: "You were supposed to hang this thing!"

"I never said that," Noble called back.

"Never mind that now!" Lord Walter snapped at his brother in French.

"Excuse me—" Gwirion tried again, but got no further because Ralf was brandishing a knife. "Christ!" Gwirion scrambled frantically to the other side of the room, Ralf behind him knocking into things and people in his rush to catch him.

"Sit down!" Noble shouted at Ralf. "Put that away! Nobody draws steel in this room, ever, under any circumstances!"

Half the men around the table gasped as Noble reached out with his unprotected hand and grabbed the bare knife blade, staring Ralf down with his mesmerizing glare. Ralf froze and the room quieted at once. "Put the knife away," Noble said slowly to the older man through gritted teeth, and released his grip. Fuming, Ralf obeyed, sending killing glances at Gwirion.

"Excuse me—" Gwirion started again.

"Not now, Gwirion, this is a crisis," Noble said impatiently, and pickup conversations returned the room to auditory chaos. "I'll send for you later. Your presence will not help right now."

Looking uncharacteristically crestfallen, Gwirion began a slow cross through the room, back toward the door, absently fingering his cowlick. Without looking at anyone, he collected the gazes of the officers as he passed by them, his very docility making them suspicious. He saw the queen from across the room and she gave him a troubled, questioning look. She knew no details of his plan to help Thomas, and had no idea if this was a part of it or an unexpected complication. Gwirion did not try to communicate with her, just continued trudging past the bank of bolted windows toward the door. He retrieved his sodden wrap from the young teulu guard and began to thank him. And then he did not stop, even to draw breath. "I do so appreciate you holding this for me," he said, speaking not loudly but very rapidly. "Especially as it's wet and malodorously aromatic, and I

hope you don't think that I equate you with a cloak peg, because I don't. To tell you the truth, I think your job is very difficult and I hope these gentlemen are treating you well, or at least better than they're treating me—well, you saw how the English gentleman was treating me—and forgive me for asking, but I can't help wondering, is it hard for you to just stand here like this and keep a straight face while they're all rattling on to each other?" The guard's mouth twitched as more of the men turned toward them and the room gradually stilled. "Or is it harder for you to keep a straight face while *I'm* rattling on to *you?* Do you ever have a chance to rattle on to somebody? I suppose it must be very difficult to hear the rot that goes on in council all day and not be able to—" When he sensed that he had everyone's attention, Gwirion cut himself off abruptly and looked at the staring faces as if just noticing them. "Pardon, did I interrupt something important?"

"I told you to leave," the king warned him in a baritone growl.

In the jot of time between the end of the royal dismissal and the recommencement of the debates, Gwirion tossed something directly onto the middle of the table. It landed with a soft clack on the layers of maps and castle diagrams.

It was the prison key.

After a startled moment, an entire room of heads—bearded, mustached, clean shaven, bald, wimpled—snapped toward Gwirion, who shrugged and turned to leave. But the cacophony of shouts to the guard, although none clear enough to understand, made him slam the door closed. Noble stood up and glowered over the table at Gwirion.

"What have you done with him?"

"I'm not prepared to share that information quite yet," Gwirion said placidly.

"Fiend!" Ralf hissed. "Whip him!" He signaled to one of his own attendants and the man took a step toward Gwirion, who ducked away from him.

"No," the king said, holding up a hand. "No whipping. Gwirion, tell me where he is."

"Whip the bastard! He's not going to cooperate!" the Norman insisted. "His impertinence alone is grounds for the block!"

"They tried that just the other day," Gwirion informed him confidentially. "It didn't take."

"Gwirion, I'm serious," the king said in a threatening voice. "Where is he? I'm sure you've rigged up some very clever gag out of this whole scenario, but you can't go through with it. Do you understand? This is bigger than you. It's bigger than *me*." He gave Gwirion a look that made it clear he was absolutely serious, with no hidden wink or grin or wagging eyebrow. Gwirion was surprised by how furious he looked—but also how frightened. It was satisfying, and he toyed with the idea of keeping His Majesty in this state for as long as possible in revenge for the mock execution, but decided there were better things to do with his morning. And in the end, this was about Roger Mortimer, who would always be their shared enemy. So he met Noble's gaze and walked toward him around the conference table. When he reached the king, he continued to look at him steadily, then nimbly leapt onto the table and took a large step into the center of it, scuffing the maps and diagrams with mud.

Noble killed the growing murmurs around them with a look, and gestured up at Gwirion. "All right, go ahead," he said in annoyance. "Give us your performance."

"The performance is for after supper. This is *serious*, Noble—have you no sense of propriety?"

"Get on with it!" Noble snarled as Ralf muttered in audible French to his brother, "I can't believe he allows himself to be subjected to such humiliation."

Taking his time, Gwirion swept the maps together into a neat pile and handed them politely to Father Idnerth. Then he sat cross-legged, facing the king, suddenly all business. Those at the table he had his back to shifted slowly toward the king's chair, unable to resist seeing the encounter unencumbered—except for the uncles, who remained tense in their seats. The queen hovered behind her husband, watching anxiously.

"I'll produce Thomas on one condition."

"You do not presume to give the king conditions!" Ralf said from behind him, but Noble waved him to be quiet and said, listening, "Go on." The Normans exchanged disbelieving glances.

"The boy realizes he was in error, and he's sorry for it. He has a new proposal for resolving the situation fairly, which I shall now share with you. You will accept it without reservation and take the first step toward putting it into action. And then I will tell you where Thomas is."

"Aren't you still in welts from the lashing the other day?" Noble demanded with quiet fury. "Do you really want another one already?"

"As you said, this is bigger than me," Gwirion answered coyly, and batted his eyelashes at the king. "My pain isn't a deciding factor."

"Maybe your life will be," Noble said dangerously. He gestured Efan toward Gwirion.

"You've already tried that threat, I'm not falling for it again," Gwirion said, laughing, unfazed by the large gloved hand closing on his shoulder.

"Gentlemen, if you will just step across the yard with me," the king announced in an annoyed voice, ignoring Gwirion's laughter. "We'll need a water tub. This should not take long."

Reassembled grumpily outside the kitchen with their mantles wrapped to protect their heads from pelting rain, they clustered around a wooden tub filled with well water that Marged's grandson had been summoned to fill. Noble pointed to the tub.

"Gwirion, your head is going in there unless you tell me where Thomas is at once."

Gwirion, the only one with no wrap, frowned at the water tub. "I could use a hair wash, is there any soap?"

Glaring at him, Noble signaled Efan. Gwirion made a pained face as the huge young man shoved him down onto his knees in the mud, then grabbed a hank of his dark hair and pushed his head completely underwater.

For a long moment, Gwirion neither breathed nor struggled,

holding his breath as they all watched. Then bubbles disturbed the surface, slowly. Finally, when it felt as if minutes had passed, the bubbles stopped and Gwirion's body jerked. The penteulu looked at Noble, who nodded, and Gwirion's head was hauled out of the tub. He was gasping for breath, painfully, but his black eyes sparkled.

"There're some trout in there that are simply enormous!" he announced.

"Where's the boy?" Noble demanded.

"I can't tell you until you've heard his new terms," Gwirion said, and took a deep breath, anticipating another submersion.

Three more times they dunked him, each time for longer. On the fourth round he began to convulse in earnest, in true distress for the first time, his hands grabbing at Efan's forearms in desperation until Gwilym grimaced and Isabel couldn't watch any longer. "Don't kill him!" she begged reflexively in French. "We'll never find Thomas!"

"Please, sire," Walter seconded. Noble immediately gestured to Efan, who was grinning; he hauled Gwirion's head out of the tub and this time pushed him to the ground. Gwirion lay purple-faced in the mud on his side, retching, gasping for breath and getting rained on. Nobody moved to help him. He appealed for no sympathy. They stood around him, their breaths congealing in little puffs, awkwardly waiting for him to get his own breath back, and when he could finally croak out a sound, he pulled himself gingerly to his feet. "Cold," he managed, hoarse and shivering. "Inside."

Noble, avoiding his eye, nodded. The group squelched back across the yard to the council room, except for Gwirion, who was temporarily dismissed to the kitchen to recover. He staggered to the door by the well, stumbling, shaking his head and trying uselessly to wipe his face dry and wring the water from his sodden, muddy clothes. Marged had watched the whole episode from the kitchen in extreme indignation, and already had a blanket and hot brew waiting for him by the stool near the fire.

He sipped slowly and mused that he was back where he'd been two days ago, only now in addition to everything else, he was freez-

ing wet. *I seem to be on a downward spiral,* he thought, and opened his mouth to share this insight with Marged, but it hurt too much to talk. Then he noticed that Marged had risen to her feet with a nervous huff and was staring over his shoulder.

His cold nose caught the hinted scent of rosewater. "What's the rest of your scheme?" said the queen's voice in his ear.

"I thought *merci* was the word for gratitude," he croaked without looking back at her, and rubbed his throat.

She blushed. "Forgive me—and thank you. Thank you a thousand times. But what happens now?"

"Now I tell them Thomas's conditions."

"Which are what?"

He made a pained face, not wanting to speak. "I'm not much good at political strategy, Your Majesty, I rely on impulse and intuition. I'll just say whatever comes into my head at the moment."

"You can't do that now," she countered. "Not with such a delicate matter."

He looked up crossly at her. "Do you have a better idea?" he whispered mockingly.

"I do, actually," she said, imitating his tone. "Would you like to hear it?"

"Not really," muttered Gwirion, and turned back to the fire.

A few minutes later, he was back in the council room, sitting on a chest against the wall. The queen had managed to slip in separately, unnoticed.

"Thomas proposes a neutrality statement," Gwirion said in a voice so husky it was hardly a voice. "He'll swear allegiance to Mortimer in matters of English politics, and to you in matters of Welsh ones." He winced and rubbed his throat, struggling with a deep breath that was as loud as speech. "But he'll also swear an oath to

both of you saying that he will not raise a hand against *any* family, neither uncle nor brother-in-law. And most important, he will not allow his land to be used as a staging point for either of you to attack the other. Since his estate is really just a long strip by Llanandras, that creates a safety buffer for you—it gives Mortimer almost no place to launch an easy attack."

Noble considered the proposal as Ralf translated for his brother. "That will never work," the king said at last.

"Why not?" Gwirion challenged, trying to suppress a painful cough.

"Mortimer will never accept it."

"Sorry, if you want the boy back, you have to agree to at least trying it. Draft a proposal to Mortimer and send it off immediately."

Ralf stood up to protest but his brother pulled him back down. "It's this or Thomas as Maelgwyn's hostage," Walter murmured in French. "If he is so deranged he'll let his parasite dictate policy, close your mouth and be grateful."

Noble crossed his arms, then leaned back in his chair and crossed his legs at the ankles, scrutinizing his friend. "It's rather ironic this is happening now, you know," he said, suddenly conversational. "Just two nights ago I was playing with the idea of making you king for a day, but I postponed it because I couldn't have you at the helm while we were navigating the hazardous waters of Marcher politics."

"Yes, another lovely example of irony," Gwirion said, smiling, but his voice and his breathing were still husky and strained. "I was explaining irony to Thomas only last night. I'm not sure he quite understood."

His eyes still on Gwirion, the king called for paper from the chapel stores, which brought protestations from some of his own men. The two uncles were caught between appalled incredulity that he was obeying Gwirion's orders and relief that Thomas would be out of harm.

Gwirion dictated the proposal to Father Idnerth, in the form of a letter from Thomas to both Noble and Roger Mortimer. The

queen penned her brother's name, and Noble signed to indicate he endorsed it. While the ink was drying, Noble sat back and asked, "Just out of curiosity, who devised that proposal?"

"Thomas," Gwirion replied promptly.

"Not Thomas," the king said. "I don't know him well but a boy sitting traumatized in a prison cell is not coming up with a new model for border politics."

"He may have had a little help," Gwirion said noncommittally, with another painful swallow. The king grinned.

He turned to the rest of the council and announced, "We've just implemented policy invented by a fool." He seemed tickled by this, almost more so because nobody else in the room found it amusing.

Gwirion leaned forward, gathering the woolen blanket about his shoulders. "Actually, sire, it's more subversive even than that," he said hoarsely, in a tone that sounded confidential but was loud enough to be heard by all. Because it sounded confidential, it caught everybody's attention immediately. "You've just implemented policy that was invented by a woman."

"A woman?"

"Your wife, sire," Gwirion answered, nodding toward the queen. "It's a *French* woman, no less." Before she could catch his gaze, he looked away and stood up. "We'll give your runner a three-hour start, then I'll bring you the boy." He met Noble's eye one final time and Isabel saw an entire unspoken conversation flash between them; she half believed Noble approved of what Gwirion had done. Gwirion headed out of the room, drawing the brychan over his head against the rain. Noble saw the Normans' attendants make to follow him, but he called out to them sharply and they did not persist. Then he stood and turned to stare at his wife.

"When did the two of you begin collaborating?" he asked, looking amused despite himself.

She laughed dismissively. "I'd hardly call it a collaboration," she assured him.

"*THIS* is why women don't make policy," Noble spat. It was two weeks later and an exhausted, filthy messenger, shadowed by the hulking young Efan, had burst into the hall, interrupting the breakfast meal to hand a rolled and sealed parchment to the king.

"What is it?" Isabel asked, laying down her oatcake and leaning toward him for a better look. Gwirion had finished eating and was already huddled near the fire, where he was restringing the gilded harp. The king tossed down the parchment with an annoyed gesture. Concerned, the queen grabbed it up from the table before Goronwy could get his stubby hands on it, and looked at the broken seal. She recognized it: her uncle Walter's. Her eyes glanced over the words and she paled.

"What's happened?" demanded the judge.

"Roger Mortimer responded to the neutrality proposal by taking Thomas hostage," Noble announced, grim. "His own nephew."

"We have to raise a ransom," the queen said in a faint voice, struggling to keep her composure. Noble stood up and turned on her, his grimness fast evolving into anger.

"Did you read what Walter wrote?" he snapped. "Mortimer doesn't want a ransom. He wants Thomas's lands around Lingen. So that he can launch an attack on my eastern border. That's all he ever wanted—it's what he was after when he asked Thomas for a loyalty pledge. It had nothing to do with deBraose or any other English baron. In fact for all I know, Thomas is not even hostage, this is all an involved pretense to make him appear innocent so they can use him as a pawn against me in the future."

"He's too guileless for that, Noble, you would have seen right through it when he was here," she countered impatiently.

"I'll have to back that," Gwirion said from the fireside. He lay the harp aside, realizing the situation was serious enough to require even his fickle attention. "The boy is hardly the model of fearless integrity but he's too simple to pull off a double cross."

Noble grimaced but made a dismissive gesture that they both knew meant Thomas was, for now, not under suspicion.

"What is going on, sire?" Gwilym asked calmly, striding in toward the high table from the kitchen.

"Our darling Mortimer is raising a hostile force near your queen's birthplace," Noble said with irritation.

"That doesn't make any sense," she insisted. "He endorsed our marriage to stabilize the border."

"No, madam, he endorsed it to give me a false sense of security!" Noble thundered, slamming his hand on the table so hard the platters rattled. Isabel started. Even Gwirion sat up straighter; he had never seen the king so publicly explosive. "Without this marriage I'd have no responsibility to that idiot brother of yours locked up in Wigmore and I'd have an entire company of defensive troops on the other side of Offa's Dyke *right now*. Clearly all Mortimer ever had in mind for this fruitless union was taking over Maelienydd." He turned on her in wrath. "And so help you, if ever I have reason to suspect you knew—"

"Noble!" she gasped, horrified.

Ignoring her, he swung around to face the steward. "Summon the council." Goronwy and the other officers still at breakfast rose at once; Gwilym did a head count, nodded, and walked out quickly, taking a cloak from a servant by the door. The other councilors followed him into the courtyard, scurrying to the council chamber.

"I'm sitting in," the queen announced, standing and gesturing to Generys for her mantle. Noble shot her a derisive look.

"You most certainly are not," he informed her.

"It's my brother!"

"It's my *kingdom*," he hissed through clenched teeth.

"It's my kingdom too," she protested.

He stared at her. "Is it?" he demanded in a menacing voice.

"Noble, don't be ridiculous," Gwirion said, his focus back on his harp, perfectly aware he was being inexcusably rude. "If she were that duplicitous, don't you think she and I would have taken to each other at once? She's never fit in because she's too artless to

be capable of anything as charmingly twisted as what you're suggesting."

Within minutes the council room was filled with the high officers of the court: bard, steward, penteulu, judge, marshal, chaplain, physician, usher, chamberlain, falconer, and huntsman. They met for less than half an hour, in a rare show of complete accord about what had to happen. Troops would go at once to the eastern border. Runners would be sent around the kingdom to convene a war council beginning in two weeks, on the first of December. A missive of official rebuke was drafted and sent to Roger Mortimer, demanding that he release Thomas, remove his men from Thomas's land, and cease any further preparation for hostile acts. Prince John would be petitioned too, although he hardly had the power to do much more than chastise, and Mortimer was already known to hold the royal family in contempt. Finally—and this was the sole source of brief debate—a message was sent to Llewelyn ap Iorwerth in Gwynedd, alerting him to Mortimer's preparations and apparent intentions. Llewelyn would have no more patience with an Anglo-Norman occupation force than Noble would. He was invited to attend the war council or send a representative, although they doubted that he would condescend to participate in something he was not leading.

Gwilym immediately settled into urgent efficiency, organizing their limited resources to host such a congress. The king, regretting his outburst against his wife, invited her to help him summon and greet the barons. Marged was informed with minor apology by Hafaidd of the meeting's outcome, and almost threw a fit at the prospect of feeding the hordes who would come just as winter and its privations descended on the castle.

· 8 ·

A Suitor at Council

Early December, 1198

 HERE WERE THOSE at Cymaron who thought things might actually be better with Norman overlordship. Nobody was stupid enough to say it, but the king knew who they were; he knew as well that they would not go against the collective will of his barons, which he could usually manipulate. Some of the barons would also be inclined toward capitulation, but he knew how to handle them. He was almost looking forward to it now that they were all here.

Gwirion's work would be simple that night, just a few tunes after Hywel's raspy recitation of "The Sovereignty of Britain." But he was fascinated by all the faces, both the familiar—Anarawd, the king's cousin, for example—and the unknown. He scrutinized the guests as they laid their weapons in a pile by the door and made their way to the dais to receive a formal welcome from their king and queen. Of the forty or so men who attended the war council, more than a dozen had brought their mates, and of them, seven or eight had young children underfoot, offspring not yet old enough to have gone to war-

dens and foster parents for their upbringing. These men were mostly from the eastern border near Mortimer, and they had chosen the inconvenience of traveling with children over the anxiety of leaving them behind. Gwirion adored the children, and even had a sentimental flash that first chilly afternoon of wanting the queen to produce offspring so he could play with them. Ashamed of himself for falling prey to such sentimentality, he banished the image from his mind. She would probably never let him near her children anyway.

MORE than one man who was meeting his queen for the first time looked into her bewimpled face with surprise, and commented that he hadn't heard her beauty praised as it deserved. At first she dismissed this as flattery, knowing the Celtic aesthetic differed from the continental, but when enough of them had said it, always after a brief, surprised stare, she beamed, beginning to believe the compliment. Noble enjoyed the glow in her tawny eyes. He still did not consider her beautiful—handsome, yes, perhaps pretty with her petite, efficient features and high forehead, but not beautiful—and he found it as surprising and flattering as she did that so many men were struck by her appearance. It made him want to gloat. They were an elegant couple tonight, matching in their heavier ceremonial crowns and long tunics of brocaded crimson silk edged with gold, she with a surcoat of velvet from England that all the women eyed covetously.

A dark-haired young man, her age or likely younger, knelt at their feet now, and kissed first the king's hand, then the queen's, before even lifting his eyes. He wore a green woolen tunic onto which had been sewn a yellow eagle *displayed,* and he was handsome, his features sharp and aristocratic. He too did an appreciative double take when he first saw her, but unlike the ones who had come before him, he seemed struck dumb. He took in a breath and finally turned to the

king with a dazzled, guileless smile. "Your wife her ladyship is the most beautiful woman I've ever seen."

"I thank you," Noble said. "You may tell her so directly."

He looked at the queen and then quickly back at the king. "I don't think I can," he said with complete sincerity.

Noble chuckled. "Conquer your shyness, lad." He kept an eye on his wife, seeking her agreement as he added, "Sit by us tonight and share our cup if you like. See if you can bring yourself to talk to her."

The young man's face lit up. He nodded his thanks, and began to descend from the dais. "What is your name, sir?" the queen asked, holding him back with her words.

For a moment, he looked as though he really didn't know the answer. Then he beamed reassuringly and announced, "Owain ap Ithel, milady."

"Owain is a good name. We say John in England."

"You may call me John if you like, milady. I would turn Norman for your sake."

Noble almost snapped at this—but seeing that the young man was obviously too flustered to realize what he'd said, he smiled broadly instead and clapped him on the arm. "Good lad, not only talking to her but flirting! We'll make a man of you yet."

Owain nodded and excused himself. While waiting for the next man to cross up to them, Noble glanced at the queen and quietly baahed like a sheep.

"That's not nice," she scolded, laughing, both of them grateful for the moment of levity between them.

AFTER the official greetings, people dispersed to dress for supper. It was crowded, and most of them would be sleeping in the hall for the duration, pushing the servants to the lower end near the door. There were curtains hung for nighttime privacy along the

outer edges of the room, and these were pulled closed now to change behind, while every pitcher and basin in the castle was collected for people to wash the road mud off their hands and boots. The custom of washing guests' feet was suspended with the understanding that there were far too many feet and not enough washers.

The king had chosen two parties to honor with the only separate apartments the castle offered visitors. One was Anarawd his cousin, the man who was still for now his heir. Although Noble found him hateful he felt obliged to honor the kinship, so Anarawd's entourage would stay in the king's snug, unadorned audience room directly off the hall. Huw ap Maredudd was being coddled for quite another reason: His large manors high on the hills near Llanidloes, although poor in soil like much of northwestern Maelienydd and therefore nearly worthless in themselves, were full of mountain passes and put him closest to Llewelyn's siren call, which he was openly intrigued by. He was one of the very few wealthy landowners with no traceable lineage to the king, and Noble needed to keep him pleased with his current sovereign; he would be staying with his wife above the steward and usher, in the quietest, most private room in the castle.

But Gwirion noticed the portly, middle-aged Huw standing now in the upper half of the hall near the fire, in personal audience with Noble as people unpacked and settled in around them in the din. The unobtrusive chandler had already lit the hall—it was dark hours before supper now, and a room with more people in it seemed to require more light. As Huw and Noble spoke, there spread across the king's face an understated slyness that Gwirion historically associated with secret assignations. It surprised him: Noble nearly always used Gwirion as his interlocutor for intimate arrangements. He supposed Noble was requesting to detain some attendant lady in Huw's retinue, but he idly wondered why the king was doing it himself instead of sending him.

Before he had a chance to glean the answer, he was conscripted into duty. The children, ten in all, were scampering through the hall, darting around the screens wreaking havoc and spreading mud, glee-

ful the journey and then the tiresome formalities were over, and a harried Hafaidd gave Gwirion the job of keeping them from mischief.

He decided to settle them by the hearth and explain to them what their parents were too busy or nervous to explain: why they were making this visit, and what the fuss was all about. He had finished his main narrative and was answering their questions when he noticed the young dark-haired baron who had been so inarticulate with the queen on the dais, his face washed and his travel outfit exchanged for a long black ceremonial tunic. He approached Gwirion and the children, and stood watching him with quiet interest.

Not noticing Owain, Isabel caught Gwirion and the children in her peripheral vision, and immediately handed the brychans she was carrying to a passing hall servant. "Take these to the men in that corner," she ordered, and headed briskly back toward the hearth. She didn't trust Gwirion with youngsters, so she was surprised and impressed to hear him engaging the children in an apparently sensible conversation, and paused out of sight to listen.

"But why do they want our land?" asked a six-year-old boy.

"I don't really know, to be honest." His face brightened. "Let's ask the queen the next time we see her—she understands all about the English, she's very fond of them. Those English seem to delight in taking other people's things." She bristled in her hiding place, but decided not to intervene. She almost hoped he'd say something worse and get himself thrown out of hall for the week.

"But why so much?" another child demanded.

Gwirion looked at their trusting, upturned faces and wondered if he should give in to a terrible impulse. Probably not, he thought.

Oh, what the hell, he thought.

"It has to do with genitals," he said gravely. "Do you know that word?" They didn't. Around the corner, listening, she assumed she had heard wrong, and tried to figure out what he'd actually said.

"When boys piss—you know how that's different from girls pissing, of course."

They all did, from the family livestock if nothing else. "You mean a penis," said a little girl, gravely.

"Exactly." Gwirion smiled. "Some men have very small penises. Roger Mortimer, for example, has a *very*—"

"*That's enough,*" two voices announced in unison, as Isabel and Owain descended upon him from opposite sides at the same moment. They startled each other more than they startled Gwirion or the children, but both recovered at once, with a formality that was almost as risible as their embarrassment. Owain bowed—gracefully, to Gwirion's surprise—and the queen nodded her head in acknowledgment.

"It's Your Majesty's prerogative," he insisted, gesturing toward Gwirion as if he were a piece of furniture.

She smiled and shook her head. "I have such ample opportunity for this particular chastisement, I've grown weary of it. Please continue, I applaud your initiative."

"They're discussing who's going to bawl me out over pissing," Gwirion explained loudly, annoyed. He glanced up at them. "May I finish?"

"No, Gwirion," Isabel said firmly, "it's—"

"But why does having a small genital make someone want to take our land?" an older girl, about seven, asked. She was pleased with herself for incorporating the new vocabulary word. "Girls have smaller ones than boys and girls don't do such things."

They all looked expectantly at Gwirion. He held up his hands. "Alas, my friends, I've just been banned from speaking to you about this very timely topic. Query the grown-ups." He lifted himself up from the hearth and walked off toward the side door with a huff of exaggerated indignation—then immediately ducked to hide behind the corner of the fireplace, where the queen herself had just been eavesdropping. Owain and his hostess were left looking at each other and the children in silence.

"So then?" one of the boys finally ventured. "Do you know the answer or not?"

The queen looked down at them. Other than Thomas she had no experience with children, and he had never demanded this kind of

explanation. "Of course we do," she said gamely. But her mind was a blank.

"Here's what it is," Owain announced, and gave her a reassuring smile before turning his attention to the children. "Men think the bigger they are there, the better they are. So men with smaller ones act the way they think men with big ones act, so everyone will think theirs are bigger too." The children exchanged perplexed looks: This was so stupid, he had to be making it up.

"So why do men with *big* genitals take over land?" the seven-year-old pressed on behalf of the group.

"Oh, but they don't," Owain assured them, with doe-eyed sincerity, and without thinking it through he added, earnestly, "I've never stolen so much as a handful of dirt." Her Majesty's surprised laughter made him blink, and then blush. He glanced quickly at the children, but they hadn't followed the logic and were already bored with him. He turned his attention nervously back to Isabel, who couldn't check her amusement. After a hesitant moment, Owain chuckled sheepishly with her and when their glances met again, they both began laughing in earnest, although the blush stayed on his cheeks.

The exchange was delightful to Gwirion until the moment he realized they were enjoying themselves. That robbed him of his pleasure, and he skulked off toward the kitchen looking for something to eat. If he had to listen to them *giggling* all evening he would lose his appetite.

NOBLE was astounded by the change in Owain's composure by the time the trestles were set up and supper served. Isabel must have taken the effort to put him at ease, and he was so guileless about his admiration of her that it was hard to begrudge him his oddly unassuming familiarity. There was nothing predatory in his attentions; he had no thought of his worship being given weight either

by a married queen or by her lord. The dais had been disassembled and replaced by the high table before the fireplace, hosting only the royal couple and certain members of the court. But none of the dignitaries sat as close tonight as Owain did, right at the queen's side and serving her from the platter they both shared with the king. She was unused to portioning food among three, and it was occasionally awkward keeping track of who wanted the mead and who the milk, but it was an awkwardness she found herself enjoying, and she laughed throughout the meal.

Owain and Isabel shared an interest in the stars, and each knew many constellations, although they ascribed different names and legends to them and it took some puzzling to figure out who was discussing what. Noble, amused by Owain's uncomplicated amiability, suggested the three of them repair to the wall walk before the end of the council week to stargaze, and they both nodded, forgetting there was a full moon that would wash out the heavens. Gwirion rolled his eyes, but nobody saw him.

The king was enjoying his wife's hilarity. Earlier in the evening she had been merely cheerful. Now she was effervescent. He had never seen her so lighthearted and he liked it. If this was the effect of her being unabashedly adored, he would have to round up lots of adorers to keep her in good humor. It could do remarkable things for his domestic life. As the tables were being cleared away he even suggested this to Gwirion, but Gwirion scowled at the idea. "And what if she falls in love with one of them?"

"Gwirion, look at him," Noble scoffed. "His voice has barely changed—he only came into his inheritance last month. I'm not sure he's even realized he's flirting."

The queen settled in her chair near the fire for the evening's entertainment, and invited the young man to sit beside her until the king joined them. Owain pointed to Noble and Gwirion's huddled conversation nearby. "And what's that about, milady?" he asked.

She shook her head. "They have the strangest friendship. I don't think I'll ever understand it, and I am not sure I care to." That was a lie. She wanted very much to understand it.

"Is he a bit off, then, that fellow?" Owain ventured thought-fully, watching them. "May I ask Your Majesty what he does here?"

She laughed ironically. "What doesn't he do would be easier to answer. He certainly doesn't do anything useful." She softened. "That's not true. He saved my brother's life a month ago."

"Really?" he asked. "I'm glad to hear it. What was it, then, an accident?"

She gave him an awkward smile. "Not quite. Mostly he pulls elaborate pranks that take weeks or months of planning, and he doesn't care about the victims as long as the prank comes off. He's insulting, rude, bawdy . . . and very good at what he does. We despised each other the first six months I was here." She was surprised, and glad, that she could put that in the past tense.

"Why?"

She didn't discuss this with anyone, even her ladies, and she knew it was impolitic to broach it with one of the men Noble needed for his mission. But she liked the easy innocence in his eyes. And she was lonely; Noble was the only one she could talk to without enduring officiousness or boredom, and his attentions had been entirely on this conference for a fortnight. "We were both mad with jealousy for the king's attention," she explained and then, oversimplifying, "It took a while to accept the pecking order."

Owain made a face of expansive sympathy. "I can see how it would be hard for him to yield up pride of place."

"He didn't."

He was incredulous. "The funny fellow comes before you? How could the king make such—forgive me, Your Majesty, but how could he make such a choice?"

She smiled tightly and shook her head; Noble was making his way toward them and they dropped the matter. When he reached them he gave Owain a warm smile of greeting, then settled between them into his cushioned chair and took his wife's hand. "That's enough gallivanting for you tonight, young lady," he teased, kissing her cheek. Her unprecedented levity made him sincerely grateful for the first time since last spring to have her as a companion. There was

something almost Enid-like about it. With Lord Huw's cooperation, he had already negotiated an early evening rendezvous, but if she was still glowing like this later on... He kissed her quickly on the lips and then turned to listen to Gwirion play, not noticing her smile waver for a moment.

It was the condescension that annoyed her, the assumption that his wife would docilely obey the marriage vows he so blithely broke. *If my receiving such attention is amusing, I'll amuse you with it until it's not amusement anymore.* What a simple plan. She should have tried it months ago.

A FTER Gwirion's performance that evening, Owain asked a dozen harried servants where to find the harpist, and finally somebody suggested that he try the king's private receiving chamber just off the hall. Owain was shown to the room and knocked. When nobody answered, he tried the latch, and the big oak door swung inward.

The room was crowded with sleeping blankets, but none of their inhabitants had claimed them yet. The usual furniture—Noble's leather chair, the cushioned settle, and the chest that doubled as a table—had been pushed to the side, and across the room was a blazing hearth. The room, with walls almost twice as thick as the solar above it, was cozy and wonderfully warm. It was a relief to be out of the crowd.

Gwirion sat curled up like a cat in front of the fire, gazing into the flames. He did not turn when Owain entered.

"Excuse me," Owain said pleasantly. Moving only his eyes, Gwirion briefly glanced toward him, then back to the fire.

"It's you," Gwirion said, as if that implied something.

"Yes," Owain said, smiling, as if he was content with whatever it might imply. "Me."

A silence. Gwirion wondered whether his ease came from stupid-

ity or cockiness. Or perhaps—although it was hard to imagine it—genuine innocence.

"Do you want something, then?" Gwirion asked, still not turning toward him.

"You play exquisitely."

"Thank you."

"Do you compose as well?"

"Ah." Gwirion uncurled and finally turned toward the younger man. "You want me to compose a song on your behalf extolling the beauty of the queen."

Owain was surprised. "Yes!" he said, pleased. "How did you know that?"

Gwirion was about to give a mocking answer but reconsidered and simply smiled. "Call it a hunch," he said. "But I can't help you."

"Why not?"

"I don't find her attractive, myself. I think she's sexless."

"How can you say that?" Owain scolded gently. "Those eyes? That smile?"

Before Gwirion could pretend to vomit, the door opened and the subject of their conversation stood in the doorway, looking slightly less elated than she had before. Because he had taken a few steps away, Owain was hidden behind the door as it swung inward, and Gwirion was backlit by the fire, his face in shadow. "I wondered if you would care to join me on the wall walk to look at the constellations," she said to Gwirion. "I have been displaced from my quarters for a little while and I thought to enjoy your company until my bed is ready."

"Oh, Christ," the harpist groaned, standing up and moving toward her so she could see his face in the light from the hall. "You're even worse than he is."

She started when she realized who it was. "I thought you were—"

"Yes, I know. He's right behind the door. Take him and good riddance. I assume you don't want a threesome."

He left. She took a step farther into the room so that she could

see Owain. "That was embarrassing," she said, not sounding embarrassed. "Did you hear my invitation?"

"Thank you, milady, I'd like that very much. But don't you think the king might like to join us?"

"The king is otherwise engaged," she said with tight finality. "He is entertaining one of our female guests." Seeing the startled look on his face, she laughed in the dim light. "I'm telling you all our little secrets. You must forgive me. I'm so desperate for somebody to talk to. And I've had more wine than usual. Would you like to come up and look at the stars?"

Owain said he'd be delighted to.

GWIRION wasn't sure what to do now. It was one thing when their guest was innocently drooling over the queen, but for the queen to encourage or return the attention drastically altered the picture, and suggesting they stargaze when there were no stars was a declaration of mischief. She must have learned that the king had gone for a "nap" and was motivated by a reckless sense of revenge. Surely she wasn't actually interested in Owain? Impossible, he decided, and dropped it. Noble had enough on his mind already. He didn't want to be a snitch.

SO it was without malice of intent—quite the contrary—that he worked his way through the crowded hall, across the chilly yard, and up the stairs to the king's chamber. As he expected, the king's massive doorkeeper Gethin was standing in the anteroom looking bored, ignoring the sounds of sexual rapture from within. Any vicarious thrill to be had from the job had worn off years ago.

"Some servant of Lord Huw's, is it?" Gwirion asked, remembering the conversation he'd overseen earlier.

"Actually it's his lordship's wife."

Gwirion looked impressed, then confused. "His lordship condoned it?"

Gethin grinned confidentially. "For a price. The king offered him a stable boy he had his eye on."

Gwirion was stunned. He forced himself to leer. "Ah. So everyone wins."

"Except the stable boy," said Gethin, and chortled. Gwirion pretended to join him, but turned his face away to hide a flash of anger. That explained why Noble had not used Gwirion as a go-between; he knew Gwirion would never broker such an arrangement, would probably even sabotage it. He sat on the floor, resting his back against the wall. It was cold down there, but the cold was numbing and he needed to calm himself.

After half an hour, the noises from the inner chamber stopped for good, and a few minutes later the door opened. A tall, graceful woman noticeably older than the king came out of the room in a very elegant russet gown that was in slight disarray. Her hair was uncovered and loose, tumbling long, dark, and unruly down the curves of her body, and she looked both sleepy and giddy at the same time. She was strikingly beautiful and exuded that rare smoky sensuality that deepens with maturity. Not noticing Gwirion, she gave the ogling doorkeeper an engaging smile as she passed him to descend the steps. Gwirion had never seen her here before today, but she must have had some arrangement with her husband to be so casual about cuckolding him. He tried to imagine the queen agreeing to such an arrangement and shook his head.

"Scrumptious," he said when she was out of earshot. "I want one." But he was still angry about the boy.

The king's voice called out. Gethin stuck his head into the room, received an order, and shut the door again, heading for the stairs down to the yard. Gwirion leapt to his feet. "The queen?" he asked.

The man nodded. Because of the horde of guests, the queen's chamber had been turned into a dormitory for the children, with her three women and several visiting nursemaids jammed in as well, so she and her husband were sharing his bed for the week no matter what his recreational intentions.

"She's not in hall, I'll get her," said Gwirion. "She's outside, it's cold, you stay snug in here." Before Gethin could respond Gwirion dashed out onto the open wall walk.

The temperature had dropped while he'd been waiting by Noble's door, and the cold hit him like a slap. He wrapped his arms around his body wishing he had brought at least a cloak. The winter night was biting but mesmerizing, cloudless, the moon so brilliant its light washed out the constellations. A hundred feet away from him, near the opening to her own antechamber, stood the queen and her admirer, each wrapped in purple cloaks, absurdly pretending to stargaze and clearly distracted by their proximity. Gwirion observed them for a moment, fascinated.

It had never occurred to him that the queen could feel desire, attraction, any independent emotion at all besides peevishness. He felt no protective loyalty toward her, but he knew he had to nip the infatuation in the bud. Their backs were to him and he could hear an unfamiliar cooing quality in the queen's voice that made him ill. Soundlessly, he drew up behind, easily visible but entirely unnoticed in their mutual absorption. As a silence settled on them and the queen smiled at her escort with an inexcusably stupid level of invitation, Gwirion lunged forward and clapped his hands together between them.

Isabel gasped and they both spun around. His teeth flashed in the moonlight.

"And how is heaven this evening?" he asked.

"What are you doing here?" demanded Isabel.

"Saving you from yourself," Gwirion replied loftily.

"You can't be serious," the queen said. "We're not even alone." She gestured to the guards standing watch over on the tower keep, a hundred yards away across the trench and twenty feet above them.

"You might have had an orgy and those men wouldn't have known of it. It would behoove Her Majesty to keep a guard with her at all times now," Gwirion retorted testily. "The castle's full of strange men. Even their allegiance to the king can't guarantee their behavior toward you. They can be very dangerous—one of them even wanted to compose a song about you."

"All right, now," Owain interjected awkwardly.

Ignoring him, Gwirion jerked his head up the walk. "He's ready for you."

Isabel looked down at her feet for a moment, stalling, pushing a stray pebble about with her shoe. "Is he in his chamber?" she asked at last.

"Better than that, in his bed. Probably asleep. Be grateful—he really worked over your proxy, she could hardly walk when she left."

"Don't speak to your queen that way!" Owain gasped, shocked, and raised a gloved hand to smack Gwirion, but she grabbed his arm and stopped him.

"Don't hurt him, it's the only hanging offense in the castle," she said resentfully.

"I'm doing you a favor coming here," Gwirion snapped. "He sent his doorkeeper for her. Do you know what would have happened if he'd had to look all over the castle for her and then bring her back with the report that she'd been alone up here with you? *Stargazing?*" he added sarcastically, waving at the moon.

"How is it any better if *you* tell him?" she demanded.

"I'm not going to tell him."

In the diffused light he could clearly see her surprise. He didn't know if she was relieved or annoyed—it must have been the latter, if she was doing this just to get back at the king for his tryst.

"Thank you," she said stiffly. She turned to Owain, bid him a polite but impersonal good night, and headed along the walk until she disappeared into Noble's tower.

Alone, the two men looked at each other in the moonlight.

"I'm sorry," Owain said, sincere and slightly sheepish. "I didn't realize how serious it was."

"Were you raised by wolves? A married woman, any married woman, knows better than to be alone with—"

"She invited me!" he insisted.

"Of course she did, she wanted to enrage her husband. You should have respectfully declined." Gwirion began to head back toward the stairs. "Excuse me, there's a boy in the stables who needs tending."

"Ah, did old Huw get his hands on him, then?" Owain asked casually.

Gwirion stopped and turned back to him. "You know about that?"

"Everyone in the western baronies knows Huw," Owain said with an awkward smile. "Not that anyone cares about Huw, but his wife . . ." He laughed nervously, then explained in a confiding tone: "She gave him three boys, but late in life, and something happened with the third and she couldn't conceive anymore. So he decided he didn't care what she did as long as she didn't care what he did. Their marriage is, mmm, well-known near the border. I doubt there's a local gentleman who hasn't . . . been affected by it."

"Are you one of them?" Gwirion demanded.

"It would be ungentlemanly of me to reveal that," Owain stammered.

Gwirion felt a wave of alarm. This cherub might be capable of things the king assumed he wasn't. "Owain, the king and queen don't have such a relationship. Her attentions toward you are not foreplay, they're to punish the king for his philandering. You're just a pawn. Don't think you're anything special."

BY the following evening, Gwirion was painfully eating his words.

· 9 ·

USES OF LOYALTY

Early December, 1198

 WAIN WAS BUSY all day in council, which was convened at the upper end of the hall since the council chamber wouldn't hold everyone. Mass had been said here as well, and when it was over Gwirion was entrusted with the children again, with admonitions not to discuss genitals. The usually unflappable duo of steward and usher were so overwhelmed with the details of feeding and housing the guests while also maintaining a presence in the war council that Gwilym, conquering his pride, asked Her Majesty for the honor of her assistance overseeing the daily operations of the household. She was delighted by both the distraction and the chance to be useful; other than the official greeting ceremony, which the king had offered her to be conciliatory, her presence was unwelcome at the war council. The sewing bevy was put out by the new assignment, although it gave them greater opportunity to cross through the hall, hurling demure glances at certain younger members of the court. They dutifully followed

their mistress into the kitchen and even kneaded bread, but they had an impressive range of excuses to refuse anything that might splatter sauce or oil on their tunics.

By suppertime Isabel was tired, but revived when they sat at board, returned to the radiance born of Owain's wide-eyed reverence. She behaved as if the awkward moment on the wall walk had never happened, and before the end of the meal, she was not merely basking in the youth's attention but actively encouraging it. She made little darting glances with her cat's eyes at him, often with a smile that bordered on coquettish. She used every excuse to brush against his sleeve or shoulder as they ate, and—apparently—a thrill ran through her with each contact. Gwirion watched with disgust, wondering when the king would correct her, but Noble seemed oblivious.

When supper was over and the trestles struck, the queen allowed Owain to follow her around the hall like a pup, trying to be helpful as she organized the servants to prepare the room for bedding down. There wasn't a thing he could do, being a guest, a lord, and especially a bumbling, smitten boy, but she encouraged his shadowing because it further publicized the infatuation and that would make it hard for Noble to ignore it. She sent a hall boy to get fresh bedding for one of the spaces that was sectioned off for privacy, and she managed very casually to herd Owain into the area that would be hidden when the curtain was pulled closed. She was reaching out for the curtain when a hand appeared from the other side of it, grabbed it, and whipped it aside. She started as she found herself looking directly into Gwirion's hard dark eyes. "People are talking," he muttered under his breath.

She shrugged, a triumphant twist in the corner of her mouth. "Let them talk," she said, and began to pull the curtain out again. He grabbed it just below her hand and stopped her. "They're not talking about you. They're talking about him. You're going to cause him trouble. To feed your pride." He gave her a knowing look.

She flushed with anger. "You're meddling," she said.

"No, milady, not." He smiled. "You are." He flashed the curtain closed again between them and was gone.

She turned around to look at Owain, who was standing near her politely waiting to be useful, or at least noticed. For a long moment she gazed at him, troubled by Gwirion's words. Owain, who hadn't heard the exchange, returned her gaze worshipfully. "Your Majesty?" he whispered at last.

"Owain." Expectant, even nervous, he took a step toward her. His closeness in the intimate space made her heart beat faster and she suddenly wanted to touch him. Instead she withdrew a step, nearly backing into the curtain, and cleared her throat. "Owain, there are certain circumstances in which men and women may be playful with each other without it . . . meaning anything." He blushed. "Apparently that's not the case here. I'm sorry if I misled you. You are a darling man and I enjoy your attention. But—" The curtain whisked open again behind her and Owain winced. She growled, "Leave me *alone*, Gwiri—" but was interrupted by her husband's voice.

"Gwirion?" he asked in an ironic tone. She spun around, inches from his chest, and he looked down at her without expression. "Gwirion is on his way to my chamber. In lieu of public entertainment, the two of you will join us there."

GWIRION didn't want to perform privately for this trio, but he grumpily made an excuse to the steward, wrapped his harp in its felt sheath, and downed a mug of ale before trudging as slowly as he could across the bailey, slushy from a wet afternoon snowfall, to the king's tower. He was the last to arrive. The king stood facing the other two in the middle of the well-lit room, a handsome, patient father hovering over his wayward offspring. He held a slender walking cane that Gwirion thought he remembered seeing earlier with one of the older visitors.

"Sit down, Gwirion, make yourself comfortable. Put the harp anywhere, you won't be playing it."

"Am I not performing?"

Noble shook his head. "No. You're here as witness. As audience. Isn't that a welcome change?"

Gwirion didn't respond. As he sat by the fire and laid his harp near him, he saw worry on the queen's face and troubled confusion on Owain's.

"Now then," Noble began, calmly and without a trace of anger. "There's no need to make a scene over this, but I want to clarify a few things. I am your king. This is my wife. Do you understand?"

Owain blushed and looked astonished. "Sire, I hope you don't think I had any intention of—"

Ignoring him, Noble turned to her. "It's not just a matter of your honor, or even my honor, it's a matter of the realm's stability. The mere appearance of impropriety from you right now is as dangerous as any reality, especially with Anarawd skulking about with his eyes glued to you. Until there is a son that is absolutely, inarguably mine, your dallying with another man will bring chaos. Even then, you are still *mine.* Do you understand that? If I see fit to dole you out to some young stud, then I will, but you don't make those decisions on your own."

She was aghast. "You may not dole me out to some young stud!" she hissed. "If I'm yours, then I'm only for you."

"That's true for my wife, but you're also my subject," Noble said evenly. "Are you not? Am I your sovereign?"

"Yes," she said impatiently.

He turned at last to face Owain directly. "Am I your sovereign?"

"Yes, sire," Owain stammered.

"Good," Noble said, smiling. "And here's a little trial to make sure we all understand what that means." He backed a step away from them. "Kiss her."

Owain blinked. "Sire?"

"I told you to kiss my wife. I know you want to and now I've ordered you to, so there should be nothing holding you back. Take a step closer to her, place your hand at her waist, and kiss her on the lips."

"Noble, don't do this," she said in a strained voice. "We understand your point, I understand it, I'll be obedient."

"If you want to show me you're obedient, kiss him back when he kisses you. Owain, begin please. Can you see, Gwirion?"

Gwirion said nothing. Owain turned to the queen and bent toward her with an apologetic expression, pecked her on the lips, and pulled away. The king laughed scornfully.

"Not like that!" he said. "A real kiss. Long. Slow. Taste each other's tongues. *Now!*" he demanded, banging the cane on the floor.

Again Owain moved toward her. She looked down, her jaw twitching.

"Chin up, madam," Noble said harshly.

Slowly she lifted her head. Any ambivalence Gwirion had had about this gathering was smashed by the heartbreaking humiliation on her face. Her skin was splotched and her expression was unbearable to Gwirion. He ducked his head away embarrassed, but he heard everything. There was a kiss, a long one, barely maintained through the queen's ragged breaths. Finally Noble gave them permission to pull apart and Gwirion heard her gasp for air.

"We're not through," her husband informed them. "Owain my lad, give me your hand."

Holding Owain's right hand in his left one, the king abruptly ripped open the front of her crimson kirtle and slapped Owain's hand onto her exposed breast. She cried out and tried to pull away but Noble's free hand held her fast. The fingers of his other hand pressed directly over Owain's and he squeezed Owain's fist open and shut around the giving flesh.

"Keep touching her," Noble ordered, releasing his own hand. "Squeeze her very small breast." Owain did, again with a profoundly apologetic expression. She looked over his head into the darkness, refusing to satisfy her husband with any reaction. "Slide your hand to the other breast," Noble ordered, and Owain hesitantly did it. "Does that feel good? Now put your mouth on her breast and suck on it like a mewling baby."

"Sire, please——" Owain began.

"Do it!" Noble shouted, furious. Owain, grimacing, kissed the queen's breastbone. "No, not there!" Noble chastised angrily. "Do what I tell you."

As if her flesh seared his lips, Owain gingerly moved his mouth over first one breast, then the other. She teetered, barely breathing.

Finally Noble announced, "You may stand up," and Owain pulled away from her, avoiding her eyes, his cheeks crimson. For a long moment there was complete silence in the room except for Isabel's unsteady breathing. Then Noble smiled at them with tremendous indulgence. "I know it's hard to believe right now, but I've done this as a favor to both of you. Oh, yes," he said in response to the glare his wife gave him. "Now that your attraction is irreversibly intertwined with humiliation and guilt, it will be much easier to resist it. I'm assisting you in averting adultery. Admittedly I have something to gain from that, as does the entire kingdom of Maelienydd except perhaps my cousin, but the real onus is on the two of you. Do we all understand why this had to happen? Do we?" he pressed when they didn't reply.

"Yes, milord," they both murmured.

"Good." He smiled. "But I want to be certain. So, my good friend Owain, you are going to do one more thing to demonstrate that you understand both your own status and my wife's." Cordially, he held out the cane to him. "You are going to beat her."

Owain stared at the stick as if it were poisonous. "I will not harm the queen," he said in a shaky voice. "She is my sovereign lady——"

"Nonsense. I'm your sovereign lord and she's my consort, the rest is all polite trimmings for minstrels to sing about. If I hadn't married her, the kingdom wouldn't even be in this predicament with Mortimer. We may be out on a battlefield together soon, my friend, and I must believe that I can trust my men to follow my orders without question. If you can't do that here, you can't do it out there, and I'll have to treat you as a deserter. You know what I do to deserters. So take the cane and hit her. Hard."

Owain looked ill as he reached out for the cane. Noble turned his shaking wife around and swept the long train of her headdress forward over her shoulder, then calmly ripped open the back of the kirtle so that she was exposed from neck to waist. Too disturbed to resist, she crossed her arms over her breasts and tensed against the blow.

Owain raised the cane to the level of his elbow. "Higher," Noble demanded. Owain raised it an inch. "Higher," Noble said, and repeated the demand until Owain held the cane far above his head. He drew a breath and steeled himself to strike.

In the hesitation before Owain's blow, Gwirion darted from his place by the fire and leapt up high enough to grab the cane from Owain's uncertain grasp. As soon as he landed he broke the cane over his knee with a muttered curse. He threw the pieces to the floor at the king's feet and glared at him, rubbing his shin.

The king glared back.

Then he burst out laughing.

"Anyone but you would already be halfway to the gallows, fool," Noble said companionably.

"If you'd kill someone over that, you're not even fit to rule sheep," Gwirion snarled.

Still the king smiled. "And you're the only one who can get away with that as well. You owe Twdor a cane, by the way." Gwirion glowered at him. "But you realize, of course, that you must balance rights with responsibility. You're allowed such behavior only because you're also obedient. Be obedient now, and kiss the queen."

"Go to hell!"

"Or I'll have you publicly whipped."

"And what reason are you going to give out? You're punishing me because I refused to molest your wife? Me, Noble?" Gwirion demanded in disgust, and throwing the door open he walked out of the room, limping a little from the cane's resistance.

They stood there a moment looking after him. Then Noble cleared his throat and turned back to his two pupils. "Well, that ruined the mood, now, didn't it?" He smiled. "All right, then, lesson

learned." Turning to Owain he said in a very deliberate tone, "I am sure we can all agree that this never happened." The young man nodded, silent and distressed, and Noble sent him away with an almost smarmy wave.

Alone, the royal couple studied each other. He picked up a blanket lying near the hearth, and wrapped it loosely around her shoulders. The gentleness of the gesture startled her, and she almost collapsed against him. He put his arms around her and helped her to the edge of the bed, then sat her down and lifted her legs onto the feather mattress so that she was reclining. He kissed the top of her head. "I'll have the kitchen send you up metheglin to soothe your nerves," he said softly.

"Where are you going?" she asked as he went for the door.

"To find Gwirion."

"Please—" She sat up, with a desperate look on her face. "Please don't punish him, Noble."

He stared at her. "You still are such a foreigner here," he said quietly, and left.

NOBLE went personally to the kitchen to order medicinal mead for the queen, and then to ask for Gwirion. "I need to speak with Huw ap Maredudd and his wife," he told another servant. "If they're not in hall listening to Hywel, they're in the visitors' tower. Tell them to meet me in the audience room."

It took longer to find Gwirion; by the time he was ushered into the whitewashed chamber, Noble had completed his business with the famously unorthodox couple, and Huw had already departed. His wife reclined quietly on one of the guests' bedrolls. She wore a dark long tunic, blending into the low-lit room. Gwirion was too busy being sullen to notice her. He cleared his throat to announce his arrival and crossed his arms, radiating sulky defiance.

"The queen asked me not to punish you," Noble said, standing in front of the fire.

"You weren't planning to punish me," Gwirion snapped back. "What do you want?"

"I have a peace offering, actually."

"Gold?" Gwirion said sarcastically.

"No, better than that. A woman."

"Your wife?" he asked with disgusted sarcasm.

"No, a willing woman. A wanting woman, even." A throaty female chuckle from near the floor made Gwirion turn to look just as Noble introduced her. "This is Branwyn, wife of Huw ap Maredudd. You intrigue her. That makes you a lucky fellow, trust me."

Gwirion recognized the siren who had exited Noble's room the night before. She was lounging in a position intended to encourage him to simply fall on top of her, and for a moment he gawked, astonished and willing to forgive the king anything. Then, unexpected and unwelcome, a wave of anger smashed against him. "Where's your husband?" he demanded.

"Gwirion, that's rude. Introduce yourself properly."

"My name is Gwirion and I want to know where your husband is."

Branwyn, amused by his brashness, purred, "He's occupied."

"Is he occupying the same boy as last night?"

"I don't know, it might be a girl tonight," she said mildly, and rearranged her limbs a little, invitingly.

"It's no concern of yours, Gwirion," Noble said, shifting with almost imperceptible discomfort.

"I saw the boy this morning. He was in bad shape."

Unconcerned, the woman shrugged. "They bounce back quickly at that age."

"That's an appalling attitude."

She had a low, throaty laugh. "It's just a servant boy, I'm sure he's used to it. You surprise me, Gwirion. You struck me as someone who'd approve of entertainment no matter what the form."

"Is Huw with the boy right now?" Gwirion demanded.

"I believe he was headed that way, but I don't spy on him."

Gwirion spun around and ran out the door. There was a pause.

"Did I scare him?" Branwyn asked.

"No," Noble said in an aggrieved voice. "He's going to the stables."

"Does he know that boy?"

Noble hesitated. "He's been that boy," he finally said, a rare note of pain in his voice.

T HE stables and smithy were across the courtyard from the hall. Gwirion approached at a run, skidding on slush, and came to a slithering halt outside the tack room. The noises coming from within needed no explanation. He shoved open the door and rushed in.

Huw had set a torch in the wall brace and what Gwirion saw made him shriek with rage. He flew at the baron and tore him off the boy, pushed the boy out of the room, and then shoved Huw to the floor and threw himself on him. Huw fell hard under his own bulk, but he was a trained fighter and collected himself immediately, and once Gwirion lost the element of surprise he was in trouble. When the king ran into the room moments later, Gwirion's face was cut and bleeding and one of his eyes was swelling shut. Huw was threatening him with a dagger, indignantly tugging up his drawers with his free hand.

"*Stop!*" the king demanded in panic. Huw checked himself with disgruntlement.

"This mongrel attacked me unarmed, without provocation! I—"

"He's not right in the head," Noble said quickly. "He's out of his wits, you can't hold him accountable for his actions."

"I was assaulted! Who's responsible, then?" Huw demanded.

"I am. Petition to me for redress."

Huw was angrily taken aback, and Noble didn't wait for a reply.

He knelt down beside his cowering friend, lifted him in his arms, and carried him out of the room, past the dumbstruck baron.

S HE had almost drifted off to sleep when a commotion outside startled her to alertness. Gethin threw the door open and Noble entered hurriedly with something in his arms that looked like a huge rag poppet. She gasped when she realized it was Gwirion and saw the state that he was in.

"What happened?" she cried as he laid Gwirion before the hearth.

"He was playing Defender of the Subjugated again but he took on a little more than he could manage," Noble said, annoyed, and stuck his head out the door, asking the doorkeeper to bring Marged up with her healing tinctures. "He'll have to stay up here tonight."

"On the floor?"

"What choice is there?" Noble said sharply, pushing the harp out of the way.

He moved briskly around the room, opening the carved wooden chests lining the walls in search of brychans and cushions. As he set about making a nest for Gwirion to curl up in, she swept the blankets off her legs and got up. "Let him have the bed," she said. "That chest is nothing but blankets, there's more than enough for the two of us."

He stopped what he was doing to look at her. "Are you sure?"

"I owe him at least that. He saved me from a beating."

"And I saved you from something worse."

"Fine. You take the bed and Gwirion and I will sleep on the floor together."

Noble glanced down. She thought it was a gesture of shame at first, then realized he was actually trying to hide a smile. "You don't have to believe this," he said, "but I wouldn't have let him strike you."

"How gracious of His Majesty not to oblige me to believe it," she said indifferently, going to the chest and flipping up the lid. She

began to pull the blankets out, tossing them into a pile. Noble lifted Gwirion up from the hearth and laid him on the bed.

"I intended to stop his hand. The purpose of that exercise was to make sure of his obedience, it wasn't to inflict pain on you. You were pained quite enough by then. I wouldn't have let anything happen."

"I wouldn't have let anything happen either."

"It was already happening," he corrected. "In front of the collected powers of my kingdom, you of all people were not treating me as king. In front of Anarawd, of all men, who would leap at any excuse to invalidate my offspring."

She paused in her activity and looked at him for a long moment. Then she turned her attention back to the chest.

THE next morning at breakfast, an uncomfortable silence filled the great hall. Everybody knew that strange things had happened the night before but almost nobody knew what, although it obviously involved the king's odd little confidant, who walked with a limp and sported an immense black eye. Huw and Branwyn avoided mass and demanded their breakfast brought up to them, and Noble followed it to their private tower room. He spent an hour placating and threatening by turn until Huw let the matter drop, and agreed to come down when the council resumed.

In the hall itself, over breakfast, Owain stayed as far from the queen's table as he could. Gwirion did likewise, unwilling to decide how nice he ought to be to her without the king around. This made it easy for Owain to approach him—or rather, to corner him, since Gwirion had no desire to speak with him, anticipating how the conversation would go. But Owain trapped him just outside the kitchen as he was peeling a hazel twig to clean his teeth.

"I want to thank you for last night," Owain began in a chagrined voice.

"You're welcome," Gwirion said awkwardly, squelching the impulse to find sexual humor in the line.

He looked shamed. "I'll always have to wonder what I would have done if you hadn't—"

"Oh, spare me, please. Spare yourself," Gwirion pleaded, chewing on the twig. "Forget it happened."

"I also know what you did later." Owain pressed on. "My man heard the servants discussing it at mass. They're all astonished. They're calling you the patron saint of stable boys."

"That's ridiculous, look at me, he ground me to a pulp," he muttered.

"I just want you to know, for whatever it might be worth, that I think you're a good Christian," Owain said, with such unselfconscious sincerity it made Gwirion himself self-conscious.

"Well, that makes everything all right, then," he answered sarcastically, clapping Owain on the back harder than necessary. He began to walk off but Owain detained him with a gentle hand on his arm.

"And I want to tell you that I envy you." His eyes had a childlike surety that unnerved Gwirion.

"You want to be the patron saint of stable boys? It's really not as glamorous as they say, and the wages are dreadful—"

"Not that. Everything else. The liberty."

Gwirion dropped the twig into the floor rushes, gleefully relishing the absurdity of this assertion. "The *liberty*? I can't take a wife or a mistress without permission of the king. I can't go anywhere without permission of the king. I can't *possess* anything, including money, and even when bighearted guests give me a gift on the side, for trifling favors such as saving them from having to flog defenseless women, say—no, Owain, it was a joke," he said, interrupting himself, as Owain immediately reached down to his belt for his purse.

Owain dropped the purse and looked back up at Gwirion. "Isn't that freeing? It simplifies everything. You don't have to worry about practical matters at all."

"Because I'm a parasite!" Gwirion snapped. "He keeps me com-

pletely dependent on him for *everything*. I live in a state of permanent humiliation. Liberty? You have no idea what you're talking about."

"You have the liberty to do what you did last night," Owain pointed out.

Gwirion frowned at him and then declared, "I'd trade that in for a chance to earn my own keep."

"Why don't you leave, then?" Owain asked.

"And do what?" Gwirion demanded. "He doesn't want me to go. The only skill I have is the harp and he'd have no trouble finding me if I were out in the world doing that. I have no other skills, I have no way to survive."

"What if somebody hired you into their household? Anonymously. You can read and write, can't you? You could be almost any official's assistant. Those are freemen positions—they pay well. If you moved up to an officer's status you might even get land."

"Who would hire me?" Gwirion asked in exasperation, more than ready to end this.

"I would," Owain said.

A day earlier, Gwirion would have laughed right in his face. But now he couldn't. He couldn't respond at all. He just stared.

"I'm new to my patrimony, I'm still establishing my household. Anytime you choose to free yourself of this place, my manor stands ready to welcome you. Not as a parasite, as a man. There is no reason for the king to ever know you're there. I'm the least of lords in the outlands of Gwerthrynion; there never was much traffic past my father's door and I don't think that will change."

Gwirion's knees almost gave out. It frightened him how seductive the offer sounded. Scowling, he asked, "That means no privileges, though, right? I can't attack pederast lords or serve arse-shaped bread loaves or insult stupid visitors, can I?"

Owain considered this. "Well, that sort of thing would likely get back to the king."

"So I'd have to give up what you call my liberty here."

Owain nodded. "Yes. In your own interest, yes."

It seemed a small price to pay for dignity.

"Thank you. I'll consider it." He leaned in to Owain. "You're a good man too," he allowed, grudgingly.

He worked his way through the hall to see if any children had finished their breakfast yet. That had been an aggravating conversation and as soon as he was free of Owain he knew the idea was preposterous—Gwirion could flee to Jerusalem and Noble would still find him. Anyhow, he would hardly know how to comport himself in the world away from Noble's side. It was the boy's ignorant earnestness that had made it seem possible for even a moment.

The queen caught his eye and gestured him over to where she sat alone at the high table. *Oh Christ,* Gwirion thought, *and now there's this one too.* Still, he flushed when her face registered anguish at his bruises.

"I heard how that happened. It was charitable of you."

"It was just stupid," he said dismissively. "Now I'll have to watch my back until Huw leaves. What do you want?"

"What was Owain talking to you about?" she asked, dropping both her voice and her gaze.

"He was singing my praises." That was all he'd intended to say, but something made him go on. "And he invited me to join his household if I want to escape this insanity."

She clapped her hands over her mouth and stared at him.

"What?" he asked, impatiently. It wasn't an outrageous proposal, and this morning she of all people should appreciate the temptation.

For a moment, she stayed looking at him, hiding most of her face behind her hands. She lowered them at last and gave him a sheepish smile. "For the longest time nothing in the world would have pleased me more than your going away," she said. "Now that there's actually a chance of it, I realize . . ." This was hard to say. "I realize you're probably the best friend I have here, and I'd miss you."

"Friend? When did we become friends?" Gwirion demanded, alarmed. Isabel straightened, looked embarrassed.

"Allies, at least. If not friends, allies. You've shown me I can rely on you and I'm grateful."

"No, no, we're not allies," Gwirion said, holding his outstretched

palms toward her and sounding almost panicked. "I don't do things for your sake. I do things for my sake. Period."

"You helped my brother—"

"That was to punish Noble for whipping me."

"Last night—"

"When something sickens me, I do what I can to stop it so I don't feel sick anymore. That's all," Gwirion said firmly. "Don't take it personally. I'm not anybody's ally—and *certainly* not a Mortimer's."

FOR days Noble spent sixteen-hour stretches huddled in the council room with smaller groups, interspersed with assemblies in the drafty hall that often became shouting matches. The queen, barred from politics and increasingly burdened with running the household, could not participate; in the evening her intention of querying Noble was checked when she realized how exhausted he was.

She puzzled about the understanding with Huw, but Gwirion's behavior confused her more. He was cold and snippish toward Noble, refusing to engage in their usual private banter at the supper table and one evening making a very public fuss about performing after the meal. Noble was gently solicitous toward him but the whispered, ferocious private conversations they had, at least once a day, appeared always to consist of Gwirion demanding something and the king, in a variety of sympathetic but condescending moods, refusing him. She was vaguely aware of Huw's continued evening activities, which she found distasteful but hardly outrageous, and supposed this was the source of contention, although why Gwirion would care about it so much was beyond her. Huw and Gwirion never spoke but glowered at each other across the hall. The entire dynamic confused Isabel, but she had no time to spare for asking subtle questions or even eavesdropping.

And when she did, it was to try to follow what was happening in the war council. Gwilym in their morning meetings would speak of

nothing but domestic matters, so her only knowledge of what was going on was what she could pick up on the periphery. The collected barons of Maelienydd were split into at least five different camps at the start of the council and Noble was by turns bullying and reasoning to bring them all into accord. A small majority followed his way of thinking: establishing a larger, permanent guard and possibly earthworks along vulnerable sections of the border, without actively seeking hostilities. The section of Maelienydd nearest to Mortimer's troops had been briefly taken by the Saxons long ago, and its reconquest by Noble's ancestors made it hard to defend because it was on the far side of Offa's Dyke, the enormous ditch that ran the entire eastern length of the country, built many centuries earlier by a Saxon ruler to keep the Welsh in Wales. The dyke had largely accomplished its task—but not in this small section of the middle March, where Maelienydd now spilled east beyond it by some two hours' ride. The area's few inhabitants just wanted to be left alone to raid black Welsh cattle or their English counterparts as fancy struck them. This was rich farmland valley, a rarity in Maelienydd, and yet privately Noble would almost have relinquished it—to anyone other than Mortimer. But whoever held it would then be perfectly positioned to launch a campaign of absolute destruction throughout eastern Maelienydd. With Mortimer's troops gathering on Thomas's land, the area had to be secured immediately. Noble acknowledged that winter was an ill-conceived time to set out on a campaign, but, he argued, it was a mild winter and Mortimer, in his slightly more temperate homeland, was in any event not going to accommodate their seasonal vagaries. He pressed that he was not advocating a military campaign for midwinter, only a preventive one. Thomas's release, he argued, should be obtained through diplomacy or not at all.

Others, led by Anarawd the Default Heir, were more traditionally Welsh and bellicose, and saw this crisis as an opportunity to push Mortimer farther east, take more farmland, and raid his thriving villages with impunity. It was, they agreed, a green winter, so supply sources would not be dire; in fact, there would be better winter fodder for the horses lower down, closer to the border. Some went

so far as to demand they besiege Wigmore Castle to free her brother, although everybody knew by now that Thomas's fate really only mattered to the queen. She silently applauded their sentiment but considered the plan a death wish. Another group, she gleaned, even thought that this was the perfect opportunity for Noble to reclaim true self-sovereignty and stop paying yearly homage to the English king, which made her want to laugh. That was *definitely* a death wish. Others just wanted to fight, with neither rhyme nor reason. Unsurprisingly, Efan, as captain of the teulu forces, was the ringleader of that group.

Still others, whose philosophy the queen was able to overhear in hall one morning after breakfast, gingerly brought up the idea of capitulation. Like Noble, they were tired of bloodshed; unlike him, they thought the best way to end it was to let the Normans claim themselves overlords and then go about their own lives, which would not really change a whit beyond higher taxes. They all detested Mortimer, but he was an excellent administrator over his own properties.

Noble smiled contemptuously at this argument. "The Mortimers have not been systematically killing off my family for the last five generations because they want to help you run your estates more efficiently," he informed them, in a mockingly gentle cadence, as if their feelings might be wounded by the revelation. He went on, slowly, speaking to them as if they were dull-witted; this same argument came up anew each day without its supporters ever acknowledging his rebuttal. "Mortimer has many relatives and retainers. He wants to keep them loyal, so he has to keep them in his debt, and what they want is land. Not just to live on, but to *own*, to collect taxes on, to work villeins on. This isn't the same as when Rhys and I would argue over Rhaeadr—that was about who would receive the land-use fee. This is about who receives the land itself and if we capitulate, it won't be you. The villeins are the only ones who wouldn't be massacred or at least left homeless, and frankly I don't think they care who's in charge as long as they get a hen and a week off from duties at Christmas."

The queen took a step into the hall from the kitchen with a de-

liberate cough, and the entire company of men turned around to stare at her. Noble shot her a furious look that ordered her to go away, but she stayed there, taking in everybody's gaze, from Owain's bemused but supportive smile to the many looks of suspicion and resentment. They saw her only as a Mortimer, she knew, and she had done nothing much to make them think otherwise. Of course he could not let her sit in on council; to them it was arguably like having the enemy eavesdropping. She would not have been surprised if they had asked him to divorce her now. "His Majesty my husband is telling you the truth," she said in a clear, loud voice, putting more than her usual effort into combating her accent. "Trusting Roger for anything will be your doom. He'll kill every landowner without compunction. You must do everything possible to keep him out of Maelienydd. Even—" Her voice nearly quavered, but she controlled it. "Even if it means removing Thomas from the issue entirely. I would be grateful for his release but he . . ." She almost couldn't say the words. "His fate is nothing compared to the fate of our kingdom. In fact," she pushed on, "although I realize much of what you need cannot be obtained with gold, half the sum of the queen's coffers will go to whatever effort His Majesty my husband deems most advisable. I challenge all the faithful among you to meet me in that endowment. There is nobody in this room who better knows the mind of Roger Mortimer than I do, not even Maelgwyn ap Cadwallon. I am telling you to trust our king." She turned abruptly and walked outside, taking deep, calming breaths in the relative quiet of the courtyard's damp grey morning.

She had not seen Noble's face change as she spoke. For the rest of the morning he was in better spirits, glancing now and then at the hall door to see if she would return. When dinner was called, he spirited her away to his chamber and made love to her with an affectionate exuberance she could barely remember ever existing between them.

There was another, final faction at council, perhaps the most troublesome, and the queen's conversion did nothing for it. This group was made up of all the men from the northwest, including Owain and Huw ap Maredudd, who was their spokesman. Llewelyn

of Gwynedd did not appear, but these border barons were intrigued by him. He had a great swath of Gwynedd under him now; he would reunite that ancient kingdom soon, and there was no reason to think he would stop there. He was phenomenally popular, his successes public mandate. His undeclared philosophy was that to defy the English invaders, the whole of Wales had to be united—under him. He had recently been wooing barons near his eastern and southern borders to align themselves with him. He had been delicate, almost discreet, with the hope that he could work his way outward through wobbling Powys and convince Noble and the scattered princes near him to acknowledge Llewelyn their overlord. Noble was faced with a bloc of fighters and landowners who wanted to throw their lot in with Llewelyn and let him decide how to use their collective resources. Noble was urged at least to marry one of his near kin to one of Llewelyn's as soon as possible. The arguments he made against capitulating to Mortimer were no good with this crowd. Unlike Mortimer, Llewelyn would not slaughter the landowners or even (it was posited) depose Noble—he would, at worst, merely demote the king to a petty prince. They said Llewelyn had an army of ten thousand men, mostly peasants but like all native fighters vicious and competent. They wanted that size host fighting with them; more important, they did not want it turned against them. Eventually, this faction argued, some form of central power would be needed to keep Wales out of English hands, some brilliant overseer to replace the remarkable, but lamentably dead, Lord Rhys of Deheubarth. It would almost inevitably be Llewelyn, so for Noble to align Maelienydd with him now, when he was offering and not ordering, was not weakness—it was savvy. Gwilym suggested asking Llewelyn to help them with this struggle, whose outcome would affect his own future, without discussing the fate of Wales as a whole (or any potential nuptials) until the border had been stabilized.

The king couldn't afford to alienate a single baron in his process of forcing consensus. His resources were too limited and his border, suddenly vulnerable on two fronts, could not afford a weak point.

The brief moment of levity from his wife's declaration had evaporated entirely by noon of the following day.

GWIRION was also busy, but his business was a mystery. More and more often, he turned the care of the children over to Angharad or Generys and disappeared. He would be spotted during the day, usually outside, in brief but intense discourse with one or another of the grooms or squires attached to the visitors. If the king had heard of this he would have interpreted it instinctively, and canceled the informal tourney that was planned to celebrate the end of council. Isabel noticed enough to wonder if she should mention it to him, but her curiosity was piqued. She couldn't believe Gwirion, for all of his recent anger, would try to undo the king's coalition efforts. Noble enjoyed any prank Gwirion came up with, and took it as a sign of affection for himself, so surely after this troubling week he would welcome a little harmless mischief.

BY the end of the fifth full day of arguing, a grudging consensus had been reached, and the forty guests swore an oath to stand behind their king and his decision. Noble would send more men east immediately, both to secure the area from Mortimer's potential raid and to scout out the weakest natural defenses in the border. He would approach Llewelyn, asking him to join him on the endeavor, but he would not consider yielding sovereignty to him as part of any strategy—nor would he offer up a relative for marriage. He would also call reserve troops to go into training should there be urgent need for an expanded army: Every healthy male of fourteen and older would be given the privilege of serving the king in arms.

After a supper that used up most of the remaining fresh meat, when the tables had been struck and the large and now familiar crowd had collected in a huge cluster as close to the hearth as possible, Hywel—and only Hywel—performed. The king had decided the tenor of the day called for serious, heroic, and patriotic recitations, and Gwirion had never bothered to learn any of these. The selection was familiar and inarguably appropriate: It was the epic elegy of the kings of Maelienydd in defense of their realm. The long climax, describing Cadwallon's murder by her uncle, did not humiliate Isabel as it had last summer. Now it upset her, deeply, and she felt a hopeless despair for the future of her two lands. "The hero has been slaughtered," droned the bard, "he who was so brilliant to behold." She had thought Roger sent her to Maelienydd so that a Mortimer heir might lawfully ascend to the throne within a generation, but she realized now that that was a diversion on his part, and romantic folly for her to have believed it. Roger Mortimer wanted Maelienydd for himself and he wanted it immediately.

She listened more carefully to the words this time, curious for a reference to Gwirion's supposed heroism. But there was nothing, only a passing comment that the brave and valiant prince had had a boon companion with him when he miraculously escaped Mortimer's assault. For a moment she was tempted to discount what Enid had said last spring, what the king himself had told her in September. But she realized that the duty of all bards was to elevate the king alone. It would not read well in the chronicles of history to know the kingdom owed its survival to a parasite.

To her side, Noble's face was wet with tears. More surprisingly, Gwirion—who had not spoken to the king for days—was on the floor beside the throne, away from her, sobbing into the skirt of Noble's long red tunic. Noble's hand brushed against Gwirion's dark hair in a vague, unconscious gesture of comfort. She suddenly understood that they were listening to a narrative whose details—or lack thereof—they themselves must have provided. She looked away, feeling intrusive.

But later in the evening, as the king was about to exit the hall, the queen saw the two men in confusing, bitter argument again. It ended with the king ordering Efan to keep Gwirion in custody until the castle had retired for the night. She tried questioning the pen-teulu, but the burly young man clearly knew nothing and lacked all curiosity.

THE next morning was sunny, and despite the cold the entire castle and much of the village turned out to watch the tourna-ment. The tourney field lay within the village walls, between the steep base of the castle mound and the lazy River Aron. It was small, the only level field for miles around and absolutely flat. There was a wooden terrace built out from the rampart below Noble's tower and Isabel had taken her accustomed place there; the wives and children of the fighters joined her bundled in mantles, cloaks, and blankets. The king, having finished an attractive but gratuitous romp around the field on his spotted Spanish charger (just to remind his people how magnificent a leader they had), arrived on the terrace, kissed his wife's hand, then stood up to declare the start of the tournament.

Most of the landowners and fighters were taking part in the mock battle, which would be fought with dulled lances and blunt wooden swords. The Welsh did not usually fight the way these men were about to. Welshmen were expert archers and spearmen and they eschewed their many chances for open battle to move, frequently on foot and without armor, through the wooded hills to surprise ene-mies who were playing by more conventional battle rules—and who, after more than a century, never seemed to learn better. That was how their fathers and grandfathers had defeated Henry of England more than a generation earlier. But it was part of any gentleman soldier's training to learn the Norman style of warfare, which was far more en-tertaining to watch than a spearing match.

At Noble's gesture, grooms held the horses' heads and the participants prepared to mount. He raised his hand so that he could signal the commencement as soon as their weight hit their saddles—but for many of them their weight never did.

It was a bizarre scene, three dozen well-bred, well-trained chargers bucking and rearing as they tried to unseat their own masters. More than half of the riders went down hard before the other half realized it was a universal problem and backed away from their mounts.

Twenty dizzy warriors stumbled about wondering what had happened to them while their grooms scrambled to reclaim the horses, most of whom shuddered indignantly, snorted, and trotted briskly away to the edges of the field. Nobody offered a solution and finally Cadwgan the marshal angrily ordered the saddle be removed from his own mare. He tore off the saddle pad, removed his gloves, and began to work his fingers around it. A moment later, he stopped, examined something he had found, and ripped it out of the blanket. He held it up for everyone to see.

A small iron spur had been embedded deeply in the blanket. The press of the saddle itself, even when firmly cinched, had caused the mare no discomfort, but the moment her rider's full weight bore down on the stirrup, the metal barbs on the spur had bitten into her back. All of the horses were reclaimed and unsaddled, and within moments every one was found to have at least one such burr in their saddle blankets. Anarawd's and Huw's had seven each. The villagers on the ground, and the castle staff high above on the wall walk, began to laugh, knowing at once who was behind it. The riders themselves were furious and began shouting at each other.

On the terrace, the amused children demanded of their nurses what had happened, as Noble shook his head and groaned softly to himself. "Good morning, Your Majesties," said a voice behind them. Everyone turned to see Gwirion, his eye still discolored and puffy from Huw's attack, wandering through the small crowd, tousling the heads of the children within reach as they called out to him affectionately. He had a grey mantle wrapped around his slender shoulders, and he settled kneeling on the floor between king and queen

without bothering to look down at the tourney. He was still annoyed at Noble and ignored him. "I overslept. Have I missed anything?" he asked the queen.

Noble clasped his hands, the two index fingers steeplelike pressed against each other, and hid his mouth behind them. The gesture usually implied suppressed amusement, but there was no amusement now. "You whoreson," he said quietly, staring down at the field. "How did you manage that?"

Gwirion peered over the edge of the railing to see what was happening. Several fistfights were about to break out among the fighters. "Oh, that was easy. The blacksmith's an obsessively devoted Christian."

"And?" Noble prompted crossly when that seemed to be the end of Gwirion's explanation.

"And you'll be needing a new silver cross in the chapel."

"You didn't!" the queen gasped, as Noble made a disgusted sound. "Gwirion, you must return that, you can't steal from the house of God."

"Oh, that's all right, I gave myself license to do it as long as I put it to good use, which I think this was."

"It's good use to infuriate the men I rely on to keep the kingdom whole?" Noble demanded, watching the collective reaction of the fighters grow uglier. "This is going to alienate—"

"I have it in hand," Gwirion said. He rose gracefully and waved his arms wide in a greeting to the crowd. There was a roar of approval from the commoners and a dawning bellow of indignation from the lords. The squires and grooms were conspicuously silent. "You seem to be having some difficulties down there," he chirped.

Among the angry cries, Lord Huw's voice boomed, "What's the excuse now, you little ass? This isn't the work of somebody who's out of his head, it's the work of somebody with too much idle time on his hands!"

Anarawd's voice, distinct and slightly nasal, added more loudly and threateningly, "What's the *king's* excuse? He binds us to an oath and then makes fools of us! Is this a man who deserves our obedi-

ence?" The rest of his accusation was drowned out in furious, loud agreement from the others.

Noble, his face like Gwirion's looking out over the crowd, leaned in close to him and whispered threateningly, "If he foments rebellion from this, I'm hanging you for treason."

Gwirion ignored the comment and held his hands up for silence, which took a moment to achieve. "Do you believe this to have been a prank? This wasn't a prank! This was a lesson! How do you think I did it—all by myself? Of course not. I had the help of everybody's grooms and squires. Everybody's. *Wait!*" he called sharply as the men, now furious at their own underlings, looked for those it was within their power to punish. "Wait! Hear me out! I asked no one to plot against his own master. I asked them all who their masters had any minor grudge with, and then convinced them they would be acting in their lord's interest to perform a small act of mischief against that person—one single, apparently harmless action. Your lads all acted in service *to you.* That's their duty, don't punish them for it. The lesson here, however, is that they were acting in service *only* to you. The spirit of this past week, all your striving for cohesiveness and unity—you haven't bothered to share that need with them. To communicate it to *your people.* Have you? And this is the result. Consider it. And now, if you don't mind, I have other tykes to enlighten—"

The children cheered behind him, thrilled that their favorite nurse had turned out to be the perpetrator of the entertainment, but the men were not going to let him go.

"You're not getting away with this!" Huw called out. "You shamed us, now you come down here and be shamed yourself!" This got everybody frantically excited. Gwirion tried to quiet them but they were too exercised.

Suddenly Noble leapt up and shoved him aside, so roughly that he stumbled into the queen. Isabel, wincing at the enormity of trouble Gwirion had just brought upon himself, reflexively held out a hand to steady him. The king held up his hands and the lords silenced themselves at once. There was a pause. "Tell me what he's done wrong, and I will punish him accordingly," His Majesty offered.

"He's made fools of us!" Huw declared in outrage from below.

"Has he?" Noble seemed to muse. "I would say rather that he's demonstrated something we should have understood ourselves. This will *prevent* us from making fools of ourselves again, when the stakes are higher. If anything, we owe him a debt of gratitude."

"Gratitude?" half the lords cried in a shared, incredulous voice.

But the king's glare was enough to silence them again. "I am your king," he reminded them, slowly. "And I'm telling you we are grateful for the lesson we've just learned. Who defies me?" There were unhappy looks and noises exchanged, but nobody spoke another word. Noble smiled down at them with all apparent calm. "Then we are all in accord, and Gwirion shall have the best cut of lamb tonight at supper for his thoughtful demonstration."

Without another word, he turned his back to the field and began to walk off the terrace, gesturing for his startled wife to follow him. He grabbed Gwirion's wrist on the way and pulled him brusquely along beside him. They stopped at the back edge of the platform and he pivoted Gwirion to look straight at him. Knowing there were many eyes upon them, he seemed to smile at his friend as he informed him between clenched jaws, "I should have killed you right in front of all of them." Then he released Gwirion's wrist and began to climb the steep wooden steps up to the base of his tower.

"That was very dangerous, Gwirion," Isabel whispered, more amazed than chastening.

"Of course it was *dangerous*," Gwirion retorted, watching Noble ascend. Despite his cocky tone, he fidgeted a little. "There'd have been no purpose to it otherwise."

"You would really risk your life just to show the barons up?"

Gwirion made a face and shook his head, his eyes still raised, following the king. "I didn't risk my life. He *should* have killed me, but he never *would* have."

"How can you be so confident of that?"

Gwirion gave her an arch look. "Apparently, Your Majesty, it seems that I'm a fool." He mounted the stairs, following the king.

ENGAGING ENEMIES

Winter, 1198–99

N THE DEPTHS of the midwinter holi-
days, Noble made the decision he'd grimly anticipated for a month.

Immediately after the war council, Llewelyn
had agreed—in theory—to go with him to confront Mortimer. Unsurprisingly, the other Welsh
princes all demurred, with the promise that if it turned into a military engagement they might reconsider.

The mild weather had brought no snow, but they went three
weeks without an hour of clear sunshine and Isabel thought she
would soon go mad. Throughout December Noble was rarely at Cymaron and hardly ever off his horse, riding hard from one section of
his kingdom to another, checking the state of the reserve host being
trained, conferring with the border troops, meeting with Llewelyn to
get a measure of the man, and vainly seeking council with Roger
Mortimer himself. The single time Mortimer agreed to meet, exactly
on the legal border at the windy crest of what the English called
Stone Wall Hill, he sent an envoy in his place. Noble recognized the

man and was convinced he had been part of the ambush twenty years ago; that struck him as something Mortimer might do, but he held his tongue and his temper for the sake of diplomacy. The envoy claimed that there was nothing to discuss. There were no hostilities planned; the troops massing on Thomas's estates were simply training for a possible Crusade—Noble was even chastised for reneging on his own pledge to take the cross years earlier. Thomas, it was finally claimed, was his uncle's honored guest at Wigmore Castle, remaining entirely at his own pleasure.

Llewelyn offered more satisfying audience. Noble was impressed with him at once, finding himself for the first time in his life in the company of a true peer. He was a great strategist and had a zeal, a focused ferocity for a united Wales that made it necessary to take him seriously. As adversary or comrade-in-arms, he was clearly a force to be reckoned with. It was almost enough to make Noble reconsider the idea of marrying their families somehow. But the price of his assistance would not be cheap: Noble would not only back him in his claims to the throne of Gwynedd, he would lend material aid for Llewelyn to achieve it. Noble demanded a written oath that the younger prince's sovereign ambition would find saturation at Gwynedd's borders, then clasped hands with him on the agreement and hurried home to Cymaron to arrive on Christmas Eve.

Christmas, beginning with the solemn predawn caroling in chapel, was understated and grim. Rituals both familiar and exotic to the queen's sensibilities were observed with lackluster obedience. Even the much heralded passing on of linen, which she had wondered about since her blunder with Enid and the kerchief, was anticlimactic. It was exactly as in her own home: She gave the court officials linen underclothes and the king gave them woolen dress livery, red emblazoned with his golden lion *rampant regardant*. The upset over the kerchief remained inscrutably stupid to her. The teulu were given their yearly gift of a pound each in coin, and every family in the village was sent a Christmas hen. All other Yuletide rituals were ignored; there was no impetus for cheer.

IT was Thomas's letter to the queen that tipped the scales toward action. Noble had been willing to keep a minimal force at the border, to train reserve troops without conscripting them to duty—until a letter arrived in Thomas's hand, addressed with sensational rudeness to Isabel Mortimer of Cymaron Castle, affectionately begging her to "join the family" at Wigmore Castle for a New Year's visit. It was neutrally worded, too neutrally worded, and obviously dictated. Her husband was not included in the invitation.

"That's not even *subtle*," Noble complained with a harsh laugh when she brought it to him. He had not seen her so upset since Adèle's death.

Once it was clear that hostilities were imminent, most of the penteulus in the kingdom begged permission to pillage Mortimer's villages on day raids and snipe his armies as they camped. The king appreciated the impulse, but refused it. His people had reacted that way for centuries and had little to show for it now. The Welsh had never been partial to diplomacy, and with Richard on the English throne the Marcher lords weren't either. Noble was determined to change that: For the first time since King Henry's reign, a territorial issue would be resolved by parley.

But parley only worked when one did not seem desperate for it, so he summoned the largest host the kingdom had ever seen, intending to bring them to the border, ideally to do nothing but sit there for weeks and look fierce. There were desperate outcries against this unorthodoxy, of course: A winter campaign was a death wish. Yes, said the envoys from the lords who protested, it had been a mild winter so far and yes, all signs suggested it would continue to be so until Lent, but winter was winter—they would all be hard-pressed for food and fodder. Noble listened and nodded and continued to prepare. Mortimer was collecting a massive army on Thomas's land and he had to be blocked from using it. Nothing else mattered.

When Llewelyn of Gwynedd agreed to join the Maelienydd host

at the border, with his own men, the protestations instantly and reverently subsided.

THE collected host, all under the charge of the king's ecstatic penteulu, was organized into five small armies. Those from the center of the country would convene outside the castle the night before setting off to the border, bivouacking on the tourney field while their commanders slept in the castle hall. The western, southern, and northern forces would join them at the eastern border, where troops had been since right after the war council. For a week before they set off, the castle was a maelstrom of preparation as rations for both the men and those who stayed behind were assigned, measured, packed, and stored or carted eastward. The baker took over the village oven to make sure there would be enough bread the first few days at camp, and brought huge stores of oats plus dozens of hens for the eggs. He left his son behind to bake for the castle household, which would have to survive on barley and rye. The butler took his wife, and three kitchen girls in training under Marged went as well. The blacksmith closed his forge and fit what he could into half a large cart; the other half was piled with tents for Noble and the other commanders. The beds the queen had brought from England were not collapsible, but the king did not even seek one that was, choosing instead to sleep like his men, on a brychan stretched over straw. Most of the castle officers went along, leaving only Marged the cook, Gwilym the steward, Hafaidd the usher, and Goronwy the judge to command a sea of pages, chambermaids, aging attendants, and villagers under temporary hire. Ordinarily in war, the queen would go on circuit for safety, but there was no precedence for a winter campaign and anyway, Noble had insisted again, it was not yet a war and hopefully never would be.

The night before the host left for the Marches, a supper of roast geese was prepared for the commanders and the teulu in the hall, and

double rations of ale were given to the men bivouacked outside. This could hardly make up for the near scandalous disruption of calling people to arms during the Christmas holidays and squelching riotous evenings of songs and caroling, but it would have to suffice. At evening mass the chapel was lit brilliantly with hundreds of candles; after the ceremony, Noble offered a week's leisure for all when they returned.

"Unless you lose," Gwirion commented later, during a quick moment alone with the king before the audience-chamber hearth.

"I've never lost to Roger Mortimer," Noble said.

"You've never faced Mortimer without Lord Rhys beside you," Gwirion said, speaking the thought Noble had been trying to will out of his mind. "But he is dead this time, you know."

"Well, now I have Llewelyn beside me, and judging by popular gossip that's even better," the king said with minor irritation. "And I truly hope it never comes to fighting."

"That's blasphemy! Aren't we supposed to be bloodthirsty?"

Noble closed his eyes, looking exhausted. "Even I have sickened of the battle."

Later in the evening, Hywel, almost doddering now, attempted to fill the hall with his shaking voice while Gwirion was called down to the field to entertain. A cozy, dull cloud cover masked the waning moonlight and made the evening mild. It was Twelfth Night, and a farmer-soldier from Llanbister had brought to camp a decorated horse's skull, a Mari Lwyd, so Gwirion traded in his harp for a pipe to lead a cheery, drunken procession around the camp. But out here there were no women to tease and no feast to sit down to—the main reasons to ramble about with a skeletal horse, after all—and when the paraders were drunk enough to fall over, he returned to the castle. It was an early night. There had been a short round of carols inside, but the usual merrymaking was canceled.

Before Gwilym the steward retired for the evening, he went into Noble's audience room to receive the great seal for safekeeping from Gwirion's mischief in the king's absence. Before he left, he made an

offer—looking slightly self-conscious but, as ever, dignified—that would once have been unimaginable.

"My duties will be doubled in your absence, sire."

"You always handle it with grace." Noble managed to smile, although he looked very stressed and tired. "As you did for my father before me."

Gwilym grimaced. "Thank you. It has always been my honor to be your deputy." He paused. "Considering the circumstances, Her Majesty will have a hard time of it here. There's little to occupy her attention—I understand construction has stopped at the abbey for the winter."

Noble gave him a disbelieving, conspiratorial look. "Are you saying what I think you're saying?"

"If it would assist to . . . maintain her current desirable demeanor, I will yield some of my castellan privileges to her. I must admit she has more than proven her potential."

It took Noble less than a second to decide what he wanted to do with this opportunity. "That's very generous of you, Gwilym. She may well take you up on that."

SHE was already pacing around his torchlit chamber when he arrived, even tenser than she had been for weeks now. He understood, more than he could afford to let her know, how difficult all this was for her. When he returned, when it was over, he would tell her how genuinely he admired her reserve, but the comment given now would likely, under pressure, somehow lead to argument. She was wearing only her silk shift and Noble's large woolen chamber robe, her braids hanging down to her waist, and as always in this outfit she looked like a child playing dress up. When Isabel heard him entering, she stopped her pacing and took a deep, nervous breath. "I want to go with you," she blurted out.

He stared at her and then laughed gently. "That's not even open for discussion, madam."

"If I stay here with so little to do, I'll go mad."

He couldn't help smiling at how neatly she'd walked into the game. "I seem to recall your poring over law books last summer with Goronwy. Would it help distract you if you stood in for me at court?"

She frowned. "But that's the steward's privilege."

"It could be yours," he said. "And so could many other things."

"Gwilym would be outraged. Goronwy would throw a fit!"

"I don't make offers I can't honor, Isabel." He raised one brow at her. "Let's play a little tit for tat. One castellan duty for every novelty you agree to try tonight."

She almost laughed, but duly made a disgusted face instead. "That's perverse."

"I need some perverse distraction and so do you, I think. Take off your things and lie down on the bed." She realized he was serious and stared at him in silence, unmoving. "Excuse me," he said in a sterner voice. "I am leaving here in ten hours to put my life at risk for your idiot brother—because of a marriage contract that has yielded me nothing that it should have. Take off your things and lie down now."

With a loud sigh of annoyance she obeyed him, pulling off her shift as he unlaced his boots and stripped off his own tunic, hose, and drawers. He sat over her on the bed, unceremoniously pushed her legs apart, wet his fingers with his tongue, and lubricated her. She made a constricted sound in her throat and growled at him, but he only gave her a mischievous smile and shook his head.

"I'm seeing you beg me to bind your wrists to the bedposts."

"I'm seeing you being mistaken," she retorted. She crossed her arms across her bare chest and glowered up at the bed canopy.

"If you'd like to be my deputy in court," he said, grinning, "you will beg me to bind your wrists to the bedposts. To start with. I promise you'll enjoy this game more if you play it with enthusiasm."

He ran his tongue across her lower belly and she gasped, then broke into frustrated, angry laughter from the sheer tension of the night.

H IS final farewell was to Gwirion, whom he scared by awakening, personally, two hours before dawn.

"Sire?" Gwirion whispered when he sensed rather than saw the familiar presence kneeling in the entrance to his closet. "What are you doing here?"

"If these are my last two hours alive at Cymaron," Noble whispered in response, "I shouldn't be sleeping through them."

"Molest your wife, then," Gwirion said, flattered by the visit.

"I already did that. She surprised me tonight, but she hasn't Enid's staying power."

"Neither have I," muttered Gwirion, but trundled the covers away. "Well then, are you coming in or am I going out? It's warm in here at least, and I don't think there's much privacy anywhere else."

The king ducked his head down and crawled into the space. Gwirion lit a candle and the two of them glanced briefly at each other in the dim light. "This is homey but it's rather tight. How did you and Corr both fit?"

"We were *very* close," Gwirion lisped precociously.

Noble cleared his throat. "I have something to say to you," he whispered, suddenly serious. Gwirion considered him for a moment, guessed what it was, and made a face of mock amazement.

"Don't tell me His Royal Highness is about to apologize," he said. "Not now! We have no witnesses, no artists to immortalize the moment, no bard to compose flowery monotony about your spiritual transformation."

"Be quiet or I'll cut your tongue out," Noble said impatiently. "I don't have much experience with this and I don't want you misunderstanding."

"My ears are yours."

Noble grimaced. "I don't care that Huw prefers partners that are half the size of his wife. And I don't care if he prefers it when they're not very eager about it."

"*You* don't even do that," Gwirion protested.

"Gwirion," the king said bluntly, "there is absolutely no difference between Huw and myself."

Gwirion gave him a disbelieving look. "There's a huge difference. Huw is bad to his partners, you're good to yours."

Noble gave his friend a didactic smile. "Only because I enjoy it. That's not a difference in morality, Gwirion, it's only a difference in taste."

"You give them a *choice*, he forces them."

Noble laughed comfortably. "And what sort of choice does a woman have when she's invited to go to the king, when she knows the king can take her anyhow?"

"Noble, you don't touch them if they're even just a little bashful. I've *been* there, I've *seen* you."

"That's a choice I'm entitled to make because I am the one with all the power."

"It's a choice you make because you're a good man," Gwirion declared firmly. "I wouldn't pander for you otherwise."

"You're confusing goodness with preference," Noble corrected him. "I take no pleasure in a woman's indifference, and certainly not in her resistance. I wrestle with enough recalcitrance in council—and with you, for that matter, although at least with you it's occasionally entertaining. I like the flattery of ready enthusiasm in *some* facet of existence. That's the premise of my gallantry—I'm simply taking what I want in the manner that I want it." He gave his friend a droll look. "That's sensual gratification, Gwirion, not goodness. In that way I'm no different from Huw." Gwirion looked stricken, almost nauseated, and said nothing. After a moment Noble, his expression softening, pressed on. "You were right, though, there's an apology in here." He paused, took a breath to collect his words. "It was not wrong of me to offer Huw those children. It was a kind of quid pro

quo—and not for Branwyn, by the way, she was just a rather marvelous perquisite."

Gwirion looked at him uncomprehendingly. "What did you get out of it but Branwyn?"

"The security of Huw's allegiance."

Gwirion blinked. "You're not telling me he swore loyalty to you because you let him sodomize your stable boy."

"He swore loyalty because we have an understanding now, that we will look out for each other's interests. That there are checks and balances, but I am the dispenser of favors, and he must be deserving of such favors if he wishes to receive them. He's seen that I will dispense with my subjects as I see fit, but he knows that applies to him as well as to a stable boy. What happened that week was a necessary transaction, and in itself it was entirely unobjectionable. My failing was in my obligation to you. You were distressed about the children and I know why."

Gwirion looked away awkwardly. "My distress has nothing to do with . . . *that*." He tugged at a fraying thread on the cuffs of his breeches.

"I thought they were killing you too," Noble said. "I thought I'd lost both—"

"We agreed not to talk about it," Gwirion insisted sharply, looking up.

Noble retreated. "Fine. That is the apology. I am genuinely grieved that what happened disturbed you. You must understand something, however, Gwirion: I'm grieved but I will not modify my behavior for it. Not because I'm a monster, but because I'm a king. I may *wish* to spare a child from trauma, I may *wish* to spare your being distressed about it, but I *need* to protect my kingdom's northwest border."

"But you do wish you could have spared him, don't you?" Gwirion demanded, sounding almost plaintive.

"My wishing something that I can't act on contributes nothing to the well-being of the kingdom, so it doesn't matter whether I wish it or not."

"Drop the king-talk," Gwirion said irritably.

"For important matters, I have no other language," said Noble quietly. "That's why your nonsense is always such welcome relief."

Gwirion said nothing for a long time. Although their faces were only inches apart, the king could not read his eyes in the dimly lit space. Finally, Gwirion looked up and met his gaze. "I accept the apology," he said aloud. To himself he kept the thought, unspoken, *You are becoming a horrible man and I must escape you.* But the native affection he had for that face, more familiar than his own, and the eyes more attentive than any mother's gaze he had ever known, made such a choice, however necessary, ultimately impossible, and he knew it.

LISTLESSNESS settled over the castle when the king and his men had gone. The exception was the queen, who (indifferent to the indignant mutterings around her) reveled in the castellan duties she had earned. There were many: Each morning after attending chapel and breaking her fast, she met with Gwilym and Marged to go over the day's schedule. Every few days she met with the almoner, the laundress, the seamstress, the interim captain of the shriveled castle garrison, the mayor of the village, and the marshal's son Ednyfed, standing in for his father, who was with the king. After the morning meeting, once a week she would sit with Goronwy the judge to listen to civil matters from villagers and other subjects who had traveled sometimes days on foot. When there were no complications, the judge would simply rule on cases; when his judgment was challenged, the matter was normally turned over on appeal to the king or his deputy to consider with the council. But it was wartime and most of the council was at the front, so the queen found herself in the extraordinary position of being a one-woman, foreign-born appellate court. Goronwy was furious at first, but Gwilym calmly backed her claim that she was replacing him as the king's deputy—and further pointed out that there was no actual law forbidding such a thing; it

had simply never been the custom. Once the judge accepted that they were not breaking any law, he rescinded his objection with almost comical speed, although most castle workers continued to cast a disapproving eye on the queen's mysterious and shocking assumption of authority. The first day of court trials, suppliants did not hide their unwillingness to receive judgment from a woman and a foreigner. She was gracious with them, offering them the opportunity to return when the king was back from the border. Most took her up on this but a few, in the end, did not, and by chance or fancy those appealing liked her judgment—the peasant who cut down a sacred oak grove; the penniless young freeman who'd just inherited his father's lands but not his title and his brother who'd inherited the title but no land; a woman accused of killing her husband's concubine. With no bias, conditioning, or instinct to control the population, she was truer to the letter of the law than Noble ever could have been and word quickly spread that the queen was a prudent, fair adjudicator. Already by the second week, people had begun to argue with the judge's sentences simply for the novelty of her attention. Native law was meticulous and complicated, and she found her eyes glazing over trying to understand all the taxation schemes for the various uses of land. For a people more pastoral than agricultural, they had rules about land use and distribution that outgarbled Norman feudalism.

She also assumed the financial burden of the housekeeping, setting the budget and keeping track of who spent how much for what. There were no fees to the crown for months to come now, which spared her from the awkward situation of accepting capital from people she knew lacked enough to spare. She had never been comfortable doing this for her brother's manors, and was glad to avoid it here. On a couple of occasions she found herself awkwardly accepting minor fees for things she could not believe Noble ought to benefit from: the loss of every maiden's virginity, for example, enriched the king's coffers even more handsomely than it did each ex-maiden's. She wondered sardonically how the math worked out when Noble himself was the responsible party.

But more than the mental gymnastics of a day in court, what left

her most uncertain was what to do with Gwirion. Normally he was forever busy at errands, performing, rehearsing, or pursuing other vague activities she had never bothered to look in to. But with the king gone, he sank into almost immediate lethargy. He would do anything that was asked of him, quickly and efficiently, from performing acrobatics for the village children to helping prepare grain for the mill, but left to himself he was like a puppet without a puppeteer.

COURIERS, running in relay along preestablished routes, came to and from the eastern border regularly. The temperature held mild, but with the mountainous terrain and unpredictable weather, it took at least a day for the fastest of them to reach the front, and much longer when there was mud or driving rain.

The only thing that put Isabel on edge were Noble's reports. They had arrived without incident, he wrote, stopping only at Pilleth's holy well for a blessing from the statue of the Virgin there. But once they were encamped near Llanandras, Mortimer had mocked them and told them to go home. They had demanded Thomas's free presence in person, and Mortimer stalled for days. The next report told her that Mortimer had ambushed and imprisoned her old coot uncles, Walter and Ralf, while they were on their way to petition Prince John for Thomas's release. Finally, Noble wrote, Mortimer had come to parley at the River Lugg, but he was cagey and indirect and at the end of the discussion, nothing at all had been justified or promised. There was no further parley.

But after five tense days, a band of teulu, going stir-crazy camped out through endless winter nights, stupidly crossed the border to raid the English village of Lingen, which belonged to Mortimer— and every day since then had seen a retaliatory counterstrike from each side in turn, skirmish after skirmish that were almost as difficult to quell as a full-out battle would have been to prosecute. The messengers came less frequently, and the queen's brow was perma-

nently creased. When news finally arrived again from the east, it came in a coffin. Hywel the bard had fallen early on, sword in hand, during the largest engagement so far: a brief battle in which Mortimer had almost effortlessly annexed the Maelienydd valley that had been the no-man's-land between the armies. He moved the whole of his force onto the richest soil in Noble's kingdom and settled them there: squatters, invaders, victors. He did not press his advantage, he did not attack the native host. He simply stayed.

When this news reached Cymaron, Hafaidd and Gwilym spent a fretful day calculating what smallest possible company could defend the castle in a siege. With the queen's sanction, they chose from among the guards those least likely to contribute much in battle. They kept these men at Cymaron to form a skeleton garrison; all the rest, they sent to the front. Years later, two old men in an altered world, they would trace the events of that winter and spring backward through time and agree that the folly of their decision was to blame for all that followed, although they could not possibly have foreseen the worst of it.

THE morning after the bard's burial, on the first day it was truly winter cold, Castell Cymaron was alerted to a sound no one had heard in years: five urgent staccato notes sounded on a trumpet, repeated many times. People looked up from their work—plucking geese, laying down new strewing herbs, fixing ploughs, balancing books, feeding horses, tending fires, hearing confession, letting blood—wondering what it meant. Then, almost as a single unit, the castle population realized they were under attack.

Panic swept the bailey and everybody instinctively scuttled into the hall, where the queen and the judge had been holding court. Gwilym, with the prescience Isabel had grown to admire, was already standing at her side. She turned to him, grim but unshaken. "The keep?" she asked.

The keep tower was intended for protection in an attack, but the castle's design required crossing over a trench to reach it from the courtyard. Since marauders were usually sighted from a distance on these high broad hills, there would normally be time to get up into the keep, but the trumpeter's signal was the code for an imminent siege; she was concerned that there would be no time to get people safely across. "I'll learn more," the steward offered, and went out to the courtyard.

Gwirion wandered in as Isabel was trying to soothe the visiting women petitioners. He had heard the alarm and imagined the queen would be hysterical, so he chose to appear with an insouciant attitude to accentuate her fear. He entered eating a heel of barley bread Marged had told him he couldn't have, chewing slowly and loudly to demonstrate how unconcerned he was about the chaos.

"Gwirion," said the queen's voice beside him, with a calm authority he had never heard and could hardly believe. "We may be moving to the keep and we'll need your assistance." She pointed to an elderly couple from another valley, at court on petition. "Help those two." Without waiting for an answer, she efficiently shifted her attention to a large man, a villager, and told him to carry a woman who was blind. Gwirion was floored by her levelheadedness; he wasn't sure whether he was disappointed or impressed.

Gwilym returned looking confused. "There's been some mistake, milady," he said. "It's nothing but a small company outside the barbican. The guards at the village gate let them in and they made their way up to the castle without incident. They're not even on horseback. I would recommend you come speak to them, Your Majesty."

"Why did our man sound the alarm?"

"We're so lightly garrisoned right now, all of the guards have been on edge." He did not add his personal opinion: Feeling insulted for being kept behind, these men were hoping for a crisis so they could prove themselves, and they were only too eager to read drama into any unexpected circumstance.

She called for a mantle and tied it closed, then stepped out of

the side door with him into the cold, grey morning air, descending the steps to the main gate. She nodded to the deputy porter, a gaunt tanner from the village who bowed nervously, flustered by her proximity. He opened the small eye-level panel in the gate to reveal an enormous jowl and moustache. "Identify yourself to Her Majesty," he ordered the moustache.

Its owner descended enough to show his face in the opening. He was about Noble's age and coloring but much rougher looking, and reddened from the cold. "Good morning!" he said to the porter as if they were old friends. "Let us in, would you? We're freezing."

"Identify yourself," the porter repeated.

The man proclaimed himself Cynan ap Dafydd, baron from Gwynedd and kinsman to Prince Llewelyn.

"Why aren't you fighting with him if you're kin?" Gwilym asked, moving closer to the gate.

"I've been keeping an eye on things at home. We're on our way to the Marches now to join my prince and his men, but we needed to warm ourselves and possibly restore provisions. We'd pay for that, of course."

"And why did my man sound an alarm?" the steward persisted quietly.

"Well, there's a lot of us," Cynan said. "The whole of my company stands outside the gates. He might have been a bit overwhelmed. It's a misunderstanding. I'm not asking you to shelter all of them, just my teulu, and there's not many of them. We need a day to regroup, then we'll be on our way again. I've got Llewelyn's seal with me if you're seeking proof."

Satisfied, Gwilym looked to the queen for instructions. "We need a moment to discuss this," she said politely, and to the porter added, "Close the panel."

"Wait, wait!" the baron called. "There's nothing to discuss. I'm kinsman to your lord's closest ally, on my way to help fight for *your* border, and we need some shelter because it's colder than ice balls out here. Open the gate."

She stared at him through narrowed eyes. "You've arrived in the morning. Why does that seem strange to me?"

"We got lost in the hills, lost our bearings. All the valleys look exactly alike around here, don't they? We didn't know we were so close until we broke camp at dawn. Please, lady, we have lads out here with frostbite. We're guests! There's a code of decency! Haven't you got that in England?"

"Why didn't you send a messenger ahead to let us know you were coming?" she pressed, ignoring the insult.

The man cursed. "We did! I guess he's lost too, then. I hope he didn't freeze to death, poor lad. As castles go, this one is damn hard to find, you know that, don't you?"

She couldn't argue that point; her wedding party had almost gotten lost coming here and she hadn't had nearly so far to travel. Beginning to shiver a little in the cold, she turned to the steward. "What are your thoughts on this?"

"Saxons," she heard Cynan mutter in exasperation to someone in his party. She forced herself to ignore it.

Gwilym had a ready answer. "Your Majesty is the king's deputy in this, but I would admit them. It's a terrible insult to Llewelyn not to. They'll leave their weapons with the porter."

"Of course we will," Cynan said, impatient at having to even discuss something so obvious.

At last, displeased, she gestured for the gate to be opened. Although a man on the barbican had already vouched that the visitor spoke the truth, she didn't relax until she saw Cynan's company for herself: a small teulu of about a dozen men, and their squires who carried satchels. "There's soldiers out that way," he said, nodding down the road out of the village. "Watching our mounts. But they'll stay there unless you have the room and inclination to house them in your bailey. They're hardy enough."

She smiled stiffly without responding, and exchanged formal greetings with him as he and his men laid their quivers, bows, and swords in a pile near the gate. To reassure the queen, Gwilym signaled most of the garrison to shadow the visitors into the hall. As they

mounted the broad stone stairs, Cynan asked if breakfast was a possibility—again, he said cheerfully, just for these men, not his entire
company. Marged grudgingly agreed to scrounge something up.

People began to drift out of the hall and back to their tasks or
(after wrapping themselves snugly) down into the village, and even
Goronwy excused himself to waddle back to his room, since court
was clearly adjourned for the morning. Some folk stayed around, fascinated by the unexpected guests; the guards tried casually to blend in
with them. The queen's focus was so intently on her visitors that she
didn't realize, until the familiar strains of "Rhiannon's Tears" caught
her attention, that Gwirion was in the room, squatting on his stool by
the hearth. She had to admit to herself she was glad of his presence.

She had deliberately neglected offering to wash her guests' feet,
and denied Cynan's request to let his men enjoy free rein of the bailey, but he simply shrugged agreeably. Still there was something
about this man she didn't trust. He was enjoying himself too much
for somebody fighting off frostbite. She excused the steward and
usher to their chamber, but she did it in a tone of voice that encouraged them to tarry in the courtyard to keep an eye on things.

There was a table by the hearth for the morning audience that
had been interrupted, and the baron and his men settled themselves
there. She sat near them, partly to be courteous but mostly to keep an
eye on them. Marged managed to feed them all cheese, barley cakes,
and ale, and everyone who saw it wondered if that would be a meal
out of their own mouths before the end of winter. The men ate with
gusto, and quickly. Cynan pushed his ale away and rubbed his sleeve
across his moustache and lips, which approximated cleaning them.
He smiled broadly at the queen.

"You have a good harp there, milady."

"Thank you," she and Gwirion said at the same moment. She
glanced at the harpist quickly; he did not return the look, just ran his
hand with deferential affection over the slightly curved forepillar and
the lion head atop it, and began a new piece.

"Excuse me, milady, but did I really hear the steward call you
your husband's deputy?"

"That's correct," she answered stiffly, wondering what to say if questioned about how that had come to pass.

"Then if you don't mind, milady, there is in fact just one quick thing I'd like to speak of with you."

"It depends upon the substance of it."

"Is your ladyship aware of my prince's interest in . . . unifying Wales under a single banner?"

"A single banner of Gwynedd, do you mean?" she said coldly. "My husband has mentioned it. He's opposed, of course. I thought the issue had been dropped."

He shook his head, grimacing. "It hasn't. My master Llewelyn would like him to reconsider an arrangement."

"That should be negotiated by the two of them personally after the current crisis is settled. This is hardly the time to resolve it."

"Well, yes, that's what I told His Highness myself, but the way he saw it, the current crisis offers an opportunity to demonstrate to your husband the wisdom of cooperating."

"How?"

"Llewelyn believes it might encourage your husband to cooperate if I brought Your Majesty to Gwynedd for a while."

She was on her feet instantly and backing away from him, but eight of the pages, hidden knives drawn from their knee boots, were already in pairs at the exits and the foot of the stairs. They'd moved with arrow-straight choreography: Someone who knew this space had drawn it out for them. Marged shrieked from the kitchen and Gwirion, leaping to his feet, banged his knee on the harp as the few green or aging guards, taken by surprise, took a moment to collect themselves, which cost them. Cynan's teulu were far better fighters and outmanned them, and had them disarmed in less than a minute as Gwirion and the queen gaped at what was happening. The four remaining pages, with almost mechanical synchronicity, pulled ropes from their satchels and had the men bound before another minute had passed, as Isabel stared helplessly around the hall. It had happened so quickly and with so little struggle that it was hard to believe there was any real menace involved. The baron's companionable ex-

pression did not change. "It's no use running away, milady, and you won't be sending anyone for help." As if on cue, the trumpeter outside began to sound the five-note alarm again, and the church bell joined the noise urgently. The baron smiled. "So your man has finally puzzled it out. My host has the entire village surrounded now. No one will get away but by my permission."

"If you hold me hostage—"

"Oh, no, milady, it's nothing like that." Cynan chuckled reassuringly. "You'll be a treasured guest of my prince, that's all, and he'll be very jealous of your safety. You'll notice we haven't hurt your men. This isn't a siege, we're simply here to escort you northward. I'll be bringing you back with me today, and my soldiers will stay outside the village walls a few days more to make sure word doesn't travel to your king too quickly. He needs to keep his mind on the enemy, you know—wouldn't want him distracted by domestic troubles." As she calculated her chances of getting past the boys by the kitchen entrance, the baron's teulu and the remaining pages dashed through the exits in groups of four to secure the entire bailey. She knew, with a sinking feeling, that they would meet almost no resistance. Even Gwilym, despite his height and general build, was too old now to be strong in arms. "So, milady, thank you for the breakfast, that was a treat, and we'll be departing at once. If one of you lads would bind Her Majesty's hands—gently, she's a delicate thing—and where is that pretty cape you were wearing?" He looked casually around the hall, as if expecting a servant to show up holding it out.

"You're wasting your time, he won't give up a thing for that one," Gwirion said from the hearth. She closed her eyes and breathed a silent prayer of gratitude. He set the harp against the wall and walked up to Cynan. "I'm the one you want."

The baron looked at him as if he were insane. "And who in hell are you?" he asked.

"I'm a person of importance to the king—isn't that all that matters? If you're taking somebody hostage to manipulate His Majesty, you'll have a lot more leverage if you take me."

Cynan turned to the queen. "Is the fellow daft?"

"No," she said, barely able to bring her voice above a whisper. "He's not. He's telling you the truth." It was a truth she never thought she'd be grateful to hear touted.

"What sort of prat is this, then?" the baron demanded. "I don't believe either of you."

"The queen's no use to him. She hasn't brought him a son, she couldn't even carry to term. And it was a political marriage designed to help stabilize the area where—in case you hadn't heard—there is now a battle going on, so obviously that part of the union didn't work either. You'd be doing him a favor, frankly, taking the thing off his hands. The rest of us wouldn't mind either, to be honest, she's an uppity woman who will *not* keep to her place. He'll let her wither away in your dungeon or wherever you keep her. She's not even a native subject! It'll be a wasted effort."

"And you? What's to be gained by you?"

"Noble would raise the heavens to get me back under his roof. Take me, don't waste your time with the queen."

Cynan curled his lip at Gwirion. "I hadn't heard about that particular predilection."

Gwirion laughed. "It's not like that, but make of it what you will."

The baron snorted again. "This is an obvious ploy, I'd have to be an idiot to fall for it."

Gwirion shrugged. "If you don't believe me, help yourself to her, but you're wasting your time and she'll be another mouth to feed for no benefit at all. She's small, but trust me, she eats like a starving pig." He walked back toward his harp. Isabel's heart thrilled with gratitude at his convincing nonchalance.

"Why are you being so helpful?" Cynan demanded.

Looking down demurely as he settled at the harp, Gwirion said in a conspiratorial tone, "Some people here think Llewelyn would not be such a bad overlord, but nobody's been able to persuade the king of that. I am happy to offer myself up for the sake of a better future."

"Is that so?" Cynan asked, with wary sarcasm. "I'm glad there are

those here with a little common sense." He studied the harpist. "If you're telling me the truth, prove it."

"You can ask anybody in this room. In the castle. In the village. In the valley," Gwirion said calmly.

"That's nothing," the baron scoffed. "That could be a stratagem you set up weeks ago."

"Naive as we are, it never occurred to us we'd need a stratagem for protection against our major ally. But if you need proof, just ask the king," Gwirion said, already sounding bored with the discussion, and picked up his tuning key to fiddle with the harp pegs.

The baron laughed. "Yes, I'll just trot over to the front lines and say, 'Excuse me, Your Highness, but I need to take a hostage and I was wondering whose absence you'd be most disturbed by.'"

"Send a messenger," Gwirion suggested casually, apparently more interested in tuning his harp than he was in the conversation. But Isabel saw a look on his face that she suddenly recognized and something inside her relaxed, trusting his instincts and knowing that things might be under control now, as preposterous as that seemed. "Send one of your messengers dressed in our livery, and have him ask the question very neutrally—tell him it's a bet we're making here among ourselves, and they need a written answer to who matters more, the queen or Gwirion."

The baron's eyes got very wide. "You're Gwirion!" he said, as if that made everything clear. Gwirion looked up from tuning, then down again in mock consternation at his own hands and arms.

"Good God, man, you're right! How did *that* happen?"

"I thought Huw had invented you!"

Gwirion and the queen exchanged looks: Huw ap Maredudd, seducer of stable boys and longtime advocate of Prince Llewelyn. Of course. He turned back to his harp, refusing to grace Cynan with a direct glance. "Will you do that, then? Send one of your boys to the king? If you've a good horse and a strong boy, he can be there and back in two days."

The baron eyed him thoughtfully. Now that he knew who the fellow was, there was actually a remote possibility he was telling the

truth. Based on stories of what the king let this man get away with, there was surely some unique bond between them. But still . . .

"Don't be daft. The lady is his queen consort and you don't even exist as a political entity."

"Noble doesn't negotiate," Gwirion lied, apparently speaking to his B-flat string. "He won't make decisions from political manipulation. He's completely self-centered, a creature of whims and fancy, and you'll get far more out of him if you appeal to his emotions than to his political loyalties. He simply has no sense of loyalty." He finally looked up at Cynan. "Not unlike your own prince."

The baron ignored the remark. Gwirion's suggestion sounded appealing. This was a warm castle, and a few days' rations at somebody else's expense was always a good idea in wintertime. On the other hand, there was the garrison to deal with. Although it was only a skeleton crew, his men could not hold all of them at bay for more than a few hours. Unless—

"Madoc," he called out, as one of his men reentered from the yard. "Look at their keep. Could we lock the castle guard into it for a few days?" That might work. It would be easy to control them, they'd be removed from the unarmed civilians, and there would be ample provisions for them there. "Is there a dungeon?" he suddenly asked. He saw Gwirion and Isabel both blanch. "I'm not interested in torturing you, I just need to hole you up somewhere until the messenger returns— What?" he demanded when Gwirion laughed.

"Together? I'd rather have the rack!" the harpist answered, and ran his fingers over the strings to check the tuning. "In any event, the only cell's not big enough to hold us both, unless you want to breed us—but from an aesthetic perspective, I really wouldn't advise it. My magnificent profile would be lost to history."

Cynan ignored the flip comment. "Is there a room we can secure entirely? No windows, one door? Her Majesty is now a guest of ours, I don't want her put out."

Nobody offered information.

"Then she shall have to join you in the cellar," Cynan said with a shrug.

"There's the king's private audience chamber," Gwirion conceded, seeing the look on Isabel's face. He tightened the third peg slightly and plucked the string, his ear pressed close to it. "That would be acceptable to Her Majesty, I think. It's snugger than a nun's loins."

"Where is it?"

Gwirion gestured toward the door in the corner of the hall before returning to his tuning, and the baron sent one of his men to check the room. A moment later, Madoc returned with the report that the keep would work. The top floor was intentionally empty, to provide refuge in a siege, and the basement held months' worth of food. The baron agreed to Gwirion's suggestion, and a courier outfit in the royal livery of red tunic and yellow hose was found to fit one of the baron's pages. The baron coached him on what to say, and Gwirion put the harp down at last, to point out where the boy's accent was too obviously of Gwynedd. "If anybody asks, say you're from the northern border—say Newtown—and you've just arrived here as a page. If you use my name, or the queen's, you should get immediate access to the king, and he'll probably laugh and write you a response right away."

"Won't he think it strange that in the middle of battle he's getting such a trivial request?" The baron frowned.

"On the contrary," Gwirion assured him, picking up his harp again. "He'll assume it's part of some bigger prank of mine. It will seem so reassuringly normal he'll forget about it within an hour." He closed his eyes and began a series of melodious descending arpeggios, smiling contentedly.

"You're an odd lot in Maelienydd, aren't you?" Cynan snorted. "Anyway, now, into the chamber with you, boyo." Isabel started slightly and the arpeggio ended in midnote as Gwirion clapped his hands over the strings, his eyes springing open: Neither of them had realized they were actually going to end up shut in together.

"I thought I was going to the cellar," Gwirion said.

Cynan gestured vaguely toward the door. "In this cold? If you're the prize we want, I can't risk your taking a chill and dying off."

Gwirion, thrown, affected insouciance and made a great show of laying the harp on its back, bowing, and fluttering an imaginary cloak as he crossed to the door and finally marched in, waving gaily to everybody as he vanished into the shadows of the chamber. Cynan turned to the queen, who had watched his parade with obvious discomfort. Silently, she allowed herself to be escorted in behind her fellow inmate. The door was pulled shut, and she heard the butler's key turn in the lock.

UNVEILED

Late January, 1199

HE ONLY LIGHT was from the fireplace and it took her a moment to adjust to the darkness. Gwirion was trembling, actually shaking with fear, and his face was almost as pale as the whitewashed walls.

"Gwirion?" she said in disbelief.

"I was so frightened," he whispered, ashamed, and collapsed hard into Noble's chair.

"I would never have known it." She sat on the chest beside him but didn't touch him for fear of making him more self-conscious. "Why did you do that?"

"To buy time. And because what I said is true." He was trying to calm his breathing.

She pushed away the immature impulse to argue with him. "So what? What do you gain from it?" He didn't answer. "You told me you aren't my ally, you only do what benefits you. How on earth do you benefit from being taken to Gwynedd as a hostage?"

The truth was, he did not know why he'd done it, and he scram-

bled mentally for any excuse that wouldn't sound chivalrous. "I can escape. I could free myself from anything they would put me in within minutes. You can't."

"But how do you benefit from that?"

"Then I'm free!" he said nervously, still jangled. "It's the perfect way to desert without having Noble's hounds on me."

"I didn't think you wanted to desert anymore. You didn't go with Owain."

He'd forgotten he had confided that to her. No, he hadn't gone with Owain. And Noble had done nothing objectionable since the end of the war council . . . except for that twisted apology the morning he left, a moment of unmasking that left Gwirion with a terrible opinion of what his friend was made of—something he could never tell her about. "That was before there was *war*," he said instead. "I don't want to be confined to a castle with this sort of nonsense happening all the time."

She shook her head. "You're safer here than anywhere else. People come *to* Cymaron for safety. You're not making any sense."

He threw her a challenging look, trying to stare her down with his onyx-hard eyes. "Why do *you* think I did it, then?"

"Because you're my ally," she said, risking a shy, pleased smile.

"Why do women sentimentalize everything?" he groaned. He leapt up and knocked hard on the door. One of Cynan's teulu opened it a crack and stuck a knife through it to discourage Gwirion's coming too near. "Excuse me," he petitioned the soldier, "would you be willing perhaps to construct a rack and keep me on it in another room for the duration?"

"You are such an ass!" Isabel said crossly, standing up. Unexpectedly, Gwirion laughed and the guard slammed the door closed again.

"Thank you," he said, his humor restored. "I don't think you've ever let yourself go with me before. This might actually be entertaining! Quick, what's the worst insult you can think of? I'll win that duel, but I'd be happy to mentor you."

She made a gesture of annoyance and crossed away from him to

the dark side of the room. "This is even worse than being cooped up with the sewing bevy," she muttered to herself. Gwirion, hearing her, gave her a gaping look of delight.

"The *sewing bevy*? Is that what you call your attendants?"

"Not to their faces," she said shortly, turning away from him.

"And you don't like the sewing bevy?" This, in a hopefully tentative voice as if he feared her answer might disappoint him.

She spoke clearly but without malice, still facing into the darkness. "They are a bunch of ninnies."

He clapped his hands together, nearly prancing. "Your Majesty, I wish I'd known you felt that way, I'd've persecuted them!" She looked over her veiled shoulder to stare at him. "If I knew someone might derive satisfaction from it, I would have paid them some attention, but I assumed you were all birds of a feather so I never bothered about them."

"You bothered about *me*."

"Of course I did, you're the top hen."

"And I threatened you," she said firmly, returning to the fireplace.

He stopped prancing, but grinned at her boyishly. "For about a day. I threatened you much longer than that, and much worse. I *still* threaten you. That's why we're in here right now, isn't it?"

She looked at him with wounded dignity. "If he answers that I'm the more important, won't that threaten you?"

"He won't say that," Gwirion assured her, impatiently, then grinned again. "Tell me what you dislike about the sewing bevy."

"Just because I think they're dullwits doesn't mean they deserve your persecution."

"I'll only do it behind their backs," he promised. "They'll never even know."

"And what purpose would that serve?"

"I'd be doing it for *you*, of course," he explained. "As a favor. You've never said a cross thing about them that I know of. You've been an angel, and you need a devil to let the bile out on your behalf."

"Oh, is *that* what you're for?" she asked ironically. He nodded, pleased that she finally understood. "Then I must assume you insult

me because Noble hates me but can't let himself say so. You're being the devil he can't let himself be?"

He looked startled at this thought, and then shook his head. "No, that's different," he said in a rare moment of utter guilelessness. "You're an outsider who's invaded my kingdom. When I insult you, I'm doing it for myself."

She crossed her arms and took a step toward him. "Why?" She wanted to finally have it out with him.

Gwirion looked blank. He stared wide-eyed at her, at the wall, at the floor, at his own shoulder, but nothing inspired an answer. Finally, with an awkward laugh, he declared, "Because it's *fun*, of course."

She made a disgusted sound and leaned back against the mantel seeking warmth, wrapping her arms around herself. "That's the most puerile thing I've ever heard."

He moved in toward the other end of the hearth. "I insult the king too! He enjoys it! Why can't you enjoy it? What's wrong with you?" he asked, overplaying the mockery to hide his discomfort.

She gave him a killing look. "You insult him as a perverse way of showing him affection. You aren't showing me affection when you ask somebody to stretch you on the rack in order to avoid my company!"

"Perhaps I am," Gwirion shot back without thinking.

There was a pause. He considered what he had just said and fidgeted in the firelight.

"Is that true?" she demanded. Her impulse had been to berate him, but if there was any way at all, ever, for the two of them to reach a genuine détente . . .

There was another pause, this one more awkward. Gwirion wanted to rescind the statement, but didn't have the energy to get into another round. And somehow, insulting her for its own sake had lost its vicious appeal; he was simply getting bored with it.

"It didn't used to be true," he said at last.

"Is it true now?" she pressed.

"Who else do you dislike in the castle?" he asked, regaining the boyish grin. In a hopeful, conspiratorial tone, he whispered loudly, "I

bet you have a terrifically twisted secret side. We might come out of this the best of friends!"

"Stop avoiding the question."

The grin faded and he turned away from her. She watched him absently brush away the hair of his cowlick as he mused, expressionless, and she decided with a certain smug condescension that he was really almost good looking when he wasn't making those ridiculous faces. Finally he turned back to her to explain in a dismissive tone: "It's just pity. I was so appalled by his treatment of you, that night with Owain, and you couldn't have gotten away with the sort of thing I did. You're still fundamentally insultable, but I had never really understood before how powerless you were."

"We're exactly the same, then, aren't we?"

He looked at her, bemused. "You mean besides the fact that you sleep in the king's bed?"

"Our only real value here is our relative worth to him. We have no independent function, either of us. That's a distinction nobody else shares." He blinked, unprepared for an insight he couldn't mock or dismiss. Finally, he nodded slowly in concession, and she added with a soft laugh, "I'm glad I did not have that thought before now. A few months ago it might have made me ill."

He leered at her theatrically. "You mean you're starting to like me?"

She mirrored the leer back at him across the mantelpiece, a mildly malicious gesture he approved of although it was startingly alien to her blunt features. "No," she said, and dropped the expression. "But I understand you a little more. I'm on shakier ground than you are, you know. What you said about my giving him a child is right. If I'm permanently damaged, he might be pressured to . . . free himself, so he may take a wife who can produce an heir." She tried to say this in a tone that wouldn't reveal how many nightmares the thought had caused her. Divorce under canon law was practically impossible, and she'd heard more than once of a man simply killing his wife to expedite getting a new one.

But Gwirion waved the idea off. "No, you're thinking like those

silly English," he said. "In Wales, any son he has with anyone, any son he acknowledges, can inherit. As long as he sires at least one bastard, you don't have to give him anything."

This did not reassure her the way he'd intended it to. "So I'm not even needed as a brood mare, I can't rely on the need for an heir as a way to make sure he keeps me. That means I'm completely dependent on his whim!"

Gwirion, for whom this had always been true, didn't understand the crisis, but he felt vaguely responsible for her agitation and in any case wanted her to calm down. "He doesn't kill people when he gets tired of them," he reassured her. "He would just get an annulment."

This didn't help either. "And that would reduce me to *nothing*," she fretted. "I would be a spinster, without power, prestige, money—"

"That's what I am now," Gwirion offered as a clumsy attempt to both empathize and distract. "Except the spinster part—but my carnal carousing is as frequent as a spinster's. If it weren't for the Spring Rites, I might still be a virgin." He pursed his lips shut abruptly.

"The what?"

"Oh, nothing," he said, too quickly and avoiding her gaze. "A . . . poem. A poem I recite that makes women weak in the knees. Shall I recite it to you now? It goes like this," he said, getting down on his knees before the fire and assuming, in his oversize clothes and featherweight stature, a mock-heroic pose. " 'In the spring, it is only right to honor my right to spring on you—' "

"Oh, for God's sake!" She strode across to the door and smacked it hard with the heel of her hand. Again, the door opened a sliver and the knife poked through.

"What?" the guard said, as if she had interrupted an important meeting.

"This is unacceptable!" she announced. "Let me speak to the baron. It's indecent to shut up a married woman with a man not her husband."

The baron had been standing behind the guard, and motioned

him to open the door wide enough to confront her. A weak grey shaft of daylight lit the air behind him. "Milady," he said politely, with a bow. "The only other place to put him is the little cell in the basement of the barbican. Do you demand that?"

"Yes!" she said at once. Seeing Gwirion's face in the firelight as he uncomfortably rose to his feet made her regret it. "Actually, no," she said, between nearly clenched teeth. That was no way to use someone who was risking his own safety for her. "But this arrangement is unacceptable. We need certain concessions or we'll both go mad."

"Such as?" Cynan asked with his maddeningly jovial smile. She saw that he was munching happily on some salted pork. It was a January morning. There wasn't enough food in the castle to justify anybody eating anything between breakfast and dinner, but she pushed her furious indignation aside to speak in a steady voice.

"We require air. There will have to be a few moments when you let us out of here, even if it is simply to walk around the hall. You may bind us and send everyone away if you like, but you can't expect us to stay in here without falling ill."

He shrugged noncommittally. "What else?"

"More light, of course. And we need a bucket to relieve ourselves and a basin of water for washing. And a curtain to have some privacy from each other when we sleep."

"And *things*," Gwirion added from the hearthside behind her. "We need *things*."

The man shifted his eyes to him. "What things?"

"The queen requires, I don't know, embroidery or spinning, have one of her women bring her something down."

"I don't care to sew," she said sternly, to Gwirion.

"Then bring her a cow to milk. I want my harp, it's lying by the hearth."

Promising nothing, Cynan shut the door. A quarter of an hour later, they were given the bucket, the basin, the harp, and a half-finished pattern in an embroidery frame. They were promised regular meals and firewood, but no exercise and no curtain; the baron didn't

see why two people asleep should need privacy from each other. He did, however, give them torches for the wall sconces, which brightened the room to its usual warm glow.

"Brute," she said under her breath when the door was closed again. "Do you think there's a way to escape?"

Gwirion had immediately curled up around his harp on the padded settle like a snake seeking warmth from a sunbaked stone. He picked up the tuning key that hung from his leather belt. "No. The air vent is far too small. Maybe the chimney, if we let the fire die down, but you could never manage it in that kirtle and I'm not sure even I could get up through it. I don't even think it's in our interest to try. If they think we're docile, then they won't be so vigilant over whichever of us they take. Would you like to hear something in the turn-string tuning?"

"Whichever of us? You said it would be *you*."

"I know. But the more I think about it, the more I wonder if I misjudged. Noble might answer the question wrong just to be perverse—"

"Not possibly because that's how he *feels*?" she demanded.

"Of course not" Gwirion said offhandedly, as if oblivious to the fact that this could hurt her. "And anyway, they might decide that regardless of his response, it's still better to have a political pawn than a personal one. So I can't *promise* they won't take you, but at least we'll have delayed their plans by several days." He looked up from tuning. "You won't faint or become hysterical, will you?"

She scowled. "I am a *Mortimer*."

Gwirion gave her a droll look. "Which means . . . what? You commit regicide? Slaughter the innocent? Imprison your own family for political gain?"

"I have never been faced with a crisis I couldn't handle," she scoffed indignantly.

"You fainted when Corr scared you at the wedding."

"That wasn't a crisis, that was a *prank*," she snapped.

"Fair enough," Gwirion said, and tested the pitch of the string he'd been tuning by sounding it against its neighbor. He tightened it

a fraction of a turn. "But please, if they do take you, don't be a Mortimer, just be docile. Do what they want. I'll say something to scare them out of trying to molest you, but I suspect they know better anyway. I'm not worried about the watch they've set up, I can slip out of here without being caught, so I'll go straight to the front to warn him." He smiled at her. "You'll be safe. But I really don't think they'll be taking you."

At once comforted and insulted by the assertion, she arranged her embroidery where there was the most light, as he began to play "Rhiannon's Tears." They passed the morning without another spoken word, but each relatively content in their respective distraction. It was a comfortable silence, not a cold one.

Gwirion could carry a tune well, and invent wild harmonies when he sang with the villagers, but he had never been trusted with romantic ballads or important poetry of any sort. He was, however, a profoundly gifted harpist, and it was pleasant to work to his music. Every now and then she would glance up at him bent close to the strings, his cheek almost resting against the curved shoulder of the instrument. The finial of a lion's head, looking not forward but back along the string arm in imitation of the royal coat of arms, seemed to be watching over him. The dozens and dozens of nights she'd seen him play in hall, she'd always been galled by the focused contentment on his face as he basked in the attention and admiration of everyone present. Alone with him, she didn't mind it so much. The pleasured expression was still there even without a crowd applauding him, and she was forced to consider the possibility that the smile was not for being publicly adored, but for the joy of the music itself. She realized, a little shamed for it, that she had considered herself the only one who could truly appreciate the beauty of it: Noble liked anything Gwirion did, and he had no ear anyhow; Gwirion, she had always assumed, was an attention-hungry cretin who had randomly been blessed with the gift to create something far more beautiful than he himself could understand. She was embarrassed to see that he appreciated it at least as much as she did. There was actually something winsome about the loving absorption he was giving to the

strings as he sounded them; it reminded her of the way Noble looked at her—sometimes—when they lay together. Trying to imagine Gwirion looking at a woman that way, she blushed and hurriedly returned her attention to the embroidery pattern.

Eventually the door opened and a platter was shoved into the room. The portions of barley bread, cheese, porridge, dried fish, and weak ale were generous enough to feed them both, but it was all mangled; the guard had investigated every piece of food for hidden messages or weapons being slipped in from the kitchen. Gwirion lay the harp on its back and brought the platter to the carved chest that lay between the settle and Noble's chair, where Isabel was sitting. The queen, although at first resenting the sewing, had become so mesmerized by her work that she continued as if she hadn't noticed the interruption. Gwirion stood watching for a moment, then ventured up to her and gently took the frame and needle out of her hands. He laid them on the floor beside her. "Come and eat," he coaxed. "Or I'll eat it all myself. You're scrawny enough as it is."

"*Dammit*, Gwirion, *why* is everything an insult?" she demanded, leaping up with an abrupt hurt fury.

He backed away from her, eyes wide. Vicious responses spewed through his mind but he stopped his lips against them. "I apologize," he said instead, quietly, and possibly for the first time in his life. It surprised him.

It surprised her too, even more than her own wrath had. "Oh," she said after a moment, and then added awkwardly, "Thank you."

She sat across from him at the chest and began eating. Gwirion had grown unused to sharing over a meal, and kept forgetting to return the cup to a place where she could reach it. Amused more than annoyed, she would tap his wrist gently and gesture, and he would immediately grab the cup and offer it to her. Sheepish about his manners, he insisted she eat all the porridge, but she refused.

Then there was a silence. They looked at each other, never at the same time but always with the same thought: How strange to be sitting here with this person. It occurred to each of them independently that although they had never been friends, they knew each other well.

The months of his persecuting and her hostility had woven their attention tightly together, braided it with Noble's life. This person sitting across the chest was someone they'd never had a friendly discussion with but still was not a stranger, and far more than a mere acquaintance. The realization amused both of them for different reasons, but for different reasons also it was not an amusement either wanted the other to see.

So when their eyes finally did meet, they each blushed, then were more embarrassed about blushing as they looked hurriedly away. And yet even the embarrassment had a comfortable intimacy to it, emphasized perhaps by invaders just beyond the door. There was almost something pleasurable about the self-consciousness of it, Isabel thought. Gwirion did not quite admit this to himself, but he was grudgingly aware there was something he wasn't admitting.

After ten minutes of silence, she ventured awkwardly, "I'm grateful you thought to ask him for my sewing. I don't know how I would make it through this otherwise."

He nodded to acknowledge the comment, a little uncomfortably, and continued to eat. They stared at each other's hands, hesitating to reach for something the other one might want. When they had finished, he placed the platter by the door, set the bucket as far away from the fire as possible for future use, returned to the couch, and picked up his harp. They resumed the morning's routine for some three hours, Gwirion pausing occasionally to tend the fire or the torches, until finally she pushed her handiwork aside. "I can't do any more of this now," she said. "My eyes are watering and my hands are getting stiff. It's soporific, doing nothing all day, and it's stuffy in here." She yawned. "Will it discomfit you if I stretch out and nap for a bit?"

He squelched the impulse to tell her this was the king's favorite place for naps and said instead, "You won't be able to sleep through the night."

"I always sleep well. Will you help me to find a cushion?" She moved toward the deerskin rug by the hearth. "I'll just rest here."

Gwirion knew where there were cushions—and blankets, and

even a quilt stuffed with goose down. This room was designated as a berth for visiting dignitaries, but the bedding got far more use when Noble indulged himself of an afternoon or evening without his wife.

He decided not to mention the bedding to the queen. Instead he took the lambskin throw from the king's chair, rolled it up, and offered it to her. She accepted it with a smile.

"Will you think it indecent of me if I take off my wimple?" she asked, reaching up to pull the band from her chin.

"Not nearly indecent enough," Gwirion quipped.

The headdress was a little involved, but she was adept and had occasionally done it herself since Adèle's death. Noble was the only man who had seen her hair loose since her wedding, but since she saw her own uncovered head every night and morning, there was nothing exotic or unusual about it to her, and she forgot it was an unknown to the rest of the castle. Her tomboyish youth had accustomed her years ago to wear her hair in braids curled up on either side of her head. But she'd been rushed this morning, and had cheated, twisting the long, tawny locks into a simple quick chignon and covering the wimple with a longer veil in case it slipped. It took only a moment to undo. She was surprised when, after laying the headdress and hairpins on the chest, she turned and saw Gwirion's expression. He was gaping at her. "What?" she asked.

"Is that what you really look like?" he demanded loudly before he could think, staring at the honey-toned cascade that fell smooth and heavy nearly to her knees. It was the glossiest mane he had ever seen. He didn't know women could grow hair like that.

"Haven't you ever seen hair on a woman before?"

Not like yours, Gwirion almost said, but didn't, because that wasn't what had floored him. What left him blinking stupidly at her was that she had become a different person. The queen he knew had hair made of fabric, with a bald face peering out chinless and neckless from it, stiff and formal. English. Standing before him now was a pretty young woman, with hair that seemed exotic compared to the coarse tresses of his countrywomen, hair that matched her pale eyes perfectly and—most astonishing to him—a woman with a neck.

Most of the castle women wore simple white veils, so seeing a woman's neck was not unusual...but seeing *the queen's neck* shocked him because it forced him to admit that the queen actually was a woman, with a woman's body. Somehow, even the time he had peeked in on Noble possessing her on their wedding night, that had never been real to him. Despite the firm, square face, she had a delicate chin and a graceful neck, which only made the revelation more disturbing. It had not really occurred to him until this moment that he was locked alone in a room with a woman, and he was distressed by it. To be shut up alone with any woman would have been difficult enough; an attractive woman made him feel even more awkward, and when that attractive woman had the gall to be *her*...

She had considered, and completely misjudged, his reaction. "Go ahead," she said through tight lips, the afternoon's peace lost.

"Milady?" he asked.

"Whatever insulting thing you're going to say about my hair, just say it and be done with it so I may sleep in peace."

He looked at her as if she were speaking Latin. Finally, mumbling, almost sullen, he managed to reply, "I have nothing insulting to say of your hair." In response to her surprised look, he grudgingly added, "It's actually...pretty." He wanted to smack himself for the admission.

Her face softened. "Really? Noble doesn't like it. It's never been complimented by a man before." She bestowed a smile on him—truly bestowed it, as a favor, beaming. "Thank you."

That only made it worse. He had to turn away from her to hide his reaction. This was terrible. How ridiculous. How riotously ridiculous. Someday he and Noble would go riding in the hills and Gwirion would confess he'd had an erection from seeing the queen's hair, and the two of them would laugh uproariously and then when they returned home to the queen and her wimple he would casually insult her. He tried to focus on that future afternoon until it was safe to turn back to her.

"Gwirion, what are you *doing?*" she asked, perplexed almost to laughter by his behavior. "What's wrong with you?"

"Nothing," he said. "Go to sleep."

Shrugging off his strangeness, she stretched out on the rug and propped the sheepskin under her head.

"Wait," he said. He couldn't stop himself from performing a gratuitous act of kindness for her, which made him angry with himself. Mostly, he decided, he just wanted her covered up so he couldn't see her anymore. Her veil usually matched the color of her kirtle, blurring the outline of her figure; her hair, such a contrast to the dark silk she was wearing, suddenly accentuated every subtle curve. He wanted to hide all of it. "We can improve on that a little." He went to the chest and lifted the top.

"What is that doing there?" she asked of the luxurious bedding he pulled out, not really wanting to hear the answer because she was sure she already knew.

"King's stash," Gwirion replied unsentimentally. "Officially for visitors, but used more often—"

"I understand," she cut in with annoyance. They spread the down-filled quilt on the floor, layered the blankets over it, and Isabel chose a cushion for her head. As she settled into the bed, Gwirion turned away hoping that once she was covered up, she would cease to be fascinating.

The opposite proved true, of course, since once she was snuggled in, she was almost nothing but hair. Hair and face—but the face, because of the hair, was a new face, not that of an adversary or a familiar nuisance. He curled up on the settle as far away from her as he could, again grasping the harp to himself for comfort.

"Sleep well, milady," he called out, trying to pretend he was far enough away from her to need to call out. He just wanted her to be asleep so he could feel alone. He ran his fingers over the harp strings without realizing it, and at once tried to silence them.

"Oh, that's lovely," she said in exactly the dreamy voice that the beautiful women of his fantasies always used when they were in bed. "Play me to sleep."

He uncurled himself and began a lullaby, determined to lose himself in the music until she was awake again. But when the rhythm

of her breath suggested that she had finally lapsed into slumber, he felt his fingers still the strings, and found himself drawn to her side. He could not get over the transformation of her face surrounded by all that hair. It was like a magic trick; he had a childish impulse to wake her up and make her put the wimple back on just so she could take it off again. Instead, he bent down over her sleeping form to stare at the hair. And without even feeling himself doing it, he reached down gently to stroke it. It was as smooth as a rabbit pelt and smelled faintly of rosewater. Hair exposed to weather and seldom groomed was never like this. He wanted to grab handfuls of it and rub it against his face, but he satisfied himself with stroking it, gently, so gently it would never wake her. He stared at the smooth young face that was so familiar and yet so alien.

Somehow, after a few minutes, his hand, on its own, without his knowledge or permission, migrated to her cheek. He saw it there as if it were somebody else's hand, and horrified, willed it to go away, but it wouldn't. It kept stroking the warm flesh, sending him sensations of dizzying pleasure even as he was begging it to move. Finally, with all the theatrical deliberation he used when performing for children or a crowd in the courtyard, he reached his other hand out to snatch the offending paw from her face, and pulled it safely out of reach above his head. The exaggerated movement threw him off balance and he tumbled over toward her, his own face inches from her closed eyes.

She stirred at the sound and he froze, praying to a God he usually ignored to spare her from seeing him. *Go away,* he ordered himself. *Go to the other side of the room and stay there.*

He couldn't. He meant to, and maybe he would have, but she rolled in her sleep and a thick lock of that hair uncoiled like a rope across his arm as he tried to stand, and he almost sank from the touch. He hovered over her again, staring at the sweetly sleeping face, the face that had the same features as the queen he didn't like and yet looked nothing like her. The transformation alone was so bewitching that even if it had been unflattering, he would have been entranced. Even her skin tone seemed different, rich and rosier, when it was sur-

rounded by the living curtain of her hair. His fingers hovered in the space just below her chin, wanting to touch her there. He could barely make out her pale, slender throat in the shadows beneath it. He could almost *smell* how soft that skin would be.

She was absolutely unlike the queen he enjoyed mocking. This was just a pretty girl, a child almost, and she trusted him enough to fall into a deep sleep in his company. It was a trust he felt unworthy of. *Don't be beautiful, you irritating creature,* he thought, pulling his hand away. He tried to be as annoyed with the sleeper as he was with her animated, wimpled counterpart. It didn't work. She was too innocent.

The key turned loudly in the latch, the door creaked open and the supper platter was pushed in. He glanced down at her but she didn't stir, and he found himself smiling at her. He didn't understand what he was feeling. He would have called it lust—in one inarguable way it was obviously lust—but lust usually made him feel like a nervous puppy, silly, forward, playful. This was calmer. He was pleased to see her sleeping safely and deeply, as if she were a child he was looking after. That's what it was, he decided, ignoring the physical reaction he was still fighting. *I feel paternal because I'm looking out for her.* Feeling virtuous, and very relieved, he gently rocked her shoulder until she was awake. She blinked sleepily and opened her catlike eyes, then looked up at him with exactly the dreamy smile that the beautiful women of his fantasies always used when they were in bed, and he backed away in distress, not feeling the least paternal anymore.

CAPTIVES

Late January, 1199

HAT WAS LOVELY," she said groggily. Gwirion pulled farther away and went to fetch the platter. Her behavior felt almost seductive to him and he didn't know if he should be angry with her or with himself. "The sleep of the Mortimers," she purred. "Only the strong of heart can rest well during a crisis."

"Sleeping during a crisis is just a lethargic way of swooning," he retorted. He set the platter on the chest and held out her wimple to her. "Here, you may as well put this back on now."

She took it from him but then dropped it onto the quilt as she sat up. "It will be time for bed soon, I don't feel like bothering." He said nothing in protest as they sat down to eat, but she was confused by how distressed his silence seemed now.

Supper was the same as dinner, with a little salted pork added; under the circumstances, a luxury. Gwirion had an even more awkward time sharing the trencher and cup than he'd had at dinner. He

was suddenly too aware of where her hands were, seemed terrified of brushing against them with his own.

"Oh, no, please," he said at least a dozen times, yielding up almost the entire meal.

"Gwirion," she reassured him, as if he were a toddler, "there's enough for two." His behavior was inexplicable to her. He nearly breathed a sigh of relief when they put the platter aside, as if some gruesome ordeal was over.

After supper they returned to the sewing and the music for a while, but it was hard to have a sense of time in a room without windows or conversation, and eventually they agreed to face the slightly awkward task of preparing for sleep. Gwirion dragged the padded settle over before the hearth, and moved the quilt and her blankets onto it. Taking a few of the woolen brychans that were left, he made a bed for himself on the rug between the settle and the hearth, then dowsed the torches before he nestled in.

T HE king had been brooding anxiously, listening to the rain on the canvas roof, already sleepless. When Gwallter the chamberlain stuck his narrow face through the tent flap with the news that there was a rider come from Cymaron, Noble welcomed the midnight distraction. He received the boy's peculiar query with warily confused curiosity, hoping whatever mischief Gwirion was up to would not overly upset the queen. Actually, though, the question was so blunt—Who matters more, the queen or Gwirion?—that it seemed almost more her style of querying than his, but the boy was too vague to give him a clear answer about its origin. A written response had been requested. He wrote it himself, and the boy, not even waiting for refreshment or dry clothes, accepted a new mount and was riding west again within an hour. The king tried to envision what prank or jest would arise from this, but his imagination failed him. Reluctantly, painfully, he returned his attention to his enemy.

He could not let Mortimer just sit there on his best soil, stalling for time, attempting no further aggression beyond keeping what he'd taken and efficiently annihilating any Welshmen who came too close. But it was an astonishingly massive army that Mortimer had planted on the Welsh farmland, and Llewelyn warned against an all-out attack, had refused to lend his own men to such an assault. This was supposed to be a *show* of force, he'd reminded Noble, not a *use* of force. Hopefully Roger Mortimer had similar intentions for his legions. Llewelyn had already lost men enough against the English in his support of other border princes.

Mortimer seemed to be taunting them with his idleness. He had enormous reserves of food and fuel, and hundreds of workers to deliver it. Spies provided unwelcome rumors: His intentions were to keep the army camped there until the Welsh froze to death, ran out of food, or just gave up and went home, and by Easter he would have lumber and stone in place to build a fortress—like Cymaron, a sturdy Norman fortress. There would have been symbolic and even spiritual satisfaction in defeating this plan in a manner that was thoroughly Welsh. But Welsh fighting was based on violent, brief surprise raids in impossible terrain and one did not stage a sneak attack on an entire army.

GWIRION was right: After her nap, however brief it had been, she couldn't fall asleep again. And she would never have admitted this, but she was a little nervous, knowing there were hostile men outside who could overpower her before Gwirion woke up, even though she doubted they would try anything that stupid. She leaned over the edge of the settle, hovering over Gwirion's sleeping form as if it somehow gave her extra protection. Ignorant of the irony, she fell into the same game he had only a few hours earlier.

She had rarely seen him relaxed, without making some grimace or setting his mouth in concentration on a melody or acrobatic

movement. This was no longer the prankster's face, it was the face of a man she realized she didn't know. It did not affect her physically the way it had her cell mate earlier, but still it fascinated her. But of course she knew him, she argued with herself, it was *Gwirion*, a force almost more ubiquitous in her life than her own husband. He was an intimate, even if a cool one. She had known, early on, that she would never have any meaningful discourse with her simpering sewing bevy, and had not even tried to be close to them. After Adèle was gone, Noble had afforded her her only real companionship, and that was certainly inconsistent. This day spent largely without words in Gwirion's presence was a gift; there was an unexpected and inexplicable sense of being with a peer.

Sometimes when Noble slept she would look at his face and marvel at the transformation sleep had wrought. Little pieces of his character poked through the mask of slumber, things that he kept hidden during the day. He slept with his mouth closed in a tight, straight line, looking grim, worn down, hopeless almost. She had never seen such an expression on his face by daylight; by day he was sometimes moody but always energetic. But the skin around his eyes was softer in sleep. His eyes were almost never soft when he was awake. Hypnotic, but not soft.

She didn't know Gwirion's waking face well enough to truly appreciate all the ways it changed in slumber, but she was intrigued to see what was before her now. He was just an ordinary man, small framed, dark hair with a cowlick and a healthy swarthiness to his skin. The scars from Huw's attack had not quite disappeared. He had a mole on the left side of his face, beneath his eye. She'd never noticed. Crinkles that seemed like part of a weathered mask when he was awake softened to very fine lines around his eyes and the corners of his lips; he looked both older and younger in repose. Her eyes traced his hairline. There was a scar on his temple—very old, probably from some childhood mishap—another one on the web of flesh between finger and thumb on his left hand. There was something else that looked like a burn wound on his throat. She wanted to touch the white skin there, but didn't let herself. She returned her attention to

his face and wondered what personality she would assume such a man had if she came upon him for the first time, without a history. There was something pleasingly familiar about him. His face was actually well proportioned and classically Welsh, an oval with strong, fine features and what she decided was an elegant chin. He warped the natural contours of his face behind the sarcastic sneers and exaggerated impish grins of his daily life. She thought about how pleasant it had been to work to his music, what a relief to have him treat her with something other than scorn. He had been so enraptured with her hair that it was possible, however unlikely, that he'd even considered her with appreciation. The thought made her stomach tighten in a strangely pleasing way.

"I like appreciation," she whispered to the sleeping man. After a deliberating moment, she tucked her veil and wimple out of sight under the quilt.

THEY both awoke in the morning to the sound of the key in the lock. The aroma of breakfast touched them: Marged was trying to send them comfort by feeding them what little fresh meat she could pull together, an unheard-of indulgence for a morning meal in winter. Isabel was surprised their guard hadn't eaten it. A second unsmiling youth of Cynan's teulu entered with fresh light for the wall sconces, and rekindled the fire. Isabel was up before Gwirion and set the platter on the chest, then relaxed into the leather chair.

"Good morning," she greeted him as he began to crawl out of the blankets.

"Put up your hair," he said gruffly in reply, not looking at her, and began at once to gratuitously change the tuning on the harp.

She stifled a laugh, pleased. She had never had this power before, and she liked it. "Oh," she sighed, running her hands through her locks with a smile, letting them fall smoothly through her fingers, "It's a rare thing to have my head uncovered, and it feels so lovely. I want to enjoy

it a little longer." She studied him out of the corner of her eye for a reaction. If she could pain him with beauty, as he had once pained her with wit, it would be such sweet vengeance, not only on him but also on Noble, who had never once given her reassurances that she was attractive. In fact, she conceded, the real impetus was vanity more than revenge. It hardly mattered what man it was who ogled her, it was good to feel *noticed*. That it was Gwirion was simply an entertaining irony. To her tremendous satisfaction, he frowned slightly and looked away. "And," she went on, "this way we're on an even footing."

"And what does that mean?"

"We are both without our protective shields. I'm without my veil and wimple, you're without the king."

He looked up from the harp pegs and smirked at her sarcastically. "Oh, very good! But I don't need the king around to be a rude, offensive ass, I'm quite capable of that on my own."

"Yes, I know," Isabel said. "Please don't feel the need to prove it."

"It wouldn't be worth the effort," he assured her.

Smiling, she began combing her hair with her fingers. She lolled her head back for a moment, pretending to stretch, exposing her neck and the underside of her chin. It was so satisfying to know he was gawking at her; she could feel his grudging attention without looking at him. Attracting him thrilled her, even though there was no love lost between them. In fact, the absence of affection made the attraction more real, more flattering: He was ogling her despite himself. She wasn't beautiful because he cared for her, she was beautiful because she was beautiful. It was so impersonal that it was almost animal. She flushed a little. She liked that sense of power and she liked him just for giving it to her. "Are you hot?" she asked, making a move as if about to remove her surcoat.

"No!" he said crossly, and put the harp aside with an agitated gesture. "And neither are you. Just eat, would you please?"

As they ate, she looked across at him. He was diligently avoiding her face, watching only her fingers to avoid touching them, so she could stare with impunity. She was enjoying this. All the things she had seen last night on the sleeping stranger's face were now animated

on the man she knew as Gwirion. Again she admitted to herself that part of her pleasure was in discomfiting him, but a larger part was in realizing how effectively she could distract a man.

Gwirion wanted to throttle her. They were shut up alone together for another day at least, and this behavior couldn't possibly make it pass more comfortably. And how *was* one supposed to act, being shut up with a woman one had an abrupt feeling of lechery for, but otherwise disliked? He wondered if he should ask to be put in the cellar.

T HERE had been a morning raid on the northern extreme of the camp, quickly repelled without serious harm to either side, almost as if Mortimer's troops were bored and simply seeking an hour's exercise. Cadwgan the marshal brought word that provisions would be gone in a few days, and Efan at once insisted that a retaliatory raid onto Mortimer's lands would be both strategically and logistically advisable.

Noble wanted to refuse. But he knew it would happen anyway, and if he was overseeing it he could at least make sure it was Mortimer's immediate stores, not Thomas's or anyone else's, that were plundered. So he agreed, ruefully, and Efan swaggered off to give the news to his teulu, who whooped with appreciation so loudly they could be heard a mile off. Noble turned his troubled gaze back to the east. He needed other options. This was maddening. He had to break the stalemate.

W ITH no other options, they spent much of the second day as they had the first, Gwirion bent close to his harp strings and Isabel sewing, her hair pouring over one shoulder into her lap like a pool of honey. He went through his entire repertory, adjusting the strings nine different times to create keys whose names she

thought he must be making up: the drunkard's tuning, the witch's tuning, the sad Irish tuning, the strange tuning.

When they needed a change, in the late afternoon, they finally risked a conversation. It began simply: She admitted how fond she was of "Rhiannon's Tears," a tune he played obsessively, and she told him her earliest memory of hearing it, in a very different form, during an English wedding dance. Gwirion promptly described English music as "the sounds of a people entranced by their own boredom," and did a cruel and witty imitation of what he thought "Rhiannon's Tears" might sound like if mangled by English musicians. Suddenly it was five hours later and they had never paused for breath.

And they had never mentioned the king.

He was alluded to. His presence hovered all around them, every moment. But they knew each other well enough now, had enough shared references, that if they chose they could forge an independent friendship, something neither of them had much experience with. At her request for a story of King Arthur, Gwirion rattled off a parody of Culhwch's quest for the daughter of Ysbaddaden, turning the characters into real people—Roger Mortimer standing in for the malevolent giant Ysbaddaden, spherical Marged the cook for his ravishingly beautiful daughter Olwen, and little Corr for Arthur, giant king of the Britons. He delivered the entire monologue in an exaggerated imitation of old Hywel's humorless melodrama, and she found herself wiping tears of hilarity from her eyes, wondering if Adèle would have banished this sort of romance from her hearing too.

"But why do the Welsh poems about Arthur never mention Camelot?" she asked.

"Who's Camelot?"

She made a face at him. "Stop that, Gwirion—even *I* know about Camelot and Adèle hardly ever let me listen to the ballads."

"What *ballads*?" Gwirion asked, incredulous. "Why would there be ballads about Arthur in *England*? He's one of *us*. He slaughtered the lot of you," he said with some satisfaction, and ran his hand over the lower harp strings to create a brief, triumphal cacophony.

"He slaughtered the *Saxons*," she corrected patiently. She'd given

up on trying to explain the difference to anyone. "Six *hundred* years ago. There are dozens of ballads in French about him and his knights and his court—haven't any of them made it to Wales?"

"In French?" Gwirion gave her a look of barely suppressed sarcasm. "Please consider that he slaughtered the Saxons. Because they invaded Britain."

"And?"

It was hard to believe such an obvious point had not even entered her mind. "*You* invaded Britain. *Recently.*"

"We've been here more than a *century!*" she protested, but Gwirion just laughed at her.

"You're as much the enemy as the Saxons are by Arthur's standards. And you're telling me your courts are full of stories about him. Where he's the hero? Where the man who would butcher all of you is the hero? Isn't that just a bit odd?"

"No," she said. "They're just entertainment, they're not political."

"*Everything* is political," Gwirion chastised her, but gently. "Arthur is *our* king. If you've appropriated him, I'll wager you've changed him too, haven't you?"

"Well, he's not as violent as your version," she began, but Gwirion cut her off with a harsh laugh.

"We don't have a *version*, milady, we have history! You have fiction!" He softened when he saw her discomfort. "Tell me about the fiction, then. Let's hear what the silly French have done to our man."

She told him then the stories she could dimly remember from years earlier, of Camelot, Lancelot, Guinevere—one of the few names familiar to Gwirion—and as many stories about the Round Table as she could recall. He lay back on the settle and listened with riveted attention, then shook his head in wonderment when she had finished.

"How extraordinary," he mused, staring at the ceiling. "We give you the greatest warrior in the history of the British Isles and you castrate him."

"Gwirion!"

"He won't be very happy about that when he comes back," he insisted, playing with her now.

"He's coming back? Is that part of your *history*?"

"Of course," Gwirion answered, straight-faced. "He's just in some netherworld somewhere getting a second wind. He'll be back to scourge the land of our invaders, meaning you, as soon as things get bad enough."

"That will be hard for him to do, considering he's *dead*," she said with cheerful smugness, understanding now that disagreement was the whole point of this conversation. "They found his body at Glastonbury about a decade ago, hadn't you heard?"

Gwirion, who had heard, theatrically rolled his eyes. "And that, of course, is not *the least* political. That couldn't *possibly* be your Norman kinfolk trying to prove to us naughty natives that we have no hero waiting to reappear to throw off your Norman yoke. Of course not. And the timing is *pure* coincidence—that his demise would *happen* to be proven just as your uncle and the others decided they wanted to step up their attacks on us."

She held up her hands in self-defense against the verbal onslaught. "All right," she conceded, slightly sheepishly. "All right. You take the honors for that round. Now what?"

"Oh, fornication I think. That's always a lark to talk about."

She narrowed her eyes at him. "I don't want to hear about any more mistresses, thank you."

"There aren't any more, milady, you scared them all away." That was a mistake, he realized too late: It resembled genuine barbs not yet far enough behind them. She looked away from him. She even picked up her sewing, which he knew she had lost all interest in. "Milady," he said in a conciliatory tone, and sat up. After an obstinate pause, she glanced at him from the corner of her eye. "I must apologize for saying such a thing." She raised her head to look at him more directly, and less sourly, but clearly expected more of an apology. He did not have the discipline. "Yes." He nodded. "I didn't mean that. You haven't scared any of them off, there's dozens of them, they're crawling all over the castle."

She threw her sewing, frame and all, right at him as he

laughed—and then she started laughing too, grudgingly, despite herself. "You are such a spiteful boor," she said with amused resignation.

"Ah, the fickle flame of flattery," he intoned. "And I am so deserving of it." He liked that they could tread dangerous ground more safely now, and decided to see what else he could get away with. "I will not say another word about that. In Enid's honor."

The amusement left her face at once, but this time she looked chastened more than angry. "I am not responsib—"

"I know," he said, and stood up to hand her sewing back to her.

There was a silence. Gwirion returned to the harp, ran his fingernail across the strings to remind himself what tuning he was in, then began to play a piece she'd never heard before. It was sweet and lilting, playful yet soft, and there were no words to it. When he finished she complimented him, and he nodded thanks.

"I learned that from Hywel. It was the first full tune he ever taught me. He was never much good for a laugh, that fellow, but he was the most learned man I ever knew and I'm sorry that he's gone."

"Who do you think will replace him as bard?"

"Oh, me, I hope," Gwirion said, brightening. "And I'll encourage much deflowering to fill my pockets with the maiden fees."

She gave him a disbelieving stare. "Not the bard as well," she said. "Don't tell me the *court bard* profits from a woman's—" Gwirion nodded cheerfully and she demanded, "What is the *excuse* for that?"

He shrugged. "He gets it for his role as chief of song, so maybe his music is credited with bringing lad and lass together, although I suspect our dear-departed sage did more for insomnia than for romance. But even so, he profits by it and that's why he and Father Idnerth clashed. They had *rather* different attitudes about the value of virginity," he explained confidingly.

Mention of the bard led them to speak of poetry and music, and they argued playfully about religion. Isabel described her pilgrimage to Compostela, the towering cities of London and Gloucester, the estate she had managed from the age of twelve; Gwirion shared decades of decadent castle gossip with her that nearly made her eyes bulge,

and recited his quirky interpretations of native legends that were so often alluded to and quoted from but had befuddled her out of context. She listened with grudging fascination as he spoke of Llew, who sanctified each oat stalk, Llew the god of sun and harvest—"in other words, of life"—the same Llew whose tales she had contemptuously ignored last August in the courtyard.

Gwirion had never had such an involved conversation with anyone but the king, and Isabel doubted she'd ever talked to another person for so long in her entire life. She knew she'd earned some special status when Gwirion listened to her tell stories of St. Milburga the revered abbess of Wenlock, a lock of whose hair she carried in her crucifix, without sneering at her for it. Despite the awkwardness at breakfast, she had the urge to say to him now, "Do you know, Gwirion, I actually like you," but she couldn't bear the possibility of his reverting to his usual demeanor and mocking her for it. And yet she could tell it was reciprocated, and thought happily of future times when Noble was back and order restored, of the three of them engaging each other as friends, which she realized with regret was what Noble had wanted for them all from the start. Gwirion was her inverse, all of the things she wasn't and yet both of them reflections of the king, and there was a sense of union there that made her want to throw her arms around him and declare him her brother.

But there was also a part of her that wanted to wring from him again the agitated attention a man gives to an attractive woman. How delicious and unexpected it would be to receive both friendship and flattery from the only man Noble would ever allow near her! Adèle had banished the *chanteur des romances* before he was halfway through his ballad, and she was ignorant of what disasters could follow from such affections.

THERE was no maniacal light in his eyes this time, but the entire army was convinced their king had gone mad. Just hours af-

ter the camp had settled in for slumber, he initiated the chain of com-
munication from his officers down to the water boys, with the news
that they would be attacking Mortimer—immediately. The afternoon
drizzle had cleared and now the full moon was brilliant, bright enough
for a simple skirmish. But the moon was inching toward the horizon
now, and even if it weren't, a surprise attack of such a scale, lit only by
winter moonlight, was surely the conception of a mind that had
cracked. Llewelyn had nearly suggested as much when he dismissed the
idea the night before. Knowing precisely what each of his officers
would say in protest, Noble did not bother telling anyone else until he
woke Efan two hours before he intended the attack to begin. This way,
he explained hurriedly, a leak was impossible—the news could hardly
reach Mortimer any faster than Noble's army would. The penteulu's
response was only the first of many times that night the king was
silently cursed. Absolute incredulity spread in waves across the sleep-
sodden, dark encampment. But when Efan finished his reveille rounds
by going to Llewelyn's tent, the northern prince agreed this time and
summoned his own officers to wake his men as well. He told Efan,
grinning, that this was the most foolhardy thing he'd done since he'd
challenged his uncle Dafydd in battle—the first of his many victories.

Within half an hour all commanders of both armies were in
Noble's tent, few fully dressed and some still half asleep; he bid
them to silence and gave them each their orders, then sent them away
again with no chance to register protest. The foot soldiers would go
in first, relying on the Welsh stealthiness that Englishmen did not
consider a battle asset. When the enemy was awake and beginning to
regroup, the archers and the horsemen would begin their work. But
what mattered most was taking Roger Mortimer alive. It was a simple plan, crude in fact—that was its strength.

"It is immoral," Father Idnerth argued moments later, when the
commanders had been sent off. The candle he held trembled in the
cold. "It's murder. You are killing men in their beds."

This had troubled Noble when he'd first contemplated it, but he
had justified it to himself. "If we don't do this, my people will have
their own throats cut in their sleep before long," he said steadily, as he

stood spread-eagle in the middle of the tent, Gwallter fastening his leather armor. "Mortimer has shown himself utterly devoid of morals and I have no chance unless I respond to him with equal disregard for decency."

"Mortimer is not the one whose throat you're slitting, sire."

"Those throats are all Mortimer's," said Noble.

Now he was waiting outside his tent for his groom to bring his Castilian charger. He surveyed the moonlit camp around him as it swarmed with quiet, dark activity in the frigid air. As his men ceased grumbling and began to follow orders, they were all surprised—as he'd guessed they would be—by how much easier it was to prepare than they'd anticipated. It was not sight that aided them in putting on their armor or stringing their bows; it was routine, and they realized now that they could, literally, do it in the dark, half asleep. They sensed their comrades by their general shape, their smell, the singular subtle noises each one made; they could assemble without sunlight. In total blackness it would have been a disaster, but Noble, when he saw he would have a clear sky, had timed this perfectly. Even if Mortimer's watch saw movement here, they would never be able to decipher its meaning; the most reasonable assumption would be that the Welsh were packing up for a dawn retreat.

He saw his groom approaching, carrying a lantern, Cadwgan the marshal beside him. Noble's eyes were so adjusted to the fading moonlight, the little fire in the lantern was almost blinding. He waved once so they could see him, and they hurried over.

"Sire," said Cadwgan, bowing. "This is irregular, but a boy was caught by the western watch trying to slip into camp. He says he must speak to you, he won't breathe a word of his mission to another."

"Unarmed?" asked the king.

"Unarmed, filthy, hungry, and exhausted. He's lame and he's spent the past two days on foot getting here from Cymaron. That's all he'll say. He's quite frantic, he's desperate to speak to you before you ride out."

"One of our boys?"

"I recognize him, sire, but I don't think he's from the castle." A

treble voice down the line, faint but growing louder, caught their attention and Cadwgan gestured. "That's him. He'll wake the enemy if he keeps that up."

"Silence him and bring him to me," Noble said. "Quickly." He took the reins from his groom, then reconsidered and handed them back. "I'll see him inside."

"Shall I stay as bodyguard?" Cadwgan asked. Noble shook his head. "I'm not worried about a threadbare child," he said, glancing toward the setting moon. "Unless he wastes my time." He drew his sword.

The boy, a skinny fellow of about eleven years with thick brown hair, dressed like a farmer's son, was unknown to Noble, but he recognized the king and calmed at once when he realized he was to be granted an audience. Noble gestured him into his darkened tent and sat him on the floor. He stood over him with his sword tip under the boy's chin. "Be quick," he said.

The boy was surprised by, but unafraid of, Noble's action. "There's a hostile force around the entire village of Cymaron," he announced breathlessly.

"What?"

"I'm from a farm in the next valley, but I was near the castle the morning before last, and I heard the siege alarm sound so I went up to the eastern hill to look. I'd seen a troop of foreigners just a little earlier heading toward the castle so I thought perhaps they had something to do with it. Things seemed quiet inside for a while, but then the main company of foreigners slipped around the edge of the village walls, and the alarm sounded again, with the church bells. They weren't attacking, it looked more like they were standing watch for something."

Noble was perplexed by this description. "And then?"

"All the castle garrison was marched across the bridge by the foreign fellows who'd gone inside the castle, and they were put into the keep, and then the bridge was drawn back from the wrong side so they were stuck in there. The castle's been taken, sire."

The king was grateful it was too dark for the boy to see how

shocked he was. This had to be a bad dream, punishment for the atrocities he was planning. "Who was it attacked?" he said, nudging the sword against the boy's throat. "Saxon? Norman? What did they speak?"

"I memorized the banner to describe it to you, but there's no need to do it—it's the flag of the other camp."

"Mortimer's?"

"No, sire, Llewelyn of Gwynedd's."

He almost slashed the boy's throat from his violent start of amazement. "What?" he demanded in a whisper.

"Yes, sire, I memorized it. The same image. I wanted to get closer in to see what was happening but then I had the thought that you would need to know, so I came here instead." He stretched his neck as Noble lowered the blade and paced to the far side of the dark tent in agitation.

"Who knows this?" Noble demanded.

"Nobody, sire," the boy answered. "I was going to just blurt it out as soon as I found anyone to talk to here, but I saw their camp first, I saw their standard in the moonlight and knew something was up, so I decided to talk to no one but you."

Noble was across the tent again at once. Instead of praising the boy's decision, he returned the blade to his windpipe, pressing hard. "Nobody? You have told nobody? If you've told anyone, boy, let me know now, and I'll forgive you the blunder. If I hear later you told someone, that will be accounted treason."

"Nobody, sire," the boy insisted, looking uneasily at the blade.

"And this is not a jest?" he demanded sternly. "Another of Gwirion's peculiar pastimes? We had a rider last night"—he stopped himself, realizing. Realizing everything—what the question had meant, what his answer would mean. "Oh, *Christ.*"

"I saw a rider, sire, a boy my age in your livery, he passed me coming and going. He left the castle right after they took it. Whatever he brought you didn't come from Gwirion, sire, it was coming from Llewelyn's men."

Noble lowered the sword. He sat down hard on his bedding, and pressed his palm across his eyes a moment, nearly cringing.

"Dammit," he whispered, and took a breath. The hand rubbed his face, moved down to his stubbled chin. For a moment he forgot the boy, the tent, the imminent attack. "What have I done," he breathed. He grimaced, then forced his full attention back to the boy and said with a focused frown on his face, "You will not tell anyone else this. Nobody, not even my closest men, are to know this at present."

"Of course not, sire, I understand."

"I cannot stress how important that is. What I am about to do requires the fiction that Llewelyn is my inviolable ally. If this were a few hundred years ago I would cut your tongue out right now just to make sure nobody else came to know."

The boy blanched in the darkness. "No, sire, I'm excellently good at keeping secrets."

"And how am I to trust that?" Noble asked.

He squirmed a little. "Well, sire, we've worked together before, in a manner of speaking." At Noble's quizzical look he added, sheepishly, "I'm Ithel, the boy who helped Gwirion train the dogs."

Noble looked at him for a moment, weighing in his mind if this meant the boy was more or less likely to be true. Finally he granted him a tight smile of approval. "So you've been trained by an expert in keeping secrets. Very well, then. Find yourself some victuals and get a little sleep. I have a Norman army to decapitate." He rose and headed for the opening.

"Sire?" Ithel cried quietly. "Aren't you going to do anything?"

"No," Noble said brusquely, barely stopping himself from lashing out in fury at the child. "From your description, they're holding all of them hostage, and they won't harm hostages. They're inconvenienced but not in danger."

"It's your *wife*, sire, your *home*," the boy said.

"Maelienydd is my home and this is how I tend to it," Noble answered.

"But, sire—" Ithel was very fond of Gwirion and was certain he'd been in the castle when it was taken.

Noble turned away abruptly. "I have a war to prosecute. Get some sleep, lad. Sleep in here if you like."

Ithel got to his feet and would have protested, but the king was already gone. The boy rushed behind him to the tent flap and stopped short in the entrance, watching. His Majesty mounted his Castilian in a smooth, liquid movement of casual athleticism, reached down for a torch from his chandler, and urged his mount through the ranks of his men.

Few of them were devout, but now all of them were praying for deliverance. Noble seemed to be looking them over, although he could not see them with the torchlight blinding the edge of his vision. But he knew they were there, and he knew they were watching him in the flickering flames, wondering if he was mad. It hardly mattered: Now that they were up, dressed, and at least half awake, their native fighting spirit was roused and it was easy to turn their irritation to battle fuel. While the whole circle of the horizon was absolutely black, his men were following him—grudging, grumbling, disapproving almost to a man, but they were following him and they were feeling their hearts pound with anger, fear, and savage raw energy in the biting dark.

"Leave a bard behind to sing about the king's folly when we're all dead—which will be in about an hour," Noble heard a foot soldier mutter, deliberately in his hearing. He smiled and ignored it. There was another torch, a quarter of a mile away, moving toward him. He turned his horse to meet the other rider. It was Llewelyn, the treacherous ally, leading his troops who were equally stupefied but equally obedient. Eyes glittering in the torchlight, the two men grasped each other's forearms in greeting—like brothers, Noble thought, like Cain and Abel—then turned and rode abreast over the black swell to the east, their silent armies rushing on foot behind them.

CYNAN had been having a pleasant stay at Castell Cymaron. He allowed his men to turn their attention only to the downstairs servants for physical amusements, but the king had stocked his

larder well in that regard, and they had been feasting. The food was also excellent, and Cymaron's hall was warmer than his own. He now considered their reason for the extended visit a sham—obviously the king, no matter how much he may have preferred Gwirion's company, could not afford to make a written declaration saying his queen mattered less than his parasite. But it didn't matter, it justified their lingering, and that was enough.

He was surprised when one of the pages came running into the hall, out of breath, from the side door near the barbican. "The courier is back, sir!" he called out, waving a rolled parchment. "He has your answer!"

The baron leapt to his feet. "In less than two days?" He frowned. "Has the fighting moved this way?"

"No, sir," the page said, dipping his head respectfully. "The roads were good. And the moon's full."

The baron took the scroll from the boy. It was closed with Noble's general seal: a lion *rampant regardant* over a red kite. He broke the seal, unrolled the rough paper, and read the six words Noble had written as his answer.

"Kings be damned," he muttered. He looked up and told the messenger to wake his men.

The boy nodded and darted off. Cynan looked at the note again to make sure he wasn't misreading it, then carried it toward the room holding his two captives.

I T was perhaps the most gratifying moment of Noble's life, finally pressing the blade of his dagger against that particular jugular vein. They were on the far outskirts of the Norman camp. Efan thrust a torch near so that the king could see his captive clearly. "Welcome to my kingdom, Roger," he whispered, smiling viciously. "But you seem to be lacking a writ of safe passage. How terribly unfortunate there is no bracken here for you to hide in."

S HE loved how the natural lessening of tension, the almost alchemical change in the feel of the room, soothed them into
cheerful placidity together. After Gwirion had pressured her for a
quarter of an hour, she finally relented and performed her secret im-
itations of the sewing bevy, sashaying and primping and giggling like
each in turn. He fell off the settle he was laughing so hard.

"You've been masquerading all these months as an English gentlewoman," he scolded, "when the truth is you're cut from a swath of
my own fabric!"

"Thank you," she said, grinning, warmed. It was as close as he
would ever come to voicing the sentiments of friendship and affection that she wanted to hear, she knew. It was enough.

They were startled out of their laughter by a knock on the door.
It swung open as they rose, Gwirion protectively clutching the harp
up to him with one hand and holding an arm out in front of the
queen to shield her. Cynan entered. With his unrelentingly convivial
grin, he waved a scroll in the air at them. "From your king," he said.
"We leave before dawn. That's not so far from now—you children
are up late tonight." He laughed, but when neither of them took a
step to get the letter, he dropped it to the floor. As if he really did
care about them getting sleep, he made a clucking sound and removed two of the sconce torches when he left, leaving the room in a
dim glow.

After a moment, Gwirion lay his harp on the settle and retrieved
the note. He unrolled it and scanned the message silently. It read:

She is replaceable. He is not.

How this would have made him crow with vicious victory a few
weeks ago, perhaps even a few days ago. Now he cringed for her sake.
Still, he was glad of it, and it was the answer he needed.

"What does it say?" she demanded, her heart in her throat.

He looked at her for a moment, feeling trapped, then quickly crumpled the message in one fist and threw it into the fire.

"Gwirion, what does it say?" she repeated, more shrilly.

"I'm going," he said quietly, and sat down on the floor by the hearth.

She took a moment to collect herself. Noble had not chosen her. The relief was greater than the hurt, but the hurt would last longer, she knew. She noticed Gwirion was not gloating. "Thank you," she said quietly, sitting beside him. Impatiently, she swept her hair over one shoulder to contain it; her earlier preening seemed silly now. Gwirion's attention was lost in the flames. "Are you sure you can get away from them?"

He nodded. Still staring into the fire, he added quietly, "I just hope they don't come back here and take you when they realize they've lost me."

"When you escape, go straight to Noble and tell him what's happened," she said.

"They can turn around and come back here in less time than it will take for me to get a message to the king."

"Just go to him yourself, you'll have immediate access." They were both whispering, as if the guards might somehow overhear them through the heavy oak door.

He looked at her. "Don't you remember? I'm escaping. From *everyone*. I can't go to him myself because I'm not coming back to Maelienydd."

Her look of disappointment and surprise only convinced him more. What to her had simply been a lovely evening of friendly conversation had been ecstatic agony to him. She wasn't the queen anymore, she was an attractive young woman and he wanted her. But that wasn't the worst problem—lust was at least impersonal, it could be exorcised by proxy. Despite himself, he'd got caught up in conversation with her, hanging stupidly on her thoughts, wanting so to impress her, to enthrall her with his wit—the very thing that had alienated the queen. Suddenly finding himself with a woman who shared his points of reference as the queen did, but lacked the queen's

usual prickly attitude, he reveled in her company almost as much as he did the king's, and he found it alarming. Affection and attraction, commingled, dizzied him—this was a new drug, and he was desperate to fight off its seductive stupor. He wanted the night to go on forever but he did not see how he could ever survive another one like it. And Noble read him so easily; if such an evening passed with Noble present—

"I'm escaping," he repeated firmly.

"You can't," she declared. "I won't let you."

"You can't stop me, milady," he said with a soft, pained laugh, avoiding her gaze.

"But we're friends now. If you stay, everything will be good. For all of us." She hadn't recognized the drug for what it was as readily as he had.

He didn't quite manage to swallow a bitter laugh. "I don't think so, milady."

"Stop miladying me. Why do you need to leave? We're not at odds anymore, and Noble's been behaving himself for months. Relatively." When he didn't reply, she challenged him. "Anyhow, you've said you were leaving before and you didn't, why should I believe you this time?"

"Please don't ask me to explain," he said, looking back into the fire.

She curled her graceful arms around her bent knees. The fire was blazing; it was so warm that she decided to resort to her threatened coquetry from earlier in the day and seduce him—chastely, of course—into staying. She stood up, slipped off her heavy, fur-lined surcoat, and sat again, in only a long kirtle that revealed more of her gentle curves than Gwirion thought he could bear to look at. She tipped her head slightly and the curtain of her hair slid down her arm, brushing against him. He tensed.

"Please put that back on, milady," he said, sounding genuinely distressed.

"I'm hot," she said, gazing serenely into the flames.

"Then please put it back on and stand away from the hearth."

She turned to him and smiled—sweetly, not suggestively. "I want to sit here. I like sitting next to you."

He looked even more distressed. *"Don't,"* he said gruffly, and stood up, moving away into the shadows. She immediately reached for her surcoat.

"All right, I'll put it back on. Come sit beside me."

"I'm fine here," he growled.

"Gwirion, I'm your queen, I order you to sit down."

"I don't obey frivolous orders."

"It's not frivolous," she insisted, with an impish grin that reminded him of Enid. "It's your last few hours as a member of my household and I want to say farewell properly." He dreaded the possible meaning of this, even as he fought to hide his body's insane, irrational delight over what the words could have implied. But she seemed completely undistressed; had she felt one jot of what he did, she would surely have been traumatized. Her very sweetness proved she felt nothing of the kind—she was too artless and too honest to manipulate anyone that way. All she meant, all she could possibly mean, was a chaste embrace and a friendly kiss. The thought of even this sent his heart to his throat. But he let himself sit beside her, grunting in annoyance to show her how put out he was by the request.

"Thank you," she said, angelic. He didn't remember her ever sounding angelic before. Why did she have to start now? She wasn't really angelic. She was really a shrew. He remembered that, in theory, although he couldn't recall any specific examples.

"So," he said when he was sitting beside her, trying to sound nonchalant. "Here I am. Farewell." He started to get up again, but she put a hand on his arm and he froze.

"Not just farewell. Farewell and thank you," she said gently. She leaned forward to kiss his cheek and he felt dizzy again. Her lips were impossibly soft, like rose petals. He was disgusted with himself for having such a hackneyed sentiment, but that didn't keep them from feeling like rose petals. He realized with a sinking feeling that he had leaned into the kiss slightly, and that she must have felt his body shift.

She finished the kiss but kept her head close to his. Their eyelashes could almost brush against each other. She had never been so close to any man but Noble. She was fascinated by the *difference* of him, his scent, his shape, the planes of his face. He had a sinewy grace, feline but not feminine, so different from Noble's muscular solidity. She remembered blushing as she'd watched Gwirion gaze intensely at his harp strings, and a shiver raced through her as she wondered how else the two men differed.

She kissed him again, this time on the lips.

He did not kiss back. He made sure not even to lean into it this time.

She pulled away, disappointed.

"Kiss me," she said.

"Is that an order?"

She almost said yes, then saw his expression. "It's a request."

"I can't," he said. "You're Noble's."

"So are you," she said, trying to smile. "I think that makes it all right."

"You don't really know him, do you?" Gwirion muttered.

"Just a kiss. I'm not asking you to put your hand up my skirt! Just a kiss to celebrate that we're friends at last."

He shook his head, looking anywhere but at her. She leaned in and kissed him again. He pushed her away roughly, got to his feet with an expression of panic on his face, ran to the door and began kicking it and smacking his hands against it frantically.

"What what what?" the baron demanded, when the guard had opened it.

"Put me in the cellar until we go," Gwirion insisted.

"I will not allow that," said the queen, in a voice of iron. Surprised, they all turned to look at her. She was standing. The glow from the fire behind her glancing off her veil of hair silhouetted her with an aura that made her look otherworldly. "This is his last night in his own home for what might be quite a while. I will not have him so insulted. Besides, it's your last night here as well and I would feel much

more comfortable having one of my own people standing watch over me in case you were tempted to perform any indecent acts."

The baron burst out laughing. "Majesty, we've got all the indecent acts we can manage out here already," he assured her, smoothing his mustache with one hand as he pretended to try to hide his smirk. He turned to Gwirion. "I don't know what your argument is with your mistress but you'll have to harden yourself to it. By the time we had you settled in it would be time to go. See you soon, then," he finished cheerfully, and closed the door.

Gwirion stayed with his face to the door for a long moment. "Milady," he said at last, sounding hoarse. "I won't kiss you because if I did I don't think I could *keep* my hand from going up your skirt."

"But that's all right," she blurted out giddily, unaware she was not thinking rationally and so happy to have his attention it seemed fine to say anything to keep it.

He spun around to face her and she was shocked to see he was near tears. "I did not want this!" he shouted.

She blinked, refusing to understand his distress. "What are you frightened of? You're not trapped, you're about to escape." She smiled, feeling generous and thrilled and believing herself to be sensible. "It's any man's fantasy, Gwirion—a night alone with a woman you want, who *condones* your abandoning her afterward."

Gwirion blushed, flustered. "You don't condone it, you tried to talk me out of it."

"I would be willing to lose you if only I could really have you first."

He gawked, and she almost laughed at her own brazenness. She'd never imagined she could talk or even think this way, and it gave her a heady feeling of power. Astonishing a man with her own will and desire fueled both the will and the desire. It was dangerously rash— no, not dangerous, for he was about to vanish permanently, and she would never find herself in this extraordinary position ever again.

"I won't be able to stay away," Gwirion stammered, red faced, trying to keep his senses. "I'd come back, and we'd be tormented,

and, and . . . besides the fact that I'm no Lancelot, Noble is hardly Arthur, especially *your* Arthur. This isn't a romantic tale. I'm flattered you chose me for your first little juvenile crush—confused, but flattered. But you don't have the luxury of indulging in it, *Your Majesty.*"

She stood up, slowly, and keeping his gaze, she again removed the surcoat, pushing it slowly off one shoulder and then the other. "Come here," she ordered calmly.

He shook his head. It was maddening how heedless she was. It made his determination to behave himself seem silly. She seemed so convinced that this wasn't wrong, it nearly eroded his belief that it was.

"Please," she said.

"I'm sorry for this," he managed to say, without moving.

She walked to him. He backed up against the door, looking cornered, but she stopped a long stride before reaching him and held out the surcoat. She looked disappointed, even exasperated, but dignified. "I didn't mean to unnerve you. If you'll help me back into this, we'll pretend it never happened." He took the coat and looked at her, distressed, but held it open for her. She gave him one last inviting smile, which he looked away from, and then she began to turn her shoulder away from him to back into the surcoat. The casual tilt of her head in the firelight was so elegant and lovely it was almost physically painful to look at her. She sensed his discomfort, and still hoping that he would relent she slid half a pace toward him and deliberately cocked her elbow so that it brushed against his body as she turned. He grabbed her arm and furiously yanked her around to face him.

She answered his angry expression with an almost giddy smile, although her heart was beating so furiously she could hardly breathe. "You're touching me," she whispered, glancing at his hand on her arm and then back up at his face. "Touch me some more."

He tossed the surcoat aside and pulled her to him, and a noise that was half gasp and half laugh escaped her as she threw her arms around him, kissing him. He kissed her too, terrified and ecstatic at the same time, trying hard to forget who she was, trying to make it an impersonal meeting of flesh.

Grinning, she led him back to the floor by the fire and they sat,

but when she lay on her back, trying to pull him down with her, he resisted. She reached up and ran her hand over his worn wool tunic, and was rewarded by his nearly collapsing against her, finally lowering his body onto hers with a shaky, resigned sigh. It felt strange to her, a man other than Noble on top of her, but thrilling. She had never been this aroused before her clothes came off, and there was an emotional intensity that had never been there with Noble at all. She wondered fleetingly if it was because he was Gwirion, or because he wasn't Noble, but the answer really didn't matter. The feeling was there and she loved it. He would be safely gone forever soon, and this would be a secret memory that she could cherish always.

He felt her body underneath his, felt her legs pressing against his, tangled in her silk skirts, felt the delicate torso under her belt, the very hips he had watched Noble grasping the night he'd spied on them. He cupped his own hands around them now. These weren't the same hips. They couldn't be. He tried to pull away, but she raised her face up to his and kissed him again. The impossibly soft lips parted for an impossibly strong tongue, and he knew that Noble had probably trained that tongue well, to do things that he tried very hard to keep from thinking about now. But maybe anything that wasn't technically fornication—

He cut his own thoughts short. He remembered what Noble had done to Owain and the queen just for making eyes at each other. And then, he simply remembered Noble. He pulled away. "We can't do this," he said, with a firm desperation that made her pay attention.

Breathing hard, she grimaced and pulled herself up to a sitting position. "Now you'll think me horrible," she said, morose, knowing the entirety of the day's joy was permanently ruined.

He choked back a pained laugh. "I thought you were horrible before I'd even met you. Now I think you're human."

They didn't dare eye contact, two disheveled people with sheepish smiles and pulses racing. There was a long silence.

"Where will you go?" she asked, just to say something.

"I have no idea." He pulled away to face her. "Listen. Let Marged be the one to tell him that I'm gone. She's the only one who's

immune to his rages, he'll traumatize anybody else who gives him the news, including you. He needs to know that I'm not really hostage, so he doesn't negotiate, but spare yourself the experience of breaking the whole truth to him. Especially if it's coming from you, he might think you drove me to it."

"There was a time when I would have," she said, fidgeting with her rosary.

"Pretend you still feel that way."

Again they looked at each other trying to agree without words what was acceptable. Regardless of their age, all the women he'd been with—many of them handed over by the king—had seemed older. This was the first time he felt older and in some strange way wiser than the girl beside him. It was a seductive feeling and yet he couldn't bear it. He wanted to be the silly, puerile prankster who earned women's amused but indifferent favors. That was familiar, that was easy.

Forgetting himself, he kissed her, the first kiss he'd let himself initiate, and he felt her tremble against him. No woman had ever responded that way to a kiss from him. The flattery of it alone pushed him beyond reason. He grabbed her closer to wrap himself around her—but the noise of the key in the lock made them pull apart, breathless and disoriented.

"It's time," the baron declared from the door, as if he were announcing Christmas morning.

A Hero's Welcome

Approaching Candlemas, 1199

RMS BOUND, Gwirion was led away well wrapped against the chill. Cynan put him on a horse, which genuinely pleased him since he was so used to his pony. Isabel had slipped him her precious rosary after taking off the relic-bearing crucifix, so that he would have something to barter for food or shelter until he got his bearings. He did not tell her what he would probably barter it for instead: He'd determined to exorcise her from his mind by finding a whore as soon as he was free.

IT was over before the sun rose, and an hour after dawn Noble was reclining on a brychan, hands clasped behind his head, his legs stretched out before him and crossed at the ankle. He grinned at his captive, who was tied standing stiffly under heavy guard. The smells of a belated breakfast wafted past. Noble had chosen to take the au-

dience this way partly to hide how bone tired he was and partly to insult Roger Mortimer with extreme informality.

"Might we interest you in a traditional Welsh breakfast?"

"Richard will raise a stink about this," Mortimer said.

"About feeding you a Welsh breakfast?" Noble answered. "I didn't know he was so particular about his lords' diets. Very well, then, how do you Saxons break your fast?" He punched the word, knowing it was rude. He was jubilant.

"I meant my capture," Mortimer said disdainfully.

Noble shook his head. "Let's not waste our time with feeble posturing, Uncle Roger. Richard won't even hear about this for weeks, maybe months, and he'll just think you were stupid for provoking me. Which you were. Of course, if you would like to be your niece's guest at Cymaron until Richard can be bothered to raise your ransom, you're welcome, but I suspect you'd be more comfortable in your own home, so let's settle this now." Through all the glibness, he had one eye on Llewelyn, studying him. The younger prince either didn't notice the scrutiny or didn't care, and in any case he gave nothing away. He was the model of a young commander whose star was rising: cocky but deserving it, respectful and obedient to Noble's seniority. "I would like to get home to your niece myself," Noble said in a light tone, and absolutely nothing was revealed in Llewelyn's face.

THE castle was physically undamaged, but the stores were plundered and the inhabitants moved about like ghosts. The serving women who had been forced to entertain the invaders clung together in the kitchen, where Marged warmed milk to soothe their nerves. The queen called the castle residents together in the hall, to warn them that there were still armed men outside the village walls who would not let anybody leave, for any reason, and she begged them not to try. The entire assembly spontaneously interrupted her with applause for her aplomb and poise in the face of crisis. She blushed and patiently ac-

knowledged their admiration, then pressed on to assure them that Gwirion would alert the king once he escaped, which evoked another outburst of approval. She did not reveal that Gwirion was not coming back, although she meant to tell Marged that night.

But night fell and she did not tell Marged because she didn't want to concede that it was the truth. As a comforting gesture, she requested the most indulgent supper the kitchen could muster, trusting that Cynan would be called to account to replenish their stores before the end of winter. But there was little fresh meat and no means to get any—the butcher, huntsman, and falconer were all with Noble.

For her brush with danger, the queen was instantly granted the status of an adored young saint; everybody wanted to be near her, to assist her, to receive attention from her. She enjoyed it but she was unused to it, and it seemed ironic that after months of trying so hard to win these people's hearts, she was successful only after being locked up in a room doing nothing for two days but entertaining adulterous thoughts.

Almost everyone offered to perform during and after the meal; the honor of playing first was awarded to an awkward young wheelwright who had been left behind as part of the guard. He sang and played the pipe, and Angharad, the oldest of the sewing bevy, performed next on the harp. The two of them, and the motley assortment of musicality that followed, all did the best they could to entertain, but the collective effect on Isabel was abysmal. In tribute to Gwirion, Angharad attempted "Rhiannon's Tears." Gwirion had played it half a dozen times in their two days of confinement. Once, to show off, he had played it—he claimed—backward. Angharad butchered it compared to Gwirion's finesse, but even if it had been an excellent rendition it would have left Isabel heart heavy. She remembered that his harp was still in the audience chamber, and asked that it be wrapped in its felt sheath and returned to the chest near the kitchen screen. She wondered when it would ever be sounded again. Without her rosary to worry, she began to fidget with the crucifix until she nearly snapped it in half. She put it in her purse, out of reach, and fretted with the edge of her veil instead.

It did not seem fair to her, or even sensible, how tormented she

was now. Being in his presence yesterday had suddenly been so pleasant, had made her feel light and cheerful, giddy even—and now his absence was a wall she could not stop walking into. Noble did not have nearly such a grip on her imagination. His absence never preoccupied her even though her well-being was more dependent on his safe return. And he was her husband, her bedmate. Why did thoughts of Gwirion, who had refused to undress her, make her feel abandoned? For the love of the saints, there was nothing to miss! She missed the conversation, yes, but how could anyone yearn more for one evening's conversation than for nine months of domestic and connubial intimacy? If she felt such longing for Noble, or at least his body, she could have excused herself. But she didn't. She longed only for something she had never even known.

Isabel slept that night in Noble's bed, unable to bear the proximity of her women. Everyone seemed pale and dull compared to the man she had nearly forced herself on the night before. She lay beside the space where her husband usually slept, imagining Gwirion there instead, and almost swooned in a hazy fantasy of making love to him.

She awoke with an empty feeling in the pit of her stomach.

IT was just after dawn when Gwirion's message reached the king. Noble was deep in slumber, a rare thing for him in any circumstance. He'd been up most of the night with Llewelyn, trying to break Mortimer's will without breaking his body—an act of charity Noble did not really think the Norman was entitled to. But he had challenged convention far enough already in this venture and he knew that to treat Mortimer as he deserved was risking censure from the English king, the pope, or both.

Ithel was sleeping on the floor of the tent, the king's mysterious new mascot whom nobody in camp was allowed to approach. He awoke first and awkwardly tugged at the king's blanket until Noble opened his eyes—and then he was instantly awake. "What?" he

demanded, and sat erect. At the tent flap stood Gwallter with a young runner wearing livery and breathing hard, his short hair plastered to his forehead with sweat. Ithel had wordlessly taken a grubby, unsealed parchment from him and offered it to His Majesty.

Noble recognized the writing and sent Gwallter and the boy away. He unrolled the scroll and Ithel watched him as he read. Noble looked up, straight at him.

"Well, lad," he said, "You were exactly on the mark." And then to himself, softly, "Christ." He had not allowed it to be real until he saw it written in Gwirion's familiar, spidery script.

"Will you send someone back now?" Ithel asked for the dozenth time. "You don't need the soldiers anymore."

"It's over," Noble said vaguely. "There was a hostage attempt and Gwirion foiled it." He tossed the parchment to the ground.

"Good!" Ithel declared. "But you had better send some troops back to be safe." Noble lay back on the brychan, eyeing the boy. Clearly he had no idea how presumptuous and disrespectful he was being, and Noble lacked both the energy and the inclination to educate him. If he was following in Gwirion's footsteps, there was little hope for improvement anyway.

"No," he answered. "And you will continue to keep your mouth shut."

The boy looked distressed. "Sire? Why?"

"We'll finish the formalities with Mortimer this morning and then we're starting for home after dinner. I'm keeping my army intact until I have a signed and sworn concession from the enemy I just humiliated. For all we know, deBraose or one of Mortimer's other neighbors is sending twenty thousand men to take us down. We are not necessarily through here, Ithel, but the situation at Cymaron is resolved."

THAT morning castle life was almost returned to normal. Queen and judge sat in hall again, and met with the villagers

and other petitioners to hear their disputes. Many of them chattered excitedly about Gwirion as if he were some heroic figure of legend, happily anticipating his triumphant return. His selfless act of bravery and cunning being undertaken for her sake only added to her new popularity, and she was dizzy with compliments and adoring glances by the end of the day. She received the subjects who had come in from the countryside and been held hostage within the gates by Cynan's outside troops, and invited those who could not find lodging within the village to come back to the hall for the night.

She had hoped there would be more talented entertainers in their ranks. There weren't. But a few well-meaning souls who were praised within their own undemanding hamlets wanted to impress Her Most Esteemed Majesty, and, of course, most of them played some painful variant of "Rhiannon's Tears." She wanted to scream.

She went to Noble's bed again the second night determined not to think about Gwirion, and failed at once. He must have escaped by now. She wondered how long it would take his message to reach Noble, worried that the baron would come back for her once Gwirion escaped him. Anxiously she lit a candle, then a wall sconce, to search for a map of the region, but of course there were no maps in the bedchamber. Defeated, fretting, she darkened the room again and crawled back under the blankets, trying hard not to imagine what it would be like to have Gwirion beside her.

She drifted to sleep and dreamt that he was lying on top of her, but he was much bigger, bigger than Noble, he had grown so huge that he was suffocating her and she couldn't breathe. In a panic, she forced herself to wake up, but the suffocation didn't lessen and she realized with a painful twist of fear that it was real.

A gloved hand was clamped hard over her mouth and nose. She tried to scream, but the hand had an airtight seal. Somebody yanked her head up roughly and held her in a viselike grip against his cold body. A knife poked into her neck right behind her jawbone.

"Don't move," a deep voice whispered in the darkness. It was a

northern accent like the baron's and she knew with dread what was happening. His breath smelled of cheap ale, and the stubble on his cheek raked her ear. "If I remove my hand and you scream, I'll send this dagger right through your throat. Do you understand? Nod." She nodded against his hand. The hand released.

"What do you want?" she demanded in a harsh whisper, praying she sounded more angry than frightened.

"Just you, Your Majesty." The knife poked a little. "Are you going to cause any trouble?"

"Who are you?" she asked, wishing she hadn't doused the torch. Now she realized how foolish it was to have lit it—that's how the man must have located her.

"An ally," said the voice, suddenly sounding familiar. The knife fell away, the grip relaxed, and she barely stifled a scream of pleasure when she saw Gwirion's profile silhouetted against the window.

"You came back!"

He pulled the glove off, lit a candle, and placed it beside the bed, avoiding her glance. "I'm not staying," he said.

"Then why did you come at all?"

He couldn't tell her the crude truth of it: That hours after he had escaped he had, in fact, found himself on a prostitute's pallet, unable to summon even lust. The whore had been genial and understanding, especially since she had already been paid. She told him that if a lass had that kind of hold on him, there was only one cure: He had to possess her. Whatever feverish and idealized image he had of being with her would make the real experience pale in comparison, and then, disillusioned, he would be free. This woman was not a romantic.

"I came to let you know it went off smoothly. And . . . to see you one more time," he said awkwardly, feeling like a cretin. "If you want that. Or I can just go," he added hurriedly.

Anticipation tickled her from her throat down to her thighs and for a moment she could hardly breathe. "Is *seeing* all you're capable of?" she whispered.

"I'm not going to become your lover," he said, more aggressively than he meant to. "This is one night. And then I'm gone for good."

"Then we must do things just right, so we may feast on the memories for years." If she was going to long for him, she at least had a right to know what she would be longing for. She was pleased with this rationale, believing herself the first lover in the history of forbidden desire to think of it. She stroked the stubble on his cheek with the back of her finger. "But first tell me what happened."

He jerked her hand away from his face, shaken by how intensely the simple gesture aroused him. He took a breath, then grimaced apologetically and released her. "It was simple," he began, willing himself to focus on speech. "We got just past the Severn, and they made camp as soon as the horses recovered from the fording. I got away soon after sunset and propped up my blankets to look like I was sleeping. The nights are so long now, I had ten hours' lead at least, I think. And I'd dropped a few hints during the day about having family in northeastern Powys, so I think they'll have wasted today heading in exactly the wrong direction. I went back over the Severn to Newtown, and sent the mayor's courier to the border to warn Noble." It was this mayor, thrilled at being invited into the annals of history, who had taken him to the village's one hostel and treated him to its one whore, who was his niece. That reminded Gwirion, wryly, of Isabel's rosary, which he took from around his neck now and draped over her hands. She set it beside the bed. "The fates seem to be with us—there's a good moon and it was clear, and there's a manned relay course from Newtown to the king's camp. The message is certainly at the border by now. If Noble can send somebody, you should have protection by tomorrow night at the latest. I've been hearing conflicting things about how things are faring there, so I don't trust any of it."

Noble's fool, the man she knew as her tormentor, was not capable of what Gwirion had just done. She wondered, if she could persuade him to stay, whether he would regress to the rascally waywardness that Noble so enjoyed. Perhaps he was afraid of that too.

"Thank you" was all she said. Then she took one of his hands in hers and drew him onto the bed.

He resisted. It was the personal betrayal, not the technicality of adultery, that troubled him. The king had betrayed his trust in many ways—*pretending to kill me, for example*—but in the end Noble's actions had been, however strangely, a celebration of their friendship, not an affront to it.

She slowly peeled away the layers of blankets until she sat nude beside him. This alone could have kept him spellbound for the night. Her skin was almost translucent. "My God, you're beautiful," he managed to say aloud, remembering she could not hear the thoughts that sounded so deafening to him. For nine months now, Noble had had this in his bed and he had never once spoken of it with appreciation.

She reached for the tongue of his belt. She knew how to undress a man, it was one thing her husband had taught her early on. Gwirion was stupefied; rarely had a woman so much as lifted the hem of his tunic. Even when Enid seduced him he was almost fully clothed and she had simply pulled up her skirt.

Her hands were small and soft, wonderfully warming on his chilled skin, but he became self-conscious when she tried to remove his drawers. "What's wrong?" she asked, smiling up at him. He couldn't manage to say anything coherent. "Are you afraid I'll be disappointed?"

"*Yes*," he said. It should have been obvious. He went on, stammering: "I'm not the lover he is. I'm not as gifted, in any sense." He pushed her hands away.

She put them back. "I'm not worried about that," she whispered, and nudged his hands aside again.

When they were both undressed there was a long, indecisive moment. They stared at each other, fascinated and desirous but also stunned that they found themselves here, when a week ago they had been grudgingly civil at best. "Please," Isabel said at last. "I've dragged you this far. You must take the next step or I'll feel as if I'm forcing you."

This was the king's bed, and Noble's blue eyes, in his mind, stared down at them unblinking from the canopy. She had given herself to a man many times here but it had always been her husband. He didn't know if Noble's image was plaguing him to terrorize him, shame him, or just intimidate him, but he tried to push it away as he laid her on the mattress and hovered over her. He was frightened of the first moment, the commencement of true sin and irredeemable betrayal. Beyond that, when it was too late to turn back, there would be a sickly kind of freedom and relief. But until then the possibility of redemption gave guilt and fear their own seductive powers—

"You're thinking too much," she whispered. "Stay here."

He gave her an apologetic smile, bent over to kiss her cheek, and then he lost himself in her.

They were tentative at first. But their lean bodies fit together beautifully, moved together with one rhythm, intertwined so naturally they could almost forget they were not one. This was the mystery she had missed on her wedding night, the sense of being let into some secret. He lacked Noble's suave assurance but his touch was a hundred times more electric. She didn't know where her Christian Lord fit into it, but she knew this was a mingling that no benevolent God could have condemned. This could not be an evil thing.

She was not indulging him, as he now realized suddenly that most other women had always done. There was some fathomless craving beyond the animal need for sex and it frightened him to feel it. It frightened him much more to sense she felt it too.

Hours later, they lay beside each other on the bed, her face buried in his shoulder, arms around each other. "I want more of that," she whispered. "More and more and more." She felt him tense.

"We can't. Only tonight. I have to get out before it's light and I can't come back." He kissed the top of her head, where her tangled hair made a zigzag part across her scalp. That silky hair that had so enchanted him for the first time just a few days ago. It seemed like another era. It was another era. "Only tonight," he repeated, kissing her. "It's better this way," he insisted quietly when she frowned. "It's not complicated. We'll have unsullied memories of each other, and

the part of each of us that belongs to him will never have to—" He stopped talking abruptly, realizing that she wasn't listening, and realizing why.

She was running her fingers over a ridge of skin near his spine, an ancient wound from the day she was born. "What's that?" she asked, and lifted herself up to peer over his torso in the candlelight. She gasped. "Gwirion! Your back!"

She was staring at the faded scars from the lashing he'd received on Halloween. "That's from my little misadventure with the dogs," he said dismissively, but she shook her head.

"No, I see those, but there's something else here," she insisted, and reached toward the patch of slick, taut scar tissue. "This is much older—"

"I fell off a horse when I was nine," he said quickly. "Let me dress now."

They stood before the fireplace. She slipped into a chemise and then Noble's long wool robe for warmth, and helped him back on with his clothes so coquettishly that by the time he was ready to go, their hands were all over each other again. "Please stay," she whispered into his neck and ran her hands down his front. "Just once more. Quickly, we'll stay dressed—"

"Do you want me to get caught?" he asked backing away, his voice rising in alarm. "If there's light enough to see someone climbing over the wall, those men will shoot to kill."

She threw her arms around him one final time, hating to let go, and he held her tightly, her face nuzzling his collarbone, her knees bending slightly to press against his legs. They stayed in this final clench, lost in each other's presence, too distracted to hear the dim noises rising from the courtyard on the other side of the tower, or even, a moment later, slippered feet racing up the wooden steps outside and low voices greeting each other on the other side of the door.

The king's doorkeeper Gethin rapped hard, and—against all custom or decorum—entered immediately, torch in hand. "Milady!" he cried, heading automatically for the bed before looking toward the now-dim fire and feeble candlelight. In that moment of delay they

dropped their embrace and leapt apart, but Gwirion had no chance to hide.

Gethin blinked in surprise to see him and forgot to bow to Her Majesty. "How did you get in here? I've been on guard since the queen went to bed."

"Scaled the wall," Gwirion said in a high voice, trying to sound casual. "I've just terrified Her Majesty." Her Majesty was too flustered to act terrified, so he babbled on. "Saw a light in the window and assumed the king was back somehow—"

"He is!" the doorkeeper nearly bellowed, grinning. "They saw him from the beacon tower and he'll be here in ten minutes or less, that's why Gwilym requested Her Majesty to come to hall. Oh, Gwirion lad, but he'll be glad you're home safe. You must both come down to greet him."

She felt him sway beside her and she took his arm to support him. "Gwirion is feeling poorly," she said. "He's had a rough journey out and back, and he's chilled. I am excusing him from seeing the king tonight."

"Oh, Your Majesty, I don't know about that. The king would want to see him if he were at death's door. Come on, lad, I'll take you down to the kitchen and see what Marged can do for you. We'll see you when you're ready, milady."

Before either of them could object, the burly fellow had scooped Gwirion up under one arm and was escorting him out of the room, radiating cheer. Gwirion managed to turn his head and give her a traumatized look of resignation before he disappeared down the steps. Alone, she leaned against the mantel, uncertain if she wanted to laugh or weep.

THE queen's chandler hurriedly lit rushes around the hall. Outside in the bailey, the castle population had gathered in the cold to shake off sleep and greet their sovereign. Noble reined in his

sweat-drenched mount, Efan and three soldiers riding up behind him looking agitated and exhausted. Everyone had tried to talk His Majesty out of doing this. The sky was clear and the moon bright enough to travel by, he'd argued. On foot, perhaps, and in familiar territory, Cadwgan had angrily admonished him, begging him not to run a tired horse through unfamiliar hills at night. The roads from Wigmore to Cymaron, Noble had rebutted impatiently, were well worn from the days of the Mortimer occupation, and traversing nothing but treeless hills, they could be trusted in dim light. Since he had no chance of changing horses along the way he would obviously not spend his mount foolishly, but he had delayed enough already and did not want to wait until morning to be gone. He'd wanted to go alone, arguing that even a single guard would slow him down, but Efan refused to let him leave the camp without an escort.

He had been supping with Llewelyn and their officers near Knighton as the armies traveled home, preparing to split off to go to their respective kingdoms the following morning and celebrating their last night of war rations by drinking as much as possible. They were cheering the settlement they'd forced on Mortimer, crowing triumphantly over Thomas's release and the terms, which were all to Mortimer's loss. Just as King Richard's benign neglect gave the Marcher baron freedom to run wild with ambition, it gave him little to fall back upon for help in a defeat. Lord Maelgwyn ap Cadwallon, King of Maelienydd, had decided all the terms.

Throughout that final supper, he'd waited. He waited as the ceremonious toasts acknowledged him the supreme and successful commander. He waited as the camp bards and the bards from Gwynedd paid him elaborate praise. He waited, barely wetting his lips, smiling and laughing with the officers who were all guzzling foul brew on the grounds that the less there was to carry, the faster they could get home. He waited until he knew everyone's attentions were truly turned away from war and toward their own homes, until Llewelyn's value as his comrade-in-arms was of substance only to the bards.

Then he had his dagger at Llewelyn's throat too fast for even the keenest guards to stop him, and cleared the tent of everybody else,

declaring that only one of them would leave the tent alive if blade met blade. However savvier a politician and tactician the Prince of Gwynedd was, Noble was a better swordsman—at least when he was cold sober and Llewelyn wasn't—and Llewelyn knew that. He chose at once to admit his mischief, and Noble, not condescending to speak further with him, called in Father Idnerth to negotiate a penalty. Ten minutes later the king was on horseback racing toward Castell Cymaron.

He wondered as he rode why he suddenly felt emotional. Gwirion had obviously escaped safely and might even be back at the castle before him. The queen was safe. Nobody was hurt. The danger was over. There was no need for him to come flying home belatedly this way; he had known something was amiss for two days and nights and he'd done nothing about it, and all had come out fine. Still his breath caught, thinking what it must have been like for them, his two dependents so completely unprepared. It warmed him that Gwirion had put himself in harm's way for his wife. It was her face that hovered in his mind's eye now, and a rare tenderness threatened to weaken his limbs. He was ashamed and furious that a fellow Welshman had betrayed her trust, and he wanted to wrap reassuring arms around her and promise her she would be safe now. And he would have a chance to do that before sunup.

His spirits were high as he flung the reins to a waiting groom and tried to dismount. But the crowd—villagers, servants, the scrawny men who'd stayed behind to guard the castle, and the petitioners who'd been locked inside the village walls—swarmed around his horse and lifted him onto their shoulders, cheering, crowing with delight at his safe return and the presumed victory it presaged. He was taken aback by the excitement but then, laughing, let them carry him. A great wobbling carpet of heads and hands, they rushed up the steps to the great hall and cheered again when they saw his wife waiting to receive him.

She was across the room, standing alone by the low embers of the fire, in a chemise and surcoat, her hair braided hurriedly and

hanging limply down her back. She was startled by the joyful on-slaught, but seeing who it carried, knelt down respectfully at once. The crowd, with the awkward grace of a collective entity, brought king to queen and slid him gently to his feet to stand beside her, before retreating to where they could all gawk and listen without crowding the couple. "Milady," Noble said, taking her hands and pulling her up. "I praise every god in creation for your safety." He pecked her formally on each cheek and then, so relieved to feel her small frame in his grasp, kissed her passionately on the lips for a moment, not noticing her tremulous response. There was a hearty caw of approval from around the room. Noble glanced at the congregation as if seeing them for the first time, then turned back to his wife, stroking her face with roughened hands smelling of leather and horse sweat.

"Are you well?"

"Yes, milord," she managed to say. "Just a bit overwhelmed by all the excitement."

"Things will be in order now," he assured her, and murmured quietly, a private message for the only one who really cared, "Your brother is safely back in his home." A small sob of gratitude escaped her and she hugged him. He loved the feel of her slender arms clinging to him, and stroked her hair, resting his chin on the top of her head until she had collected herself. Then he took her hand, turned to the crowd surrounding them, and announced, "The fighting is over. We are victorious and all our terms are met." They cheered again, ecstatically; they had no idea what the terms were, but "victorious" sounded promising. "And I've had it out with the upstart prince who subjected you all to his cousin's rude visit. We'll have no more problems from that border either." This had more immediate meaning for them, so the cheering was ecstatic and prolonged.

Noble was about to dismiss them all to return to bed, when he saw a small figure near the kitchen, nearly hidden behind Gethin's bulk and drinking deeply from a cup. The king's face lit up. "Gwirion!" he cried out, and instantly the crowd turned its collective

exuberance in the same direction. The doorkeeper, swept up in the spirit of the moment, jovially grabbed the startled Gwirion under the arms and lifted his limp form high in the air, presenting him to all like a sacred relic.

Noble broke through the crowd to reach him. Gethin lowered him into the king's strong embrace and he hung inert in Noble's arms. "It's a master politician we have here—I should make you my heir! Our little hero, and come home already!" The castle populace cheered with approval around him and he looked so joyful it made Gwirion want to kill himself. He was trapped now. Antidotal to the alarming novelty of the last few days, Noble's familiarity calmed something in Gwirion; the seductive aroma of charisma was already weaving its way around his rib cage. His eyes met Isabel's briefly over the crowd. She knew he wasn't leaving now. And she turned away, understanding it was for the king, not herself, that he was staying.

The king dismissed the collected huddle with a gesture and turned his full attention to his friend. "How long have you been back?" he asked quietly, still smiling, as the crowd dispersed.

"Just a few minutes, sire, I'm surprised we didn't come across each other outside the gates. I've been on foot and I'm chilled through, so—"

"Come up for a bit to my room. Play for me," he said, "and for the queen. What you did was tremendous, Gwirion, for the kingdom and for me, but also for her. This is the beginning of a great friendship for the three of us, I hope."

Gwirion decided then that the only way out of the situation was sudden death. "Noble," he said miserably, in a quiet voice although people had already wandered out of earshot. "I've been with your wife."

"Yes, I know, shut up in—"

"I mean carnally," Gwirion said with a wince.

The king chuckled. "Indeed? You always were a fellow of extremes. Come on up, just a tune or two—"

"I'm serious," Gwirion said in his most humorless voice. "Christ, Noble, send me away."

He only laughed harder. "I hope this is a quick jest, Gwirion, it's too late to get into something complicated."

"And what is the jest?" demanded Isabel in a too bright voice, appearing suddenly at Noble's elbow. The bottom of Gwirion's stomach fell out.

Noble merely smiled. "I don't think it's for a lady's ears. Finish it tomorrow, won't you, Gwirion? It's an excellent deadpan." He put a hand on each of their shoulders, looking between them with satisfaction. "I'm so pleased," he said. He turned to his wife. "Do you know how extraordinary it is for Gwirion to have done that?" And back to his friend, beaming: "Truly. You amaze me. You of all people."

"It's not as if he despised me," the queen protested, slightly unnerved by Noble's wonderment.

The king shook his head. "It has nothing to do with you. I'm amazed that Gwirion left the castle at all. Gwirion doesn't take to the open road, do you, my friend?" He saw the confused look she shot Gwirion, who ignored it. Noble slid his arm around her shoulders, pulled her to him, and kissed her cheekbone near her ear. "Come to bed, and I'll explain it."

"Please don't, sire," Gwirion said in a tense voice.

"Then come up with us, distract me from telling tales with a tune on the harp." He kissed her cheek again, more ardently, and murmured, "Would you like a serenade for our reunion?" Gwirion, who heard the question plainly, shut his eyes, wishing he could disappear.

Isabel managed to be equal to it. She leaned against her husband, smiling up at him. "I thought privacy might be in order." Lowering her voice suggestively, she added, "I earned castellan privileges from you before you left. Do you wish to earn them back?"

He nearly did a double take. "I don't need to earn them, they're mine to take—but is my own wife flirting with me?" He looked up at Gwirion, delighted. "I'll have to go to war more often. Come up and play."

Gwirion willed his exhaustion to visually manifest itself. "I've been on the road without rest for two days, sire, I would be a disappointment to you. I need to sleep."

Noble shrugged, then smiled lecherously at his wife. "I hope you don't need to sleep, milady, because I don't intend to let you. Take leave of your new friend for the night." He playfully pivoted her toward Gwirion.

They avoided any direct glance. "Good evening, Gwirion. Thank you. For everything."

"Good evening, milady," he mumbled in response. "It was my privilege."

SHE had straightened the bedchamber before coming down to greet him, but as he cheerfully pulled off his dusty clothes she stared desperately about to make sure no hint of what had just happened here remained.

"What did you mean before?" she asked, to cover her fidgeting. "About Gwirion never leaving the castle?"

Noble sat down on the bed to unstrap his boots. "Haven't you noticed that he doesn't?"

"He has no reason to."

"He invents reasons all the time. Whenever he's angry with me, he threatens to run off. He never has and he never will."

"Why not?" she pressed.

Noble paused, grimacing, fidgeting with the week-old stubble he was desperate to be rid of. "It's not my place to tell you."

She looked at him in surprise; he usually took as much glee in disregarding other people's proprieties as Gwirion himself did. "Not your place? You're the king. It's your place to say whatever you wish to."

"I don't wish to say what happened to Gwirion." He grinned broadly. "What I do wish is for you to undress and lie down. Let's not waste his gallantry in saving your little body from imprisonment." Her stomach tightened as he threw the blankets aside: She had

stripped the sheeting from the bed and hidden it, but had been too flustered and hurried to find a replacement.

"What's the meaning of this?" He frowned, examining the bare mattress. "Why is my bed unmade?"

If he'd asked her a question that required yes or no for an answer, she might have been able to dissemble, but inventing a falsehood at that moment was beyond her. "The sheet was stained," she said, trying to sound casual. She wrapped her arms around herself and suddenly realized that even if she could get through this moment, her body offered as much evidence as the bedding had.

He stared at her for a moment in confusion, then a look of anger crossed his face. "That whoreson," he spat. "Using my bed to rape my servants." He didn't notice her sag heavily against the bedpost as he replaced his annoyance with a suggestive smile. "Well. If the baron has desecrated our bed, then we must resanctify it, mustn't we?" He held out his hand and beckoned for her.

"You're very dusty from the road, shall we bathe first?" she said quickly, silently thanking whatever guardian angel had put the words into her mouth.

He smiled approvingly. "Lord, yes. And let's get rid of this," he added, scratching the beard. "Before I start looking like a Norman. One of those *defeated* fellows."

G UIRION retreated to his closet behind the kitchen chimney, to the warmth and privacy he thought he'd never see again, which he'd been away from for nearly four nights in a row—one of the longest absences of his life. He crawled under his blanket, comforted by the familiar space, and tried hard to pretend he didn't know what the king was doing. He was undoubtedly doing it far better than Gwirion had, which was the best reason to try to forget it was happening.

THE next morning on Noble's orders the entire castle rose late. The king, still jubilant from victory, graciously received spontaneous applause first in chapel and then again at board. The queen missed mass and when she finally appeared, to eat, she moved very gingerly toward the high table, nodding with bashful pleasantness to the many servants and villagers whose adoration she had earned over the past week. She avoided Gwirion's eyes. Noble, watching her with a satisfied grin, whispered to Gwirion, "I gave her the riding of her life, she's never had half so much ploughing in one night."

"Probably not a quarter as much," Gwirion said quietly, feeling ill and picking at his barley bread. If Noble thought it was a deliberate deadpan, at least he didn't have to fake cheeriness. "I'm surprised Your Majesty didn't choose somebody a little more exciting for your homecoming romp."

"I had romps enough at the front," Noble whispered back. "This was better than a romp. And she always smells so good." Gwirion involuntarily made a distressed expression, and Noble laughed. "Stop that, Gwirion, she's not the ogress you pretend she is. Anyhow, all she's useful for now, really, is an heir, and I need one, preferably a legitimate one. This episode with Mortimer has convinced me of that. I'll find another mother if I must, but legitimate offspring would be best, especially if we have to deal with the English in the future."

"Ah, I see," Gwirion said. "You're suspending recreational sex in favor of procreational sex."

Noble grinned. "Exactly."

"Well where's the fun in *that*?" Gwirion said, desperately grasping for something wittier to say and finding his brain turned to mush. *Sound cynical,* he thought, *and perhaps he won't notice anything's different.* He'd already retreated from the impulsive honesty that had led to his confession. His determination to be truthful had evaporated; now he

just wanted the event and all its evidence to permanently disappear, for everybody's sake.

Noble looked pleased with himself. "Oh, I've trained her pretty well by now and she's an admirably apt pupil. When you claim them virginal, you can convince them that almost anything is normal." He grinned. "You're perverse, you might take great advantage of that. What do you say? I owe you a huge favor and you're quite the hero now. I could find you a willing concubine without much trouble."

"No thank you," Gwirion said, but immediately reconsidered. Maybe that was the way to free himself from thoughts of her. "I'd say yes, but I'm so busy saving the kingdom and all that nonsense, I just don't know when I'd find the time to train her."

"I would train her for you." The king winked.

"Aren't you saving yourself for the queen?"

"For you, my friend, I will always make allowances."

"I'm deeply honored," Gwirion said in an exaggerated monotone, and the king clapped him on the shoulder.

"Is it some experiment of yours, this new delivery?"

"Yes, sire, it's so the next time you go away, I can stand in for Gwilym," he said, imitating the steward's somber diction. "And nobody will notice I'm not him."

"Gwilym is twice your size," Noble pointed out.

Gwirion leaned in close to Noble. "Not where it matters, sire," he assured him, with an exaggerated wink.

She watched them whispering together and it enraged her. Obviously Noble was bragging about his performance in bed the night before, and apparently Gwirion was making crass remarks, probably about her, because Noble was smiling and laughing, sometimes folding his hands in front of his lips with the forefingers pressed together, which was always a sign he was hiding a vicious delight. She knew Gwirion had no choice, but it hurt her. He would do whatever he had to do to make things seem normal, to protect himself, and there was no reason to think he'd spare her in the process. It was safer for both of them if he didn't, in fact, but she wasn't sure she could

survive it. Maybe he would decide to run off after all. The thought brought as much depression as it did relief.

After the meal, she excused herself to her chamber and closed herself in with the sewing bevy. These were her only safe companions now, she realized with an internal groan. She took up her old task of spinning and lost herself in the mesmerizing monotony of the work, remembering last summer when she had also turned to this for comfort. At least then she'd had Adèle. At least then it had been warmer too, and there was sunlight, even if it was relentlessly grey or at best silver. To keep out the winter chill, the windows were now sealed with waxed cloth, and nearly all the light came from the wall sconces. For some reason this didn't give the room the coziness of the receiving chamber below; it only made it feel that much more a cage.

Two tedious hours later there was a knock on the door. She acknowledged it, assuming it was the chandler coming in to check the fire. Instead Gwirion entered carrying a basket of freshly laundered rags. The pit of her gut clenched when she saw him. "Excuse me, Your Majesty, Marged wants to know if the kitchen may have these, or if they should be mended to be of use elsewhere first." He avoided looking at her as he put the basket down, even taking a step away when she approached, pretending to clean his fingernails as he waited. The rags were the remains of bed curtains, hung along the outer sections of the hall to provide nominal privacy at night. They were unstained but very worn.

"We can make sheets of these," she said. "If Marged needs some rags, she may have what's left over, there should be plenty."

He nodded once, excused himself, and left. Isabel immediately put aside her spinning to follow him out.

"Gwirion," she hissed in the shadows of the balcony. He froze, and turned back to her, almost squirming, his foot on the top stair.

"Your Majesty?" he replied as neutrally as he could.

Now she had nothing to say. "Was there a reason for that?" she finally asked.

"Yes, milady," he said respectfully. "Marged wanted to know if—"

"That's not what I meant," she snapped, and it made a bad impression on him in combination with the wimple. She lowered her voice to a whisper, afraid her words would carry down to the hall. "You know that's not what I meant. Why did *you* bring it? You don't run errands for her."

"She asked me to and I couldn't say no without seeming strange," he whispered back, which was the truth. "I was not looking for an excuse to get near you—is that what you're accusing me of?"

"I didn't mean it as an accusation. God forbid you actually try to be in my presence."

"I think God does forbid it," he answered. "I'm not much of a Christian so I ignore him. But I'm not an idiot either. We have to stay away from each other until we can behave normally and pretend nothing happened."

Everything vulnerable inside her wanted to shriek at him, but she forced herself to stay calm. "You're saying that once we've lost the desire to be around each other, then we may be around each other."

He almost smiled. "Yes, I suppose that's it."

"Since avoiding each other is logistically impossible, could we perhaps discuss alternatives?"

"Could you perhaps be more officious?" he answered with nervous sarcasm. But he stepped away from the stairs, then slipped around behind her and began playing with her veil, trying not to think about all that it was shielding from his view. He spoke in a low voice, not a whisper; whispering, if anyone in the hall happened to glance up and see them here, would look suspicious. "Your headdress slipped and I'm adjusting it for you." She nodded, picked up her rosary and ran her fingers anxiously around the outline of the crucifix. "First of all," he said quietly, "it will not happen again, you understand that, don't you?"

"*Yes*," she said with exaggerated impatience, furious that he'd said it first. Or perhaps that he'd said it at all. His touch, even in passing on the back of her veil, made her light-headed. She tugged at the shadowed side of her wimple and pulled the whole thing askew, to give him something real to do with his nervous fingers.

"And it's better for us to stay away from each other until we're each . . . calmer about it."

"We can't shun each other utterly," she insisted. "He believes us to be friends at least."

"He has no idea what a friendship between us would resemble. Considering our history, simply ignoring each other could constitute profound affection."

"Maybe six months ago, but not now. Now he would notice."

"Your Majesty," Gwirion corrected, with a grudging smile at her naiveté, "Even *I* lack the exaggerated self-importance to believe that Noble will notice *anything* in the next week but celebrating his victory and dispersing the army. He won't even open court again until Lent at the earliest. There couldn't *be* a better time for us to snub each other." Inspired—and desperate—he grabbed the opportunity to estrange her and with a harsh tug on the wimple added: "You should realize that better than I, Your Majesty—you're the one obsessed with invading the enclave of courtly power. Speaking of which, how many points do you score for ensnaring the king's top man? That must be quite a coup."

She drew a sharp, indignant breath, but caught herself and said with cutting dryness, "Kindly envision me turning around and smacking you very hard across the face." He had to duck his head away to hide how charmed he was by the retort. "I presume your silence is an acknowledgment that you were speaking rubbish," she continued. "If you said it to generate antagonism, then you're very shortsighted. Antagonism *will* catch his attention. You should know that, it's how you curry favor with him half the time."

He resented how attractive the uttering of insults made her. "Then are we agreed that an act of mutual indifference is the safest course for now?"

"No," she insisted. "It must be an affectation of friendship, if you can possibly bring yourself to be decent to me. Anything else will make him suspicious."

"A compromise, then," Gwirion said stubbornly. "Two weeks of cold shoulders followed by a month of pleasantries."

"He believes us to be friends *now*."

"Well then, he's wrong. It has been known to happen. And now I must be going, I've run out of wimple." He stepped away, not looking at her.

"Do you regret that it happened?" she asked before she could stop herself.

"Considering the consequences, of course I regret it," he whispered impatiently, moving toward the stairs, but then he softened. "If I had escaped, no, I wouldn't regret it at all." He would not look her in the face. "Am I excused, Your Majesty?"

THAT evening the king and queen, standing together, opened the hall for Candlemas and the entire village walked up to the castle carrying tapers. This holiday, in the bleakest, dullest part of the year, was a symbol of hope and renewal: The procession of candles was a collective reminder that the sun, the great god Llew, was returning to them at last. This had been manipulated by the church into the Feast of the Purification of the Virgin, a day celebrating Mary's ritual cleansing after childbirth, and her return to the church ("What church?" Gwirion interrupted incredulously when Father Idnerth attempted to give his usual brief sermon between courses at the supper feast. "Jesus hadn't yet been crucified, there was no church!")

And this year, of more import than any symbolic or religious meaning, there was a victory to celebrate: Roger Mortimer had been prevented, again, from taking Maelienydd. The queen's brother was free, his lands restored to him, and his primary allegiance sworn to Noble. Thomas would host a large, permanent garrison of Welsh fighters who would patrol the border, overseeing new standing defenses: a dyke and palisade, to be built and paid for by Roger Mortimer. Noble explained all this informally to the assembly; the people were thrilled, even with the details they did not quite understand,

and the ready flow of ale made their laughter, their applause, and their general delight ring out in peals into the night. The king also took a moment to publicly acknowledge Gwilym's selfless and unprecedented yielding of castellan rights to the queen, and to praise the queen for her able job of standing in for him while he was away. "My mother Queen Efa and all who came before her would rejoice to add this woman to the roster of worthy consorts," he declared, and she blushed, more grateful for his praise than for all the adoration of their subjects. He had never so nearly treated her like a peer—all the more remarkable now, when she knew full well that the political value of the marriage had been virtually nullified. Gwirion watched silently from the hearthside, sadly dazzled by how beautiful she was when she was happy.

Isabel feared that the hour-long elegiac poem about Cadwallon's murder would be dragged out again, but instead a young poet—sent by Llewelyn as part of his damage payment—presented a poem in progress extolling Noble's virtue in battle. Gwirion, who'd resolutely refused to speak to the queen all evening, looked trapped, almost persecuted, by a verse singing his praises for heroically defending her. He did not return to his normal humor until the applause and cheering had died away and the chaplain was halfway through the blessing in honor of the spring hunt, which would begin the next morning at dawn. In keeping with tradition, most of Idnerth's hunting prayer was drowned out by urgent whispered conferences between the villagers and castle servants concerning, for example, bets placed on chess games between the mayor and the steward.

Then Gwirion was asked to perform. He had played for them all five thousand times before, but tonight it was as if an archangel were gracing them with his artistry; this was his share of the adoring celebrity the people of Maelienydd were slathering on the three of them. Noble had offered him new clothes, but he'd refused them, saying he preferred his familiar shabby, shapeless garments. He did this entirely because he wanted desperately to look handsome to the queen and refused to let himself indulge the impulse.

She'd been able to distract her mind from the poet's incantation,

but the harp went right through her. As always, his first tune was "Rhiannon's Tears," and hearing it distressed her so deeply she had to make an excuse to her husband and leave the hall. Needing privacy and knowing Angharad and Madrun were in the solar, she slipped out into the courtyard, hiding in the shadowed niche between the end of the hall and the barbican tower. She hadn't brought a mantle with her, not wanting to draw attention by asking for one, and within moments she was shaking from the cold, but she hardly noticed. She knelt down and lifted the hem of her skirt to her face, wracked by frustrated sobs. When she had finally calmed herself, she pressed the heels of her hands against the frozen building stones until they were almost numb, then held them over her eyes until, she hoped, the evidence of her weeping had subsided.

Inside, Gwirion had finished playing and was sitting next to Noble—in her chair. Whose idea was that? Nervously, she approached the two men. They sat in their usual evening poses, Noble reclining comfortably, legs stretched out before him with feet crossed at the ankles and his fingers interlaced behind his head, Gwirion sitting upright and alert, almost pitched forward, as if he were about to be catapulted somewhere. They both noticed her approach and responded at the same moment but in very different ways: Noble, with an easy smile to her, signaled Hafaidd to bring another seat, but Gwirion leapt out of her chair as if the bottom were on fire. Realizing he'd drawn Noble's attention by his abruptness, he continued the natural arc of his movement by dropping into a cartwheel that landed him on the far side of the king. Then, as if this were a perfectly common mode of perambulating, he settled nonchalantly on the floor by Noble's seat and fixed his attention on the young bard who was performing.

"You needn't spring away like that, Gwirion, I don't have the plague," Isabel said in a pleasant voice as she sat, determined to show him how easy and preferable it was to be kindly toward each other.

"I'm sorry, did Your Majesty speak?" he said impassively, not looking at her. "I missed it."

"I said I don't have the plague," she repeated, still very sweetly,

and busied herself adjusting and smoothing her skirt to affect offhandedness.

"I never suggested that you did, milady," he said reasonably, and straightened up again, pointedly looking at the musician.

Not even a jibe. If anything, she thought irritably, he would raise Noble's suspicions by his very blandness. And Noble did, in fact, find it an odd exchange.

"Are you being short with the queen, Gwirion?" he asked warningly.

"Not as short as I am with you, sire, considering you're a good deal taller than she is. I'll be less short if you wish it, though." In a single smooth move, he leapt up onto the arm of Noble's chair, perched on the backrest—and then sat astride the royal shoulders, as Noble lurched to keep his balance from the suddenness of the action. "Now I'm far from short!" Gwirion crowed. "I'm taller even than you. In fact, if you would just stand up, I'll reach such heights that you need never fear my being short with anyone again."

"We'll see about that," Noble muttered. He stood slowly, lifting Gwirion on his shoulders, and the entire hall turned to stare at them. The bard silenced his instrument; nobody even noticed. Gwirion, grinning, waved grandly as the king took a few steps away from the hearth toward a clump of matted rushes strewn on the floor. He braced his hands just above his knees and with an abrupt jerking motion flung his upper body forward until he was bent over double. Gwirion, with a startled grunt, tumbled off the descending royal shoulders and landed on his back on the rushes, his complaints drowned out by laughter from their audience.

"I'd rather you be short, at least then I can keep an eye on you," Noble said with an affectionate smirk, giving him a hand up.

"As it pleases His Most Royal Majesty," Gwirion intoned a little breathlessly, recovering at once and giving him a very exaggerated bow. "But now, if you'll excuse me, I'm for bed." Ignoring the queen, he bowed his head to Noble and departed for his little room, acknowledging the affectionate farewells that the crowd called out to him.

"What a silly fellow," Noble said, smiling, sitting again beside

his wife, his mind a thousand miles away from the awkward moment that had birthed the silliness. She didn't reply, afraid her voice would not be steady. This was even worse than the old antagonism. Now he was camouflaging his coldness to her, not flaunting it as he had before, so there was no way to seek even sympathy from Noble, let alone reprieve from Gwirion himself.

AFTERMATH

Lent, 1199

HE KING was distracted over the next fortnight; his focus was, as Gwirion had predicted,
entirely upon security and military matters. Specific conditions for Mortimer were declared,
written, signed, and delivered not only to Roger
himself but to King Richard's court, and to the
manors of all the other Marcher lords, to warn them off interfering
with Maelienydd's borders. The army came home and dispersed,
which required days of delegating paperwork so that each man's military contribution to the crown could be measured and entered into
the rolls. Accounts of the victorious raid were written up and sent to
every manor and castle throughout Wales, an invitation to immortalize Maelgwyn ap Cadwallon in poetry and song. Congratulatory
notes and gifts poured in; these were cataloged and archived and announced at supper each night, spinning out the golden hour of victory into days, then weeks.

Of greater urgency was the settlement with Llewelyn. Noble's
first demand was freedom from his obligation to support Llewelyn's

claims against other Welshmen—and a sworn oath that he and his subjects would never have to pay obeisance to the Prince of Gwynedd in any way, even if Llewelyn should in time conquer the whole of Britain. For Cynan's offenses, Llewelyn replaced thrice over the appropriated food and fodder, and paid a massive fine that Noble split between the state coffers and his molested servants. Llewelyn sent his own envoy to apologize and swear profusely that from now on, the rising star of Gwynedd would work in league with Noble in all things. Noble accepted the proclamation graciously, knowing it to be a lie. In private, he mused briefly on a mitigating tie by marriage between their two courts, but dismissed the thought at once—a marriage bond had not staved off Mortimer's ambition, after all.

Finally, there was Huw to deal with. Assisting Cynan to plan the infiltration of Cymaron was an act of treason and treason called for hanging. But Huw's three sons were not yet old enough to claim their patrimony and there was a very real danger his cousin would seize his lands. The cousin was in Powys, the neighboring kingdom, already causing problems for his own prince, and he was a known champion of Llewelyn. So Noble grudgingly argued clemency for Huw on the grounds, ironically, of national security. The royal court fined him nearly enough to beggar him, and three of Noble's teulu were sent to his household as a permanent guard, to be at all times in hearing distance of him—and of Branwyn, who entertained more men than he did.

Nobody, including Isabel, was entirely certain if she was still Noble's deputy in quotidian matters of the realm, matters he neglected for a fortnight. So while he attended to weightier issues, the court hovered in near stasis, tentatively taking its lead from her. The council met only once to discuss domestic matters; Goronwy heard no cases; the coffers were kept closed for all but minor expenditures, all at Isabel's authorization.

That fortnight culminated in Shrove Tuesday's final huge indulgence before the Lenten fast. The village children were hired to ring the chapel bell unceasingly for hours, as inside the hall everyone in-

haled what little fresh food was left to them, smothering everything in butter, cheese, and lard. There was an air of forceful gaiety and excess to the evening, since everybody knew what was to follow come the morning mass.

Gwirion as always sat behind the king's left shoulder at the feast, managing to smile and laugh and contribute his usual puerility. He had become exhausted by the constant vigilance required in the queen's presence. Her "friendliness" was a feeble pretext for what, to him, was dangerous behavior. But he hoped that finally he had guided her to a comfortable level of coolness, in which they never spoke directly to each other (or rather, he never spoke directly to her, nor did he acknowledge anything she said directly to him), and yet they could engage in a triptych conversation when Noble was between them. Although his humor remained excessively libidinous, he made no bawdy jokes about her to her husband; in fact, he had nearly transmuted his image of her to that of a sexless curiosity who happened to sleep in the king's bed. It was a fiction he was certain he could grow accustomed to believe in time. And so by the great feast of Shrove Tuesday, he had very nearly convinced himself that everything was back to normal.

Noble rose as the final course of veal was being cleared away, and raised his cup, gesturing to his wife in her brightest veil and kirtle to stand beside him. She looked gracious and confident—even though he'd apprised her of the speech he was about to make, and it was hard for her to feel gracious about it. He gazed out over the rows of happily tipsy villagers and castle denizens, a firm but loving father. "My people," he called out, and waited for it to quiet. He spoke with unwonted formality. "You whom by the grace of all the gods I'm charged to steward. Tonight we feast together because tomorrow we bend under the solemn yoke assigned to us as faithful Christians. In addition, tomorrow my wife and I both bend under the particular yokes assigned to us by God—I by returning my full attention to the duties of the throne, she by returning her full attention to her duties as my queen and yours. I have been remiss this

fortnight, neglecting my more domestic duties in favor of settling the issues at the borders. I now turn my energies home and hearthward, so that my gracious bride, who has been so selflessly and valiantly burdened as my deputy, may now entirely return to the role that is preferred for her by God, by nature, and by her own sweet spirit—to be my consort and the mother of our kingdom's heir." He beamed warmly at her in front of all of them and she managed to return the expression, but her throat constricted at the import of the words. Then a suggestive little smile tickled the corners of his mouth and he winked at her, reverting to his usual, more personable demeanor. "In the evening's spirit of excess, I'll be particularly ardent possessing her tonight, by way of symbolically repossessing my entire court." The crowd, hardly hearing what the words were, catching only the tone that assured them he was being lecherous, cheered him, especially when he added, leering, "I admonish all my soldiers to similarly repossess your own private domains. Tomorrow let us greet the Lenten season knowing we are truly back in residence." He grinned. Gwirion had managed a halfhearted expression of approval and was preparing to top off Noble's speech with something appropriately prurient, when the king raised his voice and finished grandly: "My castle shall be under my jurisdiction again, as shall my court of law, my council, my people, and also, of course"—he gestured broadly over his shoulder—"my beloved sacrificial fool!" He laughed heartily and spun to his left, startling Gwirion with an effusive embrace as the crowd cheered approval. Gwirion smiled weakly, absolutely flummoxed how to respond to this. Isabel felt her knees almost buckle, and prayed no one was looking at her. Nobel, still radiating cheer, released his friend, who sat down very abruptly on his stool. "Yes," Noble continued to the crowd, grinning, "we are very grateful that she had good use of him in my absence, but now she must relinquish her hero so that my court can have its jester back. So come, madam," he finished with a flourish, "to my bed. We have a kingdom to restore to custom—all these good people are relying on you to give me what is mine and therefore theirs." He led

her grandly around the table and out of the hall toward the stairs up to his bedroom; she followed, looking pale.

Gwirion knew he should have made some approving, lewd comment as they departed but he did not trust himself to speak. As soon as it was safe, he forced himself to wander very slowly toward the kitchen with his empty tumbler. Then he dived into his little closet room, grateful for the privacy, trying to will Noble's comment from his head.

When the meal was cleared, the happy, sodden congregation followed Marged out to the forge, where she ceremoniously gave the smith an old cooking pot. He smashed it against his small block anvil with his heaviest hammer, crushing it.

Lent had begun. It was a time to honor discipline and deprivation.

AT breakfast the next day Gwirion felt compelled to keep up an almost constant stream of whispered witticisms to the king, about any topic under heaven except the queen. Half the time he rambled incoherently and could barely invent punch lines to justify his yammering. He resented the effort it required.

Isabel eyed them whispering over the king's shoulder in the shadows, just as they had done for at least as long as she had been alive. She felt iron splinters in her gut simply watching them. Whenever Noble smiled she winced, certain that Gwirion had somehow just sacrificed her dignity. For two weeks now he'd neatly deflected her innocent attempts at interaction, distracting the king with jokes, insults, or antics. He never once allowed himself a simple, friendly exchange with her. Clearly this was what he thought was necessary to protect them both, but to her it was unfeeling and excessive. It hurt more now than it had the first day. She had to make him stop.

]UST stop it," she begged, when she managed to make their solitary paths cross by the well that afternoon. The smith was in his
shop beside them and the echoing tenor clank of his hammer offered
them some privacy of speech.

"But that's what the king expects of me."

"And you always have to do what he expects of you?"

"You don't?" he snapped. "He wants your body and my wit. I'll
withhold my wit if you withhold your body." He fumbled, realizing
it had sounded like a wish. Before she could respond he pressed on
brusquely, "But that of course is not the proper *use* of royal fools,
now is it?"

"He meant nothing by that comment last night," she said, nervously but firm. "That was his Welsh oratory getting the better of
him in the moment."

"Of course he *meant* something by it, he was warning me away
from you. That was a threat. He doesn't even want us speaking to
each other."

"Don't be ridiculous," she hissed impatiently. "I was with him
the full ten hours after he said it and—"

"I *know* that," he sneered, appalled at himself for speaking jealously.

"—and there was nothing off in his behavior," she insisted, ignoring his interjection. "Nothing pointed, no hints or threats of
even the subtlest kind. It was only a guilty conscience that heard
more than what he said."

"It's *your* guilty conscience that needs to believe something so
naive about him."

Isabel frowned. "At the very worst," she said, in partial concession, "he suspects we might have strayed, that's all. He was making it
clear that *if* we did, we mustn't stray again. In fact, in a way it was forgiveness, because he publicly reclaimed us both."

"Your Majesty, please," Gwirion said quietly, worried that peo-

ple passing through the courtyard were noticing him upset their new darling. "We're bickering as if we were lovers, as if we were carrying on. We're not. So there's nothing more to say."

"May we at least be friendly?" she insisted. "It wasn't just lust, it was affection. We came to have real regard for each other. Can't we try to be easy in that?"

She looked small and vulnerable and he was annoyed with her for rousing gentle impulses in him. He frowned, a hard, angry expression. "No, not after his resounding proclamation," he said. "He's so possessive of us both, it's just too dangerous." But the hardness wavered. "And too ... strange," he added, sounding regretful. He walked off, briskly, toward the main gate where he had been headed when she'd stopped him. She felt her eyes smart and took a moment to steady her breathing.

Gwirion had been called to the barbican to help greet a traveling party. Although St. David's Day, March 1, was two weeks off, some folk were beginning Lenten pilgrimages to the saint's home village, far to the southwest in Deheubarth, and the occasional gentleman pilgrim asked leave to stay the night in Cymaron on his way. The flag of the approaching party, a white Maltese cross on a red field, looked vaguely familiar, but Gwirion couldn't place it—until he recognized Corr's patrons, Humffri ap Madoc and his wife. She wore images of daffodils embroidered on her veil; the real ones weren't yet available to make offerings. Humffri handed down his spear to Einion the porter and coaxed his spotted charger farther into the bailey where a groom was waiting.

A servant who had come in on a large grey pack beast at the tail end of the entourage tossed a lumpy sack of oats practically on Gwirion's head. He sputtered with annoyance and pushed the sack off him to the ground, then looked up to castigate the offender. He saw only a skirt, descending on him very fast, and he reflexively held his arms out to catch its occupant.

"You always were a gentleman, Gwirion," a cheerful peasant accent said in his ear as he got his bearings.

He looked at his burden, and with a crow of delight he

dropped her to her feet and then almost smothered her in an embrace. *"Enid!"*

AFTER Gwirion had exhausted her by dragging her all around the bailey and hoisting her onto his shoulders so she could wave to people working in the towers, Enid sat with him outside the kitchen, both of them wrapped in brychans, and they talked, their breath coming out in mist. As Noble had said, Enid had been taken from the castle, although the bit about shaving her head was an embellishment. She'd been allowed to take her clothes and a few possessions, and had even been given—at Noble's insistence—enough salted meat to last her for a month. She'd found herself at Lord Humffri's gates within a week or two; Corr had happily endorsed her abilities, and a history in the king's kitchen gave her clout. It was assumed, without ever being said, that she had been terminated because she was a favorite of the king's and therefore not of the queen's—"So I promised to keep downstairs this visit," she concluded with a grin that made her nose wrinkle. "And Corr sends greetings, of course. But I want *you* to talk now, tell me what a hero you are. I want to hear your side of this crazy tale about your risking your life to save the queen."

Gwirion rolled his eyes. "That gives it a veneer of romance that simply isn't there."

"Suddenly everyone seems to adore her—haven't you become bosom buddies with herself, then?" Enid teased innocently.

Gwirion was suddenly fidgety. "No. Nothing's changed. Nothing to tell."

"Pranks?" she asked, dark eyes glittering. "Tell me your latest prank."

He shrugged, staring at the ground. "No good pranks lately. Actually, I think he's getting bored with me." He glanced at her sidewise and leered. "Maybe he needs your sort of entertainment."

"The queen has been through enough of late without having to

endure me again." Enid laughed. "She's a sweet lady underneath it all, Gwirion; I don't want to upset her." He was looking at her strangely. "What?"

It was right here, at his feet, the perfect opportunity to embrace disaster. "She—" he stammered, "she understands him a little better now. I don't think she'd be upset if he met with you. In fact, with this new obsession he has for getting an heir of her, she'd probably like a night free from him, the poor girl." He tried hard to believe that he was only doing this to give himself a respite from the gut-twisting jealousy that convulsed him every night. He would not go to her. He would simply relax with the gratitude of knowing she too was alone.

Enid smoothed a patch of mud with the sole of her buskin, considering the proposal. She hadn't appreciated, until she'd left this place, either the flattery or the actual pleasure of the king's attentions. For all of her deliberate sunniness, her life lacked enjoyable diversions. "Are you sure?" she asked.

"I'll arrange it for late tonight. In his audience chamber. Then you're not even breaking your promise about staying downstairs."

Enid grinned. "All right." She nudged him. "Since we're on the subject, have you put any notches on your belt since our little misadventure?"

"No!" he said, too loudly and too quickly. She laughed.

"That kind of no means yes with a naughty tale behind it."

"No it doesn't," Gwirion said, looking away.

She took his head and turned it toward her, ducking down to make eye contact when he wouldn't look up. "Confess, Gwirion. Is it a girl? A boy? A horse?"

He finally looked at her, considering something. "You mustn't tell a soul." He gestured her close and whispered, very gravely, "I've decided to become a nun."

"Gwirion!" She laughed and swatted him through the blankets. "I'm serious."

"So am I. What better way to get my filthy claws into a gaggle of virgins?"

Enid gave him an affectionate smile, but shook her head. "You can't distract me from this." She looked at him appraisingly. "Something's different."

"No it isn't," he said quickly.

"Yes. Something's definitely different. I noticed it in your eyes right away."

"Feminine imagination," he scoffed, and turned his head away again.

"If you don't look at me, I'll know there's something there that you're trying to hide and I'll assume the worst," she said. "So you might as well let me have the real story."

After an obstinate and nervous pause, he turned back toward her with a false front of defiance, but wouldn't look directly in her eyes. She examined his face with the absorption of a physician, and sobered. "Forgive me, Gwirion, I shouldn't have teased you," she said softly. "What's her name?"

Gwirion gave her a panicked expression. "Can't tell you," he answered, although when he'd opened his mouth, he'd meant to deny it completely.

"Does the king know?"

"Of course not!" he said, his eyes widening. "Don't tell him!"

"Of course I'm not going to tell him, idiot. I remember what happened the last time, and that was just one night with me, as if *I* were any threat! Won't you tell me who, though? I'm not going to blab."

He shook his head, jaw set, and no amount of cajoling would change his mind.

SUPPER that night was brief and informal—and Lenten, being mostly salted fish. Humffri's bard Brychan ap Caradog, accompanying him on this pious pilgrimage, was given the honor of

performing for His Majesty, which freed Gwirion. The prankster whispered a brief word to the king, promising him a special treat and more than a little mischief if he waited in his receiving chamber after supper. Then he excused himself from hall for the night, afraid that given the opportunity his mouth might operate without his permission and let the queen know the madness he was trying not to contemplate.

He joined Enid with Marged's little stable of assistants in the warm stone kitchen where they were catching up on gossip, drinking, and belching. Enid was helping Marged close down the kitchen for the evening, since most of her attendants—using Enid's visit as an excuse—were already too tipsy. Gwirion was gaily called over to join the party, but people lost interest in him almost at once when they saw he was not in a rowdy mood.

Enid tugged his sleeve and took him aside. "What's wrong?" she asked. "You look like somebody's been practicing rope tricks with your guts."

"It's nothing. I just need an easy night's sleep, which I'm finally going to get." He gave her a grim smile. "Enjoy yourself tonight." He exited into his closet, yawning.

But lying in the dark, he could not begin to relax. Knowing the queen would be alone tonight was even worse than knowing she was with the king. He wanted to touch her so badly it made his throat dry. It was impotent, humiliating desire: All week she had been with a man who knew so much better than he did what to do with her. She must be thanking God for returning her to her senses. Between adultery with a clumsy oaf and sanctified union with an experienced lover, there could not even be a choice. He was almost nauseated with embarrassment, realizing he had let himself think that her annoying behavior this past fortnight was because she still wanted him.

But he still wanted her. He would not be able to sleep knowing there was even a slip of a chance that he could touch her. It was nothing personal, it was just that he was so hungry for a woman's touch, and hers was the only one he had known for so long that of course his desire would think she was the only possible source of sat-

isfaction. But any other woman would do. If he could find himself with another woman, obviously within a night or two this obsession would have transferred smoothly to she-who-was-not-queen. But right now it drove him toward she who was.

He decided to go to Noble's chamber. On the unlikely chance she was there, he would suffer the humiliation of being refused by her, but then at least it would be over, and official. Anyhow, she almost certainly would not appear, so he would simply curl up on velvet cushions and sleep by the fire, as he did sometimes, and tease Noble when he came back from his tryst with Enid. Just like old times.

But of course he couldn't go to Noble's room. She probably would not be there, but it would raise eyebrows—having arranged for the king to be busy, Gwirion goes to the king's room, where the queen usually retires? That would look suspicious. He couldn't go.

But he couldn't sleep. He couldn't even rest. The kitchen sounds had quieted down, and throwing a blanket around himself he stepped out of his room.

Enid was still perched on the cutting table, alert and awake, while the floor around her was covered with sleeping forms on matted reeds, wrapped in mantles and brychans, huddled together for warmth. She gave him a pleased but surprised look when he appeared.

"I thought you were asleep," she whispered.

"Couldn't," he whispered back. "Too early. Why aren't you with the king?"

"I'm just waiting for the ladies to retire. He's in his audience chamber but the queen is still talking with my mistress in hall, and I can't go to him right in front of her."

He wished she would. That was a terrible, stupid, foolish wish but he wished she would. If the queen saw Enid go in to Noble, she'd know her husband would be detained all night, and perhaps she would go not to her own room, the sewing bevy within earshot, but to the privacy of the king's chamber, and perhaps if she found him there she would not refuse him, if for no other reason than anger at the king's dalliance with Enid. He almost told her to go. No. He

couldn't. He had to keep himself from doing anything idiotic. He would walk. He would cross over to the keep and walk around all night, until he saw Noble's chandler light his room for him, until any possible opportunity for meeting her was over. He had been such an ass to arrange this assignation. His mischief was supposed to torment other people, not himself.

"Gwirion, you really don't look well," Enid was saying, trying to bring him back from whatever interior world he had vanished into. "Is it your stomach? Shall I mix something up for you?"

"I'm going for a stroll," he said abruptly. He picked his way over the sleeping bodies and disappeared through the back entrance, past the well, into the night. Enid, watching him go, noticed he was barefoot. *Something is going on with that fellow,* she thought, tickled and concerned at the same time.

THE queen finally bid good night to their visitors, who had paid her priest to perform a special late-night Ash Wednesday mass for them. Noble had earlier excused himself to finish reviewing the accounts. He told his wife he didn't know when he would be finished, and that if she preferred to go up to her own room tonight, she should do so. The temperature had dropped during supper, and she decided to accept his offer, since there was no way to cross over to his chamber without going out into the frigid night. Even the hall was chilly; the servants who slept in here had decided as a unit to attend the late mass with Humffri, simply for the collective body warmth of standing close together in the relatively airtight chapel. The great hall, for the first time in Isabel's memory, was absolutely empty.

She had taken two steps up the stairs when she saw a figure slide from the kitchen and into the hall.

It was Enid.

Astonished, her heart suddenly beating very fast, Isabel came

back down the stairs and took a step toward the young woman, blocking her path.

"Excuse me, Enid," she said with remarkable steadiness, and the girl jumped. When she saw who had approached her she squirmed noticeably even as she dropped into a deep curtsy.

"Your Majesty," she said, as innocently as she could, and explained almost apologetically, "I'm here with Lord Humffri."

Isabel fought hard to not sound flustered. "And I presume you're on your way to see the king."

Enid blinked awkwardly and seemed to be looking for an answer just behind the queen's head. "Beg pardon, Your Majesty? I don't know what—"

"Don't dissemble. Are you going to see my husband?"

Enid dropped her eyes, ashamed when she realized the queen wasn't going to stop her. "Yes, ma'am," she murmured, barely audible. "But I won't if you ask it, he doesn't know to expect me."

"Excuse me?"

"It was—" She hesitated. "Please don't be sore at him, Your Majesty, but it was something that Gwirion set up for him as a surprise."

Isabel blinked. "*Gwirion* set this up?" she asked in a fierce whisper.

"Yes, ma'am, but please don't be—"

"He knows the king will be down here tonight? With you?"

"Don't hold him respons—"

"Answer my question!" Isabel demanded.

"Yes, ma'am, he knows, he arranged it," Enid mumbled, looking down, resigned to once again bring royal disfavor on her friend. When the queen said nothing, she looked up again, and was confused by a feverish look on Her Majesty's face.

"This was Gwirion's idea?" she asked again. "He wanted to send you in to keep the king busy? You didn't suggest it?"

"No, I was surprised that he did. I won't go in there if it will cause problems between yourself and—"

"No, go in. Stay. Stay all night. Keep him there. *Please.*" She spoke

in a half whisper glancing nervously around the hall, which made her seem deranged. She looked briefly up the stairway that led to her solar and the sewing bevy, then rushed toward the main door—where, in the yard, she could climb the steps to the king's empty room. The light from her candle betrayed how much she was shaking. Enid knew these symptoms. Suddenly she knew the cause as well.

"Oh, *Christ!*" she cried aloud before she could check herself. The queen stopped and glanced at her sharply over her shoulder.

"What?"

Enid stared at her, troubled and amazed. She wanted to say something but there was nothing she could say without being whipped for presumptuousness, even if she was right. Finally she ventured a whispered plea: "Be careful, milady."

The queen froze. After a long moment of silence she nodded once in awkward acknowledgment, looking troubled, and continued toward the door.

NOBLE'S eyes were starting to cross from the amount of paperwork before him. Except for signing an official rebuke to Mortimer—who was already tardy in observing his obligations to the treaty—it all felt like busywork, but almost anything requiring ink felt like busywork to him. He wondered how long he had been waiting. Gwirion had told him to come in here and keep himself busy. He complied because he missed Gwirion's cavorting and anticipated one of his absurd old tricks, but if something didn't happen soon, he was going to give up on it for the night.

Finally there was a gentle rap on the door. He got up and walked to it, bracing himself for some harmless attack.

He was unprepared for the familiar pretty face attached to the familiar pretty body waiting for him. Weeks of stress lifted from his shoulders and for a moment he felt like an adolescent boy with a crush. "Good Lord," he said, laughing quietly.

Enid smiled playfully and stepped into the room, pushing the door closed behind her. Seeing him up close gave her a greater thrill than she'd expected, more than sex but less than love. His warm grin banished any fears she'd had that she would not be welcome.

"How did you—"

"I'm with Lord Humffri's household. They almost didn't bring me, they were afraid it might cause trouble."

"Trouble? Darling little Enid? And I have you all to myself for how long?"

Thinking of what else was probably happening tonight, Enid smiled a sultry smile and said, "All night. I overheard the queen before I came in, she's not expecting you."

"Gwirion won't be barging in on us, will he?"

She reached for the clasp of his leather belt. "I think Gwirion is already in bed," she answered softly.

S HE was sweating in the icy air. Her heart was pounding in her chest and she dropped the candle, heard it hiss out on the cold, damp stones. She kept walking, fidgeting relentlessly with her rosary, relying on the torchlight around the bailey under the magnificently star-strewn sky. It probably meant nothing. Gwirion was trying so hard to return things to how they had been, and pandering for the king had been one of his duties, so he was reclaiming it. That was all. But just in case, just in case ... she made herself smile calmly at Gethin's deputy, a rheumy-looking older man posted outside Noble's door. "His Majesty will not be coming in until extremely late tonight," she said, "but I would like a moment to waken and prepare myself for his arrival. When you see his light heading for the stairs, please rap on the door."

"Yes, milady," he gurgled pleasantly. "If I'm off duty before he arrives, I'll tell my relief, shall I?" She nodded and smiled her thanks, then went inside.

Too nervous to look around the room, she leaned her forehead against the door as the man outside pulled it closed and latched it. She stayed there for a moment, willing her heart to slow down. Gwirion didn't just know about the tryst downstairs, he had arranged it. Wasn't it possible that he had done it to see her? But he was so irritable, she was afraid to assume there was any remaining affection. And he had said, adamantly, that it was not going to continue. So then there was nothing ulterior in tonight's downstairs meeting. He was playing pander, nothing more. In fact, by using Enid, he was deliberately trying to upset her, to assure alienation. It was manipulative but it was smart. She felt stupid for having rushed here, and decided to go back to her own bed, reaching for the door latch.

From out of nowhere in the darkness, a hand touched her shoulder softly. She spun around and found herself eye to eye with Gwirion.

"Do you want me to leave?" he whispered anxiously. "I'll leave if you want."

In answer, she grabbed his arm and led him to the bed. For a long time they just sat on the feather mattress, looking at each other with troubled expressions in the light of a dying fire.

"Are you frightened?" she said at last.

"I'm *terrified*."

"But we'll never get caught. Nobody else would ever believe it."

"I hope you're right," he said. "Think of what it would do to my reputation. Everyone will stop offering me their sheep."

She shoved him playfully. And again they sat in silence, basking in each other's presence.

"Would you like to undress me?" she asked suddenly, with the incongruously untroubled pleasure of their first kiss. He had a physical reaction to this, which delighted her.

"I don't understand you. All you've ever known is Noble. He's beautiful and experienced, what could I ever—"

"Undress me." She stuck out her lower lip in a mock scowl. "I command it."

"I don't obey commands," he replied, but he reached for her belt anyway.

She had to reassure him that there was no need to hurry, they had hours, although he fretted when she insisted that they also had years. "We don't know if there'll be anything beyond tonight," he insisted nervously. "This is not an affair. I'm not your lover." She forced back a laugh, for he said this as he was pulling her shift off her with shaking hands. She wanted to stop him for a moment, take the time to engage on that other level, where they used words as well as fingertips to captivate each other, but she knew he was frightened of it. And it was no painful compromise to let the night be about physical satisfaction. She reclined into the pillows, shivering with pleasure as his warm mouth grazed all over her. "Your skin," he informed her earnestly, "has two dozen different flavors." She laughed softly and wrapped her legs around him. Her curious fingers strayed on their own toward the strange wadded scar on his back. This time she said nothing about it, only touched the smooth, unfeeling skin gently for a moment and then turned her attention to more sensitive parts of his anatomy. They were still experimenting when the guard rapped on the door just before dawn.

Gwirion, to her alarm, climbed out the window into the freezing air completely naked, tossing his clothing down before him. There were pocks in the whitewashed outer walls of the tower, he assured her, that he was as comfortable using as a stairway, and there was barely any moon for him to be seen by. He reminded her as he disappeared to put the blankets back on the bed, a task she rushed at and finished just as Noble was opening the door.

Gwirion had pleased her many times during the night, but at the moment he rushed off he had been in the middle of arousing her again, and it was with great difficulty that she managed to greet her husband without looking sodden with sex. Noble seemed happily exhausted, and she felt a flash of sympathy. Now he would make some excuse for staying up all night and she would have to accept it, although she wanted to say, "I know what you've been doing and I hope you enjoyed yourself; I certainly did." She thought of Huw ap

Maredudd and his wife Branwyn. Their arrangement, which had seemed abhorrent to her before, was suddenly enviable. But Branwyn had earned that right—she had provided her husband with three boys. If she could just give Noble a son, maybe . . .

"I thought you would be in your own chamber," he said.

"I didn't know you'd be so long."

"There was more waiting for me than I'd anticipated."

She smiled and wished that she could tell him she understood. "That's all right. Balancing accounts is exhausting. You get up close to some of those figures and they mysteriously suck you in." She gave him a smile that left him wondering whether she knew what he'd been doing all night.

·15·

STRATEGISTS

Late Winter, 1199

NID HAD BEEN given a rare privilege when the king left her: He'd invited her to sleep through the chill remainder of the night in the audience chamber, wrapped in the feather quilt from the chest, provided she was up and out before the household stirred. Gwirion did not see her in the kitchen when he returned to his warren, and guessed where she was. Knowing the castle would soon awaken, and not wanting to miss a chance to tease her, he sneaked into the darkened receiving chamber draped in a wool blanket, hovering over her dozing form with a candle. She lay in the same place and position Isabel had that fateful afternoon, more obviously sensuous, her hair dark and loose, her lips much fuller than the queen's, her complexion more hale—but it had no effect on him. He almost wished it would; he was still trying to depersonalize the attraction, convince himself it was just about a woman's body and not about *her*.

He tapped his finger on Enid's nose until she awoke with a start.

She blinked in the candlelight, laughed languidly, and relaxed back into the sinfully comfortable bedding.

"Good morning, little slut, I'm here to collect my commission."

She shook her head. "Anyone but you and I'd get angry."

He gave her a suggestive smile. "Did you enjoy yourself?"

She mirrored the smile back at him, her nose crinkling as it always did when she was especially amused. "Did you?"

His smile faded. "What are you talking about?" he asked, an edge in his voice to hide his nervousness.

"Gwirion, I know," she whispered.

"Know what?" He frowned at her with what he hoped passed for bored impatience and stood up, heading for the door. "Let's pester Marged for some breakfast."

"Don't play coy with me," Enid said, grinning. "She would have gone to her own room if she hadn't seen me coming here. If you had a good time, you should thank me for it."

Gwirion stumbled and fell into the king's chair. He stared at her with such abject fear that she made herself relinquish the warmth of the blankets to go and steady him. "He doesn't know," she said, taking the candle from him so he wouldn't drop it. She had on only her shift, so she set down the candle and picked up the quilt to wrap around herself, and they faced each other like two swaddled infants.

"I don't—" he began to protest innocence. "But how did you find out?" he asked, sheepish but alarmed.

"Ha! After your peculiar behavior, hers was easy to interpret." He looked up at her, horrified, and she patted his arm. "For *me*, I mean. He doesn't suspect. Trust me, I just spent the night with him, he doesn't suspect." He made a face and shook his head, refusing to be reassured.

"I can't believe this is happening," he whispered bleakly, frightened.

"I'm stunned myself," she admitted. "And I'm worried about you."

"Why?" he said defensively, looking away. A witness cemented the reality. It no longer existed in their shared desire—a disinterested

third party had called him to account. It was a fact now, a part of ob-
jective reality. If Enid could see it, then others could too.

"Because what's next?"

"We have to stop it," he said nervously.

She shook her head with a sympathetic smile. "I don't know that
you have a choice."

"I can't do that to Noble," he insisted. The answer was instinctual, and reassured him. Less instinctual was the assertion: "I'll just
find someone else."

She sighed, ignoring this final comment, which she knew was
meaningless. "It's like one of those long, tortured love ballads
Brychan the bard likes so much."

"Those ballads always made me sick," Gwirion said angrily.

LATER that morning, despite the snow flurries speckling the air,
the pilgrims continued on their way toward St. David's, embroidered daffodils wafting on skirts and veils in defiance of the weather.

Gwirion and the queen managed to avoid each other through the
morning, terrified of giving anything away in their behavior, but each
fell prey to that most common weakness of new lovers: stealing
furtive glances, even if the other was oblivious, just for the thrilling
reassurance of the other's continued and astonishing existence.
Gwirion caught himself at it finally, ogling the slight curve of her
hips from across the hall and remembering what it felt like to push
himself against them. He realized what a danger it was and scowled
at her the next time he felt her eyes on him, but she didn't understand
him. More than a risk of discovery, it seemed to him an invitation to
self-torture, for however resigned they were to a mutual lust, there
would be no easy way to indulge it again. That frustration at least offered him one reassurance: Since they most likely could not act again,
at least they could not be caught.

Isabel herself felt almost impervious to danger now. Between the

public's romantic affection for her and the secret thrill of adultery accomplished, she was no longer just the brood mare who had failed to deliver. She glowed all day, even when spasms of panic overwhelmed her each time she thought her husband was looking at her strangely. Caught between fearful guilt and the pleasant fluster of proximity, both she and Gwirion tried hard to dwell on neither their desire to grope each other nor their inability to do so.

The king held council after dinner, fretting over first Llewelyn and then Mortimer. He forced himself to listen to his men's cautious suggestion that he stabilize the situation with Llewelyn by joining their courts in a confederacy, ideally by marriage. These officers, the highest in the kingdom, humbly offered their offspring or even themselves to such a union, but the king considered it a useless project. "My marrying a Mortimer profited us nothing," he pointed out. "Who among you can offer a more profitable hand than mine?"

The shine of his victory was beginning to subside and he debated with his huddled officers how best to chastise Roger for his sluggishness. He invited his wife to sit in for this part of the council, and marveled silently that the entire table—most of whom had been at the front with him and had not actually seen her in her castellan duties—naturally accepted her as one of them. This was unheard of; not even his mother Efa, when widowed by Cadwallon and with a young son to prepare for kingship, had been so accepted in the court. He studied how offhand she seemed about this extraordinary status, how levelheaded about pressuring her uncle.

He also brought Gwirion to council, to play softly in the background, and he kept the harp within hearing wherever he was for the rest of the day, shooting his friend occasional warm smiles for his efforts. Gwirion was grateful for a chance to serve his monarch and his friend; in his tormented imagination, each new tune exonerated the sin of each new indecent thought he had about the queen. He had to play a lot of tunes.

That evening after supper the royal couple sat near the fire and Gwirion again unwrapped his harp to play. Because of the chill

weather, most of the castle was gathered here until bedtime. It was a welcome change from the unbroken hours of political ruminations, and there was a cozy familiarity to it—it was the first time since the king's return that there had been an informal evening party. Noble asked for many old favorites until people started nodding off. Gwirion was taking a final request from Cadwgan's daughter Gwladys when the queen abruptly brought both hands to her face to cover an enormous yawn.

"Don't become sleepy on me now," her husband said. With a private, roguish smile, he added something in a lowered voice that made her blush. The harp sounded a sour note, and the king turned to Gwirion with a droll expression. "I've never heard you miss a note before, Gwirion," he scolded. "Was it something I said? Do you still disapprove of my honoring my marriage vows?"

"It's just that you'll break my poor mare's heart, sire," Gwirion replied, picking up the melody again. "You said she was the only girl for you and she's been waiting all evening for you in your room."

"Excellent, a threesome!" He winked at his wife—who almost jumped—and then turned back to Gwirion. "Come up and serenade us."

"Only if I can mount the pretty one," Gwirion leered, his eyes on the strings.

"Gwirion!" the queen cried.

"What? She's my pony, I can do what I please with her," he shot back, and Noble laughed. With pursed lips, Isabel settled nervously back into her chair.

"Of course, if you'd rather a more conventional treatment to put you to sleep," the king suggested, "just call Gwirion up to play for you."

He nearly missed another string. "Damn harp's out of alignment again," he muttered loudly, inventing a complaint. He picked up his tuning key from the string on his belt and poured his attention into the imaginary problem.

She looked at her husband as if she couldn't quite understand his meaning. "In the middle of the night?" she said. "In my room? A man?"

"It's just Gwirion," he said breezily. "The worst he can do is pun you to death."

"But . . . he needs to sleep, surely, I can't wake—"

"Gwirion exists without sleep," Noble assured her. "Don't you?"

The harpist looked up innocently from the harp. "Pardon? I was distracted."

"I was telling my wife you wouldn't mind going to her room at night to play for her if she's restless. Provided of course that I don't need you."

Gwirion's eyes involuntarily flashed to the queen and away again, and he paled. He could not square this with what he was certain was in Noble's heart and mind. "Good God, sire, I can't do that," he said.

"Why not?"

Isabel tried to breathe calmly and look unconcerned, but her fingers were clenched around the arms of her chair. "Well, sire . . ." Gwirion glanced around the hall and lowered his voice confidingly. "It's her women. They're all desperate for me—I'm constantly beating them away and I just don't think I'm strong enough to fend off all three at once."

Noble gave him a sly look. "I'd think you'd want that, the way you carry on."

"I'm waiting for a woman with lots of livestock to keep me satisfied when she's not in the mood," Gwirion explained pleasantly. "What tune would you like next?"

The queen made a disgusted sound to cover her nervousness and rose to leave. Gwirion felt his stomach tighten. "I'm sorry, Your Majesty," he called to her quickly. "I didn't mean to insult your women. I'd be delighted if they ravished me. And I'm pleased to play for you any evening you require it." He'd managed to appear offhand.

She did not smile. "Thank you, Gwirion. I'll keep that in mind." She sounded totally disinterested.

"Of course, you won't be needing it so often," he said. "You're a Mortimer after all. You can sleep through anything."

She made a face at him that made her husband chuckle. "I'll be up as soon as you've warmed the sheets," he crooned, "my little harpy." Isabel gave him a flustered smile and walked away.

Noble and Gwirion both watched her lithe body in its burgundy silk crossing away from them. Her husband took a breath and rose suddenly. "You'll excuse me," he said to Gwirion and the few others who were still awake, "I believe we'll warm the bed together." He walked with light, quick steps after her until he was beside her. Gwirion watched as the king put his arm around her slender waist and hugged her slightly to him, gesturing to a hall servant for his mantle.

RETURNING to her own bed hours later, she sent Llwyd her doorkeeper downstairs "to fetch the harpist." Emerging from the sticky web of sleep, Gwirion was thrown by the man's inviting him to the queen's room alone and almost refused the request, but finally allowed himself to be escorted to her chamber, harp in hand, eager and reluctant at once. He desperately wished this rendezvous wasn't born of Noble's unthinking trust in both of them.

Perhaps it wasn't unthinking trust. Perhaps it was a trap.

But once they were closed in together, the great failing of this opportunity, the evidence that it was neither really a gift nor a trap, made itself plain: Her women could hear clearly through the tapestried curtain that offered the only privacy between her sleeping area and theirs. This was no recipe for trysting; they may as well have been in public, and he couldn't stop playing or he would lose his excuse for being here. So he played.

She reached up through the cold dark air to stroke his face, and the shock of it jolted him so severely that his fingers missed the

strings and he smacked his head against the harp's hollowed sound box. "*Please* don't do that," he whispered. "That's worse than not being here at all." She grinned and immediately reached up again, but he pulled his head away. "I'm serious," he hissed. "I can hardly keep the harp on my lap." He started to play again, almost desperately.

She kept beaming at him in the darkness, breathless with the dangerous pleasure of their treasonous proximity. "Then we'll meet elsewhere," she decided.

"That would be madness."

She ignored the observation. "The next time there's outside entertainment and you have the evening free, we'll spirit ourselves away from the hall and meet in the guest chamber upstairs from Gwilym's room. If it's empty, there'll be no guard on that floor. It will need to be quick but it's better than nothing."

He agreed with reluctance, still wanting not to want to be with her.

AFTER just two days and nights of fickle snowfall, two days of Gwirion devoting himself with doglike fidelity to the king's ebbing humor and two nights of Isabel being an obedient, ardent wife, they had an opportunity. The bard from Abbey Cwm-hir came to play for the king. He was fed before supper, accepting only bread and water, and performed throughout the meal and afterward. In honor of Lent he played nothing that was even remotely enjoyable, and in the ensuing torpor that overtook the hall it was easy for both Gwirion and Isabel to slip away.

But when they met in the empty tower, they were once again slapped by disappointment. The room was clammy and dark, and they dared not light a fire or even a candle, lest the sergeant, on the lookout for unexplained fires, notice something through the sealed parchment over the windows and decide to explore. The moon was not yet a quarter full and anyway was blotted out by clouds. Unfa-

miliar with the room and unable to see anything, they could not navigate to retrieve a blanket or cushion from a storage chest. They were both distressed about time, fearful of being missed in hall and then of being seen returning, and the bed, when they finally found it, was missing its blanket—there was only a dense pile of dried heather, flattened slightly from Humffri's visit.

Her teeth chattering in the cold, Isabel still let out a sigh of imperial annoyance. Gwirion took it personally, thinking of the feather mattress and warm woven blankets and billowing canopied curtains Noble offered her each night.

"This wasn't my idea," he said unhappily, rubbing his arms for warmth in the dark. "I had no way of—"

"I know that," she cut him off impatiently.

He was almost glad this was going afoul. As desperate as he was to feel her against him again, he was equally desperate to be free of that desire, and two frustrated assignations in a row was an excellent way of souring it. Noble had offered him a mistress and there was a new hall servant whom he found his gaze drifting to at meals; maybe he would ask for her. To be respectful to Her Majesty, he would wait until she herself declared their liaison over, which would certainly be soon if these frustrations kept arising. Then he would take a lover, she would return her full attention to her marriage and all would be well; perhaps they could be proper friends again. He missed those hours of conversation, locked up together in the audience room.

Defeated and unsatisfied, they left separately and took different paths back to the hall. Gwirion braved more of the cold and slush by descending and walking the long way around the inner curtain wall; the queen took the icy wall walk over the barbican across to her own room, and descended back into the hall from there. Neither of them had been missed, and they avoided addressing each other directly for the rest of the evening, but Gwirion was immensely attentive to the king.

She tried to convince herself that his behavior was prompted by either fear or guilt, but she could not deny the genuine affection that he exuded, almost despite himself, toward Noble. It galled her on

two fronts. First because, despite his sexual attentiveness, Noble had never extended to her whatever it was that made Gwirion cleave to him so; second—and worse—because Gwirion gave so freely to the king that part of him, the hidden human part, which had first drawn her to him when they were locked up alone together, and she ached for it.

G UIRION feared and hoped that the fiasco in the tower was the end of it, especially when Noble sent the queen ahead to his bed to warm it for him. So he was confused when the same sleepily whispering doorkeeper came for him in the midnight hours, requesting his presence, with his harp, in the queen's chamber.

He closed her door behind him with a soft sigh, wondering why she was subjecting both of them to this torture a second time. He would have to invent a gentle refusal if she tried it again.

The room was unexpectedly warm, the fire recently stoked and brighter than a torch. "Good evening," she greeted him with polite formality. "My ladies have asked that you play as quietly as possible, so you will continue to sit beside my bed." She gestured for him. "And you will play for as long as I require it."

He acknowledged this with a feeble smile and took his position near her head. "Why am I here?" he whispered, grateful the sewing bevy was hidden by the tapestry.

"To play the harp. For now," she whispered back. "Until they've fallen asleep."

He was astonished. "You're not thinking—"

She put her finger to his lips. "A lullaby, please."

His heart pounding, Gwirion performed every soft song he knew, every gentle song, even every drinking song slowed to a lull. He tried playing the melody with only his left hand, while droning gently on the lower strings with the right, and the effect was something

stuporous. His fingers wanted to rush through all the tunes, as if the faster they were completed the faster those women would succumb to slumber. He almost couldn't keep the rhythm of anything he played, all of it moved so much more slowly than his own heartbeat in fearful anticipation. Every few minutes he looked anxiously toward the door, expecting interruption. "I can always hear him approaching," she whispered reassuringly, but he wasn't reassured.

After almost an hour, when even he was having trouble staying focused and the fire was dying down to embers, she nodded to him to stop, and drew the curtains closed all around the bed. Except for one small opening, through which she beckoned him to enter.

He mouthed the words "Are you mad?" to her, but she only smiled.

"They sleep through it when Noble comes, they'll sleep through it now."

"How can you possibly—"

"Even if they hear something, they'll think it's him come during the night. They can't see anything."

He glanced at the tapestry that hid the women, his heartbeat quickening. To help him make a well-reasoned choice, she slid her hand along his lap toward his groin. He spun around to look at her, a wild, pleading look in his eyes.

"Why do I have to start everything?" she asked in a coy whisper. "Couldn't you just once pretend I'm irresistible?"

He blushed, and after a hesitation, he laid the harp on the floor and crawled in through the curtains. "Do you prefer hanging or dismemberment?" he asked as he straddled her.

As she undressed him, they were nearly as aware of the sleeping attendants as they were of each other, but for her it only fueled the excitement. She almost wished one of the women would call out in her sleep, just to add an adrenaline rush to her own already soaring state. Gwirion would have given anything for the surety of privacy, but her enthusiasm was contagious and he managed to put the images of hanging and dismemberment out of his mind for a while.

She radiated heat from the blankets and the pleasure of sliding against an entire female body of such warmth was nearly as intoxicating as the consummation.

"We can't do this very often," he whispered afterward.

"Of course we can!" she whispered back, absently fingering the scar on his back.

He shook his head. "My nerves would be ruined by the end of a week and I'd have a stomach ulcer the size of Wigmore."

She grinned. "It's always funny to hear a Norman word said with a Welsh accent. Do it again." She whispered even more quietly, "Say my name."

He stared at her, shook his head nervously. "That's dangerous. I might get used to saying it, I'd get sloppy—"

"We've already been sloppy," she said, sobering. He guessed that she meant Enid, and nodded. He ran the side of his thumb across her lips. Already he couldn't remember how he had ever looked at that mouth without wanting to taste it. Seeing that he was getting distracted, she frowned at him in the darkness and pushed his hand away. "What do you suggest, then?" she asked.

"I suggest losing interest in each other. But I don't imagine that will happen for a while." He glanced at her for confirmation and she pressed her nose against his cheek. "All right, then. Random encounters. When it's safe. No more than once a week." By his standards, that was decadently frequent.

"No!" she begged. "More than that!"

"Twice, then," he relented as she slid her leg over his thigh. She wiggled up against him, grinning. "Oh, Christ, as often as you want. But only when it's *safe*. Not near the full moon, people don't sleep as deeply, there'll be more open eyes around. Not if Noble's in a mood—"

"If Roger doesn't start honoring the treaty, Noble will be in a permanent mood," she sighed.

"If you don't like it, then help him out of it," Gwirion said, almost chiding her.

"That's your responsibility, fool," she retorted. "Keep him pleased so that it will be safe for you to come to my bed."

He sat up and pulled away from her. "That will never be the reason I please him," he said sternly.

NOT every night throughout the next three weeks, but often, the restless queen would excuse herself from the king's bed to her own, and send for the harp. Once her women were asleep, Gwirion would slink through the curtains and warm himself against her, amazed each time that she wanted to give herself to him after being with her husband. It was almost enough to make him religious. The need for silence forced them to find other ways to express desire and satisfaction. They learned to read each other's subtle shifts of weight and movement, the scents of the other's body changing with excitement. It was reckless of her but she actually enjoyed knowing they were never safe. It added romance and intensity to their lovemaking. Because they were unable to converse freely, they focused all their energy on physical intimacies, and he would leave almost immediately afterward, as if neither of them knew what to do with each other when they weren't actually making love.

Strangely, once they had established that they could have each other almost as often as they wanted to, the dynamics of their daily routines were undisturbed by their affair, and they were able to treat each other with friendly indifference in all but the most awkward circumstances. Perhaps this was because he never stayed with her beyond the lovemaking, and so there were two parallel worlds between them whose rules of conduct never overlapped. In one they were unspeaking carnal partners; in the other they were the king's two devoted dependents, still adored, as he was, by the populace. But there was a jealous tension between the two worlds, and both lovers noticed, with more attention than either would ever have confessed to,

whom the other one spoke with and for how long. There was no opportunity to complain in daylight hours, and the night was too precious to waste in words. So she bit her lip when he ogled the new
buxom black-haired hall maid or flirted, however innocently, with
Marged's workers, and he looked away whenever the king's hand casually touched her sleeve, her cheek, her knee, and most of all when
Noble sent her to his bed each night, smiling with royal anticipation
at the thought of warming his own limbs against hers in his comfortable feather bed. That moment was always the hardest for
Gwirion. Despite the quiet drone of guilt that filled his head, sometimes he had the sense that he was being robbed.

There were of course the deprivations that late winter wrought,
the tensions at the court from Mortimer delaying reparations, from
rumors that Llewelyn's ambition was on the rise again. Gwirion dutifully applied himself to offering distraction, although his genius for
clever mischief had gone into hibernation. A routine of sexual intimacy caused unforeseen distractions and he now found himself more
aware of women's bodies at the most inopportune of times. Not
only breasts and hips and lips and eyes, but the collarbones, elbows,
jawlines, knuckles of all his female acquaintances and friends seemed
suddenly rife with potential sensuality and he blushed more often
than he had since puberty.

For relief he would escape outside, to snow forts and vicious
snowball fights organized by Efan to train (or so went his excuse) the
next generation of potential teulu. It was a matter of debate whether
Efan or Gwirion offered more rigorous training in winter sports.
Gwirion's exercises were the more unorthodox, of course: snow
sculptures of half-size troops, dubbed as either Mortimer's or
Llewelyn's, would be overwhelmed by means of bodily fluids, leaving
melting, golden lumps of snow in the corner of the courtyard for
Elen, the marshal's wife, to grouse about to Noble.

Noble had far more pressing issues to attend to, and took to
keeping Gwirion with him almost every waking moment—sometimes to listen to him play the harp, sometimes to listen to him ramble comically, sometimes to try to interest him in statecraft or war

sports on the grounds that he was, after all, the new hero of Maelienydd and could surely find a better way to manifest it than pissing on snowy effigies of his enemies.

He kept his wife near him frequently as well, for different reasons. He continued to invite her into council, but her suggestions for strong-arming her uncle hadn't been successful, and as Roger's stonewalling increased, Isabel's value in the officers' eyes threatened to diminish. Begetting an heir was still a constant goal—and generally more pleasurable than it had once been—but until he had her with child, he could not rest easy that he had a useful marriage. Then cousin Anarawd wrote, asking after Her Majesty's health and wondering when he might have the pleasure of attending a christening. Noble frowned and burned the letter without showing it to anyone.

ONE day in early March, when the snow had receded to a negligible six inches, news arrived that Humffri's party, returning at last from their early pilgrimage to St. David's, had begged the honor of stopping at Cymaron for the midday meal before the final leg of their journey home. Noble had been cooped up in the council room all morning and was glad of an excuse to take the air: He stood waiting to receive his baron, quite informally, with his wife beside him on the hall steps, both of them in winter reds and golden circlets. Humffri's retinue was small, but he was escorted to the gate by a most peculiar and unnerving entourage, consisting of the entire village of Cymaron—carvers, weavers, wrights, carpenters, tanners, smiths, bakers, and dozens of others with their wives and children and aging parents, and finally, one skinny long-legged breathless boy in Noble's livery.

The runner, not the baron, was the focus of the mob's attention when two hundred soggy brogues, buskins, and boots stopped obediently at the gates. The crowd was well behaved and courteous of convention; they made no move to enter. Einion came out of the

porthouse, gaping. The king, startled but affecting indifference, sent Gwilym to the gate to glean the cause of this spontaneous congress. The steward brought back with him not only Humffri, his lady, and their riding party, but also the gasping courier and an explanation. It was mere chance that baron and boy had arrived at the village at the same moment. A pretty village gossip, flirting with the gate watch, had seen the boy arrive from the northwest—*the northwest*—and within ten minutes the whole of the village knew there was news of the feared, distrusted, and despised Llewelyn. They wanted to know what it was.

Noble climbed the steps to the top of the barbican, looked down on the silent, anxious crowd, back toward the runner who was too exhausted to reveal much emotion, and finally informed Einion and Gwilym that if the villagers truly had nothing better to do with their dinner hour than hear trifling tales of a petty prince, they were welcome to enter the bailey.

INSIDE the hall, king and queen took their seats at the high table with their aristocratic visitors to their right and Gwirion, as ever, behind the king's left shoulder. The villagers, obedient but dogged, had poured quietly through the castle gate, and with the collective focus of a school of fish had gone straight to the hall steps. Both doors had been opened, and the human mass split itself spontaneously in two, each half crowding around a broad threshold, eyes on the high table, waiting to hear what new pillaging of trust the powerful, dreaded Llewelyn had accomplished. Noble and his officers paid them no attention. The rest of the diners squirmed under their scrutiny.

The first course of dinner was already laid out but Noble ignored it, which required everyone else to ignore it as well. The king turned his attention to the boy and the boy handed him the scroll.

He looked at the seal on it and raised his eyebrows. "Your lover, madam," he said to his wife in an arch tone, and showed it to her. The seal was Owain's.

She said nothing, content now to let him say that, even think it. Gwirion feigned indifference as Noble signaled the hall to begin eating, but he himself began to read the missive, and nobody so much as picked up a knife. He read in silence, his face growing somber. The court officers had watched him break the seal, anticipating a call to council. He felt the collected eyes upon him and looked up from reading. "Hubris," he spat with sudden venom. "Llewelyn is creeping ever outward in his quest to conquer—pardon, *unify*—Wales. He's appropriated yet another county in Gwynedd." He threw the scroll down onto the table with a sharp, angry gesture.

There was an uneasy exchange of looks around the upper end of the hall and the crowd huddling at the door murmured as if they were watching a performance. Isabel's guard went up at once. This was hardly damning news to her ears, and had nothing to do with Maelienydd. Noble was genuinely angry and dismayed about it, but she wondered if he was not, in fact, performing.

"It may have been under Norman control," Father Idnerth observed.

Noble shook his head. "Welsh."

"He does have birthright over certain areas," Goronwy said. "Perhaps he was reclaiming—"

"No."

There was another awkward silence.

"Perhaps he seized it from a rival," said the queen.

"Owain seems to think he *convinced* the baron to yield to him. I find that more alarming than if he'd taken it by force." He got to his feet so abruptly he almost knocked his chair over, and Gwirion, who recognized the mood, asked, "Harp?" at once. Noble jerked his head once in response, and distractedly signaled ease to the other diners, who had all in turn nearly knocked their benches over in a rush to stand. His Majesty walked around the high table and into the central

area of the hall, where he began a round of long-legged pacing, deep in thought, his jaw hanging slightly slack, brow furrowed, blue eyes pensively downcast. The whole room and the entire population of Cymaron village hung in suspension, waiting on him, privileged to see the king in a moment of such vulnerable introspection. As Gwirion moved to the hearth he unintentionally swapped glances with the queen and saw plainly on her face the wariness already in his mind. It was unlikely that Maelgwyn ap Cadwallon had ever in his life suffered a bout of vulnerable introspection, and he most certainly would never suffer it in public. Unless, that is, something was very wrong. Gwirion, trying not to feel spooked, settled with his harp and began to play, not an actual melody but a series of simple descending arpeggios.

After a moment, without pausing in his movement, Noble made a sharp gesture toward his audience chamber. "Senior council," he said tersely, and turning toward Humffri, announced, "I'm appropriating your bard for the while." He nodded in response to Gwirion's questioning expression, and harpist followed steward, penteulu, chaplain, and judge into the audience room. "No, madam, don't even ask," Noble said, anticipating his wife. "How could we be so rude as to leave our guests unattended? Pardon me, Humffri, this will be short. Continue your meal. My wife will provide company until I return."

Brychan, Humffri's recently appointed bard, could not have looked less bardlike. He was short, compact, thick-necked, and red-haired, his face constructed so that he looked permanently alarmed at the prospect of public speaking, and he was barely seasoned enough to be a bard of his own standing. But bard he was, and obedient. He followed Noble's flourishing gesture with his eyes, then belatedly rushed into the receiving room after the castle officers.

Noble looked at the bizarre collection of faces stuffing the doorways, pink and splotchy from the cold. "We are going to close the doors now. Your presence is not required at this moment," he informed them, but none of them moved. He reviewed them a moment longer and then groaned theatrically. "You may as well come in, then," he declared, ironical, long-suffering. "We've lost enough of

you to war, let's not have winter claim the rest. But I'm not feeding you today." He disappeared into his receiving room as the village— voiceless, spooked, polite—flowed into the hall.

IN the receiving room, they stood. The little round chamber was always lit and heated, but there was not enough seating for the seven of them. Noble nodded respectfully to Brychan. "We lost Hywel in the Mortimer campaign, as you know. We've managed to stumble along, but what I need to know now is distinctly a bard's area of expertise." Noble looked grim. "You are, I believe, versed in all the genealogies of the royal families of Wales?"

"Yes, sire," Brychan answered, wide-eyed.

"Can you tell me if there are any marriageable women in Llewelyn's close family?" To his startled men he said, heavily, "Perhaps all of you are right, and that's the best way to control him."

"If I may, sire," Brychan stammered, bowing. "I require a meditation alone someplace to review within my mind's eye the tributaries of that family river." Gwirion almost shouted with laughter at his language but Noble, anticipating that, preempted him with a stern look.

"You may be hard put to find privacy with that silent mob outside," the king said. "The chapel is empty, but it's frigid in there now."

When Brychan was gone, swallowed at once in the eerily quiet throng of onlookers in hall, the council members exchanged solemn glances. Young Efan and old Gwilym, the two highest-ranking members of the court, shifted self-consciously. "We are all your servants, sire," Gwilym said. "But which of us do you consider weighty enough to give to such a union?"

"None of you," the king said, and turned briskly to Idnerth. "The second thing I need to know is in your jurisdiction, Father. How may a king sue for divorce under canon law?"

S H E sat down hard on the settle, holding out her hand for balance.

"Am I that disposable?" she breathed. "I thought we'd finally . . ." She had to take another breath. Gwirion continued to play the same soft chords, sitting backlit by the hearth. Noble had dismissed the council. "I thought you and I had finally come to a genuine—"

"We had," he said, gently, and sat in his chair across from her, reaching for her hand. "That's the sad irony here—you truly have become a consort worthy of Maelienydd. But your family is treacherous. Your uncle is treacherous. Our union buys me nothing that way, and the victory I just won over Roger was completely hollow. He's not going to honor the treaty, we both know that. Besides, Mortimer is not the nemesis to fear. Llewelyn is. Mortimer is just another foreign headache; Llewelyn is a native danger." That observation genuinely pained him. She wavered in her suspicion that this was just a trick. "And Llewelyn is encroaching," he went on heavily. "Roger killed off so many of my menfolk, there's nobody else to seek a marriage with but cousin Anarawd and I would never trust him to be closer knit to Llewelyn than I am." He released her hand and waited for her to speak. She still said nothing. "As I said, this will happen only if there's a match to be made that would be more useful than ours. If there is, and we divorce, I'll have no hold on you. But if your heart is truly in Maelienydd—and I believe it is now—I have a proposition that will serve us both extremely well. This is personal, would you have Gwirion leave?"

"I don't care either way," Isabel said with perfect offhandedness, her pale brown eyes artless. She was telling the truth, both grateful and resentful that Gwirion was responding so indifferently.

Noble said nothing to their musician, whose fingers moved automatically over the horsehair strings while his attention was bent entirely on keeping his own breath steady. He had no idea how

plausible or possible this scheme of Noble's was; his old fears were reignited and he was half convinced Noble had rigged the entire scenario just to test them both. Why else would he subject her to hearing such a cruel plan before it was even a reality?

But now Noble was giving her a look that Gwirion recognized for its sincerity. The blue eyes beamed beneficently; the king considered whatever he was about to propose a boon bestowed, proof that he was the most indulgent of sovereigns. "I want you," he informed her, "to marry Owain."

"What?"

"It's a happy solution for both of us. Even if I marry into Llewelyn's line, that corner of the kingdom is not secure. Owain is alarmingly naive, Huw has far too much sway over him and Huw has ambitious kin in Powys. I require an intelligent, loyal soul minding that border and you've proven you are that; you want a partner who reveres you for more than your political worth, and our little Owain has more than proven himself in that regard."

Gwirion sneezed. "Excuse me," he said gruffly, when both of them snapped their heads to stare at him.

"Our sage Gwirion sneezes at this idea," Noble said with lofty mockery. "Perhaps he will be so good as to tell us why?"

He wasn't sure yet, Gwirion decided—he only suspected. They could disarm his suspicion if they handled it adroitly; he had probably even invented this outrageous scenario as a test to let them prove their innocence. "I think after the king's bed, she'll find herself bored to tears to lie with him," he answered in a leering tone. "You've ruined her for anyone else."

Noble laughed lightly and turned back to his wife, who dutifully made a little sound of annoyed disgust. "We may always rely on Gwirion to remind us of what matters most in life," he said. "What do you say to the proposition, madam?"

She lowered her eyes. "I'd consider it if it would help you, sire, but I think I would lose my mind with boredom to spend the rest of my years in that dull corner of the world."

Noble looked as if he was about to make a sarcastic remark in response, then controlled the urge and said instead, "Your alternative would be a nunnery. Or, I suppose, you would be free to return to your beloved Wigmore."

"I have no longing to return to Wigmore."

"Well, you can't stay *here*, that would be rather awkward for my bride," he said wryly, then sobered. "You will not contest a divorce? I'll make it clear to everyone it has nothing to do with my regard for you. I won't let you be insulted by the process."

"The process itself is an insult," she said tightly.

"But you won't contest it?" he repeated, biting back his impatience. She said nothing, just stared into the fire. He grimaced. "Madam, here we have an excellent example of abusing power, which you've accused me of doing more than once. You have the power to contest this. Exercising that power suits your whim, it does not suit your people."

"Grand words if your plan were necessary for the people," she said, still staring at the fire. "I don't think it is."

He sat back and waved his hand impatiently. "Go ahead, then, make your case."

"If there is a useful match to be made between Llewelyn's court and yours, make it with someone else. Your court is full of bachelors and widowers."

"I've already considered that. Llewelyn won't waste a marriage opportunity on a mere officer. It would have to be my near kin to be of value. Thanks to your uncle, the only near kin I have left is Anarawd and I refuse to give Anarawd that kind of power, I may as well abdicate."

She suddenly knew how to pass this test. She was certain it was not about the prince of Gwynedd. "Llewelyn knows from experience who's of real value to you. Should he have a bride to offer, marry her to Gwirion."

The two men started at the same moment, and Gwirion, picking up her lead, cried, "Oh, please do, sire! I've heard about those girls of Gwynedd, they entertain themselves with stallions when their men

are away fighting. And sometimes, they say," he added, lowering his voice and speaking with a thrilled and knowing tone, "the stallions don't survive the night."

Noble laughed suddenly and hard at this, his face crinkling with genuine levity for the first time all day. The queen and Gwirion did not exchange looks this time but both of them relaxed: The test was over.

But then Noble, quieting, shook his head and the heaviness settled back upon him. "We don't even know if Gwirion is freeborn or not. He's politically unmarriageable. Otherwise, I applaud your suggestion. But I'm afraid I have only myself to sacrifice in this. And by extension, you." He stood up. "We've left our visitors too long and the stew is getting cold. Come to board with me, Gwirion. Madam, you will not contest this?"

He really meant to do it. Flummoxed, she looked down into her lap, nodding weakly, and he seemed satisfied.

"Your people thank you. Would you like a moment alone?"

She nodded again.

Gwirion followed Noble out, trying not to stagger.

Nobody was seated anymore. The meal and the day's tasks were forgotten. The news had exploded as soon as the council had adjourned and people were swarming, buzzing about it—villagers, castle workers, officers, Humffri's retinue. Again Llewelyn posed a threat to their beloved queen. That their own king's decision was to blame this time meant nothing to them—he was, after all, being forced into this sacrifice by Llewelyn's hubris. Already a crowd of those in warmer layers and slush-proof brogues had formed around the chapel door, waiting for Brychan the bard to emerge into the grey afternoon to tell them if this shocking insult to their queen was in fact to pass. A few earnest adolescents even knelt on the chapel steps praying aloud for God to smite dead every female in Llewelyn's line.

Noble took a speechless Gwirion with him through the ripple of bowing peasant heads in the hall and out to the buzzing courtyard, ignoring the murmurings—but hearing them all the same. His subjects noticed him, of course, and besides bowing hurriedly and giving

him a wide path to walk through, they were as blunt as decorum would allow. Nobody petitioned him directly and nobody spoke rudely in his hearing, but however demure they were in their language, it was clear that the castle and the village wanted to hold on to their lady. Now and then the king would raise one astonished brow at something that was said. "Can you imagine this reception last spring?" he whispered to Gwirion. "What wretched timing that they've come to love her only when I must be rid of her." Gwirion smiled politely, still trying to recover from the shock that Noble was entirely serious about divorce.

They made a beeline for the chapel. By the time they got there, the murmurings proved that not one of these xenophobic peasants would willingly trade Isabel Mortimer for some native princess. When they reached the chapel steps, the curious villagers moved to give way to them. Noble nodded a dismissal to Gwirion, and after the slightest hesitation, pushed open the chapel door to join the bard inside.

Perplexed and disoriented, Gwirion stood alone on the stone steps. He wanted to run back across the yard and into the great hall, to throw his arms around the queen to comfort her. His muscles tensed to hold himself in check. Suddenly a pair of arms had grabbed him from behind around the waist, a woman's arms but very strong.

"Gwirion," said Enid's voice softly from behind his left shoulder.

He turned fast, and embraced her hard in return without speaking. People excitedly crossed below them in the slush, gathering at the chapel steps to wait for the bard, back to the hall to see if the queen had emerged to face the news yet, gossiping and conjecturing self-righteously.

When they disengaged, Enid took a moment to peruse his face. Self-conscious, he began to speak, but she quickly held up her hand.

"Don't tell me anything," she commanded quietly. "Unless you can tell me that there is nothing to tell."

He looked down, his forehead wrinkling with distress. He'd fol-

lowed the king out here without bothering to get a wrap, and he shivered now, rubbing his knuckles up and down his arms for warmth.

"I can't say that," he whispered.

Enid reflexively reached up to touch the amulet around her neck. She gave him a look of maternal worry. "Gwirion, Christ, you're such a fool."

He grimaced. "Yes, that's what Noble likes about me."

ISABEL was terrified of stepping out into the hall, terrified of how she'd be received. If any of them still housed some secret hatred of "the Saxoness," this would be the time to gloat, although she feared indifference more. How naive to think Noble's decision was anything personal toward either of them. She wondered if Gwirion had also realized how entirely political the situation really was. She doubted it.

She straightened the gold circlet crowning her wimple, smoothed her skirt, adjusted the silver brooch on her breast and the rosary hanging from her belt, pinched her pale cheeks to bring some color to them, and pulled open the door.

She strode through the hall briskly toward the side exit, the crowd parting for her like the Red Sea. She knew so many of these faces from the passing patterns of daily life. The same wash of gazes that had once been cool to her now looked sympathetic, even troubled. She had earned their attachment, and she was about to be deprived of it. She wanted that to be the thought that most upset her. It would have been a month ago. It wasn't now.

When she reached the threshold, she looked out over the courtyard, aware that eyes out there were also turning to stare at her, that the bailey was falling silent at her appearance. Angharad appeared behind her with a red wool cloak and she nodded, allowing her attendant to tie it on her as she scanned the yard. Generys appeared on the

other side and gave her a cup of warmed metheglin, which she took with a grateful nod.

She recognized Enid by her billowing dark hair, before she even realized whom the girl was talking to. Then she saw Gwirion's face in the hazy light and felt her heart thud. Oh, God, she wanted him to come to her. She watched as he slipped his arm around Enid's shoulders to give her a gruffly affectionate squeeze, perhaps the resolution of some friendly spat between them. With no rancor toward Enid she envied the girl, that she was allowed to receive such easy, innocent affection from him publicly. More than any other upset of the past half hour, that moment made her want to weep. Even if Brychan brought a reprieve, even if he miraculously announced that there was no one in Gwynedd for Noble to propose to, she would never be allowed that casual embrace with Gwirion in the courtyard.

Around her, behind her, before her, the people waited, their attention torn between the hall entrance and the chapel. Their peerless monarch was victorious against the Mortimers; his queen had proven herself his worthy consort; together they had foiled even Llewelyn's craftiness. They were the stuff of bardic ballads. Why, went the unspoken but universal cry, should they be deprived of such magnificence?

THE king pulled closed the chapel door behind him. It was warmer here than out of doors, but not by much; the utter stillness of the air felt icier than wind. "Brychan," he said softly. The bard was kneeling before the altar, eyes half closed, his lips moving a little as he wandered through internal corridors of sacred memorization. Noble watched him for a moment, troubled.

The divorce itself did not disturb him; it was plain to all that the marriage had accomplished, and would accomplish, nothing. Isabel

had turned out to be an interesting woman, but that was not the value or purpose of a royal match. Her removal would not be a significant loss, and in some important ways would be a boon. What he did resent was having to contemplate mutual reliance on Llewelyn to ensure his own kingdom's independence. Turning to the man he knew hoped to rob him of his sovereignty, as a means to *keep* his sovereignty—it was the sort of thing that Gwirion, in an exercise of witty nonsense, might try ironically to justify. But he could not continue without allies, and allies these days did not come easily. At least a tie of marriage was not as onerous as an outright pledge of subjugation. It was, in the larger picture, the closest thing he could imagine to a panacea.

Brychan opened his eyes. Noble took a deep breath, found that he had clenched his fists.

"Tell me my future," he said quietly. Brychan opened his mouth to speak and Noble held up a warning hand. "Quickly and simply," he ordered. "I do not need a litany of the house of Gwynedd, I want only to know if there are potential brides within two degrees of Llewelyn himself."

Brychan nervously shook his head. "Not within even four degrees, Your Majesty," he said apologetically.

"Damn it!" Noble hissed, and struck out furiously at the wall he stood beside. The wall shuddered and a small wooden statue of St. Cynllo tumbled off a shelf nearby. He forced himself to calm with a long, slow exhale. "You did not see that," he informed the bard. Cowed, Brychan nodded.

Noble stared across the room at nothing for a long moment, an unreadable expression on his face.

When he turned back to the bard, he was entirely transformed: smiling, poised. "This is excellent news," he announced in his convincing, reassuring baritone, as if to an awaiting throng. "Now we are entirely free to pursue what has clearly been our intention all along, to rely entirely on our own particular strengths in ruling our own particular people." Brychan regarded him wide-eyed, and with

an indulgent smile Noble continued, polishing his act with this captive audience, "You are wondering, perhaps, what those strengths are?"

"I would never question—" Brychan stammered, but Noble silenced him with a grand flourish of his hand.

"Come and see for yourself."

He threw open the door and left the chapel, as the bard scrambled to his feet to follow him out into the courtyard. Scores of onlookers, shivering and stamping the slush from their boots, had gathered round the steps, and withdrew slightly at His Majesty's apparently ebullient appearance. The yard felt silent, uncertain how to decipher the unexpected flush of triumph on his face. Every single pair of feet shifted an inch or two closer to the steps where Isabel stood. Gwirion, with Enid beside him, risked a glance up at Isabel. Her strained expression made his heart hurt.

Without a word, Noble walked briskly down the steps and across the courtyard, the crowd parting all around him, giving him beseeching looks that he ignored. He headed toward his wife in the hall doorway, her red wool mantle wrapped around her, proud and pale, not certain where to put her eyes as the king approached her. She felt Gwirion looking at her but she did not dare look back.

When her husband reached her, he pivoted to face out over the yard, and without looking at her he took the cup of spiced metheglin from her hands. He raised the cup high and finally spoke. "A toast to your eternal queen!" he called out, as if he were proclaiming the start of a festival.

The courtyard burst into explosive cheers and Isabel nearly fainted with relief. Feeling her falter, Noble handed the cup to Angharad, and wrapped both arms around his wife, then pulled her toward him and kissed her hard and long on the mouth. The cheering grew louder.

As he pulled away from her, he kept his mouth near the side of her head. "An hour ago we were a people in crisis," he whispered, "and now we're joyfully celebrating our blessings."

"Was this just a charade, then?" Isabel asked, not believing it.

"You know it wasn't," Noble said warningly, his voice still low. He kissed her forehead, softening. "You are content with this?"

She averted her eyes. "Beyond content, sire. Grateful and obediently yours."

He looked pleased with the description. Still he asked, whispering, as the courtyard began to quiet down, "You don't regret the freedom you might have known had I divorced you?"

"I hardly consider the status of a divorced woman very free," she answered, forcing a smile.

"But, madam, then you would be free to take a lover," he said in a meaningful voice, "without it impinging on your precious popularity."

Appearing not to notice how she started at this, he laughed and nudged her affectionately with his shoulder, then took the cup from Angharad's waiting grasp to publicly salute his wife again.

By Proxy

Late Winter, 1199

SABEL SPENT a panicked week believing both that Noble knew about them, and that
he didn't care. Or if he did care, he needed her
too much now. He had made her the darling of
Cymaron, which made Cymaron that much
dearer to the kingdom at large. With Mortimer
to one side and Llewelyn to the other, it was largely force of personality that was keeping Maelgwyn ap Cadwallon on his throne, and
she was part of that mystique now, amplifying it. She played her role
beautifully for her husband through the grey, end-of-winter dol-
drums that had settled on the castle. She rode uncomplainingly for
hours with him through hellish weather for brief "social" sojourns
to remind Maelienydd's aristocracy in person how fortunate they
were to have such a powerful and charismatic first couple attending
to their interests. They made many of these visits to the south, near
to Anarawd's estates and friends. She would return from these
trips—two days out and back at most—exhausted and yet strangely

sleepless, and only the harp could soothe her nerves. Her women, growing accustomed to the noise, came to sleep so soundly through it that there were nights when they would have sworn the harpist, although summoned, did not play at all.

Mortimer was still stalling on providing the promised resources for the earth defenses, complaining that no work could be done in winter anyway, and the barons whom Noble had assigned to be his watchdogs, all of them fearful of Mortimer's wrath, were too half-hearted to demand results. And Llewelyn's rising popularity to the north, outside Maelienydd's borders, seemed unstoppable—to Noble's great annoyance, for he understood the source of it: Lord Rhys of Deheubarth had been a boon to all of Wales, lending support to almost any skirmish against the Normans. But Rhys was dead now, his kingdom in shambles; men wanted a new font of manpower and Llewelyn seemed to have it. Noble himself had shown his own army that by taking Llewelyn with him to the front. Owain reported duly that the king's northwest barons, learning Mortimer was not abiding by the terms of treaty, could not understand why Noble would not pledge himself to Llewelyn. The prince of Gwynedd was not a conqueror, he was a unifier, and asked only appropriate respect from those whose lands he would protect. In their minds, Maelgwyn ap Cadwallon's demotion from sovereign to petty prince would be a small price to pay.

As relief from these and other plagues, Noble craved distraction, but Gwirion had not been up to form and he was beginning to resent it.

But perhaps something was afoot now. The king was pleased when he saw his friend revert to old familiar habits of scuttling around dark corners of the castle, speaking hurriedly in whispers to people who later denied seeing him, and disappearing for hours at a time into dank basements. Surely he was staging an event of some sort, and he was staging it for Noble. This was all that mattered to the king. The less he could afford time for such distractions, the more he needed them.

THE morning of the March new moon, the castle awoke under a damp snowfall that melted underfoot, leaving the courtyard a mess of slush made slushier by the predawn brigade of Gwirion's bribed assistants. When the muffle of fog and darkness eased enough for light to enter the courtyard, the guards on the keep tower briefly started: There were strangers in the bailey, standing in formation as if awaiting orders. Their stillness in the face of the guard's warning calls suggested an intimidating martial discipline, and Gwirion appeared at the watch's elbows just as they realized the things weren't alive. He crossed the soldiers' palms with what was needed for them to respond as he wished and at once the trumpet sounded the five-note siege alarm. The castle population assembled, half-dressed, groggy, and shivering in the hall, already suspecting this had to do with Gwirion, because no one would be insane enough to attack in this weather. The queen had been summoned to her husband's bed in the middle of the night, and came with him now straight from his room to the hall, one of his shorter robes wrapped over her shift for warmth, without stopping to collect her jewelry, her rosary, or even her wimple from her own room. People stared at the thick tumble of her hair in the lamplight, unused to it.

The grey daylight grew, and features on the figures became discernable. That created the first buzz: All of them were dressed as women. They were effigies, enormous poppets, life-size and sometimes bigger, held upright by stakes shoved into muddy cracks between the courtyard paving stones. The mock siege alarm was called off and everybody in Cymaron, following the king and queen in their bedrobes, grabbed wraps and wandered outside into the wet, grey morning to see what strange immobile army had invaded them.

The creatures themselves were simply made, limbs of rags wrapped around branches and heads made of leather with facial fea-

tures drawn or glued onto them, but all of them wore actual clothing stolen from women in the castle. In fact—

"This is Marged!" Noble cried out with a delighted chuckle, reaching an especially short, round one near the kitchen. He took a closer look. "That's her nose!" He glanced around at the rest of the figures. "Did he make everyone?"

The sewing bevy had just discovered their unflattering statuary: three beings identically dressed and decorated with feathers. "Yes, sire," Generys said in a clipped voice, her nose running in the cold. "At least the women."

"Let me see my wife," Noble called out to the courtyard as a whole. "If someone finds the queen—"

"Here she is," Gwilym announced, his lips squirming as he tried to squelch a smile. He gestured to a small figure with an enormous metal crown hanging cockeyed over a long wimple that was one of the queen's own. There was a black-and-white belt around its waist and from it hung a remarkably good imitation of her rosary, complete with the cross housing the relic of St. Milburga. The royal couple admired it from across the courtyard, laughing.

For nearly half an hour, all activity was suspended as the entire population wandered about marveling and chortling over the likenesses. The more Noble smiled, the easier Isabel felt. For several nights now, Gwirion had not come to her, explaining only that he was at work on an enormous secret project designed to please the king. She regretted that their trysting had to be eclipsed for this to manifest, but it was necessary insurance. Her husband was still affectionate to her in court and amorous in bed, but she had become more anxious than Gwirion about his possible suspicions, and anything to alleviate them met with her instant approval. If Noble knew and felt trapped into looking away, she was grateful that Gwirion at least gave him something else to look at.

Gwirion watched them all from the highest point of the wall walk, hidden from view in the tower that housed the bridge to the keep, wearing his entire wardrobe for warmth: four tunics, two

britches, and two pair of hose, all of it too large. For the first time in his life, inventing mischief had felt like labor to him, harder not only to dream up but to find the energy to realize. He had rallied himself to do it as a patriotic duty: His king required it of him.

When he sensed the hubbub dying down, he crossed along the wall walk and descended the stairs closest to the king's tower. "Attention, people!" he cried out from the last step, affecting a dreadful French accent. He was bulky in all his layers and he'd slicked his dark hair back on his head with water and spit, although a curl from the cowlick lay obstinately askew. "My dear students! And faithful assistants! I am glad to see you here at the convocation of my school!"

Noble grinned. He was impressed with the effigies, but he'd have been disappointed if that was as far as the effort went. "What school?" he prompted.

"My dear king! You do not know about this great school I have created? Just for your men? Just for the men of this castle? You have so many beautiful virgins and so many beautiful prudes and it is so frustrating for your men. So I have invented the school of proximal fornication! Behold!" He grabbed the skirt of the nearest figure—the butler's wife—and flung it up over her head. The actual wife, standing near it, shrieked when she saw it exposed, and everyone else in immediate view had such an enormous reaction that the rest of the yard squelched through the slush to see: The effigy was crudely anatomical. The butler himself thought it was amusing, and after a moment his wife started laughing even as she blushed.

"Here we are!" Gwirion cried out happily. "In full working order—every one! I have tested each myself, only this morning, so you may have to clean up a little." The beaming teulu at once dispersed to hoist the skirts of all the figures, and found with hilarity that every one was similarly outfitted. Noble leaned against the wooden staircase to his room in the cold morning air, clouds of laughter bursting from him, and the women present were wrestling with different levels of amusement, shock, embarrassment, and fury; amusement generally won out. It was an egalitarian offense, at least, with every servant and every lady equally obscene.

The one effigy whose skirt was not upended was the little wimpled one.

"Is my wife not worthy of your lechery?" Noble called out to Efan and his band. He embraced Isabel from behind and rested his chin on her still unwimpled mane.

Efan looked extremely clumsy for a moment. "Nobody would presume to gape at the queen's private parts, sire."

"Don't be absurd—Gwirion *made* the queen's private parts." Noble laughed. Gwirion suddenly felt the need to focus all of his attention on adjusting the sewing bevy's veils, and Isabel willed herself not to tense in her husband's arms. "Go on, then, have at her."

The teulu exchanged glances, but all hesitated to take the first step.

"You silly children," Gwirion said with forced casualness, in his own voice, and ran to the queen's figure to flip up the skirt. "It's just another cunny, lads." He instantly busied himself again in the sewing bevy's veils.

Noble kissed Isabel's head quickly and went to study her double. She knew going with him would seem most natural and lighthearted, but she could not bring herself to do it. Everybody chuckled with anticipation as Noble knelt down to view the artificial copy of his wife's loins. Screwing up his face with exaggerated scrutiny, the king poked and pried, examining the artifact with such vulgar fascination that even Isabel herself, blushing, had to laugh. Gwirion was apparently having a devil of a time getting the veils to sit right on the sewing bevy, and missed the king's performance. Noble finally stood again, shaking his head. "You didn't quite capture it, Gwirion. You must study your subject in more depth next time."

The queen's blush vanished and she looked ill, but nobody noticed her reaction because Gwirion shrugged theatrically and answered, "I made them all alike, sire. Just like women really are." This brought roils of indignant amusement from both sexes and gave him an excuse to resume his French persona and push on with the prank. "Come along, students, we will be getting started for the first lesson now. Let us begin! I need a volunteer boy and a volunteer girl. If

there is no volunteer girl, I will substitute myself. I choose..." He looked around the courtyard. Madrun, the queen's youngest woman, was standing clutched and giggling beside the hall serving girl whose breasts Gwirion, with his new wonderment about the female form, often found himself staring at.

"And I will choose the fair Madrun over here..." As she squealed, he stomped through the slush to her and dragged her over to her effigy. Her face was pink from both the cold and the thrilled embarrassment. "And for the man I find..." Nobody said it but everyone knew whom he was looking for. Madrun and the marshal's son Ednyfed had been besotted with each other for months, but Ednyfed's mother Elen would not allow him to court a woman from the south; she considered that stock infected with the blood of Flemish settlers and therefore beneath him. "Aha, here is the young man I am searching..." He found the boy, blushing but hearty, and dragged him briskly toward the effigy as well. "Now this is the game we play, yes? He wants to relieve his burning desire with her. But he cannot relieve his burning desire with her. So—he has use of the proximal fornication. Pull your drawers down, lad, and make yourself at home." Gwirion flipped the skirt up and casually threw it over the effigy's face. The assembly laughed. He knew that nobody would actually strip in such weather—although he wondered briefly if there would be any takers had he tried this in summertime. "And you, fair Madrun, you will be providing the sounds! You will stand behind and mo-o-o-o-an and gro-o-o-an for all of us to hear, to make it seem more real, yes?" She covered her face with one hand, laughing and blushing, and tried to swat him away with the other hand. "No, no such gestures, only sounds. Very well. Are we ready to begin?"

For the next several hours, Gwirion teased and goaded random couples to bond over the figures. Almost everybody, including all of Noble's teulu, who came over from the keep or up from the village, took the dare at some point, although no man went so far as to drop his drawers. At one point Noble pretended he was about to engage with the effigy of Marged the cook, with Gwirion offering to provide the sound and even giving a spirited demonstration. For over

two hours, nobody touched each other, removed any article of clothing, or even made much eye contact, but Gwirion had roused as much flirtatious mirth as was usually reserved for the Spring Rites of May Day. It was an antidote to the weather, the winter, and the threat of war. *Give us this every day and I can endure anything,* Noble thought gratefully.

The hilarity might well have lasted into the afternoon if Noble had not decided to try coaxing his wife into participating with him. There was no problem with her enthusiasm—she agreed to it, and the crowd cheered and applauded her as she crossed, blushing slightly, over to her small effigy. The moment she was beside it, however, her face changed from pink to purple and she was instantly enraged. She grabbed at the fake rosary hanging from the figure's belt and snatched it away so hard the belt broke.

It wasn't fake.

"Gwirion!" she nearly screamed. *"This is my rosary!"*

Gwirion, who had almost succeeded in getting the buxom hall servant to have a go with the falconer, glanced over his shoulder and called back pleasantly, "Of course it is, that's why I put it on you."

"You had no right to take this!" she shouted. People in the path between them stepped away—this was not hysteria or whining, it was righteous wrath. She held up the chain and shook it in her fist. "You *know* what this means to me. And *this.*" She held up the cross, her hands shaking, and spoke very slowly and clearly. *"This is the relic of a saint.* You know that."

The courtyard was instantly silent and all eyes turned to Gwirion. With a quick nod he excused himself from the black-haired girl and walked to the royal couple. Even Noble looked slightly cowed by her announcement.

Her eyes blazing, she pushed the cross out toward Gwirion, daring him to further insult it. He took the rosary from her politely and examined the crucifix. "But you see, it's just an *English* saint," he declared dismissively, and handed it back to her.

Nobody laughed. People stood silent, ruddy cheeked, suddenly noticing that their boots were leaking in the slush. Gwirion looked to

Noble for support; the king shook his head slightly. "What does this mean, then?" Gwirion said, raising his voice to address the crowd. "I'm allowed to mock the men who persecute us, but not the church that justifies their doing it? What hypocrisy!" There was an uneasy shifting of legs and exchange of glances, but still nobody spoke. "Oh, for the love of ale!" Gwirion said, laughing. "It's a strand of hair! It was probably cut off some leprosed peasant who died on the side of the road near the shrine. If half the relics out there are real, the saints were all eight feet tall with sixteen legs and triple rows of teeth." The silence grew even more absolute. He had never in his life so utterly misjudged his audience. He tried to think of some way to bow out gracefully and decided that it had to be at her expense. "Surely you can afford to buy another one, if that one's been desanctified," he suggested sarcastically, and addressed the crowd again: "You do understand that's why she has it, don't you? It was a purse that earned her that little tidbit, not merit. Just a purse, and probably Mortimer's at that. But go ahead, please, be incensed on Uncle Roger's account."

It didn't get the response he'd hoped for, but there were finally mutterings that sounded more questioning than damning. She looked like she truly would have killed him if she could. "You stole something of mine," she said, quickly shifting the emphasis away from her family.

"No, I stole several somethings," Gwirion corrected with forced cheeriness, and lifting up the makeshift crown, he pulled the wimple off the effigy. "Here, you can have this back too. Would you like me to strip her for you? Or shall we ask the king to do it, he has *much* more experience than I do. In fact maybe he should strip them all!" Finally there was a very slight ripple of chuckling around the yard.

She was unappeased, and all the angrier for not being able to chastise him with the bluntness this deserved. "Adèle made that rosary for me. It's the most cherished object I possess."

"I didn't damage it, milady," Gwirion said, trying to avoid being cornered into defensiveness or worse yet, apology. "I didn't even disrespect it. I had it hanging from your belt like it ought to be—

believe me, there's a dozen other more creative places I could have set it! Shall I list them for you?" She stared at him, saying nothing, and nervousness began to dictate his behavior. "And there's a dozen other *things* I could have done with it," he babbled. "For example, I could demonstrate its essential Englishness and my essential Welshness by flogging myself with it, like this!" And he reached out to take it from her grasp. She snatched her hand away but not before his finger had caught a loop of the chain, and the length of the rosary was stretched taut between them. He didn't want to be accused of stealing it again and she did not want the chain to break under tension; they both re-leased it at the same moment and the rosary plummeted. The clear glass crystal that encased the relic in the center of the cross struck the stone paving of the courtyard first, and struck it hard.

Isabel said nothing, which was the harshest possible condemna-tion. She knelt at once without looking at him and picked up the cru-cifix, wiping the slush and dirt away on the yellow woolen robe, almost too horrified to speak. Reflexively, Gwirion got to his knees to help her, but she pushed him away, so abruptly and angrily he toppled into the slush. "Leave me alone," she said in an icy voice. "Go away. You've done enough damage." She clasped the rosary and crucifix against her chest and stood, then walked out of the courtyard without another word or glance at anyone. Everyone watched her go in silence.

The king found her in her solar, fuming, the rosary and crucifix drying near the hearth. The crystal hadn't shattered, but it was scratched. "Do not even try to defend him," she blurted out in lieu of greeting. "Even without the relic, even if there was only the fact that Adèle made it for me and he knows that—"

"I agree," Noble said quietly. "I'm making no excuses." She shut her mouth, disarmed. "I came up here to see how you were faring, nothing more." He gave her an affectionate look. In the warm light of the fire, his broad face looked paternal. "We all forgot breakfast entirely this morning, but dinner will be ready soon."

"I don't want to see him," she said.

Noble pursed his lips. "I assume you are not asking to eat in your chamber."

Instead of answering she peered through a rip in the sealed parchment covering the window, tried to make out the different hilltops an inch at a time. "Very well," Noble said. "I'll tell him to take dinner in the kitchen."

"And supper," she added at once, her eyes still on the abbreviated landscape.

"This will *not* be a return to the hostilities of last year," he announced firmly. "I don't have time to relive such nonsense now. I require the two of you to be civil to each other."

"Tell *him* that," she snapped, forcing herself to be fascinated by the little she could see out of the window.

She did not call for Gwirion that night and relished, for the first time, the power she had in their affair: He could not come to her unbidden.

G UIRION tried the next morning, after mass, to apologize. She requested him to do so formally, in front of the king and court as they broke fast, and he agreed even to this humiliation, even knowing that for the first time, perhaps ever, he was not the congregation's secret darling. He stood before the high table where the royal couple sat, feeling rows of diners' eyes on the back of his head, self-consciously penitent in stance. "What exactly are you apologizing for?" she asked sharply, when his two-word declaration—"I apologize"—was over.

"Whatever you want me to regret," he said after a moment. It was an honest response; he had no other answer.

"What *do* you regret?" she demanded severely from her chair. He reviewed the whole event mentally as king and queen waited, watching him expectantly, and finally he answered, "I regret that I released the rosary. Then it wouldn't have fallen and gotten scratched. That's the only real harm that was done—and we're equally responsible for it," he pointed out reasonably, adding in an exaggeratedly indulgent

tone, "but if you'll apologize for your part in the mishap, I'll certainly apologize for mine." This got no reaction from the hall. But Noble was making a steeple with his fingers before his lips, his signature of suppressed laughter, and Gwirion knew he was amusing the only one who mattered. He relaxed a little, reassured. There was no harm done, then—in fact, a public falling out like this, suggesting things were somehow as they'd always been between them, was strategically savvy, although he was glad it was over now and things could go back to normal. After only one night apart, he missed the feel of her hair between his fingers.

She gave him a disgusted look. "I accept your apology," she said coldly. "And when you figure out what you should really be apologizing for, I'll accept that as well. Until then, please refrain from placing yourself unduly in my presence."

FOR three days she ignored him. He did not dare approach her, even given a chance to. But he ached with missing the smooth warmth of her skin, would have been content even catching a hint of her scent at the hearthside. And yet the young hall maid seemed more attractive every hour. He found his own fickleness oddly reassuring, proof that it was only flesh he missed, and flesh could come from other sources. Hall maids, for example.

Isabel was glad he'd reminded her of just how callow he was, for she'd been teetering on the edge of real attachment, and this had helped her to collect herself. She was grateful for the affair, it had brought her pleasure and a sense of power, but Noble seemed wholeheartedly devoted to promoting her adoration and contentment now, and deserved the whole of her in kind. Gwirion would be her lover only on the physical level, and as physical levels went, what Noble offered was easily superior in both form and technique. So there was no profit to an intimate reconciliation. It was not guilt or even loyalty that prompted her decision; it was simply pragmatism.

Let Gwirion find himself a woman better suited to him, she thought, and when each was confident that the other was independently content, perhaps a treasonless friendship could mature between them. It would be a graceful and sensible resolution to an otherwise impossible scenario.

WHEN his wife had first become seized by insomnia and insisted on retiring to her own bed each night, he realized he missed feeling a feminine body asleep beside him. He had seldom kept a woman in his bed after lovemaking prior to his marriage, and was surprised to find that he had developed an attachment to it; he was not surprised to find, however, that he had no attachment whatsoever to the feminine body actually belonging to his wife.

There was a young woman who had caught his eye weeks earlier. She was black-haired, with the curves and generally wild look that he liked so much, but a sweet, almost childlike face. He asked Gwirion about her and learned that she was new to Cymaron, that she was orphaned but well past the age of consent, with a younger sister who like her worked in the hall. One night shortly after Gwirion's wan apology to Isabel, Noble saw the girl standing with a group of others, mostly Marged's assistants, listening to Gwirion play. When he had finished the tune, the king called him over. The rest of the clique broke up to return to their chores, but the black-haired girl, curious, followed Gwirion's path of travel with her eyes. Servant and queen both watched the two men in whispered conversation. Noble's gesture, and Gwirion's eyes following after, left no doubt who the subject of the conversation was. The girl, her face wide-eyed but unreadable, darted out of sight into the kitchen. Isabel felt a stab of jealous anger in her gut as she realized Noble was openly setting up a tryst; it mocked her assumption that they were working toward at least the appearance of adoring monogamy. *Perhaps I misunderstood,* she

decided with a dismissive mental shrug. *Perhaps the girl is simply meant for Gwirion.*

Suddenly she couldn't breathe.

A FTER supper Isabel excused herself to the chapel and sat for a long time in the light of a single votive, the rosary on her lap and her eyes fixed above the altar, staggered by the unwelcome enlightenment about the state of her own heart.

Back in the hall, she found Gwirion in his usual loitering spot by the kitchen screens, cleaning his teeth with a hazel twig. He made to walk away at her approach, but she signaled him to stay. Being close to him again made her palms clammy. It took her a moment to corral her thoughts into words.

"That Christian spirit you find so contemptible is coming to your aid," she finally whispered. "The moon is far from full tonight, so people will be sleeping soundly. Except perhaps for me."

He was surprised. "You don't think I'm beyond redemption?"

"Oh, you might be," she answered, still whispering. "But that's not for me to judge." She crossed her arms awkwardly. It made her look, as certain gestures did, like a little girl playing at adulthood. "I know you felt you had to do that, and I forgive you, Gwirion, but you must understand something. I don't think you realize just what an insult you committed that morning." He decided it would be best not to comment on this. "What you mocked was the very part of me that is choosing to forgive the mockery. You may find devotion absurd, but if I were not devout, I would not be speaking to you now—or ever."

"I don't believe that," Gwirion said quickly. "I'm not devout but I'd forgive you nearly anything." And then he was quiet, looking almost embarrassed.

"Then you're a better Christian than you realize." A pause, as he graciously refrained from mocking her for saying this. "I know that

nothing is safe from your derision, least of all me. I don't care, give him what he wants. But I do ask that you *hesitate*, at least, before you mock my piety again."

He grimaced for a moment, chewing on the hazel twig. "I'll do that for you, not for your piety. Good evening, sire," he went on brightly in a louder voice, his eyes widening, and she jumped as Noble's hands squeezed her shoulders from above. She whirled around to find him grinning at her.

"I see there's some progress being made here. Excellent. Life is much easier for the entire castle, frankly, when the two of you are not at odds. Is the battle over?" Both nodded, slightly sheepishly. "Who took the honors?"

They exchanged glances. "She did," Gwirion conceded.

"That's fine," her husband hummed. "As long as you don't rub off on him." The king nudged her toward the door. "I'll be up in a few moments, go and warm the bed for us."

She nodded, said good night to Gwirion politely, and left the hall. Noble turned his hypnotic gaze on his friend. "Thank you," he whispered, squeezed Gwirion's shoulder, and exited after his wife.

A N hour later, as the castle was settling in to sleep, Gwirion received two summonses at once—to play the harp for the queen, and to play the pander for the king. Grudgingly he took up his old vocation of royal procurer, a job he had once approached with a certain amusement and, if nothing else, vicarious pleasure. Now it felt seedy, even shameful—and annoying at the same time, for it was the young woman he had very nearly asked the king to give him as a mistress. He found her lying on a pile of rushes and meadowsweet not far from the hall fire. When asked, she said her name was Nest, and she seemed not only prepared to follow him upstairs, but, in fact, quite pleased about it. As they traveled through the night-fogged courtyard, he was close enough to her to catch her

scent, the kind of sweet muskiness that would have excited any man; Noble's taste was impeccable. He led her up the outside stairs to the king's chamber, pausing at the door with a nod to the bored and smirking Gethin. "Here we are," Gwirion said, and she laughed with nervous pleasure. He gently nudged her through the door and closed it behind her.

In his bedchamber, Noble lounged propped up on one elbow near the fire, throwing a few sticks into the hearth to keep the new flames hot. He heard brief, excited laughter outside, and smiled. Then the door opened and he saw the girl enter. Somebody pulled the door shut and after a moment, realizing she'd been left here, she turned and faced the king. Her eyes went very round as she saw who her companion was. She looked confused for a moment, then nervously dropped into a curtsy.

"You don't need to do that in here," Noble said expansively. "Come sit by me."

Her jaw went slack and she gave him a stupid, stunned look. "Your . . . Your Majesty has called me?"

"That surprises you? You came willingly along, didn't you?"

"Yes, sire. I didn't realize this was your room, sire, I've never been upstairs before."

"Whose room did you think it was, then?"

She swallowed uncomfortably, radiating embarrassment. "I thought the room was unoccupied, sire."

For a moment he was confused by this answer, then understanding, he lay back on the floor and shook with laughter. "That's brilliant!" he crowed. "You, my dear, are a *godsend.*"

HER women were asleep by the time Gwirion arrived and he did not even bother with the pretense of playing the harp. They were impatient to touch after days of separation; he had just undressed and they were running their hands along each other's bod-

ies with breathless awe as if it were for the first time. A moment later and he might have been too absorbed in her warmth, but he was still alert enough to realize that it was the king who was whistling "Rhiannon's Tears" as he descended from the wall walk. In barely a second Gwirion had blown out the candle, scrambled out of her bed and into the shadows near his harp. She barely had time to register what he was doing before he leapt back, pulled the bed curtains closer together and disappeared again into the shadow to frantically pull his tunic on.

"Noble!" Isabel managed to sound normal as her husband abruptly flung open the door and entered.

"I have extraordinary news," the king announced cheerfully, throwing open the bed curtains and placing his candle lantern on the side chest. His cheeks were flushed from the cold and he slid his chilly hands under the covers, pressed them against her warm abdomen.

She shrank away from his hands and gestured at the tapestry that shielded the sewing bevy. "Be quiet, you'll wake them," she shushed.

"I don't mind if they overhear," he said as Gwirion emerged, miraculously dressed. "I thought you'd both enjoy hearing that my evening's assignation failed utterly."

"What a pity," the queen said sardonically, although at this moment she hardly cared. "Why?"

"Because the girl thinks she's in love with Gwirion." Noble laughed.

Gwirion was astounded. "But she seemed eager to go to your room—"

"She didn't know it was my room. She thought it was some special bower you were taking her to for your own devious purposes. She was so adorably earnest that I decided to reward her for it. So she's waiting in your room downstairs—I promised her you'd be right down."

The two of them started violently in the darkness, and Gwirion felt a weight lift from his chest. This was the perfect solution for him, the perfect out, and he knew she knew that because when he risked a glance at her, he saw on her face exactly the look he had

wanted never to see there: fear. Anything else he could have managed—derision, amusement, sulking, even jealousy or anger. But the vulnerable look that begged him not to wasn't something he was equal to. The alternative he wanted—the safe, relatively moral, and very delectable alternative to the worst kind of adultery—was dangling within reach and the only thing keeping him from grabbing it was that look on her face. As if reading his mind, she caught herself and turned her head away, forcing her expression into a neutral mask.

"Thank you, sire," Gwirion finally managed to stammer. "Did you mean . . . now?"

"Of course now," Noble said, laughing at him. "Now and later too. I think it's an excellent long-term proposition. Go on, then. She's practically edible."

"Thank you, sire," Gwirion said again stupidly, but his legs were unwilling to move. Inexplicably he felt compelled to take her emotions into account—an alien, confusing impulse. He resented her for it but the resentment did nothing to dull his disorienting sense of duty to her.

She read his mind and forced the hardest sentence of her life out of her mouth. "Go on, then, Gwirion," she said, managing to sound like a teasing older sister. "The night's not getting any younger."

Noble chortled. He nudged her, grinning, incredibly pleased with himself. "He's stunned by his good luck." He turned back to Gwirion. "Go *on*." He wafted his hand in a grand wave of mock imperiousness. "You are dismissed," he intoned, sitting on the edge of Isabel's bed and loosening the tongue of his drawers belt. "My wife and I will celebrate your good fortune on our own."

With a terse good night to both of them, Gwirion collected the harp and left the room awkwardly. He was angry, and mostly he was angry with her. What she'd said to cover herself didn't count. He'd seen her expression, her one unguarded moment. Earlier in the evening she had been with the king, and he was being sent away so that they could be together again and she'd dared to give him *that look*?

He left the harp in the hall, and paused outside the opening to his own little room. There was a slight rustle within and his heart al-

most stopped. "Sir?" Nest's voice whispered from beyond the opening, and suddenly he remembered how good she'd smelled. He closed his eyes in the darkened kitchen, and rested his head against the stone wall a moment. Finally, with a heavy sigh, he knelt down and crawled into the space.

"Good evening, Nest," he said quietly, and reached for her hand.

THE next morning in chapel, Isabel prayed in vain to be released from the torment that had kept her awake, a fever of emotions she knew she was not the least entitled to. He was being paired off with a mistress who would be free to show him tender affection every day, in ways both casual and intimate. In front of other people. That would be seductive. Over time, Nest would win him away from her by offering him what the queen was not allowed to. Her envy of Enid paled by comparison.

At board, her angst was only worsened by a sharp slap of guilt when she saw her husband's face, as he was brooding over messengered dispatches he'd asked to read before breakfast. While she was nearly falling apart over the petty luxury of personal emotions, he was struggling to keep the state intact. Absurdly, she envied him the burden. He gave her a weak smile when she sat beside him and gestured to the scrolls he'd been perusing. "As usual. Llewelyn is doing things he said he wouldn't and Mortimer is not doing things he said he would," he said, sounding tired. "While Anarawd is querying his neighbors on the royal bed's fecundity." Then his eyes flickered to something behind her and his face brightened a little. "And speaking of fecundity, here is Cymaron's newest stud!" Gwirion had approached the table, and without a word or look of greeting, settled quietly upon his stool. Noble gave him a lecherous wink. "Entertain us with tales of your nocturnal exploits, then, you little satyr. I'm taking my wife back to bed immediately after breakfast, so you may be quite explicit."

Gwirion's face went very red and he looked into his lap. "I . . . don't think that would be gentlemanly of me, sire."

"When have you ever been gentlemanly?" Noble snorted, and his eyes were once against drawn to something behind his wife's head. Nest had just entered the hall, as unreadable as Gwirion, skimming the sides of the room cleaning up after the servants and guards who had slept here. "Never mind," Noble announced smugly. "I'll go straight to the source." He rose and ambled over to the girl. Isabel and Gwirion avoided looking at each other. While the chaplain intoned his usual Latinate thanksgiving, she watched the king approach Nest and speak to her for a moment. He patted the girl's arm with a parental joviality.

But after he'd left her and returned to the table, he paused and looked appraisingly at Gwirion. Gwirion tried to ignore the gaze and then realized it was going to continue indefinitely if he didn't acknowledge it, so he finally looked up. Their eyes locked and they maintained the silence for another moment.

"You really are a fool," Noble said. He was annoyed. Gwirion simply shrugged. Out of the corner of his eye, he saw Isabel relax and close her eyes in gratitude for a moment. She who willingly spread her knees to another man every evening was tormented by the thought of his being with another lover even once. He almost wished he had taken the girl after all, just to give Her Royal Majesty a taste of what he went through each evening.

THAT night when she called him, Gwirion almost sent back the message that he was busy with his stud duties by order of the king. But he couldn't bring himself to refuse her. He retrieved his harp from its chest in the hall, his gaze lingering briefly on Nest's sleeping form curled near the hearth.

He stopped. Even if Noble did not suspect them, even if he never came to suspect them, what had happened last night would be only the first of interminable irritations.

He turned to Llwyd and whispered, "Please apologize to Her Majesty, but I'm unable to attend to her, I've other commitments."

Her doorkeeper was confused by the obvious lie, but nodded and headed back for the stairs as Gwirion, trying to breathe calmly, watched him. There. That simply, it was over. He started back to his stone warren, imagining her as she imagined him taking Nest. For one dazzling moment this gave him extraordinary, vengeful satisfaction and then he was disgusted with himself.

And he had not, after all, actually fantasized about taking Nest this time—only about Isabel fearing it. He cursed softly to himself, understanding what the difference meant.

Clutching his harp under his arm, he turned back toward the stairs. Nest, as he passed her, slept peacefully. He intercepted Llwyd just before he reached the balcony and mumbled an excuse to go in.

He sat himself near her bed and began to play without greeting her, and played for nearly half an hour in the sad Irish tuning that he knew she liked. Then he silenced the strings and rested the harp on the dried meadowsweet that fragranced and padded the floor.

He waited for her to tug the bed drapes apart and gesture for him, as she always did, but there was no movement from within. After a long moment, he tentatively opened the curtains himself, unused to taking the initiative.

She was sitting up on the far side of the bed in her shift. She made no movement toward him as he crawled in; he left the curtain open behind him for the candlelight to come in. She looked anxious.

"Why didn't you?" she whispered.

"Isn't it enough that I didn't?" he whispered back.

She shook her head. "If I didn't care *why* you didn't, I probably wouldn't care if you did it at all. I want to know . . ." She hesitated. "I need to know how I figured into your decision." She shrugged self-deprecatingly. "If I figured into your decision."

He looked at her unspeaking for a long moment in the obstructed candlelight. "You *are* my decision," he finally said.

Her breath caught. She had so hoped for that answer and so doubted it would come. She held her palm out toward him and he

met it with his own. His large eyes in the muted candlelight made him look almost childlike.

"I thought it was a trap," he said, sheepish.

"So did I."

"But then I realized it couldn't be."

"How can you say that? Wasn't it strange, when he came in here last night? As if he was being deliberately naive."

Gwirion shook his head. "He knew you were sleepless, so he expected that I'd be up here, there's nothing odd in that. And you covered beautifully when you told me to go downstairs."

"The whole thing just felt . . . too pat, somehow. Like a well-planned game."

He shook his head again, this time sympathetically. "Noble's always playing games, it's second nature to him. You'd drive yourself to distraction trying to track every one he plays."

"What if he suspects, and he's setting us up to get caught?"

"He could have caught us last night. If I hadn't heard him whistling—"

"Exactly!" she hissed, hating that they had to whisper. "He was *whistling!*"

"Which he would not have been doing if he was trying to catch us at something," Gwirion said reassuringly, interlacing his fingers with hers. "I'm far more attuned to him than you are, why are you so nervous?"

She sighed. "He says things sometimes, gives me funny looks, that make me think he knows."

"He would have done something already."

"No, he wouldn't, he needs me now."

"Noble doesn't need *anyone,*" Gwirion said, almost dismissively. "If he wants something, he always finds alternatives. He would never subject himself to wearing horns because you'd somehow become indispensable to him—nobody is ever indispensable to him."

"We have to be more careful," she said with vague stubbornness.

He grimaced. "Should I come to you less often?"

"No!" She crawled over to him and leaned against him. This was

the longest conversation they'd had by far since their first tryst in this room, and its timbre bothered her. She cuddled into his arms, pressed against the body that she feared she now knew better than the person. "It isn't fair," she sighed. "It's so *simple* for *him* to tryst."

He hesitated. "This is much more dangerous than his liaisons. You know that."

"But I'm *damaged*," she said bitterly. "Even if he suspects my fidelity, he knows I can't conceive a bastard."

"That isn't what I meant," Gwirion said. After a self-conscious pause he added, "I meant he doesn't fall in love."

That night they lay together for hours, holding each other.

DRUNKARD'S TUNING

Approaching Spring Equinox, 1199

FTER COUNCIL the next day, the king summoned his wife to meet with him alone in the receiving room, a strangely formal request. When she entered, he was so drawn and somber he was almost grey. For one fleeting, irrational moment she was afraid this was about Gwirion's refusal to take a mistress.

"Are you indeed the Lady of Maelienydd?" he asked quietly, not looking at her, staring into the flames of the fire.

"Please don't start that again," she said.

"I have my reasons."

"Tell me what you suspect me of, Noble, I haven't the energy for games."

He looked deeply troubled. "I understand the world, but I resist it," he whispered bitterly. "Is it possible, do you think, to betray a loyalty that is deeper than blood, and not burn in hell for it?"

She swallowed, trying to breathe calmly. "What loyalty is that, sire?"

"*Sire?*" he snapped, and looked up at her, enraged. She took a step away from him, paling, and almost fell onto the settle. "I call you in here as my wife, my consort, my confidante, and you treat me with obsequiousness? Is that how you show me I can put my faith in you?" He turned back to the fire, disgusted.

"Noble, please, speak plainly," she begged. "I don't know what you're talking about."

He sighed, then looked back up at her, more civil this time but still dour. His mouth had the grim, firm set to it that she had only ever seen in sleep before. "This is about Llewelyn."

She relaxed a little. "How can your loyalty to Llewelyn be deeper than blood?" she asked.

He shook his head slowly. "I don't care about Llewelyn. I care about my kingdom. *My. Kingdom.*" He whispered both words as if they were a foreign phrase he was trying to recall. "I need you to support me if I sin against my fathers in order that my sons might prosper."

Still not understanding him, she rested her hand tentatively on his arm. "You need my support as the Lady of Maelienydd?" she asked.

Even his blue eyes had lost their spark. "I need your support as a Mortimer," he whispered at last. Then he told her what he meant to do, and would not be talked out of it.

THAT evening, Gwilym the steward and Hafaidd the usher requested Gwirion to perform for them privately in their shared chamber when he was finished playing for the king. He was fond of them both, and indebted to them for enduring decades of his rascal wit, so he cheerfully agreed. He finished his ale, offered Noble a parting good-night witticism concerning leeks and bodily orifices, wrapped a wool mantle around himself, and headed toward the door of the great hall, his harp in its sheath tucked under his arm. The queen had been crossing the hall not quite toward him through the

smoky amber light. She paused to speak with Elen, the marshal's wife. As Gwirion passed nearby, she excused herself, smoothly intercepted him and murmured, "Go up the stairs, not down, when you've finished," then returned her attention to the other woman.

He could barely focus as he played for them, at once hoping and dreading that she had arranged a tryst where they might have the luxury of real privacy. The two older men murmured unhappily together, in phrases rife with "Roger" and "Llewelyn," and sometimes "Anarawd." Gwirion's gaze drifted to the planked ceiling of their room, wondering whether she was even now waiting in the chamber above, and he was so flushed throughout his performance that they offered to damp the fire if he was too warm. Gwirion refused, with many awkward thanks, and declined to share a horn of ale before departing. The harp he left with them, on the flimsy excuse of not wanting to expose it to the cold.

Outside, the black night was thickly smudged with clouds. The mantle wrapped around him, he hesitated on the stairs before taking a step up. But the commitment of that one step seemed magically to catapult him to the floor above. He stopped at the door of the guest chamber and carefully pushed it open.

The room was sealed with wax parchments at the window, frigid, and completely black. It was too silent for her to have been here, but then he heard her voice calling quietly from what he guessed was near the fireplace, "Come here."

"They're not asleep downstairs yet," he warned, everything in his body quickening at once. He dropped his wrap by the doorway. "They'll get suspicious if they hear noise up here."

"It can't possibly be as bad as it is in my room," she replied. "It's safe to make a little noise—Madrun trysts with her lover here, I've heard her tell the other girls. I said come here. It's straight across, I moved everything that was in the way."

When he was beside her, he sank down onto a soft nest of blankets she had laid out that afternoon before the sun went down. "How did you know I'd be in their room?" he asked.

"I suggested it." She laughed a little, pleased with herself. "My

women think I'm with Noble for the night, and Noble thinks I'm tucked into my own bed with a sour stomach. I could get quite good at this."

He smiled despite his nervousness, and let her undress him. Naked, jaw clenched from the cold, he loosed the side ties of her kirtle and ran his chilly hands under it, along her body, and she shivered. He helped her wriggle out of the kirtle, and after she laid it carefully aside, he grabbed her gently by the hips and pulled her toward him, drawing the blankets over them into a cocoon. His mouth found her breasts and his hands lost themselves in the satin hair he so adored.

They were quiet, but quiet felt raucous compared to the silence they'd been constrained to in her room for weeks. Hearing each other's voices as they touched and pressed themselves together drove them nearly into seizures of affection and they found themselves almost laughing—quietly—at the intensity of their desire. She marveled as always at the difference in the two men. Noble treated their coupling, both in his satisfaction and hers, as further evidence of his sovereignty—it was another thing she was pleasantly useful for, both to his senses and to his pride. To Gwirion, physical pleasure seemed to be eternally miraculous, and she was credited for all of it. That had been strange to her at first; it lacked the manly arrogance that was part of Noble's sexual charisma, but now she cherished it.

But what she cherished most of all was that in the aftermath of conquering each other, it was finally safe for them to speak. They lay with arms and legs entwined and bodies pressed together, her hand draped over him, brushing against the scar on his back.

"Say my name," she whispered, but he shook his head. "Please." He wouldn't. "Then call me some pet name. I want to hear an endearment from your lips."

"There is no endearment that suffices," he whispered. "Words pale." He sounded almost bashful.

"You *always* have a word at your disposal."

"Not for you. You defeat me."

"Aha! The Normans win a round!" She grinned.

"You're Welsh to me," he said, with a simple sincerity that touched her until he added snidely, "Except for that ridiculous accent."

She began murmuring incomprehensible things with her lips brushing his. He smiled, but shook his head. "I have no idea what you're saying."

"It's shockingly filthy," she promised. "Worse than pagan. Something that would leave even that heathen August war god of yours speechless."

He gave her a condescending smile. "Do you mean Llew? He's not a war god, first of all, and he's Welsh, which means that *nothing* leaves him speechless."

"Of course he's a war god, all Welsh heroes are war gods."

"And I really can't imagine why we should feel the need for that," Gwirion muttered dryly, then went on to correct her, as if it were something any child would know. "But Llew is the god of harvest and the sun. I pity your people having a history that's limited to human mortals, how very dull for you. No wonder you were such a witless prune when you arrived." He quickly kissed her to stave off her protestations and kept his tongue pressed against hers until her muffled indignant growl had given way to giggles.

"Is he the one who—" She tried to remember what he'd been blathering about in the courtyard last summer. "The one who puts . . . a divine spark, isn't it, into every oat stalk?"

"He puts a divine spark into everything," Gwirion said, running his hand across her nude belly. "Except the English. He tried, but they're allergic to divine sparks."

"You!" Laughing, she tried to hit him but he used it as an excuse to grab her hands above her head and rolled on top of her again.

"Tell me what the shockingly filthy French meant," he ordered, the tip of his nose resting gently on the tip of hers.

"Would you like me to demonstrate?" she offered.

They came together again, but for most of the night they simply talked, teasing and laughing softly, saturating themselves with the intimacy they'd reached in their imprisonment under Cynan. Something within Isabel quivered nervously on behalf of her eternal soul,

but she could not abide the thought that something so joyful could be wrong. Anyhow, it was a joy she could not bear to live without now. Such genuine, immediate companionship was more seductive to her than an eternity of angels.

Before it was light enough to see, they folded the blankets up and she slipped them into chests whose locations she had memorized by feel the day before. They helped each other to dress. This took a long time, as it required stroking and tickling and hands slipping into places where they did not really belong, but eventually they were both presentable, in ragged linen and fine silk, respectively. The slightest grey glow had begun to illuminate the far horizon, but not yet the air, as they stepped together out of the room, she in her purple mantle and he in the dull grey woolen one, his arm still fastened around her waist, not wanting to relinquish her back to reality. They should have disciplined themselves, he thought, they should not have lingered until nearly dawn. By day they belonged to Noble, not to each other. And the days were growing longer.

"One more kiss," he begged, and a smile lit her face: He never asked for kisses, never bothered with parting terms of endearment. They pressed their lips together for a long moment that wasn't nearly long enough, then he squeezed her once more tight against him, whispering, "I hope you have insomnia tonight." She laughed softly, and they began to separate, she to the left and Gwirion to the right.

Gwirion turned smack into the teulu's stiffened leather breastplate, hurting his nose and jumping back in protest. She heard the noise and spun fully around, then froze. There was an awkward, horrible moment of silence as the guard stared at the two of them, eyes narrowed in his young pockmarked face, trying to imagine some acceptable explanation for what he was seeing. Gwirion recognized him with a silent groan: It was Caradoc, the catalyst for his misadventures last summer on the road with Enid.

"What's going on here?" he demanded angrily, sparing no niceties for the queen. She opened her mouth to speak but nothing came out. Caradoc took a menacing step toward them and began to draw his sword. "Answer me!" he growled.

Before the sword was out of its sheath, Gwirion darted back and snatched the queen's eating knife from her belt, threw his arm around her and held the knife to her throat. "What's going on is I've taken the queen hostage," he said fiercely. "Back off or I'll make mincemeat of her." She stiffened but said nothing as Caradoc gave him an incredulous grunt. "Endear yourself to the king," Gwirion urged. "Tell him to come out here and negotiate with me for her release. Go on—" He poked the eating knife against her neck and she had the sense to cry out in a terrified voice. "I'm a bit mad you know, you don't want to fool with me. Go on, Caradoc!" The young soldier, confused and disturbed by this bizarre turn, started down the steps as other teulu and guards around the bailey, hearing her cry and sensing the commotion in the predawn darkness, headed toward them. "Quick," Gwirion whispered urgently. "Up to the top of the tower, but make it look like I'm dragging you."

The two of them scrambled up the dark tower stairwell, Gwirion cursing quietly when he stumbled on his blanket. They burst out under the leaden sky, onto the pitched-round roof of the tower as shouts and calls began to echo around the walls of the bailey and from the lookout of the keep. Gwirion, eyes wild, sat her down on the conical crown of the roof and desperately tried to figure out what to do next.

"Is this a prank or the end of our lives?" she asked, pulling the mantle tighter around her and trying to stay calm as voices of angry, anxious protest came closer from below.

"I don't know yet," Gwirion said shortly. The tower rose a floor above the wall walk, and the only way to reach this roof directly was by the one stairway, a weakness in the design that he was acutely grateful for. There was a wooden cover for the stairwell hatch to keep the rain out. It lay on the sloped roof, and he struggled to move it into place. She slithered down the incline to help him.

"Don't," he grunted between labored breaths. "You're my captive, remember? They're watching from the keep, the light's rising and they mustn't see you help me." The cover was in place now but wouldn't keep anyone out long—it could easily be pushed up from

below. He had to secure it. To start with he picked up Isabel herself and placed her on top of it to give it a little bit of extra weight. There was nothing else up here. "That will have to do for now," he said. "Don't move, don't get off that. If they see you on it they'll be reluctant to muck with it much for fear of hurting you."

"What now?" she asked, alert but unafraid, and distractedly fingered an abandoned bird's nest wattled into a gap in the stone.

"I don't know," he snapped, almost annoyed with her for not being more distressed. He thought of sending her down on her own and barricading himself up here on some pranklike pretext, which would no doubt sound as feeble as what he'd pulled with Caradoc. That would at least separate them and possibly remove suspicion from her. But if they had, indeed, just irreversibly revealed themselves, sending her down to Noble might literally be fatal.

He sat beside her, and the scent of her softened his edge at once. "I want to take your hand right now," he whispered. "I don't dare because of the men in the keep. I think there's enough light now that they can see right down here."

She shrugged her mantle off one shoulder so that it covered both their hands, and ran her fingers over his. He took a quick breath, startled. "What else do you want to do to me?" she asked in a playful voice.

"It's not the time for levity," he insisted. "I don't know how to save you from this, Isabel."

He'd said her name without thinking and it startled both of them.

"The crazy fool is scolding the rigid Saxoness for levity?" She seemed delighted, and he decided it must be a peculiar kind of nervous attack.

"I am truly sorry about this," he said. "I wish to God there was some way I could shoulder all responsibility."

"Taking me captive is effective," she said. "Should I struggle? Do you want me to bite you?" She leaned in toward him. "I'd love to bite you."

He laughed. Then he stopped himself and shook his head to clear it. "I'm floating right now," he said, perplexed. "I've been caught

in treasonous adultery, and we're probably both about to be killed, and I'm . . . I think this is joy." She squeezed his hand under the mantle, smiling so prettily it made his eyes smart. "You don't know how desperately I want to kiss you right now," he whispered.

"Yes I do," she whispered back. "But tell me what else you would do to me if you could. If it were ever safe."

"I . . ." He winced. "I'd make an ass of myself."

"Really?" She looked gleeful at the declaration. "How?"

He blushed. "I'd make up dreadful poems about you, about your hair and your nipples and your kneecaps. I'd stare at you in silence for hours wondering what I did to deserve all the good and bad of this, and being grateful for all of both." He plucked a denuded oat stalk from the abandoned bird's nest and said softly, "I'd ask the great god Llew to fill this humble stalk with the divine spark of all my good regard for you. He would endow each straw in all of Wales with the power to bestow my love upon you."

"Good heavens," she said in a choked voice. "Is there a bad poet hidden under all of that?"

"And then of course," he went on in his normal voice, tossing the oat straw away, "I would summon the spirit of King Arthur to wrench your wretched Norman throat while I ravished your horse."

She grinned, nodding. "That's more like it," she said heartily. "That's the charming lad I lost my heart to." They laughed together. Nervously. Terrified, in fact.

HEARING from Caradoc only that the queen had been taken hostage by "the villain," who had possibly already forced himself on her, Noble had leapt out of bed and frantically thrown a woolen robe over his tunic and drawers before running down the steps and into the still-slushy yard.

Around the wall walk and the towers, fifty teulu archers stood ready with arrows on the string, waiting for the king's word.

Hafaidd and Gwilym were standing with a small crowd of servants staring up at the northwest tower. "Where are they?" Noble demanded anxiously.

Gwilym looked uncomfortable. "Up there, sire." The steward gestured with a nod of his head.

"And he'll parley?"

Gwilym and Hafaidd exchanged bemused glances: Apparently the king did not realize who the villain was. The steward cleared his throat. "Only with you, sire."

"Get his attention, then."

Gwilym nodded to the herald, who put his horn to his lips and blasted a long, steady note that silenced the yard. Immediately, a head crowned by a mop of dark hair popped up over the edge of the parapet and gazed down at them.

"Good morning!" Gwirion called out.

Noble relaxed. "For the love of the saints!" he scolded. "What are you doing? Where is my wife?"

At a gesture from Gwirion, Isabel rose and showed herself. "I'm safe, Noble," she called down reassuringly. "It was one of his less-inspired pranks. He told me you were up here waiting to show me something."

"I thought Your Majesties might like to view the sunrise with me," Gwirion overlapped, loudly, and scowled. "I was on my way to fetch Your Majesty when that idiot soldier ran into me and went quite mad—does that amuse you?" he interrupted himself, when he saw the expression on Noble's face.

The king was looking up at them with a knowing smile, his hands clasped behind him. "I was merely appreciating your most extraordinary gift for timing." As he said these words, he gestured to the door of the great hall as Thomas, Walter, and Ralf emerged from it out into the yard, in expensive but ill-insulating mantles. They followed everyone's upturned gazes to the top of the tower.

"What the *devil* are you doing to her this time?" Ralf demanded, instantly enraged.

GWIRION accepted a hand slap—a real one, in the presence of the uncles—when he had brought the queen back down into the yard. He sat quietly through Ralf's berating him in the council chamber, in front of Noble, while Isabel watched mutely; Gwirion had insisted she play the innocent. When the old man was finally out of breath, Gwirion gave him a pleading look. "Does this mean you won't be wanting me to play for you at supper? I had something special planned." But the glow Isabel had seen in his eyes when they were alone on the tower roof was gone. Just when she knew he was truly with her, he disappeared again.

This time it was for her sake, not his own. When they came downstairs into the courtyard, she had been glowing with the particular light of a woman rapturously in love, and to Gwirion's cautious eyes Noble seemed attentive, and curious about it. Their night-long tryst had been too easy and seductive; they were both dangerously close to tripping into a fantasia of something that could never be, and he would blame himself if she slammed into reality too hard too late. He could not let her fall; he would remind her, with her family's unwitting assistance, of their very narrow limits. If he had to he would make himself despicable.

GENERYS was fastening the underpinnings of the queen's wine-red wimple as Gwallter rearranged the drape of Noble's mantle over his red silk tunic. It was evening. The visitors had been sequestered all day, nursing a severe chill born of unexpected troubles on their travels. "Still they arrived a day sooner than I expected, which is excellent, it means I can begin the spring circuit earlier," Noble said.

"What happened to them? It's a day's ride from Wigmore, why did they arrive here in the morning?"

He tipped his head to the side as Gwallter fastened the draping with a brooch. "They lost their way and got in very late last night. I don't know how your entire race has managed to avoid self-destruction. The moon is not half full and it was clouded over completely, but they just kept *going*. They were halfway to the Severn when some scouts found them and brought them back south. Thank God they had my writ of safe conduct or they might have had their throats slit."

She pulled away from Generys and sat down hard on the bed, alarmed but not about that. "Last night?" She tried to sound casual. "Where did they sleep?"

Noble bent over a little so Gwallter could place the circlet on his head. "I had Gwilym put them in my audience chamber." He straightened, nodded toward the door, and waited for Gwallter to open it. "I was going to put them in the guest chamber above Gwilym's room but thought better of it. Illicit couples use it sometimes to rendezvous and I didn't want your uncles embarrassing anyone. I'll see you at supper." He left.

She reached out to grab the bedpost as the room wobbled.

"Milady?" Generys said tentatively, and reached toward the queen's half-assembled headdress. Isabel held up her hand to stop her. She desperately needed an hour alone to think; there were too many complications begging for resolution. "No wimple this evening," she said at last, pulling the barbet off. "Tonight I wear a Welsh veil."

THE family would be dining privately in Noble's receiving chamber, with a proper table set up and chairs brought in especially for all of them. This was an uncommon way to entertain visitors, but the visitors noticed nothing uncommon about it. To them

one's exclusion from the populace, not one's adoration by it, defined rulership.

The queen went down from Noble's room to the hall, where the rest of the castle population was assembling for their supper. The first servants who saw her murmured little sounds of surprise at the white veil, and their murmurs caught the attention of the entire room. As she crossed toward the receiving chamber, she basked in the fascinated attention of many dozen pairs of eyes. When she was near the door, she finally looked up and acknowledged the glances. There was silence for a moment, and a strangely intimate sensation between the people and their queen. Then one pair of hands in the back of the hall began to clap, and almost instantly the entire hall burst into applause. She flushed with pleasure and nodded acknowledgment with a humble smile. She knew where the applause had begun.

When she entered the audience room, her kinsmen eyed the veil, looking confused. Noble himself blinked once in surprise, then flashed her a private smile of appreciation, and her pulse, still racing from his parting comment in the bedroom, calmed a little.

They held conference as they supped. It was Noble's only chance to speak to the visitors entirely in private without rousing the worry and suspicion of his council, which he was beginning to suspect of housing secret Llewelyn sympathizers. Since Gwirion's presence would have been inflammatory, Angharad had been called in to play softly for them by the hearth; she was the quietest and most circumspect of the sewing bevy and above all did not know French.

Thomas seemed much older, only in part for the trauma of the past few months. He was taller by an inch or more since last autumn and he looked gaunt; he had outgrown the doughy, pallid look that made it impossible to take him seriously. And he had sprouted a real beard at last. He was still young, but he was a Norman gentleman now. The uncles seemed slightly lost, as if

they had no identity or reason for being without overseeing his interests.

Of Mortimer, they had little news but many rumors. They'd heard he was negotiating with William deBraose, whose lands bordered the southeastern expanse of Maelienydd, and that the two of them were corresponding with King Richard's brother John, now the likeliest contender for the throne. They were leery of delivering what they assumed to be unwelcome news, but Noble seemed untroubled. "John coming to the throne will be a boon for Wales," he insisted. "He understands the barons better than Richard does. He wouldn't see Mortimer overrunning us as a victory for England, he'd see it as a victory for Mortimer, and it would make Roger more powerful than John wants any one baron to be. He'll control Roger. I thank you for the news, but actually I want to discuss another matter." He paused, looking pained for a moment, and glanced again at his wife's Welsh veil. She knew what he was about to ask, knew how hard it was for him and why. She herself had tried to talk him out of it the day before, but having failed, had resigned herself to playing her role of consort and supporting him without comment. "I need your help," he said at last. "Against a fellow Welshman."

"Family problems?" Walter asked wryly. The Welsh propensity for fighting one's own was well-known to the Normans, who had exploited it for decades.

Noble shook his head. "A would-be empire builder. A man I would embrace as my brother if I didn't think him capable of fratricide."

"Llewelyn," Thomas said stiffly, and the king nodded. "I don't see how he's a threat to me."

"He's a threat to your sister," Noble said meaningfully.

Thomas flushed. "My sister? We thought . . . you . . ." He glanced at his uncles, who looked equally awkward. "We thought you wanted a divorce. We thought you were summoning us here to . . ." He hesitated. "To take Isabel back to England."

The royal couple stared at him, stunned. "What?" Noble demanded. "How could you presume—"

"We heard a rumor and it sounded plausible," Ralf interrupted bluntly. "This marriage affords you nothing, especially as your cousin Anarawd inherits if Isabel does not conceive. It makes sense that you would try to wed into Llewelyn's family."

Noble gave a short, harsh laugh of exasperation. "Where did you hear that?" he demanded. "It was never more than an idea and as an *idea* its life span was perhaps an hour!" They said nothing and he looked accusingly at his wife, but saw that she was as shocked as he was. "The rumor is unfounded," he said flatly, and rested his hand on the queen's. "I'm cleaving to your sister and she is cleaving to me. She is in fact part of the bedrock of my sovereignty now. Will you help her?"

Thomas was not prepared for this. "I don't have an army."

"Your uncle does."

Thomas blinked. "You want me . . . to negotiate on your behalf with Roger Mortimer . . . for him to fight with you against another Welshman?"

"The boy matures," Noble said with approving bitterness.

"Why would he—"

"Because it will endear him to John."

Thomas shook his head. "You've lost me."

"John will be king soon."

"Why do you say that? Richard is invincible—"

"So was my father," Noble said. "It only takes one arrow. John will be king soon. I predict within a year, two at most. Richard is about force, John will be about politics—I'm sure we're all aware of that. He won't want anyone in his realm having too much power, or in any way challenging the crown's absolute authority. Roger already has a strike against him there—he disregarded King Henry's writ of safe passage when he attacked us and killed my father twenty years ago. He'll need to endear himself to John. Llewelyn has it in him to become far more powerful than John will be comfortable with. Someone needs to stop Llewelyn before he gets too powerful, and that person will endear himself to John."

The uncles exchanged glances but Thomas's gaze never left the king's face. "That is the tortuous thinking of a man who is running out of options," he announced.

"Thomas!" his sister gasped, but Noble put a hand on her arm to quiet her.

"Yes," he said simply. "It is. I congratulate you on the exquisite education these last few months have clearly visited upon you. It may be tortuous but it's accurate. The question remains: Will you help your sister?"

"I need to consider the situation," Thomas said evenly. "I'll write you when I feel ready." King and queen exchanged glances. She still did not like this scheme, but she knew better now than to speak out against him.

"That's fine," Noble said. He was thrown, but pleased, by Thomas's transformation. If nothing else, it rendered Ralf and Walter obsolete. The king smiled politely. "Then the discussion is closed and we may enjoy the rest of our meal."

G UIRION, after spending the day penned up under guard in his closet, alternating between dozing and chastising himself for adolescent daydreams, performed that night in hall for the other diners. The visiting servants spoke no Welsh, which meant he was performing solely for the castle, and this crowd was so lenient that impropriety was never an issue. He improvised some debauched songs making fun of the king and the queen—as people, as partners, as rulers, and as would-be parents. It was a safe and harmless way to let out some of his own frustration. And he decided on a brazen experiment to determine if anyone suspected the affair: After one particularly bawdy verse concerning the many positions the king used to try to get the queen with child, he went on to sing,

"At long, long last His Majesty
Saw what had to be seen
He said, Gwirion, you mocker,
Exercise your cocker
And dick the devil out of the queen."

He felt a thrill of fear as he actually sang the words, but the response reassured him: It was such a ludicrous proposition to all of
them that they roared with mirth. He could see no looks exchanged or
elbows nudged; there was only tremendous, good-natured guffawing
and Gwirion decided to end the song with this. Young Ednyfed the
marshal's son offered him a cup of mead, and he was reaching out to
take it when a hand gloved in fine leather grabbed the cup and doused
the contents roughly in his eyes. The room uttered a brief collective
gasp and fell silent, and Gwirion, blinking in surprise through stinging drops of alcohol, found himself looking at Ralf's enraged face.

"Oh, damn," he said loudly, without thinking, and Ralf slapped
him with the back of his hand. Gwirion had been slapped too often—usually much harder than that—to flinch. He wiped the mead
away with a bored, annoyed look.

"What are you doing?" the queen's voice cried out. All eyes
turned to see the entire dining party crowded in the doorway to the
audience chamber.

"This *animal* has been—"

"That animal saved my life," she said with some heat. She
switched to French. "It's disgraceful enough he wasn't welcome to
sup with us at table—"

"Sup with us!" Walter snorted from the doorway, beside her.
"Independent of the fact that he took you *hostage* this morning—"

"That was a prank," Noble said mildly, "although I do think, my
dear, there should be limits to how you reward him for his nobility."
He did not look at either of them, but a shiver so intense rattled Isabel's spine that she had to grab her brother for balance. He misread
the gesture as a request for support.

"I have no objection to his joining us," Thomas said.

"You did not hear what I just heard," Ralf seethed from across the hall.

"Why don't you tell us, then?" Noble called out, smiling. The crowd stared at them, unused to hearing Noble speak what was, to most of them, simply the queen's native gibberish.

"It does not bear repeating," Ralf said, looking sickened. "Come, return to the room." He headed back toward his family.

"Gwirion," the queen said in her strongest voice, and went back to Welsh. "We would be honored to set a place at table for you."

This was exactly what he'd feared—that one of them would start to lose perspective of what was rational behavior. He made a sneering face. "No, Your Majesty, I don't belong there."

"I say that you do."

"Then Your Majesty has a mistaken notion of my place in the world. I would offend your venerable uncles with my manners. Like *this*," he explained, and belched into a sound hole in the harp, which made it echo resonantly. "Or *this*," he added ferociously, rising briefly to fart. The crowd in the hall cheered him on as the pleasure drained from Isabel's face. "That is my personal method for responding to English windbags. In the presence of ladies I do try to mend my ways, but this tends to be the result." He belched into the harp's sound box again, this time somehow in falsetto, which set the room to laughter again. The queen, her face stony, turned without a word and retreated into the audience room, as Walter harrumphed, "I told you he was a villain." Only Thomas appeared serenely indifferent to the insult.

When he knew his guests were safely back in the audience chamber and could not see him, Noble grinned and saluted Gwirion, who made himself grin and salute back, and the room again erupted with merriment.

LATER that evening, after the chandler had lit the way to the guest quarters for the righteously indignant visitors and the queen had retired in silence to her own chamber, Noble called Gwirion to his room. He dismissed Gwallter after the chamberlain had neatly laid out piles of traveling clothes for him; he announced that he would condescend to sort through them on his own, but while doing so he wanted only entertainment and distraction.

For a month he would tour the kingdom on circuit, spending most of his time in the northwest, a night or two at the larger castles and fortresses, watching the muster of troops, stopping by the smaller landowners along the way, and checking the border in certain key defensive areas, especially the area closest to Llewelyn. He had a three-pronged challenge facing him: first to convince barons who were weary of fighting and already well-disposed toward Llewelyn to consider a military stand against the prince of Gwynedd if he moved closer to Maelienydd; second and much harder, to consider doing it in concert with, of all people, Roger Mortimer. Finally, should this idea be utterly rejected, he had to at least press them to agree to resist Llewelyn's crusade.

He was leaving at dawn, avoiding the company of Thomas and the uncles on their homeward trip by setting off at once northward. For logistical reasons, he was not taking the usual full-circuit retinue, which included all his officers. So far he had mentioned bringing neither Gwirion nor Isabel and they had both been hoping with nervous delight that they might have the whole month together.

When Gwirion was alone with Noble, he felt so comfortable and normal that he could almost believe there was no secret, no betrayal, nothing outside this room. It always startled him when the queen interrupted them, a rude reminder that the rest of their shared life was getting very complicated.

Tonight, her presence more than startled. It provoked.

There was a knock on the door and Gwirion paused in his playing as Noble called out, "Come." She entered, still dressed formally from the family dinner, including the stony expression that she'd

worn for the last hour. Her husband looked up from the pile of clothes on the bed. "Good evening, my lovely veiled companion. This is a surprise. You didn't seem in the spirit of visiting. Come to warm my bed, are you?"

"Actually, sire," she said stiffly, "I'm here to speak with Gwirion."

"Certainly. Come in."

She hesitated. After Noble's loaded comment earlier about the guest room, she was sure that asking to be alone with Gwirion would equal a confession. So she entered the room and closed the door behind her.

"Did you lose your wimple, milady?" Gwirion asked.

She ignored his comment and perched on the end of the bed so that she could face Gwirion with her husband behind her. "Gwirion, I would like to know why you behaved that way tonight."

"I'd like to know why it matters to you, milady."

"So would I, for that matter," Noble said, looking curiously at the back of her head.

"I don't care that you insulted them," she lied. "Apparently that's why Noble feeds and clothes you. But you might have used a little wit to do it. I would like to think our friendship at least entitles me to have my family mocked with a sophistication worthy of our amity."

"I think, Your Majesty, not." Gwirion laughed. "You have a rather romanticized notion of this amity we've reached. It doesn't raise me to your level any more than it degrades you to mine. It doesn't mean that in a few years I may travel with you and your husband to visit your family and sit among you as a peer. If the king's regard for me doesn't earn me a place at table, your regard won't either." She gave him a hurt expression and he pressed on, feeling desperate. "We are irreconcilably disparate spirits and we've only become friends for the convenience of the king, not the exaltation of his fool."

"You're a better man than you used to be. I'd simply like them to see that."

Her sad, affectionate look pierced too acutely for him to con-

tinue a campaign of estrangement. The urge to comfort her was over-whelming. He chuckled nervously and insisted, "I'm no better than some old oat straw in an abandoned bird's nest, milady," as Noble, laughing behind her, said over him, "A *better* man? I beg to differ, madam! I was just telling him before you came in how annoyed I was with him for having grown so dull. Until that magnificent exhibition in the courtyard with the effigies, I was convinced we were all lost—don't you know that the fate and fortune of the country rises and falls on Gwirion's wit?"

"That's not the point I was making to Her Majesty," Gwirion said firmly. "I'm nothing, I'm just Noble's parasite to them, and they have no interest in a parasite. Why should they?"

"*We're* interested in you," she protested. "*We* see there's more than a parasite—why mightn't they?"

"Listen to that—*we*." Noble smiled, shaking his head. "How far she has come! To appreciate Gwirion is the measure of a mind. Your family simply isn't subtle enough to understand him."

"That also wasn't the point I was trying to make, sire," Gwirion said blandly. "I was speaking not of *their* limitations, but of my own." He hesitated, knowing he shouldn't continue to offer up the image, but unable to stop himself: "I say again, I'm no worthier than an oat stalk."

She blinked quickly as the meaning of the image became clear to her. Then, her back to her husband, she gave Gwirion a grudging smile. "Yes, in some old bird's nest," she said with affectionate sarcasm. Gwirion's stomach flopped over; he looked away quickly, defeated by the inability to estrange himself from her.

Noble laughed dismissively. "If we are through with the vegetative metaphors, my dear, you'd best go pack."

She grimaced, grateful her back was to him. "Pack, sire?"

"I'm bringing you with me, didn't I mention it?" Noble glanced with some disdain over the collection on his bed.

"You didn't, actually," she responded, and stood up to face him, inured by now to frustration. Gwirion plunged into a new tune. "My ladies will not be pleased to have such short notice."

"It doesn't matter, they won't be coming with us, they ride too slowly. Except Generys. You may bring Generys."

"And who else will be coming with us?" She tried to make it sound very offhand, and pointing to a side-slitted tunic on the bed she added in the same voice, "That one sits better on you when you're on horseback."

Noble picked up the tunic and tossed it onto a nearby chest where two others already lay. "Thank you. Goronwy has been asked to consult on a case near Llanidloes, so he'll be coming, but we need to cover a lot of area in a little time so we're taking the smallest possible entourage. And we'll be going to Huw's so Gwirion, for one, is definitely staying here. Huw still wants him dead—with better reason than your charming uncle Ralf ever gave." He grinned at Gwirion, who was pointedly giving all of his attention to the harp. "I'm sorry about that, Gwirion—I do still owe you a night with Lady Branwyn."

"I forfeit," Gwirion said evenly without looking up.

Noble frowned. "If you continue to pass up these delectable morsels I shall begin to suspect you of being a secret Cistercian. Or worse." Then he smiled. "I suppose I'll just proxy the night with Branwyn for you. But I'll tell you all about it if you like." He continued to sift through the tunics and missed his wife's shocked indignation, as Gwirion suddenly started playing louder and wilder, hiding behind a shower of notes.

"*Must* you flaunt that in front of me?" she demanded. "Could you not practice a little discretion in how you speak when I'm present?"

With a cascade of smothered plunking, the harp music stopped and Gwirion stood up. "This is private," he said. "I'll leave."

"Oh, sit down, Gwirion," Noble said, impatient but informal, and Gwirion, not sure if it was a request or an order, hesitated. "A sense of propriety in you is ludicrous. There are no secrets here, thank God. Keep playing." He turned to his wife and said politely, "And you were saying?"

To her, it felt like a dare. She no longer really cared what he did with Branwyn or anyone else, but admitting that now would give him more fuel for suspicion. She waited until Gwirion had reluctantly

taken his seat and picked up the instrument again, then said in a low voice, "I take no issue with your life before you were committed to me. But now—"

"Now I'm married to a woman who obviously cannot conceive, and it's in the interest of my kingdom to sow my seed more widely and in more fertile fields."

"That's a feeble excuse," she retorted. "Branwyn's free to be with you because her husband knows she can't conceive."

"That's true," Noble admitted. "In that case, I'll make sure to have a go with her attendants as well. They all looked fairly fecund." He smiled pleasantly at her and continued to pick through his clothes, tossing the desired ones onto the chest to be packed by the chamberlain later.

"Could you at least practice enough discretion so as not to insult me?"

He raised one eyebrow. "You are the most privileged woman in the kingdom. Considering the concessions I grant you, you might be the most privileged woman in Wales, perhaps all Britain. If one minor insult is pushed in your direction, I should hope you have the fortitude to survive it with grace."

"I'm an intruder here," Gwirion insisted desperately, standing again and fidgeting with the harp's lion-head finial.

"Why? We're only discussing unorthodox sexual relations, it's your favorite topic," Noble said. He threw a hearty grin at his friend. "In fact, you being an expert in the field, give us your judgment—is it unreasonable for the queen to oppose my intentions toward Branwyn?"

"Your intentions toward Branwyn had better not require taking any children along for her husband," Gwirion replied, his voice rising.

Noble returned his attention to his wardrobe. "If you insist. Huw's tastes are dictated by aesthetics, not anatomy. Anything petite appeals to him. I'll just offer him my wife."

"You will not!" she snapped. Gwirion stayed quiet, which annoyed her.

"The boy or the queen," the king mused. "A difficult choice." He

turned to her as if she were not the woman being discussed. "Let's leave it to Gwirion," he suggested cheerfully. "Gwirion, whom do you think I should offer?"

"Offer him your own damn buttocks," Gwirion snarled.

"You weren't paying attention, Gwirion—the choices are the boy or the queen." When Gwirion made no move to answer, Noble added with a sigh, his attention on the display of tunics, "It's not like you to refuse to play a game with me. Tell me what has put you out of humor. Or would you rather that I guess?"

"Of course not, sire, I'm your devoted player," Gwirion said quickly, fighting not to clench his jaw. Isabel tensed.

Noble gave him an approving smile. "I'm glad to hear that. In that case, whom do you propose I offer up to Huw?"

"It's detestable to dole out sexual favors as a means of ruling a kingdom," said the queen in a faint voice, already knowing she would not be listened to.

"Is it?" challenged Noble, archly. "Loyalties are forged by kinship. Huw is not kin to me, Llewelyn seduced him ideologically and although he returned to the fold I need some enterprising way to keep him there, as he is dangerously close to straying once again. So I must offer him power. But what power can I offer him?" He shrugged. "Land? It's too small a kingdom. Gold? It's a poor country, I have to keep a tight hand on the coffers. Security against the English? Llewelyn has a better offer. The only other forces that have universal power are sex and death. I can't free him from death or— for now—kill him, so sex seems the obvious choice. And now Gwirion will tell us precisely how I'll do that."

For a moment the two men stared at each other in a way that reminded her, unpleasantly, that they already shared more memories than she could ever have with either of them.

"Obviously," Gwirion said suddenly, in a strained attempt to sound rascally, "if the purpose is political expediency, you must give him what is of the greater value. I assume that would be your queen and not your stable boy."

"Gwirion!" Isabel cried out. When both men looked at her curi-

ously, she stammered, "The man who is . . . who is an *oat stalk* has no right to say such things about his queen!"

"While the man who is the king's fool has an *obligation* to," Gwirion said, fumbling with his tuning key.

Noble looked satisfied. "Well, that's settled, then," he said in a chummy tone. "I'll just trundle Isabel off to Huw's bedchamber when we get there."

"No you won't! There must be statutes against prostituting one's own wife!" said Isabel furiously.

The king laughed, lips pulled back coldly at the corners—and when Gwirion realized Noble's eyes were boring into him, he forced himself to fake a laugh as well. "No statutes that apply to me. But this was just a little pastime—I don't intend to act on it, Isabel, don't get hysterical," Noble said. "However, I must say I'm very glad to see that Gwirion stands ready to play with me."

"It is the very reason I exist," Gwirion said wearily, in a voice unctuous with sarcasm.

Noble smiled at him with a paternal warmth. "Yes," he informed him affectionately. "In fact, it is."

·18·

SNARE

Early Spring, 1199

OR WEEKS the royal couple, a few immediate attendants, and the teulu were out of the
castle. As usually happened when Noble was
away, Gwirion became lackadaisical, doing always what was asked of him and absolutely
nothing more. Gwilym often asked him to play
for the household after supper but quickly despaired of any other
satisfaction from him—as always, his wit went into hibernation in
the king's absence.

But unlike other periods of ennui, he had a new preoccupation.
In a castle not much given to higher learning, he had found a book.
It had been at the bottom of a chest in the storage room beneath the
great hall, where he with his uncanny memory recalled its being
tossed fifteen years earlier. He spent every free moment wrapped in a
velvet mantle he'd inherited from Noble, his nose to the brittle pages
of the codex, muttering to himself, but he was possessive and secre-
tive about it. Nobody ever managed to get a clear look at it, and
from what Marged's workers could glean from a quick glance at the

cover, the letters were put together in odd, insensible ways. The rumor quickly spread among the servants that he was studying sorcery.
Because it was Gwirion, this did not bother them much—if anything, they were looking forward to seeing how he would supplement
his pranks with a bit of magic. Each night after their dull Lenten
supper of salted trout, oat bread, and ale, the castle workers would
beg him to practice spells for them. He would intone strange-
sounding words and phrases with intricate arm gestures, and then inform them all that somewhere in Scotland a pig had spontaneously
combusted, or that he had prevented a boat from capsizing off the
Isle of Mon. Nobody was sure whether he was serious or mocking,
but they would always ooh and ahh respectfully. He would swap wry
glances with Gwilym or the other officers, barely keeping a straight
face as he resumed his seat and returned his attention to the book,
which had been written for Prince Maelgwyn when he was eight years
old. It was a primer of the French language.

A week into the circuit, after damp but gleeful spring equinox
rituals that he could barely rouse himself to join, Gwirion was
summoned to play for the royal party at Owain's manor. It was to
celebrate the king's birthday—which, Gwirion's own birth date being a mystery, was always celebrated as his own as well. He was not in
a celebratory mood and a trip away from Cymaron generally made
his stomach sour with tension. It was a long day's journey, a dreary
exodus on a muddy road between clouds so low they seemed within
reach, and treeless hilltops carpeted red with last year's dead bracken.
The air was wet and chilling and they had nothing to eat along the
way but salted trout. Everyone was sick of trout.

Owain's manor was a hillside, wood-framed compound in an in-
hospitable part of the kingdom. The soil was poor, but the manor
was ingeniously built so that a small tributary of the extreme upper
Wye River, almost at the Severn, meandered through the courtyard,

and there was a plentiful supply of trout. Gwirion and his escort of teulu arrived during supper and took their meal, mostly trout, in the kitchen.

Noble and Efan were dining in private conference with their host to discuss the ruins of a Roman hill fort on Owain's land. This fort overlooked a difficult pass into Maelienydd from the northwest. The king and his chief soldier wanted it refurbished and garrisoned with his own men—but at Owain's expense, on the grounds that Owain would be the first to be affected by a "visit" from Llewelyn. Gwirion pressed his ear to the door in time to hear Owain's polite rebuttal, which brought nothing but derisive rebuke from his sovereign. The hill fort was centuries abandoned because the pass was extremely challenging to cross, Owain explained, but more important, the land was simply too impoverished to support a garrison without imposing beyond reason upon his shepherds and farmers.

"I don't want to challenge my sovereign," Owain ventured, "but it really should at least be my own teulu up there, they're my kin and all sons of the local freemen. At least there would be ties of blood and affection to mitigate the burden." This was met with equal contempt. Gwirion grimaced and walked away. He did not hear the rest of Owain's quiet reasoning: "If Your Majesty forces troops onto my lands, just to scare off someone who may not even be an enemy, Huw and all the others in the area will be up in arms—they'll call you a tyrant, and they'll use it as an excuse to go over to Llewelyn."

Coming from anyone else, it would have been a threat; from Owain it was merely a regrettable description. But Noble's expression darkened and stayed that way through supper. By the time he rose from the table he knew, annoyed, that he would have to force the issue.

WHEN Gwirion arrived, Isabel was closed up with Owain's mother and sister, who wanted to practice their atrocious French. He wanted desperately to catch a glimpse of her but didn't dare

try too hard for fear of seeming suspicious, especially when he heard that Noble had himself left his supper conference in search of her. Gwirion retreated and spent a little time peering about the homey wooden manor house, imagining the life he would be having here if he had taken Owain's offer at the December war council. He could not, even now, make himself regret his choice, although the young man had not exaggerated: He could easily live out his years anonymously in this godforsaken corner of the kingdom. It was the first time in twenty years the royal circuit had even bothered stopping here.

Owain's hall was stuffy and Gwirion, seeking fresh air, eventually slipped out into the central yard. The moon was a night short of full, and with the slight cloud cover the sky had a silver-midnight haze bright enough to cast vague, unnatural shadows across the wet grass. To Gwirion's surprise, Owain had come out here too, leaning heavily on the railing of a bridge that crossed the stream, fidgeting with a small, dense fishnet that he'd pulled up out of the water to repair.

"Good evening," Gwirion said.

Owain spun around. "Oh, it's you," he said, relaxing. "I thought it was His Majesty come to torment me some more."

"Is he still on you for what happened during the war council?" It was unlike Noble to waste effort on a grudge.

"No, he's after the hill fort," Owain said in a tired voice. "He doesn't understand his own people. They can barely survive the winter but they're peaceable, they help each other out. They haven't the time or the inclination for any sort of skirmish. What I'll have to ask of them to maintain a garrison will push them beyond the edge—they'll end up desperate and resentful and they'll be a bigger problem than the supposed enemy the soldiers are being sent here to watch for in the first place."

" 'Supposed'?" Gwirion frowned. "Llewelyn's not the enemy?"

The two dark-haired, slender figures considered each other for a moment in the half-light, and then Owain looked away. "That depends on who you are," he said uncomfortably.

"If you're the king, Llewelyn is the enemy," Gwirion said, and

added bluntly, "which means if you're the king's subject, Llewelyn must also be the enemy."

Owain made an evasive gesture and tried to smile. "Come inside with me. I have a flagon of brandy wine, if you care to share it. Then we'll get the harp out for you. It was my father's, it hasn't been played since his funeral, six months ago."

They crossed the damp lawn toward the cellar where Owain kept his butlery, but as they passed a side gate that opened into the stable yard, they saw and heard something that brought them to an instant freeze.

The sound that made them turn was Isabel's voice, and the scene that brought them to a stop made Gwirion shudder and Owain gape. Noble had brought his wife outside into the night and had her pinned between a barrel and the side of the stable. Beneath his red woolen cloak he wore only his tunic; beneath her lighter linen one she was naked, and he was possessing her. Her face was unreadable in the muted moonlight, but every movement he made against her stood out in sharp relief, lit by the flames of a freestanding stable-yard brazier.

In unison, the two men automatically turned away and then immediately looked back again. Owain made an embarrassed sound and dropped the fishnet without noticing. Gwirion thought for a moment that his knees would give out, and instinctively he grabbed at Owain's sleeve.

"Yes, I see it," Owain whispered, misunderstanding the tug on his arm. He blinked and shook his head slightly, as if he could not make himself believe what he was seeing. "Why—"

"I don't know, but look away," Gwirion said in his ear. "We're just playing into his hands if we stand here."

Owain nodded and walked away. Gwirion started to follow, but his eyes, against his will, strayed back to the stable.

Noble had pulled her away from the wall and laid her on her back across the barrel, her mantle in a heap on the ground by her head. As he began to climb on top of her, he murmured something too quietly for Gwirion to hear, and she made a feeble cry of protest in response. Gwirion stiffened. *You have to go away*, he told himself fu-

riously. *Leave. There is nothing you can do.* He managed to lower his eyes from the scene, and saw the little fishnet Owain had dropped. He felt himself bend over to pick it up. *Don't,* he ordered silently. *You're not going to do it.* But then on the other side of the gate, she cried out again, louder this time, and Gwirion saw red.

HIS wife cried out as he had told her to, as if she were in pain, and then a second time, but the bait was obviously not luring. Seeing her shivering and tensed against the late March air, Noble was about to offer her a hand up and his own mantle for warmth. He ran a finger down her trembling abdomen—when he heard her gasp in surprise and then the world went black.

Somebody shoved him hard from the side and threw a foul-smelling rag over his head, twisting it tight around his neck and knocking him off her. He stumbled away from the barrel, reaching for his throat as his assailant shoved him again, knocking him to his knees. He leapt up at once and tore off the sack—it was actually a net—but the attacker was already fleeing. Following Isabel's astonished face and the sounds of speeding footsteps toward the inner yard, he rushed to the gate and saw the slender dark-haired figure as it disappeared into the great hall. He uttered an oath of infuriated triumph, then turned back to the queen as she scrambled to wrap her mantle around her. Confused and traumatized by the charade, she braced herself, afraid he might strike her, but he followed Gwirion. She sank to the ground, too exhausted to be frightened, almost relieved that the end had come.

YOUR Majesty?" Owain cried incredulously, confused. He had been brought under guard before Noble at the hall hearth, and he stared stupidly at the net. "Yes, that's from my stream, and I

had it out there with me, I was about to repair it, but I didn't . . . I would never assault—"

"Did you see me with my wife?" Noble demanded, his eyes an intense unnatural blue. He was standing near his captive in only his tunic, his hair in wild disarray. The queen was seated behind him, looking down. She had retreated long enough to don a long wool kirtle and surcoat. Her braids were disheveled and she was shivering from cold; at Noble's order Generys was fetching her mulled cider.

"Yes, sire, I saw you. I . . . went inside afterward." He cleared his throat awkwardly.

"Do you have any witnesses?"

"I was with Gwirion. He can back me up. I invited him in for a drink."

Noble made a dismissive face, but he signaled one of the teulu to summon Gwirion. His wife remained exactly as she was, her face grim but otherwise unreadable, her posture stiff. She did not glance up as Gwirion walked past her to stand before the king, and he made no attempt to communicate with her.

Noble stared at Gwirion. He stared back, his face the epitome of innocent curiosity. "Sire?" he asked. "I was just searching for the moon, they seem to have misplaced it. Is it time for the birthday celebrations?"

"I was assaulted," Noble said. "Tonight. I was by the stables—"

"I know where you were, I saw you," Gwirion said in a quick, tight voice, so cold Isabel thought Noble must realize at once who his attacker really was. Gwirion nodded with his head toward the shackled young man. "And you think Owain did it?"

"We are already aware of his extreme partiality toward my wife. And I was nearly strangled by that," Noble said, pointing to the netting on the floor. "He admits he had it out there. And I saw him flee."

After a flicker of hesitation, Gwirion said calmly, "No, you didn't. You saw me."

"You?" Noble smiled as though this was the beginning of some new game.

"What's amusing about that? You don't think I'm capable of assaulting you?"

"Of course not," Noble said with maddening affection. "But I'll indulge you. How did you get the netting?"

"He dropped it," Gwirion said promptly. "Ogling you. He left it behind when he went into the house."

Noble glanced at Owain. "How much did you bribe him to cover for you?"

Owain looked affronted. "I didn't, sire," he protested. "I don't know if Gwirion attacked you, but I swear it wasn't me."

"Well, it certainly wasn't Gwirion, so if it wasn't you, who else could it have been?" Noble demanded. He gestured, elegantly and vaguely, around the hall. "Who else in your household has your general build and coloring?"

"I would have to think about that, sire."

"Yes, do that. You'll think more clearly if you're not distracted, so to keep you from distractions you'll be put in prison overnight. You have one here, I presume?"

Owain's face contorted with disbelief. "Sire?"

"Your Majesty, may I speak with you alone?" Gwirion said through clenched teeth, taking a step closer to him.

Noble signaled Efan to bind Owain's hands. "Find out where the cellar is and take him down. Goronwy and I will decide on his punishment in the morning."

"*Sire,*" Gwirion growled urgently.

"In a moment, Gwirion. Efan, see to the watch yourself. Bring the prisoner to us after breakfast."

"What are you going to do to him?" the queen's voice said suddenly in the dark hall. She had risen stiffly to her feet but was still staring at the floor.

"I'm not a tyrant, Isabel, I do observe the rule of law. He'll have a fair trial in the morning, with the judge presiding." Noble glanced around at the random manor servants, guards, and teulu who had collected nearby to watch the drama unfold. "You are all dismissed.

Our birthday observations are canceled." Efan, towering over Owain, began to lead him from the hall. "Gwirion, we will not be using you tonight after all. I regret you troubled yourself with the journey for nothing." He turned to leave.

"Sire," Gwirion said again, barely getting his voice above a whisper. "I require an audience in private."

"Of course you do," the king sighed. "Come along, then." He gestured for his wife to follow them out into the misty yard. She stayed as far from Gwirion as she could without it seeming obvious, and resolutely avoided looking at him. He obeyed the unspoken edict.

Noble nodded toward the door to their room. "Go in, my dear, I'll be right along." Still without a word or look for Gwirion, she turned awkwardly away and went inside. The king glanced at him. "Yes?"

He hated that his breath was visible in the diffused moonlight, it would reveal his anxiety. "I did it and I know you know I did it," he said, his eyes feeling glued open. "I don't know why you're doing this but please don't bring that boy into it, he's innocent."

"Nobody is innocent," Noble said with a soft, bitter laugh.

"He didn't do it, Noble, I did."

"What you must understand, my perennial crusader against sexual predation, is that I don't need you to have done it. I need Owain to have done it. Therefore, Owain did it. You will not confess to it. Do you understand me?" Gwirion stared at him, shocked. The king frowned as if he was hurt by the look. "I'm not a monster, Gwirion, I am a monarch. I think you afford yourself the luxury of forgetting that sometimes." He patted his friend on the arm. "Get some sleep now. I think they've made a bed for you in hall." He walked through the dewy grass after his wife.

Guirion found his ability to meddle suddenly stymied. He wrapped a brychan around himself and squatted in the

moon-illuminated yard outside the king and queen's ground-floor sleeping chambers, as close to their small shuttered window as he dared, to eavesdrop. He heard Isabel insist Owain was innocent, but she would not name another culprit in his place, and anyway, the king seemed entirely uninterested in her protestations. Then Gwirion, slipping inside and down a staircase, tried to speak alone with Owain in the cellar—a room far larger, drier, and more habitable than the cell at Cymaron—but Efan the penteulu refused to cede them any privacy.

Gwirion tried, quietly, to share his wisdom with the imprisoned young baron despite this: He did not know what Noble's plan was, but he was certain that the way to foil it was for Owain to do the one thing Noble would never expect him to do: make a false confession. "Say it was a mistake, that you thought it was a vagrant harassing one of your servants, and when you realized whom you'd attacked, you panicked and fled. That makes it an accident, not treason."

"That's a stupid risk," Owain whispered, nervously, through the iron bars.

"He knows it wasn't really you," Gwirion whispered back. "His scheme, I think, depends upon your claiming it wasn't you. So if you *admit* it was you, somehow you will undermine his scheme."

"If I admit it was me, I will be *hanged*," Owain insisted. "If I claim innocence, there will be a trial and I'll be acquitted."

"That might be true if you weren't dealing with a tyrant," Gwirion muttered despairingly. Efan heard him use the word "tyrant," and with glowering eyes chased Gwirion from the cellar.

THE following morning after breakfast, Noble ordered one of the trestle tables left up, and he sat behind it, with porcine Goronwy to one side and Owain's own chaplain holding a quill to the other. Across from them stood the prisoner, hands bound, un-

shaven, unwashed, and generally the worse for his night in the cellar. Gwirion perched near Owain's household workers and the rest of the retinue. The queen was placed directly behind Noble, so that she and Owain could not see each other. She folded her hands in her lap and kept her head bowed, barely hiding how furious she was.

The simple questioning of the evening before was repeated for Goronwy. Owain quietly maintained his innocence, and Gwirion testified that he'd seen the baron leave the yard without touching the king. The warning look Noble shot him kept him from making an actual confession again. But then, it hardly seemed necessary: Within ten minutes the judge had acquitted Owain, who smiled with relief. "Now, Gwirion," Goronwy continued, "as you're our only witness—"

"Just a moment," Noble said, stretching and yawning in his chair with a deliberate informality. "We're not quite done with Owain."

"He's been acquitted, sire," Goronwy said.

"As the plaintiff, I'm questioning your judgment," Noble announced. "And so in keeping with the custom and the rule of law, it shall be decided on appeal." He swung his smiling face directly front toward Owain. "By your king."

Owain gaped at him in disbelief.

"That's outrageous," the judge announced, slamming the table with one stubby hand before he could stop himself.

"I'm certainly outraged," Noble said agreeably. "People shouldn't wander about attacking their sovereigns with fishnets. Owain, on appeal, based on the information available to us, I find—"

"I did it!" Gwirion said desperately. "Stop it, Noble!"

Noble gave him a sardonic look. "Don't interrupt, Gwirion, it's rude. Owain, I find you, on appeal, guilty of treason. Assault per se is only punishable by fine, but treason, as I suspect you know, is a capital offense. According to the law I would, ordinarily, have no choice but to hang you. But this being my birthday, I am inclined to indulgence, so I have decided to spare your life."

"Thank you, sire," Owain said in a voice choked with relief.

Gwirion, although confused, relaxed a little. But Isabel pursed her lips, waiting for the next twist, a twist she suddenly realized she should have seen from the beginning.

"However," the king continued, sounding very pleased with himself, "there is still the fact that you are capable of performing an act of violence against my royal person, and I must be protected against that. So your life is spared, thanks to my graciousness, but you are hereby banished from Maelienydd." Owain looked up sharply, horrified, and half the room cried out in shock: Banishment was almost worse than death.

Isabel, hardly knowing she was doing it, leapt to her feet and opened her mouth to protest. Noble glanced over his shoulder at her. "Yes, madam?" he asked in a lazy voice. "Is there something you would like to tell us regarding this travesty?"

She stared back at him, trying to calm herself. *Don't do this,* she wanted to beg him. *You will turn every baron against you.* But she realized with a sick feeling that she was too compromised to say anything at all. She shook her head once, hurriedly, and sat again.

The king nodded with approval and returned his cool smile in Owain's direction. "As you will be in Ireland—a kinder sentence, you must agree, than sending you to England—there is the matter of your property. As you have no immediate heir, since I doubt you've ever had an emission in your life, it will of course come to the crown, and the crown in turn is awarding it to the brotherhood of Abbey Cwm-hir. Seeing as that will make it church land, our friend Llewelyn is less likely to come trooping through it than he would if it were yours. However, against the unfortunate chance that he might stoop to such a sacrilege, we will write at once to the head of the brotherhood in Bordeaux and ask for a church-financed company to refurbish and garrison the old hill fort we spoke of earlier. They at least will certainly not be seduced by Llewelyn's siren call. Do you have any final words before you go to pack, Owain?"

Owain looked as if he would be permanently speechless. Goronwy was furious but silent; the king had done nothing outside

his lawful warrant. Gwirion shuddered and sat down as steadily as he could.

Owain muttered something under his breath.

"What?" Noble asked. "Speak up, man."

"I said I didn't recognize you in the torchlight," Owain said, still mumbling. "I didn't recognize either of you. I thought you were some vagrants using my stables for unsavory activities. I . . . I attacked you and then I recognized the queen's face, and realized I had made a mistake, and I was frightened and confused, so I fled. I apologize for attacking Your Majesty, especially at a . . . moment of intimacy. I'm prepared to accept whatever punishment you see fit, but I hope you will bear in mind that it was an honest mistake. It was ignorance, not treason."

Noble rose in annoyance, and above the muttering that whirled round the periphery of the room, Goronwy quickly announced, "There will be a retrial with this new testimony." He sat up straighter and asked Owain, "Have you been coerced into making this confession?"

The young baron answered with a pained smile, "Only by experience, Your Honor."

"I hope that is the same experience that has suddenly convinced you to invite a garrison of my men to your hill fort," Noble growled.

Owain hesitated and glanced at Gwirion, looking torn. Gwirion felt the king's eyes on him too and his impulse was to turn and leave; the last thing he wanted was to become anybody's strategist, especially against the king. He knew no details, only that it was Noble's will against another's, and his was a conditioned response: He looked at the king for a moment, then glanced back to Owain and nodded.

There was the briefest pause and then: "The garrison will be welcome, sire, whenever they appear." Owain spoke in a voice of depressed capitulation. "I'll make sure my fellow barons know that your men are there by my own invitation."

"Yes, you will, and you will counsel your fellow barons against supporting Llewelyn."

Owain appeared to physically grow smaller. "Of course, sire."

"Thank you," Noble answered, instantly serene again. He resumed his seat. "That is a generous birthday gift. This has been a remarkably productive twelve hours. I'm only sorry," he added in a quiet aside, over his shoulder to his wife, "that Gwirion came all the way out here for nothing."

He gave her a knowing smile that froze her blood.

TYRANT SPRING

April, 1199

WIRION WAS SENT back to Cymaron, and the rest of the circuit was a blur to Isabel, a rushing bustle of public audiences in strange manor houses interspersed with private moments with her husband. Each time they were alone together she was certain he would finally confront her. He never did—but he adopted, at least in her imagination, an air of constant private amusement and she was certain he was gloating over her unease. He remained affectionate in bed, which confused her more than reassured her, although at Huw and Branwyn's he flauntingly spent each night in their hostess's bedchamber. His wife, too frightened to object, remained demurely silent. *He needs me*, she reminded herself with growing anxiety, *he needs me to secure English aid against Llewelyn*. In this corner of the kingdom, it seemed unlikely that anyone but the English would assist him to deflect the prince of Gwynedd: Huw was not the only baron to insinuate that it was solely Noble's pride hindering the bounty of Llewelyn's generosity. Noble needed his Mortimer wife. That was her security.

Gwirion, returning home directly from Owain's, retreated at once to his French primer with a sense of furious impotence. Without Noble's presence demanding his humor or Isabel's inspiring it, he was, he knew, a disappointment to the villagers. The days extended and the Easter feast passed without the usual antics of Cymaron's favorite comedian. The whole of the village and castle climbed up the high slope to the east of the castle, to breathlessly salute the sun with spiced bragawd cider at dawn on Easter Monday. Except for Gwirion. This was more than his usual mental hibernation; it was spiritual retreat.

When the royal party's return was trumpeted through the bailey, when the usual hustle began to fly the flag and strew the roads with daffodils, Gwirion simply disappeared.

He had not been discovered by the time the royal party made its celebratory entrance through the barbican. The castle and all the village turned out to cheer home their handsome king and his beloved bride. Noble was on his grey charger and Isabel behind him on a bulkier but smaller dun palfrey, her face veiled up to the eyes behind a linen travel kerchief. Even with the cold dust of the road on it, the king's garnet-studded circlet, the crown he wore for all but the most important state occasions, gleamed. His famous blue eyes blazed with a fatherly affection for his audience, barely masking ragged exhaustion. After their retinue had ridden entirely into the bailey and children had thrown flowers at the palfrey's feet, and finally the cheers had subsided, Noble relaxed in his saddle and asked for Gwirion. "I don't know where he is, sire," Gwilym said. "We summoned him an hour ago and I've had Marged's Dafydd looking for him."

As if on cue, the boy popped out of the stables, darting comfortably between the tired horses that stood waiting to be freed of their riders. He bowed hastily to the king and turned to Gwilym. "I can't find him, sir, but the pony he rides is missing as well, and all her gear."

The crowd murmured as Noble's eyes, and the queen's behind him, widened. Looking automatically back to the gatehouse, he saw the herald up on the wall walk start slightly at something just

outside the bailey, something apparently on the road up to the barbican. The king reined his grey charger around to face the gate, and the crowd shifted with him. The trumpeter, after gaping at whatever had startled him, slowly brought the instrument to his lips again and sounded a few hesitating notes of fanfare.

Through the gateway, up into the courtyard, and straight to Noble's charger trotted Gwirion's little mount, with her rider standing upright on the saddle, bobbing with her gait and gripping the leather with his callused unshod toes, his arms held out to the crowd in mimicry of Noble's public greeting. This alone would have been a mild but risible gesture of mockery. But Gwirion had done something that changed the timbre of it dramatically: He had spirited himself into the king's coffers and was wearing the heavy crown that Noble saved for solemn ceremonial events. He'd also donned one of the king's red silk outfits, identical to the riding costume the king himself now wore. He looked absurd, the clothing too big and fine for him and far too regal for anyone to wear while standing on a pony.

"Thank you, my loyal subjects!" he crowed. "How kind of you to lay down your useful labor to spend an hour feeding my pride. You'll each receive a chicken for Christmas." There was a nervous titter from the crowd. Noble was thrown for a moment, then decided he liked the cheekiness of it.

"You do know that impersonating the king is a treasonous offense, don't you?" he said.

"Then you'd do well to stop it before I decide to have your head!" Gwirion said in a menacing voice. Although the charger was hands higher than the pony, Gwirion standing up found his head above the king's.

Noble gave him a droll look. "You're the real king, are you?"

"Of course I am," Gwirion announced loftily. "I have the bigger crown. And my head is higher."

"Your head will be a *lot* higher if you don't watch yourself," said Noble, straight-faced. He pointed beyond the curtain wall to the exalted keep tower. "Up there. On a pike."

"But may I keep my crown?" Gwirion said with sudden childlike

eagerness. He took it off to admire it. "I would sooner have my head on a pike than give up my crown."

Worried anger flashed across the royal face and Gwirion realized his mistake: To the king's wary ears, it had sounded like veiled criticism, a suggestion that his insistence on retaining his kingship would make his kingdom suffer. Even Gwirion understood that was not for joking, and tried to change the tenor of the comment. "And why must it be my head?" he asked, loudly. "Impale me through the arse, milord, that would at least give your people something prettier to look at."

"What an excellent idea," the king said. Relaxing, he finally granted his friend a small grin. For Gwirion, the impromptu jest was over. He was about to dismount when Noble's grin mutated into a grimace. "Is that *all?*" he demanded. "Gwirion, you're hardly up to form. Spin it out a little longer, won't you? Perhaps do something with the queen."

"Pardon?" Gwirion said lightly.

"If you've stolen my crown you may as well abduct my wife," Noble said in a reasonable tone of voice. And smiled again.

The crowd guffawed in its unsuspecting, collective personality as a huge unseen hand squeezed Gwirion's guts and he blanched. He reached down to the pony's neck for balance and slid into the saddle, willing himself not to look at Isabel.

"I . . ." He brightened, relieved by the rare chance to be honest. "I already have! The day before you left! You had to bring her family all the way from England to rescue her, remember? Please don't press me to do it again, it truly was a *chore.*"

Noble laughed. "Very well, never mind, then. Cadwgan!" He dismounted and turned his attention easily to other matters, and the invisible hand relaxed its grip on Gwirion's guts.

THE queen was somehow spirited through the hall and into her room before he even caught an indoor glance of her. Des-

perate for contact, he brought wine up to her solar. The door was closed as he approached carrying the small clay flagon, and the phlegmatic Llwyd stood to bar his way.

"Her Majesty has not asked to see you," he intoned.

"I haven't asked to see her either," Gwirion retorted. "I'm only here as wine bearer, under orders from the kitchen." That wasn't entirely a lie. He had been standing in the kitchen when he gave himself the order.

"Wait a moment, then," the man growled, and opened the door slightly. There was an indistinct exchange of voices and Gwirion blushed just hearing the muffled intonation of her accent. Finally Llwyd pulled his head back out and gestured lethargically for Gwirion to enter.

Gwirion stepped into the room, pulling the door closed behind him. Isabel had her back to him and was looking out the window over the russet hills, her hands clasped around her rosary. Gwirion, after a nervous pause, set down the flagon near her bed and went to her. She turned at his approach but did not move toward him; she looked startled, almost frightened, like a cornered deer. Gwirion pulled from his belt the silly, meager gift he'd made: a braid of oat stalks. Sheepishly, he took her left hand and placed the little token in it.

"The great god Llew and I have missed you very much," he said. In French.

She smiled hearing it, especially the way he mangled all the vowels. Then she burst into tears.

They were frightened tears and he hugged his arms around her to steady her and calm the sudden shuddering of his own heart. Her anxiety surely wasn't for their safety: Not even Noble could have affected such levity in the courtyard if he knew about them. He kissed her ear, brushed the side of his thumb across her lips, wished a primer for a prepubescent boy might have included even a single word of romantic endearment.

When she had calmed enough to speak, she nestled herself deeper into his embrace and said in a fatalistic voice, "He knows."

"No," he said reflexively. "I'd be able to tell."

"You haven't been near him for over a fortnight."

"Exactly, so there's been nothing to reveal us."

She looked up at him. "He knows you were the one who at-tacked him, Gwirion, he'd have to be an idiot not to know why."

He enveloped her in his arms again, gave her a reassuring squeeze, and smiled. "No, no, thwarting rape is in my bag of tricks. He doesn't question why I did that. In fact he was *relying* on my doing it."

"Yes, because he knows about us!" she insisted impatiently.

"No, because he knows about *me*. I hardly knew that stable boy, but I went to his defense, remember?" He tilted her head up to look straight at him, and said with quiet confidence, "I was just a pawn in his game against Owain. So were you. Please trust me. Every time his behavior makes you think he knows, I promise you, there's some-thing else at play. Owain's was a perfect example. You don't appreci-ate his subtlety, you think he's playing one very simple game with us, when there are half a dozen games he's playing all at once with the world at large. Like marrying into Llewelyn's family—"

"That was a bluff to test us," she said firmly.

He shook his head. "No it wasn't, there was much more going on. And in the end, he cemented your popularity—he wouldn't have done that if he wanted to get rid of you."

She shook her head. "He did that for a reason and the reason isn't working. Even his most faithful are intrigued by Llewelyn now."

"You're still an asset and he won't squander that. Doesn't he need you for that repulsive scheme of his, to fight in league with the devil—I mean your uncle?" He gave her a tentative peck on the tip of her nose, wishing he could will away the little crease between her brows.

"I'm scared of him, Gwirion."

"Everyone's scared of him, he's the king."

"He's not acting like a king, he's acting like a tyrant. Roger Mor-timer looks benign in comparison. I shudder to think of what he's become capable of."

With every atom of his being resisting it, he offered, "I'll stop coming to you if it would—"

She clamped her hand over his mouth, looking miserable. "I

know I should say yes, but I hate that you can even make that offer." She removed her hand and kissed him impulsively, slipped her arms around him, almost clinging to him. He was heady with the rareness of this, the simple act of standing up together fully clothed in daylight hours, embracing. Noble was an idiot, he thought bitterly, an utter imbecile, for estranging the woman whom he had a right to enjoy this way.

There was one loud rap on the door and they leapt away from each other, Gwirion frantically trying to remember his excuse for being here. He scuttled for the flagon just as the door opened and the king entered the room.

"Sire," they both said at once, sounding hollow. Gwirion stood upright, holding the vessel before him to make sure Noble understood the reason for his presence. Noble nodded to his wife, then crossed his arms and gazed at Gwirion with his head tilted to one side. "That was witty, what you did in the courtyard earlier," he began. "And you know that I would never curb your wit. But, Gwirion." He hesitated. "These are difficult days. It's fine for you to mock my office as long as everybody else understands that they mustn't. This is not the time for that."

"You're censoring me?" Gwirion asked, incredulous.

Noble looked very annoyed. "I've just told you I'm having trouble holding on to my kingdom and that is your response?"

He was instantly contrite. "I'm sorry, sire, but I don't see you having trouble. What you did at Owain's—"

"What I did at Owain's would never have been necessary if I were secure," Noble interrupted. "You have a wide array of targets, Gwirion, I'm requesting you choose one other than me for now. Content yourself with something safe, like fornication." He left the room.

The queen shot Gwirion a troubled look, but he waved his hand dismissively. "That was just a passing comment. Is *that* the sort of thing you take as evidence he knows? That's so . . ." He risked an impish grin. "So *French*. The preoccupation with romantic distress and all that. Think like the Welsh, milady. We're ferocious and verbose, but we're always very practical."

BY day Noble became more and more insistent on the company of each of them, and they were both diligent in attending him. But the hours they gave themselves alone were what they lived for now, and for a week they were together every night. Isabel was still cautious and often troubled; she grew daily more convinced that Noble was aware of them, daily more adept at reading double meanings into his expressions—and yet daily more needful of her time with Gwirion to calm her. It was frightening, ironic, that she felt safe only in the arms of the one person whose proximity was dangerous. Their silent lovemaking was as intense as ever, but her craving for his nearness was almost independent of that—there was something soothing in his presence. When close to Gwirion, she felt more *known* than even God could know her.

She tried to believe his insistence that the king's behavior toward her had not changed. Certainly in bed Noble was as affectionate as ever, a detail she did not share with her lover. And during the day, he continued to encourage her popularity at court, among the local population, and at the abbey. Perhaps Gwirion's argument was sensible; perhaps her worries were all a trick of a guilty imagination. Perhaps, she fretted, but likely not.

Gwirion himself felt almost reborn, impervious and undyingly grateful to the God he'd never before taken heed of. That there could be no future, no development, in what they had together meant nothing; they had it now and now was all. They learned that they could speak in silence by mouthing words against the other's ear. One night they didn't even make love but simply lay together looking at each other in the candlelight, bashfully seeking expressions of regard. They knew better than to arrange another tryst out of her room, and reestablished their many silent ways of making love.

At least, they hoped their ways were silent.

THEN one rainy evening, Angharad was relieving Gwirion at the harp; the queen reclined alone on a pelt rug before the fire, pretending to do needlework and waiting for Noble to join her for the evening entertainment.

Madrun very awkwardly approached her. "Your Majesty," she stammered, "we have a request and are uncertain whom to petition."

"A request for what?"

Madrun gave her a sheepish smile. As the only member of the sewing bevy with a lover, she had been deemed the most apt to discuss these things, but she was also the youngest and most easily flustered. "We would like to hang a second set of tapestries around our beds."

"Is it too cold? Shall I have the chandler build a larger fire?" she asked, giving up on the embroidery.

"No, milady it's for . . ." She lowered her voice and blushed. "It's for the noise."

The queen started. "The harp?" she said hopefully.

Madrun shook her head. "After the harp, milady. When . . ." The girl lowered her voice. "When His Majesty comes to you at night."

She could breathe again. That had been close but safely avoided. And it was to her own advantage to grant the request, as long as she didn't have to explain it to Noble—whom she suddenly realized was standing right over them.

Seeing them in huddled, conspiratorial conversation, he instantly dropped down to his knees to join in. "Good evening," he said, and grinned at Madrun's blush. "I was coming over to talk politics with my wife, but apparently I've interrupted something far more interesting." He examined the girl's embarrassed face with avuncular amusement. "Is this the talk of women? Is the fair Madrun suffering an ill-mannered love?"

"No," the young woman said, smiling shyly. "Just an ill-insulated sleeping chamber."

"I'm seeing to it, Noble," Isabel said firmly, holding her hand out. He gave her a funny look.

"This is a secret? How very intriguing."

"It's not a discussion for mixed company," Isabel insisted, desperately adopting the air of being Madrun's protector.

But Noble only smiled more broadly. "Then I *insist* upon hearing it." He grabbed a nearby wooden stool and perched on it, so that his head hovered very close above theirs.

"Madrun, you're excused," the queen said with a look at her husband. "I will explain the situation."

The girl bowed her head and began to rise, but Noble grabbed her arm and held her in place. "Oh, no, no, no." He grinned. "Half the fun is in watching her squirm. She's adorable." He looked beyond their heads at the figure who had been eyeing them from a careful distance, and beckoned. "Gwirion, you bore, come here and enjoy this with me."

The queen's hand moved instinctively to her rosary, and she had to fight the impulse to pray aloud as Gwirion joined them with a forced smile of anticipation. "Yes, sire?" he said, settling onto the rug across from Noble, a woman to either side. He nodded politely to the queen. As he lowered his eyes he noticed her hand fidgeting nervously with the rosary beads and he looked up quickly, examined all three faces. "What's going on?"

Madrun was by now that particular shade of scarlet achieved only by redheads. "Have you ever seen anything like that?" Noble asked, delighted, as if she were an exotic animal. "She knows a secret and my wife doesn't want her to tell us what it is. Go on, Madrun."

Gwirion hesitated for a moment, trying to grasp at once all the possible calamities that could arise from this encounter, to determine if his presence or his absence would be preferable. His hesitation cost him the choice, as Madrun began to speak, haltingly, cheeks flaming with embarrassment.

"We only wondered if you might like more privacy when you come to the queen's bed late at night, sire."

Noble started violently.

Then by turn he looked alarmed, enraged—and terrifyingly controlled. "Ah," he said shortly. "I see. We're making too much noise, are we?" He looked sharply at the queen. The queen looked down at the rosary in her lap.

Gwirion had to choose between fainting and scheming and almost made the wrong choice. But he pulled himself together enough to utter one short sentence. "What exactly do you hear, Madrun?" He had no idea if he sounded panicked, amused, or merely curious. The fact that he could speak at all was a miracle.

"Those . . . those sounds. Hard breathing. The bed moving." She was bright red again.

"Oh, *that*," Gwirion said with what he hoped sounded like a dismissive laugh. He brushed his hand in the air to show how blasé they should really be about the issue. "And maybe sometimes stifled groans with it, no doubt." She nodded, wide-eyed. "That happens all the time when I play for her. First she can't sleep and then when she does she has nightmares." He turned to Noble. "That's all it is. No offense, milady, but it's rather unbecoming, to be honest. I'd wake you but that would be presumptuous of me." He laughed nervously. "Perhaps the problem is my playing."

Noble looked narrowly first at Gwirion and then at Isabel. "You've never had a nightmare in my bed," he said.

She forced herself to meet his eye, and then harder yet made herself say, "That's true, sire. I wonder if you might allow me the pleasure of staying the entire night with you from now on."

Good girl, Gwirion thought, even as it wrenched him. Noble, still looking hard at her, nodded very slowly. His face relaxed gradually, shifting from anger to calm to something strangely vulnerable. He looked touched by her request and reached out to grasp the hand that had been fingering the rosary. With a small smile, he brought her fingers to his lips and brushed them with a kiss.

"I would like that," he said softly. "My apologies for thinking—" But she graciously waved it away.

"Well, thank the saints," Gwirion said after a brief pause, in a

voice that managed to sound lively. "Maybe now I'll catch up on my sleep and capacitate my wit again."

"I hope a little sleep is all it takes," Noble said dryly. "Or I'll have to put you out to pasture."

"I always did like sheep," Gwirion said agreeably, feeling himself die inside.

"Is it sheep now? I thought you had a predilection for your pony—what is her name?"

"Jenny," Gwirion echoed, sounding wistful. "I once had a mare named Jenny, she was worth a pretty penny. But *then*, I met a ewe named Annie, and she had *quite* a darling fanny."

Madrun giggled, turned bright red again, and covered her face. Noble chuckled. "I hope you appreciate how quick his wit is, madam, however lame," he said pleasantly to his wife, and then back to Gwirion, "Keep going."

"I don't actually have a close acquaintance with much livestock, sire," Gwirion fumbled. He could see how shaken Isabel was by the king's comment, how clearly it seemed to have a double meaning to her. But he knew those looks: Now the king was in a purely impish mode. He wished that he could reassure her.

"What about girls, then? I can think of many girls you've known." Noble smiled. "Let's see—I think there was a Breila—"

"I once knew a girl named Breila . . . it was great fun to defile her."

"That was rotten," Noble said, making a face. "Yes, you do need sleep."

Madrun's face lit up: Young Ednyfed her lover, the marshal's son, had entered the hall. She rose tentatively. "Sire, do you require my presence any longer?"

Noble followed her gaze, saw what fueled her glow, and smiled approvingly. "No, run along. But, Madrun"—he held her back with his voice, and gestured for her to lean in so that he could speak softly to her—"you will not mention your mistress's nightmares to a *soul*, do you understand me? I don't want her embarrassed for it. Tell Angharad and Generys, and then do not discuss it even among yourselves again." His

expression was unnervingly serious. Finally she realized she was expected to nod, so she did so, earnestly, and departed. He turned back to Gwirion and Isabel. The queen was the color of plaster.

"Gwladys," Noble said in a conversational tone.

"I once knew a girl named Gwladys," Gwirion tried shakily, "Whose . . . buttocks were loved by all the laddies."

"That's dreadful," Noble declared. "Go along to bed, then. I expect a full recovery by morning." He kissed his wife on her ashen cheek. "From both of you."

Gwirion was standing first. "Good night, then, Your Majesties," he said. He bowed and left as quickly as he could without actually fleeing.

"Isabel, are you ill? You're pale as fog." She stared at him, her fear too raw to hide or even control. She wanted to confess, it would be less terrifying than his toying with her like this. With a silent prayer for deliverance, she opened her mouth, and found she could not speak. "Isabel? For the love of God, what's wrong? Shall I call Madrun back?" She was about to faint. He took both of her hands in his, looking very concerned. "Let me take you up to the room. Can you walk?" She nodded, spastically, but had to lean against him to keep from falling over.

IN his room, Noble finally stopped asking about her health. Ignoring her peculiar fevered stare, he gently helped her out of her kirtle, which was already wet just from crossing through the rain-drenched courtyard. He slipped in beside her under the blankets. For actual sleep he usually wore shirt and breeches, like any Welsh warrior trained to be forever at the ready, but tonight he stripped entirely and wrapped himself around her gently as she lay facing him, without pressing further intimacy. The gesture was physically soothing, almost mothering, and finally, as he seemed about to fall asleep himself, she began to relax.

Isabel draped an arm over his torso as they lay facing each other,

and her fingertips rested against the sleekness of his back. "Your skin is smooth," she murmured, grateful to have something natural to say. He had to know, it was too obvious for him not to know. But for some reason he was electing to be gentle with her now, and even if he was setting her up for a harder fall later, at this moment his behavior was genuinely comforting and she was in need of comfort. He made a purring sound of contentment and pulled her closer to him, tucking her head under his chin. The skin of his neck had the warm scent that had nearly drugged her with lust the first few weeks of marriage. That attraction had never truly diminished, it had just become dwarfed by all of the other things between them. She pulled back to look at him. In the candlelight she ran her eyes across the wide span of his shoulders, his beautiful broad lion's face, the well-muscled chest. He was a magnificent creature in a way that Gwirion wasn't, but Gwirion's touch incited something in her Noble's never had, something more personal than lust.

"Do you know," he muttered sleepily, as if they had been in the middle of a conversation, "how Gwirion saved my life?" He went on in a rambling tone as if he were talking in his sleep. "He distracted your uncle. Long enough for me to hide safely in the bracken. Then Mortimer tried to draw me out . . ." He paused so long she thought he had fallen asleep. She was about to pull away to roll over to her other side when he took a breath and went on, ". . . by hurting Gwirion quite a lot."

She stiffened. "Are you accusing Roger of torture?"

"Judging by the wounds," he continued, eyes still closed, voice still muffled and rambling, "they used everything they happened to have with them—he had been cut, and lashed, and burned, and beaten. And other things." The recitation was so casual he might have been discussing crop rotations. "He still has scars from it, old now, faded. But there's one spot that was lacerated badly, the skin was torn away, it was such a mess they couldn't sew it up quite right, and there's still scar tissue dense enough to feel. It's in the spot you're touching," he finished placidly. "You would feel it if you brushed your fingers over his back exactly as you're doing now to mine."

She stopped breathing and her hand despite itself pulled away from his skin. He said nothing, and she forced herself to return the hand, forced herself to draw a gentle breath, and waited for the next move in the game, to see in what droll manner he would finally confront her. She wished Gwirion were here for the unmasking, then was glad he wasn't. But she wished that she could warn him.

She turned her attention back to her husband in anticipation of the worst, and found that he had fallen asleep.

G WIRION feared that the king and queen actually sleeping together would bond them in a way that would make him redundant—not to the king, as he had feared nearly a year earlier, but to the queen. Since her return from circuit, the hours with her had been thrilling and sweet, and he relished recent memories all through that first night of many that he would no longer be called to her room. It was the innocent moments that nagged at his attention, not what made them lovers but what made them fond: the tilt of her head in the candlelight, the rosewater scent of her hair, her nervous amusement when he tried to stifle a sneeze, all the foolish little things he used to mock lovers for. He ached for them, but there could be no nighttime trysts now, and privacy in daylight hours was impossible.

The next morning, awake but still curled up in his blankets, he steeled himself for what would be the hardest thing now: that although he could not touch her he would be forced to be around her all the time because Noble wanted them both near him almost constantly. Gwirion cringed. It would be torture. He pondered morbidly on the new state of things. If they would never make love, never spend time alone together, never show affection or share intimacy in any way, then by definition, it would seem, they were no longer lovers. He felt unexpectedly disoriented by this revelation; he couldn't rest with it.

The king and queen were crossing to the high table to break bread after mass, casually acknowledging the morning bows of servants, when Isabel saw Gwirion from the corner of her eye and almost started crying on her husband's arm. The only sane thing for him to do was to dismiss her; she promised herself not to blame him for whatever coldness he had to show her. She gave Noble and their congregation a vague smile as the royal couple neared their chairs.

Noble released her arm, moving around the table to his seat, and Isabel blinked, stared at her own seat, then sat beside him carefully. She leaned back against the object that had caught her attention, hiding it from view: a single oat stalk, no bigger than a straw, had been placed neatly on her cushion. Gwirion did not otherwise acknowledge her, but she glowed with a private smile all through breakfast, and later wound the stalk gently around her rosary.

But as days wore on, the little crease between her brows became etched into her skin. He thought and hoped it lessened each time he was in her company. Still he worried for her; she grew paler and more withdrawn each day, bedeviled in a way that the king either did not notice or did not mind.

Noble had his own bedevilments to contend with. There was no word from Thomas yet, and rumors reached them that Mortimer, in defiance of the newly crowned King John, was gathering troops again within striking distance of the border with Maelienydd. The chaos of Powys and Deheubarth moved daily closer, and although Noble's barons had men to reckon with it, it was a constant tax to the collective manpower of the kingdom. Anarawd wrote several times, asking after the queen's health.

And then there was Llewelyn. The great Llewelyn, already both rebel folk hero and entitled aristocrat, Llewelyn who promised the Welsh a unified land again, entirely free of the English. All Noble need do to protect his people was to offer up his sovereignty. Gwirion wrestled no such demons; knowing that the king genuinely needed him, he unstintingly forced himself to perform his prancing wit, even when Noble listened with his wife upon his lap caressing him.

O NE chill sunset well into April, while the trestle tables were being set up for supper, Gwirion sat down at his tripod stool by the fire to play. Out of habit, he ran his fingers across the harp to remind himself what tuning it was in, but he arrested the movement as he neared the higher strings. One of them had some thin filaments wrapped and tangled around it. With a cluck of annoyance he began to unwind it—then realized he was holding several strands of Isabel's hair. He rested his head against the shoulder of the harp, tucked toward the fire and away from the hall so nobody could see him blink back tears.

During supper that night, a courier from England was admitted to the hall bearing a scroll with Thomas's seal. It was addressed, very formally, to Maelgwyn ap Cadwallon of Maelienydd. Noble eagerly received it in his chair by the fire as Isabel and the councilors hovered near.

He scanned it quickly and naked shock washed across his face. He read over it at least three times, the alarm in his eyes rising, then stood, flung it furiously to the floor, and stormed toward his audience room. At the door, he turned back into the hall, irritated. "*Gwirion*," he said impatiently, as if Gwirion should have known to follow. The harpist leapt up with the harp and rushed after him. When the door slammed closed, the queen picked up the scroll, read her brother's message, and nearly panicked.

In the audience chamber, Gwirion curled up near the hearth on his usual cushion and began to play the descending arpeggios that were normally so effective at calming the king's wrath. Noble hardly seemed to hear them. Gwirion had never seen him so enraged—he stormed across the room, kicking aside the pelt rugs that lay in his path, and as he passed the settle he grabbed it and violently upended it, sending it smashing against the wall. He kicked the ornamented chest, growling, and threw himself with aggravation into his leather chair. But he couldn't sit; in a moment he was up again, knocking the

chair angrily across the room as well. "That *whoreson!*" he shouted, "That weasly bastard *puppet!*"

"What's wrong?" Gwirion asked nervously, almost afraid to hear the answer. "Did Mortimer refuse to help against Llewelyn?"

"*No,*" the king spat. "He couldn't refuse because Thomas never *asked* him. Thomas went straight to John."

"And?" Gwirion prompted, not seeing the problem; surely having England's royal army on their side against Llewelyn would be helpful.

"He proved himself a loyal and useful subject by offering his services to John, to act on John's behalf—*diplomatically*—with Llewelyn, should the need arise. He explained that he was the best man for the post because he not only spoke Welsh, but he had firsthand knowledge of Welsh culture, as his sister was married to"—he was so angry he almost laughed—"his sister was married to a minor Welsh chieftain."

"Oh Christ." Gwirion winced. He had stopped playing, but Noble didn't notice.

"There's more," Noble went on, righting his chair and trying to sit, but still too agitated. He began pacing again. "He did, *generously,* tell John that the minor Welsh chieftain had offered to participate in limiting Llewelyn's progress, but," and here he impotently oozed derision, "they discussed it further and decided it was not in *England's interest* to accept the offer. They don't feel it would be appropriate to interfere internally, they want history to take its course. In other words they want to wait until one of us has subdued all the others, then ride in and demand that the victor submit to England. Thomas has just joined the growing ranks of those who *want* to see Llewelyn overwhelm me. The next time he sets foot in Wales it will be not as my ally, or her brother, or even Roger's nephew, but as King John's lackey." He sighed heavily and finally came to a stop. "She's absolutely useless now."

"What?" Gwirion asked, trying not to sound alarmed.

Noble shrugged with resignation. "I've done everything I can to keep her politically relevant, to squeeze some semblance of utility from the marriage. She's lost any believable value as the potential

mother of my heir, but I thought she'd have some pull getting Thomas to work with me on Mortimer." He shook his head and settled into his chair. "That opportunity is gone—Thomas sold us to John's vagaries and he sold his sister with us. She's worthless."

"Your people love her. You made her beloved."

"That was probably a mistake," Noble said wearily, rubbing one temple. "I wanted to secure popular sentiment for the throne, and I did that, but I've also taught them that an outsider deserves their good regard. If they could come to love a Norman woman, they could surely come to love another Welsh prince." He leaned his elbow on his knee and rested his head in his hand, looking exhausted.

"They could love a Norman woman because she proved herself lovable," Gwirion said carefully. "Llewelyn has done nothing but enrage your subjects."

"That's only true here at Cymaron," the king corrected miserably.

There was a gentle rapping at the door and at Noble's weak nod, Gwirion admitted the queen. She looked fragile. This was the closest he had been to her in days; he could smell her scent and had to take a step away to keep himself from touching her.

This situation was, she knew, as dangerous to her safety as adultery was. Seeking something to say, she finally managed to stammer, "I'll estrange myself from Thomas—" but she stopped at an enervated gesture from her husband.

"That's useless, it does nothing but chastise him. He's not a boy anymore, Isabel, he doesn't care about chastisement." There was a long silence. "If I don't get a child soon, Llewelyn is becoming an option by default," he said at last, grimly.

She hurried nervously across the room and knelt on Gwirion's cushion, near the king. "What option is that?" she challenged. "You give up your sovereignty to him so that your people are absorbed into his united front, which will be broken up by John as soon as it's too powerful?"

"What is my alternative?" he demanded with quiet harshness.

"But Llewelyn isn't actually conquering by force," said Gwirion with a small grunt—needing something to do with his hands, he had

begun trying to right the settle. "He's using personal persuasion. Make it clear to him you're not one to be persuaded and send him home. It's not as if he's planning an armed assault, it's not as if he poses the sort of danger Mortimer would."

Noble looked up at Gwirion in amazement. "Your grasp of politics makes *Enid* sound well educated," he announced irritably.

"What's wrong with what I said?"

"He won't have to use force against me because he'll find a way to win my people to him."

"Your people love you, they won't break with you," Gwirion declared, as if that ended the discussion, and dragged the bench back into the middle of the room.

Noble gave him the slow, hypnotic stare. "Won't they?" he asked. "You would be amazed, my friend, by what seduction can achieve."

Gwirion, afraid that Isabel would hear this as some sort of threat, hurriedly changed the subject. "Independent of my understanding politics only as well as Enid—"

"Not quite as well as Enid," Noble corrected tonelessly. In a dry attempt at levity, he added, "But then sometimes I think women have a deeper understanding of what it means to be overtaken."

"Noble," Isabel interrupted from the cushion. She took his hand, looked up at him. "Let me be useful. Tell me what to do."

He considered her for a moment, gave her a sad, paternal smile and planted a kiss on the crown of her veil, resting his chin on the top of her head. "End the treachery," he said quietly.

Gwirion sat down very hard on the settle, certain the queen would faint. Isabel tensed and barely kept herself from leaping away from Noble. She held his large rough hands between her own petite ones and said, with frightened resignation, "Tell me how to do it and I will."

"Oh, for pity's sake, Isabel," he said breezily, as if she were naive. "I was being ironic. Gwirion seems to have misplaced his own ironic powers, so we are trading roles a little, he and I."

That night it terrified her to even undress before him, but he was

very natural with her, caressing her as always and holding her against him. He was the same considerate lover who had taken her virginity, who had gotten her with child, who had taught her everything about making love except what love was. His physical presence was so unthreatening that each night her internal siege alarms were calmed. If he knew, her body whispered to her mind, he would be too hurt and angry—nobody that angry could have been so gentle to vulnerable flesh.

THAT Llewelyn would finally send an emissary surprised no one. That the message would be a request for a sworn "alliance" was assumed, however odd it might be to ask it of an established ally. That it would be worded to present Llewelyn as de facto overlord was equally expected. What nobody foresaw was that the bearer of the message would be Cynan.

He arrived on a sunny morning a few days shy of May Eve, without his full teulu, only an honor guard of four swarthy mountain men. Gwilym was summoned by the porter; the steward came to the gate and discovered, to his disgust, that the baron from Gwynedd was entirely unchanged from his January infestation. He inhabited the bailey, large and jolly and this time well dressed, in an elegant blue silk tunic, red hose, and expensive leather knee boots. Those who recognized him either fled or skulked after his party in outraged disbelief. The castle children armed themselves with hoof picks, skewers, and flinty rocks, spying on him from a safe distance and earnestly believing themselves ready to spring on him to save their queen.

Poor diplomatic Gwilym envied the children the liberty to be enraged. His face an inexpressive mask, he grudgingly led Cynan into the great hall. By the hearth sat the king and queen in their high-backed, carved oak chairs, listening to Hafaidd's and Marged's plans for the May Day supper feast. Steward and baron made a peculiar

duo as they crossed the hall: Both men were tall, but Gwilym moved with a sleek efficiency of movement in a direct line toward the hearth while Cynan, twice as large in girth, meandered energetically behind him, of a speed with Gwilym but covering far more lateral ground along the way. Hafaidd and Marged, recognizing him, took several steps back from the throne almost in unison; hall servants froze in shock.

"Milady!" he cried joyfully when they approached, before Gwilym could intercept with introductions. "You are a vision of beauty in your sweet Welsh veil!"

The queen turned an unpleasant color and her jaw dropped open. Noble, who had never seen the visitor before, glanced curiously from one to the other. Isabel closed her mouth and pointedly looked away, but she clenched her fists so tightly that her arms shook. Then Gwilym formally presented the grinning visitor and Noble closed his eyes for a moment, calculating how to handle this, enraged. He could imagine the prince of Gwynedd chuckling as he thought of it, and he wished he'd slit Llewelyn's throat when he'd had the chance. He opened his eyes again to study Cynan—Cynan who was waiting, knowing exactly what Noble was debating and determined not to let the moment ruin his pathologically chipper mood.

"It's an honor to finally meet you, Your Highness." He beamed.

Isabel caught the nuance of his comment and corrected him at once. "My husband is a king, Cynan, not a prince," she said stiffly. "You will address him as Your Majesty."

"Of course I will." Cynan smiled, and finally bowed. "Your Majesty." Noble looked at him unblinking. Cynan met the gaze comfortably, unimpressed.

"You must excuse the chill reception you're receiving," Noble said at last. He reached out and took one of his wife's fists from her lap, rubbed it between his palms to try making her relax it. "We have long memories in Maelienydd and your last visit left a sour taste in everybody's mouth for introducing us to the concept of betrayal."

Isabel shuddered. She was almost getting used to these com-

ments, these potential threats, but she wished Gwirion had heard that one so he would understand that she wasn't hallucinating the danger.

"If you're worried about loyalty, Your Majesty, you might want to mind your northwest border," Cynan suggested off handedly. "Did you know your young Owain ap Ithel is in league with my lord Llewelyn?"

"What?" Noble demanded, stiffening, his own grip tightening around Isabel's clenched hand.

Cynan grimaced cheerfully, reeking with mock regret. "It seems Owain was quite panicked, having some difficulty feeding troops— yours, apparently—who for some peculiar reason have been visiting a hill fort on his property. His concerned neighbor Huw ap Mare- dudd mentioned it in passing to my prince, and Llewelyn was pleased to lend Owain some provisions—in fact, I delivered them myself on the way here. Lovely lad, Owain. Not well stocked above the ears, if you'll excuse me, but your soldiers are very grateful to have their bel- lies full again." He smiled at the king, who had gone pale. Cynan raised his voice a little. "You see we're prospering in Gwynedd under my lord Llewelyn, we've grown used to hearty meals when our bellies growl. Even after I paid the fine you levied against me for our silly little misunderstanding, my pantries and cellars were full to bursting through the winter." He looked around the hall and boomed to all the hovering servants, "Do you like the sound of that?"

"You will not address my people," Noble snapped from his throne. He released Isabel's hand, almost throwing it away from him- self, and leapt to his feet, barely in control of his mood. "You must excuse our rudeness, we have neglected to offer you proper hospital- ity. Hafaidd," he said tightly, and the usher stepped toward them again. "Find someone to wash the baron's feet. If you will excuse me, Cynan, I need a moment with my councilors."

"Oh, certainly, Your Highness—"

"*Majesty,*" the queen corrected, glaring.

"Certainly, Your Majesty, but you haven't even heard my mes- sage yet."

"Yes I have," the king said evenly, and gestured with his eyes to Gwilym.

For an hour the senior council met behind the heavy door of Noble's private audience chamber. Cynan, eternally amused by circumstances, wandered comfortably about the hall affecting interest in the well-being of certain female servants he remembered. Quiet, child-faced Nest had the misfortune of being assigned to wash his feet. Watching her, Isabel was overwhelmed by an uncomfortable combination of guilt and protectiveness, and when Nest had finished her task the queen excused her, and every other female, from the hall. Cynan at once turned his effusiveness entirely on Isabel.

She had never been fond of Efan, but she wished he were out here and not locked away in the audience chamber with Noble. The penteulu was the only man at Cymaron big enough to overpower Cynan; although Cynan had never lifted a hand to her in violence, she felt terrified of him. His breezy chatting distressed her as much as any threat would have, and by the time the audience-room door opened, she was severely dyspeptic.

They filed out somberly: king, steward, penteulu, judge, chaplain. "No bard?" Cynan queried from the middle of the room, and added helpfully, "We have an excess of bards as well in Gwynedd, if you need a good one."

Ignoring him, Noble crossed to his chair. He gave his wife's hand a reassuring squeeze, then sat straight-backed and silent, looking abstractedly into thin air. Cynan sauntered through the hall again toward him to resume his friendly conversation, but Gwilym stepped in front of him to stop him. The steward managed to present an officious-looking smile, hardly his natural demeanor. "You will speak to me, sir, not to His Majesty," he informed Cynan.

"Pardon?" Cynan said, surprised, but made no effort to push past him.

"His Majesty has many appointments to attend to. I will hear your petition in the receiving room and bring it to His Majesty's attention. Should I find it worth his while."

Cynan leaned back on one heel and crossed his arms with an appraising grin at Gwilym. "But my message is for the king," he said.

"If your prince needs to discuss matters directly with my king, he will be welcome to Cymaron at any time. If the matter is trivial enough to send a deputy, my king appoints a deputy as well. I have the honor of that office." The steward, without shedding his dignity, still looked uncomfortable. This was easily the longest speech he had given to an outsider in his life. "As a messenger of Llewelyn's, you are of course a welcome guest. Castell Cymaron certainly has the resources and the spirit to embrace you—and then to send you safely back to your very distant home."

Cynan laughed and asked over Gwilym's shoulder, "Did you compose this for him, sire?"

Without acknowledging the question, Noble kissed his wife's hand rather ostentatiously, rose from his chair, and walked through the hall toward the yard, Efan trailing him. "His Majesty does not have time to receive you just now," Gwilym explained politely. "He is organizing a supply train to his baron Owain's, now that you have been good enough to bring the message that there is need of it, for which we thank you. Will you speak with me, or would you prefer to tell your prince that my king is pleased to receive him in person?" His voice was uninflected and yet almost timorous.

"I would prefer to tell my master that your master refused to receive me." Cynan was pleased to hear the king's footsteps stop abruptly on the threshold at this declaration.

"I am receiving you on His Majesty's behalf."

"I wasn't sent to speak to you."

"Your posturing is childish," Isabel said sharply from her chair. From the doorway, Noble gave her a warning look and she pursed her lips angrily but said no more.

Cynan, to nobody's surprise, would not agree to waste his breath on one he deemed to be subordinate. Nonetheless, before beginning his journey home, he convivially invited himself to dinner, an invitation Noble graciously seconded. Isabel choked back her indignation, understanding her husband's choice and yet resenting it. The tension

of the moment was making her begin to feel genuinely ill. She took Noble aside by the kitchen screens to ask to be excused from the meal for fear of being sick in public. He would not allow it.

"We want to slight him, don't we?" she argued. "My absence at table surely does that."

"We want to *invalidate* him," Noble corrected her. "Acknowledging that he has the slightest effect on any of us works against us now. You are the Lady of Maelienydd and you will not be cowed, enraged, or in any other way affected by a baron of Llewelyn's." He put his hand firmly on her arm and led her to the table.

Dinner was almost unbearable. She couldn't count, let alone name, the blur of emotions Cynan's presence provoked in her. Noble placed him with the lower officers at table, a subtle insult Cynan blithely refused to acknowledge. He was boisterously social with the room at large, and Noble in turn was unfailingly civil and charming to him throughout the meal. Isabel, although too shaky to mirror the king's suavity, forced herself to participate in chitchat. This was at first more to show up her husband than the baron, but Noble's obvious approval and appreciation calmed her spirit, if not her stomach. By the end of the meal, although she still would have preferred to be almost anywhere else, she sensed that she had carried some of her husband's burden for him. Even given the warped circumstances, it was reassuring to know that they could work together.

When the ordeal of the repast was behind them the royal couple accompanied their unwelcome, indulged guest outside to the bailey. The silent communal alarm over Cynan's presence was still in full force and people clustered around the courtyard, waiting for him to appear. Somebody tried to start a rumor that he would shrivel and die in direct daylight.

It was a spring day, still cool but windless and unusually dry and sunny; Isabel wished she had the presence of mind to appreciate it. The king had dismayed her by inviting Cynan to stay through the afternoon and overnight, suggesting that he might like to hear their marvelous harpist play. Cynan said, smilingly, that he was aware of the harpist's many talents, but he was eager to return to his beautiful,

fair Gwynedd and his beloved prince. That was the first moment Isabel realized Gwirion had been absent since Cynan's arrival. She wondered if he'd heard they had a visitor.

His appearance, moments later, made it clear he hadn't.

The circumstances of their meeting were so perfect for catastrophe that half the castle workers in the yard were openly choking back hilarity: Just as Noble and Isabel were escorting Cynan down the wide wooden stairs into the bailey, Gwirion, doing the huntsman a favor, was exiting the kitchen carrying a large wooden pail of bloody meat scraps for the dogs. He stopped short when he saw Cynan and even took a small step backward, gaping. Everyone watched him, fascinated to see what he would do. He did nothing. He stared at the visitor without expression but unblinking, saying nothing, doing nothing. Cynan grinned and waved. Gwirion did not respond.

"We have a visitor," Noble called out unnecessarily. "An old friend of yours, to whom you owe your recent popularity. Why don't you come to greet him."

Gwirion, with difficulty, collected himself. He took a step toward them and Noble added, dryly, "Without the bucket, Gwirion."

Gwirion's eyes glanced from Noble to Cynan and back again. He began to lower the pail of meat slops. Then he looked between them at the queen and stopped lowering it. "Her Majesty is not well," he said with genuine concern, barely hiding how distressed he really was by her appearance.

"Her Majesty is absolutely fine," Noble said in a voice of deliberate offhandedness. "As are we all." His expression explained the entire situation to Gwirion as plainly as spoken words would have—especially the fact that Gwirion was not, under any circumstances, to misbehave.

"Christ, sire," Gwirion urged. "Let her go. She looks as if she might vomit on him."

"You're mistaken, Gwirion," the king said serenely. He turned to the baron. "We have so enjoyed your appearance, however brief. Do accompany your prince when he has the leisure for a visit. Are your horses ready? Put the bucket down, Gwirion."

Gwirion glanced briefly at the bucket as if he hadn't realized he was holding it. "Sire, are you implying I'd dump this gore all over him, simply because he's deserving of abuse? What do you take me for, a fool?"

"There is no license for fools today, Gwirion," the king said in a slightly strained voice.

Gwirion mused thoughtfully. "What about avenging angels?"

What happened next seemed physically impossible, but Gwirion did it. Still holding the bucket, he continued walking toward them, then tripped so elaborately that he either flipped or turned a handless cartwheel—nobody was ever certain which—and landed on his feet much closer to the three of them, the gory contents of the pail miraculously in place. There had been a collective gasp when the trick began, and then nervous laughter when he seemed to right himself. And then, in another move nobody ever quite deciphered, Gwirion himself was suddenly, spectacularly, wearing the contents of the bucket. Fat trimmings, gristle, stringy bits of rabbit flesh, and bloody juice covered his hair, his face, his tunic, his legs, and splattered onto the paving stones around him. It was somehow not so much gruesome as farcically outrageous, and Isabel almost started laughing from sheer nervousness. Instinctively she backed away from the three men.

"Oh, dear," Gwirion said quietly, blinking in the sunlight he'd just cartwheeled into and using a gory hand to wipe at his gory face. "I've made a mess of it."

He avoided Noble's outraged, killing glare and began, apparently, to seek something with which to wipe his face clean. The king immediately stepped in front of Cynan, but Gwirion nimbly veered around him and went straight for the long side-split skirt of Cynan's riding tunic. Grimacing, the baron pulled away, but Gwirion held tight and kneaded the smooth blue silk with his bloodied hands, then lowered his face to wipe it clean on the skirt panel. He had not actually gotten that much gore on it, so he blew his nose into it as well. Cynan tried in startled disgust to shunt him off, but Gwirion calmly grabbed the loose hem of his sleeve and coughed into it fluidly, leaving gobs of sputum, while everybody stood watching in

stunned silence. "I suppose I ought to change before this dries on me," Gwirion said matter-of-factly, and trotted back into the kitchen dripping meat juice.

The king, using every jot of self-discipline to control his own fury, turned to Cynan with a forced smile. "You must forgive Gwirion, he's terribly clumsy, he's forever bumping into things."

Cynan's gaiety was replaced by a sour sneer. "I see." He nodded. "That would explain why the queen's gown was so askew after we'd shut them up alone together."

Noble's knife was at Cynan's throat almost before he'd finished speaking. The king threw an arm around the larger man, a violent, mocking gesture of camaraderie, although his face was a mask of calm. "Rephrase that statement."

Cynan glanced down at the knife, his humor instantly restored, delighted that he'd unnerved his host.

"If you don't rephrase that statement, I will give my good friend Gwirion the pleasure of opening your well-fed midriff," Noble informed him sternly. "You slander him and you slander the woman he risked his own welfare to protect." Cynan said nothing, just kept grinning down at the gleaming blade. "Gwirion!" Noble called out, and several of the servants near the kitchen excitedly went in to search for him.

Cynan sighed. "The light was dim," he said in a voice of concession. "Perhaps her gown was not askew."

"That's not enough," Noble said, and pressed the knife into his flesh.

Cynan gave a grunt of pain. "Her gown was definitely not askew. Her gown has *never* been askew."

Noble pulled the knife away and avoided looking at his wife, who had first blushed and then turned very pale. He shoved the blade back through his belt and slipped one arm around her shoulders with a private grimace, pulling her away from Cynan. He looked at their guest with a smile that was little more than a lifting of his upper lip. "I'm so glad we cleared up that misunderstanding," he said in a voice lifeless with civility.

He kept his arm around her even when she was revived, offering Cynan the picture of marital and state stability. Finally, after more supercilious ceremony than Noble engaged in when he really was sorry to see a guest depart, the baron was gone.

In silence, the king led the queen back into the hall, where Gwirion, cleansed and changed into one of his other cast-off tunics, was seated calmly by the fire tuning his harp. His hair was wet, and he had managed to steal some of the queen's rosewater so he smelled unusually floral; otherwise there was no evidence he had done anything this morning but rise from bed, get dressed, and settle into his usual routine.

The royal couple took their seats, which had been moved near the hearth across from Gwirion. There was a tension to the quiet: the deceptive, heavy calm before a storm breaks.

Gwirion nonchalantly sounded one string against its neighbor. "Is Her Majesty feeling any better?" he queried innocently.

She opened her mouth to answer him but Noble cut her off. "Yes, thank you, she's much improved. We established the source of her unease and she is now recovering from it."

"And what was that?" asked Gwirion, smirking into his harp. "An ugly visitor? A rude visitor? A villainous visitor?"

"Oh, no," Noble said pleasantly. "It was much more domestic. Her gown has been askew."

USES OF SOVEREIGNTY

May Eve, 1199

T THE DEADEST hour of the night before the dawn of May Day, Gwirion was summoned to the king.

Since Cynan's departure two days earlier, nothing had felt right. Noble hardly spoke to either of them, had not called Gwirion to play for him or make him laugh, never once expressed affection in public, or private, toward his wife. There was an oppressive, airless cloud around the king. Gwirion had been trying not to panic, trying to convince himself that this was the passing mood of a beleaguered monarch.

Marged's grandson, almost sleepwalking, stuck his head through the hole in the wall to wake Gwirion on behalf of the king, who sat writing by the hearth in the great hall.

"Sire?" Gwirion whispered as he stumbled out, cautious and befuddled. "What's wrong?"

Noble was reclining in his cushioned, high-backed wooden chair, across his lap a broad oak board that he was leaning on to write. "Nothing's wrong," he said. He carefully underlined something he'd

just written. He was already dressed for May Day, elegant in the long green-and-gold tunic he'd worn a year ago to celebrate his wedding. He'd thrown a light green cloak around his shoulders for warmth, and as if color had a spiritual dimension, the brightness seemed to have affected him: He looked more relaxed than he had for days, perhaps for weeks.

"Shall I do that for you, sire?" Gwirion asked. Noble hated writing.

"No," Noble said offhandedly.

"Sire, I don't mean to pry but it's the dark of the morning and you rarely write your own correspondence and when you do, you do it in decent light in your audience chamber. What's wrong? Is this about Llewelyn?"

Noble looked up and smiled at him casually. "No. Nothing's wrong," he said. "These are just instructions for Gwilym about some minor changes in the May Day celebrations. Christ in heaven, I'm looking forward to an occasion free of politics." He returned his attention to his work. "Play for me while I finish, won't you?"

Some two dozen servants were trying to sleep, either beside them or in curtained cubicles, exhausted from the wild romps of May Eve around bonfires enormous enough to blaze despite the intermittent spring showers. Gwirion chose quiet melodies. He tried to convince himself that this was like any of the ten thousand evenings he had passed with Noble; the king seemed utterly oblivious of the tension of the past few days. A small part of Gwirion hovered upstairs, wondering which room the queen was in and wishing there were a way to escape Noble's attention just to be alone with her for a moment.

The queen's doorkeeper Llwyd descended into the hall, the man who for months had escorted him to her side believing that he was merely fetching her a lullaby. When he saw that Gwirion was already engaged, he crossed to them and bowed. "Excuse me, sire," he said woodenly, "but the queen has requested the harp. Perhaps when you are finished with him, he might go to her chamber?"

"I'm never finished with him," the king said. "But if I feel like sharing she'll be the first to know."

"Her Majesty is not in your room?" Gwirion asked, hoping he sounded disinterested. "I thought she wanted to stay with you because of her nightmares."

"She hasn't had them for some time now and she wanted to see how she might sleep alone." He elaborately added his signature to the letter, laid the quill aside, and blew on the ink to dry it.

Gwirion picked up his tuning key and slipped it over one of the pegs, hoping he did not look too blatantly delighted with the news. He sounded the string very lightly as he lowered it half a tone, and dissembled, saying, "I'm concerned about Her Majesty. If the nightmares prove to continue, I'm honored to be of service to her but I believe she'll need more than I provide."

Noble smiled a lazy, leering smile. "I think you're right about that." He folded the note over without sealing it. "To start with, tonight she needs a final good rutting to tire her out. So come along," he said, rising from his chair and gesturing to Gwirion to follow him.

"Sire?" the harpist croaked, staring, his stomach in his throat.

"Between the two of us, let's see if we might help her sleep."

"Sire?"

Noble gave him a puzzled expression as if he couldn't imagine what Gwirion was protesting. Then he grinned. "You filthy-minded little swine," he said approvingly. "I meant you be her bard, I'll be her lover."

"At the same time?" Gwirion asked feebly.

"Of course, like the old days."

"Those women were different. I don't think the queen would welcome—"

"Really, Gwirion, you must give her a little credit!" Noble laughed. He signaled toward the lower hall, and Gwirion was surprised to see tall, quiet Gwilym, who never showed himself in hall before mass in the morning. He too was already dressed in his bright May Day outfit, but he was hardly in the spirit of revels; in fact, he seemed quite wretched about the early hour. When he approached them, Noble handed him the note. "As we discussed," the king said lightly. "Ignore it otherwise." Gwilym took the note, wordlessly, and

bowed. He did not acknowledge Gwirion; Gwirion thought he was too tired to even see him.

Noble nodded toward the stairs. "Come along," he said to Gwirion with a smile of anticipation. He hoisted a rush light out of a wall brace near the bottom of the stairs and began to ascend. Gwirion followed miserably, willing himself to faint if not expire. For nearly a month, he'd dreaded what was about to happen.

But then the king paused. He mused on something for a moment, and finally handed the torch down to Gwirion. "Go up without me, there are some more logistics I must see to here. Send her women down to Gwilym, would you? I'll be up in an hour or so."

Gwirion shook his head, confused. "You want her women down here? Now? It's hours until dawn, sire, why must they rise so early?"

"And when did you become the guardian of their best interests?" Noble retorted. "The steward has years of organizing May Day rituals. You do not. Please send them down, and tell my wife to be awake for me when I come up in an hour."

WHEN the grumpy, sleep-fogged sewing bevy had been dismissed to hall, Gwirion and Isabel looked at each other in silent amazement, thrilled and yet afraid to act on the opportunity. Finally she held out a hand, smiling in the torchlight, and he nearly threw himself on her. He straddled her, bent over her, covered her face with kisses, and nuzzled his nose into her hair as she squeezed him to her. Nothing in his life had ever felt so good to him. "An hour alone in a room with you and a bed," he whispered ecstatically into her ear. "I'm the most blessed man alive."

"Why just an hour? It's ages until dawn."

He tugged at her shift while she wriggled under his weight; she grinned and ran her hands through his hair, trying vainly to tame the cowlick. "He's coming up here in an hour," he murmured, and kissed her earlobe.

She froze, then with genuine terror pushed him up and away from her. "What?" she demanded.

"I was just downstairs with him, he said he'd be up in an hour."

"Are you daft?" she cried, pushing him away with something approaching sudden hysteria. "It's a trap! Get off the bed—get out of here, leave the room! It's a trap! You *idiot*—get off the bed!"

Gwirion stared at her, confused. She pushed her shift back down around her legs and sat up in the bed, straightening the blankets, trembling. "It's not a trap," he said at last. "Noble's traps are subtle. That would be too obvious."

"He's counting on us to think that," she insisted, slapping frantically at his legs to make him back away. "He sent me to my own bed tonight. He sent you up here alone, and he called my women away. And he let you know we'd have an hour. It won't be an hour, it will be any moment now, as soon as he hears incriminating noises."

"If he knows," Gwirion insisted, "he wouldn't bother staging something like this."

"Of course he would, it's more distressing for us that way. *Leave*, Gwirion, that's an order."

Instead of leaving he took a step closer to her and she tried to draw away, but he snatched her hands in his and sat on the bed beside her. "I gave you the wrong impression," he said in a soothing voice. "He was coming up here with me—he stayed downstairs at the last moment."

"That was staged," she said firmly.

He gazed at her pale face in the candlelight and sighed. "If his goal is to distress you, he's succeeding. And if his goal is to distress you by keeping you eternally on edge, do you think he'd ever actually confront you?" She rolled her eyes in agitation, but when he reached out to brush his thumb against her lips, she let him. He kissed her cheek. "We haven't been alone together for a month and you're still terrified every day, I see it in your face. I swear to you I would never do anything to give you more cause for that fear." She looked down and shrugged, a little reassured by his calm, trying to control her breathing. Tentatively, he perched on the edge of the bed and put an

arm around her, rocking her against him. Her little body was warm and familiar in his arms, and he felt too glad to speak. She closed her eyes and let herself collapse against him.

He smiled down at her. After a moment, he reached under the blankets with his free hand and began to lift the hem of her shift, his pulse and breathing quickening. She stiffened and pushed the hand away, but he threw his arm around her, trapping her in his embrace, and rolled over until she was beneath him. Her face flashed fear again.

"Get off of me! You fool, it's a *trap.*"

"We just had this conversation," Gwirion whispered, and kissed her on the lips. Isabel uttered a smothered sound of despair and yielded. His kiss, after weeks of missing it, erased the world. She reached for his bed tunic and he at once tore it off, while she fumbled with the string to his breeches belt and pushed the blankets away. They made love silently but frantically, an almost violent act unlike any coupling of theirs had ever been, his slender body driving against her bare legs and silk shift.

Afterward, at her insistence, Gwirion immediately drew away to dress, but safely clothed again he returned to her side and held her, rocking her. For a very long time, they sat in silence.

Then abruptly, whether it was nerves or gladness, Isabel began to giggle and Gwirion, because it soothed his soul to hear it, joined her.

They settled back into a comfortable silence.

He nuzzled her cheek with his nose and whispered affectionate obscenities in an exaggeration of her accent. She tried to teach him the French erotic phrases Adèle had never wanted her to know. He invented elaborate stories about all the livestock he claimed to have seduced since they'd last been together, and she laughed again. She rubbed her head against his chest and reached up to stroke his hair. "You should take a lover," she said. "I feel childish for resisting the idea of Nest."

"It's too late. You've spoiled me, I can't settle for anything less now."

"I'm serious, Gwirion. You need more than this, and it will throw him off the scent."

"Oh, yes? And he's ardently *on* the scent now, is he?" Gwirion asked.

"I'm telling you, this is intended to be a trap."

"How original," Gwirion mused archly. "To make us think we'd have an hour, and then giving us nearly two. That cunning lad. Whatever is he up to, do you think?"

"It hasn't been two hours."

"It's been at least an hour and a half. If the plan was to surprise us before we were expecting him, he's slightly tardy. And that, madam," he added, imitating Noble's affectionately condescending tone for the epithet, "is not the sort of error he would ever make."

Isabel sat up a little straighter. "I was wrong?" she breathed, relieved but incredulous.

A few moments later, they heard Noble's voice outside the door cheerfully bidding an early good morning to her doorkeeper. In one move, Gwirion slipped to the floor grabbing for his harp while Isabel pulled the blankets back over herself. They were a picture of innocence when Noble entered, carrying a second torch and smiling.

"Did you keep her awake for me?" he asked, closing the door. He rested the torch in a sconce near a window. "What a nuisance all these ritual details are. I couldn't wait to be up here at last."

Gwirion braced himself as Noble tossed down his cloak and moved to the bed. But he remained fully clothed as he slid casually under the blankets to lie beside his wife. "Ah," he sighed contentedly, warming his hands against her upper arms. She shuddered from the cold touch. "That's much better. Play us something, Gwirion. Play 'Below the Ford.'"

"Below the Ford" was the tune Gwirion had always used after supper to signal to Isabel that he would be available if she called him.

"I'm in the wrong tuning for that," he said quickly.

"We'll wait."

As Gwirion retightened the string he had lowered downstairs, Noble reached under the sheets and then up under Isabel's silk shift to stroke her hip, moving his fingers toward her groin. She stiffened and he stopped, looking mildly disappointed. But he wrapped an

arm around her outside the sheet, spooning her to him in a half-reclining position, and she nestled in against him, reached down to kiss his hand. When "Below the Ford" was over, Noble called for "Rhiannon's Tears" and then two other tunes. Gwirion, to avoid looking at them caressing, played with his face bent so close to the harp that his hair nearly brushed the upper strings. Noble nuzzled his wife's ear. There was such a sweetness to the moment: the mildness of the damp spring night, the warm flickering of the torchlight, the dancing cadence of the harp, the silent presence of his dearest friend, and the soft, yielding, milk-smooth body of his wife beside him. And best of all, Llewelyn, Mortimer, and the rest of his concerns locked outside the door.

There was a comfortable silence when Gwirion finished the final song.

Then Noble ruined the mood.

"Gwirion," he announced genially, "I've decided you'll lead the Spring Rites this year."

His wife had no idea what this meant, but after a glance at Gwirion she knew it wasn't good. He had said it in an affectionate, indulgent tone, so she guessed it was something disgusting and perverse that Gwirion would once have leapt at.

"Why?" he asked, when he could finally find his voice.

"What are the Spring Rites?" she asked, looking back and forth between them. She had heard the term several times before, especially recently, and surmised it was some spring folk festival, probably involving large-scale, drunken debauchery, but the speakers—even Gwirion—always seemed sheepishly determined to avoid details.

"Don't be dim, Gwirion. Because of your derring-do with Cynan in January. You've earned it."

Gwirion looked completely at a loss. He moved his harp from one spot to another on the floor, fidgeting with it, trying to balance it upright and taking particular interest in the grain of the wood where it rested on the floor. "I don't think I deserve that honor, sire," he finally said with a nervous, self-effacing laugh.

"I make that decision, Gwirion, not you. You can't be telling me you don't *want* it."

"What are the Spring Rites?" she asked again.

"It just seems unfair to the girl," Gwirion stammered. "After all—who am I? She's expecting the king."

Isabel sat bolt upright, the blankets almost falling away from her. "One of you tell me what you're talking about," she demanded.

"Gwirion, you explain," Noble said, easing her back down against him.

Gwirion used his finger in a futile pretense of dusting out the lion's tiny ears at the top of the harp's forepillar. "We have a . . . tradition of sorts here."

"Don't tell me there's a ritual deflowering of a virgin," Isabel said.

"No, no," Gwirion said hastily—then hesitated. He continued swabbing the lion, trying to sound casual. He really did not want her to associate him with this story. "Well, that is, it doesn't *have* to be. What's important is that she seems . . . appropriately . . . fulsome. Fecund. For her night. With the king."

"What?" she said sharply, and pulled the sheet up to her neck, breaking out of Noble's embrace.

"Perhaps that sounds worse than it is," Gwirion said. He couldn't bring himself to look at her. "The girl is always willing—in fact, everyone makes a big fuss over her. She's *chosen*. No one's ever *forced* to it. It's just . . . something that's always been done."

"They say it guarantees a better harvest," Noble said, conspiratorially playful.

"That is the most superstitious, backward barbarism I've ever heard of!" Isabel declared. "That's absolutely *cretinous!*"

"What do you think *you* were?" Gwirion said impatiently, trying not to snap from the tension.

She gave him a look. "I was the king's *bride*."

Noble laughed. "What was the date of our wedding, madam?"

Her eyes widened and she turned to stare over her shoulder at him.

"Not a coincidence." He smiled.

She was disgusted. "But it's not the same at all!"

"Oh, of course not," Noble said lazily. "You came here willingly to partake in an ancient ritual that would culminate in our bedding together for the good of the kingdom, but it's not at all the same."

For a moment she couldn't even speak.

"It's considered a huge honor for the girl," Gwirion said, trying to be helpful.

"Oh, yes, I'm sure it is!" she sneered, and elbowed her husband away as he tried to nestle up closer to her.

"Tell her the rest, Gwirion," he ordered, smiling.

"There's more?" she said, appalled.

Gwirion desperately wanted this conversation to be over. He was actually blushing. After an awkward pause, he explained, "Um. Yes. Afterward. There's a bit of a free-for-all."

"Oh, is that all?" she said with sarcastic offhandedness. "I had pretty much expected *that*." But she sobered. "And you participate?" she asked Gwirion, then added hurriedly, to cover, "All of you, I mean—everybody?"

Noble laughed beside her in a tone that made both of them wince. "There have been years at a time when May Day has provided Gwirion his only stab, so to speak, at female flesh."

She looked away. There was nothing she could say in front of Noble, but Gwirion read her silence and it made him heartsick. He rested his head on the shoulder of the harp as if it were a person who might comfort him.

"However, this year," Noble continued grandly, "he takes the honors." He leaned down over her and murmured in her ear, "King's prerogative, to appoint a proxy for the main event, when there's a deserving champion."

Gwirion immediately protested, "Sire, I told you that I don't want—"

"I visited the girl tonight," Noble went on, as if Gwirion hadn't spoken. "She's staying with Cadwgan's family. She's very pretty, a little like that hall servant who took a fancy to you, but more flirtatious. I'll—"

"Thank you, sire, but I am respectfully declining the honor,"

Gwirion said, and lifted his tuning peg from his belt again to fiddle with the harp pegs.

"No you're not," Noble informed him, his cheeriness abating slightly. "This isn't a dinner invitation, it's a sacred tradition."

"It's not *sacred*," Gwirion said. "It's actually *profane*."

"That makes you the perfect acolyte," Noble retorted. "You're profane."

"I'm working on that," Gwirion muttered under his breath, fidgeting with the peg of the lowest string.

"Yes, I've noticed, and I wish you wouldn't, it makes you a dreadful bore," Noble said. "But you see, *I* mustn't do it anymore." He looked down at Isabel with a sly expression. "My wife resents it when I stray."

"I would make an exception if you strayed for the proper reasons," she said with forced levity.

Noble pushed her shoulder down, twisting her supine onto the bed. He hovered over her with an intrigued expression. "Would you?" he said, imitating her tone. "And what would you consider a proper reason to stray from the royal marriage bed?"

She blanched and stammered up at him, "Whatever is in service to the throne, sire. We know I'm damaged and you need a son. Don't let my harping on monogamy come between you and our people's expectations." He looked impressed by the response, and she continued, a little more confidently, "If you really consider it imperative that Gwirion stand in for you, I've no objection and I can't fathom why he would, but I would think the need to get a royal heir comes before offering Gwirion an hour of pleasure he seems too squeamish to accept."

He gave her a searching look, seeking something beyond her words. Finally he released her and smiled, patiently. "Well spoken. Gwirion, you will simply participate as you always have in the bacchanalia."

The chance to be alone with her again—while the entire castle was distracted—was too tempting. "I don't want to do that either, sire," he said cautiously. Noble started.

"No, Gwirion, that is going too far! It would hardly be worth it without you there." Almost out of the side of his mouth he told his wife confidingly, "Gwirion at such a gathering is a thing of wonder."

"I'm sure I'd like to see that, sire," she said with a wan attempt at humor.

Gwirion hesitated. "You must excuse me, sire, I've no desire to participate at all."

The king stared at him. "Yes you do," he said sternly.

"No, I don't." He tried to meet Noble's eyes as they bored into his but he couldn't, and turned his attention again to fidgeting with the harp pegs. Somehow, he had to pass this off as his usual contrariness.

Noble suddenly sat up and threw the sheets off himself with such vehemence that he almost uncovered his wife as well. She scrambled to reclaim a blanket, passably pretending to be shy of Gwirion's eyes upon her. Noble leapt up from the bed, and with quick, controlled steps swung down around the foot of it to stand over Gwirion. "Listen to me," he said in a threatening voice. "You will attend tomorrow. Of your own volition. You will enjoy it."

"Is that an order?" Gwirion asked with an edgy laugh, still pretending to tune.

"It shouldn't have to be—don't make me order you," Noble said. "You ass. Do you know what thin ice you stand on right now?"

"No, but I'll retreat at once to solid ground," Gwirion offered with nervous pleasantness. "And pen myself up in the kitchen tomorrow night."

"Why are you being so contrary, Gwirion?" Isabel asked in the most offhand tone she could affect. She risked a pleading glance at him but he didn't see it.

Noble's expression darkened, but she saw a flash of desperation behind the anger; then it was brushed away. "Aren't you man enough to handle it?" he taunted.

"Aren't you man enough to handle it without me?" Gwirion taunted back as if they were playing at bickering. "Why are you so desperate for my presence?" He fluttered his lashes at the king. "I'm hardly equipped to receive your particular attentions for the evening."

"That is not the point!" Noble thundered. He snatched the tuning key from Gwirion's fingers and hurled it furiously across the room. "You don't know what you're meddling with! For the love of the saints, behave yourself!"

"Is that an order too?" Gwirion prayed for any graceful way out of this standoff. He hoped his frantic pulse was not actually audible.

The king stared at him for a moment, looking troubled. Then: "I am leaving now," he announced with deliberation, his voice trembling with tension. "You will remain here and play for Her Majesty. Later today, you will attend the Spring Rites with me."

"And if I don't?" Gwirion asked, desperately clinging to the pretense of banter.

Seeing Noble's eyes widen with annoyance and frustration, Isabel immediately announced, "You will attend, Gwirion," but the king turned on her, outraged.

"*Be quiet!*" he ordered. "Ignore her, Gwirion! You will not choose to go because *she* told you to. Do you understand? You are not to do her bidding. This is your own free decision and your own free decision is to attend."

Despite the strain, Gwirion laughed nervously at the absurdity of this. The laughter snapped some final string holding Noble's fury in check; he lunged at the harpist and snatched the harp from his hands. He clutched it high over his head and for a moment seemed about to smash it down on Gwirion. Gwirion stopped laughing at once and cowered.

Noble turned and in three long, sure strides had crossed to the window—and hurled the harp out into the grey dawn air.

Gwirion leapt to his feet in disbelief and cringed as the sound of splintering wood and snapping strings echoed faintly up to them from the bottom of the castle mound. He raced toward the window but Noble stepped in his way and caught him, an outstretched hand grasping each arm. "Now," the king said, devoid of all expression. "I am leaving. You will remain here and play for the queen and later today you will attend the Spring Rites with me. *Do you understand?*"

Isabel did, and shuddered, drawing the sheet up around her as if it could somehow give protection, but Gwirion just looked confused. "How can I play?" he cried plaintively. "You just destroyed my harp!"

"My harp," Noble corrected at once, and pushed him back toward the bed, shoving him down so that he nearly fell on Isabel.

Gwirion sprang back scowling. "Bastard!" he spat. "That was your father's harp, Noble! *Bastard.*"

"Come with me to the Rites and I'll give you a new harp."

Again Isabel thought she saw desperation behind the firm expression in her husband's eyes. "That sounds like a fair exchange," she said in a cajoling tone to Gwirion.

"That harp was irreplaceable!" he protested furiously.

"Dammit, you idiot!" Noble shouted, and grabbed him by the high collar of his tunic, shaking him. He jerked the fool toward him so their faces were very close; they could feel each other's breath. "I don't care if you sit in a corner and sulk the whole time, you must attend!"

Gwirion twisted away from him, shrugging and shuddering as if his touch were repellant. "*Why?*" he demanded.

Noble abruptly slammed the back of his hand against Gwirion's mouth. Isabel cried out as Gwirion collapsed to the floor, both hands cupped around his jaw. Noble grabbed him like a shepherd would a wayward sheep and hauled him impatiently onto the bed. "Because," the king hissed through clenched teeth, inches from his face, "you are *expected.* If you do not attend, people will talk. If you do not attend because you are in this room, people will do more than talk—people will *know*, and, Gwirion, I am trying very hard to keep people from knowing. Do not further rob me of incentive." Then, very softly, almost a whisper: "And *damn you*, Gwirion, for bringing me to this."

They both stared at him in horrified silence, Gwirion dumbfounded, Isabel resigned and pale. Noble sighed, looking both exhausted and annoyed. He released his captive and took a heavy step away from the bed.

Gwirion cradled the side of his face, his tongue feeling thick in

his mouth. He swallowed and made the mistake of playing innocent. "What do you mean, sire?" he asked timorously.

Instantly ignited again, Noble whirled around, grabbed the front of Gwirion's tunic and hoisted him up until he teetered on his toes for balance. "You have one opportunity to cease insulting me."

"But how am I insulting you?" Gwirion babbled, tasting blood behind his teeth. Isabel closed her eyes in defeat.

The king's jaw clenched. "You have now wasted the opportunity," Noble informed him. "You stupid wretch." He shoved Gwirion hard onto the bed, glaring at him, then pulled his dagger from his belt and smacked it against Gwirion's chest, pressed the point hard against his heart. Gwirion stared down at it, stunned, not quite believing this moment had arrived. Noble looked at him furiously— but far more than that, with sorrow, and for a moment Isabel, watching them, thought she was looking at the face of amnesty. Then, too fast for her to see it happen, the blade flashed up and cut into the skin of Gwirion's temple, exactly where the childhood scar was, the scar she'd noticed the first time she'd watched his sleeping face. As badly shocked as pained, Gwirion clamped one hand to the wound, cursing. He stared in disgusted terror at the king.

"Is that not both poetic and economical of me?" Noble demanded with satisfaction. "The first wound you survived and the last wound you'll survive, on the same small patch of flesh? You will *not* survive another wound from me."

Isabel tore at her shift, ripped away a piece of silk from the skirt and pressed it hard against Gwirion's bleeding forehead. Noble slapped her harshly and she recoiled. Gwirion, dazed, tried to move between them to protect her, but the king pushed him aside. "*You* are a very foolish child," he told his wife angrily. He settled on the foot of the bed, facing them, and sheathed the dagger. His taut face transformed immediately, unnervingly, into a personable, almost chatty aspect. "Shall we begin negotiations for surrender? There's so much to consider and dawn will be here soon." Only his breathing, shallow and quick, betrayed his real mood now.

For a long moment there was silence. She gave Gwirion the piece

of silk to press against the wound himself. "Move away from him," Noble suggested in a conversational voice, which under the circumstances was more distressing than an outright threat. She retreated several feet, still under the blankets.

"How long have you known?" she asked at last.

Gwirion could not speak. His distress, Noble noted with grateful satisfaction, was much more complicated than hers was. He, at least, still loved the man they'd wronged.

"A long time," Noble answered. "But you knew that, of course, I made it very clear to you." He gave her a chill smile. "And then, sometimes, I didn't."

"What gave it away?"

"I suppose Gwirion *telling* me the moment I returned from the front raised my suspicions—"

"You didn't believe me," he objected in a reedy voice.

"True," Noble said. "It took at least three minutes of watching you both gawk stupidly at me to wonder if there might be something to it." He saw the expression on his wife's face, outraged castigation aimed at Gwirion. Noble smiled at her. "But, my dear," he went on, "the honors for giving it away go all to you. I offered you a cure for an insomnia you'd never had—and suddenly you had it nearly every night."

She pursed her lips. "Why did you do that?"

He shrugged. "I was curious to see what would happen—you cannot deny the inherent fascination of the situation for me. I was sure the whole thing would explode in your faces, and once it was safely behind us I could tease you about it. But it didn't explode. And then I realized it was more than merely lust. Which is when it all became so interesting. You're each in your way the two most honest people I know—Gwirion to the point of cruelty and you to the point of boredom. Two honest people being dishonest is a fascinating thing to watch. Most of the time, I was impressed, and I was almost always entertained. I had some brilliant moments along the way myself, driving you to distraction."

"And what did it serve to do that to me?" she demanded.

He gave her a smile of private meaning. "It was a *whim*."

"You said you never indulge whims."

"Usually I wouldn't. Usually I wouldn't indulge cuckoldry either. Obviously I made exceptions. I did what I required to keep myself sane—I've had a kingdom to tend, you know, we haven't all had the luxury of making this adultery the center of our lives. But generally, I've been having a grand time with it. I could have kept it going for years, maybe forever."

"Then why this now?" she asked.

"To begin with, you're both becoming sloppy, and I can't risk that any further. You might at least have practiced enough discretion so as not to insult my office—if I may paraphrase you, my dear. But far more urgent, to be honest, is how you're ruining him. I can't condone that any longer. The Spring Rites were suddenly upon us and I realized that would be the touchstone, so I had to act." He made a gesture that was at once self-deprecating and self-satisfied. "I believe His Majesty has been a paragon of thoughtfulness. I deliberately gave you a final hour alone together tonight—I do hope you took advantage of my generosity. And I never once succumbed to the obvious temptation of making him watch us, I never once summoned him to serenade our mating—although believe me, I have considered it almost every evening." He turned his complacency on Gwirion. "This is hardly a significant detail, but my male pride compels me to inform you that nothing matches the ardor of an unfaithful woman trying to distract her husband from her unfaithfulness. I've been very satisfied by her this month and I have satisfied her greatly in return." He smiled at Gwirion and concluded, "While you have not."

"What are you going to do with us?" Isabel asked before he could prolong the taunting.

"With *us*?" he echoed, amused. "Are you under the delusion that the two of you are a unit? I shall do something with you and something with him, but there is no more *us* between you as of this moment. Is that understood?" He took Gwirion's face in one hand and lifted it toward him. "You understand that, don't you?" Gwirion

stared at him, still too distressed to speak. After a moment, satisfied, Noble nodded.

With a small flourish, he again unsheathed the dagger and displayed it to them like a child revealing a personal treasure. "This small piece of metal," he informed them, "goes by many names: dagger, stiletto, dirk, dudgeon. It's intended to rend flesh. Human flesh. It is not a hunting knife, nor is it used to slaughter livestock."

"We know what it's used for," Isabel said impatiently. She pressed the torn bit of silk more firmly to Gwirion's bleeding forehead; he had forgotten it entirely.

"This particular dagger," Noble went on, gazing at it fondly and ignoring her, "was given to me by my father a week before he was cut down by your despicable uncle. I held it sitting in the bushes nearly twenty years ago wishing I could slit Roger's throat. It was forged by the grandfather of our current smith, and despite its simplicity there is a genuine grace and elegance—"

"For the love of God!" she snapped. "If you're going to kill us with it, just—"

"Not *us* again," Noble said with a chastising smile. "I told you, no more us. You may say, 'If you're going to kill *me* with it—"

"If you're going to kill me with it, just get on with it," she said between clenched teeth. Angrily, she slipped her shift off, pushed the sheets away, and kneeled upright beside him, nude, her arms at her sides, her hair cascading heavily behind her and her head held back slightly. "Here's my heart and here's my throat. I'm sick of your Celtic verbosity."

Noble laughed with genuine affection and glanced at Gwirion, who was still staring at them both slack jawed. "She's quite marvelous, isn't she?" He looked back at her. "Since you offered, you may assist my presentation. If I were to use it this morning, I would have a variety of options. Sit."

He pulled her down so that they all faced each other in a triangle, but he kept his free hand cupped hard around her arm. "The uses of a dagger," he intoned didactically, regarding with dreamy rev-

erence the one he held. "First, of course, there is the resource of the cutting blade. This would most commonly take the form of slitting the throat." He whipped the dagger up toward her bare white neck and Gwirion impulsively grabbed at it. Noble pushed him away without effort, elbowing him in the stomach so that he staggered back against the edge of the bed trying to breathe. "It's just a demonstration," Noble said. "Don't become hysterical." He turned back to her and lightly drew the blade across her throat where a lethal slice would be made. She took a sudden breath when she felt the metal cold against her, but did not flinch. "There is also the tip, which offers us a number of options. First, the straightforward piercing of the heart, which might have a certain poetic appropriateness here." He rested the tip of the blade against the meat of her left breast and pressed it just enough to dimple the flesh. Gwirion sat staring, worried that any gesture at all from him would push the king too far. Isabel didn't move. She did not look at the blade, just gazed at Noble with a look that was both calm and vulnerable.

"Of course," Noble went on, removing the dagger and turning her to sit with her profile to them, "an approach with greater resonance would be the stab in the back." He pointed the blade just to the left of her spine, and pushed a little harder this time so that blood rushed to the skin. She winced slightly, which made Gwirion sit up in alarm. Noble lowered the dagger. "You handled that very well," he announced as she turned back to face them. "I was quite tempted to go ahead with it."

"I know," she replied. "But since you didn't, would you please tell me what you are going to do instead?"

"But you are hard!" he said with feigned dismay. "When did you come to be so hard?" She waited, unspeaking, and he nudged her. "Tell me your preference." She said nothing. "Let me guess, then. You with your dreary English artlessness—you would just want a straightforward direct hit, wouldn't you? Obvious and efficient."

"I doubt you're capable of straightforwardness," she replied. "I am still waiting for an answer."

"Answer?" Noble frowned. "Ah, yes—what am I going to do

with you? Let me ask you the same question: What were you planning to do with yourselves if I hadn't interfered?" Neither of them spoke, and after a moment he sighed with apparent satisfaction. "Well, at least there was no full-scale conspiracy going on. That puts you on a *slightly* higher plane than those whose betrayals are merely political. I must admit that's reassuring." Without relinquishing his flip exterior, he sobered a little. "I, on the other hand, am somewhat organized. We must consider the situation in a larger context, beginning with an enumeration of each sinner's sins. Not that you are devout, Gwirion, but the commandments are not to be broken lightly. Thou shalt not covet thy neighbor's wife. Have you heard that one? Thou shalt not bear false witness?"

"Thou shalt have no other gods before me," Isabel interrupted. "Which is really the only sin he can commit against you."

"Tut, my darling, you verge on sacrilege," Noble said mildly. "But certainly, an examination of your sins gives us more cud to chew. You've taken a lover out of wedlock. You've compromised the sanctity of the womb that is supposed to conceive my heir. You've stolen the affection of my closest friend. But really, at the end of it all," he concluded, a little smile creating the passing deception that he might forgive her, "your worst offense, madam, has been your womanly effect on him. I warned you last September not to become the agent through which I could ever lose him. As I said, I might have been willing to endure the infidelity if you hadn't ruined him in the process."

"I haven't ruined him," she argued. "He's a man, Noble. He used to be your puerile little shadow and now he is his own man."

"What good is that?" Noble demanded. "My court is full of men, why couldn't you have taken one of them? Did you ever consider that I might *need* him as a puerile little shadow? Why did you have to *mature* him?"

"I matured myself," Gwirion protested, finally finding his voice.

"Ha!" Noble said with amused disbelief. "The maturity of dumping meat slops on oneself to defend the honor of one's mistress." He turned his full attention, his glittering blue eyes, back to Is-

abel. "So, madam, those are your sins. As I still have some regard for you, I would prefer to find a way to absolve you of them, and with that in mind, it seems to me that it is in your best interests—and mine too, perhaps—for me to free you of the bonds of matrimony."

She gaped at him, and even Gwirion drew in a breath. "Free me?" she asked.

"If you were not my wife, then most of those offenses would fall away."

"But can you . . . do that?" she asked. "The church won't grant a divorce."

"Welsh law would. What a pity you insisted we be married under canon law." He shrugged. "We must try a different course."

"Annulment?" she ventured, trying to understand his meaning.

"Do you desire that?" he responded.

"Annulment?" she repeated. What had once terrified her was suddenly a panacea. "How? Will the church agree?"

"If you and I both desire it, as royal citizens of a true state of Britain, there are steps we may take together to enact our own annulment, so that the church will have to acknowledge our uncoupling. But I need your full willingness."

"We would be annulled?" she said, as if she could not get the idea to stay in her mind. "You would agree to it?"

"I certainly agree to take steps toward it," he answered. "We began this in good faith, but it seems to have brought nothing but trouble for everyone." He smiled gently at her and brushed the back of his hand against her cheek. The gesture was so uncharacteristic, so intimate, so simple and sincere, that Gwirion looked awkwardly away, feeling like an intruder. "And I'll make sure you're taken care of. You will never go hungry or homeless, you have my word."

"What are the conditions?" she asked, as a year of seasoning prodded her to be skeptical.

Noble shook his head. "No conditions. I want Gwirion to stay with me, not go with you, but that is his choice too."

Gwirion was stunned. "If I chose—" he began, but hesitated. Noble nodded, grimly.

"I have little experience in granting you freedom, but I want to redress the failing. So it will be your choice."

Gwirion blinked in amazement, but Isabel warily pressed on. "And how do we go about initiating this annulment?" she demanded. She tried not to sound too eager. It could not possibly be this simple.

"We don't petition the church," Noble answered. "We go directly to the source." She frowned at him, uncomprehending, until he said: "God loves beauty, and I doubt He can resist a pretty face. So you are going to petition him directly." He smiled at her with a sudden intensity that unnerved her. "And you are going to do it now."

"No!" Gwirion screamed, understanding, but she frowned in confusion even as Noble rushed her with the dagger and sank it through her breastbone. As she realized what was happening, it was shock more than pain that washed over her face. The king made a strange sound between a cry and a laugh and kissed her hard on the lips.

Gwirion, after a moment of horrified inertness, leapt at Noble to pull him away. Like an enraptured acolyte in some arcane religious ritual, Noble pushed the sagging body against Gwirion's chest and intertwined their arms, propping her up as Gwirion frantically embraced her. He pulled the dagger out of her and hurled it away; as the wound began to spurt he tried, uselessly, to stop it with his hands. Sobbing, screaming, he kissed her, then pulled away again to see her face, trying desperately to make eye contact, trying to pull her away from death with his look. She couldn't focus on him but she knew he was there, and a sad smile tickled her lips as her head lolled forward onto his shoulder and she was still.

"Apparently God said yes," Noble said, wrestling with hysterical, triumphal laughter. "Would you rather join her or stay here with me?"

Gwirion thought he screamed and threw himself at Noble in a blind rage—but when he came to himself he realized he had not moved. He was holding her body. Her head was still resting on his shoulder, tucked against his neck. The blood had seeped from her and soaked the sheets; it was all over him, he was lying in it, slipping farther into it. With a cry he leapt away and fell off the bed and onto the wood floor, his tunic heavy with her blood.

Noble had calmed completely, retrieved his dagger, and crossed to the window, staring out over the hills. Gwirion's commotion in ripping his blood-sodden tunic and drawers off, wiping the blood from his naked limbs in a frenzy with the bed curtains, made the king look over toward the bed, serene and expressionless.

"Please dress yourself properly," he said. "I am not through with you." He looked back out the window.

"Sire," Gwirion said in a small, horrified voice. "Noble. Look what you've done."

Noble, without looking, nodded, facing out. "It's very final, isn't it?" he said pensively. "In the field, you have so many opponents, you have more than one chance to get it just right. In politics, the dance can last for years as you refine it. This is different." His eyes still gazing in abstraction out the window, he held his hand up and away from him to reenact the movement. "One jerk of the wrist and it's over."

Gwirion stared at him aghast. "Is that all this means to you? You've just *murdered your wife*." And as if speaking it finally made it real to him, he caught back a cry and scrambled around the bed to cradle her body from the far side. He avoided her open, sightless eyes, but he touched her skin, still soft and pliant but unnaturally still, and his breath caught raggedly.

"If you must continue to paw her, at least put on some decent clothes," the king insisted. Gwirion looked about unsurely, and Noble pointed across the room. "If I'm not mistaken, you'll find some just inside the door." Gwirion took a hesitant step toward the threshold. Lying there neatly folded was the black silk outfit Noble had worn the day before. Beside it was a large basin of lukewarm water and a pile of washrags.

"The note to Gwilym," Gwirion said quietly, understanding, feeling his body turn to lead.

Noble nodded.

With one traumatized eye on the king, Gwirion sponged the blood off himself and then began to dress. He realized as he pulled on the long-sleeved tunic that somebody had taken the seams in; it fit

him almost perfectly. Just like the last time he had faced his execution. The king had seen to every detail of this production.

"When you've finished dressing, open the door," Noble said calmly. "We shall continue this in a slightly less intimate setting."

"May I have a moment with her?"

Noble shrugged. "Very well."

"Alone?"

"No," the king said immediately, and settled into the tapestried cushions of the window seat. He looked untroubled, exquisitely regal, in the sunrise.

Gwirion put on the rest of the clothes, pressed the bandage from her torn shift to his wound again, and returned to the side of the bed. She was paler and already cold. The blood had long stopped. With a knot in his throat, he reached out and gently pressed her eyelids down so that they covered her unseeing tawny eyes. He stroked her cheek and the seductive silky hair, said her name, and sobbed.

Noble waited, basking in the early light at the window, marking time patiently by the shifting shadows of a cloudless morning. He was willing to go slowly now. Despite the game with the dagger, his fury had barely found relief in her quick dispatch, but he was weary and there was still so much he would have to wring from Gwirion to be satisfied. He could wait.

After what felt to Gwirion like weeks, his tears dried and he settled from a rage of grief to the exhausted numbness of resignation and mourning. "Now," Noble said gently. "Open the door."

One hand still pressing the fabric to his temple, Gwirion nodded dully and obeyed.

He was shocked to find a small crowd clustered on the landing, waiting for the door to open. Beside the usual morning doorkeeper there was the sewing bevy, the physician, the queen's priest, and Efan, shadowed by another soldier from the teulu. The women's eyes were red from crying; the men were somber and would not look Gwirion in the face.

He stumbled back in surprise and spun around to Noble. "What is this?" he demanded. "This isn't anybody else's business!"

"This is everybody's business, Gwirion," said the king, rising from the window seat and nonchalantly retrieving his cloak. "These good people are here to take care of her. It's time for you and me to quit her."

"No!" Gwirion yelled automatically.

Noble raised the dagger. "Yes," he countered placidly. "Downstairs. We'll conclude this where I'm almost certain it began."

Efan stepped into the room, avoiding Gwirion's gaze. He had the doleful awkwardness of one who had intended to gloat over a fallen adversary but found he couldn't. The same was true of his fellow soldier, who—on Noble's orders—happened to be Caradoc.

Gwirion, staring at Caradoc, muttered to the king, "Your sense of spectacle is relentlessly perverse."

"I consider it poetic," Noble said with serenity. The guards each clapped a hand on one of Gwirion's shoulders. They pushed him gently out of the room, onto the darkened balcony and toward the stairs.

As they descended to the hall, Gwirion grew more and more astonished: Most of the castle had gathered near for the shameful promenade. Everyone looked stunned—and yet no one looked surprised. *They all know*, he realized, feeling sick, and once again he remembered the note to Gwilym. Even plump, protective Marged, standing discreetly near the kitchen screens, obviously knew now. He gave her a distressed stare across the hall and her response was to shake her grey head helplessly and shrug. She had not known for long enough to warn him.

He looked down, but some of the eyes upon him were so intense he felt their attention as physical slaps. He never knew their actual expressions, only that they stared. Marged's grandson Dafydd. Madrun's beloved Ednyfed, his mother Elen, his father Cadwgan the marshal. The butcher and his son. Nest, and all the other hall servants, all the kitchen workers, all the teulu. Einion the porter. Father Idnerth. Gwilym. Hafaidd the usher. Goronwy the judge. All the other officers. The stable boy whom Gwirion had saved from Huw. And there were dozens more.

The silence, in such a crowd, was unbearable. As Gwirion reached the bottom step and pivoted toward the round white audience chamber, he glanced at the collection of faces and announced, loudly, "Thank you all for your petitions, but we've already selected our chief fool."

It wasn't witty but it broke the awkward silence, and they released their collective breath. Nobody—except Gwirion, who wasn't looking—could fail to see the king's affectionate expression. Surely, the castle denizens thought as one, surely the king would punish him but then forgive him. She had come to them as an outsider, and however worthy she had grown in their eyes, she'd lived among them only a year—but Gwirion was nearly the only constant in the king's life since infancy. He could not be so rudely dispatched.

WHEN they were inside and the door had been shut and locked from without, Noble tossed down his cloak against the wall and casually settled, lolling, into his comfortable leather chair. All the sconces were blazing brightly; the room looked far too cheery. "May Day is not off to a promising start," said the king.

"She didn't wrong you," Gwirion said mournfully. "I did."

"I know you wronged me," he answered calmly. "But so did she."

"I wish you had punished me for both our sins," Gwirion said.

Noble looked up near the ceiling, an unreadable expression on his face. "The irony here is that your only sin is saying that."

"I don't understand you."

"Gwirion. Anything I have is yours. If you wanted her, you had only to ask me for her. I would have found that rather titillating, in fact."

"You're disgusting. That's not what I wanted."

"Yes, it took me a bit to realize that. I threw far more tempting

morsels in your direction and encouraged you to nibble, and you never did. That was the real problem."

"The sin wasn't sleeping with your wife, it was falling in love with her?"

"It was falling in love with *anyone!*" Noble shouted. He leapt at Gwirion and grabbed him round the neck, hurling him to the ground and bashing his head against the wood floor. "How could you do that? Traitor!"

Gwirion grabbed at the king's fists trying to get them off his windpipe, hearing his own breath rattle in his ears. He forced himself against instinct to let go of his clutch on Noble's hand to swipe at the king's face. Noble pulled away for a moment with a curse, taking one hand from Gwirion's throat, but before Gwirion could twist away Noble was clutching him again, now really clutching, hard, and shouting. Gwirion's legs flailed the air, trying to find something to kick, striking nothing. He saw blood snap across his vision every time Noble struck his head to the floor, and imagined that the gurgles of his constricted breathing were bubbles of blood seeping into his throat to drown him. He couldn't hear what Noble was saying anymore, couldn't even see the frenzied face and contorted mouth. A metallic taste in the back of his mouth calmed him, and although he knew it was the first taste of death, he relaxed with it, grateful to escape.

Almost too late, Noble realized what he was doing and released him. There was a horrible silence and the body lay inert. Then Gwirion convulsed and began gasping for air.

When he came to, he found himself lying on the settle, the king regarding him intensely from his chair.

Gwirion took a moment to regain his senses, and struggled slowly to his feet. He stood, dazed, trying to remember where they had come from, why they were here, where the queen was—and then he had to face it all over again. "What have you *done?*" he shrieked, and hurled himself at Noble.

Noble was ready for him with quicker reflexes than Gwirion's, and they were snarled up together tearing at each other—for a few seconds only, until Noble pulled the dagger from his boot and had it at Gwirion's throat. Gwirion stopped, tried to leap back, and smacked into the chest. Noble moved forward just enough to keep the blade at his throat.

For a long moment they stared at each other, breathing hard, the knife hanging between them. "Why don't you just *do* it," Gwirion spat.

"I've always believed in delaying satisfaction."

"That's not what your wife told me."

Noble smacked him hard across the face even as he burst out laughing. "That's the lad I miss!"

"You won't get him back by slitting my throat."

"I know," said Noble. "That's why you're alive right now. You have a chance to save yourself, if you choose to take it."

Gwirion's laugh was brittle and sarcastic. "I won't like it, will I?"

"No, it's simple," Noble assured him with vicious cheerfulness. "Just give me what I want."

Gwirion fluttered his lashes at the king and lisped, "But, Noble, you know I'm not a loose woman."

Again, the king smashed him across the face and laughed.

"Please hit the other side next time," Gwirion said, forcing his voice to stay calm. "I want to keep the bruises symmetrical."

"Remember what it was like before we ever knew her," Noble whispered earnestly. "That's all I want."

Gwirion looked from Noble to the blade. He felt the blood trickling again from the cut at his temple. He knew he couldn't win a physical fight, and he wasn't even sure he could win a mental one now. He didn't trust himself to outsmart the king's fury, and he was too tired in his bones to win back his life with laughter. He thought of the dead woman upstairs and wondered what she would do in his place. She was so direct, so artless. He had never tried artless.

"Would you let me live freely?"

Noble hesitated. "I would let you raise hell. I would let you

shock and insult me and everybody around me. I'd let you put my reign in peril with your pranks. I would sooner lose my kingship to your scheming than to Roger's or Llewelyn's."

"That's not what I asked. I want to know if you'd let me live freely—for myself, and not just for you."

Noble shook his head. "That's what you did when you fell in love with her and nothing good came of it for any of us. I'm offering you your life so things can be as they were between us."

"Then, sire, the answer is no," Gwirion said softly, meeting Noble's eyes comfortably for the first time in months.

Noble blinked in disbelief. "What do you mean, no? This is a dagger, Gwirion." He spoke with slightly exaggerated diction. "I'm holding it at your throat and I'm going to kill you with it unless you say yes. Under the circumstances, one says yes."

"I am saying no," Gwirion replied calmly.

"Don't test me, you whoreson."

"I'm not. I expect you'll kill me." And he slipped under the blade as Noble, with a roar of fury, stabbed at him.

They were wrapped about each other again, Gwirion trying to hold Noble's right arm back and leaping away as the dagger slashed toward him. Gwirion bit at the knife hand, but Noble shoved him off and tossed him across the room, then threw himself after him. Gwirion scampered from under the assault and was up and around, throwing himself on Noble before Noble realized where he had gone to. Gwirion's teeth sank into the flesh of the king's hand, until he felt something grainy give way under his teeth and he tasted blood. Noble cursed and dropped the dagger, pushing Gwirion away from it as it fell to the floor. But Gwirion, smaller and more agile, twisted away from the king and lunged for it. Picking it up, he made an awkward stab at Noble. Noble ducked and tripped on his long tunic, and Gwirion threw himself on top of him, landing astride his chest with the dagger against Noble's throat.

Noble looked up at him and laughed sarcastically. Gwirion was white and his hands were shaking.

"You're going to let me live as I want to," he rasped.

"No I'm not," Noble taunted. "You'll have to kill me if that's what you want."

"Don't be stupid," Gwirion ordered in an unsteady voice. "I have only myself to think about, you have the entire kingdom. You have to save yourself for them, they need you. You *must* agree with me."

Noble shook his head. "As much as I resent it there are others who might rule the kingdom, Gwirion. There are no others who might be my fool. Or my friend. If you want the life you spoke of, kill me."

"Don't make me do that," Gwirion begged, losing any pretense of bravado.

"You can do it," Noble prodded in a seductive whisper. "It's easy. Just reach under my chin and slit my throat. I'll go quickly. It will hardly hurt. Llewelyn will be good to my people. And you'll be free."

"I can't do that!" Gwirion screamed, sobbing, trying to hold the point of the knife against the king's throat.

"I know," Noble whispered, gently now. "So take the dagger away from my throat and put it in my hand."

Gwirion closed his eyes with a sob of resignation as he lowered the dagger, slackening his grip.

THE king had told them not to open the door under any circumstances, but the inhuman shriek alarmed even the teulu and brought people running from all over the castle. The sound dissolved into a wailing moan, the voice of a fatally wounded animal abandoned by its pack. As if there were no need to draw breath, the moan went on and on, a furious lamentation from a bellowing set of lungs unused to grief. Like a caterwaul, it grew worse and more frantic rather than dying down, and finally Marged demanded that the door be opened.

Efan threw it ajar and Caradoc thrust a torch into the room, but it wasn't needed—all the sconces were lit and the whitewashed walls had an almost gaudy brightness to them.

Piled together against the far wall were the king and Gwirion. One of them was screaming. Blood was splattered in a bright, sparkling arc just above them, dripping down on them. Madrun, who had come down to ask about funeral proceedings, fainted at once. Elen gasped and ran out of the room. But the others stayed where they were, staring at the tangled mess of limbs and clothing. Gwilym covered his face with one broad palm.

Oblivious to the intruders, the mourner keened on. He was so animated when he gasped for breath that both bodies seemed to heave for air, and at first they thought and hoped both men were still alive. Finally, he quieted, lay limp for a moment in his friend's rigid arms, and then began to disentangle himself.

It took a few moments to get free; he was gentle and respectful, moving the royal limbs until Noble sat still and peaceful against the wall. As a final gesture, Gwirion took the king's green cloak, kissed it in homage, and draped it high across Noble's shoulders to hide the gaping neck wound. With the wound hidden, the king looked as if he were sleeping. Gwirion pulled himself up to his feet and the onlookers, finally registering what had happened, grasped each other in horrified shock. They stared at Gwirion and Gwirion stared back at them, blinking the last of his tears away, rubbing the blood from his forehead.

"Are you going to kill me?" he asked the steward, in a tired voice.

Gwilym shook his head. He folded and unfolded the letter Noble had written hours earlier. "He said that if he allowed you to survive, we were to do the same."

"I see," Gwirion sighed. Hesitantly, he walked toward the door.

"But I must ask for the weapon," Gwilym said uncomfortably, stepping in his way.

Gwirion looked up at him. "Apparently I am the weapon," he said quietly. "But the knife is with the king."

They all turned to see. Noble's hand clutched the knife in a death grip. Nobody spoke.

Gwirion turned toward the door again and walked out of the room.

HE stumbled through the great hall, where dozens of eyes peeked at him in fear from the corners. He pushed the great double doors open and walked out into the yard. The bells were ringing. The early-morning sky was bluer than he had ever seen it, bluer than the best of their days out riding. He took the few steps to the unattended barbican, walked through the gate and down the castle mound into the village.

People were huddled in small clusters in the open air, staring toward the chapel tower where the bell was ringing, wondering what disaster was unfolding and when the news would reach them, debating if the villain of the hour would be Mortimer, Llewelyn, Anarawd, or Thomas. Many turned to him, expecting him to fill his frequent role of herald, but he walked past them as if he didn't see them.

When he came to the village gates he paused. He had never passed this spot alone before. The guards, sensing it would not do to question him, moved aside and he walked out, the sun warming his back and the road lying before him, offering him everything and nothing.

AUTHOR'S NOTE

aelgwyn ap Cadwallon, ruler of Maelienydd, really existed. But this story is a work of fiction, and takes creative license with some well-established historical facts for the sake of crafting a tale. To honor what really was, I would like to acknowledge the more obvious and egregious ways I have played with history. Almost without exception, every change I have made has been in the interest of simplifying an extraordinarily complicated political scenario, and I've done this by removing certain real-life figures, consolidating kingdoms, and telescoping the time line.

The land I call Maelienydd was known in earlier times as both "the land between the Severn and the Wye" and Cynllibiuc. In the 1190s, the region was made up of a few smaller kingdoms; the largest of these was Maelienydd, and I have consolidated them all into one kingdom with one ruler. Maelgwyn ap Cadwallon actually died in 1197. At the time of this story (1198–99), Roger Mortimer had control of Castell Cymaron and Maelienydd; he had taken Cy-

maron in 1195 and Maelgwyn spent the last two years of his life fighting, with the help of Lord Rhys of Deheubarth, to try to win it back. I have fictionalized nothing about the intensity of the Mortimer feud with the native ruling family, and the assassination of Cadwallon (the prologue) is factual. Isabel and Thomas, however, are both my creations, and by extension so are all political and military activities predicated on their existence.

The historical figure most clearly warped by my alterations is Llewelyn ap Iorwerth of Gwynedd, later known as Llewelyn the Great. His trajectory of power did indeed go from a small part of Gwynedd to an enormous swath of Wales. He did not, however, accomplish this in a year, as I have him doing—it took many years and the consistent mandate of the people; by the time he was a real force to be reckoned with in Maelienydd, Maelgwyn was long gone. Accelerating his rise to power as severely as I have risks presenting him as Machiavellian (particularly considering some of his actions in the story)—but he wasn't. Gwywynwyn of Powys does not appear by name in my story at all, but was a formidable figure of the time. Maelgwyn had brothers and cousins, some of whom ruled small sections of the area I call Maelienydd. I have either ignored them or diminished their significance, for simplicity's sake. Maelgwyn actually had sons (and daughters), although none of them ever had the chance to rule. There are many other simplifications. In general, in the era of this story, the land between the Severn and the Wye was not as cohesive, safe, or stable as I've depicted it.

Although most Welsh rulers of the time were, in written records, known merely as lords or princes, Cadwallon was referred to as "king" by at least one English chronicler, and I have taken the liberty to pass that honor on to his son—who may have been called "king" by his subjects, regardless of what the English called him. Abbey Cwm-hir really existed, including its enormous church; it was founded by Cadwallon. Gerald of Wales (chapter 4) was real, as was the book of his to which Isabel refers—and so was the encounter Maelgwyn had with him.

Depictions of the court, council, laws, and customs are based

upon real medieval Welsh law (with very occasional creative license); obviously, both Isabel and Gwirion constantly fly in the face of established convention and get away with it. All folk rituals and formal ceremonies, with the exception of the Spring Rites, are true to life. What we today call "Celtic Christianity" had died out by 1198, but certain core beliefs and values predating Christianity were still deeply imbedded in the popular mind-set. People would have seen nothing heretical about blending native beliefs and myths with Christian dogma into one fairly seamless belief system, which they would have considered fully Christian.

Gwirion is not only fictional, but historically improbable, as the Welsh court had no known position corresponding to the concept of a European fool or jester. The word "gwirion" means both "innocent" and "foolish," but beyond that is based on the root word for "truth."

R